Praise for

In the Midnight Room

"A beautiful novel about families and love and complications of human relations. . . . Superb."

—*The Daily News*

"In the opening pages of Laura McBride's new novel, June Stein dives off the Haverstraw Bridge and straight into the reader's imagination. I love how June, and the vivid, complicated women around her, often fail to act in their own best interests while they still win our affection and admiration. And I love how McBride brings to life the fast-changing city of Las Vegas through their intertwined stories. . . . A passionate, gripping and beautifully written novel."

—Margot Livesey, author of *Mercury*

"Laura McBride reminds us of the invisible threads that bind us together as she weaves the stories of four very different women into a haunting tale of love, loss, and the power to endure. A compelling, transporting, and deeply wise novel. I was enthralled from the first page. Laura McBride is a stunning storyteller."

—Patry Francis, author of *The Orphans of Race Point*

"When Laura McBride starts a novel, her characters lead the way."

—*The Denver Post*

"The novel's ending . . . is a heartfelt nightcap to a tale that runs the gambit from adventure to tragedy."

—*St. Louis Post-Dispatch*

"Through outstanding character development and beautifully crafted storytelling, McBride uses the stories of four seemingly insignificant women to weave her tale into the readers' heartstrings."

—*Deseret News*

"Gorgeous, engrossing, moving, and at times wickedly funny, this brilliant novel pulled me in and didn't let me go until the shattering final sentence. This is the novel you need to read right now."

—Joanna Rakoff, author of *My Salinger Year* and *A Fortunate Age*

"McBride crafts passages of sterling imagery and diction. . . . Mostly, though, she tells an honest Las Vegas tale about life and fate, with characters, not caricatures."

—Nevada Public Radio, "Desert Companion"

"McBride has achieved the difficult feat of keeping her book fast-paced while realizing her characters' complex and nuanced emotions."

—*Washington Independent Review of Books*

"An exciting new novel . . . filled with independent, heroic women whose lives resonate with ours today."

—*Focus Daily News*

"Las Vegas itself is a character in this immersive novel that effectively exhibits the changes to the city throughout the decades. This is a tale of love, loss, and the unexpected, unheralded ways that lives meet around blackjack and roulette tables."

—*Publishers Weekly*

"Laura McBride braids a compelling, heartbreaking narrative of four women— June, Honorata, Engracia, and Coral—whose lives are transformed by the El Capitan. . . . McBride is skilled at handling multiple narrative threads, but more simply, she knows how to do what Vegas does: lure a passerby in, hook them with a good story, and leave them wanting more."

—*Shelf Awareness*

Booksellers everywhere recommend
In the Midnight Room

"Taking readers from the depths of grief and then sending them soaring with emotion . . . an awe-inspiring novel that deserves to be on the bookshelf of every avid reader."

—Pamela Klinger-Horn, Excelsior Bay Books

"Had me from page one and held me until the final sentence."

—Sarah Bagby, Watermark Books & Café

"This is good reading of the highest order."

—John Evans, Diesel, A Bookstore

"A satisfying tale of community, the strength of women, and hope."

—Deon Stonehouse, Sunriver Books & Music

"One of those books that as soon as I finished it, I went back to the beginning to reread the first couple of chapters. . . . I cried at the ending that was so touching and so right."

—Julie Dickerson, Barnes & Noble

"McBride shines again in her second novel set in Las Vegas. A cast of characters, all of whom you know to the core of their hearts as she did before, go about living their lives. There is love, loss, redemption, and ultimately hope."

—Valerie Koehler, Blue Willow Bookshop

"McBride outdoes herself in conveying her depth of understanding of the heart and soul of individuals of various backgrounds. This story will remain with you for a long time after you close the book."

—Vicki Burger, Wind City Books

"There are authors you read because of their stories and others their use of language, and then there are the masters that deliver perfection. Thus we have books like McBride's that leave us breathless, satiated, and moved to the core."

—Jesica Sweedler DeHart, Neill Public Library

"I loved falling into the world of June, Honorata, Engracia, and Coral. The characters are so richly drawn that you'll be sad to say good-bye to them when you finish the book."

—Suzie Mulligan, Tattered Cover Book Store

"It was a profound and thought-provoking read."

—Maxwell Gregory, Lake Forest Book Store

"Spurred on by love, fear, hope, or regret these fabulous characters play the cards life dealt them with an honesty that will resonate with any woman trying to make her way in the world today."

—Luisa Smith, Book Passage

ALSO BY LAURA McBRIDE

We Are Called to Rise

IN THE MIDNIGHT ROOM

PREVIOUSLY PUBLISHED AS
'ROUND MIDNIGHT

LAURA McBRIDE

TOUCHSTONE
New York   London   Toronto   Sydney   New Delhi

T

Touchstone
An Imprint of Simon & Schuster, Inc.
1230 Avenue of the Americas
New York, NY 10020

Copyright © 2017 by Laura McBride

First Touchstone trade paperback edition August 2018

TOUCHSTONE and colophon are registered trademarks of Simon & Schuster, Inc.

For information about special discounts for bulk purchases, please contact Simon & Schuster Special Sales at 1-866-506-1949 or business@simonandschuster.com.

The Simon & Schuster Speakers Bureau can bring authors to your live event. For more information or to book an event, contact the Simon & Schuster Speakers Bureau at 1-866-248-3049 or visit our website at www.simonspeakers.com.

Interior design by Jill Putorti

Manufactured in the United States of America

10 9 8 7 6 5 4 3 2 1

The Library of Congress has cataloged the hardcover edition as follows:

Names: McBride, Laura, author.
Title: Round midnight / Laura McBride.
Description: First Touchstone hardcover edition. | New York, NY : Touchstone, an Imprint of Simon & Schuster, 2016.
Identifiers: LCCN 2016032682 (print) | LCCN 2016054552 (ebook) | ISBN 9781501157783 (hardcover : acid-free paper) | ISBN 9781501157790 (softcover : acid-free paper) | ISBN 9781501157806 (eBook).
Subjects: LCSH: Casinos—Nevada—Las Vegas—Fiction. | Interpersonal relations—Fiction. | Life change events—Fiction. | Las Vegas (Nev.)—Fiction.
Classification: LCC PS3613.C284 R68 2016 (print) | LCC PS3613.C284 (ebook) | DDC 813/.6—dc23.
LC record available at https://lccn.loc.gov/2016032682.

ISBN 978-1-5011-5778-3
ISBN 978-1-5011-5779-0 (pbk)
ISBN 978-1-5011-5780-6 (ebook)

Originally published in 2017 as 'Round Midnight in hardcover by Touchstone.

For my mom

JUNE

The one who fell in love

MARCH 11, 1960
In the Midnight Room

Coming in the casino's main entry, the Midnight Room was on the right. A scantily clad ingénue waving a golden star in front of her torso—its two jeweled points artfully covering the money bits—adorned the neon marquee above the door. Below, a man in black tie greeted those lucky enough to have a ticket, and escorted the ones who slipped him enough cash to the better seats in the room.

It was a straightforward showroom: a hundred-foot stage, with a narrow apron, about four feet above the main floor. There were twenty or so small round tables, and chairs with red velvet seats. Along the back wall were a row of booths, higher even than the stage, and the velvet there was closer to maroon, and the stained glass lamps cast a warm but not revealing glow on the table where the drinks would sit. The sound system was excellent, and the lighting was standard, and there was room for a pretty good-sized band on the stage if someone wanted it.

That night, there was a man playing the piano, another playing the sax, and a third on the drums. When the curtain parted in the back, a top light rotated to catch the singer's face. He'd been doing this awhile; he swung to the light intuitively and let it accent the plane of his cheekbone, the hollow of his eye, the curve of his lip.

He was thinking he might never play there again.

He knew what was coming later.

And when he saw her, sitting at the back, at the booth she always sat in—still he was startled, it had been a long time, she had not said she was coming—he signaled to the band to quit playing. He thought he might say something, just say it, put it out there, but in that split

3

second in which he would have had to decide what to say, in which he would have had to find the courage to say it, he suddenly remembered the first time he'd seen her.

He'd had no idea who she was. He was new in town, didn't know anyone at all. And of course, she was the only white woman. She'd looked up—damn, she was good-looking—and the horn player had sounded a note, and he'd swung his hip, just a little, instinctively, and her breath had caught—he'd actually seen that; he'd never forgotten it—and right that minute, maybe he'd fallen in love.

So tonight, four years later, when it was probably the last time he would ever sing for her, he lifted his finger to Jamie, who played the sax, and when the note sounded, he closed his eyes and remembered the rotten little bar, the white woman's face, the flick of his hip, and he let his body take over, repeated the one instant of that fateful night, and as he did so, he remembered, he thought of her face, the intake of her breath. He remembered, even though of course she would not.

1

To celebrate victory in Europe, June Stein dove headfirst off the Haverstraw Bridge.

A few months earlier, she had bought an eighteen-inch silver cigarette holder on a day trip to the city—snuck into the shop while her mother was choosing a hat next door—and spent the spring flicking ashes on the track as she smoked behind the stairs of the boy's gym. In April she wore stockings to school, and bent over the water fountain to highlight the brown seams running along the backs of her legs. Leon Kronenberg said he had touched her breast. When Mr. Sawyer came back from the summer holidays with a goatee, June Stein breathed in, licked her lips, and shuddered.

She was bad for the neighborhood.

Things happened to other girls because of June Stein.

When she married Walter Kohn at nineteen, most people figured she was pregnant. June Stein would get her due. She'd be stuck in Clinton Hill for life; Walter Kohn was going to be bald in three years, like his father and his uncle Mort.

But at twenty, June Stein disappeared.

She was gone for six months.

When she came back, Walter Kohn had become something of a catch. People thought it was wrong that his wife had left him.

They said she'd gone to Reno, gotten a divorce, that she'd never been pregnant, she had just wanted to have sex, and now that she'd had it, now that she'd used Walter Kohn—who did have beautiful blond hair and the bluest eyes—she'd gone and left him, and who knows what man she might try to take up with next.

June Stein returned a pariah.

It was a role she had cherished, but at twenty-one, she found it less amusing.

She had not gone to Reno.

She had gone to Las Vegas, and the lights and the shows and the desert air, the dust and the heat and the way one felt alone in the universe, were more appealing in memory than they had been when she lived them. There had been only a handful of Jews in town, and none she found interesting, so while she was waiting for the divorce, she hung around a different crowd: locals mostly, born and raised Nevadans, and some that had come in for the gambling boon. And they rose in stature after she moved back to her parents' house, after even her friends expressed sympathy for Walter Kohn—who had taken the newspaper into the bathroom with him each morning—and there was the way her mother looked at her in the evenings, and the way her father kept asking if she would like to take a stenography course. One day June Stein packed a suitcase, including the eighteen-inch silver cigarette holder, called a taxi, and flew all night from Newark to Las Vegas.

She didn't even leave a note.

But that was June Stein.

Prettiest girl in Clinton Hill.

And the only one who ever dove headfirst off the Haverstraw Bridge.

2

"June, you shouldn't be on that ladder. You look like you're going to fall right off."

"Don't you think I would bounce if I did?"

Del laughed.

"I mean it. Get down. What are you doing up there anyway?"

"There's one of those atomic bomb favors in this chandelier. You can see it from that side of the room. It's been bothering me for a week."

"Well, tell Mack to take it down. Why would you climb on a ladder when you're eight months pregnant?"

"I did ask Mack. Three days ago. He really doesn't have time. And I'm bored to death. Even the baby's bored. He's been kicking me like a trucker."

"A trucker? I don't think our daughter's going to be a trucker."

"Well, then, our daughter's going to be dancing with the Follies down the road."

June jumped backward to the ground from the second rung of the ladder. She had meant it as a graceful note, but her weight was unwieldy, she landed on the side of her foot, and caught herself awkwardly before she could fall.

Del darted forward, and June grinned.

"I'm fine. Maybe it'll get labor started."

"Okay, just try to be reasonable this week? I need help. The hotel's booked solid for the holidays, and Ronni wants to visit her dad, who's sick. We're short everywhere. If you feel like going through the applications in the office, maybe we could get some folks started this week."

"Hmmm. All right. If you're sure I can't help Mack hammer at things. Baby and I love hammering."

June reached up to give Del a kiss, her belly snug into his, and he distractedly returned it. He didn't notice her puzzled gaze, or the way she walked with a slightly duller step toward the office.

Cora was already there. She was sitting at the table where June usually did the books, with one cigarette between her lips and another smoldering in an ashtray, her long legs stretched out in front of her—an old lady who looked as if she had once been a showgirl.

"You looking for people to hire too?" June asked.

"Odell's single-minded. How ya feeling?"

"Fat. Bored. See if I let your grandson knock me up again."

Cora smiled at June. Her language, her sultry ways, did not bother her. These were the qualities that had left June needing Odell. And without June, Odell's life would be different in ways that Cora did not want it to be. Cora had given up a lot for her grandson. She didn't regret it. When her son and his no-account woman had dropped Odell off the last time—his bottom covered with neglect sores, and the marks of someone's fingers on his thin arm—Cora didn't waste any time making her choice. She and Nathan had picked up what they had, locked the door on the little Texas house the Dibb family had lived in for ninety years, and headed to Vegas. There was a railroad job there for Nathan, and a new world for Odell. She and Nathan had done some things well and some things poorly, but in the end, the only thing worth taking out of Texas was a two-year-old child.

June was even prettier pregnant. Everything about that girl was pretty. Her hands, her feet, her skin, her hair. When she spoke, her voice trilled as if she were about to laugh. You listened to her in the same way you couldn't stop looking at her. Cora figured that if everything went to pieces, June might stand in as the club's entertainer. If she could sing a note, she'd make it.

Entertainment was why the El Capitan was a success. That was why she and June were going to spend the afternoon reading through letters—pages and pages of them, some handwritten, some done up on an Underwood (with all the *n*'s and *l*'s faded to a slightly lighter gray), some folded around photos. All these people, young and old, wanting to start a new life in Vegas. Yep, the El Capitan was a hit. And it was the showroom that brought people in—or more to the point, Eddie Knox. Eddie Knox and those atomic bombs.

There had been a bomb detonation every five days all summer and fall. Operation Plumbbob. June called it Operation Plumb*rich*. Tourists flocked from all over the country, from Canada, from Mexico. People who wouldn't have come to Las Vegas otherwise. But everyone wanted to see an explosion. Ever since *National Geographic* had described a bright pink mushroom cloud turning purple and then orange, spraying ice crystals like an ocean surf in the sky, people had been coming. They drove up the dusty road to Charleston Peak and leaned against their cars to watch the white dawn burst against the night, or they crowded into tiny Beatty and asked the locals if the air was safe.

Afterward, they returned to Vegas, to the air-conditioned hotels and crystal-clear pools, and giddy with the awesomeness of the power they had witnessed, with the strange menace of invisible rays, they gambled more than they might have, ordered another round of drinks, splurged on a second show. When the showgirls came out wearing mushroom-cloud swimsuits and headdresses that looked like explosions, they hooted with glee, and cheered when Eddie ended his set, dead silent, and then one word: Boom.

It was fun and dare and newness. If danger lurked, the Russians, a nuclear bomb, polio, distant nations and foreign religions and dark skin, then there was also the thrill of a mushroom cloud, the sound of doo-wop, Lucille Ball, the clickety-tick of dice rolling on a craps table, feather and sequin and mirror, red lips, breasts, Mae West onstage with muscled men in loincloths, anything goes, anything went, a small town in the middle of nowhere, and already, eight million people a year coming to see what was happening.

Cora herself had little to do with the El Capitan's success. Odell and June were doing it on their own. She would help them out by going through a few applications this week, but for the most part, she stayed away from their business and their marriage. She liked her little apartment downtown, liked her habits there, and if she had learned one thing from her own son, it was that it would be better for her to leave June and Odell alone. There would be no option to rely on Cora Dibb when things got tougher.

They would get tougher.

Cora could see this already.

June didn't seem to see it. How could someone so quick not see what was coming?

Well, life was hard. For pretty much everyone. June Stein had made her bed long before she married Odell Dibb. And in the long run, marrying her grandson was going to be the best decision June ever made. Though it might be awhile before she understood that.

"I'm going to find Del. I need a backrub."

Cora thought it unlikely that her grandson would stop what he was doing to rub June's back, but he might. She hoped he would.

June left the office and headed upstairs to the casino floor. Del might be there, but she wasn't really looking for him anyway. She liked to spend time in the casino, watching the players, listening to the dealers calling for chips in, tracing the pattern of lights that swirled against the hard surfaces as the machine wheels spun dizzily. She could wander around there for hours, her stomach wobbling in front of her—a little startling to the patrons that did not know who she was—and it was good for business, her wandering. She noticed which dealers got the best action, or when a customer headed off to the bathroom at an odd moment, and whether or not the girls were getting drinks to the right gamblers.

From time to time, surrounded by the swirl and stir and smoke of this new life, June's former life would come back to her: the look of low-slung clouds as she walked down the block to school; her mother singing the blessing on Friday night, her father's hands over her head; later, the way her body had melted into Walter's, and how for a while they would couple over and over, and she would wonder if everyone could see this, in her gingerly walk if nothing else.

When she moved to Las Vegas, she was free of her marriage, free of certain expectations (not just those of others, but also her own)—free of a past she had never fully shouldered. And it was Vegas in the fifties, when it was a small town and a big town, when no one she had ever known would be likely to visit, when a young

woman who enjoyed men and adventure and the casual breaking of conventions was something of a community treasure. For a
while, this life had been entertaining—entertainment was high on
June's list of values—and when it had become less so, when June
started to notice the long, slow slide that some of the older women
had embarked on, Del was there waiting. Persistent, loyal, unlikely
Del, someone you wouldn't notice on your first pass through a
room, but who lingered in the mind later—who showed up at unlikely moments, and always with the right drink, the right idea, the
right equipment for the task—his charms grew on her.

Also, Del had a plan. He was hell-bent on running his own
casino, and he knew how to make it happen, and for some reason,
June was part of his vision. They would revamp one of the old casinos, right at the center of the Strip. They wouldn't try to compete
with the new places, but their games would be fast; he had a way
to run some tables without limits. Certain gamblers looked for
these joints. He would talk to June about it, a bit flushed, excited,
exposed in a way she never saw him exposed to anyone else. It
caught her attention.

Little by little, Del's dreams became her own. Perhaps Del was
right that they could make one of these joints go, perhaps she
would be good at it. She knew what people liked, she knew the
atmosphere they wanted, she knew what they were trying to escape and what they wanted Vegas to be. This desert, this odd town;
maybe they were June's future too. It wasn't what she had imagined for herself, but then, what had she imagined? Did lives look
sensible if you were outside them, and startling if you were in? Or
was it that some people stayed in the groove in which they were
born, while others skittered and skipped and slid unexpectedly
into a new groove? She, June, was one of those.

June and Del gave the El Capitan everything they had, and by the second year, it was growing faster than their wildest early hopes. Not every tourist was hot on the new carpet joints: the Dunes and the Flamingo and the Sands. Some liked the old-time feel of the El Capitan, especially now that she and Del were cleaning it up, now that Eddie Knox was as good as it got when it came to nightclub entertainment. Yes, Eddie. Eddie had made the difference.

She and Del had known what good entertainment would mean—how a really great act could draw people in, create the right buzz—so they had gone to Jackson Street to see who was singing in the clubs. At the Town Tavern, a pretty good singer named Earl Thurman had invited his friend Eddie, just in from Alabama, to join him onstage. And Eddie had come up, soft-shoeing across the floor, and before he had opened his mouth, before a single note came out, he had swung his hip, a small move, in perfect erotic time to the horn behind him, and June's private parts had clenched, and she had known. Known that Eddie Knox would make them all rich. She grabbed Del's hand and squeezed. This was it.

And then, the voice.

People started whooping, calling out, a woman stood and lifted her arms above her head; he wasn't even through the first verse.

After he finished singing, June and Del waited while he was introduced around. June saw the women watching Eddie, noticed that he had his arm around one and was keeping her with him even before he had stopped meeting folks, even while Earl the pretty good singer was back at another tune, and nobody was listening to him, because all the energy in the room—all the hope and buzz and sex—was already around Eddie Knox. That's the kind of impact he had.

But June and Del were there first. The only white folks in the place. The first in town to hear him. Del said he would like to talk to Eddie. They had a nightclub at El Capitan, they were looking for a regular act; could he stop by the next day? And Eddie said, "Sure, that sounds good," but June knew he might not come, because he was brand-new to town, he didn't know the lay of the land, and how could someone like Eddie Knox not know that plenty of offers would come his way, of one sort or another?

So she named a figure. An amount per week. Plus a percentage. She could feel Del about to protest, so she pulled his elbow tight into her rib, and they were friends enough, real partners, that he trusted her even though her number had surprised him. She added: "The offer lasts twenty-four hours. Come tomorrow if you want it."

June Stein. Barely twenty-seven years old. Too pretty and too featherbrained to have managed such a thing. In a crowded room, on the wrong side of town, with nothing but chutzpah to make her think she could do it. But then, she had also dived headfirst off the Haverstraw Bridge.

And Eddie was there the next day.

They pulled Mack off the kitchen, which badly needed renovating, and they put nearly the whole budget into the nightclub, into the lights and the sound and the velvet-backed booths around mahogany tables. June handpicked the girls who would serve the drinks, served some herself the first months, wearing a ten-inch silver skirt and a studded headband and a sort of bra made of a thousand tiny mirrors.

The first time Del saw her in the outfit, he drew in his breath, and the sound of that breath played in her mind for months, even years after, because she could hear the desire in it, and because it told her that Del could feel that for her, that he could be knocked off his reasonableness, his deliberations, his kindness; if she had not been in the middle of the casino, with employees around, she could have had him on the floor, right there, her way.

And they had all made money.

The figure she named for Eddie was doubled in six months. Plus, he had a take. Which was easy because they liked each other. Sometimes it even seemed like Eddie was in it with them, that he was just as much a part of the place as she and Del were. They spent so much time together, into the dawn hours after his show closed, and at dinner, which was more like breakfast for Eddie, before the act started up again.

Eddie liked to gamble, mostly on the Westside but sometimes at the El Capitan, at the back when the tables were slow. Negroes weren't allowed to gamble on the Strip or downtown, they weren't allowed in the shows, no matter who was playing. Once in a while, someone came in and said he was a friend of Eddie's, and then Del told Leo just to seat him in booth nine, where he and June sat. Del got away with these things. They were done quietly, and he had grown up here, so he had a little room in which to work.

And, of course, women liked Eddie. Sometimes he liked one of them long enough to bring her to dinner or for a drink after the show. They would sit in a private room at the back of the bar, June and Del and Eddie and whoever-she-was: a Jewish woman, a white man, a Negro singer, a colored woman. They would sit there, laughing and trading stories and sipping one another's drinks, and maybe that's why June didn't understand how things really were in Vegas; what it really meant to be Eddie or the girlfriend or any of the people working in the back of the El Capitan.

June overheard the doorman say that Vegas was the Mississippi of the West; she listened when the California tourist told his friend that even Pearl Bailey and Sammy stayed in a boarding house off the Strip, but she didn't pay them much attention. Del had grown up here, and his closest friend was colored; he and Ray Jackson had lived on the same block on North Third Street, had gone to the same elementary school, had worked the same job hauling wooden crates at the back of a downtown casino when they were about twelve. When she and Del married, at the county office in the middle of the night, laughing and excited and with a little whiskey to make them do it, Del had stopped to make one phone call. June figured he was calling Cora, but he had called Ray, and Ray made it there while they were still filling out the papers, with a ring of his wife's that he said June could borrow as long as she liked. So what the tourist said, what the doorman thought, it wasn't the whole story. She knew for herself that Vegas was not as simple as that.

Usually June's new home made the rest of the country seem slow. Hung up. Here there was money and music and gambling and sex and drinking late into the night. And all of that was the center of town, was the domain of the prosperous, was what the town celebrated; it was out in the desert sunshine, not in the back-room alleys and dark bars of New York or Chicago or LA. To June, this world felt free and fast and stripped clean of the conventions that had closed in on her in New Jersey. Hollywood stars came to Vegas to play. The richest and the newest and the most beautiful, and they were there every night; they flocked to the big casinos, and they came to the El Capitan pretty often too.

Las Vegas was the future. She saw this in the entertainment, in the way people lived, in the way the town kept growing; the future was there in the atom bombs and the magnesium plant and in the dam south of town. To see that dam, one drove a winding road up the side of a steep treeless mountain, and when June looked out the car window, down a thousand feet to an angry Colorado River, she imagined the people who had come to this desert before her: the ones who had taken the measure of Black Canyon, narrow and deep and forbidding, scorching hot, and decided that they could stop that river, they could turn it aside, they could conquer these sheer rock faces, pour three million cubic yards of cement in a raging river's path. It was extraordinary, it was inspiring—surely humans could do anything. That was the lesson June learned from her new home.

But then what about the Negroes? Cora said the bad times for colored people started when that dam got built, during the Depression. Workers poured in, from all over the country, but especially from the South: sharecroppers and farm laborers, some Negro and some white, and all dirt poor. Southern white folks brought their ideas about colored folk with them. A quarter century later, if you were Negro, you shopped and ate on the Westside, your kids went to schools without windows or floors or chalkboards, and you worked in the back of a casino as a driver or a maid or a janitor. Or your band played in a casino, for huge money, but you couldn't spend it in Vegas, because there was nothing you were allowed to buy, no place you were allowed to go. It was 1957, and some people thought things were changing in the country, but in Vegas it had gone the other direction.

Anyone could make it in Las Vegas, anyone could be a winner, just by being smart and playing the game the Vegas way. And most of the time, the Vegas way left tired old ideas in the dust, but not when it came to Negroes. When it came to Negroes, Vegas was worse than New Jersey, and June did not understand how that could be.

But even so, she and Del and Eddie did pretty much what they wanted in their own casino.

3

Three months after Marshall was born, June and Del flew to Cuba. They brought along Cora, and she watched Marshall as June learned the mambo from some dancers she met at the Tropicana, and Del talked business. By day, they sat next to the pool at the Sans Souci, or on striped loungers dug into the white sand of the beach. The air was moist and salty, and the baby was happy in his little cave created of an umbrella and a towel. People called Havana the Latin Las Vegas, and Del was thinking about the growth of the El Capitan; to June, the whole world seemed open and lovely and possible.

When they returned, Marshall got sick, and June stayed home with him and did not go to the casino at all for a week.

Del walked in mad on Thursday.

"Eddie didn't get the house."

"What? I thought it was already done."

"Owner backed out. Said his kids had gone to school with the neighbors' kids, and he just couldn't do it. Couldn't sell the house to him."

"Can he do that?"

Del didn't answer. Eddie wanted his own house. He was sick of paying rent for a shack made from wood stolen from Nellis Air Base;

for the same money, he could own a new house almost anywhere in town. But every time Eddie tried to buy a house in another part of the valley, it went off the market. All his money couldn't buy Eddie a house with hot water, or an indoor toilet, on a street that didn't turn into a muddy creek in the August rains. "Negroes like to live together" is how June heard it said. Del said, "Negroes'd like to have hot water and a decent school." But that's all he said.

It had looked like Eddie was finally going to get a house. He'd told the owner he wasn't the fathering kind, wouldn't be having any kids to send to the schools, and maybe that's why the guy had considered it long enough to tell Eddie he'd sell it to him, long enough for Del and Eddie to get the cash together. Cash deal. High dollar. But it still hadn't worked.

In the meantime, Eddie had taken to staying in the apartment at the back of the El Capitan. Del had offered it to him for nights when he didn't want to drive home, but bit by bit, Eddie had started staying there most of the time, at least the weeks when he was playing. When he wasn't playing, he was mostly out of Vegas. He flew to New York, he drove to LA, he liked to show up at a club in Baltimore, where friends from Alabama had a combo.

And he talked about Cuba. He wanted to know everything about June and Del's visit there, what they thought of the Sans Souci, who was playing at the Montmartre, what the people acted like, on the street, in the cafes, on the beach. Eddie liked to say that Cuba would be his bit of heaven.

June figured that Eddie stayed in the apartment because he'd had too many girlfriends, and the 'Side was a small community. She'd heard some of the blackjack dealers grumbling about him being at the El Capitan; how a Negro shouldn't sleep anywhere in a Strip hotel. But she didn't say anything about this to Del, and the employees got quiet when they realized she was around, and soon she never heard anything said at all. It wasn't worth telling Del and making trouble.

Also, June liked having Eddie nearby, especially now that she had Marshall. She brought the baby to the casino every day. Del had suggested that maybe she would want to stay home, join a mothers' group, meet some of the ladies in the houses nearby. And June had laughed. Having Marshall hadn't turned her into someone else, hadn't turned them into some other couple; she loved the El Capitan. So she and Del had switched offices, and she had set up a playpen and a basket and a little set of drawers in the larger one, and Marshall was growing up there with them. Several afternoons a week, when the sun shone straight in from the west and Marshall started to get fussy, she would head upstairs to Eddie's apartment at the back. Usually he was just getting up.

Eddie might not want kids, but he was a natural with a baby.

"Eddie, you're so good with him."

"Honey, I'm good with everybody. Babies, women, children."
He rubbed his nose on Marshall's chin, and the baby laughed.

"It's a black thing? Black men are good with babies?"

"Black men? We're good with everybody."

June laughed.

"Actually, I got four little brothers. And an older sister. You didn't know that, did ya?" Marshall reached up and pulled at Eddie's lip and ear. "Bertie helped Ma with the cooking and the washing, and I took care of the babies. We had some adventures, my brothers and me, because I didn't have no sense with the first ones."

"You have four brothers? Are they all in Alabama?"

"Most of 'em. We lost Jacob. He died just before I came out here."

June waited, wondering if Eddie would tell her, but not wanting to ask. Not sure she could ask.

He lifted Marshall into the air.

"How you doing, little guy? You gonna grow up in a casino, with your pretty momma and your rich daddy? You gonna run this place someday, Marshall Moses Dibb? You gonna be the rich daddy?"

Eddie was talking to Marshall in a low rumble that was almost a croon, but he didn't look at June. He didn't offer any more information about his brothers, about Jacob.

June sometimes thought that Eddie was probably just about as far from home as she was. Del belonged here. He grew up here, watching the casinos grow, seeing people move to southern Nevada from all over the country. So he was rooted in, part of the landscape, but she and Eddie, they had left different lives behind— so different that they were hard to imagine from here.

"Vegas is really different, isn't it? I mean, it's not like home."

"I don't know about that. Vegas is a hell of a lot like Alabama some days. A hell of a different, and a hell of the same. That's what I think."

June was quiet. Vegas wasn't like her hometown. She shook off the thought, and danced a few steps toward Eddie. "Want me to show you the mambo?"

"You going to show me the mambo?"

"Yeah. I got pretty good in Havana. At least, that's what people said."

She smiled her devastating June smile, and Eddie laughed. He whistled a little mambo rhythm, and she took Marshall from him. The baby laughed and waved his arms wildly, trying to clap, or catch his fetching mom's cheek. She rubbed her nose on his face, and he opened his mouth and slobbered on her chin.

"Marshall, that move is not going to take you very far."

She held the baby in front of her and swung his feet from side to side as she stepped and turned. Eddie sang a few lines. June was happy.

After awhile, she stopped dancing and set Marshall on her hip.

"Let's go home, baby man. Let's go home and make some dinner for Daddy."

Eddie looked at June straight, held her eyes a minute, but she simply shifted Marshall's weight, winked, and left.

She and Del were working late when the call came in. The count was down at the poker tables, and Del was worried that someone was running a game while he was busy at meetings in Carson City; it would be bad if one of their own dealers was in on it. All this left Del quieter and cooler than normal. He wasn't one to get worked up, but June knew he was bothered; that his mind was spinning. She had returned to the El Capitan after dinner to keep him company, and even though Marshall would have been asleep for hours by now, she was anxious to get home. When the phone on Del's desk rang suddenly, she felt slightly irritated, not alarmed. Then she heard him telling the operator that yes, June was here, go ahead and put someone through.

Del's voice dropped lower. He was asking questions. He shot a look at her across the hall, and her heart dropped. Something was wrong.

It was her father. Dead beside her mother in bed. Maybe a heart attack. Or a stroke. No sound at all. Her mom had just tried to give him a push, move him from where he had rolled in the center of their bed, and he was gone. Her mom was confused on the phone; she'd called the police, she was about to call June's aunt. She said she could hear the siren coming down the street, and hung up before June could take the receiver from Del.

June's body turned to stone. Tears trickled down her cheeks as Del repeated what her mother had said. She concentrated on the possibility that this was not true. Her mother panicked easily—how many times had she panicked at something June had done?—so perhaps her father was not dead. When the ambulance driver examined him, perhaps he would be revived. They would laugh together at the fright her mom had given her.

Del reached out to hold her, but June stood stiffly. To fold into Del would be to believe it was true, and she did not believe it. Her mom was in shock, it was the middle of the night for her, she had called before the ambulance even arrived. Del stroked her head. "June, I'm sorry," he said, and then, "June, it's true," because of course he already knew what she was thinking.

She stepped back then, and Del said he needed ten minutes before they could go home. He had to take something to the safe. He would make the flight arrangements from the house. June thought she could not bear to be alone, even a moment, but she nodded yes, and then she walked upstairs, to the back of the casino, and knocked on Eddie's apartment door.

He was getting ready for his late show, and a woman was with him. When June told him, he wrapped her in a big bear hug, and rocked back and forth. June shuddered there. She saw the surprise in the woman's eyes.

"You're going home, June. You're going home, but you'll be back. You'll be okay."

"He never saw Marshall."

She could hardly get the words out.

Eddie held her. And he hummed as he did it. Just a soft hum, and a rock.

"I didn't take him home, Eddie. We went to Cuba. But I didn't take him home."

Eddie didn't reply. Just the hum, the rock. They stood that way for long minutes, June collapsed into Eddie's rocking, and eventually the woman looked away from them, and then she left the room. When June stepped away from Eddie, they were alone. She looked at him—the tears had swollen her eyes nearly shut—and Eddie looked back, his eyes moist, and June thought that if not for Eddie, maybe she wouldn't have stayed in Las Vegas after all. Maybe she didn't like running a casino that much, and what did it mean that Eddie Knox was the person who held her while she cried on the night her father died?

4

June and Marshall were in New Jersey for two months. Marshall learned to crawl there, and June tried to share this with Del.

"How's our little man?"

"He wants to crawl. I'm trying to keep him from doing it. But if I set him on the ground, he rolls on his tummy, sticks up his bottom, and starts waving his arms and legs to get going. When I'm holding him, he flips down and reaches out to the floor. He's just set on it."

"Why would you stop him?"

"I want you to see it. I don't want you to miss this."

"It's okay, June. It's good for your mom to see. And I've got a lot going on here."

Sometimes June wasn't sure quite what Del meant. She tried to shake off the way her husband's voice on the phone made her uneasy. Del loved her, he loved Marshall, they talked every night. But there was something in his voice; some distraction even when he was saying he loved her. What did Del feel?

Marshall crawled across her mother's kitchen, started to pull himself up on the chairs, grew out of the overalls June had brought with her. And still they stayed in New Jersey. Still Del did not insist they come home. Lying awake at night, with her son asleep beside her, June thought often of her father. She remembered how it had felt to hold his dry, bony hand, and how his brow would wrinkle when he asked her about what the teacher had said, about what the neighbor had reported, about what her best friend's mother had suggested.

"June," he used to ask, "what are you thinking?"

And sometimes June would feel bad, and she wished she knew what she had been thinking, or why she had done what she did. But other times, she would flash her blinding smile, laugh, say, "Poppa, it was fun."

June's father was an amateur photographer. He had built a darkroom in the basement and spent his evenings there. When she was very small, she hadn't even known he was home. She thought he went to work after dinner the way he did after lunch. Later, when she knew he was in the basement, she'd been afraid to follow him down into it. An eerie red light glowed when he opened the darkroom door, and often it smelled as if he were striking matches, so in June's mind, the darkroom was associated with fire. In second grade, a new girl in school told June about hell, and when she described the fires where sinners would burn, howling and howling without ever being incinerated, June thought of the basement, and pictured her father, with his sore red hands, as the flaming miscreant. It made her cry. Hazel, the new girl, took this as the sign of a guilty conscience, and for the next four months, until she left the school as abruptly as she had arrived, she called June "sinner" under her breath.

Hazel frightened her, because by eight, June already had the sense that she wasn't quite good. Why couldn't she wear a dress that her mother had carefully sewn and pleated without tearing the skirt or getting ink on the pale cotton? How did she lose her book on the way to school, and why did pencils break and cups drop and pages get ripped whenever she came near? June was easily distracted by the sense of things: the rub of a neatly stitched hem on her thigh, the round, hard smoothness of that pencil, the sound of paper fibers splitting one from the other, the intoxicating scent of a pink flower shooting out of a crack in the sidewalk. The idea that her parents had somehow ended up with the wrong little girl—one who was hapless and pell-mell when they were deliberative and precise—had already formed vaguely in her mind.

The great work of her father's photography was June's own childhood: hundreds of two-inch black-and-white squares, carefully documenting a little girl with perfectly combed hair sitting at a piano, a baby lifting her dark head to stare at the white muzzle of a whiskery dog, three children dressed as Indians with feathers stuck in their headbands, a toddler resting a fat finger on the base of a flickering menorah. Her father's photos were perfect. In seventy years, they would still be detailed representations of a time hardly anyone remembered, but to June, even as a child, they spoke to her mostly as depictions of how she was meant to be: clean and silent and still, instead of rumpled and impetuous and inclined to pull at any stray thread.

And yet she had been loved. Her quiet, careful parents, not given to demonstrative acts, had somehow made this clear. She was loved.

So how could she have gone so long between visits? How could she have left them at all? She didn't know. If there was any answer, it was that she hadn't done any of it—as she hadn't knocked over the cup, as she hadn't lost her sweater—she had merely lived, from this moment to the next, in this day or that, and there had been so much to attract her gossamer attention. June didn't think forward and back in quite the way that her parents did, but when this caught up with her, when she had made some error she would never have chosen to make, if she had thought it possible for her father to die without seeing Marshall—for her father to die at all— then she grieved her lack of foresight. And again she felt like the little girl who broke the pencils and snorted at the teacher and said the wrong thing when the rabbi asked what it was that a child should do.

"June, what are you thinking?"

"Poppa, it isn't thinking at all."

So she stumbled through this time, with Marshall doing something new every week, and her mother thrilled with every sound and gesture. Now and then, her mom would pull out a jacket and say, "Would you like to take this to Del?" or "I'm going to give these shoes to the auxiliary; is that fine?"

Their days filled up with visits. Nearly everyone she'd ever known was still in Clinton Hill, but they didn't ask about her life in Nevada. Perhaps Vegas was a taboo, embarrassing to ask about, like whether or not she was a virgin when she and Walter got married (of course not) or whether Leon Kronenberg had really felt her breast (he had, more than once).

It rankled her that people found it awkward to talk about Vegas. She imagined that they looked at her and thought instead of the showgirls in Minsky's Follies. They disapproved, when topless dancers were not that big a deal, though it was amazing when they all walked out in a line, their backs to the audience, and then spun around in unison, pasties whirling. All those beautiful girls, tall, with long legs and false eyelashes—the effect was dramatic. It did surprise one.

Of course, people here would not approve of the way she and Del lived, the things they did: Marshall in his playpen in a casino, the late nights in a club, the drinks and the cash and the energy of it all. June wanted not to care about this—nobody would ever expect she did care—but it lingered in her mind.

Finally, she bought her own ticket back and didn't tell Del or her mother until after it was done. Once she had made the decision, she could feel sad about leaving Clinton Hill. Something in her responded to this place: to its gray sky, its squawk of seagulls over the bay, its light, its air, the way people talked, even the smell of the tanneries in summer. These all moved her, they were so familiar, and yet it was impossible. Vegas was her home now.

Del picked her up at the airport.

June was anxious, so her hands shook. She walked down the stairs from the plane with Marshall in her arms. He looked suddenly like a little boy, wearing red pants and a blue jacket. He had on shiny cordovan shoes, with laces, which June had bought him in New York. She was wearing a brown-and-white dress, with a wide patent belt, and a small hat pinned on the side of her head. She had given a lot of thought to their appearance. She was rarely nervous, but here she was, about to see her husband, to show him his adored son, and she felt light-headed and wondered if they were wanted.

Del was standing in the sun about twenty feet back from the bottom of the jet stairs, just behind a woman and her two children who were waiting for someone else. He looked uneasy too. He had his hat in his hands, and when he saw them, he raised it high, as if to wave them in. June relaxed and held up her hand, and Marshall dug his face into her shoulder and kicked his new shoes into her stomach. Then Del was holding them both, and he was kissing her head and kissing Marshall, and Marshall was not sure whether to laugh or cry, and June couldn't remember why she had been afraid; why she had imagined that Del had not missed her.

"Well, my grown-up man. What tricks have you got to show your dad?"

Del had Marshall in his arms, he was grinning, and Marshall seemed to remember him; he dropped his face toward Del, and their heads cracked together, like a shot. Marshall started to cry, and June made a sound, and Del rubbed his head ruefully. Then June reached up and kissed Del, and he kissed her back, and she felt the warmth of it right through her middle, and knew she was right. This was where she belonged. Where Marshall belonged. She was so glad to be home.

5

On the day Ray Jackson was killed, June was at the house with Marshall. When the door opened, she expected Del to be bringing ice cream, but instead, her husband stumbled in, looking raw and panicked in a way she had never seen. He wrapped his arms around her and cried. When he finally spoke, his words were almost unintelligible. Just for an instant, June wondered how Del would react if something ever happened to her.

He choked out that Ray had been shot—by some lousy drunk, a drifter—and June thought that Ray must have had the night's take with him. When he was in town, he took the money to the bank for Del. *It could have been Del.* It could have been Del who was shot. Later, June questioned this thought. Cora slipped that Ray had been on his way home from the bank when it happened, and Leo told the pit bosses not to bring their kids in to swim for a while.

That didn't sound like a drifter.

But that first day, when she barely recognized her husband for the enormity of his grief, June kept silent about the relief that flooded her, imagining that it had been a drifter after the take, and that somehow, incredibly, it had not been Del with the cash that morning.

Del's friendship with Ray was part of the life he had lived before her. She knew how much he meant to her husband, but she didn't really know him. He was on the payroll. Security. He went back and forth between LA and Las Vegas. Whatever Ray did for Del rarely put him at the El Capitan, and when he was there, he was formal with June. He called her ma'am, in a way that made her feel silly. She didn't want him to treat her this way, and yet she hadn't known how to make him stop. The few times she had tried, smiling or laughing or offering an inside joke about Del, he had been quiet, and she had felt embarrassed.

Ray had the capacity to be still. Twice, June hadn't even realized he was in a room with her. He was large and very dark, and June had seen him dance, sinuous and graceful. He spoke softly, even when everyone around him was excited, or in the middle of a casino floor, with the racket of dealers calling bets and coins dropping into bins. There had been only one time when Ray had treated June with any familiarity. She was pregnant with Marshall, and unexpectedly, he had placed a thick finger on her stomach and then leaned in to whisper how glad he was that she and Del would have a child. This gesture had moved June; somehow he cared for her baby.

Of course, Ray had children of his own—two or three; she wasn't sure. In all these years, she and Del had never had him and his wife to dinner, the two had never joined them at their booth in the Midnight Room. This seemed strange now, that June would not know someone Del loved so deeply, that she would have met Ray's wife only once, that she would not know his children's names or exactly how old they were. When she returned his wife's ring a few months after they were married, June suggested to Del that they all go out to dinner, but Del looked at her oddly—where would they have gone?—and said that he would send the ring over with one of the casino hosts. June should pick out some flowers, and perhaps a hat. Ray's wife liked hats.

So June had ordered an extravagantly expensive hat from New York, and she thought Del might comment on the price, but instead he simply thanked her for choosing it.

In the weeks that followed, June worried about Ray's wife and his children. She asked Del if they could do something for them, and he answered sharply that of course he already had.

"How's Augusta?" June asked, the name unfamiliar on her lips.

"Not very well," he said, in a clipped way that hurt June. After that first day, when Del had sobbed against her, he had not shared his feelings about Ray. It was as if he were angry at her for not caring in the way he cared, though she had done everything she could: sent flowers, attended the funeral, dressed Marshall in a navy-blue suit though the church was small and hot, and he had struggled fiercely to get out of her arms.

Ray's oldest child, a girl, had jumped into Del's embrace after the funeral. This startled June, and Marshall had burst into tears, so June had walked away to console him without learning the little girl's name, without getting a chance to talk to Ray's wife. She wondered if this is what had made Del angry.

If it wasn't a drifter, who was it?

Who would kill Ray Jackson? Who would kill anyone associated with Hugh?

Hugh had put up the money for the El Capitan. He lived in LA and didn't come to Las Vegas because there had been some problem in the past; some reason he couldn't return to Nevada. Ray handled things with Hugh.

June didn't like Hugh, and she had been grateful that it was Ray who took care of what the man needed, and she wondered whether Del would now be the one to go back and forth to LA to see him.

She wanted to ask her husband about this—to ask Del what Hugh knew of Ray's death, to ask him what Hugh might do in response—but Del was closed and angry these days, and she didn't dare. He had asked her to stay home with Marshall for a few weeks until things quieted down—whatever that meant—and working at home, doing the books while the new maid, Binnie, made Marshall's lunch or set him down for a nap, June wondered about Hugh.

Eddie had once asked Del about him. They'd all been drinking—even Del was a little in his cups—and Eddie asked how Del and Ray had ended up working with Hugh. June was surprised when Del answered. He never talked about Hugh, and sometimes he didn't even acknowledge that he knew him when his name came up in conversation.

Del told Eddie that it started when he and Ray were just kids, maybe twelve. Hugh had come to the casino where they worked. He was in his midtwenties, and he'd been on his own awhile. He already had a reputation.

"How much this place pay you?" Hugh said to Ray.

"Thirty cents an hour."

"And him?"

"Forty."

Hugh looked from Ray to Del and back to Ray again.

"You're bigger than your friend. How come you making thirty cents?"

Ray didn't say anything. Kept his head down.

"Shut up, Hugh," said Del.

"Shut up? You telling me to shut up?"

"Yeah. Shut up."

"Those are dangerous words, *Skinny*." Hugh moved closer to Del, near enough to speak in his ear. "You think you're safe 'cause of your friend? Your friend who isn't making as much money as you are?"

"Ray and I split our pay."

Hugh whistled. "Is that so?"

Neither Del nor Ray said a word.

"That true, Ray? He give you a nickel for every hour he works?"

"Yup."

Del stepped away from Hugh, then leaned down to pick up another crate and go back to work.

"Well, that's another thing altogether."

Ray joined Del. Hugh didn't move, just watched the two boys.

"How'd you guys like to make a dollar an hour? Each?"

"Yeah, right. You gonna pay us a dollar an hour, Hugh?" Del was mad. He didn't want any trouble with Hugh, and his grandmother would take a belt to his backside just for talking to him.

"I might. If you're up to it."

"What we got to do?" said Ray.

"Collect some tickets. That's all. Just the tickets. No money."

And June gathered that that was how it all started. Del and Ray collected the slips of paper on which people wrote down their bets, and dropped them off with Hugh at night. Somebody else collected the money. It wasn't until Del got a lot older that he ever collected any money.

By the time Vegas got too risky for Hugh—by the time he was well known for a short and dangerous fuse—he and Ray and Del had been working together for more than fifteen years. Hugh was making a lot of money, running a lot of games. But the county and the state were cracking down. They wanted to keep the feds out of Nevada, and guys like Hugh made that tougher. It was Hugh who figured out that the real money was going to be in the legal casinos; that Del should get one of the new gaming licenses, that he was the only one of the three who could.

So Del had applied for the license, and eventually Hugh put up the money for the El Capitan. Mostly he stayed in California, where he was safe from the Nevada authorities, and it was Ray who attended to whatever Hugh wanted done. For years, June had seen Hugh only in the middle of the night, in their living room, and always with a couple of men standing bodyguard.

Very early on, though, she'd met Hugh in more ordinary circumstances. He'd come to a show when she and Del were dating, and after they said their good-byes, just as he started down the street, Hugh turned and called, "You bet, Del. She's perfect. She's gonna be just perfect!"

It irritated her to remember this. The way he'd spoken as if she weren't there. Who was Hugh to say something about who Del was dating? And why had Del let him?

"I don't like Hugh," she had told Del that night. "I don't like him at all."

"Well, that's good. He's not someone you should like. But don't worry about it. You're not gonna have to worry about Hugh, darlin'."

She had liked the way Del said "darlin'."

6

At lunch, Shirley said that it was nice how colored people could sing and all, but that didn't make it right that white and colored should mix in a restaurant. Nancy said that nobody did anything when Harry Belafonte swam in the Thunderbird pool, but that the Flamingo had burned Lena Horne's sheets after letting her stay in a room. Shirley said it all came back to money: that the casinos made so much money on the colored performers, they would let them do anything. Sleep in the hotels, play at the tables; Lena Horne's kids swam in the pool all day long. Colored entertainers used to always stay in one of the rooming houses on the Westside, and then some of them had refused. They brought in so much money, what could the casino hosts do?

And there was going to be trouble, Nancy said, now there was that colored dentist saying he was the head of the N-A-A-C-P in Las Vegas. She drew out the offending letters slowly, enunciating each one, and hitting the final two sounds slightly harder.

June was silent. She was silent more and more now. Now that Del had made it clear he wasn't going to hire any Negroes for the front of the house. Del said he couldn't. It was wrong, but he couldn't fight every battle. He had to keep the El Capitan going. A lot of people's jobs were at stake. And what about all of the people that worked in the back of the house? June wouldn't be doing much for them if people stopped coming to the El Capitan.

Eddie was out of town more than he was in. Hadn't even showed up for one of his weeks in the showroom last month, and didn't even bother to explain when he came back. He looked bad. June didn't want to know what he was doing, or what he might be on.

But when he was at the El Capitan, the days Eddie stayed in the apartment, she went and found him there. Sometimes, she brought Marshall, who was two now and called Eddie "Master Knox." June didn't like this, but Eddie thought it was funny. June had wanted Marshall to call him Uncle, but Eddie had looked at her as if she were daft, so she had told Marshall to say Mister, which he had turned into Master. Now he climbed on his knee, put his fat white hands on Eddie's cheeks, and told Master Knox about the rabbits in the park.

Eddie was good with Marshall even when his eyes were shot through with red, and his clothes smelled and his hair, and even when he couldn't keep down anything June fixed.

And Eddie was good with June, too.

They didn't talk about their troubles. June didn't tell him that things were different with Del; that she was alone most of the time. Eddie never told her what was bothering him—what the women troubles were, or the money problems, or how damn sick he was of living in a town like Vegas.

June could guess. Eddie probably guessed. But what they did was race trucks with Marshall on the floor, smoke, play some fierce games of canasta, and listen to Cubop or mambo. Celia Cruz, Dizzy Gillespie, Compay Segundo. Eddie would listen to the same six measures a dozen times in a row, and then Marshall would hum the notes as he packed his toys into a basket or sat and splashed in his bath at night.

Sometimes, listening to a singer like Olga Guillot, June would lean her head onto Eddie's chest, and he would step back and say, "No, June, you're a death sentence for me. For you, it's fun. For me, it's the end."

And she would knock it off, because of course she desired him—she liked men in general, and all women liked Eddie. Also he was her best friend, and he loved Marshall, so of course she sometimes wanted him, and even thought about tempting him, because she was sure she could. But something held her back, had held her back for four years. Maybe it was Shirley and Nancy at lunch.

Del came home for dinner that night.

He didn't always. He said he had to go back to the El Capitan later, that maybe she would want to go too, catch Eddie's show. He didn't know how much longer Eddie was going to hang around; didn't know how much longer the El Capitan could keep him.

That was Del's way of telling her, she supposed.

She knew that Eddie would go—he would have to go—and she would be left here in Vegas; the place she had chosen, her place. She had cut every tie, but the bloom was off the rose, as they said. She was lonely. She was lonely and she felt stranded, and somehow it all had to do with Del, even though there was nothing she could put her finger on exactly.

"I want a baby."

"What?"

"I want another baby. I'm ready. And it will be good for Marshall."

Del was quiet.

June didn't care. She felt a little wild all of a sudden. Maybe because of what Del had just said, or maybe the way Eddie had looked that afternoon, or maybe just that she couldn't think of anything else to say. Something big enough to balance what was happening to them.

In fact, the thought of having another child hadn't crossed her mind.

It would be pretty hard to do, given that Del hadn't touched her in weeks.

He wasn't mad. They didn't fight. The other night, she had slipped into bed naked, and when he came in late, smelling of smoke and casino—the way he always did, even though he never smoked—she laid her narrow warm body close against his, lifted her leg over his hip, reached her hand around to his middle. And he stood up. Apologized. Said it had been a long day.

Well, Marshall was already in bed. Binnie never came out of her room once he was asleep.

June didn't have anything to lose.

And she didn't really want to have a conversation with Del; she just wanted him to touch her.

June smiled slyly at her husband.

"*Only you . . .*" she sang, with a slight tease.

It was the smile that worked. It always worked.

And probably Del didn't want to talk about things either.

June unzipped her dress, slid it partway up her leg, kept her eyes on Del.

She could feel his ambivalence, that resistance that was always there—that was Del, but no other man she'd ever known—but he also felt a pull. She knew that too. He smiled at her.

June ran her hands through his hair, then her finger in her own private area.

She licked.

And the deed was done. Del took her there, on the dining room rug, which felt great, which felt mad, which didn't last long, but at least they had coupled. At least she could still move Del. Later, June said she would go back to the El Capitan with him. She hadn't been in the nightclub, hadn't heard Eddie sing, in a long time. And Del thought that would be terrific, though he wouldn't be able to join her for the show. Should he send someone to their booth to sit with her? She said no, it didn't matter one way or the other. She was fine on her own.

Leo saw her before she entered the room.

"Mrs. Dibb," he said. "The boss told me you were coming. Let me take your coat. Here's your seat. Will Mr. Dibb be joining you?"

"Maybe."

"Gimlet?"

"Yes. Please. And a second."

"Of course, Mrs. Dibb. Eddie was in good form last night."

"That's nice to hear."

Eddie wasn't out yet. The band was playing low, and June watched as Leo seated the guests; the women wore long gowns and the men wore jackets and ties, handing their hats to the coat check girl as they walked in. Leo was a master at filling a room. There was an art to it: to knowing who would want a quiet booth, who would laugh and play along with the band from a front row table, how much cash someone might be willing to slip a maitre d' for special consideration. Leo's bald head shone with the effort and the heat from the stage lights, but his face was relaxed; his compact body moved easily through the crowded room.

June wondered if Eddie had a warm-up act tonight. He liked to mix it up; didn't like to be held to a plan. She and Del figured out early on that they might suddenly have to pay a singer they hadn't known they'd hired, or a bill for a set of instruments they'd never ordered. It had worked out. Their partnership with Eddie had lasted longer than most shows on the Strip, and when you figured what Eddie might have made somewhere else—how big some of those rooms were in the newer casinos—really, she and Del owed Eddie a lot. Maybe even all of it. Because Eddie Knox and the El Capitan were just a *thing*: something everyone who came to Vegas knew about, something a lot of people wanted to try. And the three of them had done it together, keeping it kind of easy, just making one another happy most of the time and not planning too far ahead.

Eddie came out alone.

The music stopped. The crowd quieted.

He looked right at June, lifted a finger to the horn player, and swiveled his hip in time to the one long horn note—the exact note, the exact swivel, of the first instant that she had seen Eddie Knox four years earlier.

Her whole body leaped.

And then he stood, silent, the horn silent, the room silent, still looking at June.

And she knew. She knew right that minute.

She loved Eddie Knox. She was in love with him, had been in love with him, would always be in love with him. She was doomed. Eddie Knox was not the man to love.

But it was total, and it was absolute, and the only thing that was notable was that she had kept it from herself for so long.

He was singing now.

A little bebop song, lips into the mike, flirting with a row of women in the right front.

He didn't look at her again.

She barely heard the show.

He was great. She could hear that. He was Eddie at his best. Not Eddie of the bloodshot eyes, not Eddie rail thin, not Eddie puking into a toilet. But Eddie as he had been, and Eddie as he was, with everything he'd learned in four years of carrying a nightclub, carrying a casino, carrying a whole certain kind of dream, night after night after night.

He was better than they'd even known.

And he sang and sang. He brought up some women to dance with him. He let an old man croon three verses into the mike. For a while, he sang from a booth on the other side of the room. And the audience knew it was a special night. They were all with him, pulling with him, hanging on his every note; they would talk about this night for years.

When it was over, nobody in the room got up to leave. They just sat there, waiting, watching. June could feel the longing. She caught Leo's eye, and he walked her out the door at the back. Her body was trembling, and she did not dare see Eddie.

Leo had a security guard drive her home; said he knew Del was working late and that she would not want to wait for him. June let him tell her what to do. She couldn't think about her husband; she didn't want to see him. Had they actually been on the dining room floor that night? Had Marshall been sitting on Eddie's lap that day? Her world spun and spun, and all these ordinary parts of it, these things that had made perfect sense, did not make sense at all. What was she doing? And what would she do now?

She didn't get the news until late afternoon the next day.

Del told her. Came home from work early again. Came in and put his arms around her and told her that Eddie had been beaten the night before; that it was bad, that it had happened behind the El Capitan. He was in the hospital, and he would probably make it, but he looked real bad.

7

They'd taken Eddie to Las Vegas Hospital on Eighth. He was at the back, in a room with six beds, and the nurse who showed June where to go mentioned that there wouldn't be much privacy. It was hard to tell what she was thinking. Perhaps she disapproved, perhaps she wanted June to say who she was, perhaps she was just a fan of Eddie Knox.

June said nothing. She wore heels and a narrow skirt and a jacket with wide lapels that she had ordered from the Bloomingdale's catalog. Eddie's bed was in the corner, and it was the only one partially obscured by curtains.

"Hey, Eddie."

He looked at her, one eye fully shut, the other open just enough for her to see his pupil rotate toward her. He looked worse than she had thought he would. As bad as she had imagined, it was worse. There was no way to tell he was Eddie, his face was so swollen, and his mouth caved in a bit where his teeth were gone. She had meant to be cheerful, but it was all she could do to hold back the shock, to keep the tears in. She sat on the small green chair next to the bed, placed her fingers oh so gently on his arm, leaned her head near his face, but did not touch. He did not move or make a sound, and it was a few minutes before she could speak.

"I'm sorry. I'm so sorry."

He mumbled then, and she strained to hear him. "Go away. Stay away from me."

"I'm not going away. I'd never go away."

"This is my doing, June. Please. You can't help me."

"I can help you. I can. Del can."

Eddie made a sound then, when she said Del's name, but she didn't know what it meant. She couldn't tell if he agreed that Del could help or not.

"Have they given you enough pain medicine? Can you eat?"

Eddie didn't answer.

June didn't try to keep talking. She laid her head on the pillow near him, her body bent awkwardly from the chair, and she stayed there, quiet, inhaling Eddie's hospital smells: antiseptic and gauze and sweat and something it took a minute to recognize as blood. Eddie didn't move to push her away, he didn't protest. They lay there, head near head, silently, a long time.

June heard someone, a nurse, an orderly, pass nearby. There was the sound of breathing, a sharper step, a slowing step. She didn't care. She didn't care what they thought, didn't care what they said, didn't care what happened next. She had been naïve about all of it, about what Eddie was up against. She hadn't spoken out when she should have, and it wouldn't have made a difference, and still, she had sat silently at lunch with her friends, she had picked this town, she had seen the Westside, she had gone to all the big shows, many times. She knew as much as anybody could know. And she had known nothing.

She had been too stupid even to know what she felt.

But this was the man she loved, and if he were lying here, in pain, in this bed, in this place where not even Del could get him a room on the second floor, then she would lie here too, and they could all say anything they wanted. She didn't care.

The nurse's voice was brusque.

"He needs rest. And he doesn't need someone laying on his pillow."

June sat up. The nurse glared. June had given birth to Marshall in this hospital. She had a private room with a window that looked out over downtown and toward the mountains. The nurses brought her apple juice with ice chips every time she asked, and they brought the baby in too. He slept in the nursery, and every three hours or so, he came in to nurse, and afterward, Del would sit in the chair and hold his boy. The sun would stream in, and the white of the bed covers and the white of the baby clothes and the blue of the sky out that window fused in her mind, and felt like happiness manifest. Until today, June had loved this little hospital with its adobe walls and its red stucco roof, and she had loved that her son was born here, in Nevada, in the West.

"He's had enough visitors for today. You're not the only one."

June sat up, pushed the green chair back from the bed, and went to stand in the corner. The nurse placed a glass thermometer in the side of Eddie's mouth, laid the palm of her hand expertly on his forehead, lifted his wrist and watched the second hand on her watch to count his pulse, then wrapped a tan rubber cord around his arm. She inserted the needle with practiced efficiency, drew two vials of blood, carefully marked each with his name, and placed the purpling beakers in a basket marked "Lab—Colored."

"He needs to rest, so you're not helping him just standing around here all day. That's what I told the other woman too."

At this, June almost laughed, and she saw Eddie's lip curl upward. He wanted to laugh too, knew what she was thinking, and so June smiled brightly at the nurse, who was, after all, good at her job, and the woman just shook her head and walked out.

June angled back to Eddie's bed, tilted her head near his battered face, and said again, "I'm so sorry."

"It's time to go."

"I want to stay. I don't care what they think."

"Please go. Please."

"Eddie, I . . . I didn't . . . I want . . ." Tears welled in her eyes, obscuring Eddie's face. She didn't know what she wanted to say. Just didn't want to leave.

He turned away. Shook his head slightly when she said his name again. And June left.

In the lobby, she picked up a newspaper and sat down to collect herself. There was another article about the NAACP. They wanted the casinos desegregated. Negroes would be able to gamble, eat, stay in the rooms. There were rumors of a march. Inside, a small notice: "El Capitan Headliner Eddie Knox Beaten, Recovering in Hospital." There was no indication of what had happened, just that the performer had been found hours after his show by a security guard from the El Capitan, who had rushed him to the hospital.

June folded up the paper and set it on the chair beside her. She didn't want to think about who had found him, how long he might have lain there. She considered the front page story instead. The casino owners would hate a march. Would hate the publicity. Del said that there were some who would die before they would serve a black man. Others remembered watching their biggest headliners take off for the Moulin Rouge at midnight, had seen people flock to the Westside casino for the six months that it was open in 1955—paying customers who walked right out of their fancy carpet joints to see a third round of late-night shows, and to play and gamble and drink in an integrated hotel. Those owners wanted the business.

"I visited Eddie today."

"I heard."

"He's bad, Del. It was bad."

"I know."

"Who did it? What happened?"

"It's complicated. I don't know, exactly."

"Exactly?" She wanted to shake him, he was so calm.

"Hey, I'm not the enemy. Eddie's been taking a lot of risks; he's been out of control for a long time. Something was going to happen."

"Out of control? Whose control?"

"June, I can't talk to you if you're going to be this way."

"What does that mean? What am I not getting? Eddie Knox was beaten to a pulp outside our hotel. *Eddie.* He could've died."

"Yeah, he could've died."

"Please. Tell me what's going on."

"It's better if you don't know."

"Can't you protect him?"

"He's gotta get out of town. He's gotta stay away."

"Because you can't protect him?"

"Obviously I can't."

"What about Hugh? Have you talked with Hugh?"

She and Del never talked about Hugh. For a split second, he looked startled that she had said his name. Then he shook his head.

Looked straight at her and said slowly, "Hugh isn't going to protect Eddie Knox. That's the last person to protect him."

June did not want to dwell on Hugh. But Del had to understand.

"We have to do something. We owe Eddie. After all the money he made for us. And . . . he's Eddie."

Del didn't answer right away. June knew she was pushing too far; that he was composing himself because he was angry.

"I don't owe Eddie Knox. We had a business deal, and we both made money. He made his own choices after that."

"I don't even know who you are. A business deal? That's what you call it?"

"That's what it was."

"I know you care about Eddie. I know he's not just a business deal to you."

Del said nothing. Got up and walked out of the room. June heard him talking to Marshall, offering to go outside and toss him a ball.

Leo told her what he had heard about the NAACP threatening sit-down demonstrations, but he said nothing about Eddie. Nobody said anything. Not if it was drugs. Not if it was gambling debts. Not if it was a woman. Not even if it was Vegas. Eddie was always going somewhere on the weeks he was off. And June didn't care, really. It didn't matter what it was.

Every day, she visited him at the hospital.

Some days he was glad to see her, and other days he asked her to leave. Told her that she was making it worse. That he had earned what he got, and she had to stay away.

After two weeks, they were ready to let him out. Eddie didn't want to tell June what his plans were, just that he was going away, would lay low awhile. Del had already negotiated a new headliner act, a band that had appeared at the El Capitan before. But Eddie was really banged up, both his arms were broken, the vision in one eye wasn't back yet. He couldn't take care of himself; he couldn't move somewhere on his own.

June approached Del after dinner, when he was reading the paper and sipping a whiskey sour.

"I've told Eddie to come back to the apartment for a few days. He can't leave yet."

"That's a bad idea."

"What do you suggest?"

"He's got family in Alabama. He can go there."

"I've already told him that we agree. That he can come to the apartment."

"And he believed you?"

"He said he would come. He said he'd be out of there fast, that he had to be."

"Okay, June. You're on your own here. He stays there. He doesn't come out. He doesn't come out of that apartment until he's headed out of town."

"I'll tell him."

"And Marshall doesn't visit him."

"Marshall loves Eddie."

"Marshall's never going to see Eddie again. That's a deal breaker. Marshall does not go to that apartment."

She had gotten as much as she could. And she hadn't really thought about Marshall and Eddie anyway. She didn't want him to see Eddie the way he was now. But what Del said: that their son was never going to see Eddie again. Never. She couldn't think that far ahead; couldn't think about next month. June needed to take care of Eddie right now. She couldn't bear that he would leave, and she would never have any chance to show that she understood—that she finally understood—what he meant when he said she was a death sentence; what it meant that Nancy and Shirley didn't want to sleep in a hotel room that someone colored had slept in. She had known all of this, she had known all of it, but she had not understood what it meant.

And that's where it happened. Maybe that was predictable. But it wasn't what June was expecting, it wasn't what she had planned, it wasn't why she brought Eddie to the apartment for those days.

He needed a lot of help. He couldn't get dressed on his own. Couldn't wash himself. Del didn't say anything when June had one of the maids take a night shift in Eddie's apartment. He didn't say anything when she left Marshall with Cora all day, and when she disappeared most of those days into that apartment.

In Del's mind, this was a problem that would go away on its own, that would disappear when Eddie did, and one of the reasons he was so good at running a casino was that Del didn't take on problems that would solve themselves. He kept the focus on what he needed to do. If Del wondered what June was doing, he didn't say it.

At first, June felt uneasy in the apartment with Eddie.

She had spent so much time there; she and Marshall had spent hundreds of hours there.

But now it was different.

Different because Eddie was vulnerable, different because he needed physical help, different because he had been beaten, and he was afraid, and he did not sparkle with energy and optimism and confidence—everything that had made him Eddie Knox, and everything that was probably the reason he was sitting there, broken, defeated, unsure.

But different as well because June had never been this close to Eddie when she was in love with him, or when she had known she was in love with him.

Had she ever been in love with anyone? She loved Del. She loved him even now. But had she ever been in love with him? Had she ever trembled with the possibility that he did not love her? Had she ever felt the terror of being in love with someone, knowing what one would risk for that feeling—for an instant of that feeling?

Until now, she had thought that love felt like power.

They were talking about Marshall. June told Eddie that her son had decided to become a robber. He said he liked robbers better than soldiers, better than pilots, better than cowboys. He said he would grow up and be a robber and steal all the money, and he would be rich, and he would give some to June and to Del and to his grandma. Also, robbers used swords. So everything in the house had become a sword. A towel could be a sword. He would plant his feet wide apart and challenge his dad to fight with "*sowds.*"

Eddie laughed.

"Jacob liked to fight with swords too. Almost took my eye out once, when he was about five."

June felt the tears in her eyes. She didn't know why. Eddie hadn't mentioned Jacob with any sense of pain, he hadn't ever told her anything more about his brother. But everything felt fragile right then, everything important teetered, a rounding drop about to fall, glistening with light, an instant before dissolution.

Eddie reached over, caught one tear with a finger that emerged from a graying cast, and June leaned in, and finally, after four years, they kissed. It was as sweet and demanding a sensation as June had ever experienced. And if their lovemaking looked awkward from a distance, with Eddie's casts, and his bruises, and the difficulty in finding just how to move, just where to embrace, it didn't feel awkward. It felt tender and absolute, exhilarating and unyielding, inevitable, glorious, terrifying, gentle. And when it was over, they lay tangled on Eddie's bed, and they kissed more, and they tried to say words, but then they kissed, and they made love again, and this is what they did, pretty much all they did, in those hours—for those days—in which June was in that apartment, and Marshall was at his great-grandmother's, and Del ran the casino.

June knew that it would end, though she told herself that something would happen. There would be a way; she would take Marshall and go with Eddie. Something. It was not possible that she would never see him again, and they did not speak of it. Then on Friday, Del asked her if she would like to have coffee with him before she went to see Eddie, and Mack asked if she had seen the plans for the new card room. By the time she got to the apartment, Eddie was not there. Some of his clothes were gone, and his wallet; and he was gone too. No note.

8

She was five months pregnant.

It might be Del's.

She and Eddie had been careful. She and Del had been on the dining room floor. The doctor's due date split the difference between these events—a perfect split, though she had given him no dates.

It had to be Del's.

They planned as if it were Del's.

Del never asked her anything about Eddie.

Of course, she had asked Del. She had gone straight to Del when she found Eddie gone, demanding to know where he was, whether Del had shipped him off, why he had asked her for coffee that morning.

Del had been patient, and then been annoyed, but all he'd said was that they both knew Eddie had to leave—there was never any doubt about it—and didn't she realize he could have ended up dead?

"Is he alive? Do you know he's alive?"

"He's alive."

"Where?"

"I don't know where. But he'll start singing somewhere. We'll know."

"Will you tell me?"

"Yes."

And six weeks later, Del had told her. Eddie was in Cuba. Things were a little different there than they had been, but Havana was still a great place for him. He could work. He'd do well. He'd been smart to get out of the country.

And that's all Del would ever say. He made it clear he would not speak of Eddie again.

And maybe June could have chipped away at that resolve, but by then, she knew she was pregnant and she was calculating the odds, and wondering whether Del would ask, and wondering what she wanted—what she really wanted—except she knew. She knew the baby had to be Del's.

She wrote Eddie a letter. Mailed it to a casino in Havana after she overheard a guest saying he was appearing there. She didn't say much in the letter. Just wanted to know that he would get it, that they would be able to stay in touch.

She thought about the letter every day. Where it might be, what day it would arrive in Cuba, how long it might take to wind from the casino's mailroom to Eddie. Did he have a regular gig? Had he appeared only once? Would they know how to forward it to him?

But one day, Del dropped the letter on the desk in the study.

"You can't write him."

"How did you get this?"

"No letters."

She stared at the envelope. It hadn't been opened. She'd put it in the mail slot to be delivered; how had Del gotten it? But, of course, he could get to any mail in the casino. If he were watching it, if someone at the hotel were watching it. Her face flushed hot.

"I'm not messing around," Del said. "Eddie Knox is out of our lives. No letters, no phone calls. Don't cross me on this."

Don't cross him? Del had never spoken to her in this way. It was a tone of voice she had heard him use only in rooms with men talking about cardsharps. He had no right to speak to her like that. Hot fury coursed through her.

"You're going to have a baby." Del's voice was strained, in a way June almost never heard it. "We have Marshall."

Was it a threat? Did he also wonder about this baby inside her? Even as they repainted the nursery, even as they told Cora that a little girl would be named for her, even as he ordered bottles of champagne?

She had betrayed Del.

She had betrayed him, and he might know it, and he had allowed it, and maybe even he had understood. And that was worth something. But still, he didn't have the right to stop her letters. He didn't have the right to speak to her in this way.

She took the car and drove.

It often relaxed her to drive without knowing where she was going: to get in the Chrysler and drive west, toward the mountains (she might not stop until the sea); or north, toward the proving ground (she might watch a nuclear bomb explode); or east, toward the rest of the country (she might go home to her mother). Today June drove up Charleston until the road turned to dirt, and then aimlessly back on Sahara. She crossed over the Strip, and turned on Maryland Parkway before remembering that a school was right there and the children would be leaving now. Sure enough, a nun in full habit stood in the street holding a stop sign. June turned at the corner before the walkway, thinking she could avoid stopping, but it was not a street, just a drive into a small parking lot. She turned off the car. A giant oleander bush, with its hot-pink flowers finally fading and wilting and starting to drop, blocked her view of the building. She breathed in and thought.

It was possible that Del knew about her and Eddie. How could he not, when she had been so wild last spring, when she cared not a whit what anyone thought; when the sight of Eddie lying un-recognizable in the hospital bed had driven her mad? Del was not someone who needed to share what he was thinking. Of course he knew. He must have known then. He had said nothing.

What sort of husband would say nothing?

It was unbearable to think of never seeing Eddie again. But what other choice was there? She and Del owned the El Capitan. They had Marshall. She was pregnant. There had to be another choice.

There wasn't another choice.

The fury with which she had taken the car and started to drive had already begun to ebb. Now, in this strange little parking lot, with pink flowers draped lasciviously across her window, June felt a thick heaviness descend. For an instant, she wanted to close her eyes and stop. Stop everything. Sit in this car until something forced her to go. Anything not to move.

There was only one way to play this hand, and Del had already figured that out. She had trouble gripping the steering wheel. Del had known before she did. But he was right. She would have to accept this.

June started the car and nearly backed into a man walking be-hind her. She heard his startled "Whoa!" and saw him in the rear-view mirror.

"Oh, I'm so sorry. I didn't look."

"No harm done. I hopped."

He was young and very good-looking. He wore a priest's collar, and June realized that the parking lot probably belonged to the church or the school next door.

"Thank you. I was thinking about something. I'm really sorry."

"Do you need anything? Were you here to see someone?"

"No. I . . . I pulled in because the children were crossing the street. And I got distracted. "

"It's not a problem, but if you wanted to talk with someone, I'm here. Father Burns, at your service."

His blue eyes twinkled.

June couldn't think of anything to say.

"Or you could talk to Father Fahey?" He seemed embarrassed that he might have been forward.

"Oh, no. I'm Jewish. I didn't even know I'd pulled into a church."

"Well, we're happy to talk with anyone. Even Jews." He smiled when he said this.

Why would someone who looked like him be a priest? She hesitated a moment, because suddenly she *did* want to talk with someone. Someone who would hear the whole story; someone who might understand. Weren't priests sworn to secrecy?

He waited.

He was so young. No. She didn't need to talk to a priest. She was June Stein. She knew what she had to do.

"No, I just made a wrong turn. Thank you, though. Sorry." She was starting to babble.

"Sure," he said easily. His eyes flitted to her rounded belly, and June thought, maybe he could bless the baby. Which was a strange thought, and unsettling. She drove away quickly.

If she hadn't had those days with Eddie, then she might never have noticed certain things that Del did. The way he answered the phone in the study, even if the hall phone was closer. The way that Leo or Mack sometimes told her where Del was before she had asked. Even the smell of sweat, of salt, on his skin: some nights she noticed it, some nights it caught her attention, but she couldn't put her finger on why.

And one day, when Mack offered to drive her home because Del would be late, June asked.

"Is he in a meeting? Do you know where he is?"

Mack wasn't expecting this, and there was a split second between her question and his answer, a second imprinted on his face; a moment where he recalibrated what she had just asked and how he would reply.

"He had a meeting with some guys from the golf course. It's a charity event for that new school on Sahara."

June didn't answer. She didn't look at Mack. He was loyal to Del, and she didn't want him to know what she had seen in his face. When he drove up to the house, she said lightly, "Marshall's going to be so excited. Del told me your car was a rocket, and Marshall thinks it *is* a rocket."

"Should I give him a ride?"

"He'd love it. Let me go and get him."

She tried to decide if it mattered to her. What she felt. She wondered how long it had been going on. She'd noticed things only in the last month or so, but the truth was, she hadn't been looking for anything. Before having her own secret, June hadn't considered what a secret looked like.

But who?

Del didn't seem to pay particular attention to anyone at the hotel. In fact, she couldn't remember any time when she had noticed Del notice someone. She had noticed Eddie notice, from the first night she met him. It was an instinctive part of being around him, the way women looked at him, the subtle ways he indicated interest back. She'd practically done a study of it, long before she had admitted she cared. She and Del had sometimes mentioned it; heck, she and Eddie had laughed about it. So June tried. She tried to remember a time when Del had suddenly noticed a woman, and she could not.

Nor did she see it now. Now that she was watching for it.

He was a cool cat, Del. He played a long game, following beginnings out to their possible endings, and adjusting course before his competition knew the race was on. June knew this about him. Perhaps she hadn't fully considered what it might mean for her.

Well, he wasn't tougher than she was. She could play a long game too.

And did it matter if Del was seeing someone? Maybe it mattered if he were in love. But if he were, he'd missed his opportunity to move June out. And it wasn't like Del to miss an opportunity he wanted.

So who was she?

June smelled something, a different salty, sweaty something, on his skin.

9

June's pregnancy stretched into the long, slow months, and she experienced the world as simultaneously leaden and diaphanous. There was the not knowing whose baby she carried, there was the knowledge that her husband was capable of hiding things from her that she would not have been able to hide from him, there was the small boy who chattered at her side, there was the extraordinary sensation of a new person shifting within her. And then there was Eddie: the way his face had been swollen, how his skin had tasted, the words he had said, what she had felt in that room with him. All of this echoed in her mind, night and day.

In November, Cora stopped by the El Capitan to have lunch with June. They sat outside because the weather was warm, and June arched her neck to feel the sun on her face. Del's grandmother wore an olive green hat and carefully positioned herself in the shade, though her deeply lined skin revealed decades lived in the desert.

"Del's pleased about the baby. He thinks it's a girl." Cora slipped a cigarette between her lips, offered another to June, then placed the pack on the table where she could easily reach for it.

"Yeah, he's sure it's a girl. He says I look different than I did with Marshall."

"I don't see that, really."

"I feel different. I feel bigger. Like a car."

"You carry your babies right up front. From the back, you don't even look pregnant."

"Well, from the side . . ."

"From the side, you look pregnant."

"I look like a car."

"Or a train."

June snorted. Cora could make her laugh.

She was huge. Twice, she'd hit her stomach on the side table. She grew so fast, she couldn't figure out where her body started and stopped. Marshall could crouch directly under her belly, and she couldn't even see him. She'd told him this, and after first saying "I don't like it, Mommy, I don't like to be inbisible," he decided it was funny. He would slip underneath her and yell, "Daddy, look! Mommy can't see me here."

And then he would peek out, give her a long sideways glance—his lashes so lush they looked fake—and say, "Hi, Mommy. It's your Marshall."

In the evenings, June sometimes lay next to Marshall in his bed. Stroking her belly with his fat, soft fingers, he placed his ear on her stomach and said, "Can you hear me, baby? Can you hear me, my brother?" One time Del was there and whispered, "What if it's a sister?" And Marshall said, "It's not."

Which was why June tended to think it was a boy too.

She did feel different this time. Not just wider. But different. She was queasy every day.

Still, it seemed as if Marshall might know. Her son was so aware of the baby. He would talk to him while he played with his cars, or ask if the baby liked what June was eating. Maybe almost-three-year-olds had some special knowledge. From the day he was born, June could sometimes look in his eyes and think that he saw things, that he knew things, she didn't see or know.

"Daddy, is Chuck coming?"

"Chuck?" June asked.

"A runner at the Sands," Del told her. "He brought some papers here last week. You were home."

"Oh, yeah. I didn't see him."

"Chuck has red candy, Mommy."

Del winked at June.

"That's right. He had candy. He gave Marshall a piece. I might have told him not to tell you."

June smiled. She had thought there might never be a time like this again. And yet here it was. Even after Eddie. Even after Ray. An easy moment, just the three of them. It was Marshall who made this possible. And maybe there would be more moments like this. Maybe they would come more often. She placed her hand on her stomach and found the lump of her baby's foot. *Please*, she whispered to herself, *please*.

Marshall stood up on the bed and jumped.

"Hey, little man," Del said. "Let's read a book."

"*I Know a Lot of Things*! Let's read *I Know a Lot of Things*."

"That's just the one I was going to get. Up you go."

And Del carted Marshall off to the big chair where they liked to read, and June got up and poured herself a glass of wine. Then she straightened up the kitchen, and thought about two little boys, riding their bikes, and kicking a ball, and going off to school hand in hand.

Her pains came early.

The baby was Del's.

That was her first thought.

She waited with them through the day, and when they seemed to ebb at dinnertime, she didn't mention them to her husband. She'd had contractions for a month with Marshall, and it was early. Del put Marshall to bed, June ran a bath. Getting into the tub was a bit of comedy; things like this made her laugh. She concentrated on her balance as she stepped in, but from the corner of her eye, she could see the absurd watermelon of her stomach, and the dark line that divided it vertically. It was funny being human.

It happened all at once. The baby kicked, her belly contracted sharply, her foot slid on the damp tile floor. Painfully, bent forward, June started to fall, grabbed wildly at the air, caught her legs on either side of the bathtub rim, and slipped sideways into the tub. A surge of water landed on the floor. She could not catch her breath. Her stomach hurt, her private parts hurt, she had twisted her back, she was panting heavily, afraid. She gripped the edge of the bathtub and pulled herself upright, willing herself to relax. Breathe. Relax.

A contraction came again, so sharp she let out a sort of whistle. This didn't feel the same as Marshall. She'd had an easy birth. He'd come quickly. Dr. Bruno had said she was made for giving birth; that not many women had such a simple time with a first child.

Again, a contraction.

"Del!"

"Del!"

Where was he? He couldn't have left. Had he fallen asleep next to Marshall? Suddenly Marshall's new room all the way down the hall seemed like a terrible choice. They couldn't leave Marshall on the other end of the house. What if he cried, and they didn't hear him? Another contraction. June gritted her teeth and watched it grip its way across her belly. It was something separate from her, this force that kneaded her from within, that was making it so hard to breathe.

She couldn't stay in the tub. Were babies born in tubs? Hadn't she read that? Well, she couldn't stay in. She'd drown if she slipped underneath; if she loosened her grip on the rim. June was beginning to panic, the panic was rising in her, she couldn't stop it. She could drown, the baby could die, was the baby coming, why was this so different from Marshall, where was Del, couldn't he hear her, if she tried to get up, she might fall, she would fall, she could hit her head, what would happen to the baby? And another contraction. And another. What was this? Her body was bucking in the tub, and she was screaming, and holding onto the side, and suddenly, finally, there was Del.

"June! What's happening? Is it the baby?"

"The baby's coming! I feel his head. He's coming right now."

"He can't be coming. You haven't even been in labor. Just breathe. Take a breath. I'll get you out of the tub."

June screamed.

Del lifted her, wet and slippery and awkward, her belly bucking again, again, from the tub. He wrapped his arms around her shoulders, held her upright, half carried her, half walked her toward their bed, murmuring, "It's okay. It's okay, June. We did this before. I'll call the doctor. I'm going to set you on the bed, and I'll call Dr. Bruno, and you're okay, we did this before."

The bathtub was pink and red with blood, her legs ran with blood, there was blood on the floor, there was blood on Del's light-brown pants. June closed her eyes. It was too early. It was too fast. Something was wrong. She had never felt this kind of terror.

Del laid her on the bed and piled the pillows behind her. When the contraction came again, he held her shoulders with his hands and stared right into her eyes. He said, "You can do this June. It's okay. We're having a baby. It's going to be okay." And she was hoping he was right: they were having a baby, this was somehow normal, but she was also afraid, and she had lost control of her body, and this baby wanted out, and Del needed to call the doctor, and she needed to get to the hospital, and how would she possibly get to the hospital? Would they take her in an ambulance? Oh, the pain. Would the baby be born in the ambulance? Was the baby okay? This was not what she had planned. Why was this happening so fast?

"I'm scared."

"I know you are. But you're okay. I'm going to call the doctor. I'm just going to the hall. I'm calling the doctor."

Another contraction came, and this time June felt the head. She remembered Marshall's head, and there was no doubt: she could feel the baby's head.

"He's coming! He's coming now."

"June, I'm just going to call the doctor."

"Now!"

And she arched her back, and gave one great long push, and the baby's head was out; she could see the wet black crown between her legs, but not his face, and she was crying, and Del was saying, "Oh! Oh!" and he was holding the baby's head, and now he was afraid—more afraid than she was—and she pushed again, and the baby turned slightly in Del's hands, and then his shoulders slipped out, and then one last push, and he was free: a glistening, perfect Negro girl.

The next seconds were all feeling—exhilaration (a baby), shock (this was not Del's baby), chaos (June's body was still heaving, she was pushing, there was everything else to be born)—and Del was gripping the wet, slippery baby, and he was crying, and he was holding the cord and watching as everything else came out. He looked at June, and there was so much there, in that look, in that instant; June would never forget it. And then the baby hiccupped, and Marshall opened the door, said: "Mommy, I'm scared."

Somehow, Del put the baby in her arms, and he hoisted a fascinated Marshall on his hip, and went to the hall to call Dr. Bruno, but he didn't call an ambulance. And Dr. Bruno, who had known Del since he was a child—since Del's grandfather Nathan had helped him lay pavers in his carport—came by himself. He cut the baby's cord, and he washed her gently, and squeezed something into her eyes, and estimated that she was small, perhaps six pounds, but healthy. He left the baby at June's breast, with Marshall asleep on the pillow beside her, and he and Del went in the living room. June could hear the low rumble of their voices, and the doctor giving Del instructions, and Del saying something else. The conversation lasted awhile.

For three days, June and the baby stayed in the bedroom. Del did not go to work. He took care of Marshall, and of June, and of the baby. They didn't say anything about a name. He didn't call his grandmother. Nobody from El Capitan phoned, at least that June heard. She wouldn't have thought it possible that the three—no, four—of them could live entirely in a bubble alone, even for three days, but they did. Dr. Bruno came each afternoon. He was cheerful. He said nothing about the baby's skin, her hair, her face. He didn't ask her name. He came to see June, and he checked her carefully, and he was kind to all of them, but he didn't say anything.

Marshall stayed in the room with them for hours. He brought in all his cars, and his stuffed animals, and his favorite books. He chatted to his "brother sister" as he always had, telling her which car was fastest, which one she could drive, how many races he had won. He liked to watch the baby while she nursed. He would stroke her head, and say, "Did I do that, Mommy? Did I eat you too?" And June would pull his blond curls away from his forehead, and nod, and say yes, Marshall had done everything just like baby.

Marshall seemed to think her name was Baby, and did not ask for any other.

Del was the most surprising. He held the baby tenderly. He sat and rocked with her in the chair in the nursery, and June could hear him humming, and she could hear him talk to the baby while he changed her diaper, while he carefully washed the skin around her cord, while he jiggled out a burp.

He did these things with love.

This was what June remembered.

This was what she would cling to for all the years after. How Del had loved the baby. How Del had been tender.

And for three days, they lived in this way, and Del did not say anything about how the baby looked or about Eddie, and June began to believe that it was going to be okay—that as impossible as it seemed, this too was going to be part of the deal between her and Del.

Perhaps they were never going to speak of it. Perhaps it would just be this little girl, a little bit different, who was their daughter, who was Marshall's sister. Would they name her Cora? Did Cora know yet?

On Sunday June dared to hum to the baby. Until now, she had cared for her almost in silence, talking with Marshall as he played, answering Del's questions about what she needed, but caring for the baby, holding her, nursing her, dressing her, washing her, in silence. It was as if her voice could break the spell, and she couldn't risk it. But by Sunday, she'd begun to relax. She loved Del more than she had ever imagined she could love him. And even the love for Eddie seemed small, seemed tawdry, next to this: next to a husband, a proud man, who was singing to their baby girl—their Negro baby girl—in her nursery.

But that night, Del came into the bedroom with a basket. She had never seen it before. A baby basket, with a beautiful pink blanket. And her heart stopped.

"No."

"There's no other way, June."

"No! Never. This isn't the Middle Ages. You can't take my baby."

"I can take Marshall."

June was standing, her body swaying, unsteady beneath her.

"Del, you can't possibly mean this. You wouldn't do this."

"What do you think we should do, June?"

"Keep her. What do we care what people think? What do you care?"

"What about Marshall?"

"What about him? I don't want him to be like these people anyway. You don't want him to be that way."

"That's not the point. What about Eddie?"

"He's in Cuba. He doesn't even have to know."

Del shook his head then. He looked away from her as she said, "It's better if he doesn't know. It's safer for him."

"Nothing's safe for him now. Not now. Not with her." He motioned to the baby. "This he would not survive."

"But why? If you accept it?"

"It's not what I accept. It's the way it is."

"No. No, Del. I will *not* give her up."

"You will, June. You will. We will."

"No!"

She was crying, she was shrieking, she was holding on to him, with the basket in his hands, with the baby now in it. Marshall wasn't home. He had taken Marshall somewhere. He had known how this would go.

But Del didn't take the basket out the door while she was crying, while she was screaming.

Like a man shot, he folded. His back to her, he was standing, holding the basket, and then suddenly, he set the baby on the ground, and folded to the floor. She could hear him start to cry, and then to sob. His sobs came in convulsive bursts, and June crumpled to the floor next to him, and they sobbed until they were spent, until the baby woke up. Until one of them—it was Del—lifted her from the basket, and she nursed, and they cried together watching her.

And then Del took the baby from June, and he bundled her softly in the basket, and June watched, depleted and desperate and silent, and then Del kissed June's head, and her tears came faster, faster, and he stood, and he took the basket out the door.

Dr. Bruno came the next morning and showed her how to bind her breasts. He had kept Marshall for the night; he had known what Del was going to do.

The day after, the doorbell rang and the first of the bouquets arrived. "In Sympathy." "For the Loss of Your Baby." "In These Sad Times."

Cora came over, but June drew the line. She told Del that she didn't care what he said, what lies he told, but Cora could not come in. Nobody could come into the house; she would see nobody. She let Cora take Marshall for a few hours every day.

June understood that she owed it to Marshall to stay alive; the thought of him without a mother was unbearable. But for now, that was all she could do. She was not capable of anything else. She didn't want Del to tell her what he told people about her, she didn't want him to tell her how Marshall had reacted, she couldn't bear to think of the questions or the answers.

One day, she was able to ask Del where their baby was.

He said it would be better if she did not know.

She said that she could kill him as easily as look at him.

He didn't flinch. But he told her. The baby was in Alabama. With one of Eddie's brothers. He was a nice man. It was a nice family. They hadn't asked many questions. Del had given them money. A lot of money. He would give them more.

"Then Eddie knows."

"I don't know. They haven't talked to Eddie in years. But they know she's Eddie's daughter. And they're nice people. Two little boys."

And June thought about the two little boys she had imagined. Riding bikes. Playing ball. Heading off to school hand in hand.

10

"Baboooppboop booopp booopp."

That was good. That felt good.

He could hear it. And the little heat in his veins, that was good too.

The room tilted oddly, faded and blurred, moving. That was okay too. That was like being in the bath. Warm and woozy.

And someone was yelling.

"Eddie!"

"Eddie!"

"Eddie, shit."

Stop yelling at me.

"Eddie, damn it."

"Eddie, again?"

"Goldarn it, Eddie."

Someone was always yelling. Women were always yelling.

Mama. The teacher. Wanda and Bertie and Patricia, and on and on and on. Some woman. Mad at him.

He didn't want to hear those voices.

He took another drink. Another.

The room tipped the other direction.

His blood still ran warm. It was good.

He could feel his pants, wet where he had probably pissed himself, and his shoulder against something that protruded hard from the wall, but these didn't matter. He felt these things, but they didn't bother him. Like the voices: he heard them, but they didn't hurt.

"Eddie, your daddy gonna get hanged. That's what my daddy says. Your daddy gonna hang."

Not that voice.

"Eddie, Daddy's gone away. Daddy had to go away."

Not that one.

"You nigga shit. You think you something? You think you can sing?"

Not that voice.

"Get your hands off her. Get your hands off before I count one, or you're a dead man."

"Eddie, don't go."

"Eddie, don't leave me."

"Eddie, I'm pregnant."

"Eddie, he'll beat me."

"Eddie, stay."

"Eddie stay, Eddie stay, Eddie stay."

"God gave you that voice, child. God gave you that voice."

"Whew. That cat can sing. That is some singing."

"Eddie, can I sing with you?"

"Eddie, sing in church."

"Eddie, that is the Lord's voice."

"Eddie, what you singing with that voice the Lord gave you?"

"Eddie, where'd you get that? Where'd you get that money, where'd you get that bottle, where'd you get that girl, where'd you get that dope, where'd you get that voice, where'd you get that face, where'd you get that song? Eddie, where'd you get that?"

"Eddie, where you been?"

"Where were you all night?"

"Don't come around here, you gonna be singing that stuff."

"God gave you that voice, and you give it to the devil?"

"Eddie, can you sing for me?"

"Eddie, will you sing?"

"Eddie, make it better."

"Eddie, I got something for you."

"Eddie I got money I got pussy I got champagne I got money I got dope. Eddie, Eddie, Eddie, will you sing?"

11

Marshall refused to go to school. He locked his feet against the floor of the car, wrapped his hands around the loop over the door, and elevated his six-year-old body like a two-by-four above the seat. Everyone in the drop-off zone heard him screaming. "No, no, no! I won't go! I'm not going to school, Daddy!" Plenty of them heard Del begging Marshall to calm down, offering him a new GI Joe tank, threatening to spank him. There he was, Del Dibb, in a white Cadillac, arguing with his six-year-old son in front of John S. Park Elementary School, and wondering if he could wrench him out of the car without hurting him. And then what?

Marshall had picked a really tough day. Binnie had gone to help her sister recover from a surgery. Cora was in Texas, visiting a cousin Del didn't remember having. He had meetings scheduled all morning, and he had to be at the county commission hearing that afternoon, and he was already late, since he wasn't expecting to have to fix Marshall his breakfast and take him to school.

Of course, June was home. She was swimming. Had wandered downstairs while Marshall was eating a bowl of Cocoa Puffs. "Good morning, Mommy!" Marshall had said, but June looked at him as if she had never seen a child before, and then said, wearily, to no one in particular, "I'm late to start my mile, and I wonder if there will be any fish in the water."

Del had not thought to look at Marshall's face.

What Del had noticed was that June was calm. It was a relief that she was calm.

So he had raced, trying to get Marshall ready, on the phone with Leo about how to handle his first appointment, feeling a little sorry about the Cocoa Puffs, though Marshall was pleased. He had said, "Thanks, Daddy!" in his sweet, high voice, and then a rich brown stream had slipped out of his mouth and onto his pale-blue shirt.

But now Marshall was lodged in the front seat of the car like a stick in a cog, and Del was out of options. He couldn't leave his son home alone with June.

"Okay, Marshall. You'll have to come to work with me. But I have meetings, so you'll have to stay with someone else."

"No, Daddy, no! I'm not going to work! I'm not going!"

"Marshall, what are you doing? What do you want?"

"I don't want to go to school! I don't want to go to work! I won't, I won't, I won't!"

"I have to go to work today. Grandma's in Texas. Binnie's sister is sick. So you have to go to school, or you have to go to work with me. Now which is it?"

"I want to go home!"

"You can't go home!"

Marshall screamed. He screamed so long that he started to choke, and then he threw up, brown Cocoa Puffs all over the clean shirt and his pants and the front seat of the car.

Del gave up.

"Okay, Marshall. We're going home. It's okay, buddy. It's okay. We're going home."

Marshall pulled his knees to his chest, and rode home with his cheek resting on his knees, looking at his dad.

"Buddy, I know it's tough. But you got to pull it together. A man has to do the right thing. He has to go to school, he has to go to work."

Marshall just stared at Del, expressionless, his eyes rimmed in red. He didn't look away.

When they got home, Del called Leo and told him he wouldn't be in. Send Mack to the commission meeting. Tell him to handle things the best he could. Things at home had come to a head, so he didn't know when he'd be in. Screw it. He'd make this up to him. Then Del sent Marshall in to find clean clothes, and walked outside looking for June. She was there, stretched out on the lounger, her body still wet from her swim.

"June."

She didn't answer, didn't open her eyes.

"Marshall wouldn't go to school today. He's upset. You didn't say anything to him this morning."

June didn't open her eyes. He couldn't tell if she was listening.

"Did you notice him? Did you see him sitting there?"

She opened her eyes, staring at him blankly.

"What are you on? What'd you take?"

His wife rolled to her side, facing the wall.

"Miltown?"

She said nothing.

"Where'd you get it? One of your friends?"

She moaned, rolled back over, and looked at him.

"Well, I'm not waiting for it. I'm not sitting here, with Marshall, waiting to find you dead. My son is not living his whole life with what you are doing to him right now. You were better—I thought you were better—but today . . . today it ends."

She sat up.

"There's a place in LA."

She shook her head slowly.

"I've called them, and as soon as someone's here to watch Marshall, we're going. You don't need to pack. You won't need anything."

"I don't want to go."

"It doesn't matter. You're going."

"You can't make me go. You can't make me do anything. You can't just do anything you want."

Her voice was rising, reaching a squeak. It was an old argument. They had both heard it, over and over.

"I can make you."

"No!"

"I'm going to take you to this place, and if you refuse to go in, I'm going to leave you there at the door. I've already drawn up all the paperwork. We'll be divorced in six weeks. And you won't see Marshall. There isn't a judge in this town that will let you near him."

"There's other towns."

"Try it."

She puckered her lip and spit at him, but she was so wrecked that the saliva simply dribbled down her chin. Del felt sick.

But that afternoon, June went with him. He was afraid he would have to restrain her in the car, but she sat without moving, staring blankly out the window for most of the five-hour ride. As they drove onto the clinic grounds, down a long drive with walls fringed in bougainvillea, she finally spoke.

"When it's over, let me come back."

"I'll let you come back."

June hadn't recovered from the loss of the baby.

That's how the world understood it. That her baby had died, and she had never been the same. Del supposed that Cora guessed there was more, but she didn't ask him. His grandmother had never asked him about any of it. About Hugh. About Ray's death. Any of it.

Of course Dr. Bruno knew about the baby. He was the one who had given June the pills first.

"These will help her through, Del. She needs some relief."

Damn.

And, really, losing a baby was what *had* happened. June had lost a baby, and afterward she had fallen down some hole, gone down so deep that some days he couldn't even remember who she had been. And then, when he had more or less given up—was actually wondering if committing her was the one option left—she had crawled back up. He and Marshall had lain down at the lip of that hole, with their arms outstretched, reaching for her, for June, for Mommy, for the woman who had once been so joyful, and almost, almost, they had pulled her up. They'd had her fingers in their hands; they had all been smiling.

They'd had eight months of the old June. Looking back, it was moving that had made her better. Selling the house and buying another one on the other side of the Strip. A house where no baby had been born and lost. A house without neighbors who had noticed June, too drunk by ten in the morning to get to the mailbox without tripping, or who had heard her boozy "Haaaaayyyyrrooo!" to the newspaper boy and then watched her fall down laughing at how funny the word came out. A couple of those neighbors had even seen June climbing the ash tree, sawing off the branches as she went up, dressed in a pink silk robe and singing "Yankee Doodle Dandy." Binnie was there that day. It was the maid who had noticed that Marshall was alone out back; that his mommy had climbed up a tree. After phoning Del, she bundled the boy off to his bedroom and read him stories while the drama at the front of the house played out.

So they moved. Del hadn't known what else to do. The psychologist didn't help. The pills Dr. Bruno prescribed: they definitely didn't help. (It took him awhile to persuade Dr. Bruno to stop giving them to her, but then it was so easy for her to get more. He couldn't plug every damn hole.) Del had moved without any hope that it would actually make a difference. But it had. June had seen her chance. She had made Marshall her captain, and they had planned and painted and purchased: the new house a project that worked when doctors, when pleading, when medicines did not. For eight months, he had his little family back.

And then, just like that, for no reason that he could figure, she had disappeared back down the hole. One evening he came home from work—it was Binnie's day off, but June was fine being left alone with Marshall then, they were all so happy—and as soon as he opened the door, Del heard the dog barking, smelled something burned in the kitchen, knew something bad had happened.

He found June passed out drunk by the pool. And where was Marshall? Where was Marshall? The pool? Thank God, no. He started yelling "Marshall! Marshall!" and he shook June. "Where is he? Where's Marshall?" and the dog barked faster, and Del was frantic, racing through the house: not in the kitchen, not in his bedroom, not in the bathroom. He dashed to the front door, ran halfway into the street, grabbed Mrs. Walkenshaw: "Have you seen

Marshall? Did you see Marshall outside?" She looked alarmed and then said, "I'll help you look," but already Del was running back to the house. Where was he?

A neighbor called the fire department, and it took an hour, but someone finally found Marshall huddled in a cabinet in June's dressing room. He had closed the door on himself, and Del hoped he had fallen asleep curled up in the dark, but he thought probably his son had just sat there, having seen or heard whatever he had seen or heard to send him there, and unable to answer all the people, even his dad, calling his name.

And that had been the beginning of it all over again. Only this time, Del didn't believe she would get better. And Marshall was different too. The little boy who'd weathered all that had come before, who had seemed cheerful and loving and marvelously obtuse about his mother's behavior, disappeared. In his place was a nervous six-year-old who would throw fits in public places, and who had night terrors, and who crawled into their bed and slept curled against Del night after night, sucking his thumb and shuddering in his sleep.

Del never knew what made June fall back down. He would lie in bed, listening to Marshall's light snoring and to June's footsteps as she restlessly roamed the floor below, and he would remember. He remembered holding June's hand—so tiny, such thin fingers—in that bar on the Westside. He had been able to feel the excitement coursing through her. It hadn't bothered her to be the only white woman there; she was not uncomfortable. She liked the pulse of the place, everyone a regular, the bartender sliding drinks over without needing to be asked, three couples dancing, their feet whirling. That was the night they met Eddie Knox.

And he remembered June laughing, spilling the night's take

on the table as he and Eddie and some woman—who was she?— drank champagne and sang "Bye Bye Love." They had sounded pretty good, drunk as they were, with June and Eddie taking harmony, he and what's-her-name taking the melody. There was a moment—there was often a moment on those nights—when Del felt perfectly happy, perfectly at ease, when the four of them singing and drinking and celebrating felt like everything that could be right in the world.

One night, he had taken Eddie to the vault to get him some cash. They were sloshed, of course, and June had gone to bed. After Del handed him the money, Eddie got sentimental. He told Del he'd never had a friend like him before, pulled him into a hug, and Del's body, flat against Eddie's, reacted instantly. Del should have been horrified, but he was on fire, he couldn't bear to move away from him. And Eddie waited, still, just a second, and then said, "Sorry, man. Man, I'm really sorry." Eddie stepped back. Del looked away. They left the vault, quiet.

And from then on, Eddie knew it all, knew what Del kept secret. He knew it all, but he didn't do anything with it—at least not then, at least not for a long time. If only Eddie could have left it that way. If only Eddie hadn't threatened Hugh. If only Del hadn't been the one with the gaming license, the one who couldn't be guilty of a crime. Eddie was smart, but not smart enough to figure out how dangerous a thing he knew.

Del remembered other moments.

Laying his palm on June's belly and waiting for the flutter-kick move that was the first sign of Marshall. Then later, June's belly would roil so fiercely, and he could make out the shape of Marshall's foot rolling from one side to the other. They hadn't known it would be Marshall. It might have been Marilyn.

And the girl. The real baby girl.

Del had known the baby would be Eddie's.

He'd pretended that it could be otherwise, but he'd been planning, thinking, calculating all along. He had thought he would have to pay off the nurses at the hospital, so he'd kept a roll of cash in his coat pocket that whole last month. Weeks earlier, Dr. Bruno had helped him with the arrangements. There was a place in California, near Anaheim. It mostly took in unwed teens, but it also placed babies.

Of course, nothing happened the way he had planned.

Because Del hadn't known he would fall in love. He hadn't known that the color of her skin, the awareness of who she was, wouldn't make any difference. He would fall in love with her, just as he had with Marshall. She would be born, and there would be the instant of shock, of sadness, and then, without warning, there would be that same mad total falling in love that he had felt when Marshall was born. And maybe knowing who she was, seeing this tiniest, newest human being, knowing how things were going to go for her, made the experience more intense. Del couldn't bear to take her from her mother. He couldn't bear not to set her on June's breast. Poor thing. She needed her mother.

No, Del had not imagined he would feel this.

From there, the plan just kept unraveling. Because he didn't feel the way he thought he would. Because he loved her mother and maybe he had loved her father, and mostly, he loved the baby. He had thought there was nothing he could not do, if it needed to be done. But that turned out not to be true.

And this is why he put up with June. This is why he continued. Because what had happened to June shouldn't happen to anyone, and not just Eddie, not just the baby, but him, Del. *He* shouldn't have happened to June. Marrying June had made everything possible for him, but she was a calculated choice, and she had not known, and Del was not such an operator that he did not appreciate the magnitude of that betrayal. It was not June who had betrayed Del.

What she wanted, what she begged for, what he would not give her, was to know where.

Where was she?

Wherewasshe, wherewasshe, wherewasshe.

How could he tell her?

He would never be able to tell her. That was the mistake he had made, when he was driving around with a baby in a basket, when he drove past the spot where he had agreed to bring her—drove past it one time, two times, three, thinking all the while, What could he do? What were the other options? None of them was possible, all of them were worse, because what if Hugh found out? Hugh would not tolerate this risk. And then the baby had started to make her little mews, her little scratchy yowl, her hands and feet pushing the blanket into a storm of pink silk and cotton beside him, and he was out of time, she was hungry, she had to eat.

He had wished he could talk to Ray. He had wished Ray were next to him, in that car, with that baby. Ray would have known what to do. Or Ray would have told him to stick to the plan. And Del would have listened. He would have listened to that deep, soft voice, to the one person who knew everything there was to know about Odell Dibb and who loved him anyway. He could have taken care of things if he'd had Ray next to him.

So that's how it happened. How Del made the choice he did. How he went to the one place he should not have gone. How he put them all at risk, when risk was what he had been trying to avoid.

This was what he couldn't tell June. He couldn't tell her where the baby was, because it would be piling error on top of error, because he wouldn't ruin another mother's life, because Hugh was a dangerous man. There was no way to predict how Hugh might react, and Del couldn't risk finding out. June had the right to know where her husband had taken her baby, but Del would never be able to tell her.

He had tried to help, but he'd made the worst choice of all.

HONORATA

The one who got lucky

and

CORAL

The one who always wondered

OCTOBER 19, 1992
In the Midnight Room

The priest noticed the woman, but she did not notice him.

She was small and dark. Asian, maybe Filipino. She had on evening clothes, a silk dress beaded at the front and gold sandals with heels that seemed too high for her tiny feet. She was carrying a plastic bucket of coins, and it was heavy; her shoulder drooped slightly with the weight.

He had noticed her the night before, dressed in a similar way, carrying the same heavy bucket, wandering disinterestedly from one area of the casino to another. He often noticed the people in the casinos where he played. The regulars. The tourists. It was an occupational hazard to wonder who they were, what brought them there, whether they were having a good time, whether they believed this place would change their lives. He could think like this—he could think about other people gambling and how foolish they might be, how vulnerable—but he couldn't stop himself from playing, couldn't stop thinking about the whir of the reels spinning, the lights, the feel of the heavy metal ball in his hand as he pulled on the machine's arm. No, he couldn't stop thinking of these things, even as he sat and listened to a confession or helped an altar boy lift the heavy book to a stand.

He was sorry for his weakness. Sorry and embarrassed and discouraged. He tried to make up for it in other ways.

The small woman stopped to read the playbill outside the Midnight Room. Father Burns had seen the show: it was a "Psychedelic Sixties Revue" whose pulsing lights and electronic sounds had only made him want to play more, so here he was hours later, in this dark corner of the casino, sitting at a machine that had not hit in a long time. An employee slowly moved a carpet sweeper back and forth, an older woman with a cigarette turned mostly to ash stared blankly at the reels of her own machine. The Filipino woman studied the poster of the 1960s revue, opened the door that led to the nightclub, and looked inside for a moment. Then she turned and walked unsteadily toward the oversized Megabucks machine just a few feet away.

Megabucks was even more of a sucker's game than the slot machines to which he and ash-lady were tethered. He watched her climb onto the slightly too high seat; he saw her look for a place to set down the bucket, and then decide to balance it between her knees, with the silk dress stretched along her thighs. She played slowly and without enthusiasm, mechanically dropping in three one-dollar coins, lifting them from the bucket one by one, letting each one drop and settle before adding the next. Then she leaned forward, reached out her hand as far as it would go, and pulled down the oversized arm. She did it again and again. The priest could have set his watch to her methodical motions, and somehow it transfixed him: the tiny woman, the huge machine, the drop-drop-drop of coins, the body stretching to catch the great arm and pull it down.

When the machine hit, when the lights and the bells and the horn sounded, the woman reared back as if there had been an explosion. The still-heavy bucket slipped and fell to the floor. Coins rolled. The woman with the cigarette yelled. The employee dropped the handle of the vacuum. Father Burns jumped to his feet. And the woman looked stunned, afraid, confused.

People started running toward her, toward the machine. Before the crowd descended, the priest saw the words and the numbers running across the top of it.

"Jackpot! $1,414,153.00! Winner!"

12

Of course, they had sex first. They went directly from the airport to a room at a nearby hotel. He had paid someone to take her things: the gray plaid suitcase her mother had given her and the small leather-like one that had belonged to her uncle. And when the sex was over—when he had showered and then offered his cock for a blow job after (it surprised her that he could do this, as fat as he was, as pale and large and soft as her uncle's old couch)—after that, he called someone on the hotel phone. A few minutes later, a man in a round hat, such as a young boy might find in the boxes left by missionaries, brought the bags to her room. Jimbo said she could take a shower, that she could change her clothes, but not to unpack anything; the car would be coming to take them home in an hour.

So it was done. She was going to his house. According to her uncle's agreement, he would marry her now. Just as he came—the first time, his heavy body pressing the design of the bed's brocade cover onto her skin—he had cried out that they would be getting married in Las Vegas, that he had already made the arrangements, that his friends at the El Capitan would show her a wedding she could write home about.

He also mentioned the ring, as if he might give it to her then.

He had showed it to her at O'Hare. Not two minutes after she had emerged from customs, hungry and disoriented, still in shock that this thing had happened to her, that the whole string of impossible, unlikely, unbelievable events had occurred one after another (as if some diabolical cherub had been given control of her fate and was wildly stacking the least likely scenarios on top of one another, laughing as the madcap pile teetered and grew), right then, with her fellow passengers still bunched around her, looking for whoever had come to meet them, he had caught her eye, called out her name, and held open the small black box with the ring in it. When she walked up to him, he closed the lid of the box and handed her only the receipt, which showed exactly what he had paid to a jeweler on East Walton Street.

The ring was her trump card. At least her uncle thought it was. He thought it was why she had agreed.

"You'll be wearing a five-thousand-dollar ring," her uncle said. "You can walk away anytime. It's yours, and it's on your finger. You'll both know what that means."

Honorata tried to imagine five thousand dollars. One hundred thirty thousand pesos. In Manila, she had laughed when Kidlat told her about the businessmen who paid fifteen hundred pesos for dinner in Makati. At the *tinapayan*, she made three thousand pesos a month, and gave a third to her mother in Buninan. It had been her mother's whole income.

"I don't want a ring."

"Silly little fool. Do you think it was easy to talk him into that ring? Do you think it was easy to persuade him to give you something you could walk away with? You're pretty, Honorata, but you're spoiled meat. You think you'll get another deal this good?"

She'd never known it was possible for her uncle to talk like this. She'd never known any man to talk like this, and certainly not her uncle, who walked with her mother up the hill to where the priest said Mass on Sunday mornings, and who had come to Manila after Kidlat disappeared, telling her that even after all this time, after everything that had happened, her family still wanted her; she should come home to her village.

She showered quickly, her body like a thing tethered to her. She wished it were something she could unhook and release, something that would slide off her and down the drain, something to be dispersed into the sewers beneath the airport. She didn't bother to change her dress when she finished. It was wrinkled and limp, but even the tiny act of choosing another one seemed too much in that moment.

In the car—a big black sedan, with a driver wearing another one of those stupid hats—Jimbo brought up her name.

"You can't be Honorata here. We'll call you Rita."

For an instant, something rose in her. The deal did not allow him to choose her name. Then, what did it matter? It wasn't her body that had slipped down the hotel room drain, but her name.

He had not given her the ring.

She wondered when he would give it to her. If she would have to wait for Las Vegas. The car moved slowly in traffic. Outside the air was cold, there were heavy clouds, white and black and gray. She could only occasionally glimpse the lake, but it looked metallic and angry. She could not see more than a few hundred yards in any direction.

Next to her, Jimbo busied himself with papers in his briefcase. There was a phone in the car—her left knee kept bumping the plastic cradle that held it to the floor—but Jimbo had his own phone, with an antenna that extended rigidly from the top, the sight of which made her slightly sick.

She was starting to feel as if she might not be able to ride calmly after all. Her head ached. She had not eaten in at least twenty-four hours. All that had happened to her in the last two days was brewing in her now: kneeling on the dirt floor with her mother before the statue of the Sacred Heart; kissing her mother's frail, sad face good-bye; her uncle's clipped instructions, vaguely threatening; the long flight, and the smell of the man sitting next to her, who eyed her from the side, pressing his knee into her leg; the speed with which her uncle's deal had been consummated. It was all brewing and stewing and fermenting in her to the rhythm of the phone's wagging antenna as Jimbo talked and leaned forward and dug in his case for something the lawyer, the accountant, whoever it was on the other end, wanted.

What kind of name was Jimbo?

The black car pulled into a curved driveway and stopped. Jimbo kept talking on the phone. When the driver opened the door, she stepped out.

"Be careful, ma'am. The stones are wet."

The stones were wet. Wet and slick and uneven. Not far from her was a mound of what she realized must be snow—so dirty, not pretty, not what she had imagined. She tottered unsteadily in the narrow strapped sandals that had seemed right back home. The driver offered his arm.

"I'll do that," said Jimbo. And there he was, at her side. The mass of him was alarming. She thought of the neighbor boy, the one with the Nike shirt, who brought his basketball to the park near where she and Kidlat had lived. "Kidlat, you are *matangkad at mataba*," he would say. Jimbo was *matangkad at mataba*. Thinking of his size made her dizzy. She wobbled in her ridiculous shoes, and Jimbo steadied her.

"It's okay, Rita. I've got you."

He said it softly, kindly. Rita. That's not my name, she wanted to say.

"Martin. Miss Navarro is hungry. Please ask Gina to prepare her something."

Honorata steeled herself. The slight note of kindness in Jimbo's voice was worse than what had come before. She was very close to losing control, to beginning to cry; she imagined herself dropping to the cold wet flagstones, begging for mercy. The driver, Martin, was still there. She could feel him looking at her, and this kept her upright. Already, so many men had stared at her today. It was as if she were wearing a sign—who she was, what she had done—and that imaginary sign was blood in the water. The man next to her on the plane had smelled it. Jimbo smelled it. The driver, the bellhop at the hotel, they all smelled it.

Jimbo held her arm as she climbed up the two steps, and then just as she was about to enter through the door, he squeezed her waist.

"This is your home now. I hope you'll be happy here."

His arm held her body. She did not look at his face.

There was a huge vase of flowers in the entryway: orchids and sampaguita, gumamela. Flowers from home. The container looked like the one her mother used to catch rainwater. Honorata felt dizzy. Was she being welcomed?

"You're tired. Let me take you to your room."

It was too much to imagine she would have her own room, but she did. It was larger than the apartment she had shared with Kidlat.

"I bought the bedding to match the dress you wore in the photo you sent."

Honorata could not speak.

"This door leads to my room."

She looked at the heavy door on the far side of the sitting area.

"I'm very tired," she finally said. "I'm so tired."

It was not the right thing to say, but it was all she could manage. Jimbo looked at her, his thoughts hidden, and helped her sit on the bed.

"Gina will bring you a tray. You can sleep. I'm going to go out, and I'll see you when I return."

"Thank you," she said. She didn't want to thank him, but it was bred in her: to thank someone who had been kind.

That night, the woman named Gina woke her for dinner. She said that Mr. Wohlmann would like her to dress for their first evening together, so Honorata wore the green sheath her uncle had given her.

Later, Jimbo knocked on the door between their two rooms and then entered immediately. He was carrying the small black box.

"This is yours," he said without ceremony.

When she looked in his eyes, he opened the box, and reached for her hand. Slowly, he slipped the ring, studded with diamonds, onto her left hand. She had narrow fingers, but it fit perfectly. She wondered how her uncle had managed to find her ring size; whether he might have measured her finger one night when she was sleeping. Anything was possible; nothing made sense. She was caught in some other life: one that disconnected her from everything she had known; a world in which her once-pious uncle might indeed be an incubus.

"You're older than your uncle said."

Honorata trembled. She had no idea what her uncle had said.

"But you're more beautiful in person. Even more beautiful than your photo."

He undressed her then, and they had sex. Honorata fell asleep after, but when she woke up, he was lying next to her, awake. Without speaking, he rolled her over and entered her from behind. Only then did he get up and go through the door to the room Honorata had not yet seen. Lying alone, she stroked the ring on her finger. A bitter taste rose in her throat, but she did not cry.

Their days settled into a rhythm.

Jimbo woke her every morning before it was light. He left when the first timid rays of dawn peeked through the curtains. They had dinner together, sometimes at the house, prepared by Gina, and sometimes in a restaurant downtown. Afterward, they came back to her room. They watched television, sitcoms like *Cheers*, or Jimbo read to her from the book he was reading: a crime story about a woman who had been raped and murdered, which Jimbo read as if it would mean nothing to her. Some nights, he would ask her if she wanted a bath, and her trembling excited him. He liked to wash her back, rub soap over her small body, and then lift her up and take her to bed still wet and slippery.

He was not, however, a cruel lover. He liked to talk. He could talk without stopping, about his work, about Las Vegas, about mystery novels, about his time as a young man. The army had sent him to Japan, and he had gone to college late, when he was twenty-five. He despised rich college students. Often, his talk washed over her. She would lie in bed after he left, back through the door to his own room, and be unable to remember anything he had said.

On the weekends, they sometimes played cards. Jimbo liked blackjack and poker and pinochle; Honorata found a cribbage board in a drawer, and they played this instead. She liked the language of cribbage: 15-2, 15-4, 15-6 and nobs is seven, your cut, in the stink hole, his nibs. She would call out "Muggins, I'll take two!" in the tickatick rhythm with which she spoke, and Jimbo would play game after game with her, though at first he had said that cribbage was dull. Sometimes when they were playing, sitting in the room that Gina called the study, with the game laid out on a heavy oak table and the light coming from the stained glass sconces and a ray of sunshine striking the leaded bottles of scotch and whiskey that Jimbo kept on the sideboard, sometimes, Honorata was at peace.

There were no locks on the doors. Jimbo was away at work all day, and on Tuesdays and Thursdays, Gina did not come, and so she had the house to herself. Martin came each morning and drove Jimbo to work. She wondered if her fiancé—if that was the word for him—knew how to drive.

In any case, Honorata didn't know how to drive and didn't have a car. She was free to go where she wanted, and she often took long walks in the neighborhood, lacing up the heavy boots that Gina had bought her. She had found a grocery store—a big American one—with pale leaves of lettuce and tall stacks of canned food, which seemed as if they might collapse on top of her when she hurried down the aisle, but she didn't have any money. She fingered the ring, realizing it was not quite the same as money.

Jimbo had never invited her into his room on the other side of the door, but she had gone in there once. She was surprised to find that his room was smaller than hers. There was no sitting area, and the bathroom was in the hall. Honorata liked the room better than her brightly colored one. The walls were a deep gray, and the mix of gray and tan and chocolate colors calmed her. Honorata looked at everything in the room carefully—she stared at Jimbo's things—but she didn't touch anything, didn't open a drawer, or move anything sitting on his dresser.

After awhile, the days became more difficult than the nights. There was nothing for her to do. She didn't know anyone and didn't have anywhere to go. Gina took care of the house and the food. Trembling, she asked Jimbo if she could buy some groceries and cook dinner. At first, he said that she did not need to cook, but the next day, he left a hundred dollars in an envelope and told her to take a cab home from the store.

Honorata carefully smoothed out each bill and studied it. She thought about the pesos she had sent to her mother and wondered if her uncle was giving her mother money now. She had let her uncle tell her mother that she had fallen in love with an American, that she was leaving with him, and she had not written her mother since. There was no phone in Buninan, and she could not have risked hearing her mother's voice anyway. She knew she should write, but Honorata could not find the courage to tell her mother that she was fine, that she was happy, that she was rich. This is what she would have to write, and even thinking about it made her cry. No, she could not write her mother.

Instead, she went to the American store and tried to find what she needed to make a meal. The rice was dry and fell off her fork when she tried to eat it, but a customer pointed her to tamarind one day when a clerk said that they did not carry sampalok, and another time, a man gave her directions to an Asian market not too far away. The market was mostly Chinese, but she found good rice there.

That night, Jimbo asked her if she liked the ring.

"It's pretty," she said.

She didn't know how to answer his question.

"Do you know why I gave it to you?"

Honorata thought of her uncle. She thought of Jimbo's house, of Gina, of Martin taking him to work each morning. It didn't seem likely that he had given her the ring because her uncle had bargained for it.

"I gave it to you because your uncle asked for it. Because I wanted you to be happy."

She trembled involuntarily.

"I didn't trust your uncle. But here you are."

Honorata began to shake, and tried to hide it by wrapping her arms tightly across her chest.

"I wasn't sure you would walk off the plane."

Tears filled her eyes, so she lowered her face. She could feel him waiting, waiting to hear what she would say, but she could not speak. The silence stretched out, and Honorata knew that she had to look up, she had to speak, but before she could, she heard him turn and leave the room.

"Good night, Rita."

Jimbo didn't come to her room that night. He didn't give her a bath, he didn't have sex with her. Honorata was relieved. She crawled into bed and pulled the covers completely over her head. In the blackness, hot and without enough air, she slept deeply.

A few mornings later, after Jimbo had finished with her, he brought up the ring again.

"It's an engagement ring. I have the band that goes with it. Would you like to go to Vegas?"

How strange that he would ask her this. What did he imagine?

"I've never been there."

"Of course you haven't."

They sat quietly.

"Are you wondering why I want to marry you?"

She looked up at him. She didn't want to say anything, but she stared straight in his eyes. She didn't often look at him this way, though she already knew it moved him.

"I want a wife. I know my money . . . I know that you are here because . . . because your country is poor. I understand that. But I want a wife. I don't want a whore."

Honorata noticed that his foot was shaking as he spoke, though his voice was measured, matter of fact.

"I want a family."

She looked in his eyes still, not answering.

"You'll have to sign papers. I'm not giving away my money. But I'm a generous man. When you're my wife, those papers won't matter."

Honorata looked down then. Her heart fluttered with the faint memory of the woman she had been, the girl. She saw Kidlat's face, the smile she had known her whole life, the narrow plane of his back, and the knees that rounded out too large for his calves. She thought of her father, before he died, and the lime green of the rice fields, and how her stomach had lurched when she had taken the jeepney up the Mountain Trail with him. For a moment, she remembered the soft island air on her skin, the slap of wet fronds against her thighs, the slosh of water running through the fields, the trill and mutter of birds, and the squawk of the rooster being beaten for *pinikpikan*.

She should never have gone to Manila. But she had loved Kidlat. And how would her mother have lived if she had not gone to the city?

Jimbo was waiting. Honorata said nothing but pulled him back toward her pillow, buried her head in the thin strands of hair on his wide chest, and flicked her tongue against his nipple. He moaned. This was the only way she knew to avoid answering.

13

"*I had a rooster, and the rooster pleased me,*" sang Coral, after stepping through the arch of paper flowers that festooned the door of the kindergarten classroom.

"*Cock-a-doodle-doo!*" yelled Faraz, which Coral ignored. Sara dropped her box of crayons, and Coral ignored that too. The rest of the children hurried to put away their things—the construction paper to the middle of the table, the crayons and scissors into the slots of their desks—and two boys raced to be first to sit on the color block mat.

"*I fed my rooster on a green berry tree.*"

The children on the mat joined in.

"*The liiiiittttle rooster went cock-a-doodle-doo, dee doodly doodly doodly doo.*"

"The duck!" called Aaron from his desk near the bookshelf. Coral ignored him.

"*I had a cat and the cat pleased me.*"

More children were on the mat, singing now. They wiggled a little, scrambling for place, and Coral slowed the tempo of the song, without quite looking at any wiggler.

"*I fed my cat on a green berry tree.*"

No more wigglers, and even Aaron was putting his art project in the correct spot on the bookshelf.

"*The liiiittttlle cat goes meeeeow, meeeow, the little rooster goes cock-a-doodle-doo dee doodly doodly doodly doo.*"

By the time they got to the duck, all the children were assembled, each on his or her own color square, and Coral had motioned for Aaron to sit cross-legged next to her. They finished the song with the lion, roaring with wide-open mouths, and just after the last doodly doo, Coral paused, raised her hands high, and then all together, in perfect time, every child clapped once.

"Hoorah! Mrs. Barrosa's class, you are on top of the world today."

"Hi, Miss Jackson." "Hello, Miss Jackson." "Miss Jackson, are we doing the love song today?" "Yes, the love song!" "Can we do the love song?"

Their voices came in an excited rush, but nobody jumped up or shouted. They sat eagerly waiting.

"We can do the love song today. But first, can anybody tell me what we are learning about music this month?"

"About music writing!"

"Yes. About music writing."

Coral held up a card with a treble clef.

"And what's this?"

"It's an *S*!" "It's a cliff." "It's the high voice sign."

"Good. It's a treble clef." Coral sounded out the two words carefully. "Let's say it together."

"Treble clef."

"And again?"

"Treble clef!"

"Three times, like bells ringing."

"Treble clef, treble clef, treble clef!" the children sang out, pitching their voices even higher than they were naturally.

"Perfect. Does anyone remember the name of the other clef?"

"Basic clef!" yelled Faraz. "It's the basic clef."

"Good! *Bass* clef. Let's try that one together."

"Bass clef."

"Three times, like a choo-choo train."

"Bass clef, bass clef, bass clef!" the children chanted, puffing out their chests in the effort to deepen their voices.

On Tuesdays, Mrs. Barrosa's kindergarten had music right before their day ended at 11:40, so Coral would stop five minutes early to line them up; she was the one to give each child a high-five good-bye and to watch until everybody had left the playground with an adult. The children who spoke Spanish had someone waiting to walk them home, but most of the rest walked or skipped to a designated pick-up area, where a driver with a van marked Happy Daze Care or Kids Korner waited. Last week, one child had been left after all the others were gone. Coral wasn't sure why, but she had already decided whose turn it would be for the love song today.

"We have five minutes left," she said to the class.

"The love song!" "It's love song time!"

"Yes, it is. And today the love song is for Melody. Do you all know that *melody* is a music word too? It means a series of tones that we like. Melody, did you know that?"

Melody shook her head shyly.

"Do you want to have the love song today?"

The little girl nodded.

"Do you want to tell us someone who loves you?"

She shook her head.

"Well, then, we'll start with me." Coral sang, *"You're the one that I love, I love, I love, you're the one that I love, sweetest one of all."*

The children joined in. *"You're the one that we love, we love, we love. You're the one that we love, sweetest one of all."*

Melody was wearing a faded purple T-shirt, with a peeling green Baby Bop on the front. "*You're the one that Baby Bop loves, Baby Bop loves, Baby Bop loves, you're the one that Baby Bop loves, sweetest one of all.*"

Melody smiled and touched the hem of her shirt.

"Butterflies," she said so quietly that Coral almost didn't hear her. "*You're the one the butterflies love, butterflies love, butterflies love, you're the one the butterflies love, sweetest one of all.*"

The children sang brightly, beaming at Melody as they picked up their cues from Coral, and when she motioned for them to stand, they kept singing, more quietly, as they found their backpacks and unhooked their sweaters, and the ones who were going to day care retrieved their lunches from the shelf near the door. Melody stood on the mat the longest, listening to them sing about her, and saying softly to Coral, "Minnie Mouse." "Puppies. "Mrs. Barrosa."

Coral watched the children line up and thought about how her life might be if she had not come home last year; if Augusta hadn't casually mentioned how many teachers the district was hiring; if the thought, initially so ridiculous, hadn't grown on her—after an argument with Gerald, after she had washed her favorite sweater three times and it still smelled like smoke from the club, after her check for the PG&E bill bounced, after Tonya mentioned that she had seen Gerald at a bar in Bernal Heights, on a night that Coral thought he had driven home to help his aunt replace her water heater.

Little by little, the option her mother was suggesting took hold. Coral had her teaching certificate, she'd never intended to become a singer. Singing had started as a dare. They were all at a club in San Francisco for someone's twenty-first birthday, and there was an open mike call. Some of the guys started chanting "Sing! Sing! Sing!" until, laughing, she and Tonya went onstage. After that, it happened fast: someone in the club offered them a gig, for tips, and soon after that, there was another offer. Tonya dropped out to manage their bookings—that surprised Coral—but Coral kept going to school, showing up first to class and then to her student teaching bleary-eyed and hoarse. Whether she had done so because she wanted to finish college or because she would never have dared tell Augusta that she'd quit, she wasn't sure.

And was that whole life a detour? For most of the six years that Coral had sung with Tonya and then with the band, she felt like she was doing exactly what she should be doing—that the music, her voice, the way people responded, the songs she wrote in her head, over and over, all the time, this was who she was and who she was born to be. And what did it mean that she could simply drop out of who she was born to be? That one day she would wake up and realize she was so tired; so tired that not being tired didn't even seem like a real state. That she would wake up and know she had fallen in love with the wrong man, and that she wasn't strong enough to fix this. She would wake up longing for a morning, missing daytime; she was so damn sick of living at night, of a pink-fingered dawn meaning it was time to go to bed. If she didn't get out of there, if she didn't get away, she'd go under. Music or no.

She wasn't Tonya. She wasn't Gerald. She was weaker than they were. And she needed her mother. She needed to go home. Coral laughed when she told her friends that she was back home living with her mother—she was careful to make it sound like a drag—but, really, she had been so grateful for the sound of her mama in the next room, for the blue sofa with the lumpy pillows, for the wooden swordfish Ray Junior had made in shop class hanging on the wall, for the mesquite tree dropping spinners on her window sill, for the suffocating, sweltering, clean, dry heat of a July noon. It was all beautiful, it was all home, it was all the way the world felt right.

So when the principal at Lewis E. Rowe offered her a job teaching music, she didn't hesitate, she didn't waste any time worrying about what anyone else might think of her decision. She said yes. And from the first week—when she couldn't find the fourth-grade classroom, when the air-conditioning hadn't worked, when the fire alarm had gone off just after she'd sent one small child to the bathroom—from the very beginning, it seemed to Coral it was a pretty good choice.

Still, not everything about coming home to Vegas was easy. Just this morning, she had woken to that old sense of something not right. Coral kept her eyes closed, but the pressure was there: an emptiness so vast it had presence, pushing against her like a force, daring her to wobble, lean, tumble in, tumble back. If she didn't open her eyes, she might fall back asleep, the pressure might go away: it might not be there waiting when she woke again.

This was a Vegas feeling, as old as she was, a feeling that stretched as far back as her own memory. How many mornings had she felt it? This dread or sadness or longing or fear—she was never sure quite what. When she was small, perhaps five or six, she had asked her mama:

"Who is it that sits on my bed in the morning?"

"Who sits on your bed?"

"On my chest. When I wake up, and I can't breathe."

"You can't breathe?"

"I can't breathe. And then I try really hard, I think about how I want to get up, and she goes away."

"She?"

"The person, sitting on my chest."

"Do you know what she looks like?"

"No."

"I sometimes come in the morning and look at you. I might even give you a kiss. Do you think that's what happens?"

"No. It's not you, Mama. I would know if it was you."

"Hmmm. Well, I think it's a dream, Coral. I think you're not quite awake. It might be a nightmare that you have."

"It feels like I'm awake."

"Yes. I'm sorry. It must be scary."

"It hurts."

"It hurts?"

"Yes."

Years of practice had taught her to get up as quickly as possible. The impulse to lie still, to fall back asleep, could ruin a morning. She sat up and swung her legs over the side of the bed. The sun slanted through the slats in the windows, striping the pale carpet with bands of light and shadow. Long ago, she had shared this bedroom with Ada, and they had made up a rhythm to step on these stripes of light. Coral placed her feet carefully along them now and stepped the rhythm again, remembering her sister's raspy voice and the way she would suddenly pinch Coral at the waist to try to make her lose her footing.

Their twin beds were still covered with the same blue-and-yellow blankets. Some of Ada's dolls were lined up on top of the chest of drawers, and the teddy bear that their older sister Althea had won at the Clark County Fair still sat, slumped and dusty, in the corner. When Coral reached the door, she leaned down and touched the bear's nose. Then she turned to look back at the room. It was almost time to leave her childhood home. She'd never live here again—and that was good—but still, it ached a bit.

That was another thing about living in Vegas. Houses were cheap. She'd already saved up enough for a down payment. She never could have bought a house in California, but here, even with 10 percent interest, it didn't make sense to rent. The realtor suggested she wait to buy until the first houses were built in the northwest, next year, but Coral didn't think she would like a master-planned community or a neighborhood filled with the thousands suddenly arriving each month from Ohio and New York and places farther away. Vegas had always been a boomtown, but things were changing much faster now. At her interview, the principal had said that Steve Wynn's new casino would need to make a million dollars a day just to stay open; that a hundred thousand people would live in Summerlin alone; that eighty-nine new schools were going to be built.

When she drove across town, Coral could see that the vast vistas of her childhood—rock and hill and sky—were already disappearing, replaced with rows and rows of red stucco roofs, the sky above blue and streaked with the puffy white plumes of commercial jets or the slowly twining ribbons left by F-15s flying in formation. When she was growing up, the streets had simply ended in desert. And there was a certain odor—dusty; maybe it was creosote or another plant—but Coral almost never smelled that now. Sometimes, if she were way out by the dam, there would be a whiff. When she was a child, the neighborhood would flood—

though there might not have been any rain in the valley, just in the mountains—and everyone would put on swimsuits, moms and teens and toddlers, and race outside to splash in water that seemed bewildering, almost mystical, though it was crowded with bits of trash left in the desert and the dead bodies of pocket mice and shrews. Once, there had even been a gray rabbit, soaked to half its size, with its ears absurdly long by comparison.

Memories like these could make her feel unsteady again.

What would Augusta say if she knew what Coral was thinking, here in her childhood room? If she knew what really brought Coral stumbling downstairs for a coffee, for a sniff of the way her mother smelled, for the sound of the voice that made the world shrink back to its proper size and made Coral feel safe just by saying hello? Did Augusta know that her daughter still woke up with a heartsick feeling, that her thoughts turned so often to what her mama had told her a dozen years earlier? Did Augusta guess that her youngest child didn't feel quite solid at the center?

The other day, a first grader raised his hand and asked not if he could go to the bathroom or if they were going to sing about alligators, but what color was she: black or white? Coral started to laugh, and to tell him that she was the color of a milkshake, or a malt ball, but just in time, she caught the expression on the face of a little girl at the back, her hair in tightly-braided rows, and so Coral answered directly, "I'm black."

And the little girl smiled, carefully looking down at her desk as she did so. This feeling, too, Coral remembered.

14

It was summer in Chicago before Jimbo asked about the letters.

"Rita, did you write these?"

"What?"

He stood there in a striped silk bathrobe; a giant with a packet of letters in his hand. She could see bits of pink stationery, words in blue ink handwriting, a couple of airmail envelopes. She had never seen any letters. She went blank, and then, in a flash, realized what they must be. Her face must have shown her shock.

"You didn't sign them, either?"

The magnitude of her uncle's betrayal loomed. That's how it was done. That's how it was usually done. Manila pen pals. Poor women who wrote letters to rich men, in the States, in Russia, other places. They wrote letters back and forth, and the women always knew what was coming; they wanted out, the letters were their chance.

But Honorata had never written a letter.

Honorata had never been one of those women.

Is this what her uncle did? Was this the job that made him travel to Manila? Did he find the women, find the men for them to write to, negotiate the deals?

He had planned it all. He had written letters for her.

Except her uncle didn't even know how to write. He would have had to pay someone to write those letters. Did the same woman write all the letters, for all the girls?

How long had he been planning for her trip to Chicago?

Honorata knew enough about Jimbo to know that her uncle would not have let him slip through his fingers. Big fish. Her uncle liked big fish.

The scope of his betrayal, of his scheme, made her dizzy. He had come into the bakery one afternoon as if he were just dropping by. Then he whispered that he knew about the movie she had made, about *Filipina Fillies*. He said he had come to help her; to take her back to the village for a while.

"Is anything in them true? Did you write any of those things?" Jimbo demanded.

Honorata couldn't speak. She looked down. For the first time, he became angry.

"I'm asking you a question. Answer me."

His enormous white hand gripped the edge of her chair. He leaned toward her, but he didn't touch her.

"No."

"You refuse to answer?"

"No, I didn't write the letters. I don't know about any letters."

There had been no time for letters. Her uncle had come to the bakery on Sunday, and by the next Sunday, she was boarding the plane to Chicago. It had taken twelve hours to go from Manila to her mother's home in Buninan, and eleven hours to return. The days in between had been desperate: her mother thin and sad; her uncle's story about Kidlat, about the people who'd come looking for him; and then the VHS tapes, everywhere in Manila, even in Bayombong and Solano—where the bus had broken down—and even in her uncle's home, though he had no television. She hadn't known these tapes were possible; these tapes from what was until then the worst time in her life: a time that changed everything, a time that ruined her relationship with Kidlat, which was why, she supposed, he had disappeared. She had made the movie to help Kidlat, because he had said a man would kill him if she didn't, that everything was special effects anyway, and the movie would be shown only in Canada.

She had gone to Manila with Kidlat eight years before. She had chosen him over her family because Kidlat did not want to live in a village—not his, not hers—and her mother would never have given her permission to go with him unless they were married. But Kidlat would not get married. Kidlat said that in America, people had stopped getting married. And if leaving the village was a choice Honorata had made, it hadn't felt like one; there had been no thinking at all, just feeling: longing and sorrow and then sudden joy (this, then, was what it was all about). After that, there had been nothing left to do but go with Kidlat, whom she loved, and who knew what he wanted, and what he was willing to do or not do, better than she did.

Always she sent money home. Sometimes her uncle came to get the money from her, sometimes someone from the village came, and sometimes she mailed it with the letters she sent every week. By the time she returned home, by the time she finally saw the thatched roof and wood posts of her family home in Buninan, by the time she saw her mother again; running away with Kidlat meant nothing. The movie—the movie she'd never seen and never would see—meant everything.

It had not all been special effects. Did Kidlat know that?

"So what did you know?" Jimbo asked. "If you didn't know about the letters, what did you know?"

Honorata said nothing. There was no way to explain. She didn't know what had happened, but now she knew it had started a long time before her uncle came to get her at the bakery in Manila.

Jimbo grabbed her then. His fingers dug into her arm. They were fleshy and strong. She stared at those fingers, at her own arm, without being able to look away. He saw her staring at the arm, and silently, without looking at her, he twisted her elbow back.

Honorata gasped in pain. But she didn't look at him.

He released her.

"Whore," he snarled, and stood up abruptly.

Honorata sat without moving, afraid to be heard. If she could stop her own breath, if she could will herself to stop breathing, she would.

He'd shocked himself. Grabbing her arm. Bending it backward. He'd almost kept going.

The rage and repulsion and roar he felt was a physical thing: a wave. Jimbo's body dripped sweat, his jaws gripped painfully, the room pulsed with the realization of how Rita's uncle had played him.

Ramon Navarro was a nasty man: insipid, pandering, unrelenting. He operated independently, no agency, and his clients had to be referred to him by someone he knew. A salesman in Miami had made the connection for Jimbo. From the first approach, Jimbo had had no intention of working with Rita's uncle. He'd told him to stop calling, to stop sending letters, but when the man asked him to read just this one letter, this one very special letter, Jimbo had done it.

"I go to the bakery at four in the morning, before it is light. The streets are not quiet even then, and they smell of all the people who live

here, and sometimes I feel so sad for someone sleeping on the ground, right in my path, that I am tempted to wake him up, to take him with me to the bakery, to give him one of the rolls left from the night before, but I know this would be dangerous, and so I step around him, careful not to wake him up."

He was a fool. A sucker. And her uncle had played him.

He had worked with Honorata's uncle only because her letters had been so different, and because Ramon had told him that this was his niece; that she did not correspond with anyone but him, that she was not one of the women who had come to Ramon for help.

What a fool.

A pathetic, fat, sweaty fool.

And from eight thousand miles away, Ramon had known.

For months, there had been no photo. Usually the photo was the first thing to come: a half dozen photos, each with a name and a short introduction. But everything about corresponding with Honorata had been different. The letters were sent directly to him, and he wrote directly back to her. Jimbo used his post office box, of course, but the letters did not go through Ramon.

He bit his tongue remembering this, realizing.

So there had been no photo, and after awhile, Jimbo wasn't sure he wanted one. The niece was likely misshapen, there was something wrong about her—he imagined acne scars, dwarfism, obesity, a birthmark, what could it be?—but as they became friends, as he found that he was able to tell her the most intimate details of his life, the slights he kept hidden, the embarrassment he felt, he realized he didn't care what she looked like. It was absurd, that this mail-order bride idea might actually work, that he might actually have met someone he could love and who would love him. He hadn't really believed it was possible.

And he would help her family. They could visit whenever she wanted. She wouldn't have to leave them all behind. Maybe he would buy a vacation home in the Philippines, something on the beach; it would be a place to go in the winters.

When the photo finally came, in a brown envelope with Ramon Navarro's name scrawled across the back, Jimbo was dumbfounded. How could Honorata be this beautiful? Why would such a woman write to him? For a while, he had once again doubted the uncle. So Ramon Navarro had explained. About *Filipina Fillies*. About the way his niece was taken and forced to make a movie that ruined any chance of a normal life for her. How this experience had nearly destroyed her. How it had been months before she would leave the one-room house of her mother. How afraid she was that Jimbo would find out.

His niece had been naïve, and Ramon was sorry that she was not a virgin, but could Jimbo understand his predicament: a beautiful niece, his sister's only daughter, no one had known what to do. He hadn't meant to introduce her to men, but when he had learned about Jimbo, he had thought maybe this would be an answer; maybe his sister would trust his judgment and agree. He should have explained it all to Jimbo from the start, but he hoped Jimbo would understand why he could not. In the interest of honesty, he felt he should give Mr. Wohlmann the name of the movie, *Filipina Fillies*.

He was stupid, ugly, useless slime. And her uncle had known it. He'd watched the movie.

Not right away. He'd waited awhile. Spent days thinking about it, knowing he shouldn't watch—that Honorata deserved better from him—but, of course, he had watched it. He had seen horror in the way her body shuddered, fear in the way her lip trembled, sorrow in those wet brown eyes. It was terrible what had been done to her. And he could not get any of these images out of his mind. He read the letters, and he watched the movie, more than once, and after he made himself return the movie to the porn store, he imagined her in it over and over.

That had almost been the end. He stopped writing to her, ignored the two letters that arrived, did not return the calls that came to his office in the city. He had sickened himself, and he felt overwrought, and he wished it would all go away.

Then a telegram arrived from Ramon Navarro.

Honorata was ready to leave the country. She could come very soon. It was important for her to get away quickly. And insanely, Jimbo had said yes.

When he thought of the day she arrived, of how it had felt to wait for her, of how he had made Gina work to get ready for her, of the way Gina had looked at him, surprised, and then—most powerful of all—when Rita had stepped out of customs, and he had seen the wolf look of the man walking behind her, the rush of tenderness and desire, of caring and lust, that he had felt in that moment.

That first time in the hotel room, it was . . . it meant . . . it was sacred to him. That's how it felt in his mind: sacred.

But she had known nothing about him, had taken him with the expertise of any paid hooker.

It was not to be accepted. He wouldn't accept it. He wanted to hurt her. Of course he had twisted her arm back. Of course he was enraged.

The only thing to do now was leave the room.

Jimbo didn't return in the morning. She didn't see him for two days, and she didn't know whether he went to work or not; she stayed mostly in her bed, slipping out to eat some chicken left in the fridge and pretending not to hear Gina when she asked if she had any laundry to do.

On Tuesday, a bouquet of flowers arrived for her. She ignored the card, left it unopened on the table, and Jimbo continued to stay in his room.

The next day, more flowers arrived. No card.

The evening after that, Jimbo knocked on the door between their rooms. For the first time, he waited for her to say he could come in. Then he stood in the doorway, looking smaller.

"May I come in?"

She shrugged.

"I'm sorry. I won't hurt you."

She looked down.

"I thought you'd written the letters. I thought you'd agreed to come here."

"I did agree."

He said nothing.

Honorata thought about her uncle. Her uncle saying that the tape was killing her mother—that running away for love had been one thing, a devastating thing, but this, this tape, it would kill her mother.

How could her mother have seen a tape? Where would her uncle have taken her to find a television? A VHS player?

Honorata still felt the hands of the man on her, her eyes still blinked at the white light of the camera; over and over, she heard the noises of the men who had watched.

"I'm not that kind of man," Jimbo said at last.

She looked at him then.

"At the airport. I thought you'd written those letters. I thought you knew me. I thought you'd chosen me."

For the first time, Honorata's eyes teared. She looked down quickly. She wanted him to leave her room.

"I wasn't looking for a prostitute. I made arrangements for a wife. Your uncle assured me, he . . . the letters . . . what you said . . ."

Honorata focused on breathing. One breath in, then one out. Her stomach knotted, turned.

She didn't look up. She stared at the floor in front of his feet, and imagined his hand coming down hard on her back, knocking her forward. But he didn't hit her. There was silence in the room, and then she heard him move, heard the door open. He was gone.

All night, Honorata lay in bed with bile in her throat. "At the airport . . . I thought you knew me . . ." The room dipped, turned, she would be sick. She thought of herself as a little girl: the yellow dress she'd worn for her first communion, the red frogs the children caught in pails, her mother's voice, singing *bahay kubo, kahit munti*. Her grandmother had called her lucky. In the Spanish that no one else spoke aloud, Lola had said, *"tienes suerte"*—"You are lucky"—over and over. So often that when Honorata was four, she told her new teacher that her name was Hono*suerte*.

Honorata didn't remember confusing her own name, but the story was family lore. And she did remember a teacher's strangely angry face, and a child's giggle, and she remembered hitching up her skirt so that she could rub a finger across the stretched elastic of her faded blue panties in a way that soothed her—in a way she would repeat right now, if it could still soothe her, if she could still feel that sudden enveloping calm that would come over her the instant that her sensitive first finger slipped across the softened elastic edge. Honorata also remembered the teacher leaning in to her ear and whispering that she would not be so lucky if she lifted her skirt in school like that again, and that the word was not *suerte*, but *lucky*. In the Republic of the Philippines, one said lucky.

For a week, Jimbo avoided her. And Honorata avoided him back. But then one night he slipped into bed beside her, and gradually they returned to something like their former routine. They didn't discuss the letters; Honorata never saw them again. Jimbo still spoke to her with tenderness, but the sex was rougher. Once, he left town for five days without telling her he would be going. And after that, he was gone more and more: a night here, three days there. Honorata eavesdropped on Gina talking on the phone and learned that he was going to Las Vegas.

Jimbo didn't say anything to her about these trips. He didn't speak about Las Vegas anymore, he never mentioned gambling. He also said nothing about a wedding. One night when they were naked, he slapped her bottom hard, and another night, her cheek. Now and then, he told her a dirty story.

Honorata spent hours roaming the streets surrounding Jimbo's home, her eyes averted, imagining that Jimbo had someone watching her. She walked dully, her knees aching with the miles traversed, timing the speed of cars passing on the busy road. Timing them, estimating when they would pass her, thinking about what would be possible. The awareness of what she was doing would rend her nauseous, weak limbed. She would think carefully, *It's not true that I've missed my last chance.* Her father used to say that tomorrow might always be better than today. He had said she was a strong girl, that God did not forget his children. And what would *Tatay* think of his daughter now?

Tatay had told her lots of stories about his parents, who had died in a bus accident when she was only five. They had gone to Manila and ridden on the top of a double-decker bus all the way down Roxas Boulevard. But there was an accident—her father never learned exactly what happened—and the bus flipped on its side right near the church. Many fell out of the top, but only Lola and Lolo were killed. Every year, Tatay went to Manila in June and prayed for his parents. When he came back, he would tell Honorata again the stories he knew of them and of how they had grown up. How Lola had been an orphan and lived on the streets. How Lolo had met her when he was in the army. How they had come back to his village, and, at first, the family had not accepted Lola, who was not from the mountains, but when she died, the whole village had mourned her.

In this story was something about Lola's past. Even as a child, Honorata had known it. But she didn't know what Lola had done or why the villagers mistrusted her initially. Tatay had wanted her to know about his mother. Maybe not everything, but the important thing: that once she had been shunned and then she had been loved.

Honorata thought about this story, and about Tatay telling her this story, nearly every day.

In October Jimbo came to her room excited.

"We're going to Vegas tomorrow. Martin will be here to take us to the airport at seven. Bring that green dress."

She looked at him, surprised.

He didn't say anything more, and she didn't ask any questions. He took her from behind on the bed, her face pressed into the flowered satin, and then he left.

"Be ready at six thirty."

That night, Honorata packed the small bag her uncle had given her. Jimbo hadn't said how long they'd be gone. She packed four dresses and several pairs of sandals. She packed a swimsuit. Was it always hot in Las Vegas? She added a white sweater. She didn't have any identification. Jimbo had taken her passport when she arrived, nearly a year ago now. The passport her uncle had ready and waiting.

15

Years ago, when Coral was a junior in high school, her mother had kept her home—on a day she had a world history test—to go to the funeral of Odell Dibb, who owned the El Capitan on the Strip. It was a crowded service, but they had arrived an hour early and had seats even though many others stood or waited outside. Coral had never been in the First Congregational Church, and the only thing she knew about Odell Dibb was that her mother thought he was a good man. She didn't know why her mama had made her attend the funeral; she didn't like to miss school, and Ray Junior could have gone instead.

They weren't the only black people, though. There were quite a few, and the Reverend Sherrell, from Antioch Baptist, was one of the men who spoke. He said that Mr. Del Dibb had been good to the African American community, had been part of the deseg-regation of the Strip in 1960, one of the negotiators of the Moulin Rouge pact, and even before that, he had been a champion and a fair man to whom plenty of local people owed a debt. There were other speakers too, and Coral shifted around in the hard pew, thinking about whether she could make up her world history test at lunch the next day and whether or not the teacher would be annoyed at her.

There was a large photograph of Odell next to the casket at the front. He was a white man, tall, with fine blond hair; the only interesting thing was his tie, which was fuchsia with narrow silver stripes instead of plain navy or red. Coral gave him credit for the tie. She glanced at her mother, who would not appreciate knowing her daughter's not-very-solemn thoughts. Sometimes, her mama could tell what she was thinking, but Augusta just sat there, large and calm and elegant, with a black hat and the small white Bible she always held in church.

There weren't many young people there. Why had Mama brought her? Mr. Dibb's son, who looked about her age, sat with his mother at the front. They faced out, toward the congregation, which struck Coral as cruel. She gathered that Mr. Dibb had died suddenly, maybe a heart attack or a stroke. People kept saying he was only fifty-four, which didn't seem that young. Anyway, his son was trying hard not to cry, and his face had a strained, purply look to it. He had wire-rimmed glasses and the same blond hair as his father, and Coral felt sorry for him. She'd never had a dad, but it would be terrible to lose one, and maybe Odell Dibb was a pretty nice guy, because his son was so upset. Mr. Dibb's wife wore a hat with a low brim, and sunglasses, even in church, so Coral couldn't tell what she might be like. She was small, and even though she had to be old too, she was wearing high black heels. She did not move the feet in those heels, even once, even a twitch, in all the time that Coral watched her.

When the service was over, Augusta nodded her head to one or two people but hustled Coral out quickly. They did not walk over to the reception hall afterward and they obviously weren't going to the burial.

"I'll drop you off at school. Then you'll only miss half a day."

"I don't want to go to school in this dress."

Her mama just looked at her, with one eyebrow raised.

"I already missed my world history test. I really don't have anything I have to do there now."

"Well, I'll let you figure that out, Miss Coral, whether you have anything to do with your afternoon in school."

Mama was mad. That sort of thing made her mad. Fine. She'd go to school, in a dress, but she was taking off these nylons as soon as she got there. Mama would never know about that.

It wasn't until a day later, after she'd told her friend Monica that her mama had made her go to a funeral even though she had a test, and Monica had asked, "Well, who's Odell Dibb to you?" that Coral had wondered. Monica hadn't said anything more, but Coral had the feeling that she was going to and then thought better of it, and that had made her suspicious more than anything.

She'd known for a long time that she probably didn't have the same dad as Althea and Ray Junior and Ada. There were photos of Ray Senior all over the house, and her mom talked plenty about him, always telling them how hard he worked, what good care he took of his family, how he'd grown up in Vegas—one of the only African American men in town back then. She'd met him after she'd come from Tennessee, and they'd fallen in love at a dance at Carver Park when Augusta was only fourteen. Coral knew all that, and everyone could see that Ray Junior looked like him, and Althea too, but what nobody said, not even Ada, who loved to tease, was that Ray Senior was just as dark as Augusta, and just as dark as all the kids, except her. This wasn't talked about in her family. How Coral was born after he died, how Augusta must have known another man, how it would have been when Ada was a baby; how else could Coral exist?

She couldn't really remember the first time someone had said to her that she was a halfie, a zebra, salt and pepper, or that her skin was cafe au lait, caramel, high yellow. By first grade at least. And not long after that, the faster kids, the rougher ones, they made it more explicit. "Your mama's black, so who's your daddy, Coral?" "Who gave you that white girl name, Coral?" And of course, she'd come home crying, and Augusta had told her to stop crying, to be proud of who she was, and to ignore an ignorant child who didn't know what he was saying. Ada had punched a boy in her class—she could punch hard—and Ray Junior had told every kid in the lunchroom that Coral Jackson was his full 100 percent sister, and anyone who didn't believe it could talk to him about it after school. She was a full 100 percent Jackson, and her skin, well, her skin just didn't make any sense, and nobody ever explained anything about it.

One thing Coral never told anyone was that she had overheard a conversation between Althea and Mama when she was only seven. She hadn't really understood what Althea was asking, but it had worried her, and for a long time, she had jumped out of bed and checked the locks on the doors before she fell asleep.

"Mama," Althea had said, "Ray Junior and Ada are too young, but I was seven years old. I knew where babies came from."

"Well, maybe, you don't know everything about where babies come from." Mama's voice held a warning note. "But you'd better stop talking like this. You want to lose Coral? You want someone to take Coral from us? If I ever hear you talk about this—if I ever hear you say one word about it, to your friends, to your brother—I will take a switch to you. Do you understand me?"

"Yes, Mama. I'm sorry."

"Oh baby, I'm sorry too."

Augusta had wrapped Althea, so thin and awkward then, in her arms. "Honey, this is a harsh world. And there's plenty of mysteries in it. But Coral is our baby girl. And it's just gotta be something we don't talk about. I ain't never talked about it, not to anyone, not to Reverend Cole, not to anyone. It's better this way, Althea. People accept something if you just don't give them anything else to think."

But what had her mother meant? That they could lose Coral? That someone could take her away?

A few weeks after Odell Dibb's funeral, Coral finally asked her mama about him. They were alone at home. Ada was in Reno, visiting the university. Althea was already married. Ray Junior had decided to enlist, and he was at the gym, getting ready for boot camp.

"Did you love Odell Dibb?"

Her voice cracked like thunder out of her mouth, even though she'd meant to say it quietly, and after, the room was still and silent, like a stone.

"What?"

Coral could not repeat the question. She had meant to ask if Odell Dibb was her father, but in the seconds when she was trying to say it, trying to spit out the words, so many possibilities flashed through her mind—that Augusta had been forced, that Augusta had loved him, that Augusta had cheated on Ray Senior—and somehow, this other question had just come out of her mouth.

Mama moved about the kitchen, sliding the broiler pan into the drawer under the oven, and setting some glasses to dry on a towel.

"Child, that is quite a question."

Coral did not look at her.

"I had to take you to that funeral. God knows I would rather not have done it. But there's things that are right to do. They just are."

She was going to tell her. Augusta was going to tell her.

"Come on in to the living room. Let's sit here together, and talk about some things."

So they sat down on the sofa, and Coral put her head on her mother's shoulder, and Augusta stroked the side of her head for a bit.

"I didn't love Del Dibb." Her mother's hand rested on the side of her head. "I loved Ray Senior, and I never loved anyone else."

Then it was going to be bad, what came next. Coral wished she hadn't asked, didn't know why she had.

"Coral, you're my child, you're my daughter, I love you exactly the same as Ada and Althea and Ray, do you understand?"

It was going to be really bad. Because why would Augusta need to say that? The air left her chest like someone had pounced on it. She couldn't breathe.

"I don't want to hear anymore," she choked out. "I don't want to know."

Augusta spoke anyway.

"Coral, I didn't birth you. I'm not your mother that way."

What?

This couldn't be. Of course she was Augusta's daughter. Of course Augusta had given birth to her. What did she mean? Nobody had ever said she wasn't Augusta's daughter.

Coral bucked her head, jamming it sharply into her mother's chin, and for a second, they looked at each other stunned. Coral's hand flew to touch Augusta's face, and then she drew back, looked down. Tears were spurting now.

Her mother wrapped her arms around Coral and settled her back onto her body. Coral kept her eyes down. She would ever after remember the heave of Augusta's chest and a small yellow button that jiggled there, when she thought of this conversation. Mama spoke softly.

"Del Dibb and Ray Senior were good friends. Real good friends. From childhood. And after Ray Senior died, it was a terrible time. I was distraught. I didn't know how I could live with what had happened."

Augusta paused.

"Mr. Dibb helped me out. He gave me money. Ada was just a baby. He put down the payment on this house."

Coral wanted to move. She wanted Mama to stop talking. She wanted to be somewhere else. But her body was solid, like a plank, and she sat perfectly still.

"He came over and visited us too. He showed Ray Junior how to ride a bike. He bought a dress in Los Angeles for Althea to wear to her first day of school. He told the principal that Althea was like a daughter to him. That all the Jackson kids meant the world to him, that he would be watching out for them."

Augusta wanted Coral to understand. She wanted her to believe something.

"This meant a lot to me, Coral. It meant a lot to this family."

Coral watched the yellow button and did not move. Her breath stuttered in and out, and her heart pounded in a lopsided rhythm; she was still afraid of what was coming. If she wasn't Augusta's daughter, who was she? This was worse than she had ever imagined. Why had Monica asked her about Odell Dibb? She hated people. Mama had always taught her to ignore what people said.

"One night, it was a Sunday. It was December, and Althea had a holiday program at school the next day. She was so excited, I had a hard time getting any of the kids to bed. And I was just sitting in that chair, missing Ray and feeling sorry for myself. Those were dark times. I heard a knock on the door. I almost didn't answer it. But when I did, it was Mr. Dibb. He was standing there, crying. He didn't say anything. I asked him to come in, but he shook his head."

Coral was afraid of what was coming. But she couldn't stop listening.

"Mr. Dibb said, 'Augusta, I need your help.'

"'Sure, Mr. Dibb. I would do anything for you. You know that.'

"'This is a little bit more.'

"'Please come in.'

"He shook his head. Then he turned and went back to his car. I thought he was going to leave, but he opened the door, and lifted out a baby basket.

"And that baby was you."

Coral started to cry then. She cried so hard, she got the hiccups, and then her head hurt, so Augusta did not say any more. She slept in Augusta's bed that night, for the first time since she could remember, and in the morning, at breakfast, her mama told her what else she knew.

Del hadn't said whose baby it was. He told Augusta that he would never be able to tell her anything about the child. That was not negotiable. But he had money. He had money to raise her, and to send her to college, and he would take care of everything legally too.

"I don't know where else to go," he had told her. "I know I can't ask you this, but I don't have anyone else."

"Why did you say yes, Mama?" Coral asked. "You had three babies."

"Well, I thought about saying no. I had said I would do anything for him, but I don't think that did include taking on a child."

Coral closed her eyes. What if Mama had said no? Where would she be? What would have happened to her?

"Mr. Dibb was awfully broken up. And you started to fuss. So I picked you up, because he was too upset. You were a pretty little baby, and you had on a pink silk nightie. I still have it, upstairs in the closet. You were real small; smaller than my babies. But it was the way you looked at me, straight into my eyes, I'll never forget it.

"I fell in love with you. Right there. My mind had been racing, thinking how I was going to tell him it wasn't possible, that I couldn't take another child. How could I explain another child? How could he ask me for this, with all I'd been through?

"And I knew he meant it, that he wasn't going to tell me who you were. And who was your mama? Where was she?

"But I also knew that he wouldn't have brought you to me if there was anyone else to take you. And I could see you were mixed. I knew what that meant.

"So I just looked at you, this tiny little girl in a pink silk nightie, and I knew you were meant to be mine. Whatever happened, you were my fourth baby. God works in strange ways, and you came to me after Ray Senior died, but you were our baby, sure as Ada and Ray Junior and Althea.

"So I said yes."

That was all Augusta said that morning, but the next day, Coral asked her, "Odell Dibb never came to see me?"

"No." Augusta's eyes filled. "He never came to see you."

"Do you know who my mother is?"

"No. I tried to figure it out. Las Vegas wasn't very big in 1960. Our community was tight. I couldn't think of any woman who was pregnant, who had lost her baby. We were living all the way over here then, but I asked around in the 'Side, people at work. I had to be careful."

"What did people say to you about me?"

"They didn't say nothing. I introduced the kids to you the next morning. Althea was all broke up, because she had to leave for school, but I told her she had to go and the baby would be there when she got home. I just kept everything real normal. Just didn't let anyone ask me anything.

"I brought you to church. Folks said, 'Who's that baby you got?' And I said, 'This is my daughter Coral.' And nothing else. And I don't know what they thought. Maybe they just thought I was a big woman and they'd missed something. Maybe they figured it wasn't their business.

"But that's one thing I learned from Ray Senior. You don't owe an explanation to anybody but the Lord, and most people will stop asking if you act like you won't be telling."

"Do you think she's alive?"

Coral couldn't bring herself to say "my mother," but Augusta knew what she meant.

"I don't know. I have wondered and wondered. I think he must have known her somewhere else. Mr. Dibb traveled a lot. You could have been born anywhere."

"You mean, you think he just put me in the car and took me away? When I was born?"

"I don't know, baby girl."

Augusta hesitated. Coral waited.

"You weren't brand new."

"What?"

"You were new, you still had some cord, but it was all shriveled up. Getting ready to fall off."

"How old was I?"

"Well, I figured you were about a week old. But when your birth certificate came, it listed the Thursday before. So maybe you were just three, four days old."

"Where was I before?"

"I don't know."

"Did he take care of me?"

Her mom looked down. "I think your mama did."

It might have been the way Augusta's voice dropped, but Coral suddenly felt as if she might cry.

"You wouldn't take a bottle. You cried so much."

"So?"

"So I think you were nursed. I think your mama nursed you those days."

Augusta was silent then, and Coral was too. She didn't want to imagine her mother, herself: newborn. She didn't know how to imagine them. Couldn't get any picture in her mind at all.

Suddenly Coral stood up.

"My birth certificate. What does it say?"

Augusta pursed her lips.

"It says I'm your mother. It says you were born at this house."

"But Mama, that's my birth certificate. It has to say who I am."

"Yes."

"That's wrong, Mama. I'm a person. Someone just can't make up my birth certificate."

"I know, baby girl. I know."

To this day, that's what Coral knew about it. That was everything she knew. Who her mother was, what the story was, Augusta never learned. Augusta saw Odell Dibb only a few times in all the years after, and always by accident. He didn't come around and play with the kids anymore. He wasn't there for Ray Junior's first day of school. But there was always money; things always worked out in town for the Jacksons. Even after Mr. Dibb died. Ray Junior had gotten that good job, Ada was chosen for a scholarship, things like that.

And though Coral and Augusta had talked it over many times, although her mother had repeated the details she knew as often as Coral needed them repeated, in the end, they hadn't talked about it with Althea or Ada or Ray Junior. When she first learned the truth, Coral had wanted to tell her sisters right away. And Augusta had said that it was her story—she could tell anyone she wanted. But she had also said that she had kept it quiet, that she had never told the truth to a soul, so that Coral would be free to keep it a secret too. She always had the option to tell someone, but she would never have the option to keep it a secret again.

Coral had said, "Althea and Ada won't tell. They'll keep the secret."

"They love you, and they'll keep your secret. But life is long. There's a lot of ways for a secret to come out. If you tell someone, it might not be your secret anymore."

"But why should I keep it a secret? Are you ashamed?"

"Oh baby girl, I'm not ashamed. I kept it a secret at first because I was afraid of what would happen if I didn't. Mr. Dibb made that clear. That something bad could happen if anyone knew who you were."

"Could something bad still happen?" Coral felt a jolt of fear.

"Oh, I don't think so. This isn't 1960. I think he was afraid of something that would never happen now. There's no reason for you to be afraid."

"Well, what would have happened?"

"I don't know. Those were strange times. Maybe he was just worried about his son, his wife. Maybe he was worried about your mother. I don't know. But he wouldn't have told me that just to protect himself. He had a reason. I just doubt that it makes any difference now."

This had frightened Coral enough not to say anything to her sisters, and even now, she wasn't sure what Althea or Ada or Ray Junior might know. She supposed they believed what she had once believed: that she was a half sister, that she had a different father, that he must have been white, or nearly white, that she certainly wasn't Ray Senior. They all knew that Augusta had a secret, but which one of them would dare ask her to reveal it? Or did Althea know something none of the rest of them did?

How strange that Coral didn't know.

As strange as the real story.

16

Marshall was in love. June could see it on his face, flushed. Some of that was wine, but not all of it. Not that giddy smile, that funny laugh. It surprised her. She hadn't noticed anything special about this girl, who worked in reservations and looked like all of Marshall's girlfriends: doe-eyed, dark, thin.

She had never seen Marshall in love. At least, not since he was a sophomore in high school and lost his heart to a senior girl who had simply wanted a good-looking date, some easy fun. It hadn't gone well. Marshall was besotted, but she dropped him three weeks before the spring dance to date someone in her class.

Del had been alive then.

He had tried to talk with Marshall, and June had tried, but their son had sat stony-faced and red. Stayed in his room, playing Lynyrd Skynyrd and eating Butterfinger bars. The candy stuck in her mind; at sixteen, Marshall already looked like a man, but was still a boy.

After that, Marshall figured things out. Waited awhile to date, but had a steady girl all through college and ever since. At first, June had sized up each one, observed their relationship, wondered if this one would be part of their little family. She had liked one in particular: her name was Kari, and she'd been around awhile;

stayed at the house for a few school breaks. Now, a decade later, June had stopped paying much attention to who was dating Marshall, to what woman he brought to what opening, or to whether or not she was the same one who had come before.

This could annoy Marshall.

"Mom, you've met Sheila before."

"Oh yes, hi, Sheila. You're a lawyer, right?"

But no, Sheila wasn't a lawyer. Marshall would tighten his lips, June would give him a smile. Really, Marshall could play all the games he wanted, and June did not mind, but she wasn't going to play them with him.

Del had never gotten to see this grown-up, confident Marshall.

He had waved good-bye to his son, driving off in a car packed with skis and a sleeping bag and a bike strapped on top, the extra things that Marshall had decided would fit in his dorm room after all. And they had waved until the car turned the corner, standing in the street, knowing they looked foolish. And June had been just about to say something funny, something about how sentimental they had become, when she saw the tears in Del's eyes; when she saw how very close he was to losing control.

Had he known?

Had he sensed that he would never see Marshall again? That six weeks later, someone from housekeeping would find him slumped at his desk?

What would they have done differently if they had known?

What would she have done differently, had she known?

There were two ways to look at this question: you could size up your life and yourself, and think that you would not change a thing. After all, the tough spots and the mistakes were as much a part of who you were as anything else. June didn't disagree. But to say that it all led to where one was struck June as a bit smug, a bit of a punt. What about that second option? To spot the change that would have made the difference. To know the choice that set the rest in motion.

She could have stay married to Walter Kohn. Or she could have divorced him but returned to Clinton Hill and led an entirely different life. She could have moved back to Vegas but resisted Del's intentions, met someone Jewish, walked a more predictable path. Could she have admitted that she loved Eddie earlier, and gone away with him—before Marshall was born? They could have gone to Cuba.

No Marshall?

And what about Eddie's women?

Or Cuba?

Should she have grabbed her daughter and run out in the night and returned to New Jersey with a second, more surprising child? This is the fantasy that had played in June's mind, over and over, until she imagined that it occupied an entire territory of her brain: all the images and dreams and stories she had told herself about her daughter—a daughter who learned to laugh and crawl and talk, who took up dancing and read *A Tree Grows in Brooklyn* and won the seventh-grade spelling bee.

But then always, what about Marshall?

Could she have found a lawyer? Could she have persuaded him to take her case? Could she have fought Del for their son? Eventually she would have won. The world came her way. How many years would it have taken?

Del was not the one who had made the mistake. It was not Del who had risked Marshall's world. And how far is one obliged to carry the weight of a single mistake?

Because she had been wrong. She had risked Marshall's world for the love of a man who would not have loved her for life (as Del, in his way, had) but it was the world's cruelty, its inanity, that had amplified that mistake. It was the world that had put June and Del and Marshall and a little girl in Alabama in a hold they could not break. Or was this the real issue at the heart of everything else in her life? That she could always blame something other than herself?

Once she had been the girl smoking on the high school track; once she had let Leon Kronenberg touch her breast; once she had run away to Vegas; once she had opened a casino; once she had believed that the world could become new again, that the right people in the right place could make up any rules they wanted. And none of that was true. They had all paid the price. And, really, where was the moment that should have happened differently? Which was the choice that had set all the others in motion? And would a different choice have been the right one?

June and Del had been good partners at the El Capitan. She and Marshall were good partners there now. They made a lot of money; Del had been right about the opportunities he saw. But how long would it last? For all the millions they had spent, for all that it seemed there had always been something under construction, something being added, some area being renovated, the El Capitan was tired and small and old now. The Strip was moving south, the El Capitan was at the edge of being in the wrong part of town, closer to Circus Circus and the Stratosphere than to the empty land that would surely be the grand casinos—the carpet joints—of the next century. If there had been a niche to carve out for the El Capitan three decades ago, it was not clear that there would still be one for three more.

Already, she was fighting to hold on to their cash cow: to the entertainment that drew everyone in. She had stuck with the formula that she and Del had initiated. Four months after he died, she had signed a brother-and-sister magician act from Belarus, paying them twice what anyone else would have offered. And once again, her instinct for talent had been true. The act grew into that salary and past it, and the pair lured the gamblers, the drinkers, the players, the shoppers, the eaters, the lookers. Casinos were all about people and how many hours you could keep them in your joint. What they did there really didn't matter, because sooner or later you always made money from them. All you had to do was get them in the door and keep them too distracted to walk back out.

And she owed her life to this challenge, she supposed. To this simple trick that was not simple at all: how to keep people coming in, how to make them stay, how to keep up in a town that raced and bucked and reared and roared, ever forward, ever faster. You had better be ready for the ride, because Vegas wasn't for the weak and it wasn't for the cowardly; if you really wanted to win, you had better take off your hat, wave it to the crowd, and smile like an idiot. You had to make it look fun. Would any other life have sucked her up, taken her in, kept her going, held her fast? Would an easier life have kept June Stein Dibb alive?

Could she have climbed up on any other steed and survived the moment when Del walked out with a basket trailing a soft pink blanket and weighted with six pounds of her soul?

It had not been easy. She had fallen off again and again.

For weeks after Del had taken the baby, June had refused to see anyone. For years, she had stumbled through her days, death-eyed with pills, with gin, with crazed antics that had finally forced Del to sell the house and buy on the other side of the Strip. There was the time the man next door called Del to say his wife was naked on the street; the time she had terrified the newspaper boy with a pair of kitchen shears; the time when Cora, in her eighties by then and already sick with cancer, had run from house to house, from the park to the school to the wash, trying to find Marshall, who had wandered out on his own, looking for help with his mom, who was passed out on the stairs.

She didn't remember Marshall's first day of school. She might not have been there. She didn't remember him learning to ride a bike, or catching his first baseball, or sounding out words in a book. Those years were gone for June. Del had done it all: run the El Capitan; taken care of Marshall; hired the sitters; managed his grandmother; held a sobbing, vomiting June; and found the center that she had finally agreed to try—where she had gone for the spring that Marshall was in the first grade, and where she had finally, finally, come back to herself.

She had come out of rehab just in time for summer.

Every day, she and Marshall would swim in the early morning and in the evening. He wouldn't leave her those first months; didn't want to play with friends, didn't want friends coming over. So they canceled day camp, and they ignored the phone, and they spent those months—that hot, blistering summer—together. Seven years old, and he drank his mother's nearness like a wilted plant sucks water. Del came home often, running in for an hour in the middle of the day, and leaving work early most nights. He made Marshall laugh by jumping in the pool in his dress pants and tie, by wearing his shoes with his swimming trunks, by banging off the low diving board and cannonballing in to swamp June when she was trying to keep her hair dry.

If there had been three years of misery, there were then three months of joy. And after, it was true, there were years and years of a good life. They had been to hell, but they had come back. You could say what you wanted about what they each did, about the choices they made—she and Del and Eddie—but in the end, her little family had been happy.

Still, when Del died, the first thing June did after calling Marshall and arranging a way for him to come home, was to go to her husband's office and dig through the one cabinet that he kept locked from her. She didn't want Mack or Leo or his attorney to get there first. But there was nothing about the baby. There were some papers about Hugh, which she knew would be there. There were receipts; she didn't look at the ones for hotels in other places. There were cards, and quite a few letters from someone named Charles; she looked at one of those because she saw Eddie's name on it, but it didn't say anything more than that they had met, not long before Eddie left. There were records having to do with Augusta Jackson and her children. Del had stayed true to his word and taken care of Ray's family. But there was nothing from Alabama, no record of those receipts, nothing from Eddie, no birth certificate, nothing about a school, nothing about expenses, nothing personal, nothing official.

How could that be?

There had been times, in those first terrible years, when June had doubled over with the fear that her daughter was not alive. In the middle of the night, strung out, it was possible to imagine that Del had done something insane. And June could not stop the thought from slipping in then, as she stood in Del's office hours after he had died, the long-watched key in her hand, and all those files, all that paper, with nothing, nothing. But it was unimaginable. This Del could not have done. He was capable of dismaying acts; his life was not simple, and she knew it. But she had heard him singing to that baby; she had known who he was with Marshall. He had promised that her baby was alive and that she was safe. He had promised over and over. But never, in the great cruelness that was somehow also possible for Del, had he told her where she was.

Of course, she had written to Eddie despite Del's ultimatum.

She had mailed the letter at the post office herself.

He had not replied.

She had written again, several times, in the years when it was still possible to send mail to Cuba. She had asked about his brother in Alabama, she had begged him to send her word. And Eddie had never replied.

He was gone now too.

Died in a fight or in an alley—the stories were not clear. One newspaper had said it was a love affair gone bad. Another mentioned a husband. A third said gambling debts. She had showed the articles to Del, and he had said he knew about it. He also said that Eddie never could get past his own history; never could take the success the world wanted so much to give him.

"I'm sorry, June."

"I'm sorry."

And they had held each other then, and she had cried, and he had cried, and later they had even played some of Eddie's records: the song he had made famous at the El Capitan, and the album that must have made him very rich after. Eddie's music played all the time in Vegas, and mostly it had lost its power to bring June and Del back to any other moment. But that night, curled up on the sofa, listening to his debut album—with its scratch on the third track that made the word *cheer* repeat, repeat, repeat—his voice took them back to how it had been when they were newly married, when they first heard him sing at the Town Tavern, when they used to eat dinner and share drinks in the private lounge behind the Midnight Room.

Months after Del died, after she'd signed the magicians from Minsk and after Marshall returned to college, June had traveled to Alabama on her own. She had not told anyone where she was going or why. She flew to Mobile, and rented a car, and drove to the tiny town where Eddie Knox, the singer, had been born. There was a hardware store, two bars, a record store, kept in business, she supposed, by tourists; there were three intersections but no stop signs.

She asked at the hardware store first, but the greasy-haired kid sorting nails said he didn't know anything about Eddie Knox's family, and she stepped away from the record store when she heard one of Eddie's songs on the loudspeaker. That left the bars, so she chose the closest one: a dilapidated shed that looked like it might have been standing there a long time.

"I'm looking for information about Eddie Knox."

"Yeah? You buying a drink?" The bartender wasn't much past fifty, but he looked older, lined and sallow with ropey veins on the backs of his hands.

"I'll buy that bottle. The scotch."

"A whole bottle? You got a lot of questions?"

"A few. But I don't drink. You can share it with the house."

He nodded. Looked around the almost empty room, at the one customer seated in the corner, apparently asleep. Then he set the bottle aside and leaned on the counter, looking at her.

"I'm looking for his family," June said.

"Yeah. Not much left. Around here anyway."

"Who is here?"

"Well, his brother. Jacob."

"Jacob?"

"Yeah, that's Eddie's brother. I think he had a sister too, but she's long gone."

"I thought he had four brothers?"

"Eddie? Yeah. He told that story sometimes. But Jacob's his only brother. I lived here my whole life. I knew the Knox family. The sister was a lot older. But Eddie and Jacob, they were pretty close in age. About the same as me."

"Did you go to school with them?"

He looked at her without speaking.

Of course: he was white. They would not have gone to school together.

"So where's Jacob? Do you know his kids?"

"Jacob's kids? Jacob hasn't got any kids. Not that he knows of anyway."

"He doesn't have kids?"

"No. He's a drunk. Always has been. He lives in a shack pretty close to the old property. Course they lost it. They say Eddie tried to give him money, tried to buy him a house, but Jacob can't hang on to money."

June felt dizzy. She was going to be sick. She bolted up suddenly, left a fifty on the counter for the bottle—three times what it was worth—and got outside before she started to heave.

She made it back to the rental car, sat there stunned and dismayed and thinking about a drink for a few hours at least. But she did not take a drink. She did not go back to the bar. When it started to get dark, she turned the key in the ignition and drove all the way back to Mobile.

There wasn't anyone she could tell about what she had learned. There wasn't anyone to ask. Del was dead. Eddie was dead. Marshall had never known. Whomever Del had told, whoever had helped Del, was probably alive. But who was it? Leo? Mack? If they knew, and as much as they loved her, they wouldn't let on. Not if Del had told them no. Not even now. How would she ever know? She had never felt more alone.

June flew to Vegas that night. Went straight to the El Capitan from the airport. She had always thought she would know someday. But Del had taken care of that. Why? Would he ever have told her?

Somewhere a sixteen-year-old girl did not know how long her mother had been looking for her, how much she wanted to find her, how hard she had tried. Somewhere, a sixteen-year-old girl could not know that her mother's heart was still broken.

That trip to Alabama was a long time ago now—a dozen years at least—and mostly June did not let herself think about it. She had learned how to let go, she had learned what she could not control. It had been that or die, and in the end, she had loved Marshall enough to live.

17

It was the second house on the cul-de-sac. Coral chose it because it was on the east side of town, not far from Augusta and near Rowe Elementary. Out back was a pool, which she hadn't wanted, but Althea brought her kids over to swim the first day.

"Auntie Coral, I'm going to the basketball game!"

"You are?"

"Yeah. Rob got me a ticket. It's been sold out since last summer, but I get to go."

"That's so cool." Coral high-fived her nephew, who then raced to join his sister at the pool. She looked at Althea. "Rob?"

"Don't say anything. He's just a friend from work."

"Who gave your ten-year-old son the hottest ticket in town?"

"Malcolm was in the office with me. And he was going on and on about how the Rebels are the best college team in the country. How they're going to win the whole tournament. So Rob just invited him. They're going together. It's an exhibition game, Friday night."

"Wow."

"Yeah, Keisha's whining, of course."

"Is there anything interesting about Rob?"

"You mean other than he's the accountant?"

Coral laughed.

"How about you? Mama said you went on a date with Paul Ormsby. Didn't he take you to prom?"

"No, he didn't. We went out Saturday, but it wasn't a date. He teaches at the high school, and, you know, we just had a drink."

"Okay. Well, Mama's very interested in your dates. You better be careful."

"Should I tell her you're dating Rob?"

"I'm not dating Rob. This fine woman's done with men, whether Mama believes me or not."

"She doesn't believe you."

"Well, I'm counting on you to distract her. I need some relief."

Augusta walked in from the backyard. "That child is mad for those Rebels!" She reached for the beach towel Keisha had left on the counter. "You'd think a college basketball team made the world the way he talks about them. Larry Johnson. Stacey Augmon."

"Yeah, isn't that ridiculous, Mom? Almost like someone who had to be taken to the ER after a certain team lost to Indiana?"

"That was a different group, Althea. My Freddie scored thirty-eight points that game."

"Remember the Oklahoma game? Mama called me and would not stop talking about that two-point shot."

"His foot was behind the line. It was a three."

Coral and Althea laughed at the same instant.

"Well, I'm not doing that anymore. The Rebels are a great team, but I'm not having a heart attack for them. They're so good this year, they oughta win. That's not the same."

"Right, Mama. We don't care if this team wins or not."

"Well, we care. We can care."

Coral wrapped her arm around her mother, and the three of

them went out back to watch the kids swim. She was glad she'd picked the house with a pool. Glad to live in Vegas with Mama and Althea and her kids.

Coral didn't want her mother or her sister to know some things about the life she'd lived in California. About Gerald, for example. The sort of boyfriend he'd been.

Gerald was the one person Coral had told about her birth. The only time she had ever choked the words out of her mouth, the only time she'd ever repeated the story her mama had told her, was to Gerald one night, very late. And, of course, he'd made it worse. He had focused on Augusta. Why had she kept it a secret? How much money had Odell Dibb given her? (That was a big one. He brought that one up a lot.) Was any of it even true? Perhaps Coral *was* Augusta's child—and the story a way of keeping secret whatever had happened that had made her pregnant. After all, that's what Coral's birth certificate said.

Coral had started to cry as Gerald was spinning these scenarios, one after another, as if it were a movie plot and not her life—not her own most personal truth, something she had shared only with him. Finally, she had reached a kind of wail, screaming "Stop it, stop it, stop it!" But he didn't stop, so she kicked at him in her rage, and he just laughed to see her so out of control. Yet even then, even after that, she continued to live with Gerald.

This was a private shame, one of many things Althea and Augusta didn't know.

At twenty-nine, the story of her birth didn't loom quite as large for Coral as it had at sixteen. It was true that her heart could still skitter unevenly if she thought of the instant before Augusta said yes to keeping her. It was true that it still nipped at her not to know how she had come to be, how her hair and face and feet had formed. And sometimes, the thought that this was a mystery to her but not to someone else galled her; didn't she have the most at stake in knowing this particular truth? But the empty space at the core, the blankness she had spent years not thinking about— even the way she had felt when she first moved back home with Mama last year—it surprised her that these feelings were starting to fade. Or fading wasn't the right word. She felt them still. They just didn't hurt as deeply as they once had.

Maybe it was getting older. Maybe it was teaching: seeing a lot of children in ruinous situations. Maybe it was having nieces and nephews, watching her brother and sisters raise their kids, seeing all the different ways a childhood might play out. She had been lucky to be a Jackson.

Still, she wondered about the woman who bore her. She felt loyal to that unknown person—who might have been afraid, who might have been treated badly, for whom her birth might have been tragic.

Who was her mother?

Had Odell Dibb loved her? Had she loved him? Had he forced her to give up their child? Could he have raped her? Where was she now?

Augusta thought Coral should let go of these questions. There wasn't any way to find her mother, there wasn't anyone alive who knew anything, and why did she have to imagine such terrible things? Why would Mr. Dibb have asked Augusta to take the baby if he hadn't cared about her mother? Why would she have been dressed in a pink silk gown? Why would he have been so upset? That was Augusta's hole card: the way Odell Dibb had cried the night he brought Coral to her. "A man doesn't fall apart if he doesn't care; if you aren't a love child. He doesn't ask someone to take a baby, to keep a secret, if you aren't important, Coral. A man like Mr. Dibb doesn't risk me knowing this about him, me having this over his head, unless you are someone very special. That's what you should think about your birth."

Coral saw the sense in Augusta's words, but she felt things too. Felt her mother deep down, in her skin, in her bones. These were things she couldn't explain to anyone else, but it was as if she owed her birth mother something, or her birth mother exacted something from her; she really didn't know which.

And what about Odell Dibb?

A long time ago, Coral had done what research she could. She'd sat in the Clark County Library on Flamingo, squinting at microfiche that listed where he had given his money, how much he had paid in personal taxes, who was listed on his private trust. Once she had seen a photo of him standing outside a bar called Le Bistro. He wasn't identified, but Coral recognized him from all the other pictures she'd seen.

And it caught her eye, that photo, because of the way her father was standing. He was smiling, maybe just about to laugh, and he held a cigarette a few inches from his mouth—about to take a puff or just having taken one, there was no way to tell—and his long frame was relaxed; his arm rested slightly on a smaller man to his left. That photo stayed in Coral's mind. You wanted to look at Odell Dibb in that photo: something about his stance, that hint of a smile, even his fingers in the air. It was arresting.

There were lots of records to find, articles about El Capitan, donations to various charities, things he had said in response to one local issue or another. People thought highly of Del Dibb. He had been influential. He had treated his employees well. And yet Coral never felt much in these records; never got a sense of him from all the photos wearing black tie at galas, nothing like the way he leaped out of the photo in which he was not even identified.

Now that she was older, now that she'd had her own experiences of love and sex and the wrong choices one could make, Coral sometimes imagined Odell Dibb differently than Augusta had described him. What sort of man had he been? Why did his face leap out from that one photo? How had he ended up with a baby in a pink silk gown?

Still, the questions about her father didn't burn in her as the questions about her mother did. She knew who he was, and years ago, she'd figured out that what really mattered to her about him was that he'd given her to Augusta Jackson. To Mama, who had allowed the rest of the world to believe whatever it would about her: to believe she had given birth to a mixed race child while married to a dark black man; to believe she had a secret life, a lover; to believe she was raped; to believe she had sold her body; to believe anything it wanted—any possibility at all—for how Coral had come to exist.

Augusta was proud. And she was a religious woman, a churchgoer; she stood for something. And still, to protect Coral, from the first instant—even without knowing anything about her, where she came from, who might have a claim to her—she had sacrificed that. She had given up being known for who she was. She had carried the secret by herself, she had done this for Coral.

That's what Coral knew of her own origins. She knew what her existence must have cost Augusta, and she knew what Augusta's choice had meant to her.

So if she got frustrated teaching at the school sometimes, if there were parents who thought music class was a waste, if there were children who showed up with bruises, if there was a little boy who kept stealing food from other kids' lunches, if the local paper ran an editorial railing against the benefits given to teachers, if the principal could not find money for supplies, if some days being the only music teacher in a school with 654 children seemed Sisyphean, then Coral always had her own mother to inspirit her: she could live how she wanted, she could take the actions she believed in. It didn't matter whether anyone else understood, it didn't matter that others did not see the value in the choices she made. She was Augusta's daughter, and this was Augusta's legacy to her.

For Christmas, they all came to Coral's. It took Ray Junior and Lynda fourteen hours to make the ten-hour trip from Fremont because Lynda's morning sickness was so bad they had to stop every hour, and because four-year-old Trey had an ear infection that made him cry whenever the Tylenol started to wear off.

"Never again," said Ray Junior.

"Do you promise, Daddy?" said Trey.

Althea wrapped her brother in a hug, while Coral took Lynda to the spare bedroom so she could change. Coral nearly twirled down the hallway; she was so excited to be hosting Christmas this year. They had always gone to Augusta's, but her mama had asked if they could move it to Coral's. Augusta said that four adult children, five grandchildren, but just one in-law (this with one eyebrow raised) was getting to be too much. Coral knew this wasn't true. Moving Christmas to her house was Augusta's way of anointing Coral's home.

Coral had been buying and making gifts for weeks, and she and Althea had picked out one of the biggest trees on the lot. Malcolm insisted on colored bulbs, and Keisha had persuaded her aunt to buy a string of plastic lights in the shape of candles. It had taken seven strings of lights, and dozens of ornaments: all of the ones Coral remembered hanging on her childhood tree—including the green star with her second-grade face on it and the angel Ray Junior had carved one year when he went to Camp Lee Canyon—and some that the younger kids had made. When he was seven, Malcolm had carefully written "Mery Christmas Momy" and "Hapy New Yere Grandnan" on two cards that now hung at eye level.

In the middle of one night, Coral heard a loud bang and came downstairs to find the whole tree lying on the soaked carpet. She didn't leave it for morning; she found a screwdriver, a hook, and some wire, and hung the whole thing from a beam in the ceiling. It was the first thing Ray Junior mentioned when he looked around her new house.

"Nice job with the tree, Coco."

Coral laughed. "It fell over. In the middle of the night."

"I could have guessed that."

"Well, it won't fall over now."

"Nope."

"Come on! You never had any trouble getting a tree to stand up?"

"Oh no, I always have trouble. I've tied trees to the wall, piled sandbags on the base; the year Trey was a baby, the tree fell over twice. I threw it away and bought a smaller one."

Lynda grinned. "Yeah, and what was Trey's first word that Christmas, Ray?"

"*Darn*. It was *darn*, right?"

Everybody laughed.

On Christmas night, with Teenage Mutant Ninja Turtles strewn the length of the house, and Keisha's talking bear Teddy Ruxpin put safely to bed—"If that thing tells me his name again, he and I are going to have some words," said Ada—Coral and her siblings sat around drinking rum brandy punch. Lynda had fallen asleep with Trey, and Augusta had taken the three older kids to see *Home Alone*.

"What was it that Ray used to say when he got dressed up?"

"Ain't I trassy!"

"Yeah, ain't you trassy, Ray?"

"I have always been a classy guy."

"You is trassy, brother. You is definitely a trassy guy." Ada and Ray clinked glasses.

"Remember when Althea said a boy was going to come over to study with her?"

"And Ray went in her room and pulled all the underwear out of her drawers, and hung her bras from the bedposts?"

Their brother snorted. "Mama took a belt to me for that. I got one belt for going in her room, one belt for embarrassing her, and one belt because I better not be looking at any girl's underwear."

They all laughed.

"Hell, I lived with three sisters. How was I supposed to not see any girl's underwear?"

Ada stood up. "Remember when Ray murdered my doll for his Halloween house?"

"Oh yeah, I remember."

"I walked in the garage, and LilyBelle was covered in ketchup with a knife stuck in her chest. I had nightmares about that for years. I might still have nightmares about that."

"I was nine years old. I didn't know you'd be so upset."

"Yeah, and I never told Mama. Which was lucky for you."

"I kept so many secrets for *you*," Ray retorted. "If I hadn't messed up that doll, you'd probably have a whole different life. Mama would have figured you out and set you straight when you were young."

"Nobody was ever going to set Ada straight."

"That was Coral's job," Ada explained. "She was good enough for two of us. Right, Coral?"

"I spent my whole life hoping you guys weren't going to get in trouble."

"Oh yeah, remember how Coral would cry when any of us got a beating? She'd cry so hard, Mama would stop hitting us."

"Can I get a thank-you for that?"

"Remember when Coral came to breakfast, all upset because she was going to be late for school?"

"Yeah, and she told Mama, 'How can I be on time for school if Althea is occuuupeeing the bathroom?'" Ray winked at his youngest sister as he mimicked her eight-year-old voice.

"The best was when Althea decided to teach Coral to drive—"

"And the cop pulled them over—"

"And asked Coral if she would drive off a cliff if Althea told her to do it—"

"And Coral said yes!"

"You bet she said yes!" Althea poured another shot of brandy. "When I told Coral to do something, I meant it. And I didn't tell her to turn down the street the wrong way. I told her to turn left into the inside lane, and bam, she just drives straight into traffic."

"I slammed on the brake when I saw the headlights, and then it was a police car." Coral took the glass Althea offered. "The officer flipped his siren on. I about passed out."

"I was grabbing the wheel and telling you, 'Move over! *Move over!*'"

"But I turned the car off!"

They laughed again. Lynda walked in, her rounded stomach showing through the buttons of some red flannel pajamas, and curled up next to Althea on the couch.

"What's so funny?"

"Oh, we were just remembering old times. Kid stuff."

"The talent show!"

"Coral's talent show!"

"Coral had a talent show?" Lynda looked at her sister-in-law.

"No, it was Althea's game. We used to play it quite a lot. We'd set up a stage in the dining room, or outdoors, and then everyone just performed whatever talent they could think of."

"Remember when Greg next door popped his shoulder out of the socket?"

"Yeah, that was his talent! He could do 'weird shoulder.'"

"Weird shoulder! That was a great one."

Lynda shifted position, trying to get comfortable on the couch. "So why was it Coral's talent show?"

"Well, Coral was little. Maybe three?"

"Yeah, I think she was three."

"And her talents were always pretty odd."

"Oh yeah. Remember her feet talent?"

"'My feet have names!'" the siblings said in unison. "'This one is Petey, and this one is Noodle-ah.'" Ada hooted.

"I don't get it."

Althea saw Lynda's skeptical look and explained, "That was her talent. Her feet had names."

"But I was really little then."

"Oh, yeah, you were small."

"And that was Coral's talent show?"

"Oh no. That was later. She was three, and she said she

wanted to sing something, so she stood on the dining table, and she belted out . . ."

All four siblings started to sing: "*So won't you plee-eze . . . Be my, be my, be my little baby? Say you'll be my darling. Be my baby now-ow-ow. A-whoa oh oh oh!*"

They could sing. Lynda tapped her foot to the beat.

"I mean, she belted it. We'd never heard her sound like that."

"She could have been a Ronette. Remember the way she was swishing her hips?"

They all started singing again. Ray stood up and camped his way toward his wife, and Ada took Althea's hand and pulled her from the sofa to dance a few steps. When they stopped, Ada spoke.

"Yeah, I think that's the first time I figured out Coral was different from the rest of us."

Coral shrugged her shoulders. "Come on, stop it. I hate that."

"I know, but I mean, Coral, your voice was unbelievable."

Althea wrapped her arms around her sister. "It's okay, Coral. Ada has wanted to be the baby of the family her whole life."

"It's true. I did want to be the baby of the family."

Coral blurted it out: "Someone gave me to Mama. When I was four days old."

There was silence. Althea squeezed Coral a little tighter, but nobody said anything, not even Lynda.

She realized they already knew. It had been so hard not to tell them, not to talk about it, all these years. And they knew.

"Mama told you? She told me she didn't."

Nobody said anything for a minute.

"Mama never told us anything. She didn't have to."

"But . . ."

"Mama wasn't pregnant." Ada's voice went up a notch. "Althea was seven. She would've known if Mama was pregnant."

Coral was crying now. Althea was wiping away the tears with her hand, and Ray had let go of Lynda to sit down by Coral's feet.

"You're a one-hundred-percent Jackson," he said. "That's what we always knew."

"But when did you know? Did you all talk about me?"

Her voice cracked. Of course they had talked about her. She talked about them. Still, she couldn't stand it. Althea was crying now too, Ray looked sick, and even Ada was bouncing on her toes and shaking her fingers the way she did when she was upset. Only Lynda sat quietly, watching.

"Coco, we didn't talk about you. It wasn't like that."

"I mean, we all knew that there was something. We always knew."

"Always?"

"Well, for a long time. And we didn't talk about it. Ever. You know how Mama is. She told Althea not to talk about it, and Althea told us, and that was it."

"And then Ray was here a few years ago, and he was telling us what you were like singing in that club, and we were all so proud of you."

"And Ada just brought it up."

"Hey, I'm not the bad guy here!"

Coral looked at Ada, who had tears in her eyes now.

"Coral, it wasn't like that. It just came out. I just asked Althea if she knew about you, where you came from."

Tears spurted from Coral's eyes at these last words.

"Honey." Ada was piled up on the other side of her now. "Honey, that doesn't sound right. I just thought Althea would know."

"Did you?"

"No. I asked Mama when I was younger."

"I heard you."

"You heard us?"

"Yeah. For years, I thought someone was going to kidnap me—take me back."

Ray laid his head on Coral's knees. It was all she could do to ask, "Did you talk to Mama?"

"We wanted to talk to her, we always say we're going to ask her, but—"

"We don't." Ray Junior and Althea spoke in unison.

This made everyone laugh, as they sat huddled around their youngest sister.

Coral spoke: "My father brought me to her in a basket. He was Daddy's friend. But he wouldn't tell her anything about my mother."

She could feel the question in the air, feel how they wanted to ask about her father, but she didn't want to say his name. She had carried the secret so long. It was too much. They all sat there, wrapped up together like one unit: Althea petting her cheek, and Ada holding her hand, and Ray's head on her knee. Nobody asked Coral for anything more, not tonight, and Coral didn't say anything more. And then Trey called out in his sleep, and Lynda leaned over to kiss Coral's head before checking on him, and Ray said again, "You're a one-hundred-percent Jackson, Coco," and they sat like this, quiet and entwined, for a long time.

18

A man wearing a jacket that said "El Capitan" met them at the Las Vegas airport. They rode in a limo that was as long as a tourist bus; it reminded Honorata of a black cat. In Manila, she had often fed a cat with a particularly long body. At the El Capitan, the man who greeted them said, "Welcome Mr. Wohlmann, Mrs. Wohlmann. Let me take you to your suite."

The suite, on the seventeenth floor, had a living room, a den, a bar, a bedroom, and floor-to-ceiling windows overlooking the Las Vegas Strip. There were fresh flowers, champagne in a bucket, a plate of cheese and grapes. Everything in the room was gold or black or mirrored.

Jimbo was effusive. He called the man Denny, clapped him on the back, handed him a small roll of bills. Honorata assumed they would have sex. Instead, Jimbo told her to put on the green dress and the gold sandals; he had some things to show her. When she was ready, he pulled out a long white box in which a necklace with a large emerald nestled.

"The hotel gave this to you to use for the weekend."

She put it on.

Jimbo leaned forward and kissed the stone of the necklace.

They left the room and took the elevator to the casino. Honorata had never experienced anything like it. Lights twinkled, glowed, flashed, there were machine sounds of dings and whistles and whirrs, coins clanking in trays, voices calling numbers, people talking, the whish of air moving: cacophonous, psychedelic, disorienting, galvanizing. Beside her, Jimbo seemed to expand; she could feel the transformation as he lifted on the balls of his feet, his chest swelling, eyes lifting. He took her to the back of the room and walked casually through an entryway where a woman stood at elegant guard; they nodded to each other slightly. This room was quieter, there was more space between the tables, and the people playing sat in concentrated silence. Jimbo introduced her to someone named Richard, who smiled. Then he pointed to the people playing and said the game was baccarat. There was poker too, behind the curtain. A woman brought him a glass of scotch, which he drained quickly. He told Richard that his wife would have a gin and tonic; the woman brought it immediately along with another scotch for Jimbo.

Honorata did not react to the word *wife*, as she had not reacted to *Mrs. Wohlmann*. Jimbo had said nothing about marriage. It was conceivable that he would surprise her with the once-promised wedding, but she doubted it. The conversation about the letters, the act of having gone directly to the airport hotel when she arrived from Manila, told Jimbo that the wedding itself was no longer necessary. He could call her his wife when he liked, he could present himself as a married man when he wanted, but the marriage itself would not happen.

This made as much sense to her as it did to him.

Jimbo had said he would show her around, teach her how to play some games, but he couldn't resist stepping up to a table when someone left. He told Richard to give Honorata some tokens, so Richard handed her a bucket filled with a hundred or more heavy gold coins marked with the El Capitan logo. It made her almost dizzy. She hadn't held money since arriving in America.

"Do you know how to play?" Richard asked.

He had a lovely voice, slightly accented.

"No."

"I can have someone show you. Perhaps roulette?"

"No."

"As you wish."

"Can I walk around? Can I go out there?" Honorata gestured to the casino floor.

Richard looked at her. Honorata saw something flash in his eyes. Then he smiled and said, of course, she could do anything she liked. Mr. and Mrs. Wohlmann were guests of the hotel, and she could go anywhere, she could order anything she liked, she need only say her name.

My name is Honorata Navarro, she thought.

"Thank you. I think I'll just walk around."

Honorata kept the bucket of coins with her for three days. She put a few coins in some slot machines, pulling the long handle and staring as the spinning figures spun into lines of color and then slowed . . . and stopped—never giving back even a single coin. She liked the feel of the bucket in her hand, the shake of the coins, so she stopped throwing them away like this. She supposed someone would give her more coins if she ran out; at least they kept giving her other things: drinks, round glasses filled with shrimp, a private table at the buffet. She never had to say who she was. They all seemed to know her, and many of the workers were kind.

She saw Jimbo only when someone from the casino came to get her, politely indicating that Mr. Wohlmann was looking, and

would she mind returning to her room? When she did, he undressed her or bathed her or offered up various parts of his body
to her. His moods varied. One time he talked rapidly, the next time
he was distracted—sullen, even. Honorata lost her sense of time
quickly. She came back to the room thinking that it was time to
go to bed, and was startled to see from the windows that the sun
was just setting. Jimbo seemed hardly to sleep at all. From time
to time, she wandered by the exclusive area of the casino where
he played. She would see him sitting there, oblivious to anything
but the cards, or once, laughing with a woman bringing him chips.
The woman wore a skirt of gold metal that barely skimmed her
bottom, and she had the largest breasts Honorata had ever seen.

During the fourth night, Honorata could not sleep. Her body
had begun to rebel, and she turned restlessly in the king-sized bed.
She thought that Jimbo would come in; she hadn't seen him in
hours, and when she had, he'd said they might be going back to
Chicago in the morning; she should be ready to go if he decided
to leave.

Honorata didn't want to be alone in the suite. If she opened
the blinds, then the lights of the Strip made the room bright as
day, but sitting with them shut made her feel claustrophobic. She
had not been outside once. She thought about going down to the
casino. At night, the play was more serious. People stayed longer at
the same machines, they were less likely to look up when a leggy
woman brought them another drink. There was almost always a
group of loud young men.

She turned from one side to the other, bunching up a pillow
against her stomach, and then throwing the pillows aside, lying
spread eagle without a sheet over her. Honorata checked the clock
beside her bed: 2:18. She got up, drank some water, picked up one

of the chocolate coins left every night on their bed, set it down again. She tried sitting on the chaise near the window. She had already examined everything in the room. Finally, as if it were a talisman, she picked up the bucket of El Capitan coins and shook them slightly. They weren't money; they'd be useless in Chicago. She might as well play them now.

Downstairs, she turned away from the side of the casino where she thought Jimbo was. She walked toward an older area of the floor, marked by a lower roof and a general sense of abandonment. The space was nearly empty, and Honorata wondered why the El Capitan had not updated it; why it didn't look like the rest of the gleaming, throbbing casino. Maybe some people liked this sort of thing, but Honorata could almost smell the sadness in the place. In the corner, a man wearing a black shirt played a poker machine. Nearby, an older woman played another; she was smoking a cigarette and a half empty pack of Camels teetered at the edge of her seat.

There was a showroom over here, which Honorata had not noticed before. A sign read "Psychedelic Sixties Revue, Playing Nightly in the Midnight Room." She wandered over, and pulled on the door to see if it was open. It was, but when she peeked inside, the room was dark, and the air smelled of dust and smoke. Behind her, the luminous face of a Megabucks, one of the giant slot machines that was almost always in use, stared blankly. Honorata had watched hordes of people play these, feeding their coins in quickly or slowly, kissing their fingers or their wives, rubbing a button, a penny, a rosary before pulling the handle.

She knew Megabucks was for fools. But Honorata didn't much care. She would play out the coins. It would take awhile, and perhaps she would get tired. She was far from Jimbo. It was quiet, and she didn't feel like talking to anyone. No one had even come to bring the smoker a drink.

She hit on the fourteenth pull.

Forty-two tokens in.

The machine exploded. A round light on the top spun like a police car flasher. There were bells, horns, dings, the whooping sound of a siren. Honorata cracked her knee as she jumped up; her first impulse was to flee.

Within seconds, people started running toward her: a cocktail waitress, a valet attendant, the woman with the cigarette, two young men—the collars of their pastel shirts turned up, one with a cigar, the other with flushed cheeks—all running at her. She heard excited yells and then someone clapping. She looked at the machine: "Jackpot! $1,414,153.00! Winner!" flashed across the top. She heard someone say "Get Mr. Wohlmann, in the VIP room," and time stopped, sound stopped, the room went pale.

There was a huge bouquet of flowers, champagne, the hotel photographer. The owner of the hotel hurried in, his hair sticking up and his tie slightly crooked, as if he had not stopped to shower when he got the call. He was young. He knew Jimbo. He kept saying things like "No problem, man. We'll have this worked out." And then he would look at her, give her another hug, ask her how she was feeling, again, again, again.

The shock of the initial excitement was wearing off.

She had been dizzy with the chaos of it. With the intensity of everyone's interest: the people who worked at the casino, the ones who were gambling, the boss who had clearly been home asleep. Jimbo had gotten to her side within minutes. And right away, she realized that something had changed. He hesitated before he gave her a hug. He seemed uncomfortable.

Everyone was calling her Mrs. Wohlmann. She heard a casino employee spelling out her name for a reporter: "R-i-t-a W-o-h-l-m-a-n-n." Honorata said nothing. The casino owner called her "Mrs. Wohlmann" too. He said that Mr. Wohlmann had been a special guest for twenty years, that it was exciting that the El Capitan's first Megabucks hit had been for a patron they valued so highly. His mother would want to say hello too.

Honorata stayed quiet, but she let them drape a mink coat over her shoulders. "For the photo," someone said. Honorata was not sure what was going to happen, but she could feel Jimbo's fear. Like a tide pulling at their feet. The casino's print department made a large check, five feet long, which said that one million, four hundred and fourteen thousand, one hundred and fifty-three dollars would be paid to Rita Wohlmann. Rita and Jimbo posed with the owner, and the photographer took that shot, and then another just of her.

At six in the morning, a small woman, only slightly larger than Honorata, entered. She was elegantly dressed, in a pale-pink nubbly suit, with an ivory silk blouse and tall ivory shoes that showed off her narrow heel and the bone at the top of her foot. Her hair was a neat, dark bob, and she did not look like she had just gotten out of bed. Her makeup was perfect; she smelled lightly of perfume.

"Marshall, did you get up out of bed to come here?"

"It was three o'clock. Yes, I got out of bed."

The elegant woman lifted her face to her son's, and he kissed her cheek lightly.

"Thank you, honey. I really appreciated that sleep." She turned to a man wearing the casino's black-and-gold uniform.

"Carmine, get us some breakfast. We can eat at the back of the club. I want to congratulate our winners."

She stepped forward then.

"James. It's always lovely to see you. And this is your wife? Is this your first time in Vegas? Did you have beginner's luck?"

Honorata nodded her head, but she felt suddenly overwhelmed. They all knew Jimbo.

"Please, will you join me for breakfast? You must be very tired, but you can sleep all day." She turned to Jimbo. "Are you still planning to fly out today?"

"I don't know. We're a little discombobulated, June."

"Then stay for breakfast. That will give Marshall time to do all the paperwork. Winning Megabucks does not protect you from Uncle Sam, you know."

Honorata felt the fear rise in Jimbo. With every minute, she felt stronger, cleaner. Something had changed. More than the money.

Marshall was talking to Jimbo.

"Sir, thank you for the identification cards. The feds are really strict with us. Since your wife is a native of the Philippines, and her name is different on her passport, I will need to see your wedding license. That's the only way that I can deposit the money."

Jimbo explained that they were engaged, but not yet married. "Is that a problem?" he asked.

"Of course not. Technically, the money is hers. If she wants to take it and go, we can't stop her. We'll just need her account information, and she can sign the paperwork."

"She doesn't have a bank account. We'll set one up now. We can go to a bank here and do it."

"Okay. Well, sure. We'll deposit the money as soon as we have an account with her name on it."

Honorata was too far away to hear what the young owner was saying to Jimbo. After breakfast, he had collected their passports from the front desk and given them to the owner. She had not known that her passport was in Las Vegas—had not seen it since that first day in the Chicago airport.

Jimbo came over.

"We'll have to go to a bank, Rita. You'll need to set up an account. We can open a joint account, which they will do for me very quickly."

Honorata said nothing. Her heart beat faster.

Just then, the other owner, the woman called June, walked up.

"Rita, may I speak with you a moment?"

Honorata stepped forward, and Jimbo started to catch on to her arm, but dropped it when June looked at him. The two women walked to a door nearly disguised by the swirling wallpaper that covered it; behind the door was a set of offices. June chatted idly about the weather, about Chicago, about the good time Marshall had had there last summer. The largest office was hers.

"Please sit down."

Honorata sat.

"Is your name Honorata?"

"Yes."

"Honorata Navarro?"

"Yes."

"And you're a citizen of the Philippines?"

"Yes."

June said nothing. She looked down at her desk for a moment.

"Does that mean I can't win? Because I'm not American?"

"Oh no. You've won, Honorata. You pulled the handle, and according to the Supreme Court of the United States, the person who pulled the handle has won the jackpot."

Honorata tried to calm herself.

"The thing is . . . Are you married to Mr. Wohlmann, Honorata?"

Honorata stared at the floor. Jimbo was an important person in this hotel. She'd had most of a week to see how important. She thought about how nice everyone had been, how they had all known her name, how they had known what she was doing at all times.

She was alone now. She didn't know how to get back to the casino. Who would help her anyway? She felt dizzy, unmoored.

"Ms. Navarro, are you okay? Please don't be afraid."

Everything swam in front of Honorata. She was going to be sick.

June stood up and asked someone to bring some water. She placed her arm on Honorata's back, making her flinch. A woman brought in the water, and June closed the door firmly behind her.

"Honorata. I can see that you're upset. I think that you're probably afraid. But there is no need to be. I'm not going to let anything happen to you. If you're not married to Mr. Wohlmann, the money's not his. It's yours. It's yours alone. And nobody can do anything about that."

Honorata started to cry. She gulped in air and sobbed.

Later, June and Marshall met to decide what to do.

"Mom, Jimbo Wohlmann has been coming to the El Capitan since I was fourteen years old. I can't simply send him home without her."

"You can. And you will. And if James never returns to the El Capitan, then good riddance."

"It's not like when you and Dad managed this place." Marshall ran his fingers through his hair, a gesture that always reminded June of Del. "Our investors are different. They look at our take every month. Jimbo has dropped millions here. We could practically make him a line item in our budget."

"The El Capitan may not be the same as it was. But it's still my casino. So I say, and the law says, that Honorata Navarro has won over a million dollars. She's a single woman, and she's the sole owner of that money."

"Jimbo isn't after her money. He doesn't need another million dollars."

"He doesn't want Ms. Navarro to have it. And we both know why. Now, I don't know what you're thinking, Marshall, but we're not going to be part of keeping that money from her. Whether it is the law or not."

"You've known Jimbo for decades. He's not a beast. She's not a slave. Why can't we extend the courtesy of a few days to him? He says that's all he needs."

"Because we are not going to extend the courtesy of a few days to him. He's going to leave our hotel, and if he wants to go down the street and stay in another one, he most certainly can. But Ms. Navarro is staying here." June rapped the table with her pen. "She's staying here until she has her money, and her passport, and then we'll take her to the airport, and she'll go wherever she wants."

"You act like I'm the one getting in the middle of this. *You're* the one getting involved. You're the one orchestrating this."

"I'm not discussing this for another minute. I'll talk to James myself. Do you think your father would have given him a couple of days to persuade that woman that she isn't free to leave? James had his chance with her, and if she doesn't go back to Chicago, I'm sure he'll know why."

"Mom, that's not fair. Don't throw Dad at me that way. I'm not evil here. I'm trying to keep the El Capitan going. Which I remember as being pretty important to Dad too."

"Honey, we'll keep the El Capitan going. We should have a line of people waiting to play Megabucks tomorrow." June smiled.

"Like that'll help."

"You're going to get your chance to make all the decisions. And you'll be great. But this is my call."

The woman had offered Honorata a new room in the hotel. The minute she was alone, Honorata lifted her dress over her head, and crawled beneath the sheets. When she woke up, she was disoriented. The sky above the Strip was dark; she had slept all day. She didn't remember getting into bed; she barely remembered coming into the room. Little by little, though, everything returned to her. Tossing about in the bed alone. Going down to the casino. Climbing onto the high seat of the Megabucks machine. It couldn't be true.

She sat up. Where was Jimbo? Did he know where she was? Honorata struggled to get out of the tightly wound sheets. What would she do with the money? Could her uncle get it? Would Jimbo call him? She stepped onto the thick carpet. Was someone watching her? Could she leave? She didn't have any money. She didn't even have her passport. Her heart rattled in her chest. Honorata was alone, and maybe she was worth a lot of money. And Jimbo, who mattered to these hotel people, was going to be angry.

She had only dresses to wear. Sandals with heels. She had a lipstick in her clutch, and a tissue. Nothing else. She looked around the room, frantic for something more useful. A basket of fruit and cheese was on the table. Next to it was a note, two hundred-dollar bills, and her passport. "Honorata—I didn't know if you had any cash. Call and ask for me when you wake up, and we can make arrangements to have your winnings placed in an account. You're welcome to stay here as long as you like—June."

She leaned against the table and let herself cry.

The next morning, someone at the hotel took her to the First Interstate Bank and waited while she set up an account. Later, she walked in her sandals to the Fashion Show Mall, which appeared much closer than it was. At Bullock's, Honorata stood and looked at the mannequins wearing low-cut metallic dresses and long blond wigs, then bought two pairs of pants, three blouses, and flat leather shoes. She found a travel agent in the mall, and booked a ticket. The agent had to call the bank, because she had only temporary checks.

Jimbo phoned on Thursday. The hotel operator asked her permission to put the call through. She trembled but said yes. She would not have been able to say no. Also, Jimbo knew her uncle. Her uncle was with her mother.

"Rita. Thank you for answering."

"My name's Honorata."

"Honorata. I'm sorry. I thought you'd like Rita."

She was silent.

"I'd like to see you. I don't want it to be like this. Could we have dinner?"

She didn't want to have dinner. She wanted him to go away, and she wanted to imagine that he had never existed. But she said, "Okay."

"I'm staying at Caesars. There's a beautiful restaurant here. I could send a car. At seven?"

She wanted to say that she would get there herself. But even these words would not come out of her mouth.

"Yes," she said finally.

Jimbo wanted to get married.

"I always wanted to get married, Honorata. We got started badly. Your uncle . . . your uncle cheated us both. But I'd like to start over. Please."

When he spoke, she was afraid. Her lungs swelled as if they would burst from her chest, and yet she felt as if she couldn't get enough air. She struggled to speak.

"I don't want to marry you."

The room swayed around her, and everything looked blurry. It was a physical effort to say this. To resist. Her heart beat frantically.

"I understand. I'm older than you. I'm not very good looking. But I'm a kind man. I want a family. We could have a family."

Honorata closed her eyes because she did not want to look at him.

"I don't want a family."

"But you said—"

"I didn't write those letters. I didn't say anything. I don't want a family. I want to go home. I want to see my mother."

It was easier now. Now that she had started. She didn't have to do what he wanted. She didn't have to please him.

"You should go home and see your mother. Then come back. There are so many opportunities in the United States. It would be easier for you to stay if we were married. You could bring your mother here."

"I want to go home."

"Of course you can go home. I can make the arrangements tonight. But after, please, Honorata, please give me another chance."

He looked stricken. Honorata didn't know how he could be saying these things. They frightened her. She wanted to forget the months in Jimbo's home, the sound of him opening the door to her room, the squeak of the bedframe as he climbed in. She remembered his hands, slippery on her back in the bath. She heard his steady snoring, asleep beside her. The gap between the shutter and the sill would slowly lighten, from deep gray to silver to white, and he would get up, or take her one more time and then get up. How could he imagine this meant something to her? How had she endured it?

"I love you, Honorata."

She looked straight at him, but in her mind she was thinking of the woman in the casino, of June, in her pink jacket and high ivory heels.

"I never want to see you again."

He stared at the ornate candlestick on the table, and she slowly removed the ring from her finger. Her voice trembled.

"If you contact me, I'll . . . " She didn't know what she would do. "I'll call the El Capitan."

She said this, and the floor did not crack open, the ceiling did not fall, he did not stand and strike her. He looked at his plate, and he fingered the leather folder that held the bill, and it was possible that his eyes were wet. Honorata didn't know, she couldn't look, she could hardly breathe. She had said what she wanted to say, and she got up fast, leaving the ring beside the plate, afraid to hand it to him. Then she walked as quickly as she could across the great glittering room; she wouldn't be able to say it again, she had never said something like that before in her life. Would he rise up, would she take it back, would the planet stop spinning? She, Honorata, had dared to resist.

19

Coral had been teaching for four years, so she both was and was not surprised at the letter. It arrived in July, and explained that the district would be adding portables to her school, and that she would now be teaching music in portable number five. The unit was undergoing renovation, but all expectations were that it would be ready for occupation a week before school started.

She called the district and tried to get someone to tell her a little more. She was pleased to hear it would be large—larger than the music room that had doubled as a stage in the cafeteria—but sorry to hear that it had been built "thirty, well, at least thirty" years ago. She asked about air-conditioning, and from the careful way the woman answered, she gathered that the unit had a swamp cooler, which "works really well in our desert environment."

Whatever.

Still, she was unnerved when she saw the unit. There were six portables, and number five was set down right where the kids played hopscotch, four-square, and cat and mouse. The top of the hopscotch frame—a rectangle with the word *Home*—angled out from the bottom of the unit, giving one the slight sense that the portable, like Dorothy's house, had fallen from the sky. It was a dirty beige color, with dents in the aluminum sides, and a rickety-looking set of stairs leading to a pressboard door that was also painted beige. The whole unlikely heap appeared as if it had been dumped in a vat of dun paint; there wasn't a pipe or a hinge or a fitting that was not the same drab color.

That night, Coral met her friend Paul and some of his buddies for a drink at the Elephant Bar. The place was loud, and Coral tried to avoid the glass eyes of the gazelle head mounted on the wall near her. Paul's college friend Koji was in from Tokyo—he was going to be doing some work in Vegas—and the guys were in high spirits. Coral told them about the beige portable, and though she meant the story to be funny, her voice shook, and her eyes started to water.

"Okay, that's one drink too many for me."

"They'll do anything to kids here," Paul said. "My nephew just got told that he'll be in double sessions until at least December. He has to get up and go to school from six to noon, but his sister is at the elementary school from nine to three. So my sister has a week to work something out with her boss."

"Can you paint the portable?" Koji asked.

"Great idea!"

"I don't know," said Coral. "I've never seen one painted."

"I could design something for you. I'm here till Wednesday. You could paint it this weekend, before school starts."

"Koji's a designer. He does work at all the casinos," Paul explained.

"I'm pretty sure I couldn't get permission to paint it by this weekend. It's okay. The building really doesn't matter. It was just upsetting to see it. I mean, who chooses beige paint for little kids?"

Paul wouldn't drop it.

"Let's do it anyway. What's the worst that could happen?"

"I get fired?"

"Come on. For making it beautiful? I think the worst thing that could happen is that we have to paint it back."

"Listen, I don't even know who to ask."

It went on like that for a while, with Coral's protests getting weaker and weaker, and the guys getting more and more excited about doing it.

And that's how P5 came to be the sunflower portable. The whole thing was covered in huge yellow blossoms that draped over the sides from the top, and down the rickety stairs, and across the door. It made one smile just to see it.

Three months later, she got a call from Koji.

"I don't know if you remember me?"

"Remember you? Are you kidding? The sunflowers are incredible. I'd love for you to see it."

"Oh, I'd like that. I'm going to be in Vegas in two weeks. That's why I was calling."

"Are you in Tokyo now?"

"Yes."

"What time is it there?"

"About noon, Thursday."

"It's Wednesday night here."

"I know. Is it a bad time? Are you eating?"

"Oh no, it's fine."

"Well, I'm going to be in Vegas, and I have tickets to this show. It's a preview of *Mystère*. Have you heard of it?"

"Of course. I loved Cirque du Soleil last year. In the tent? It was amazing."

"Yeah, that's it. This is a Cirque show, but it will be permanent. Treasure Island built a theater for it."

"I read about that."

"So, umm, *Mystère* opens Christmas day, but there's a private showing for special guests on the twenty-third. I have two tickets. I was wondering if you'd like to come."

Coral felt flustered. She couldn't remember very much about Koji, other than how wonderful his design for the portable had been, and she certainly hadn't been thinking about him as a date.

He filled the silence. "It sounds like maybe the answer's no. Sorry."

"No."

"Well, it was nice talking to you."

"No. The answer's not no. I just—I'm sorry, that was stupid of me. I'd love to go. It sounds wonderful."

"Really? Well, great. I get into town the twenty-second. I'll call you, and we can figure out the details?"

"That sounds good."

"Thank you, Coral. It was nice talking to you."

And just like that, he was off the phone. She hadn't asked him why he was coming to Vegas, or more important, told him how the kids had reacted that first morning of school. One mother started to cry. Some children had jumped in the air, yelling "flowers!" The principal didn't even get angry. She told Coral that the district wouldn't maintain it, that Coral should have gotten permission to change school property, but she didn't say anything about changing it back, she didn't ask Coral to tell her who had painted it. Coral was taken aback. She'd been steeling herself for some sort of formal discipline, wondering whether the union would back her or not.

But the sunflowers were terrific. The kids were proud of P5. Coral watched them crossing the blacktop from the main building in their mandated rows and saw them grin as they approached the sunflower portable. Students were always suggesting ways to paint the rest of the school. Some fourth-grade girls had started a petition to have every portable painted as a different kind of flower, and Coral overheard children talking about the various ways they would paint the school or their classroom or their own homes. The portable became so popular that the kindergarten teachers started walking their kids out there for music class even though Coral had always gone to their classrooms instead.

At the end of December, Koji picked her up in his hotel limo, and they rode to the Strip a little bit awkwardly. Coral couldn't quite remember what he looked like, and she had hesitated before choosing her highest heels. She wasn't particularly tall, but would she tower over him? Would he care? The Strip was wildly crowded, and there were so many people jammed onto the sidewalk to watch the pirate show at Treasure Island that the driver dropped them off a block away, and Coral tottered on her heels as she and Koji wove between the cars and the tourists to get to the casino.

It turned out that Koji's company had something to do with the huge drums that anchored *Mystère*'s musical score. He explained to her that the largest one had to be built on the stage and that there wasn't a door big enough to remove it. The casino surprised Coral. Treasure Island really was all about pirates, and it looked more like Disneyland than Vegas, but it was fun. Everything about Vegas was fun right now. The whole city rocked with the energy of the casinos, bigger and better and wilder every year. A lot of money was being made, and people were popping between LA and Vegas like it was a morning commute; anything seemed possible.

Mystère had its own lobby, filled with locals for this performance. Coral saw Althea's boss Ed near the bar with a woman who looked like she couldn't be twenty-one. Some Cirque performers, wearing skin-tight suits in green and orange and black, catapulted off the stairs leading to the balcony seats, and there was a little scurry of movement when Kevin Costner walked in. Koji excused himself and came back with a glass of white wine for her. She had barely started it when the doors opened, and people rushed to see the theater.

Inside, the room was filled with giant, abstract shapes in dark blues and greens. Coral craned her neck, looking to see what was above and behind. Koji pointed out the largest drum, the ō-*daiko*, high above their heads. He said it weighed a thousand pounds. All around her, she could hear the chatter of other people pointing out one inventive detail after another. They had excellent seats, and Koji smiled at her pleasure.

"Americans are so brash. They have fun. I love it."

"Well, I don't know if Vegas is very typical of America."

"I think it is. I think it feels quintessentially American."

"When I lived in California, my friends didn't like Vegas. Most of them said they'd never even come here—'cept maybe to see me."

"I bet they'd like to see this."

"Yeah. I mean, people visit from all over the world."

Koji grinned. "Yes. We do."

There was a reception after the show, and Koji had been invited. Coral was uncomfortable there. She hadn't realized Koji would know so many people, and she felt conspicuous; not Coral out on a date with the friend of a friend, but a young black woman on the arm of a Japanese businessman. It made her self-conscious. She excused herself to find a restroom, and coming back, she saw Marshall Dibb.

She knew who he was, of course. He was running the El Capitan now, with his mother. She tried to ignore the presence of the Dibbs in Las Vegas; told herself she had no reason to know anything about June or Marshall. From time to time, a story ran in the paper. The El Capitan was a classic, and the Dibbs kept it up even though the big casinos were corporations now, and everyone said the small resorts were on their way out.

Odell Dibb had been dead a long time.

Still, technically, this was her brother.

Marshall was fair and tall, and Coral was slight and dark. He looked like his father. Which meant that she probably looked like her mother, and even now, this thought hurt. But Coral had seen Marshall on the local news, she had studied him once when they were in the same restaurant. And as before, she saw herself in the way he moved, in something about how he was jointed, in the shape of his ears, in the way his hair lifted off his forehead. It wasn't a resemblance a stranger would remark on, but it was unmistakable if one knew.

Marshall Dibb looked her way and smiled. He must have noticed her staring. She smiled back awkwardly and turned abruptly, looking for Koji. He was nearby, watching her.

"You're not having fun?"

"Of course I am. It was an amazing show. The music, the drums, they were incredible."

"But now, here, you're not having fun."

"I'm ready to go home."

"I'll call the car."

"Thank you."

In bed that night, Coral pulled a pillow over her head and tried not to think about Marshall Dibb.

How could he be her brother?

She felt no connection to him. He didn't know she existed. And here they were, in the same small town if you were a local, and she might be running into him for the rest of her life.

Seeing Marshall made her feel like she didn't have a home. Las Vegas was his town. He was practically royalty. Son of a casino family. Still, it was her town too. She'd grown up here. Where else would be home?

And that old feeling, that deep pressing emptiness, rushed back. The sense that she didn't have a place, that she didn't belong, that she had somehow been cut adrift when she was four days old, and also that, somewhere, someone wanted something from her.

"I'm a Jackson. I'm a Jackson as much as Ada and Althea and Ray Junior. Augusta Jackson is my mother." It was ridiculous to say these things aloud, and yet doing so made her feel better.

Would she ever tell Marshall Dibb her story?

Would she ever sit down with him and say, "I think you're my brother"?

And what would be his reply? Would he see the proof in *her* walk, in her ears, in the rise of her hair?

Could he know that she might exist? Could someone have told him?

That was the thing. She didn't care if Marshall Dibb ever knew who she was. She didn't want him for a brother. She didn't want to live in Las Vegas as the bastard black child of a casino pioneer. She had thought through this scenario before, and while Althea and Ray Junior and Ada now knew everything that she and Augusta did, nobody else knew. Augusta had kept her secret for her, and if she could have a life in Las Vegas—a life separate from the mystery of her birth; a life that was hers and had nothing to do with the Dibbs; with all the people that would find her birth fascinating, a story worth telling, even a story about Vegas—if she had any chance to live free of that, it was possible because Augusta had kept this secret so well. Augusta and Odell.

But what if Marshall did know she existed? Or knew she might?

What if Marshall was the one person in the world who might know who she was?

Over the years, Coral had come close to contacting Marshall. She knew odd bits of information about him: the telephone number at his office, that he had bought a home the year after she bought hers, that he wasn't married, that he played in a recreational baseball league. She didn't want to know these things about him—didn't want to think of Marshall Dibb at all—but each time she had considered reaching out to him, each time she had prepared herself for what he might say, she had learned a little more. And every time, she had changed her mind. There was more to lose than there was to win. Why would Del Dibb have told Marshall about her, if he had worked so hard to keep her a secret all these years?

Still, the desire to know something about the woman who had given birth to her never quite went away, and remembering Marshall Dibb's casual smile in her direction made her scrunch the pillow down on her head and kick her feet, and finally stand up and find a movie and slip it into the VHS. There was the whir of the tape being pulled into the machine, and the clicking sound of it dropping into place, and then the film started: *North by Northwest*. It would be as good as anything else right now.

20

Going home was not as Honorata had imagined it would be. It took two days to get to Manila, and when she arrived, the airport smelled of gumamela, which made her think of Jimbo's house instead of the bubble paste that she and the other children had once made from its flowers. She panicked in the airport—tired and dehydrated, of course—but more and more, she found she couldn't settle down, she couldn't rest still, she was stricken with moments of coursing emotion, when she felt she had to bolt, or scream, or twist the neck away from the head of an animal. These moments were terrifying in their suddenness and in their violence, but nothing she tried made them easier. Honorata found an empty room down a long hallway, and there she put her head between her knees.

From Manila, she took a jeepney to Mayoyao. When it stopped to pick up passengers in San Jose City, she got out and threw up in the bushes. She shuddered there until the driver honked, and then she wiped her mouth with some leaves and stumbled back onto the jeepney. It smelled of sweat and *lumpia* and cassava and garlic. Some children at the back argued about who was sitting by the window, and a group of young girls experimented with lipstick in purple and magenta and black.

Everything leapt at her: the colors, the smells, the sounds. After San Jose City, the brightly painted bus began to climb into the mountains, and the fields were so green, the sky so blue, the air so soft; it was even more beautiful than she remembered. And yet already Honorata felt strange. She was wearing pants, and the other women were wearing skirts. She wanted to lean out the window and look down the valleys—see the road hanging off the side of the mountain, and the river far below—but she could hardly keep her eyes focused on the seat in front of her. She felt sick. She didn't want to throw up again, and every lurch and jostle of the jeepney threatened the possibility.

She had not told her mother she was coming, because she didn't want her uncle to know. She hoped that he would not be in the village; that he would be in Manila. It hurt to think of him in the city, what he did, the women he found, the letters he had someone write for them. But she could not do anything about her uncle. She had traveled without stopping for days, and she wanted *Nanay*.

The jeepney let her off about a mile from her village. Honorata started to feel better as she walked the familiar route, even if her suitcase felt heavy. Coming around a bend, she saw her uncle standing with two other men. She stared at him, but to her surprise, he did not acknowledge her. He turned and left the path, and she did not see him again while she was in Buninan.

She had come to take her mother back with her. This is what she had decided. This is why she had come so far, so abruptly, without telling anyone she was coming, without stopping to rest, without stopping to think about what had happened in the middle of one night, in a casino, in Las Vegas, in America, in a place impossible to describe or quite to remember now that she was back home, in a world entirely green and quiet and fresh. If her mother was with her, Honorata would know what to do.

But her mother was not ready to leave her home, not ready to cross an ocean when she had never been more than fifty feet off its shore, and even that was only once, when she had traveled very far, perhaps a hundred miles, to the sea. In Honorata's lifetime, her mother had never been to Manila. She did not want to go with her to the United States.

Still, what her mother knew, she knew well.

She knew instantly that Honorata was pregnant, which is how Honorata knew that it was true.

She knew quickly that Honorata would not return to Buninan.

She understood that the baby was not Kidlat Begtang's, and that it belonged to a different world.

She could not know what her brother had done—she might never believe this—but she knew somehow that Honorata should not see her uncle.

And in knowing that, everything was settled.

Because one could not live there and not be fully of the family. She could not live near her mother and avoid her uncle. There wasn't any way to separate family like this.

Perhaps in her mother's mind, the choice that Honorata had made so many years before—to leave Buninan with the boy from the village across the fields—was the only choice that mattered. Everything else came of it, and her mother, who had never lived anywhere but Buninan, accepted that life was to be played forward. She taught her daughter this.

But Honorata's mother didn't know everything. Honorata had not left the village, the place where her father's bones were kept, because she had been rebellious or unhappy. She had never dreamed of going away as a girl, and she hadn't wanted any other life than the one she had known. She had run away to Manila because one day she had gone into a field with Kidlat—one day she had made a sudden and unexpected and defining choice: so human, so universal, so absolute in its impact—and after that, there had been no way back to the life she had lived or intended to live. The life with which she would have been happy.

Of course, another girl would not have had to leave. These things happened, even in Buninan. They were an ordinary fact of life: perhaps Honorata was one of the few girls unaware of this. But other girls had not fallen in love with this boy. Kidlat had an uncle who had lived in America. He had a cousin who had been to Jamaica, and a friend who worked in Taiwan. Kidlat was not willing to play his part in the village script: the one that would have allowed Honorata that afternoon in the field. Kidlat would not marry Honorata and take her home to his village. If Honorata wanted, she could come to Manila with him. They could have a new life there. That was the option he offered.

So she, the precious only daughter, the one who had never wanted to leave, she, Honorata, thick with regret, with longing, in a kind of shock but also wild with desire, with love, with the feel of Kidlat's touch as vivid in her mind as it had been on her skin— insatiable skin—Honorata had followed Kidlat to Manila. And everything that came after, all of it—the tiny apartments; the city friends; the nights wondering where Kidlat was, and if he would come home bruised or even, once, burned; the movie; the bakery; her uncle; the flight to Chicago; Jimbo; the El Capitan; the coins clinking in the plastic bucket; the lights whirling and horns sounding when all the wheels spun to the same Megabucks logo (lucky Honorata—Honosuerte); the young men, drunk, running toward her in their polo shirts; the baby (not Kidlat's) now inside her—all of it, came from that instant. It was that instant after she'd thought Kidlat had stopped loving her, after he had gone to Manila when they were seventeen and come back wanting nothing to do with her, after she had mourned losing him, and then bumped into him, and neither had expected to see the other, and their attraction was so strong, their bodies drawing nearer—as if they were each on one of those moving walkways she had not yet known existed—angling toward each other, magnets propelling to their own fates, their shoulders actually bumping when they finally met, so out of control of their forward movement to each other that they did not quite recognize when they had reached the same spot. They had bumped and then turned and walked forward, shoulder not quite grazing shoulder, elbows not quite touching, and casual words spoken: "I haven't seen you." "Will you be at the festival?" And before them, the field, so green, so silent, and nothing else said and nothing else thought, but knowing nonetheless where they were going and what they would do, even if the actual words would have startled her and stopped her and sent her to a different fate entirely.

After a few weeks, Honorata left the village. She had sobbed, wanting her nanay to come with her, and her nanay had held her tightly. It was true, she agreed, Honorata must go to America, but no, she would not go with her. She would not walk onto a plane, fly across an ocean, speak a language she did not know. It was not possible for her in the same way that living where she could see her uncle was not possible for Honorata. Somehow the world had dropped between them—Honorata and Nanay—and how it had happened did not matter. Life could not be reversed.

In the days after Honorata accepted that this was true, at least for now, everything about her time in the village felt precious. She sat underneath the wooden floor of her mother's home, her back against one of the four thick trunks that held the house well above the ground, and remembered the games she had played there. At night, the rain fell softly on the grass roof. She walked about touching things, smelling them, rubbing against her cheek the dented pot her mother used for cooking and tasting the leaves of the bush with purple flowers. She did not know when she would return to Buninan or who she would then be. As she left her village, as she walked along the road to catch the jeepney, sipping the *salabat* her mother had said would ease the sickness, she imprinted every sensation: the shape of branches against the sky, the smell of rice growing, and the sounds: of birds, of children playing *luksong-baka*, of a cloud rat startled from its branch. In Chicago, she had heard the whistle and chug of busses, the honk of car horns. In Las Vegas, there had been clanking and bells, the crashing of coins into trays.

From Buninan, Honorata went first to a hotel in Manila. Not a grand hotel in Makati or Ortigas, but still her room was big and there was no garbage piled next to the building. At night, the shops closed, and the streets were quiet. She stayed there another week, looking for Kidlat, trying to find out where he had gone, if anyone was in touch with him. Finally, she found Rosauro, who told her that Kidlat had gone to Mindanao, that he was headed to Davao City, or perhaps he had changed his mind and found a way to Palawan.

Rosauro had been with Kidlat when he had found out what

happened to Honorata. Kidlat had shouted and said he would hurt her uncle, but they both knew that he would not hurt him. Kidlat and Rosauro already knew what her uncle did in the city; they had known for a long time, but Kidlat hadn't thought there was any reason for Honorata to know. Nobody had imagined that her uncle could do what he did. Did Honorata need anything? Rosauro asked. Kidlat was his *kuya*. He would do anything for Honorata.

She left Manila the next day.

She had not given up on bringing her mother to the States, and she thought that her nanay would come eventually, after the baby was born, after she accepted what her brother had done to her daughter. But Honorata had given up on finding Kidlat. Too much had happened; it had been a mistake to want to find him. Perhaps she had thought that Kidlat would persuade her to stay in Pilipinas, perhaps she had thought he would have a way to shield her from her uncle, perhaps she had imagined the life they would live with all her money. But seeing Rosauro brought it back: the way it was, not the way she pretended. There was the movie, what had happened, that she had done it for Kidlat, and that he had then left. There was her uncle, there were the months with Jimbo, and, strangely, there was the woman who had helped her in Las Vegas. All of this made not just Buninan, but even Manila—not just her village, but even Kidlat—wrong for her.

The Honorata who had lived in Manila did not exist anymore. Sitting on the edge of the bed, in that clean hotel room larger than any apartment she could have imagined a year ago, Honorata shook with this idea. For an instant, her teeth clenched, her muscles contracted, she wanted to strike something, she wanted to hit someone, she would not be able to bear it; the anger was a cold-hot rush of necessity. Then she inhaled, once, twice, she put the thought carefully aside, she unfolded her fingers and closed her eyes. She sat perfectly still for a long time.

If that Honorata did not exist, the one sitting on this bed did.

Nanay was right. The only way to live life was forward.

When she was fully calm, when she could take in air without hearing it, she repacked her suitcase, bumped it down the stairs of the hotel, and walked along the crowded street until she found a taxi. "To the airport," she said, and as she rode, with the car lurching and the smell of exhaust making her sick, she thought about the possibilities. She thought about what she had learned of the United States, about the snow in Chicago, the lights on the Strip, the grocery stores with their long aisles of boxes and cans. She thought of the television shows she and Kidlat had watched in the bar where he worked: *Charlie's Angels* and *The Brady Bunch* and *L.A. Law*. She remembered the way America looked in those shows, the blue skies and the ocean and the houses so new and big. She pictured the women—their long feathered hair as they sped away in a car; or the mother with the short bob, smiling as everyone in her family did what she wanted.

When she got to the airport, she didn't hesitate. She didn't hesitate because she wasn't the Honorata who had left Buninan for Manila a decade ago. She wasn't the Honorata her uncle had put on a plane a year ago. She wasn't even the Honorata who had sat in this airport, head in her hands, just weeks ago. She was on her own, and there was no one to protect her, and she did not need protection. She had won a jackpot, and she was pregnant. Hono*suerte*. She had a passport, and she would buy a ticket to Los Angeles. *Bahala na.* Come what may. She would live in the city of angels.

She took a room in a hotel near the Los Angeles airport, and a taxi driver showed her the nearest hospital. At first, the man at the hospital was reluctant to help her. She couldn't register for a birth without a doctor, and how long would she be staying in LA? Did she have a permanent address? So she went to a Catholic church, and there the woman in the office helped her find a doctor, and also asked where she was living and if she could afford an apartment. With her help, Honorata rented a furnished apartment in Inglewood, not too far from the hospital. She told the woman at the church that she was planning to buy a house, before the baby was born, if she could. The woman gave her a puzzled look but did not ask any questions; instead, she gave her the name of a congregant who was also a realtor.

"We don't have a large Filipino community here," she said. "You might be more comfortable in Eagle Rock. Or West Covina. The realtor will know."

Honorata thought about these words. The enormity of what she had done, leaving Pilipinas after she had found a way back, felt like a wave sweeping her out to sea. She could not think about this now. She couldn't think about whether she would buy a house in Eagle Rock or Inglewood, couldn't imagine driving the maze of roads she had seen from the window of the plane, all those neighborhoods, all those people, all those communities—some with Pinoy and some without—and did she want to live with them? Would there be tamarind and pandan and lemongrass for cooking? Would her child speak Pilipino? Would she always be shunned, a mother without a husband?

It overwhelmed her, and the plan that she had worked out carefully—that she had written down and repeated to herself over and over as she flew all those hours—no longer seemed so clear. What was she doing in LA? She didn't know anyone here. She didn't know anything about the city. She couldn't buy a house and set down her life, her child's life, without knowing anything. It was too big. It was too much. Why had she thought she could do it? Where did she belong?

Honorata spent the months before her baby was born in the furnished apartment, ricocheting between days she felt strong and days she felt weak. There was almost never a day in the middle, a day of balance. She was super Honorata or she was disgusting Honorata, and the seesaw nature of her own temperament exhausted her. She began leaving the apartment only to attend morning Mass, or to talk quietly to the priest in the dark confessional stall on Saturday afternoons, or to buy food and the things she would need to bring a baby home. She didn't call the realtor. She tried to avoid the woman from the church office, though the woman looked for Honorata sometimes and stopped to ask how she was feeling, if she needed anything. One day she brought a box of new baby supplies to Honorata's apartment, and Honorata blinked back the tears as she showed her the diapers, the sterilized bottles, the baby wipes, and the blanket with a matching cap that a parishioner knitted for all the new babies.

"Do you have someone to go with you, into labor?" the woman from the office asked.

"Yes," Honorata said.

The woman seemed to know she was lying, but she didn't say anything. The next Saturday, after her confession, a priest came out from the sacristy, wearing street clothes, and waited until she was done praying, until she had awkwardly shifted her belly and pulled herself up from the kneeler. Then he reached over to help her stand fully upright. He asked if she had a minute to talk, if they could walk outside, and when Honorata went with him, he invited her to join a young adult group that met on Tuesday evenings. "Some people have children, and others are single," he said, "but they will be people your age. You might enjoy it."

Honorata did not commit to going, but she noticed that the priest was also about her age, that he had very large ears and that he walked gracefully, as if he might suddenly turn and spin. He wasn't particularly earnest, which she appreciated.

Her contractions started in the morning.

They continued all day, and when she called the doctor's office, they asked her to time them, and when she said they were coming every three minutes, they told her to go to the hospital, not to delay, and did she have a bag ready?

She had a bag.

Honorata had had little to do but prepare for this day for months, so she had a bag for herself and another for her baby, and on the top of that bag were the blanket and the cap the parishioner had knitted. She called the number of the taxi company she always used, but when she said she was having a baby and needed to go to the hospital, the dispatcher hung up. Frantic, she found the phone book someone had left under the brown leatherette couch in the main room. The front cover was ripped off, and Honorata was not sure how old it was, but there was an ad for a taxi company on the back cover. Shaking, she dialed it carefully.

When the dispatcher answered, she gave her address slowly, said she was ready right away, but not why she was going to the hospital. Then she stood outside on the sidewalk, and waited, and the taxi came in just minutes. The driver, from some African country—she couldn't quite understand what he said to her: something about the baby, something about his wife—dropped her off at the emergency entrance, and she walked in by herself, doubling over when a contraction came, and carrying the two bags, one in each hand, like ballast.

The birth was easy.

Nanay had told her it would be easy—that her births were easy, and her mother's too. When she said this, a look had passed across her face, and Honorata knew she was thinking that Honorata's baby might be different, might not be like any other baby they had birthed. Her mother had this thought and decided not to say it, but Honorata had seen it, and her mother had seen her see it, and they said nothing of this to each other.

So Honorata was not counting on an easy birth, and yet it was.

Malaya was born just after midnight. When the nurse, a Pilipina, handed her the baby, already wrapped tightly in a pink blanket, with a pink bow fastened to a lock of hair that looked quite black, with her eyes squeezed narrow—from the antibiotic, the nurse said—and her face wide and red as a beet, Honorata experienced something she would later think of as the only true religious moment of her life. It was awkward to hold her, lying there almost flat in a bed, and the baby's body wrapped too tight to fit naturally against her own, and yet the instant that she had the weight of her in her arms, the moment she looked into those ointment-smeared navy eyes, Honorata felt her own body begin to grow, as if the edges of her were expanding and then loosening, wavering, shimmering, dissipating; as if she were not held inside her body at all but existed everywhere and enormous and without shape. She was at once formless and formed: holding her baby carefully so there was no chance she would fall, though her physical body—her arms and shoulders and back—were weak and tired.

And that was the moment in which Honorata let go of the fear that had gripped her in the furnished apartment, with its stained tan carpet and its cream-colored walls and the plastic flower in an orange pot in the corner. That was the moment in which she knew she could do it, that she was free, that she had a daughter and a purpose and the strength to do whatever it would take. She was not a foreigner, an outcast, a sinner, a whore; she was a mother, and, incredibly, she had her own money, and nothing that came after this would be as hard as what had already been. This was the revelation.

They kept her in the hospital for two nights, bringing Malaya to her every three hours to nurse and also when she would not stop crying. Honorata could not get her to stop crying either, but it didn't matter, it didn't frighten her. In the village, there had been babies that cried all the time and babies that did not, and at a certain point, they all became children just like any other.

From the hospital, she sent a telegram to the church for her mother so that she would know she had a granddaughter, and then, in a moment of inspiration, she sent her a second telegram. She had decided to move to Las Vegas. She would buy a house there, and there would be a room for Nanay. Her mother could not live eight thousand miles away from her granddaughter, and as soon as possible, Honorata would be home to fetch her for a visit. Nanay would have to learn to fly.

21

A woman had moved into the house at the top of the cul-de-sac, but Coral had been unable to say hello. She often heard her neighbor drive in, because she braked and then revved again as she managed the slight incline to her garage, but the woman kept her door shut and picked up her mail quickly, without looking to see who else might be on the street. Finally Coral left a plant and a note at her new neighbor's door. The gift was gone the next morning, but nobody stopped to acknowledge it.

It was another week before Coral realized the woman had a child.

On Saturday, Coral saw her pushing an elaborate stroller toward the park. She watched her go by, and when she noticed her returning, she stepped out the front door and said hello.

"Hello," the woman replied. She didn't look directly at Coral.

"My name's Coral. Welcome to the neighborhood."

"Thank you."

She looked down, uneasy. Coral thought she must be shy.

"May I see your baby?"

The woman looked up and flashed a small smile.

"Her name's Malaya."

"What a lovely name." Coral walked to the stroller, and looked at the little girl. She was asleep, her cheek flushed, and one curl, moist with sweat, was pasted to her small pink ear.

"Oh, she's beautiful."

At this, her new neighbor smiled fully, and her face, which had seemed still and severe, was suddenly open and pleased. She reached out to move the brightly woven blanket off her daughter's shoulder, and as she did so, her fingers lightly caressed the infant's soft skin.

"Did you make her blanket? It's so intricate."

"My mother made it. In Pilipinas. Where I'm from, we make this cloth."

"It's wonderful."

The woman didn't speak, but she also didn't move away. She stood there, gazing at her baby, and Coral shifted awkwardly. It was sweet, the way this mother looked at her baby, but intimate too, as if Coral should not be standing right next to her. She started to step away from the stroller, and the woman spoke.

"My name's Honorata. I move here from the Philippines."

"Well, welcome, Honorata. I hope you like it."

"Have you lived here long?"

"On this street? Nearly three years. But I grew up not far from here. I'm a native."

Coral was used to people commenting on this fact, but, of course, Honorata was too new to know that native Las Vegans were rare.

"So you choose this neighborhood because it's a good one?"

"Well, I like it. And it's close to the school where I work. I'm a teacher. I teach music."

"At a Catholic school?" Honorata asked.

"No. At a public school. Just a few blocks that way."

"I'm going to send Malaya to Catholic school."

The baby stirred then, and made a little noise, like the bleat of a calf. Honorata stroked the child's cheek, and made a shushing noise with her lips slightly parted. Coral turned to go back inside.

"It was nice to meet you. Let me know if I can do anything. Just knock."

Honorata looked at Coral.

"Do you like that house there?"

"That one? With the dead grass?"

"Yes. Do you like it?"

Coral wasn't sure where this was going.

"Umm. Well, I wish they still had the water on. Nobody's lived there for about a year."

"Oh. So not good house?"

"I don't know. The house's fine. I'm not sure what happened to the owner."

"You don't want to buy this house?"

"That house? No."

"I might buy it. The realtor told me that rental homes are good investment. Lots of people to rent homes here."

"Oh. Probably. That's cool."

"So, okay with you?"

Coral paused.

"I don't want to buy that house. It's nice of you to ask me."

"Okay. I find out about the owner."

"I think if you call the county, they'll tell you who owns it. Or you can ask your realtor."

"Thank you. Very nice of you to tell me."

Honorata smiled at her.

"You're a teacher?"

"Yes."

"You look young."

"Actually, I'm thirty-two."

The baby was fussing now, and her neighbor moved the stroller back and forth, trying to get her to settle. Still, she didn't move on.

"That's very good. Be a teacher. Have a house."

Coral laughed.

"My mama agrees with you. It was nice meeting you, Honorata. Take care."

"Bye, Coral."

At this, the baby let out a cry, and her mother bent quickly toward her.

Coral didn't see much of her neighbor after that. On weekends, she sometimes saw Honorata pushing the stroller toward the park, and when the evenings cooled off, she could hear her singing to the baby, in a language Coral couldn't make out, in the backyard. In the spring, an older woman came to visit, and when Coral stopped to talk with Honorata, she learned that her mother had come to live with her. Coral had never seen anyone who might be the baby's father on the street, but she didn't pay close attention. It was possible that there was a father; that he visited Malaya at times.

One day Coral's niece Keisha came over to play, and when she saw Honorata and Malaya on the street, she rushed out to say hello. The child was learning to walk now, pitching one foot forward at a time and swinging like a pendulum from her mother's hand. She was a beautiful baby, fairer than her mother, but with her mother's bright, plump lips and dark-fringed eyes.

Coral watched from inside the house as Keisha crouched down

and began to talk to the little girl. Malaya laughed at something Keisha did, and Coral saw Honorata smile and then show Keisha how to take the baby's hand, how to steady her as she threw one eager foot in front of the other. After a little, Keisha came running in.

"She says I can go over and play with Malaya one day!"

"Really? That's great."

"I told her I wanted to babysit, but she said that I would have to get older first."

"Yeah. Playing with her is a good way to start. She's learning to walk?"

"She's so funny. I tried to let go of her hand, but she just sat down on her bottom."

Althea came by later to pick up Keisha and stayed to eat dinner. Malcolm was at basketball practice, and then the team was going to the coach's house to eat pasta so the players would be ready for the middle school tournament the next day.

"I can't stand the coach. He loves Malcolm, of course, and I appreciate that. But he says these things that make my skin crawl."

"He asked Malcolm if he was planning on a basketball scholarship," Keisha piped up. "That's why Mom's mad."

Althea raised an eyebrow at her sister.

"Did your mom tell him Malcolm is planning to be a doctor?"

"Malcolm told him."

"And he clapped him on the back and said he really liked to see a kid dream big." Althea sounded like she might spit.

Coral looked at Keisha. "I wouldn't want to be Malcolm's coach and step on your mom's toes."

Keisha laughed.

"Don't say those things to her, Coral. You just wait till you have a son."

"Auntie Coral's going to have girls, Mom. Did I tell you I get to play with the baby down the street?"

"What baby?"

"My neighbor at the end of the street." Coral rinsed off the cutting board and handed it to Althea. "She has a little girl. Learning to walk. Keisha ran out and met her today."

"That's great, Keisha."

"I asked her if I could babysit."

"You're too young to babysit."

"That's what she said. But she said I could play with her."

Althea turned to Coral. "Keisha's planning on you having a daughter."

"Well, that might be a bit complicated."

"Are you still dating that guy? From Japan?"

"Sort of. He's only here a week or so a month."

"Well, do you know what he's doing those other three weeks?"

"You mean, do I think he has a wife and kids in Japan?" Rising on her tiptoes, Coral pulled down the cow pitcher that Keisha liked to use as a glass for milk. "No, I don't. But he might date someone there. He said he wasn't dating anyone in particular. I haven't told him I wouldn't go on other dates."

"And do you?"

Coral shook her head. "Now you sound like Mama. No, I'm not dating anyone else. I like Koji."

"Okay. Just be careful. This is Vegas. A lot of guys come here once a month."

"I don't think it's like that."

"And a lot of time can go by."

"Now you really sound like Mama."

Althea laughed and wrapped her arm around Coral's shoulders. Keisha was there, so they didn't talk about it anymore. Coral knew why her sister was concerned. You didn't grow up in Vegas without knowing the possibilities. Still, Koji was important to her.

The day after Keisha had gone out to play with Malaya, there was a knock at the door.

It was Honorata.

"Hi. Do you want to come in?"

"I was wondering if you could help me?"

"Sure. Is something wrong? Is your daughter okay?"

"Oh yes. Thank you. She's with my mother."

Honorata didn't seem to want to come in, so Coral stepped outside and sat on one of the chairs at the front door. Honorata took the other. She was nervous.

"Would you like a cup of coffee? I have some ready."

"No. I just have a question. I want to change my daughter's name. And I want to get a trust. I thought you could help."

"Me?"

"Yes."

"I think you have to go to a lawyer."

"Yes. You grew up here. Do you know a lawyer?"

"Umm. Well, sure. A friend of mine's a lawyer. He grew up here too. He probably does this sort of thing."

"What's his name?"

"He might be expensive. He works for a pretty big firm."

"That's good."

Coral assumed that she meant the big firm.

"His name's Darryl Marietti. And he works at Lionel Sawyer. I can contact him and tell him you'll be calling."

"Thank you."

"Sure. I'll do it today." After a bit, Coral asked, "What are you naming your daughter?"

"Naming her? Oh. No, I keep her name. I'm changing her last name to Begtang. Mine's Navarro."

It didn't seem right to pry, but Coral wondered if her neighbor would say why she was changing her daughter's name. She didn't.

"Keisha was thrilled to play with Malaya yesterday. She's getting so big."

Honorata smiled. "Yes. She's almost walking. Eleven months."

"That sounds early."

"The doctor says she's very bright."

"Well, that's great. It's so nice that your mother's here too."

"Yes, now she's here, I'm going to get a job. At the church over there. In the office. Four mornings a week."

"That'll be convenient."

"Do you know I own three houses? On this street? I bought that one too." Honorata pointed to the house next to her own.

"Wow. I noticed the sign was only up one day. Will your mother live in one?"

"My mother?" Honorata looked confused. "No. She live with me." Then she thought for a moment. "Your mother? Does she want to rent house?"

"Mama? Uh, no. She has her own house."

"Okay. Very convenient. To have your mother on the same street."

Coral laughed. Ada would love this conversation.

"Yes. Very convenient. Listen, I'll call Darryl. Let me know if it works out."

Honorata never said anything about the name change, but Darryl mentioned it once.

"That woman you sent me? Your neighbor?"

"She's a character, right?"

"She's loaded."

"Really?"

"Yes."

"Was she married? I've seen her mother. I don't think she has any money."

"She didn't tell me where the money came from. Said she was never married. Just wanted to change her kid's name. Freaked out when I told her we had to publish it in the paper. We had to put it in the *LA Times* too, because the baby was born there."

"So, bad-dad story."

"I guess. Or maybe she's a sex worker."

Coral choked. "She really doesn't strike me as a sex worker."

"Well, she got that money somewhere. And that kid. You never know, Coral. It's not as if there's a sex-worker type. She's very good-looking."

"Honorata?"

"Drop-dead. Did you even look at her?"

"Yeah, I mean, I guess she's pretty. She's so nervous when I talk with her, I didn't really notice."

"I'm a man. We notice."

"*Ohhh*-kay. Well, so did she do it? Change her daughter's name?"

"Yeah. She was pretty upset about the advertisement, but I showed her how someone would have to be looking pretty closely, and she made a big deal about it not being anywhere but here and LA. After that, it was just a verified petition in family court."

"Did it go through?"

"Well, no dad showed up. The judge could have refused it, but that's rare. Hers was fine. Kid is Malaya Begtang."

Coral raised her glass.

"Daughter of a sex worker."

"Or a drug smuggler."

"Card cheat?"

"Romance novelist?"

Coral laughed out loud. Whenever she saw Honorata after that, hurrying in and out of the neighborhood, wearing her lace veil on Sunday mornings, she smiled.

22

Virginia asked Honorata what she thought of the priest's sermon.

This was something of a ritual. Molly said they were like Monday morning quarterbacks, calling the shots after the game had already been played. This made no sense to Honorata, but Virginia tried to explain it.

"A lot of games are played on Sunday, and then everyone whose team loses tries to figure out what the coach should have done to win. It's called Monday morning quarterbacking."

This was not helpful to Honorata.

"It means that after the fact, people try to call the game differently."

Honorata didn't particularly care if she understood Molly's reference or not, but she wanted to seem interested. Molly had been working there only a few months.

"Is the quarterback the one who guards the goal?"

"What?"

"I think that's a very hard position. Because if he keeps the ball from going in, the game just goes on. And if he misses, everyone is upset. I wouldn't like to be the quarterback."

"I think that's a goalie. Like soccer."

"Oh."

Honorata looked down. She didn't know why she had started

talking about soccer. It was on her mind lately because there was a player in the news named Wohlmann, and the name made her jump. He wasn't even American, though. It had nothing to do with James Wohlmann. Still.

"Anyway, what did you think of what he said? About joy?"

At Mass, the priest had said that Catholics should be joyful. He said that joy was the natural expression of faith, and that the parishioner who followed all the rules but didn't feel joy was missing the point of a faithful life.

What Honorata thought was that the priest didn't know that much about life. He'd never lived in another country, he'd never been with a woman. He didn't have children, he didn't even pay his own bills. She didn't think she would say this to Virginia.

"I thought . . . I thought he wrote it very carefully."

Virginia laughed. "Carefully!"

"What did you think?"

Virginia might think anything. She was very surprising. She'd worked in the office for years, and she was devout, but she could be irreverent. Honorata didn't quite know what to think of her.

"I think he's got his head up his ass. Telling people to be joyful. Like that's something on tap."

Honorata wasn't sure what to say. It was very unusual, someone who worked in a church office and said "head up his ass."

"Doesn't it make sense, though?" she said. "That God would want us to be joyful?"

"Oh, what's God got to do with it? We're talking the Catholic church. Sex is joyful, but only if you're married and ready to have eight more babies. If you're one of God's chosen ones, which means you're also a man, then you can't have sex at all. Where's the joy in that?"

Honorata didn't answer. She didn't want to tell Virginia that when the priest was talking, she'd been thinking about how little he could know about her life. He looked at her and saw a little Filipina lady, something like her nanay, which was fine with Honorata—which was the way she preferred that he see her—but still, how could somebody who couldn't tell the difference between Honorata and her nanay tell her how to feel?

"It's very American," she said at last.

"It's American? That's interesting. What do you mean?" Virginia leaned forward and waited for Honorata's reply.

"I mean, telling someone what to feel. A feeling is . . . A feeling isn't . . . I don't think you can tell someone what to feel."

"Exactly! Feelings aren't on tap. Only a priest could come up with something like that."

Honorata didn't know what "on tap" meant, but she did know that Virginia was big on what priests didn't know. She said it had something to do with her parents naming her Virginia, for the Virgin. Also, she believed the problems in the church came from ignoring women.

Molly asked why Virginia worked at the church if she thought it was such a mess. Honorata knew what Virginia would say. She'd heard it before. Virginia said that she was a true believer, and that she was quite sure God was happy to have her in the church, encouraging it from the inside.

Honorata thought about the other things the priest did not know about her.

He didn't know about her village. He didn't know what it was like to grow up as if one were part of the earth, the way that she and the other children were part of the green leaves and the rain and the sky. He didn't know about the ladder she climbed into her home, or the way that home was dark and close and smelled of the rice stored under its thatched roof. What could the priest know about what it had meant for such a child, one who ran naked in rain or sun, and made the other children laugh by bobbing her head sideways like a *tamsi*, to move to Manila, with more people than even a teacher could count, with its tin-sided shanties, and human waste running down mud roads?

More than this, how could the priest know what Honorata felt about what had happened to her: about the men who had made the video, about the one who had violated her, about the way her uncle had watched that tape? What could he know about the months in Chicago and the fat American man in her bed every night? How she still felt about all of this, how the feelings came to her at night, how they made her want to scream, how she would never be sure of herself again, of who she was, of what she might do. Could the priest imagine that the little girl who had lived in that village—who was *herself*—seemed almost otherworldly to her? Even with a daughter of her own to help her remember, a sturdy American child, Honorata could not quite summon up what it was like to have once been that little girl in a green world.

Still, with everything the priest could not know, she didn't like the way Virginia talked about him. He was a kind man, the priest. He had been kind to her, and he was kind to the people who came to the door, looking for help, and to the people in the parish, so many of whom were old and had no one to look out for them. That was one thing about America. A lot of old people were left all alone.

Americans went bonkers if a child was left alone, but if you worked at the church, then you knew that all sorts of old people—

just as helpless as a child, some of them—were alone. And nobody seemed to care too much about that. But the priest did. And actually, Virginia did too. She was as kind as the priest.

Last week, Honorata and Nanay had attended a program at Malaya's preschool. It was the first program of the year. And since it was Malaya's first year of preschool, Honorata had not known what to expect. She dressed her daughter in a gold satin dress with a white lace neck, which Malaya kept pulling at; before the night was out, the lace was torn, and Malaya was saying "That feels better, that feels way better!" to anyone who looked at her. Nanay said she could fix the lace.

The room where Malaya had preschool was filled with so many toys and so many bits of colored paper hanging from the ceiling and plastered to the walls and piled on the teacher's desk that it had made Honorata feel dizzy. She wouldn't be able to think calmly in such a room. When they arrived, Malaya wanted to play with her friends on the jungle gym. Honorata made her stay and greet the teacher, but Miss Julie said, "Oh, let her play. That's what all the kids are doing." So Malaya had run outside, and Honorata had seen her sliding and trying to hang from a bar and turning a somersault in the dirt with her underwear right in the air.

In her remarks—that's what they were called in the program, "Miss Julie, Remarks"—the teacher stressed the importance of being independent. She said that at Sunny Days Preschool, four-year-olds hung up their own backpacks, four-year-olds took themselves to the restroom, four-years-olds solved sharing problems on their own. These seemed like very unusual remarks to Honorata. What else would a four-year-old do?

Miss Julie also said that she encouraged children to think

their own thoughts and to stick up for their own ideas. While she was saying this, one of Malaya's classmates, a boy, was yelling "Bang! Pow! Shazam!" Honorata looked around to see if his mother was coming to get him, but everybody sat smiling on the very small chairs. Nanay was one of the ones sitting and smiling. She couldn't understand a word. Honorata thought about asking what Miss Julie would do if the child's idea was not a good one, but she decided against it. She didn't feel comfortable speaking.

After the teacher's remarks, the parents were free to wander around the room. A man wearing a blue T-shirt said hello.

"My name's Mark. Father of Adam. You're Malaya's mom?"

Honorata was not sure how he knew this. She nodded.

"I'm a single dad. I feel sort of awkward at these things. You?"

Honorata wondered if he was insulting her. How did he know she was a single mom?

A ring. She didn't have a ring. She wondered if it would be lying to wear one, for Malaya's sake. She gave the man a discouraging look and turned away.

Later, he tapped her on the shoulder.

She didn't want to talk to him.

"Hey, listen, I'm sorry. That came out wrong earlier. Miss Julie's my sister, so that's how I know you're Malaya's mom. She told me Malaya didn't have a dad, so I was just trying to be friendly. I didn't mean to scare you. I'm really sorry."

He did look like Miss Julie.

"I'm sorry that Malaya doesn't have a dad. I know that's bad." Her voice didn't come out strong, as she intended.

"What? No. That's not what I meant. Hey, no big deal. Like I said, I'm a single dad."

He hadn't seemed mean, more like a puppy, but Honorata had walked away, and when she could persuade Malaya to leave the sandbox, she and Nanay had gone home.

Virginia was still talking about joy, and Molly had apparently stuck up for the priest.

"Molly," Virginia said, "the problem is not with the idea, it's with the command. Of course, we should feel joy. Of course, we are meant to enjoy this world."

Was that true? Were we meant to enjoy this world?

Did Honorata feel joy?

When it was the morning of Malaya's birthday, when Honorata had impulsively pulled over at the pet shop, a dirty little place, not at all reassuring; when she had gone in and seen the gray kitten, fluffy and blue-eyed, and known that it might not be healthy, that getting a pet from one of these stores was not a good idea, that in any case Malaya couldn't be relied on to care for a pet yet, that a cat would shed hair and snag its claws on the silk fabric of the dining room banquette; when she had thought all these things and brought the kitten home anyway; when Malaya had stood there, shocked to absolute stillness, with tears pouring down her cheeks, so surprised and so happy, and yes, so utterly joyful; hadn't Honorata felt joy then? Hadn't she laughed and sat down on the floor, and set the kitten near her daughter's feet, and watched while Malaya bent her knees and squatted in her Swiss dot dress and gently, oh so gently, stroked the kitten with one small finger?

Surely that was joy.

And was it not joy when she walked the three short blocks

from her home to the church office, and let herself in with the key, and poured the honey over the *pandesal* she had baked that morning, and brewed the coffee, and opened the blinds, so that when Virginia and Molly and the priest walked in, they would know the day was starting right?

Wasn't it joy when she spent the afternoon in her garden, wiping the bugs off the rose petals with her fingers and wrapping the sweet pea vines on the trellis? Wasn't it joy when she and Malaya stopped at the Blockbuster to choose a movie, and then walked to the Dairy Queen for an ice cream dipped in red candy, and then sat in a heap on the couch with Nanay while Malaya shrieked in delight as an enormous dog shook mud all over his owner's bed or stood on his hind legs to eat the Thanksgiving turkey? Malaya used her whole body to watch a movie—jumping to her feet to bounce up and down when something funny was about to happen, or throwing her arms out wide to sing "roll over baked oven" whenever the music started up again.

That was joy.

Honorata wanted to say something about joy to Virginia and Molly. She wanted them to know that she felt joy, that her daughter did, that joy was possible even if there was also a great deal of pain, but she couldn't find the right words. She wasn't quick enough, and Virginia always spoke so fast.

What Honorata said was: "Malaya has a kitten, and even when he scratches us, we love him."

Virginia looked at her quizzically.

Molly said she loved cats, and that she'd had her cat YoYo since he was three weeks old. She'd fed him with a bottle, and he still crawled in her lap every time she sat in the one particular chair that she'd fed him in.

Just then, the priest walked in.

"So, Virginia," he said. "What was wrong with my sermon?"

"We were talking about cats," said Virginia.

The priest laughed. "I bet."

Honorata didn't know how they had ended up talking about cats. She had started it, but it wasn't what she meant. It would have taken her a long time to explain what she meant, and it wasn't really that sort of conversation, this Monday morning quarterbacking. It was more like a ritual, like a way to start the week, and it didn't matter too much what anyone said. It had taken her quite awhile to figure this out.

It was confusing, being in America.

It wouldn't have occurred to her to think about whether she felt joy or not.

What occurred to her was whether or not she was doing the right thing each day. Whether she was using the money in the best way, whether she was raising Malaya to be a good person, whether her nanay was happy, whether she was a fair landlord to her tenants, whether her work at the church was correct.

She liked Americans for thinking about things like joy, even if she thought that someone should have made that little boy stop yelling when the teacher was talking. And the man, that Mark. Maybe he was just being friendly, and there wasn't any reason to feel afraid of him, and maybe he hadn't meant that he knew she was not a nice woman. Maybe he didn't think things like that at all.

But Honorata did. She regretted the mistakes she had made, how foolish she had been. It didn't seem fair that she had won a jackpot and that she had a daughter, and that her nanay was here with her. She didn't deserve these things. She tried to be as good as she could, to make up for everything she had done wrong before, but she knew that it wasn't really like that. People didn't get what they deserved, you couldn't hold off bad luck by being good, you couldn't say you earned your good luck. You just got what you got, and did the best you could, and tried not to be afraid of what might happen next. At least, that's how Honorata did it.

23

She found out at her annual appointment.

"Coral, are you aware that you're pregnant?"

She was not.

She was thirty-six years old, and she had always used birth control. No wonder the school nurse's perfume had seemed so pungent.

Pregnant?

Her heart fluttered dangerously.

What would Koji say?

Their relationship was, well, unconventional. He wasn't even in town most of the time. Augusta had stopped asking Coral what their plans were. The answer was that they didn't make plans.

Two years ago, she and Koji had traveled to Japan. Coral had assumed she would meet his family; that he was bringing her home for that reason. But he didn't introduce her. They'd had a wonderful time. Koji took her to his favorite places—temples and ball fields and gardens and the sea—and each morning, he carefully assembled a tray and fed her *natto* and pickled vegetables before she dressed. But she never met his father, his mother, his younger brother. It wasn't difficult to decode what that meant.

After the trip, Coral had decided she needed to move on from

Koji. Althea had been right, way back when. A lot of time could go by; a lot already had. For several months, she spent the weeks when Koji was not in Vegas living as if they had separated. She allowed herself to go on dates and told her closest friends that she was looking for someone with whom she could have a family. But each time Koji arrived in town, she accepted him right back. He was always so pleased to see her, he had one suitcase filled with food he would cook for her, he wanted to hear about everything that had happened in his absence again, even though they had often talked about it on the phone. Also, he had a present to celebrate Malcolm's MVP award at the high school championships; he had found a kimono for Keisha that she might like; had the little girl in the fourth-grade class come back to school or not?

After awhile, Coral accepted that she didn't want to meet anyone else, that she didn't want another life, that she loved Koji even if it wasn't the life she had imagined. She wasn't ready to let him go. Still, she knew she should tell Koji how she had felt in Japan. How she had waited to meet his family, how she had started to realize she might not, how she had not known what to do, how she had lain awake, heart pounding, wondering whether everything she thought was true between them was not true. What if he had a secret life? What if he didn't care about her in the same way she cared about him?

For months, she promised herself that she would talk with him on his next trip to Vegas, but each time, she found a reason not to do it. Finally, on a day when puffy white clouds foiled an impossibly blue sky, and the sweet smell of star jasmine hung in the air like a kiss, she asked him.

"Koji?"

He laid his head on her shoulder.

"I wanted to meet your family. We never talked about this."

He was silent. His head was still on her shoulder, but the weight shifted subtly. Coral felt tears start in her eyes. She concentrated on staying calm, on not thinking ahead of this minute. Koji shifted and sat up, but he didn't look at her. Instead, he looked at the pool, at the vines snaking up the stucco wall behind it.

"My family's very traditional."

Coral said nothing.

"I don't care what they think, Coral. It's never mattered to me."

Coral kept her eyes averted.

"I wanted you to meet them."

What did he mean?

"You'd really like my brother. His wife would love you."

Coral concentrated on being perfectly still.

"I didn't want them to hurt you."

She tried not to think about what he was going to say.

"My parents wouldn't understand, Coral. They've never left Japan. They don't like how their country's changing."

She knew what was coming.

"My father lost his brother in the war. He hates America."

Breathe in, breathe out.

"They don't believe in mixing races."

There it was.

And Coral had wept. The pain had burst out of her in great gulping sobs, and Koji had said, "I'm sorry, I'm sorry, I'm sorry," and held her and wept too. And when it was over, when they sat huddled on the bench under the glorious sky on the beautiful day, they had not talked more about it.

Coral couldn't bring herself to talk about this. It wasn't Koji's fault. It wasn't anything he could fix. But the pain was so fierce and so hot and so unbearably personal, it reached so far inside, to so many other experiences, to so many memories, to classmates calling her "halfie" and "zebra," to saleswomen standing just outside the dressing room door when she needed a new pair of jeans, to certain things that had been said to her late at night in those nightclubs where she and Tonya had sung, to a thousand other moments, uncountable memories, whispers and intimations and slights so subtle they couldn't register as slights, and yet they built up, they piled one on top of the other until the weight smothered one, until the thought of just one more assumption, one more stupid comment, one more sidelong glance, made her feel as if she would never stand again.

Not long after that morning, Koji asked Coral to marry him.

And Coral said no.

She remembered how very stricken he had looked. His face on that day was seared in her mind. But she couldn't marry someone who might just feel terribly guilty.

Gradually things got easier. It had been a year and a half, and Koji still came to Vegas as often as he could; if anything, the relationship deepened. They settled into a partnership, one that was almost the same as a marriage.

Now Coral didn't know what Koji would say when she told him she was pregnant. He had mentioned children when he proposed. For the last year, Coral had told herself, over and over, that she was probably already too old.

Apparently not too old.

Coral told Ada first.

She felt closer to Althea, but it was easier to talk with Ada about some things. Her sister was an hour away in Pahrump, living with some guy who grew marijuana for a living. Nobody said that, of course. Russ was a "farmer." Grew vegetables for some of the restaurants on the Strip. They said stuff like that. But really he grew marijuana, and Coral pretended not to know, and Ada pretended that a multi-ton marijuana operation was some offshoot of the way she'd lived when she was young: when she had followed around a couple of bands and lived in a house where nobody cared what color anyone was, or who slept with whom; where they all raised one another's kids, and laughed about which ones might be blood related after all. In Ada's case, it didn't matter. Her two kids both looked exactly like her, and whoever their dad was (dads were?), he must have hardly had any genes, because Serenity was Ada's double, and Alabaster—Alabaster, for a black man—was Ada if she'd been a boy.

Ada came to town to bring Augusta flowers. She had filled the back of her car with them, and she called Coral to bring over more vases. It was a crazy Ada idea, but they had ended up laughing harder than they had in years. Coral came right over and got things organized. She separated the flowers by stem length, nipped off the ends of each one, and then filled every pot and glass and bucket in the house. There were bowls of flowers all the same color, and vases filled with daisies and roses and asters. She had tall, spikey arrangements, and flat, floating ones, and little sprays of wildflowers to set by the beds. She was showing Augusta her work, wondering where Ada was, thinking that she'd spent an entire Saturday afternoon finishing one of Ada's projects, when Ada finally poked her head in the door.

"There you are," said Coral. "Well, it's done. They look beautiful. They do. Extravagant—and beautiful."

"Done?"

Ada stepped through the door, her arms full of more blooms. And they both laughed. Because here was Coral, with the problem all resolved, and there was Ada, with no problem at all.

They ended up giving the rest to the neighbors.

And later, after Augusta had fixed some dinner, and they had sat and talked about Ada's kids—after Augusta had said she'd turn in early, she was an old lady now, and Ada had said, "Old lady my ass" and Augusta had reminded her kindly not to swear—then the sisters found the cognac left over from Easter, and they sat in the back, in the hot comfort of a summer night, and that's when Coral told Ada she was pregnant.

"I probably shouldn't be drinking this."

"Why, you pregnant?"

Like everything with Ada, it didn't go as Coral might have predicted.

"Girl, you got pregnant at thirty-six—we'd all about given up—and now you're going to have a baby. It's fantastic news. Wonderful. Why haven't you told Mama? Why aren't we dancing?"

"I'm afraid to tell Koji."

"Of course you are. I mean, what are you guys doing? You're together, you're not. What's your deal?"

"Wow, Ada. Easy on the judgment. When did *you* ever have a normal relationship? With Russ, the drug dealer?"

"Hey, let's not go there. Come on. We're having a nice time. You're drinking, and you shouldn't be, so let's not waste it. This isn't about me. What I did. What my relationships are. I just don't understand your relationship with Koji. I mean, we all treat him like he's part of the family, but he's here, what, one week a month, and you don't go there, and he doesn't move here, and what are you doing? I mean, what's it been? Four years?"

Coral thought about Koji's family; about why she didn't go to Japan. Ada would understand this, but she didn't want to tell her. She didn't want to tell anyone. She didn't want Ada or Althea or her mother to know what Koji's family thought.

"It's complicated."

"It's always complicated, Coral. Give that up. Give up that thing you do."

"What thing?"

"That Coral thing. That everything-has-to-be-right, my-life-isn't-messy thing. Speaking of judgment."

"I don't judge you."

"You've judged me my whole life. And maybe I deserve it. But I'm just telling you, let it go. Whatever's bothering you, whatever's holding you back, let it go. Life's messy. Big fuck."

Coral looked down at her hands. Ada continued.

"I don't know what's going on in your head right now, but this baby's a beautiful thing. I know you want her. And I want her. And Mama wants her." Ada stood up. "What we should be doing right now is celebrating!"

So they did.

Her sister hadn't even stopped speaking, and the euphoria washed over Coral like a wave.

She was pregnant. She was going to have a baby. She, Coral, would have her own baby. She whooped. And Ada flew out of the chair, and wrapped her arms around her, and they both cried. Ada started it—she started the crying—and she said, "Coral, Coral, Coral, I am so happy for you."

Augusta heard them and got up to see what was going on, so they all sat there, late into the night, talking about Coral's baby, and what sort of baby Coral had been, and how Ada used to crawl into the crib and make her sister laugh by barking and neighing and mooing in her face.

On Monday, Coral called her doctor for a prenatal appointment and picked up a bottle of maternity vitamins at the GNC on Flamingo. Her mind was full of thoughts of the baby, of whether it would be a boy or girl, of what the nursery might look like, of whether it would be fussy or calm. The baby would be born near Christmas, and with maternity and sick leave, she could probably stay home three months.

She talked with Koji every night, as always, but somehow she kept the secret. He would be home in two weeks, and she needed to tell him in person. She needed to see his eyes, his face. If she didn't, she might never be sure of what he really thought. She tried not to think of what he would do, of how they might live, of the changes they would make. She was sure of Koji, but she was afraid too, and this fear was deep inside, and she had to be with him in person when he heard the news.

She started to bleed two days before he arrived.

It was a hot gush, unmistakable, in the middle of lunch duty. She made an excuse and ran out the door, leaving behind everything, even her purse. She raced to the emergency room at Sunrise, but it was too late. The baby was gone.

"Miscarriages at eleven weeks are not uncommon. I'm sorry, Ms. Jackson, I'm really sorry. You should talk to your own doctor about when to start trying again. She knows your body best."

And Coral had cried.

She had sat in the open exam room, nothing but a flimsy cotton curtain, not quite shut, between her and the child with the seizure, the old man with the chest pain, the woman who had been vomiting for days, and she cried. Her cries were great gasping shudders, mortifying cries, which she desperately wanted to stop, but she could not stop them. She sat and cried in this horrifying way, and everyone there could hear her. After a bit, a nurse said she was sorry and asked if there was someone she could call. And Coral said no, and got up, and then remembered that she didn't have any money, she didn't have her purse, so the nurse walked her to a quiet hall and gave her a quarter for the pay phone.

Two days later, Koji flew in. He always stayed with her, but she asked him to take a hotel room. She said she was sick, that she would see him in a couple of days; there was no sense in him getting it too.

"What do you mean, Coral? If you're sick, I want to help you."

"No, Koji. I don't want you here. I just want to sleep."

She knew she'd hurt his feelings, and that he had no idea what was happening, but she was wildly angry at him, afraid of what she might say if he were right in front of her.

She couldn't think what to do with herself, so she called her sister.

"Ada, it's Coral."

"Yeah, how ya feeling? Any fever?"

"No. I'm fine. I mean, my body's back to normal. The doctor said it would take longer, but—"

"Did you tell Koji?"

"No."

"Is he there?"

"No. I told him to get a hotel. I don't want to see him."

"You have to tell Koji."

"I know."

Coral hung up, but she didn't call Koji. She got into bed and tried to sleep. The next night, he rang the doorbell, and when he came in, when he took her in his arms, when she started to cry, when *he* started to cry without even knowing what had happened, she told him the story.

And then she said, "I think we should break up. I love you, Koji. I always will. But I don't want to do this. This isn't the life I want."

Koji looked at her, shocked.

"It's just not what I want. I thought it was okay. But it's not. It's not okay."

"What *do* you want?"

"I don't know. But it isn't this."

"You're mad at me because I was in Tokyo?"

"Yes."

"You didn't call me. You didn't give me a chance."

"What difference would it make?"

"I would've come."

Coral almost started to cry but steeled herself. "And that wouldn't have made any difference."

Koji didn't answer her then. He looked down at his hands, for a long while. Coral said nothing. She was thinking that she might never see him again, and that she had never loved anyone more than she loved him, and still, that she could not do it. She could not have a lover one week of the month; she couldn't keep living this way. She would not.

Finally, he spoke.

"I don't know what you want. But I do know what I want. I want you. I'll leave Japan. If you'll marry me, I'll marry you. We can live right in this house. I can get a job here in a week. And we can have another baby. That's what I want. That's what I've always wanted. Please. Say yes."

24

"Everyone plays soccer! Ashley, Brittany, Divya. They all get to play, *Ina*."

"Why do you want to play this game? It's a boy's game."

"It's not for boys! It's for girls."

"You'll get very dirty. And kicked. People will kick you."

"I like to be dirty."

This was true, to Honorata's chagrin.

"I don't like you to be dirty, Malaya. And I don't like soccer. You could take another dance class. You could try ballet again."

"No! No, no, no! I hate ballet!"

"Don't yell. You didn't hate it last year. You loved your pink leotard."

"No, I didn't. I don't want to take ballet. I don't want to take tap. I don't want to take any dance class."

"You can't just quit your dance classes because your friends are playing soccer."

"Why not?"

Honorata didn't know why not. She knew she wanted Malaya to stop arguing. She was only in second grade, but already she fought so hard against her mother. It was these American schools. But Nanay was no help. When Honorata asked her what she thought she should do about Malaya, Nanay said, "Well, she's an American. She should do American things."

What did that mean?

Why didn't Malaya like the dance classes Honorata paid for? She had taken ballet and tap, and each year, there were at least four beautiful costumes for the spring show. Last year, Honorata had bought the largest and most expensive photo of Malaya in the package deal. It showed her daughter, right hip jutted out, hair pulled tight across her scalp, a red flower over her ear, and a little red-and-black costume with a short swirl of skirt and a rhinestone belt. Malaya's lips were red and her cheeks pink and her lashes so full they looked as if they were fake; the teacher had let all the mothers use her theater makeup to get the children ready. What little girl would not love that costume? That photo?

Honorata had the photo framed at Swisher's Frame Shop, with a little gold plaque that said "Malaya Age 6," and it hung over the dresser in her bedroom. When Honorata looked at it each morning, she felt pleased with her daughter, and with herself, for giving that daughter a childhood with dance recitals and lessons and all the things a little girl living in the mountains in the Philippines could not even imagine.

But soccer? Why did Malaya want to do something like this? The specter of Malaya's father, the one who was a secret, flickered in Honorata's mind. She didn't want Malaya to be anything like this man. At times she asked herself, *Who is this little girl?* When Malaya wanted to play a boy's game; when she jumped in the puddles in her brand-new shoes and got mud straight up the back of her pressed white blouse right before she was to go to school; when she sat rigid and screaming in the shopping cart at two years old, furious because Honorata would not buy her a tray of Jell-O chocolate pudding cups (how did she even know what they were?); when the school office called and said Honorata would have to come in, that Malaya had called another child a word the woman could not repeat on the phone; when these things happened, Honorata wondered where Malaya got these qualities. Why did she do these things?

And this is why it was so good that her mother lived with them, and it was right that Honorata send her daughter to Catholic schools, even if it meant she would have to ride a school bus, and why it was so important that she watch what Malaya did, and the choices her daughter might make without knowing what it was inside her that made her choose them.

Even when Honorata had betrayed her family and run away to Manila with Kidlat, an act far more horrible than anything she could imagine Malaya ever doing, even then, Honorata had not been like Malaya. She had been in love with Kidlat—madly in love. But Malaya? Malaya was willful when there was no particular reason to be so. Malaya was not submissive as Honorata had been, Malaya did not want to please Honorata the way that Honorata had wanted to please Nanay and Tatay. Malaya had a wildness that came to her from somewhere else—that came to her from the man. That was Honorata's fault. But she would do what she could, she would protect her as much as she could, and maybe Malaya would change; maybe she would grow up. This did happen. Some wild children became serious adults.

And perhaps it was these fears, these unknown possibilities, that tipped Honorata over some days. Perhaps this was why she would occasionally wake up, after a year—or even longer—of perfectly normal mornings, and the light would shine in acidly, and the sound of a cup rattling on the tile would grate, and she would feel it about to happen, an instant before it did, and then it would be there, full on top of her, and unbearable, and no way to lift herself back up. There was nothing to do but wait, and take one leaden step after another, until one day, just as inexplicably, the light would shine clear again, and she would hear the three-toned trill of a bird out her window. Honorata would stand up, startled at how easy it was, at how gravity had somehow shifted, and how she did not have to press against nothingness, but instead almost lifted, almost elevated, with each step she took.

On those dark days, everything would stretch out impossibly. She would pick up her toothbrush, and the puddle of whitish gel at the bottom of the cup would accuse her: you can't even keep this clean. She would step out the door, her fingers gripped a little too tightly on Malaya's, and her daughter would protest: "Ina, stop touching me!" She would make herself a cup of strong, sweet coffee and allow herself to sit in the thickly padded wrought iron chairs she had bought for the patio, and she would not be able to push the chair into any position at which the sun did not shine too brightly, or in which she was not looking at something left undone, or from which the pool did not beckon like a siren: come in, come here, give up, give in, sink, forget, sink. So she would not sit down but would go to her desk and finally call about the outside sprinkler that still did not have the correct water pressure, even though she had paid a garden service twice. And when she talked to the receptionist, her voice would quiver, and then she would bark angrily at the young man who was not sure which house she meant, and then she would hang up the phone and feel mortified at what they must be thinking, what they must be saying, about the crazy Pilipina with all the houses on Cabrillo Court.

And day after day, it would go on like this. After awhile, her mother would start making Malaya *suman* for breakfast, and she would hear Malaya say, "Lola, I don't want *tuyo* in my lunch," and she would hear the murmur of her mother's voice, "*Ang pagkain na ito ay mabuti.*" Then Malaya would call, "Mommy, get out of bed!" But Honorata would not. She would lie there, tight like a stick, and she would hear the door open and close, and then awhile later, hear her mother return, and Honorata would not answer when her mother called to her. Only when the house was completely quiet—when she had counted dully to a thousand and then two hundred more—would she get up and dress and follow the to-do list she had made for herself the night before, exactly.

And then one day she would get out of bed when Malaya called to her, and she would thank her mother for helping, and she would make a peanut butter and jelly sandwich for Malaya's lunch, with an apple and two pieces of candy. And when they walked out the door to the bus, her fingers would rest lightly in her daughter's hand, and Malaya would tell her about the boy at school who could do a backflip, and about the teacher who had been to Rome and seen the Vatican, and about how she might grow up and sing onstage like Madonna. "Isn't Madonna a pretty name? And her dresses are beautiful, Ina."

And that night after dinner, when Malaya would wrap one of Nanay's scarves around her middle like a sari and totter into the kitchen in Honorata's heels, singing, "*Nothing like a good spanky*"— and Nanay, her English suddenly much better than it had ever been in the supermarket, would ask, "What? What is she saying?"—that night, Honorata would laugh. She would laugh until the tears leaked down her cheeks, and Malaya, delighted that she could make her mother laugh, would sing louder and louder, "*I just wanna hanky panky!*" And Nanay would look more and more dismayed, and Honorata would think that probably she should not be laughing, and that this might be one of Malaya's bad choices, but she would not be able to help herself. The laugh would boil up from somewhere far below reason, and it would bellow out of her, unstoppable and cleansing and bringing with it a joy she had so recently believed she would never feel again.

And what was this? How was it that she could not predict these feelings? Or direct them? And what did it matter, if right this minute she could feel this elation, she could look at her perfect, improbable, irrepressible child, and know suddenly that if she had not been so irrepressible, she would not have existed at all? It was all part and parcel of one thing: the fear and the horror inextricable from the beauty and the joy, at least for her, at least for this family. And really, if she had been given the choice—the whole choice, the good and the bad, the pain and the glory—she would have taken it. She would have said yes. Who knows, maybe she *had* been given that choice; maybe there was a reality in which she had chosen this life, somehow, someway, in that realm in which the truth was grander than anything one could know with the mind, but which did not, for Honorata, have anything to do with religion or a church or the way in which people spoke of these things.

ENGRACIA

The one whose heart was broken

MAY 8, 2010
In the Midnight Cafe

There was a bill on the floor of the almost empty Midnight Cafe. Arturo could see it through the bars of his cashier cage, and since it was slow, he watched it flutter in the slight breeze from the air-conditioning, and wondered who would find it. His guess was that whoever picked it up would immediately put it into a slot machine, probably Megabucks, since there was one nearby. To a gambler, found money was lucky money.

It was one of the maids. She looked tired, coming off the night shift. She had stopped to get a fifty-cent cup of coffee, and the old man watched as she lifted her eyes from the Styrofoam cup, spotted the fluttering bill, and then leaned over to pick it up. It was more than a dollar; he could see it in the way she straightened. But she didn't play the money. She tucked it into a pocket of her pale-blue dress.

She leaned against a pony wall that separated casino cardholders from the regular line when the cafe was busy, which wasn't often anymore, and finished her coffee. Then she shifted her purse, large and cracked, with an oddly bright buckle at the center, and dug around in it for her ID and an envelope. She approached the cashier cage.

"Cash check?"

"Small bills? ¿En billetes pequeños?"

"Sí."

"Una noche difícil, ¿eh?"

She looked startled that he had spoken about something other than her check. She must have worked alone all night. The hotel was even slower than the casino.

Her eyes caught his, but she did not speak.

She was young. She hadn't looked young, stooping for that bill, but she was. Arturo wished he could say something to her. He was an old man now, and he knew what it was like to work in a hotel, to work all night, to move from room to room with a heavy cart—and here was a room trashed by someone on a Vegas binge and there was a guest, weaving down the hall, drunk and unpredictable. And all night long, she would have worked silently; she would have observed and been mute. Perhaps she had felt nervous, perhaps she had felt irritated, perhaps she had simply moved through it all, leaden, as she looked right now.

Why did his eyes water as he stamped her check and opened the till to count her cash? Getting old had made him foolish. She was lucky to have a job, and there was nothing wrong with working as a maid.

"Gracias," she said, taking the small stack of twenties.

"De nada, Engracia. Gástalo sabiamente."

Spend it wisely. Why did he say things like this?

"Voy a comprar un patín para mi hijo."

A skateboard. For her son. She was old enough to have a child with a skateboard.

"He'll be happy."

"Sí. Eso espero."

She had a wide face and when she smiled, her eyes narrowed into deep-set black ribbons. Arturo smiled back, pleased to think that she had a son, that she could buy him a gift, that the boy would be happy.

He had worked at the El Capitan for forty-three years. Had known Odell Dibb, and worked for June when she doubled the size of the place, and then for their son, Marshall. Now the Dibbs had all left, and the El Capitan should have been gone too. Marshall had sold to a Chinese investor who immediately announced that the casino would be torn down. But the economy fell apart, and everything in Vegas just stopped: overnight it seemed. There was a huge empty lot down the street where the Stardust had been imploded, but the El Capitan hadn't closed and hadn't disappeared; it just sat, and nobody, not even the rich people, had the money to get rid of it. Most of his carnales had gotten out while they could, but Arturo figured he'd just ride the ship down. There weren't any jobs anywhere, and who would want an old Mexican guy with bad lungs?

Of course, they all had bad lungs after a lifetime inside casinos. The word now was that it was best not to go to a doctor, not to do anything; the doctors wanted to operate, wanted to confirm cancer. But of course it was cancer. All that smoke, all those nights. Surgery just stirred things up, made you die quicker. Marge said that she'd had black spots on her lungs for nine years, and she would not let a doctor touch them. Just leave those spots sit, and if you were lucky, your own tissue would encase them—that was Marge's idea. She was a tough old broad, and she'd been right about a lot of things. She could be right about the lungs too.

Arturo didn't know. He didn't like doctors much, and he didn't know anything about his lungs. The world was for young people, like this maid, anyway.

25

Engracia struggled to unhook the head of the vacuum cleaner from its notch on the canister. Cleaning Ms. Navarro's house was different from cleaning a hotel room, and she got tired of doing everything a different way in each house. It was strange how trivial things could bother her, when, in fact, she cared nothing at all about what she was doing, or how her day went, or whether something got done. Even now, if the plastic bit of this vacuum snapped off, she would feel bad to have done it.

Sweating, struggling to wrench the pieces apart without making a sound that might draw Ms. Navarro near, she cracked her elbow against the washing machine.

"*Mierda.*"

Ms. Navarro appeared in the door.

"Do you need help?"

"No. I'm fine. I—I fix it."

Ms. Navarro had followed her around the first two times she had come. She wasn't used to having a maid, and had given Engracia the job only because one of the priests had asked her to do it. This made Engracia nervous. She wondered what she sounded like to Honorata. An idiot, probably. Her English was fine but not when she was rattled. Diego had chattered away in English, and she had understood perfectly. She hadn't even told him to speak in Spanish, as most of the other mothers did, because it pleased her that he could speak so well.

Diego.

"I'm making something for Malaya. She'll be home in a while. Can I fix you a plate?"

"No. Thank you. I'm not hungry."

Ms. Navarro's daughter had purple and green stripes in her hair and a tattoo that looked like a serpent winding up her neck from somewhere inside her shirt. Engracia rarely saw her but found her a bit alarming. She could not imagine letting one's child look like that.

"I make the beds now."

"Don't worry about my mother's room. She's staying with a friend who had surgery this week."

Engracia nodded and started up the stairs with two sets of sheets, thinking that she could be done with Malaya's room before she got home. Sometimes the girl would skip school, and when she did, she would stay in bed until well past noon. Her room got the morning sun, and Engracia was amazed that she could stay asleep, swaddled in blankets, with the sun beating in and the second floor so warm that Engracia would feel slightly nauseous as she scrubbed out the shower.

Someday she would return to the El Capitan to work. They had told her she could have her job back any time she wanted, at least if the El Capitan was still open. Engracia was thinking about it. She didn't like working in homes, and while she appreciated that the padre had gotten her these jobs—that he understood she needed something to do every day—eventually she would go back to the El Capitan. It was just hard going back, as if her life were still the same.

Malaya's room had a deep-orange wall and a poster of Manny Pacquiao on it. Diego had been wild for boxing too; it was something he shared with his dad. Juan was in Las Vegas twenty years ago when Chavez fought Taylor—it was the first time he had crossed the border—and he and Diego had spent hours watching old fights on YouTube and hashing out why Chavez was the greatest Mexican fighter of all time.

This is how it was for Engracia, day after day, alone with these memories, these thoughts. She supposed it would be like this until she died—until finally she died—because she agreed with the padre: she did not have the choice about how long she lived.

Engracia snapped Malaya's sheet expertly under the mattress. She tugged the comforter up straight, and placed the girl's collection of pillows and teddy bears back on the bed. The room was a sort of archeology of girlhood: a row of puppets on one bookshelf, a doll-sized American Girl dresser and bed in the corner, a pile of CDs with titles scribbled in blue and green marker: *Aimee's Mix, Road Trip 1987, Don't Listen to This Sober*. There were photos of little girls on soccer teams and at Fern Adair dance recitals; there was a dried-up corsage, a Homecoming Court banner, a collection of flip-flops, tangled necklaces hanging from a metal stand, and a leopard-print padded bra on top of the bureau.

Engracia flicked a feather duster across these surfaces. She thought about Diego's room, for the short time they had lived in Las Vegas together. It was a closet, really, but there was a small window and room for his bed. Apart from that, there had been almost nothing in it: just an old jacket of Juan's spread on a stool and a small pile of books from the school book fair.

When Juan was detained, Engracia knew she would have to leave Pomona. She told Diego that it would be better if they were far away; that her papers might also be inspected, that they would have to lay low for a while. Her friend Pilar had suggested Las Vegas. It was cheaper than California, especially now, because the economy was so bad. And there were still jobs in the casinos, if you knew someone, and Pilar did: Engracia could work as a maid in one of the old hotels. Engracia didn't want to move because Diego was happy with his friends, and this was the only world he'd ever known.

But she couldn't reach Juan. The only reason she knew he was still in jail, just sitting there, was because Ramón had told her. Ramón knew things, knew people everywhere. Engracia had asked him when Juan would be back, but Ramón had not replied. He had shaken his head, said times were tough, and that Juan had been caught already twice before. Engracia did not tell Diego that Juan was still in jail, that he was waiting to be deported, or that she was running out of money and could not afford their apartment.

That night, Engracia tossed and turned, and then finally threw up in the toilet. This was why Pilar had talked about Las Vegas. She had known that Engracia would be on her own, would need someplace easier than Pomona—cheaper, with steadier work. Engracia resisted, but only for a few days. This was not the hardest thing she had done. It was easy to do hard things for her son.

She had crossed the border when she was sixteen, with a friend of a friend of Juan's. Engracia had found out she was pregnant, and she had known she didn't have much time. If she was ever going to leave, going to follow Juan, she would have to do it now, before the baby was born. And so she had. She had done this enormous thing on her own, without telling her mama or her papa, without kissing her little brothers good-bye. She'd given birth in a hospital filled with women like herself, and the nurse had not concealed the anger she felt at what Engracia was doing, and Engracia had had to force herself not to care about the nurse, not to need her, as her body twisted and gripped. In her mind, she thought that this pain could not be right, could not be normal, but of course it was normal, and she gave birth to a perfect Diego, who waited to cry until the doctor rubbed his feet, and then stopped crying the moment that Engracia took him in her arms.

Afterward, Engracia asked for a piece of paper and a pen. She wanted to write it all down, everything that had happened, so that she could send it to her mother. This is how tired she was: she knew her mother didn't have a phone, but somehow forgot that she didn't know how to read. Engracia could not send the letter. If she sent a letter, someone would have to read it to Mama. Her brothers were still too young yet, so it would be someone from the village. It would embarrass her mother to hear someone read aloud Engracia's words: about what it had been like to give birth to Diego.

Juan had not been there. He was working, moving farther and farther north, but he had made it back in time to take her and their son out of the hospital, to bring them, carefully and solemnly, to the little apartment in Pomona. She had been so proud of Juan, who had gotten them a place to live, just one big room, but all theirs. They had not shared it with another family. And this is where they had lived for nine years. She and Juan and Diego. By the time that Engracia left, the apartment was unrecognizable from the room they had first taken. Juan had painted the walls yellow, and Engracia had made everything herself: the curtains and the bedding and the flowered cover on the couch where Diego had slept with his thumb in his mouth, and the sound of his suck, suck, suck like an ocean lapping.

They had been happy. She had known Juan since before her *quinceañera*—they had met at the parade for Nuestra Señora de Guadalupe—and as soon as she turned fifteen, he had made the long walk from Jerez to her village to find her. Juan was older, and he had already been to the United States, already worked a few seasons in a raisin plant. He was full of ideas for what they could do, for how they would live, for the lives their children would have. In the meantime, they could send money back to her family.

And this was what they had done.

Engracia was proud to help her parents, proud that her brothers could go to school, proud that her papa, who had hated working in the States, could stay and grow peppers on the land on which he had always lived. These were not hardships: she and Juan enjoyed the life they had made. They liked being in a city—in an American city. They liked taking Diego to the park, and watching people on the streets, and buying ice cream on Fridays when they got paid. Diego was a funny little boy, and he made them laugh. They would play on the floor with him for hours. Juan used to invent silly songs, and Engracia was not too shy to dance in the park, or to run wildly down the beach with her arms above her head on the days when they took the bus to the ocean.

There were all those good years to shore her up, and if she had been capable of crossing a border and having a child and making a home when she was sixteen, then she could certainly find a way for her and Diego to live until Juan got out of jail. This was not even hard, it was just life. She still had the rent in the box they kept hidden. Engracia had ignored the landlord pounding on the door, ripped the sheet of paper from the door without reading it. She would have to go quickly, and she was sorry that there would be no time to let Diego get used to it. She picked him up at school on Friday, after getting his records from the office, and told him they would be moving to Las Vegas on Sunday. Even though Diego was already nine, he cried, and begged to stay a little longer. But because he would be afraid if he knew how little money they had, she did not explain why she refused.

Her son was subdued on the ride up I-15. They stopped at McDonald's, and she bought him everything he liked: the double cheeseburger with bacon and a Dr Pepper and a hot fudge sundae. They sang *"Hay un hoyo en el fondo de la mar"* for miles, and she made sure Diego beat her each time. For a while, it was fun, but as they got farther from Pomona, after they crossed the Cajon Pass and drifted down and past Victorville, even Engracia felt daunted. She pointed out the giant thermometer in Baker, which didn't seem to be working, and Diego looked out the window, at the desert stretched brown and barren and relentless as far as the eye could see. Cars were strung along the freeway like seeds on the backside of a fern, and the sun beat down even though it was January. They finally saw what they thought was Las Vegas in the distance, but it was merely a collection of overeager casinos at the state line, with a huge roller coaster in the parking lot, and just after that, a low concrete building, ringed with barbed wire, in the middle of nowhere.

The drive was sad, and the move was harder.

Diego was not happy in their new home, and he did not like his new school. Pilar's friend had gotten Engracia a job at a casino called the El Capitan, and she had told her about the apartments near Maryland Parkway, where everyone spoke Spanish and she would not need a deposit. But the neighborhood was rough, much rougher than where they had lived in Pomona. All night long, Engracia heard loud talk and fighting, sudden shouts, and the undulating whine of police sirens. She did not let Diego outside after dark, and she worried about the kids he walked home from school with, even while she was grateful that another mother had invited Diego to have breakfast at her house when he woke up alone, hours after Engracia had left for work.

Engracia did not think the school was so bad. She had gone to a meeting for Hispanic parents, where a man in a suit and tie talked with them about college. His Spanish was very good, and he told them there was a lot of money for Hispanic children who wanted to go to college. They could go to the best schools in the United States. And then a woman, a *mexicana*, spoke. She explained that the children who got this money had to go to school every day, had to take AP classes when they got to high school, had to join the debate team or the math club, and stay after school when they could be home taking care of younger children. Engracia heard one father say that he did not want his child to leave home, and he did not understand a college that preferred math club to a child who helped his family, but Engracia did not feel this way. This is what she wanted for Diego. This is why she had left her family, so that Diego could live differently.

It had been Juan who had first felt this way about America, who had given her these ideas about their children. But when he finally called, the day he arrived back in Jerez, he said that maybe they should all go back to Mexico. Life was so much easier there; one didn't need very much money to live in the village. Engracia was shocked. They had never considered returning to Zacatecas.

After the meeting, she wandered the school, looking at the walls filled with children's art: watercolor paintings and origami sculptures and brightly colored maps that showed small children in different cities around the world. Peering in the windows of a classroom, Engracia saw a row of computers and three book-shelves stacked with books—even though the school had its own library where the meeting had just been held—and plastic cups filled with markers and paintbrushes and rulers.

Engracia had gone to school. It was a long walk, very hot, to the next village, and the school had been just two rooms: one for the younger children and the other for the older ones. There was a little building in the back, with three pit toilets, and in between there was a dusty field where the children played at recess. The teacher, Senorita Consuela, was from Mexico City. She had been to the national museum filled with stone figures too heavy for fifty men to lift and also to the house painted blue where the artists had lived. Engracia had liked school.

Weeks went by, and still Diego did not thrive. He gained weight. He pretended to be sick in the mornings. He would call her at work and beg not to go to school, saying his stomach hurt, he had a fever, he could not get out of bed. And she would make him go to school, not listen to his pleas, and wonder at how long that would last. How long would he relent and do as she asked, and when would he figure out that there was nothing she could do if he did not go?

One night at dinner, Diego was animated. A scientist had visited the fourth grade. He had dipped a rose in nitrogen and made it freeze. He had showed slides of Death Valley and told about the Indians who had lived there, and the giant boulders that rolled mysteriously, leaving tracks in the dry earth, even though no one ever saw them move and they were too big for any living thing to push.

"Can we go see them, Mama?"

"The boulders?"

"Yes. They're sailing stones. And where the Indians lived. And the castle."

"Maybe, *papi*. Maybe in the summer, if you get good grades."

"Could Papa come?"

"I don't know."

She regretted telling him that they might go to Death Valley. She was afraid of this place. She didn't want to go there without Juan. "Do you still like to skateboard? Maybe we can get a skateboard for summer."

Diego's face dimmed.

"*Si*, Mama," he said slowly.

At this thought, Engracia dropped Ms. Navarro's laundry basket to the floor.

The clothes at the top rolled onto the floor, and she heard Ms. Navarro walk to the bottom of the stairs to see if something had happened. Engracia did not call down to her. A tight band stretched across the bottom of her rib cage, and squeezed. She doubled over, trying to breathe. Padre Burns had said that it was good to remember, that she had to let her feelings out, but she couldn't bear to remember; it took her breath away. But then, what difference did it make if she could breathe? And as soon as that thought came, her body relaxed, the cinch around her middle eased, and air filled her lungs.

She picked up the clothes that had fallen, and the basket, and started down the stairs carefully. Ms. Navarro wasn't standing there anymore—Engracia could hear her in the kitchen—so when the bell rang, she set the basket carefully on the bottom step and hurried to open the door.

The man was large, and older. His face was quite red, as if it were always that color, and at first, he seemed nervous.

"I'm looking for Honorata Navarro. Is she here?"

Engracia hesitated. Perhaps she shouldn't have opened the door. She struggled to find the right words.

"Just a minute."

She started to close the door to look for Ms. Navarro, but he put his foot in the jamb and then said calmly, "I'd like to speak with her if I could."

Engracia looked from his foot to the door to the empty hallway behind her. "Ms. Navarro!" she called.

As soon as she spoke, the man entered the doorway. He didn't move farther into the house, but stood on the entryway floor, waiting.

Engracia's heart beat faster. Why had she answered the door?

"She's not here," Engracia tried. "I'm sorry, she's not home right now."

"I'll wait."

"No. You can't stay here. You have to leave."

Her voice was weak, but at least she was finding the words she wanted.

Just then, Ms. Navarro rounded the corner. Engracia was looking at her, past the man, and the shock on her face, it actually went white, made it clear that she should not have opened the door.

"I'm sorry. I try to tell him to leave . . ."

"Rita," said the man.

"Honorata," said the trembling Ms. Navarro.

26

Life perfects us, if we let it.

I have reached a moment in which I might be almost pure. I don't wish for things. I think I finally see life: how nature is, what it means to live and die, how there is nothing at all, nothing, except in what one might do for someone else.

I've reached this place at a time when I am something like an old dog. My fur is pocked with bald spots, my skin spotted with twisty disturbing growths, my teeth smell of rot; there is always a whiff of urine or feces about me. In short, I live to do something for others, and the people around me are busy steeling themselves, summoning the courage, to do for me. Marshall tries so hard to be loving, and I know the effort it costs him, now that I am slow and dribbly and unreliable and more or less mute. It's ironic, of course. A divine sort of joke. Almost, but not quite, I even see the reason why it should be so.

"*I thought you ought to know my heart's on fire.*"

"Singing again? You sound happy."

"*The flame it just leaps higher.*"

"Oh, June, you're wet. You know where the bathroom is. Why'd you do that?"

"*I've got my love to keep me warm.*"

"You have to try to keep up. It's not nice."

Helen is a lovely person, very competent. Del would have hired her in an instant. She's not as much fun as Jessy, though. Jessy will put on a record and dance with me, or bring me a bit of the dessert she made the night before. When we walk, she doesn't seem to care that I am slow, and she brings along a little vase, with water, and collects a nosegay as we go. I can't tell you how this pleases me. (Actually, I really *can't* tell you. Isn't that funny?) I sing and sing as we walk along, I can't stop myself; it makes me so happy when she finds a flower, especially if I have spotted it first and am hoping she will see it.

"Today's physical therapy. Matt will be here in ten minutes, and now you have to change your clothes. Come on."

"*I can't give you anything but love, baby.*"

"All right. I'll just bring your clothes in here. And then you change, okay? You have to hurry, June."

"*Scheme awhile, dream awhile.*"

I'm not trying to frustrate Helen, though she thinks I am. If I wanted to make her mad, I couldn't. I can't seem to make things work the way I intend. Words are the worst, and eating is hard, but even getting dressed. I'm thinking about putting my pants on. Fifteen minutes ago, I was thinking about getting up and going to the bathroom. There's nothing wrong with my legs. I'm slow, but I can get up, I can move. It's just that if I try to do one thing, something else happens. And then when I feel something about that, a different feeling comes out.

It's caused a lot of misunderstandings.

Marshall comes to dinner when he is in town, and begs me to eat. He cuts my food smaller, and talks about how tasty it is, how it came from this restaurant or that chef, what the ingredients are, and I sit and look at him with a silly grin on my face, but my hand doesn't go to the fork, my mouth doesn't open. When he tries to feed me, I tighten my lips and shake my chin, and the food falls on to my lap.

"Mom," he says. "Please try. Just eat one bite."

And I remember saying the same words to him when he was too small to talk, and I wonder if he was thinking something other than what I thought he was. Probably he just wanted to play, probably peas tasted bitter to him, but now I see everything differently. I see all the moments of my life differently now that I am actually trying to open my mouth, trying to neatly take the food my son offers, trying not to make him feel mocked by my mysterious grin. And purse go my lips, and shake goes my chin, and twinkle go my eyes, as if I have annoyed him for fun.

"That's good," says Helen. "Thank you for getting dressed. And you wrapped up your wet clothes. I'll take them."

That's how it works. If my mind is distracted, if I'm thinking about Marshall, then I am also putting on clean pants and neatly wrapping up the dirty ones. Only I didn't know I was doing it. I'm more surprised than Helen to see that I'm ready for Matt.

"Howdy, Mrs. Dibb. How are you today?"

Matt always says howdy, but he doesn't look like a cowboy. More like a dancer. I smile at him, and apparently I really do, because he smiles back.

"Ready to work hard?"

"Nine little miles from ten-ten-Tennessee."

"Okay, sounds like a yes."

It is a yes! I feel good today. Matt asks me to stay standing, so my knees buckle and he catches me under the elbow so that I don't fall. I want to laugh about this with him, but of course I can't, so I try to get my mind to rest. My trick is that I think about nothing, that I pretend there is nothing around me, there is nothing for me to do, and then, sometimes, my body will be a little less of a rebel.

"Matt," I say. "Nice day."

"It *is* a nice day. That's really good, June. Thank you."

My eyes water, I am so pleased with myself.

He keeps me firmly by my elbow, and without telling me what to do, he walks me slowly down the hall and toward the back door. I like to have my exercises outside, even if it's hot. I've always loved the sun. Just before we walk outside, my legs lock. I push back against him, as if I don't want to go.

"She's in a mood today, Matt. I think she wants to stay inside."

Matt doesn't listen to Helen. He hums a little tune, something I don't recognize, but I try to get it. What is he humming? And just like that, we are out the door and in the sun. I love Matt.

"That's probably enough for today. Are you tired?"

I'm not tired. I want to keep going. I don't want to go in the house. I don't want to watch television. I don't want to take a rest. But Matt is already leading me back to the door. I, of course, am walking along as fast as I have all year.

"*So here I am, very glad to be unhappy.*"

When I sing, the words I want come out. Sometimes, anyway. I don't know how it works. I can sing the lyrics to songs I don't even remember knowing. I never know what I will sing until I hear my own voice. But a lot of times, the lyrics make sense. Isn't that crazy? Believe me, it makes me a lot crazier than anyone else. One thing I can't control, though, is how I sing them, so right now I sound as cheery as a little bird. But I don't want to go inside.

Matt grins. "*Do you still believe the rumor that romance is simply grand,*" he sings. Matt sings in a trio at the Venetian. He'd like to be a musician full-time, but it hasn't worked out yet. Isn't that amazing? That I would get a physical therapist who sings? It's not, really. It's how the world works. If we could just see it.

"*Since you took it right on the chin, you have lost that bright tooth-paste grin,*" I sing back. I know I'm smiling now.

"*I did it my . . . way!*" Matt belts out.

And I laugh.

Which is exactly what I wanted to do, and sometimes happens, especially with Matt. He leads me inside, so our session is done, but I am happy. I look at the ground and think as little as I can, so that I feel this.

"You tired her out." Helen comes over and touches her palm to my cheek. She does things like that when someone else is around.

"Maybe. She's pretty tough. Right, June?"

I shimmy with my shoulders and wink. I can just imagine what that looks like, now that I'm eighty-two.

"There's the spirit!"

"Okay, Miss June. I think you're ready for a little rest now."

I wish I could give Matt a hug, but my head flops forward and shakes a bit, I don't know why, and he puts his hand on my chin and says he will see me on Thursday. And then, like he does every time he leaves, he sings:

"*S'wonderful, s'marvelous, that I should care for you.*"

And my head flops further forward. I can't even see him leave, which is for the best, because I am crying.

Marshall will be fifty-four on his next birthday. That's how old Del was when he died. He thinks of it, I'm sure. Partly, he's just a bit of a hypochondriac. Goes to Scripps for daylong medical testing and all that fuss. Marshall knows more about his hormone levels and genetic profile than I know about my own hair.

Not that anyone wouldn't wonder.

His dad drops dead without a hint, and his mom ends up a raving idiot. Singing Christmas carols at a Jewish wedding and asking the cute young man at the table on the other side of the restaurant for a dance. He thinks these things mean something— that they express deep down desires I no longer have the ability to repress—but if they mean something, I sure as hell don't know what. They feel as random to me as they do to anyone else. I try to laugh. I mean, I *would* laugh if I could do what I intend. I think I must have had something to learn about humility, and now I am learning it.

Of course, Marshall's hoping to avoid ending up like Del or me. I hope he doesn't end up like this too. But the game's rigged: there's no way to win this one. It's possible to play in an entirely different way if you really see that. That's what I wish I could say. That's what I wish I knew how to share. This is a game you can't win, so don't play to win. Play to play. Play to keep everyone else in play. That's the long game here. That's what I want to tell him.

Marshall moved to Santa Monica after he sold the El Capitan. He and Janie bought a condo years ago, and the kids spent all their vacations there, so it made sense to make a permanent move. When he visits, he asks me if I'm ready to come to California. He says there are some nice assisted living programs, or I could live in the old condo, with caregivers, just as I live now. He seems to think that I'll go downhill if he moves me out of this house—this house and all its memories.

I don't know.

I don't feel like the house is me at all. I wouldn't mind going to California and seeing the kids once in a while. But I don't have a way to tell Marshall what I want, and I don't try. I don't empty my mind or start singing or make any effort to communicate what I think at all. This way, Marshall will choose what he wants. He'll leave me here if he doesn't really want me that close, or he'll take me there, and I'll live in the condo or in assisted living, and it will be what he wants.

But I do like seeing him. I love the kids.

I know that it's not fun for them to see me. I don't think there's much in the experience for them. So I don't want to want it. But I do.

I have hours, days, months to think about things.

I think just fine.

I think about my childhood. I think about my *bubbe*, and how she talked to me in Yiddish, and how I must have understood when I was small, even though I didn't later. I think about the cabin at Kittatinny Lake that we shared with our neighbors two weeks every summer, and how it felt to have my back hot with the sun and then how cold the water was. I think about my neighbor's dog Pal, who would come to the lake with us and then go with me as I rambled farther than anyone else in the woods. Momma would say that it wasn't safe, but Poppa would say, "She's okay. She has the dog."

There were ponds all over that country, and Pal and I would find one, and then I would throw sticks, and he would chase them, over and over. I can almost feel those summer mornings, the smell of the water and the trees, the quack of northern shovelers in the reeds, the heft of a good solid stick in my hand. There was one pond Pal didn't want to go in. He went in once or twice, then whined and barked and wagged his back end trying to get me to follow him away. "Come on, Pal!" I said, "Fetch!" And I hurled the stick as hard as I could, and Pal wiggled and waited and plunged in and jumped back out without fetching, and just as he barked again, loud, there was a huge sucking sound, and the water spun, and Pal barked madly while I watched, frozen, as a whirlpool formed right in the center of the pond. And like that, with one huge roar, all the water disappeared down into it.

They were old mines, those ponds, and if Pal had been in the water, he would have gone down that whirlpool with it. I ran all the way back to the cabin, yelling about what I had seen, and after I had finally gotten out my story, so that everyone could understand me, Momma started to cry. She kept saying, "Thank goodness you didn't go in! For once, June, you thought before you acted." She said it over and over, kissing me and crying, and Lew, who was my neighbor and in fourth grade with me, hugged Pal and said he was a hero, and looked at me and said, "Why did you take him? He's our dog. He could have been killed." And even now, more than seven decades later, I hear Lew saying this, and I hear the cracked fear in my mother's voice, and I remember how it felt to see that water begin to turn and to hear the sound it made, and the way the pond disappeared.

I think about other things too.

I think about how my son called himself "Hammerin' Marshall" after he hit a home run to win the opening game in Jaycee Park when he was thirteen years old. I swear he actually grew taller thinking about that hit, and a few years later, I remember the suddenly deep sound of his voice when he asked his dad whether he was also worried about Hammerin' Hank Aaron, whether Del thought maybe something was going to happen to Hank that winter, when he was one long ball shy of Babe Ruth's home run record. I couldn't even look at Del when he answered Marshall, couldn't bear all the memories our son's enthusiasm brought up. There were so many people who didn't want a black man to surpass Babe Ruth—he got death threats—and so many people who did. Hank Aaron had grown up in Mobile, and, of course, every time that fact was mentioned on the nightly news, I thought of Eddie.

I think about the first years running El Capitan. I think about Del. I think about Cora. I think about my mother and my father. How someone once vivid, vibrant, present in this world, can suddenly and absolutely be absent from it. Sometimes I think the joke is about to be revealed, that Del or my father will suddenly come around the corner, and how we will laugh and cheer and feel as if we will explode with joy in discovering that of course the impossible *was* impossible: that the people we loved have not disappeared completely and forever, lasting only in my memory, which is nearer and nearer to not lasting at all.

What if we could just see each other now and then? A quick hug, one dinner, a sunny day? What about that? It would be enough, wouldn't it? If we all got to shimmer in, here and there, and feel the cold rush of sea wave against bare ankle, the whisper-soft skin of our grandmothers, hear the low rumble of my poppa reading a bedtime story, or an eight-year-old Marshall singing "Zip-a-Dee-Doo-Dah" under a tree? It doesn't seem too much to ask of a universe so vast, that the absolute be a little less absolute, a little more bearable, a little more as it really feels: that the people I love are still present, are still real, are still near me.

"It's time for dinner. I've cooked a piece of salmon." I'd forgotten Helen.

We'll have dinner, and then she'll go home. Jessy will be here tomorrow. There's no one with me at night. Everyone worries about this except me. I might fall, I might do something I don't mean to do, it isn't perfectly safe. But I hope Marshall doesn't hire someone to be with me at night. I'll miss that little bit of privacy, even if I mostly sleep through it.

"It's only a paper moon, sailing over a cardboard sea . . ."

"Take a bite now, while it's warm."

"But it wouldn't be make believe if you believed in me."

I pick up my fork and tap it on the table to the rhythm of the song. I am feeling good, and I mean to eat, but this is what the fork does.

27

Engracia should not have opened the door.

Ms. Navarro and the man stared at each other for a long moment. Then he said, "How could you? How could you keep my daughter from me?" and his voice squeaked, as if he were a child, a tiny, high voice in a huge man's body. Ms. Navarro did not answer. She turned quickly, but before she could move, the man rushed forward and grabbed her; he held Ms. Navarro between his arms and refused to move.

"Call the police!" she said to Engracia.

Engracia stepped toward them, and the man wrapped his arm tighter around Honorata, lifting her tiny body a few inches off the ground. "Stop!" he barked. "Nobody is calling the police."

Engracia saw his great arm wrapped around Ms. Navarro's thin neck. It seemed that he could snap it as easily as she snapped a sheet onto a bed. She froze, unsure what to do, and then he gestured, using Ms. Navarro's body as a sort of pointer, and Engracia stumbled into the study next to the entrance, the only room downstairs with a door.

Behind her, the man half carried, half dragged Ms. Navarro into the study. Her face was curiously slack. She neither struggled nor screamed.

"I have a gun," he said. "I don't want to use it. I don't even want to get it out. But I will."

And he moved his jacket aside, so that Engracia could see it, resting there against his soft, heaving belly.

"I want to talk. I want to talk with Rita. And you'll have to stay here and listen."

Engracia nodded her head, her eyes glued to Ms. Navarro's face, which remained oddly calm, removed.

Then he turned back to Honorata. "I'm going to let you go. Don't scream. Don't run. We're going to talk."

Sweat poured down the man's neck and into his shirt collar. He was panting, looking around, trying to figure out what to do.

He released Ms. Navarro, and she stumbled to the nearest chair, sunk into it, looking like a child more than the intimidating woman she had seemed an hour earlier.

"My name's Jimbo," the man said to Engracia.

"Engracia."

"What? What's your name?"

"Engracia."

"Sit down there. Just be quiet. I don't want to hurt you. I'm not going to hurt anyone."

Engracia tried to take a breath, but her lungs were constricted; she could not seem to inhale. Which was strange, because she didn't care if she lived or died, and she had already had the thought that perhaps this strange man—this sweating fat man, too old to be breaking into someone's house, with his gun, and his belly, and the hair limp on his head—was the answer she had prayed for.

Still, the body resists destruction. She knew that.

Her heart pounded, and she tried again to breathe, but her

chest did not fill. The room looked to her as if someone had blown red smoke into it.

"I don't know what you're talking about," Ms. Navarro said. "You're going to go to jail."

The man stared at her but said nothing. Engracia expected him to erupt, she expected to see fury in his eyes, but instead, she saw pain. He looked as if he might cry.

"You won't get away with this. I know you've been looking for me. I've been here all along, all these years. And you never found me? You can't even find someone easy to find."

The man looked confused. Ms. Navarro kept speaking.

"Why are you here now? Why did you come now? All these years. I thought you had stopped looking."

"I never looked for you."

And again, Engracia saw that he was not angry, that the violence with which he had grabbed Ms. Navarro, ushered them into this room, was somehow not there. The terror of those few seconds was still present, though. Even her skin was alive with it.

"You never looked?"

"I never looked."

"Why are you here now?"

And at this, the man let out something between a wail and a cry. And he threw his hands to his head, and his whole body shuddered. When he lifted his arms to his face, Engracia saw the gun again, a black handle, the glint of metal. The gun gleamed there, waiting. He spoke.

"How could you?"

"I don't know what you're talking about."

"Malaya. *Malaya.*"

The name came out the second time like a wail. Engracia could see that the man was losing control.

Ms. Navarro did not react to her daughter's name. But she spoke anyway.

"What are you talking about? What Malaya?"

Engracia watched silently, trying to understand the game these two were playing, remembering what the man had said already, that Ms. Navarro had kept his daughter from him.

The man grabbed Ms. Navarro's arm. His fat white fingers dug into her skin, and she called out, but he did not release her. He held her arm, and looked at her, staring into her eyes, and Ms. Navarro shook all over and turned her eyes away first.

Malaya was his child.

Engracia could see it.

She could see it in their eyes, in the way they interacted, in what was not said. Slowly, she reached into the deep side pocket of her pants, where her cell phone was. She'd had the phone for only a few months; she could still remember the salesman explaining how to call 911, that all she had to do was open the phone and hold down the 9 button, that a chip in the phone would bring help to her.

The salesman had showed her this feature, and Engracia had cried, tears dripping down her face, at how wrong he was, at how little he knew of what phones could or could not do in an emergency.

But this was different.

This was Las Vegas, and her cell phone would work. If she could find a way to press the 9 and hold it, someone would come.

Her fingers fumbled, searching, searching.

"What are you doing?"

His voice was loud and panicky. Sweat ran in rivulets down his face.

Engracia said nothing. No English words would come. She opened her mouth, and nothing, no sound at all, came out.

"Call the police, Engracia."

"Shut up!" Jimbo turned back to Engracia. "Don't call anyone. That better not be a phone in your pocket. No one is calling anyone."

Engracia placed her hands on her lap, still unable to think of a single word in English. Taco came to mind. Taco Bell, Taco Time. Nothing else.

"I never looked for you. I respected your wishes. I thought you were in Manila, or back home. I never looked for you. I never even came back to Vegas. I never tried another woman. I never tried again."

Ms. Navarro would not look at him. She stared stonily at the floor, ignoring his fingers still buried in her arm, her body trembling, trembling. Finally, he released her arm and stepped away.

What was she thinking? Why was this man here?

"You knew I wanted a family. A wife. A child. How could you hide her from me?"

Now Ms. Navarro's voice cracked out of her.

"I didn't hide her. She's not yours."

At this, he reared back, looking as if he might slap her. But he stopped, turning his head and gritting his teeth so that his jaw jutted out from the fat fold near his neck.

Engracia put her hand back in the deep pocket of her pants.

"Don't lie. Please don't lie."

"Don't lie? Why shouldn't I lie? Who are you to tell me anything? You barge in my house. You show me a gun. You throw me in this room. If I got up now, you would shoot me. You would shoot me! This is respect? This is respecting me?"

Her voice rose hysterically. She stood up, enraged. And the man did not move; he did not make her sit back down. He stood against the wall, several feet from her, and now his shoulders slumped.

Engracia slid the phone from her pocket, and slipped it quietly behind her in the chair.

"Rita."

"My name is Honorata."

"Honorata. How could you hate me this much? How could you have done this to me?"

"I do hate you. I hate you! I have always hated you. What do you mean, how could I hate you? I hate you, I hate you, I hate you!"

Ms. Navarro was screaming, her hands scrunched into fists, her small body leaping closer at him, like a mongoose at a cobra.

Engracia silently opened the lid of her phone and slid her fingers slowly across the face of the phone. She had to be sure of the button.

The man looked at Ms. Navarro, and tears welled in his eyes.

Engracia stopped what she was doing, just for a second, engrossed by what she was witnessing.

"All I wanted was a family."

"Well, you can't buy one. You can't buy a person."

"I didn't buy you."

"You thought you could buy me. You thought your money, your man, your white, these bought me. You took me from everything."

He looked at her, still crying, and reached out his hand, as if to touch her arm.

"Don't touch me!" she screamed. "Don't touch me! Don't be in my house. Get away from me! Get away from here!"

"No!" he said. "No. She's my daughter. She's my daughter too. I will not leave."

"How do you know of her?"

"How do I know that Malaya is my daughter? That you hid her from me? That it's you who had no respect for me?"

"This isn't true."

"Of course it's true."

Ms. Navarro glared at him.

"It was Malaya who found *me*."

Engracia heard the shuddery sound of Ms. Navarro breathing. Otherwise silence.

"I got an email from a teenage girl who said she'd found me on the Internet, and she was pretty sure I was her father."

Ms. Navarro sat motionless, only the unnatural stillness of her face, her body, belying the shock she felt.

"She sent me a photo."

"Malaya sent you a picture of herself?"

"A photo of you."

Ms. Navarro's jaw tightened. Engracia could feel her rage. So could the man.

"You write to me. You ask me to marry you. You live in my home." He was angry now. His voice was like a knife, and Engracia's body lurched; the desire to run was so great.

"And then you win money. And I beg you to stay. But you go. And I let you. I never look for you. I leave you alone."

The man stopped and looked down. His back shook. It was three times wider than Ms. Navarro.

"And all . . . this . . . time." He drew the words out slowly. "All this time, you have our daughter."

"She's not yours."

"She's mine."

"Malaya's a young girl. She gets big stories in her head. She even has tattoos. She's not easy. She thinks you're her father, I don't know how she found out about you, but you're not her father. If she had asked me, I would have told her."

Engracia thought Ms. Navarro was probably lying, but the man was apoplectic.

"Stop lying!"

"I'm not lying. You haven't even seen her. You see a photo. She looks half white. You think you're her dad. You're not the only white man in the world, you know."

"Stop lying. Please, Rita, stop lying."

"I'm not lying."

Engracia was amazed at her defiance. She had started to calm down. She could think more clearly. The man was angry, but he was not paying any attention to her. Engracia waited to push the button on her phone, thinking she might be able to leave the room; that she might get a chance to tell the operator what was happening. If the police barged in right now, anything could happen. The gun was right there. Engracia had already noticed Ms. Navarro looking at it. Ms. Navarro wanted the gun.

"Do you think I flew out here, barged into your home . . . with a *gun* . . . because a seventeen-year-old girl thinks I'm her father?"

Honorata did not reply.

"We got tests. Malaya and I. We did the tests. She's my daughter, and you've always known this."

The air came out of the room. Engracia pushed the button.

In one motion, Ms. Navarro turned, screamed, and lunged at Jimbo's gun. He was a big man, but quick, and he dodged her easily. He clamped his hand on the gun but did not take it out of his waistband. Ms. Navarro slipped, banging her shin on the table and cracking her side into the chair, as she struggled not to fall. Engracia slid off the chair and made a run for the door.

"Stop!"

She kept going.

"I'll shoot."

"Run, Engracia, run!"

She couldn't see him, didn't know if he had the gun out. She had her phone; she could hear something on the other end of the line. English. She couldn't think of any word in English. *Taco*. Did he have the gun out? Was she going to die? "Gun. Man," she said, and closed the phone. She wanted to die, but she didn't want to be shot. She stopped and turned. He did not have the gun out.

"Why didn't you run? I told you to run!" Ms. Navarro's face was red with anger.

Engracia looked at the big man. He seemed stunned, just as she felt.

"Did you call someone?" he demanded. "Is that your phone?"

Engracia did not answer. Honorata shrieked, "You're going to die! You're going to jail! We're all going to die! What about Malaya then?"

The man turned pale, and Engracia wondered if he was well. Perhaps he would faint. He would collapse right there. He looked right at Engracia, right into her eyes, and with his big, fat, fleshy hand, he motioned for her to return to the study. She couldn't think. Her mind was flooded with what was happening, with how she might have been shot, with how she might have made it out the door—would he have shot Ms. Navarro?—with how she still might be shot, with how she wouldn't have to live. Her heart was pounding, she couldn't think. He motioned again with his head, and Engracia walked back into the study.

As she did, a memory so vivid came over her that for a moment she forgot there was a man, there was Ms. Navarro, there was a gun. She was in a field with her mother, standing between two neat rows of beans. She had let go of her mother's skirt, and walked along picking bugs off the leaves and smashing them between her chubby fingers exactly as she had been taught. She was much slower than Mama, in the row just next to her, so when her mother reached the end, she doubled back and walked toward the child, picking off bugs as she went. Each time they met, her mother made the sign of the cross on her forehead and said "*Que Dios te bendiga.*" Engracia heard her mother blessing her, as clearly as if she were in the room then. And so she knew she would die, because her mother had come to say this blessing again.

She looked around. The man still didn't have the gun out, but he told Honorata to sit down—that they were all going to sit down. Nobody seemed to know what to do, but Honorata sat, and the man did, and finally Engracia. The three of them looked at one another.

28

He said he had never looked for her. He thought she was in Manila or home in her village. Was that possible? That he'd never looked?

For years, Honorata had trembled anytime she was on the Strip. She had avoided the El Capitan and Caesars Palace. If the newspaper ran a story with a picture of either hotel, if there was mention of the woman who had helped her—June Dibb—she squinted her eyes and tried to make out everyone in the photo; every shadowy person in the background. Was Jimbo there? She didn't think there was any way the Dibbs could know she was in Las Vegas. The worst part of coming here, of leaving the sad apartment in Los Angeles, had been the risk that somehow Jimbo would find out.

So why had she done it? Why, in that first rush of courage that swept in with Malaya's birth, had she chosen the one place where Jimbo might also be? She was never going to play Megabucks again. She wasn't interested in gambling. But all alone in that hospital, sending a message to her mother about her daughter's birth, it had seemed to her that Las Vegas was the only place where something good had happened. Even before she had won the money, everyone in Vegas had been kind, everyone in the El Capitan had looked at her as if she were a person. She understood that they cared about her because Jimbo gambled a lot of money, but she felt it had been more than this. They had looked at her, and they had been able to guess who she was—what was happening to her—but they had not disdained her. They were kind.

That's why she decided to move to Las Vegas.

She had never seen any of those people again. She had never once seen anyone she met in those strange days at the El Capitan. Jimbo had not found her—she had changed Malaya's name, just in case—even though she had always believed he would.

He said he had never come back to Vegas.

He had never been here.

That was why she had never seen him.

And now he was sitting in her house—bigger and older and redder—with a gun jammed in his waistband and a fold of fat flopping over it, smearing sweat on the metal, and she was afraid and she was repulsed, and it didn't seem possible that he was Malaya's father. Though of course he was.

An image of Malaya—slim and taut and golden—wearing nothing but a T-shirt and boy shorts formed in her mind. Those boy shorts had astonished Honorata. They'd bought them together, and Honorata had been relieved when Malaya had not even asked to buy the tiny, lacy bits of underwear displayed on the main tables. Instead, she wanted cotton underwear that looked quite modest to her mother, so they had bought them in several colors. But the next Saturday, Malaya had wandered downstairs from her room wearing nothing but those underwear and that cropped shirt, and the boy shorts had been anything but modest.

Malaya was a freshman that year, and Honorata wondered how she had known what those shorts would do for her slim little figure. She saw too, for the first time, the body Malaya would have, how pretty she would be, how that little bit of Jimbo would fill out the curves of her slight bone structure. It was simultaneously pleasing and terrifying. She loved her daughter. She loved her beauty. She was not ready to think of Malaya in this way.

Also, seeing Malaya in those boy shorts had brought back her own adolescence. The wild desire she had felt for Kidlat even before she hit puberty, long before she had the words for what she was feeling. How old had they been? Maybe eleven. Two lean, narrow bodies, hardly different from each other, though one was a girl and one was a boy, and even then, being around Kidlat had set her skin to tingling, her heart to skipping.

They had gotten older, and their bodies had become different, and everyone knew that Kidlat and Honorata were in love, in adolescent love. Holding Kidlat's hand would make her feel slightly lightheaded, and they would spend the times when they were alone together—which were not that easy to get, because everyone in each of their villages watched them—they would spend that precious time talking and laughing and gasping whenever a hand touched a thigh, or bare toes twisted together. And when they could, they would kiss—such innocent kisses, really—but they would nearly knock Honorata to the ground.

And this is how it had been until Honorata was seventeen, older than Malaya when she came down in the boy shorts, and then Kidlat had gone to Manila with his father, and when he came back four months later, he was not interested in Honorata. He said hello to her coolly and made no effort to talk with her directly, much less be alone with her. It was crushing. She wanted to die. She couldn't understand it, and finally, one day when they met accidentally, she blurted out, "Kidlat, what happened? Why don't you want me anymore?" And Kidlat looked embarrassed, just for a moment, and then he said that he was not a boy; that in Manila he had been with a woman, really been with her, and he wasn't interested in Honorata anymore. He was trying to find a way to move to Manila.

It was unimaginable, what Kidlat had said.

He had been with a woman? Her Kidlat?

How could he have done this? It was horrible. It was a sin. It was disgusting to imagine. It could not be imagined. For weeks, she grieved, and she did not eat, and she avoided seeing Kidlat, and her nanay kept asking, "Honorata, what happened? Is it that boy? That Kidlat? Forget that boy."

She had not forgotten him.

When she saw him again, he was preparing for the Imbayah Festival, lying on his back and leg wrestling with a friend. There was a group of boys watching, and everyone was laughing. When Kidlat won three in a row, he jumped up, and the boys yelled, "*Imbayah! Imbayah!*" while he grinned and slapped his friend on the back, the other boy smiling even though he had lost. Kidlat spied her watching, and, giddy as he was with winning, he came over to her. Then he waved away the younger boys, and after a few moments, she and Kidlat walked down the road and toward the green fields alone.

Honorata shook away this memory.

How could she be thinking of Malaya's pubescent body, of her own first delirious forbidden ineffable experience of a man, there in the field with Kidlat, after months of not talking, not touching, months of imagining him with someone else, her heart so broken and then so full? Even now, it was a memory that could engulf her. And Malaya? Malaya in the boy shorts? That had been only the beginning. The boy shorts seemed innocent now, compared with the rainbow hair, the black clothes, the tattoos: all these ways that her daughter did not look exactly desirable—at least not to Honorata—but did look dangerous, the opposite of innocent.

Malaya's father knew none of this. He was not part of her life. She would not let him see Malaya.

No matter how much Jimbo frightened her, no matter what he did, she would protect her daughter. She would die here in this room, she would die, but she would not let him see Malaya. She would not let this man, this man who had haunted her thoughts, this man whose badness must be why Malaya had the peculiar hair, the serpent tattoo; she would not let this man see her daughter.

She felt sorry for the maid. Why did she have to be here today? Why was the world like this, that today, of all days, the maid should be here when Jimbo finally found her?

29

Coral had not gone in to school. She'd caught something when they were in Japan and wanted to shake it before Koji and the boys got home on Friday. The time change would be hard for them, and they hadn't done the homework they'd brought along. Gus was already worried about whether his coach would ever let him play again. There wasn't anything to be done about it. Koji's brother was very ill, and they couldn't wait for summer to see him.

Coral and Koji hadn't been prepared for how hard Isa would take this news. Coral thought the fact that their uncle lived so far away would buffer the boys a bit; that Koji's brother being ill would not upset them too much. But Isa, the namesake, was upset. He said he didn't want to be the only Isamu Seiko in the family, which was a funny way to put it, and Coral had been careful not to smile. It moved her that her youngest child would feel so deeply for Koji's brother. They were good kids, these labrapuggles of hers, avid for baseball and video games, at ease talking hip-hop with their cousin Trey or politely raising their hands to ask a question in Japanese at the *gakuen* on Saturdays. Would they remember her mama? Augusta had loved them so much. Coral wanted them to remember her; she could barely stand that Augusta had not seen

Gus puffing out his cheeks to blow on his trumpet or Isa playing with Althea's new puppy.

At five o'clock in the morning, Coral had turned off her alarm, called into the automatic message that notified the district to find a sub for her, and fallen into a thick, anxious sleep. By nine, her room was flooded with light and warm, even though they had replaced the air conditioner last month—one of many repairs—and while she knew she needed the sleep and would feel better for it, she did not feel better right then. She forced herself awake, and then wrenched free of the hot, wrinkled sheets. With her head clogged and heavy, she sucked in a deep gulp of air. A hot shower would help, but she didn't have the energy to take it. She'd make some coffee, lie on the couch, try to rest.

Coral turned off her phone, so that she wouldn't start reading her email, and tossed it in a basket on the shelf. It took half an hour to make coffee and a piece of toast, distracted as she was by everything lying uncared for in the kitchen. They had left for Japan quickly, and when she got back, she had spent every minute at the school, trying to get things ready for last night's music program.

Her body ached, and she moved slowly. On an ordinary morning, Coral would make oatmeal for breakfast, pack three lunches, and start something for dinner, all before seven. She and Koji alternated kitchen duty: on his weeks, he packed the boys' lunches carefully the night before and picked up fresh food from the market for dinner.

Even thinking about a normal routine made her tired. She walked over to lie down on the couch and then drifted in and out of sleep all morning, her raspy cough jerking her awake now and then. Coral finally got up to take a shower around one, and felt better after. She rubbed her body with a silky lotion, something that usually took too much time, and slipped on her favorite cotton pants, a soft old T-shirt, and flip-flops. She looked around the living room. There was Trey's guitar, and Coral thought of him, on the night before they left for Japan, showing Gus how to play a funk riff on an acoustic.

Gus and Isa loved having their cousin back in Las Vegas. It pleased Coral too. Her boys had so few links to her childhood, now that both Malcolm and Keisha had moved out of town, now that Alabaster and Serenity were not coming to visit Augusta. Of course, the Las Vegas her children lived in was almost nothing like the Las Vegas in which she had grown up. She and her siblings had lived in the middle of a desert—chasing lizards and making playhouses out of old sofas that washed in with the floods—but Gus and Isa lived in a metropolis. They did not walk onto barren earth and see a million mysterious stars above, they did not turn away from a glowing Strip to see a night as black as pitch. The sky her sons knew was never black: the glow of today's Strip could not be made to disappear with the mere turn of a shoulder.

Trey had lived with Coral and Koji nine years ago, when he was fifteen. It had been a difficult year. Her boys were one and two then, and she and Koji were juggling full-time jobs and diapers and two kids setting records for serial viruses—all without sleep, of course. Then there was Trey: a teenager with a big loop of silver chains, heavy jeans draped around his knees, furious at having been shipped off to his aunt's.

Ray Junior had called late one night, his voice thin and strained, and asked Coral if she would take Trey, right away, before it was too late. A boy had been murdered, shot dead by another student as he walked out of Trey's high school. Coral never learned whether Trey had any particular connection to the boy who was killed. It didn't matter. She and her brother both knew how fast it could all move, how families put it together afterward: who their son knew and what he was doing and how he had ended up at the wrong place at the wrong time. Then you had all the time in the world to figure it out, to see how useless it had been, how trivial—the small details that had cost your son his life.

Ray Junior had seen the signs. He called Coral, and then packed his son into the car and drove ten hours straight to Vegas. Coral would never forget the morning they arrived, and how, just for a moment, she'd panicked, wondering if she could do it. Koji had seen this on her face; he'd given her a wink, and then reached up to give his nephew—already a head taller than he was—a lop-sided hug.

Now they could laugh about that year, and look what it meant to her boys to have Trey. He took them to UNLV games at the Thomas & Mack, and showed up at their school events, tall and good-looking and hip. On Saturdays, he drove them to Japanese school and did the end-of-day jobs usually assigned to Coral: washing off the chalkboards and sweeping the floors and taking down the Las Vegas Gakuen poster that temporarily concealed the Clark High School sign in the gymnasium. When Isa introduced Trey to his Japanese teacher, he said he was his brother.

Coral smiled, thinking of this, and then looked around for her phone. What time was it? She'd spent the whole day on the couch. She walked to the study, looking for her phone, and was surprised to see a wash of red light reflected in the hall mirror. What was that? She looked out the window, to the street. A police car in the cul-de-sac. That was unusual. Coral turned away, not interested enough to look further. As she did, she saw the black and white of a second car, then, was that a van? A SWAT van? On Cabrillo

Court? She peered out the living room window and was startled to count three black-and-whites, and what was indisputably an unmarked SWAT van. What was going on?

Coral opened the front door, moving slowly, waiting to hear if someone called for her to stop. She stood in the shadow of the entry, where it would not be easy to see her, but where she had a wider view of the street. Two of the cars had officers in them, and two more officers were standing at the mouth of the cul-de-sac, looking at a laptop. She couldn't see anyone in the van and stayed very still, looking.

Across the way, Mr. Eberle opened his door and stepped outside. The police officer in the car in front rolled down his window and motioned for him to return to his house. Her neighbor looked confused, and then stepped back in and shut his door. Coral didn't see him go to the front window, though she imagined he was there, crouched down or standing in a shadow, watching just as she was.

The street was oddly still. No motor started, no dog barked, no child rode a bike. There was an air of waiting, and Coral waited too. She couldn't tell which house might be the problem. A few minutes went by, and then a maroon car pulled slowly up next to the officers on the street. One of them nodded toward the driver of the car and looked back at his laptop. The car sat, silent, but nobody got out. After awhile, one of the cops approached it. Coral saw the window roll down, and the officer lean in slightly, then gesture up the street toward Honorata Navarro's house before walking back to her companion with the laptop.

The maroon car did not move.

What could be happening at Honorata's house? Was it something to do with Malaya? Honorata and her daughter were going through a difficult year, and although the boys still asked if Malaya could babysit, she was rarely available anymore—and sometimes Coral was relieved. She loved Malaya, but she was not an easy teenager, at least not now. Coral felt sorry for Honorata; she tried so hard. She owned four houses on the street: her own and three she rented out. And she was a good landlord; her renters almost never left, the yards were neat, the cars were kept in the garages. It was probably because of Honorata that Cabrillo Court looked mostly untouched by the housing crash. A block in either direction, and every street had houses standing empty, with yards turned to flash dry tinder, and bits of trash lodged in the brown branches of dead euonymus shrubs and spikey pyracantha.

Coral shifted position in the entry and peered up the cul-de-sac to her neighbor's house. It looked as silent and still as the rest of the street. A curved concrete bench stood in Honorata's front yard—an oddly welcoming detail for a woman who didn't make friends easily—and the only movement on the street was a mockingbird resting on the back of the bench, his tail upright, and his body weaving a bit as he looked to and fro.

Coral looked back at the police officers.

There was a third person now, perhaps the driver of the maroon car, and Coral studied him, thinking it might be her friend Tom. Tom Darling wouldn't be here unless something big was happening. He might come out if there was a negotiation. Was that what this was? The man turned, and it was Tom. Coral had met him in a Leadership Las Vegas class nearly a decade ago. They were paired for the shift in a patrol car, and Tom had needled the officer driving them. "Hey look at that lowrider. Think his plates are right?" And the officer had thought Tom was serious, but Coral knew that Tom was being ironic, messing with the patrol officer to see how he thought. Or maybe he was trying to make a connection with her, a black woman riding in a white cop's car. She hadn't really known, even then, why Tom had needled their driver or what he really thought. Who was he making fun of? Maybe himself.

Still, Coral liked Tom. What was he doing here?

Coral almost went back inside. She wanted to get her phone. Maybe there was something on the news. But she was looking at Tom, thinking about whether she might go tell him she was there, when she saw the flash of the school bus pulling away in the distance. She looked at her watch. Three thirty. Malaya would be coming home.

30

Ms. Navarro had stopped talking.

The man had told her about the paternity test, and at first, she kept protesting. She yelled out, "You don't know Malaya! She gets these cockeyed ideas. She's very wild. She's tricked you, gotten some blood. You don't know how wild she is."

And the man stood there. Listening. Not saying anything. Not moving.

It was obvious that Ms. Navarro was wrong. This man, this huge man with a gun and a ring larger than her wristwatch, was Malaya's father. And Ms. Navarro did not want him to know. Had somehow hidden the child from him.

Now here Engracia was, with memories of her own child filling every cell in her body, in this ridiculous moment, with a man who might kill her, who might kill Ms. Navarro, who might kill himself. Who really, after all, had some reason for what he was doing. Because who would not hate the person who had stolen your child from you?

She thought of Juan, and of how Diego had missed him, and, for some reason, of a time when Juan was galloping around the little apartment with Diego on his shoulders, and somehow galloped too high and banged Diego's head on a low section of the ceiling. Diego started to cry, and Engracia was annoyed. Then she saw Juan's face, crumpled and aghast. Diego saw it too, and the boy stopped crying to lean over and kiss Juan's cheek, saying, "Papa, it's okay. It didn't hurt. Papa, it's okay."

"Rita," the man was saying, "My lawyer phoned you as soon as Malaya and I did the tests. He sent you a letter. It was certified mail. I know you got it."

"I threw it away."

"You threw away a certified letter? Without opening it?"

"It was from Chicago."

"Did you listen to his messages?"

"No," she shook her head. "But you *did* look for me. You said you didn't."

"Malaya gave me your address. I didn't look for you."

Honorata stared at him defiantly, but all he said was, "You hated me this much?"

"Yes."

His voice was very soft. "I didn't hate you. I missed you."

Ms. Navarro looked at him, and Engracia could see the tremor in her back and her shoulders.

"I never meant for you to feel like that about what happened," he went on. "I thought you wanted to come. I thought you chose me."

The pain that crossed Ms. Navarro's face was unguarded and intense. Engracia understood that she could not speak.

"I'm not what you think I am. But I know why you feel that way. I've had years to think about it. To think about what I did. To think about how you felt."

Engracia looked from one face to the other. What had happened between these two? She thought of Malaya—that odd girl with the striped hair and the tattoo. This man might be surprised by Malaya.

"It didn't matter what you wanted. It was what you did."

"I know. I know that, Rita."

"Honorata."

"*Honorata*. I know what I did. I've spent seventeen years thinking about it. About your uncle. About how angry I was. About how I didn't care what that meant for you."

"She's not your daughter."

"She is."

"No. No!"

Engracia watched Ms. Navarro fold over then, her face in her hands, and she saw the tears leak out from her fingers, and she saw the way the man watched those tears, watched Ms. Navarro. And the room was very quiet.

The telephone rang.

Engracia jumped.

"Don't answer it."

They had all been sitting, frozen in place, for a while. Ten minutes? Half an hour? It was impossible to tell. Engracia's mind wandered. She felt her mother near, though she knew her mother was in the village—she would be making tortillas, and talking with one of the other women while she waited for her sons to come home—and yet Engracia could feel her presence, as she had longed to feel her presence when Diego was hurt, as she had tried to feel it night after night in the months since. But her mother was here, somehow, now.

The phone stopped ringing. And then started again.

They all ignored it.

Engracia shifted her position, and the man said, "You have to stay here. We stay here until we figure this out."

Engracia settled back into her seat. Ms. Navarro did not move, the man did not move. It was not clear what would break the stillness.

"Honorata, I'm not here to hurt you. I tried every way I could to reach you."

"That's why you bring *a gun*? To my *home*?"

The screech in her voice startled all of them. A vein in Engracia's temple throbbed. She looked at the man.

"I shouldn't have brought the gun."

"Get rid of it! Get it out of here! I'm not talking to a man with a gun."

"Will you talk with me if I put it in my car?"

Ms. Navarro stopped speaking again.

The phone rang.

"Honorata, I don't want this gun. I shouldn't have brought it. I wasn't going to bring it in. But I—I don't know, I couldn't reach you. I've been sitting in that car, outside your door, all morning. I got—I got crazy. Sitting there. Thinking."

Ms. Navarro would not look at him. She had moved inside herself; Engracia could not guess what she was thinking or feeling anymore. Had anyone heard her say "Gun. Man"? Was there anyone who had an idea something was happening here?

Engracia was not afraid—or not completely afraid. Her body still shook; she feared the rip of the bullet. She feared how death would happen. She waited for Honorata to grab the gun. She waited for the struggle, the sound. How much would it hurt? Dios had put her here. He had put her here for a reason. So she would pay attention. She would be ready. She would be grateful for these last moments, how it felt to see and smell and hear, how her skin tingled, how she could sense her mother—but not Diego. Her son was too young, she had decided, too young to let her feel him.

Just a few months ago, Diego had asked her about a gun.

"Mama, have you ever held a gun?"

"No, Diego. Why are you asking me this?"

"Mateo says his brother has a gun, and he got to hold it."

"Diego, you must not go near that gun. Mateo shouldn't be touching a gun."

"I didn't touch it. I didn't even see it."

"Guns are very dangerous. Where does Mateo live? Who's this brother?"

"Forget it, Mama."

"I will not forget it. I'm very serious. You mustn't go near that gun. If Mateo has it, you go away. You leave. *Entiendes*?"

"*Sí*, Mama."

That conversation had kept her awake for weeks. Diego walked home from school with Mateo. She didn't know the boy's mother. How could she have moved her son into this neighborhood? To Vegas? Juan would have known they should not live on this street.

Juan.

She had called him from the hospital, because he was still in Mexico.

"It's Diego," she sobbed. "He's hurt."

"Where are you? I'm coming. I'm coming now."

She didn't know how Juan had done it, how he had crossed the border, how he had gotten to Vegas so fast. But the next morning he was there, in the lobby of the Children's Hospital, and when she went down to get him, to explain to the receptionist that he was Diego's father, that he could come with her to the special room for family, he had started to cry, and his tears came so fast they soaked the collar of his shirt, and he could not speak, and she could not speak, and they had stood in the middle of the room, with people everywhere, some silently engrossed in their phones and others rushing by, wearing pale blue scrubs. She and Juan had stood there, collapsed in each other's arms, and sobbed.

The phone rang again.

It rang and rang, and finally, Jimbo answered.

"Hello?"

His face was alert. Then surprised. He looked out the window and moved closer to the wall, peering up the street.

Engracia looked too. She saw the red glow against the stucco wall of the neighbor's house. There was a police car out there. Someone had heard her say *gun* and *man* after all.

Her heart quickened its already skittery beat.

She looked at Jimbo's face. Was he angry?

He looked startled more than anything. Startled, and strangely vulnerable.

"I . . . I don't know what to say. It's not what you think. That's not what's happening."

The man was listening to someone on the line. Ms. Navarro stirred, and he looked over at her abruptly.

"Help!" she called. "Help!"

The man cracked the phone into the receiver and whipped around toward Ms. Navarro.

"Stop it!"

Ms. Navarro stood up, enraged now. She scared Engracia. She might do anything. Anything could happen now. Anyone might live or die in the next seconds and Engracia, who knew what would happen to her, was having trouble concentrating. She thought of Juan, sobbing at the hospital, and she remembered the doctor asking them about the organs, and then, the night after the burial, when Juan drank glass after glass of whiskey.

Diego had gotten hurt in Engracia's care.

Juan had drank all that whiskey.

"Ms. Navarro."

Her voice came out small, and at first, Ms. Navarro did not look at her.

"Please sit with me?"

Ms. Navarro looked confused, and even Jimbo seemed unclear about what Engracia had asked. He started to say something, but stopped. Engracia motioned to the seat beside her, and Ms. Navarro stood a moment there, looking from Jimbo to Engracia, looking at the spot where the gun was hidden beneath his shirt, looking at the phone behind him. Then, awkwardly, as if she had not quite committed herself to the act, she stumbled toward Engracia and sat where the younger woman had indicated.

Engracia took her hand. Her bones were small, smaller than Engracia's, smaller even than Diego's, and Engracia could feel the beat, beat, beat of Honorata's heart through her skin.

Taking Ms. Navarro's hand helped Engracia.

At almost the same moment, she and Honorata looked up at Jimbo.

He looked back at them, and for a moment, Engracia saw it in his eyes: he was wondering what the hell he was doing. How had he gotten here, in this room, with a gun, and two women cowering beneath him?

"I'm sorry, Honorata."

She did not reply.

Engracia could still see the red glow of the police cruiser against the stucco of the house next door, and she noticed that the man stayed near the wall, out of reach of the window.

"Where's Malaya?" Jimbo asked. "I'd like to see her."

He did not say it, but Engracia thought that even Ms. Navarro must be thinking it: he wanted to see her before he died.

Silence.

Ms. Navarro was silent, and Engracia was silent, and the man did not ask again. Instead, he leaned against the wall and lowered himself slowly to the floor.

"Why didn't you read my letter, Honorata? Why didn't you give me a chance?"

He sounded sad, and resigned. Engracia wondered if he would kill himself there in front of her, and, for a moment, she closed her eyes, not wanting to see.

Ms. Navarro made a startled noise. Engracia opened her eyes, and Jimbo looked up.

"Is it Malaya?" he asked. "Is she here?"

Ms. Navarro glanced out the window, to the street. Engracia wondered if she could see the police car; if she knew what the red glow meant.

"Is she outside?"

The man stood up, peering toward the window. "I just want to see her once. Please."

Ms. Navarro said nothing. She pulled her hand away from Engracia's, sat up straighter on the couch, perched, alert and waiting and without speaking.

"I could have seen her, you know. She wanted to meet. I came here today to tell you I knew; to tell you we would be meeting. I didn't want to go behind your back."

Honorata stared at him then, her face a mask.

"I don't know why I have this gun. I don't know why I came in this way. I got so worked up. Waiting. I was so mad."

His voice trailed off, the enormity of the error he had made—of the consequences it would bring—becoming clearer.

"Did you call the police?"

"Yes," said Engracia.

"You were right. Of course. You should've called the police."

The man sounded sad more than anything else, and his fingers reached inside his jacket. He touched the handle of the gun, re-assuring himself it was there, or wondering if it was, or deciding, perhaps, what he should do now.

The phone rang again.

31

Coral grabbed her phone and her keys, and raced out the door. She heard someone yell, "Hey, lady. Stop!" But she did not stop. She ran straight for Tom Darling, her eye on the school bus, and the girl who was just now getting off it.

"Tom, it's me, Coral."

"Coral?"

"This is my street. I live here."

"Well, this isn't a good time. If you just go back inside, everything will be fine."

"No, Tom. The girl over there. She lives in that house. She's coming home from school."

"Shit."

Tom radioed to a patrolman at the end of the street.

"That girl. Hang on to her. She can't come up this street."

Coral saw the police officer look around, spot Malaya, and head toward her. She saw the girl see the officers, then the patrol cars, then look behind her toward the spot where the school bus had just idled. She would be afraid.

"I know her, Tom. Can I go to her?"

Tom looked around. Saw the girl's startled stance, saw Coral's concerned face.

"Yes. But don't say anything."

"I don't know anything."

"Get her off the street. Your house is too close. Ask the officer where to take her."

Coral turned and walked toward Malaya, who was talking to one of the policemen and had her backpack half off her shoulder, as if she were about to drop it and flee.

"Rick," Tom said into his radio, "my friend Coral is coming at you. She lives on this street. Knows the girl. Take them somewhere together. Keep her close by. And get the girl's cell phone. Make sure you have her phone."

Coral could hear Tom's voice on the officer's radio as she approached, and when Malaya looked at her, Coral tried for a reassuring smile. The girl simply stared, her eyes darting to her house, to Coral, to the officer. The backpack slid farther down her arm. Coral knew she wanted to run, was calculating which way to go, if she could get away. They wouldn't shoot a girl—they wouldn't—but Coral wished Malaya looked less wild. She had pulled her hair all to one side to reveal the shaved scalp above her ear and the tongue of the tattooed snake that twisted toward her neck.

Malaya had been such a beautiful little girl. Honorata used to dress her in elaborate dresses on Sundays, with a bow tied in her silky brown hair, and during the week, Malaya would walk to the school bus in a plaid skirt and a crisp white blouse. Even then, she was a funny child, knocking on Coral's door and selling Girl Scout cookies while carrying a small stuffed deer whose name was Horns. "Horns likes the shortbread cookies the best. That's the one Horns eats." Trey had adored her. Called her Malaysia, which had made Malaya angry the first time he said it. "Don't call me that . . . *Fatboy*," she had said at eight years old, her feet wide apart.

Fatboy! Trey had laughed and laughed. "Okay, Malaya, I won't call you that. But I meant it as a compliment. Malaysia is a very beautiful country." As if Trey knew anything about Malaysia. Or even where to find it on a map. He was always quick, though.

"Well, it's not my name," Malaya had said, much more amenably.

"Oh, I know that. I won't get it wrong again." But the next time Trey had seen her, he called out, "Hey, Malaysia! How are you today?" And he had given her his big Trey grin—he towered over her, fifteen and already six foot three—and Coral had been sure Malaya would be angry, or worse, cry. But instead, she laughed and said, "Hi, Fatboy!"

And that was that: the little girl and the almost man were friends that year. Trey introduced her to his high school friends as if she were a peer, and Malaya brought him drawings she had made at school, or things she found in the patch of undeveloped desert behind their cul-de-sac. Even now, on the rare occasion that Trey came by and Malaya happened to be out, they greeted each other fondly. He still called her Malaysia, and she called him Trey; she allowed him to gently tease her about the black clothes, the laced-up boots, the zany hair, and the gold chain hanging from her belt loop.

"Malaysia, you're scaring little kids. Why do you wear that stuff?"

"You scared of me, Trey?"

"Of course I'm scared of you. You're covered in black and chains, and you got that freaky tattoo. How'd you get your mother to say yes to that? You're too young."

"Well, I got friends. They think I look twenty-one, not just eighteen."

"Yeah, well, take it from me, baby girl. Those might not be the friends you need."

"Come on. You gonna get all over me too? I got a mom for that."

"Nah, I'm not saying nothing. You always beautiful to me, Malaysia."

In the house, Trey would ask Coral what was going on, why Malaya looked so wild, but Coral didn't have an answer. Malaya almost never came by this year, and Coral worried about her. She walked with her head down and a hunch in her shoulders that had not been there before.

"You think she's gonna be okay?"

"Oh, I hope so Trey. High school can be tough, right?"

"Yeah. Her mom should get her away from those friends."

Coral smiled at this.

"I love that kid," he added. "She makes me laugh."

"I know you do."

Coral nodded to the police officer and set her hand on Malaya's arm.

"Come with me. I'm not sure what's going on here, but these guys are good. We just have to lay low a bit and let them take care of this."

"Why are they here? Where's my mom?" The girl was panicking. Who wouldn't be?

"I don't know. But I know that man. He's a good guy. It's going to be okay."

"Is this about my dad?"

"Your dad?"

"My dad. I have a dad. He said he was going to visit me. Is this about him? I want to see him."

"I don't know. I didn't have time to ask about anything. I don't know if it's about your dad."

Of course it was about her dad. If anything would bring a SWAT team onto a neighborhood street, it was a domestic issue. They wouldn't take a problem with a dad lightly.

Malaya had never said anything about a dad.

All those years ago, when Honorata had asked for help changing Malaya's name, and Darryl had thought she was a sex worker, Coral had just assumed Malaya's father could have been anyone. But obviously that wasn't true. Malaya knew who her dad was.

Where had Honorata gotten the money for those houses? Who was Malaya's father?

One of the patrolmen led Coral and Malaya to the far end of the cul-de-sac, where another officer was setting up a shade canopy, like the ones Althea used to put up for Keisha's soccer games. They were getting ready for a long stretch; no one would be hurrying this.

"Honey, you hungry? I can ask someone to get us food."

"No."

The girl didn't say anything else, and Coral stood there, wondering how bad this might get.

The officer pulled out two lawn chairs and motioned for Coral and Malaya to sit down. Malaya was nervous, popping up and down on the balls of her feet, and Coral placed her arm around the girl to encourage her to be still. She didn't want the officer to think Malaya was on something—her appearance was incriminating enough. And it wouldn't help Malaya to get worked up before she even knew what was happening. They sat down in the chairs; the girl let Coral take her hand, but turned and stared off toward where the bus had been.

An image of Malaya a year or so earlier, standing in Coral's kitchen with a plate of *biko* that her grandmother had made, came to mind. Coral was talking with Malaya when Isa came running in the door, shouting, "Mom! Something bad happened!"

Coral's heart beat faster. Her youngest son held something in his hand, his eyes teary.

"What is it?"

"A toad. Do you think it's Ichiro?"

Gus had found a toad in the parking lot at school and brought him home in his shirt. He'd lived in the backyard for months, and Koji could do a pretty good imitation of his low *bwrrracking* call, but nobody had seen or heard him for a while. Now Isa held out the slightly rotting body of a toad that had been run over by a car.

"Isa, put that down. It's not clean."

Isa set it on the kitchen table and ran to put his arms around Coral. Gus walked in, dropping his backpack next to the toad.

"Mom, I told him to leave it in his glove."

"It's okay, Gus."

"Do you think it's Ichiro?"

"No. I don't."

"How do you know?" Isa choked out.

"Well, Ichiro's bigger."

"Are you sure?"

"Yes."

"And he'd be even bigger if he were smashed like that, right, Mom?"

"*Gus.*"

"Can we bury him?"

Malaya said she would help, and Gus found a Mickey Mouse T-shirt that was too small for either boy. Her sons wrapped the toad carefully in it before digging a hole near the plum tree and burying him.

"Can we sing a song?"

"How about 'Froggy Went A-Courtin'?'"

Coral gave Gus the warning eye, but Isa said, "That's a good song." And so the four of them sang it. When they finished, Isa said, "Bye, Ichiro's friend. We liked you." And Malaya took the little boy's hand and told him that he had done a really nice thing for the toad. Gus said he had helped too—he had done most of the digging—and then they all went inside to try the sweet rice cakes that Malaya had brought over.

Was that the day they had the conversation about physics? Malaya had surprised Coral, talking to the boys about her high school class.

Gus had started it.

"My teacher said that because of quantum physics, being happy isn't just good for the person who's happy, it's good for everyone else. For the whole universe."

"Because of quantum physics?" Coral was pleased to think this had caught Gus's attention.

"Yeah. Everything affects everything else."

"So being sad makes everyone else sad?" Isa asked.

"I don't know. Maybe."

"We talked about that in my physics class." Malaya flipped her long hair to one side. "It has to do with the forces that connect elementary particles, like electrons."

Gus looked at Malaya, pleased that the older girl knew what he was talking about.

"Yeah, it's physics. That's what my teacher said too."

"I don't know what physics are," said Isa.

"It's a science. It's the study of atoms and things."

"Oh."

"Somebody in my class asked if one sad person made everyone else sadder"—Gus jumped up and sat on the kitchen counter as he spoke—"and we had a whole conversation about how something good might make the whole universe better, and something bad, like war or murder, would make the whole universe worse."

"I feel sorry for the sad people," said Isa.

"That's just what I thought," said Malaya. "Like it's not bad enough that they're already sad, but somehow they make everything worse too?"

Gus frowned. "I don't think that's what my teacher said. She just said the thing about happiness."

Now Malaya wound her hair on top of her head, and stuck in a pencil to hold it in place. "Well, I thought about it a lot—and I decided that it's really about love. And hate. I think that loving something makes the universe better, and hating something makes it worse. So if someone is sad because they love someone, then they are still making the universe better, because it's really about love."

Coral remembered the way Gus had scrunched up his face and shifted in his seat when the older girl said the word *love*. And she remembered the way her own eyes had filled, and how she'd wanted to say something—something that told Malaya what a lovely thought it was, something that made Gus more comfortable—but she was afraid to try to speak right away, so it was Isa who had replied:

"Then our toad helped everyone, because he made me feel sad, and I love him."

Malaya laughed and lifted Isa high in the air.

"That's right, Isa monster!"

And Isa had laughed and said, "Put me down," and they had all taken another piece of *biko*.

Now Malaya stood up from the rickety folding chair, nearly banging into the police officer behind her.

"I don't want to sit here."

"We have to stay here. They might not tell us anything for a while. But it seems really calm. That's a good sign."

Malaya looked at her, and Coral waited to see if she would say something, but the girl just sat back down.

They stayed there, quiet, until Tom came over.

"Hi. Malaya Begtang? Is that right?"

Malaya looked at Tom and nodded yes.

"Listen, I know this must be scary for you. Things are going fine, though. We just want to go real slow, make sure there's nothing happening. We don't have any indication that anything is, and I'm sorry to scare you like this."

Malaya's lip quivered. Instantly, Coral saw her as she had been at four, at seven. She looked tough, but of course she wasn't.

"This doesn't look routine, but it is routine in some situations. And we're always happy when we've overreacted. Okay?"

The girl nodded, but did not say anything.

"Just sit tight with Coral here. You couldn't be in better hands right now."

Malaya looked at Coral doubtfully, but Coral smiled, and the girl tried to smile in return. She was trembling now, and getting close to tears, so Coral waved Tom away and looked right into Malaya's eyes.

"It's going to be okay. I'm right here with you."

"Do you think my dad's there?"

"I don't know, honey. Why do you think he might be?"

"Because I found him. And because he said he would visit me. And I told him where I lived."

There was a pretty good chance that this was about her dad.

"I really don't know anything at all. I just saw the police cars, and I came out because I know Tom. And then I saw you."

"He didn't seem like a bad man. My dad, I mean."

"Well, we don't know anything. Let's just stay right here, with what we do know."

"I just wanted to meet my father."

"I understand that."

Coral's voice caught, and she batted back tears that rose in her eyes. Incredible. That she could still feel this pain, after all these years.

"I know how you feel."

Malaya looked directly at her; she'd caught the change in Coral's voice. She waited.

"I don't know who my mother is. I mean, I had a mother, she raised me, but she isn't my biological mother. And nobody knows who that was. You're only about the fifth person in the world to know this about me."

Malaya did not seem exactly surprised.

"Does it bother you? I mean, do you want to know her?"

"Yes. I've spent my whole life wanting to know who she was. But there isn't any way to find her. I've tried. Or I did try, for a long time."

"I'm sorry."

I'm sorry. It made Coral want to cry.

"Thank you."

Coral didn't speak for a while then, and Malaya held her hand, squeezing her fingers ever so gently, and Coral struggled with the lump rising in her throat. She was supposed to be the one helping Malaya.

"I found him on the Internet," the girl said.

"Yeah," Coral managed to reply. "That makes sense . . . How did you know where to look?"

"I didn't. I just looked up my mom, and there was a thing about how she changed my name when I was little. I used to be Malaya Navarro, but now my name is Begtang."

"I knew that."

"You did? Well, I thought my dad must be named Begtang all the time, but the notice was for my father, to tell him my mom was changing my name. So that made me think she was trying to hide me."

"Hmmm. Okay. Then what?"

"Well, it was kind of an accident. I was looking in these old newspapers, and I couldn't find anything about my mom, so I was just looking for anything about someone from the Philippines. Which was sort of stupid. But there was an article about a woman who had won all this money. She won it at a casino, and she had only been in this country for like ten months. So it was a big story. And I just read it, because it was kind of interesting, even though it was too old. It was before I was born."

Coral was really interested now. This Malaya was surprising in so many ways.

"You found this on the Internet?"

"Well, it wasn't easy. Because the search engine in the paper isn't very good. So I went to the library on Flamingo, and the librarian helped me."

Coral thought of her own trips to that library, straining her eyes to see the faded microfiche records of Del Dibb's life.

"That was smart."

"Anyway, this article about the Filipina who won the money, I just read it for fun, because I wasn't finding anything. But there was a picture of her."

Coral knew what she was going to say.

"It was my mom."

Unbelievable. Incredible story.

"Her name was Rita Wohlmann. And she was married to this guy James. From Chicago. It was really easy after that. I just Googled him. He runs a big company, and I sent him an email."

"Wow. Wow! That's really an amazing story."

"Yeah. Like, did you know my mom won more than a million dollars?"

"No." She felt almost giddy listening to the girl. Malaya had done it. She'd found her dad. It made Coral want to jump up and cheer, even in the middle of this—what?—incident.

"And she was married. I mean, like, I've spent my whole life trying to explain to people why I don't have a dad. And there was this real asshole kid in fifth grade; he said I was a bastard. Which is stupid. Because half the kids I know are bastards. Just not the ones at my school."

Coral reached over and hugged Malaya awkwardly in her chair. She was so proud of her, and she was sorry about the fifth grader who had called her a name.

It was unbelievable that Malaya had actually found some record of her mom in the paper. With a different name. That's what it took. Some luck. At one point when Coral had been hunting for her mother, when she'd been doing research yet again, she had gone into some chat rooms and talked with other people looking for their parents. Usually straight-up adoptees, whose records were sealed. And the ones that found them—the mothers who found their babies or the children who found their parents—they almost always got lucky. There was one stray detail that turned out to be true, wasn't part of the standard story, and that detail led to everything else. My mother had eight siblings and was over six feet tall. My mother was an identical twin, and her brothers were identical twins too. Stuff like that.

And with genetic testing, all you had to know was that it was possible you had the right person. From there, if everybody agreed, you could actually be sure. She wondered if James Wohlmann really was Malaya's father. The girl was young. Honorata could have been married, but that didn't mean he was Malaya's father.

"What did your father say when you emailed him?"

"He asked me for a photo. Of my mom."

"And you sent it?"

"Yeah. And then he asked me if I was willing to do a test. To prove it. He sent me a kit, and then I sent it back to the company, with my blood and stuff."

"So, you're sure."

"Yeah. He's definitely my dad."

"Did he know about you?"

"No. He didn't even know my mom had a baby."

"You were a big surprise."

"Yeah. I guess so."

"Does he have a family? Kids?"

"No."

"You're the only one?"

"Yes."

Coral saw Tom walking toward them again, and he signaled her to meet him.

"Malaya, I see my friend Tom. I'm going to ask him if he knows anything. Okay?"

"Sure."

"I see a cooler over there. I think you can probably have a Coke if you want it."

"Okay."

Coral walked to the back of the canopy and then over to the next yard, where Malaya could not see her talking with Tom.

"Tom, what's going on?"

"We're not sure. We think there's a situation, and we've got a visual, but we haven't seen a gun. Nobody seems to be being held."

"Have you knocked on the door?"

"Not yet. That's the next step. We called, and a man answered once, but he hung up pretty quickly. We're just taking our time. No need kicking it up a notch too early."

"It's her father."

"Yeah? What's the story?"

"Malaya found her father online. He didn't know she existed. He had her confirm it with tests, and then he told her he was coming to see her."

"Okay. That's helpful. Know anything about the relationship? With the mom?"

"Not much. They were married. She's from the Philippines. He's from Chicago. They came out here, and she hit a jackpot. Malaya says she won a million dollars. So I'm guessing that was the end of the marriage. And he never knew she was pregnant."

Tom whistled.

"Yeah. That's a bombshell."

"Only in Vegas, right?"

Coral glanced over at Malaya, who was talking to a police officer who looked barely older than she was. "Any idea how long?"

"Not really. I mean, I'd like to talk to him on the phone first. Get a sense of the guy before I knock on the door. But if he won't answer, that's the next step."

"You haven't heard anything in there? Is something happening?"

"So 911 got a call. Couldn't make out much, except some woman who said 'gun' and 'man.' We sent a patrol over, and he got a visual just from the neighbor's yard. Two women. One man. No visible gun. No ropes. Looks like a tense conversation. It's not a lot to go on. But your information helps."

"The other woman is her grandmother. She lives with them."

"I don't think so. She's young. Looks Hispanic. Maybe the housekeeper?"

"Oh." Coral was surprised that Honorata had a housekeeper. "Well, I've seen someone get off the bus before. But the grandmother lives there too. You haven't seen her?"

"No. Damn. I have to ask the girl about her. Where the grandmother's room is. I don't want to scare her, though."

"Malaya?"

"Yes?" The young officer walked away, avoiding Tom's gaze.

Coral knew Malaya would be frightened by Tom's question, so she put her hand on the girl's thin back. Coral could feel her trembling even as she looked up at Tom defiantly.

"You have a grandmother? She lives with you?"

"Lola? Is Lola okay?" Malaya looked to Coral with fear.

"I'm sure she is. I was just confirming that she lives in your house."

"Yes. But she's not here right now. She's staying at her friend's house."

Coral and Tom looked at each other. She could see his relief.

"Do you expect her to come home today?"

"No."

"Okay, thank you. That's all I need right now."

"Is this about my dad?"

"Coral told me about your dad. That helps us. But I don't know. Listen, nothing's happened. We're being very cautious. It's really helpful if you just stay here."

Malaya looked at Tom, and Coral hoped she would not get angry. She had heard Malaya and Honorata shouting more than once. Tom reached out and took the girl's hand. "Thank you. You're doing great here. I really appreciate it." This calmed Malaya, and she shook her head and dropped to the grass in one fluid move.

"Whatever. My mom's going to be really mad if it's my dad. And she's crazy."

Tom looked down at Malaya a minute, as if he were about to say something. Then he thought better of it, nodded to Coral, and walked back toward the police officers in the cul-de-sac.

32

"*Mi shebeirach avoteinu*," June sang as sweetly as a child in a choir.

"Oh, Miss June, that's beautiful," said Jessy.

"*M'kor hab'racha l'imoteinu.*"

Her voice was clear and strong today, as if she were a younger woman.

"I wonder if you could teach me your prayers? I could sing them with you."

June banged her hand sharply on her knee.

"Do you think Miriam has a songbook? Or that you could bring one home with you from services this week?"

Her leg jutted out straight.

"Arf!" she said.

Jessy laughed.

"I'll mention it to Miriam when she comes by later, so she can help you get it."

"Ruff!"

"Can you sing it again?"

June flopped her head toward her stomach.

"Oh, I'm sorry, June. Let me hum the tune for you."

She had a pretty good ear, Jessy. She had the tune right, all the way through, though of course she had heard only the first two lines. She hummed it over and over, and June pushed the puzzle pieces around on the jigsaw puzzle, and knocked the one border that was finished to the floor.

Jessy bent down to pick up the pieces while still humming, and June noticed the red glare of a police cruiser's light flashing in the street. She watched it in a sort of dazed way. It made her think of Christmas, and of the neon lights of the El Capitan's Christmas display, and then of the dripping red and white stripes of a candy cane already licked.

"Ooooohhhhhhh!" she called.

"It's just a police car, Miss June. The light's out at Eastern, and there's an officer directing traffic. It was like that when I drove in."

"*Oh doctor, I'm in trouble,*" sang June.

"*Well, goodness gracious me,*" sang Jessy.

Jessy beamed at June, and June wished she could tell her how beautiful she was—how gloriously beautiful—though she supposed that Jessy did not think she was pretty at all. What Jessy thought of herself was there in her clothes. Today she wore a long-sleeved black cotton T-shirt that bunched up awkwardly under the lightweight fabric of a flowered halter-style dress. She wore black spandex shorts under the dress, and her heavy red-splotched legs disappeared into inexpensive maroon ankle boots, with a sharply angled heel that made her wobble as she walked. These clothes touched June.

Sometimes Jessy took her on excursions, to the indoor garden at the Bellagio or the Barrick Museum on UNLV's campus. And on the way home, they would stop at a convenience store for Diet Cokes, and sometimes for Diet Cokes with chocolate donuts. Jessy would lead her in and carefully fill two giant Styrofoam cups with ice and soda, and June would look around and wish that she could make herself say hello to the little girl touching all the bags of Doritos or to the old man with the SpongeBob backpack and the plaid pants.

It was the sort of place Marshall would never believe his mother could be, where no one else she knew would ever take her, or imagine that she had been, and June loved these trips. Sometimes the stores reeked of smoke and were filled with signs forbidding things: no debit cards for purchases under five dollars, no checks cashed, no standing near the machines, no loitering, no change available. In these stores, there was almost always someone with hollowed-out eyes waiting to buy a pack of cigarettes, or jutting a hand into June's face and asking for a dollar. The Cokes cost twice as much in these places as they did in the cleaner stores, the ones with cheerful clerks and a display case of fresh donuts and a clear plastic box where you could leave change for the people at Opportunity Village.

One time June noticed a woman give a dollar to someone begging outside a store, and then she saw the panhandler walk in and buy his own jumbo soda—the day was so hot—for eighty-five cents. And the cheerful clerk, with a broken tooth and her hair pulled back over a broad bald patch, asked the man if he would like to leave his change for Opportunity Village. The panhandler looked at the clerk, and then at the photos of the middle-aged men who worked at the training center, and then at the change in his palm. He tipped the nickel and the dime into the plastic box. "Thank you!" said the clerk, to which the man replied, "Of course."

Seeing this made June shake her head violently and caused her to bump Jessy, and there was a little fuss about the spill and her dress. June couldn't explain that her head shook because the man had given away the coins in order to help someone else, and because she never would have seen this if Jessy had not taken her into the Circle K—into the place that someone like June would never go.

On Friday evening, a van picked up her and Miriam and took them to services at Congregation Ner Tamid. June had known Miriam for almost fifty years, and while they had not really been friends, time had knit them together. Now they were both widows, they were both old Jews, they were both longtime residents of the same declining neighborhood, with wide, low-slung houses far too large for them and yards that stretched a hundred feet in every direction. When they made their way to the van on Friday nights, they passed through sunken living rooms and marble entryways and chandeliers weighted with crystal drops that coruscated light and memories as if they were the same thing.

It was Miriam who had asked June to donate to the campaign to build a synagogue in their neighborhood decades ago, and Miriam who had persuaded her to make a much larger donation when the synagogue decided to move to the suburbs years later. June had given the first time because it was easy, and because she and Miriam saw each other at school gatherings, and because her father would have been pleased to know she did it. She gave the second time because, at a certain point, after she had mostly retired from the El Capitan, after Marshall was busy with his own family, after she had started to recognize the first symptoms of whatever was wrong with her now, she had taken to stopping by Ner Tamid from time to time.

Initially, she simply walked in the garden or by the wall that proclaimed itself to be the Moe B. Dalitz Religious School, and the staff got to know her and called out her name when she went by. Finally, she started to come to services on Friday nights.

It was a reform synagogue, and the call-and-response in English surprised her at first, but the prayers were the same as she had always known them. The Hebrew came back to her effortlessly, easier almost than English sometimes, and the standing before the ark, the mournful sound of the Sh'ma—not a mournful prayer at all—and the little children who padded up to stand around the bimah when the rabbi called them up each week; these all moved her. When she was a child, the rabbi did not invite the children this way. She had tried to be quiet in synagogue.

But the congregation built its new synagogue and moved miles away from where June lived. The old building was a Baptist church now. The rabbi's assistant sent a van for her and Miriam each Friday night, and it stopped at the Sunrise Villas, and then, with the seats usually full, made its way to the new Ner Tamid on Valle Verde Drive. June had been determined not to like the pristine building, in spite of having helped fund it, but it was impossible not to appreciate the warm cream of the Israeli marble, the flicker of green palo verde leaves through the glass on either side of the bimah, the drape of the heavy velvet cloths that surrounded the arc. Too, the seats were comfortable, the sound system excellent, and the same rabbi and the same cantor led the services each Friday night.

Of course, June was not the same as she had been.

Miriam had always been as petite and small as June, and she was too frail to help her friend make her unsteady, unpredictable way into the temple. Usually the bus driver helped June down, and then one of the members of the men's club took her arm, and danced with her, back and forth and tipping giddily away from wherever she intended to go, until she was seated with a heavy and unreadable siddur in her lap. She suspected that the usher handed her the prayer book in the hope that it would provide ballast. June hoped the same, though she had learned not to count on it.

Tonight she made it all the way to the Mi Shebeirach—the prayer for healing—without attracting any attention to herself. She longed to sing, though she could rarely get any sound to emerge for these prayers she had known her whole life. This evening was no different. June concentrated on thinking about something else: her breakfast that morning or the outfit Marshall had worn to an Easter egg hunt when he was four. Sometimes this allowed her to sing. She would hear her own voice, slight but on pitch, as if it were someone else's. Now the sanctuary's lights were dimmed. Small twinkling bulbs had been strung through the potted trees, and the rabbi read out the names of those in need of healing, while the cantor prepared to lead the Mi Shebeirach, and some people behind her stood and said the names of people who had not been on the rabbi's list.

"Michael Jackson!" June yelled.

The rabbi nodded her way.

"Salvador Dali!"

The rabbi nodded again and then turned slightly to look at the cantor. The woman at the piano began to play the first haunting notes.

"Mu'ammar Gaddhafi!"

June could not stop. She was standing now, and this bizarre list of names was flying out of her mouth, louder and louder. Miriam tugged on her elbow, and the usher from the men's club hurried toward her, and she wished he would hurry a little faster, the old bum, and at this thought, she erupted into laughter. At least June didn't call out any more names, but her hilarity was so absolute and so infectious that at first the rabbi gave a gentle smile, and then he nodded encouragingly to the usher—the man really was slow—and then suddenly, June heard the cantor give a snort, and someone to her left laughed, and then there was a titter and another laugh, and a whole row broke down, and then some member of the choir. Finally, the cantor was laughing and could not stop, and the rabbi, who had great control, gave in and started to laugh as well.

When it was over, when the usher had her firmly by the arm and near the door, when Miriam looked away whether because she could not bear to see June like this or because she might start to laugh again—there was no way to know—the rabbi said, "Well, there's nothing more healing than laughter," and the congregants clapped, and June did that damn shimmy thing with her shoulders—good grief, there was no humiliation too great—and the service went on. June sat next to the usher on a padded bench in the hallway, which is where she ended up from time to time and did not mind so much. She could hear everything.

June thought about asking Jessy to come with her to services next Friday night, so that she could hear the cantor sing the prayers all the way through. Then, too, maybe it would make her laugh if June pulled such a stunt again. It would be good to see Jessy laugh.

33

The phone rang six times, but Jimbo did not answer it.

Ms. Navarro sat back on the couch without saying what had alerted her; what she had been listening for. But she was thinking about something. Engracia could see that her attention had shifted. What was it?

She still held Honorata's hand in her own. She squeezed it lightly, but Ms. Navarro did not respond. She had not responded to Jimbo's questions either, or to what he had said about Malaya. About how he could have already seen her. About how he had come to tell Ms. Navarro that he was going to see Malaya. He hadn't wanted to go behind her back.

"If you'd just opened the letter. You would have known she found me."

"This isn't my fault."

"Isn't it?"

They sat silently again, the red glow of the police cruiser on the wall outside, the sound of the phone, ringing, ringing, still in their ears.

Malaya. She would be coming home from school now. Engracia couldn't see a clock, and she didn't have a watch. But the light in the window. It would have to be about the right time. What would happen if Malaya walked in now?

These were, perhaps, the last moments any of them would be alive. They all knew it, and they were all afraid, and somehow the experience linked them: the woman who had lied to the man, the man who had a gun, the woman who did not know if she wanted to live or die.

Jimbo was still sitting on the floor, his back against the wall with the window. Honorata leaned into the couch, but Engracia could feel her alertness. It was one thing to wonder if she wanted to die, it was another to imagine a teenage girl walking through the door right now. Engracia could not bear it that Malaya might walk in. That something might happen to her.

"*Mi hijo* died," she blurted. "My son. Diego. He died."

Her voice came out cracked and accented. Engracia concentrated. She would have to say this in English. They would have to hear her.

"He was ten years old."

Ms. Navarro let go of her hand. Engracia did not move. Out the corner of her eye, she saw the man looking. She stared at the table in front of her. The wood was ornately carved, with a thick slab of greenish glass in the center. Through the glass, she saw her own foot in its dirty white sneaker. She could see her heel and then, under the glass, the rest of her foot, as if it had suddenly grown larger.

"I have only one child. He died."

Silence.

"When he was a little boy, he told me that when he grew up he would give his money to everyone on the street, to everyone who was hungry."

Ms. Navarro shifted slightly in the seat next to her. Engracia saw that the red glow of the police cruiser was also reflected in the greenish glass, just at the edge, a sliver of red.

"He said he didn't know why people walk by people who are hungry, who ask for food. 'Why do we do that, Mama?' I told him we do not have enough money to feed everyone. That my job was to feed him. And he told me that his job was going to be to feed them."

She inhaled deeply. Her heart thudded dully in her chest, and her stomach, fluttery and unsettled for the last hour, cramped. Still, it was not as hard as she thought to speak. Engracia had no one to tell about Diego now. The padre. Mary from work, who had come to see her. But she wanted to talk about her son. She wanted someone to know who he was. And she wanted these stupid, stupid people, who had their daughter, to stop it.

When Diego was small enough to swim in the bathtub, he had put his face in the water and said he could see Dios. When he was three, Juan took him to the Los Angeles County Fair, and they came home with two fish in plastic bags. Diego named them Hombre and Nacho. One time in first grade, he jumped out of line before he was supposed to leave the teacher and came running up to Engracia: "Mama, I can write in Spanish! Not just English. There are words in Spanish too!" Even then, he liked to crawl between her and Juan in bed, and sometimes, if he thought she was asleep, he put his thumb in his mouth and stroked her cheek with his small, gentle fingers.

Remembering the feel of his fingers on her skin nearly choked her. As always, she wanted to cry, she wanted to scream, she wanted somehow to force the universe back on the track it was meant to be on. But nothing, nothing that she did, nothing that her body could do physically, could express the horror of what was true, of what could not be changed. Even tears, the instant they fell, or screams, at the moment of sound, became nothing at all, worse than no movement, no sound, because they were so much less than what she actually felt and so much less than how utterly unbearable this fact was.

"He wanted to go to Death Valley. A scientist came to the school, and told him about the sailing stones. He wanted to see them."

She stopped. This was hard: what Diego had wanted and what she had done. Engracia listened for any sound in the room, her eyes not leaving the coffee table with her foot, distorted by the green glass, beneath it. Ms. Navarro and the man still said nothing. It was as if time had stopped. There was no gun. There was no argument. There was no girl about to walk in the door. There was just this moment, with Engracia hanging in space, concentrating, trying to tell them. She had to tell them now. Before Malaya came in.

"When the scientist came, Diego was happy. He didn't like Las Vegas. He missed his papa. But he liked the scientist."

Engracia heard the man sit down flat against the floor.

"I wanted Diego to go to college. I told him to study hard. Maybe he could be a scientist."

There was no other sound. The phone did not ring.

"Diego was afraid here. Without his papa. One boy even had a gun."

Honorata made a sound.

"And I was afraid. I was afraid of the boys here. I was afraid of the men on the street."

Everything was coming out all wrong. She wasn't making sense.

"He wanted to go to Death Valley. But I was afraid to take him there. By myself."

Engracia closed her eyes. She could not tell this story. She could not talk about what she had done. She could tell them something else. Something about Diego.

"His name was Diego Alejandro Juan Diez-Montoya. He was born in *Abril*, in San Diego, the United States, on the eleventh. Every year, I decorated his cake with flowers."

Out the window, the stucco continued to glow red. Engracia looked up and saw a shadow move—a man on the wall, perhaps.

She heard Jimbo stir, as if he were getting up. Maybe the man on the wall would shoot him now, before she had told them, before they understood. She had to tell them.

"He wanted to go to Death Valley, and I was afraid to take him, so I bought him a skateboard.

"But he was disappointed. He still wanted to go to Death Valley.

"So I told him I would take him to Red Rock, to the trails there, and we would look at the paintings the Indians made a thousand years ago. And on a different day, we would go and see the sailing stones.

"I told him we would go on Saturday, when I came home from work.

"But first I had to sleep that day because I work all night. So I told Diego to watch the television and to wake me at noon. I told him do not take the skateboard outside. Because his friends are too crazy. And he does not know how to ride it yet."

Engracia shuddered. *Por favor Dios mío, ayúdame.* Help me.

"Diego woke me at noon. And we got in the car right away, so we would have lots of time to find the paintings on the rocks.

"And he was quiet. Tired. I say, Diego what's the matter? But he say he is fine, he is happy, he wants to see the rocks.

"I know something is not right, but I think it is these boys, his friends. Or maybe he watched the news on the television, and something happened. I wait, because he will tell me when he is ready."

Ms. Navarro shifted in her seat, and, very gently, she put her hand on Engracia's back. Engracia accepted this because she knew Ms. Navarro wanted to help, and she knew she was sorry about Diego, but also, she did not like it. Because even now, nothing anyone did ever helped. And also, Ms. Navarro hid her daughter from her papa.

"I turned on the wrong road, the one before the Red Rock, and we drive a long way, looking for another sign. And Diego is very quiet. He says, 'Mama I am sick. My head hurts.' And then he throws up. In the car."

"'Diego,' I say. 'You should tell me you're sick. It's the car. It's too hot.' But Diego is not listening to me. His eyes don't look at me, they are not looking at anything, but there are tears. I see tears in his eyes."

Engracia saw that the man was no longer looking at her. He was holding his head in his hands, staring at the floor.

"I know he is sick, and I don't know where I am, so I try to call an ambulance. I stop the car, and I get out my phone, and the call doesn't work. I say, 'Diego, Diego, wake up. What's the matter?'"

But Diego did not reply. He leaned his head on the window, with the mess from the getting sick still in his lap, and he did not answer, and he did not look at her.

"So I start the car, and I turn around, and I drive very fast. There is no one on that road. It's not going to Red Rock. And I keep dialing and dialing, and my phone does not work."

Diego threw up again. Engracia tried to hold him, tried to pull his head under her arm while driving with the left hand, and pushing on the buttons on the phone with her chin. She couldn't do it. She couldn't hold him and drive and phone. Diego was limp now, so she put his head in her lap, and she drove the fastest she had ever driven. Finally, there was the road she needed. She stopped.

And the phone worked. And someone must have seen how desperate she looked, right through the window, because a car stopped and then another, and everyone tried to help.

Was it better to drive him to the hospital? To wait for the ambulance? In the end, she left her car on the side of the road, and a man in a Mercedes drove her and Diego very fast toward town, and when he saw the fire engine, sirens blaring, coming toward them, he pulled over. One paramedic worked on Diego and tried to rouse him, and another paramedic asked her questions. Before they put them both in the ambulance, the first paramedic said, "Where did he get this bruise? Here, behind his ear?"

And that was when Engracia knew that he must have fallen, that he must have taken the skateboard, that he must have gone outside when she was sleeping. And, of course, he would not have told her that he fell, because he would not have wanted her to know that he had disobeyed.

"He died in the hospital. Two days later. When they asked me if they could turn off the machine."

Engracia could not say more than this. She could not keep speaking, even if these idiotic people, who had their daughter, did not understand. She had tried. She and Diego had tried. If this is what Dios wanted, she had tried.

There were tears on Ms. Navarro's face now. She stretched her arm all the way around Engracia's back, and when she squeezed, Engracia could feel how her body had changed. Her breathing was ragged, but her body was no longer rigidly on alert. Instead, it was soft, heavy, pressing into Engracia.

"I didn't know. I'm so sorry."

Engracia relaxed into Honorata's arms. She was a mother too. Engracia knew that the other woman had spent seventeen years afraid of just the thing that had happened to her.

A horrible sound erupted from the man.

He was crying. He was crying, and he was trying not to, and his face was hidden, and his big, fat body shook. Engracia thought that he cried like a child, without any ability to hold himself back. He snorted, and his nose ran, and he could not catch his breath, and his body twisted and shook. She was grateful for how deeply he suffered. He suffered for her, for Diego, and, somehow, this helped.

Just then, the doorbell rang.

At first, nobody moved. It rang again, and there was a loud knocking.

Engracia looked out the window and saw a man crouched on the wall and another across the street. They were wearing helmets and military gear, though surely they were the police. They were watching her in the window, and they were looking toward the front door—toward whoever was ringing the bell.

Jimbo looked up.

"I'm sorry," he said. "I'm sorry, Honorata."

And then he looked at Engracia. "I am so sorry."

Engracia saw in his eyes that he had given up, and she thought that he might shoot himself now, but that he would not shoot her and he would not shoot Ms. Navarro. They looked at each other, the man's face swollen with his tears, and red, like the glow of that light on the stucco.

"I'm sorry about your son."

Engracia looked at Ms. Navarro, who was watching them, her face stricken, no longer angry.

Engracia leaned over to the man. He had been sitting on the

floor, and she was on the couch, so when she leaned over, and he put his arms around her, they met in a kind of crouch near the floor. He put both his arms around her, and as he bent his head near her face, she said, "The gun. Give me the gun." He didn't reply. She didn't know if he had heard; if he understood. Engracia wondered if there was a gun trained on the two of them now, someone out there waiting for some distance between her and the man, someone trying to understand what was going on in here.

"The gun."

She said it with urgency, because there wasn't much time. The person at the door was knocking loudly now, and he was yelling something, though she wasn't sure what.

Jimbo gripped her shoulders tightly. Engracia slowly moved her hand forward, toward his soft body, toward the gun stuck in his waistband. The man said nothing. And then she had the gun in her hand, and before she separated from the man's embrace, she dropped it in the deep pocket of her cotton pants.

"Open up! Police!"

Engracia and the man separated, and they looked at Honorata, who was looking out the door of the study, toward the hall.

Almost at once, they all stood. Engracia waited for the shot, the bullet that would come through the window.

"This is the police. Open the door!"

Honorata moved out of the room, toward the door. There was no shot, and so Engracia and the man followed. She didn't look at Jimbo, she didn't say anything; she could feel the gun against her leg, pulling the band of her slacks lower.

Honorata opened the door, and the policeman said, "Ma'am, is everyone all right in here? We've been calling you. We had a call earlier. What's going on?"

And Honorata said, "Everyone's fine. But I want this man to leave my home. I want him to go."

"Has he hurt you? Is there a gun?"

Jimbo and Engracia stood behind Honorata, the three of them all staring at the police officer. Except for his size, Jimbo looked the least frightening of all. An old man, older than he had been two hours before, with his eyes still swollen, and the sweat beaded in his hair and beneath his ear and along the collar of his shirt.

"I'm ready to go," he said.

"Well, ma'am, what's going on here?" the officer repeated. "Has this man been holding you? Has he hurt you?"

And there was a silence, while Honorata looked at the police officer, and Engracia looked at Honorata, and Jimbo looked down at the floor.

"No. He didn't hurt me. He didn't hold me. I just don't want him in my house anymore."

"Are you sure about what you're saying? We can hold him. We'd like to ask all of you some questions."

Honorata drew herself up—she was not much more than five feet tall—and she said firmly, "This is my home. I didn't call you. I want this man to leave, and he's ready to leave. I want you to leave too. I didn't call the police. I don't need you."

The police officer turned around and looked at another man standing a few feet behind him. That man shrugged his shoulders and raised an eyebrow.

"Someone called us, ma'am. There was a 911 call from this address."

Honorata did not answer.

"Ma'am, we understand these situations can be really complicated. But we want to be sure you're safe. We don't want something happening to you later. Do you understand?"

"I understand that this is my home, and I didn't call the police, and I haven't done anything wrong."

"Nobody thinks you've done anything wrong, ma'am. We just want to make sure you're safe."

"I'm safe. But my daughter. She should've come home by now. I heard the school bus. Do you know where she is?"

Engracia felt Jimbo go rigid. He looked up, out the door. The police officer saw him look.

"Sir, what are you doing here? How do you know this woman?"

"We're old friends," said Jimbo quietly. "I was in Las Vegas, and I came to see her."

The man standing at the edge of the yard, behind the police officer, came forward then. He said, "Mrs. Navarro, is that right?"

Honorata nodded yes.

"I'm Tom Darling. I'm a lieutenant in the Metro Police Department. We got a 911 call from this house a couple of hours ago, and we've been watching you pretty close. We have your daughter just on the next block. She's fine. But we didn't want her to come home until we knew that everything was okay here."

Honorata nodded. "Thank you."

"So, before we let anyone go, we'd like to talk with each of you. Just for a minute. One by one."

Honorata turned and looked first at Engracia and then at Jimbo. Their eyes all caught, and their faces did not move. They stood silent and immobile, and an agreement was made.

"Okay. Would you like to come in?" Honorata asked.

34

When Coral and Tom talked a few days later about what had happened, he said that they had gotten lucky; the waiting had paid off. There was no doubt in his mind that there'd been a gun, that the man had been holding the two women; the whole thing could have ended in a very different way. But the gun got ditched somewhere. They patted him down; they searched the room where the three of them had been waiting. And what else could they do? The two women insisted there was no gun. Honorata Navarro wanted the police off her property.

Family fights were dangerous. Things could go any way at any time, and in ways a police officer couldn't predict. James Wohlmann didn't seem like too bad a guy—no record—but Honorata had taken a risk by letting him off, by not telling the police what happened. Not one of the three had been cooperative. Tom didn't know what had gone down. But Coral was right. The man was Malaya's father, and he hadn't known she existed. It didn't look like her parents had been married, though. There was no record of a marriage.

Another strange thing that stood out: the housekeeper hadn't been working there very long. None of the three knew each other very well. And yet, the two others, they were protective of her. It was just a feeling, but he and the investigator had both picked it up: how Honorata and James had each been careful of the house-keeper.

By the time she and Tom spoke, Coral knew what had happened. She knew what Tom and his colleague had sensed, and why. Malaya had knocked on her door the next evening, and again a few days after that. So Coral knew what Honorata had told Malaya, and she knew why they were protective of the housekeeper. She also knew a little about why James Wohlmann had come to the door, though she didn't know if there had been a gun. Malaya had not said anything about a gun.

When it was all over that day—after the police cruiser had escorted Mr. Wohlmann out of the neighborhood, after the SWAT team and two of the patrols had left, after the young officer had started to take down the canopy and smiled at Malaya when she jumped up to help—Coral had walked with Malaya down the cul-de-sac. Before they got to the end, Honorata had come out running, and she and Malaya had embraced. They were both crying, and Coral thought about how difficult the last year had been for them, about Malaya asking to spend the night after babysitting so she wouldn't have to go home, about Honorata saying that American girls didn't listen to their mothers. It wasn't easy raising a teenager, and maybe it was harder for Honorata, who was mostly alone and who had grown up somewhere so different.

Coral said good-bye to Malaya and gave Honorata a hug, and then watched the two of them walk into their house. She had been going to offer Tom a drink, but when she turned to go back to her house, she saw the small form of the housekeeper, waiting at the bus stop on the road.

"Tom, I'll call you this week. Okay?"

"Sure. Thanks, Coral. You really helped us out. No days off for the weary, huh?"

"Yeah. Give me a school music program any day of the week."

"Yep. This is one peculiar town."

"See ya, Tom."

And Coral had grabbed her bag from the kitchen counter where she'd left it hours earlier, eased her car out of the garage, and driven over to where Engracia stood, looking, from behind, like an old woman.

"Hello?"

"Yes?" The housekeeper looked startled.

"My name's Coral. I'm a friend of the Navarros. Malaya was just with me, while you were in the house?"

The woman looked about anxiously. The bus wasn't coming. There was no one around.

"Listen, I don't want to scare you. I just thought you might want a ride home."

"No. No, *gracias*. I take the bus."

"Please. You've got to be worn out. You don't have to talk. I'll just drive you wherever you want to go."

The woman hesitated.

"Look, it's after six o'clock. The busses don't run very often now. You could be out here a long time."

Engracia looked at Coral, pulled her thin sweater together at the front, and then said yes, she would be grateful for a ride.

But Coral hadn't taken her home. The woman, who said her name was Engracia, asked to be taken to the Catholic church, St. Anne's, on Maryland Parkway.

"It's close to my home. I can walk from there."

So Coral took her to Saint Anne's, and watched while she

pulled open the heavy door and stepped inside the sanctuary. They'd said very little in the car. Coral had asked her if she could get her something to eat or drink, and Engracia had refused. Coral had explained that she was the choir teacher at a high school, had taught music at an elementary school before that, that she had known Malaya from the time she was a baby.

To this, the housekeeper said very little.

"Listen, what happened to you today. It might have been pretty traumatic. It might come back to you. And if so, you should talk to someone. The priest or something."

Coral felt foolish saying this: it was none of her business, and she didn't know why she'd said it. She just wanted to say something. It had to have been terrifying, and this woman seemed so forlorn.

Engracia looked at her strangely.

"Today?"

"Yes. I mean, I don't know what happened, but—well, it must have been frightening."

"Today didn't scare me. Today doesn't matter."

It was a strange reply. Sad. Coral didn't know what to say in return.

"Okay. Well, I'm sorry. I'm not prying. I wish you well."

"Thank you for the ride."

"You're welcome."

Coral still felt foolish, but she was glad she'd driven Engracia. The bus really might not have come for hours. And it was much too far to walk.

It wasn't until the next evening, after Malaya had told her some of what had happened, that she understood what Engracia's strange words had meant.

35

The man stood at the door a long time before ringing the bell.

He had walked up the steps quickly, with confidence. He had been about to push the bell, and then paused, his hand just inches from the button. He stood there, thinking, hesitating. And then he dropped his hand to his side and stared at the door.

Unless the person inside was watching for him, there was no way to know he had arrived. It took him a long time. More than five minutes. Maybe ten. His chest heaved slowly, in and out. Who knows what he was thinking. Whether he was afraid. The minutes, the years, he might have been reliving.

He rang the doorbell.

Jimbo was wearing a suit. A very nice navy suit, with a white shirt and a narrow mustard-colored tie. His shoes were expensive, of course, and recently polished. He looked good. Not old and red and fat, as he had looked that day.

"Honorata."

He handed her a bouquet of white roses and a box of croissants from Bouchon. He must be staying at the Venetian. She started to say his name, to say hello, but seeing him so soon after the way he had terrified her, even though she had invited him to come this time; suddenly Honorata didn't trust herself to speak. She took the flowers and motioned him to come inside.

Jimbo did not look at the study as he passed it. He followed the line of her arm, directing him to the table in the kitchen. It was a sunny nook, and outside the bay window, the wisteria was thick with its violet blooms and the door to the backyard was open, so that they could hear the bees buzzing, delirious in their lavender nirvana. An old woman, very tiny, sat with her eyes closed and her face to the sun near the far wall. Rita's mother. He set the pastry box on the table. Honorata opened a cupboard and found a vase.

"I'll just put these in water."

"Sure."

"I've made coffee."

"That'll be nice."

And he stood there, so large in her kitchen, too large for the narrow wooden chairs, and he didn't seem to know what to do, whether to stand or to sit, what to say.

"Please sit."

He looked around, perhaps wondering where Malaya was. Honorata did not say she was upstairs, probably listening.

"Here are some plates. And napkins. I'll bring you coffee."

Jimbo nodded his head, but did not risk speaking. He pulled out a chair and settled himself into the seat gingerly. Honorata's kitchen made him feel like crying. There were embroidered curtains at the window over the sink and a red wooden frame where cups hung crookedly. A small ceramic tiger, made by a child, sat in the kitchen window, along with a dusty popsicle frame surrounding the faded photo of a small girl. There was a set of brightly decorated canisters for flour and sugar and tea; there was a teakettle on the stove. The yellow-and-blue mat near the sink was folded under at one corner; Honorata straightened it with her foot while she clipped the ends of the roses.

It was everything he had wanted, everything he had hoped for, everything he had finally put aside that night at Caesars when this very woman had told him she never wanted to see him again. A wave of bitterness passed over him, a taste like bile, but almost immediately, he felt remorse. It wasn't her fault. He knew this. He had known it a long time. But he had wanted a family. There had been so much loneliness. And when Malaya had found him, he had almost gotten them all killed. He wanted, suddenly, to be out of this kitchen, away from her. He pushed his chair back from the table.

"Do you want cream and sugar?"

He paused, about to stand.

"No."

And too, there was the way she had yelled, "*I hate you! I hate you!*" over and over. All these years later. She still hated him. Had anyone ever hated him before? Jimbo wasn't the sort of person people hated. Usually he was someone people did not notice. Old and fat and somehow unappealing; for as long as he could remember, he had sensed the way that he was slightly repellent to others. He didn't know why. He kept himself very clean. He wore good clothes. He spoke respectfully. But it had always been there, like a pheromone that repelled.

"Thank you for coming," Honorata said quietly. "I know you could have met Malaya without me. She would have gone with you."

Jimbo said nothing.

"But my mother's going with you tonight. You understand?"

"Of course. I'm glad she'll come."

"I was wondering what you're going to do. Where you're going to go with Malaya?"

Jimbo had given this a lot of thought. All he really wanted was a chance to see her, to listen to her talk, but he wanted her to enjoy it too.

"I thought maybe we would see Celine Dion tonight. Or *Jersey Boys*. Has she seen those?"

Honorata looked taken aback.

"You're taking her out?"

Jimbo was equally flustered.

"I'm not taking my *daughter* out. I just want to do something nice. I'm sixty-six years old. I don't know what Malaya likes."

Upstairs, Malaya was startled. Sixty-six? She didn't know anyone whose father was sixty-six. Courtney's dad was almost that old, but Courtney was part of his second set of kids. Courtney's mom had been friends with one of his older daughters when both girls were in grade school. That was pretty creepy if your mom had been your dad's daughter's friend. Courtney had to explain it three times to Dani, who just could not get it.

Well, whatever. Jimbo was definitely her dad. And after all this work, she was going to meet him. She looked herself over critically in the mirror and then started down the stairs.

"Hi."

They hadn't heard her coming.

Honorata was surprised to see her daughter looking so pretty. She'd brushed her hair long and straight, with a clip in the back, and she was wearing a buttoned shirt that covered most of that horrible tattoo. Her makeup was pretty too. A little mascara. Pink lipstick. Had she taken out her nose ring?

It had been a long time since Malaya had looked like this.

Maybe as far back as that dance sophomore year, when she had worn the royal blue dress they found at the Fashion Show Mall. Malaya had actually whooped when Honorata agreed to buy it for her; she was so sure her mother would not let her have it. And then they had gone together to a salon to have Malaya's hair put up and her nails done in a bright contrasting pink, and she had been so pretty, so happy.

Had Honorata actually worried about that dance? Worried about the boy and the party bus and the group of friends all dressed up, posing for photos in the park? It was so innocent, compared with the friends Malaya had found the next summer, compared with the way she had started dressing after her job at the movie theater; after the boyfriend, Martin, who was so thin it had to be drugs, with his shaved head and his chains and those ridiculous boots. "Mom, you don't know anything about who's nice and who's not!" Malaya had yelled at her. "You don't have any idea what kids are like!" And Honorata had remembered how distressed her own mother had been when she kept disappearing with Kidlat, and so she had not put her foot down, but she should have. She should have stopped Malaya; at least she wouldn't have that tattoo.

Jimbo thought he had never seen a more lovely girl. She was taller than Honorata, and her face was a bit like his mother's. His eyes watered. He wanted to say hello, but he was trying very hard to stay composed. He stared at her and then looked down. He was helpless.

"Malaya. This is Mr. Wohlmann."

Everyone seemed uncomfortable, and still Jimbo could not bring himself to look up. This was terrible. He was the man. He was the father. But he didn't want to lose control. He didn't want to embarrass her.

"I'm glad you came."

Her voice was familiar, from the message she'd left on his phone. He had played it over and over, but he had not called her back. He had been afraid to chase her away, without ever getting to see her.

He took a deep breath and stood up.

"Hello, Malaya. It's an honor to meet you."

He was funny. An honor. And he looked like he was crying. Which was sort of embarrassing. But it was nice to think he cared that much. That he really wanted to meet her.

"Malaya likes movies. And she's very good at dancing."

Her mother was so awkward. Malaya was annoyed that she had said this.

"Not really. I mean, everybody likes the movies. And I just take dance lessons. It's not like I'm going to be a dancer or something."

Honorata was surprised. Malaya always said that she was going to be a dancer, whenever she told her daughter that this was not a job, not a career, not a practical plan for a smart girl.

"I'm sure you're a very good dancer."

This was the first thing he said to his own daughter. And it came out oddly. He knew what Honorata thought of him: that he was some sort of sex monster. Which was about as far from the truth as something could be. But he was going to make it all worse. He didn't know what to say to this girl, to this very young girl in front of him. He felt sick.

"I like science too."

"Really? What do you like?"

"Chemistry. My chemistry teacher's pretty good, and everyone thinks she's too hard, but I like that it's hard. And I like being in the lab. I might study chemistry in college."

Honorata did not recognize this daughter. She had said she hated chemistry and that Honorata should not be surprised if she failed, because the teacher was a witch.

"I studied chemistry in college," Jimbo offered.

"You did?"

"Yes. I'm a chemical engineer. Or I was. I started my own company a long time ago."

Malaya didn't say anything.

"Do you want some pastries?" Honorata asked. "Mr. Wohlmann brought some."

Malaya shook her head. And they all stood there, uneasy.

"Do you want to take a walk?" the girl asked. "Just down the block?"

Jimbo looked at Honorata. He saw her freeze, and he knew that even now she was afraid. He was about to say no, to tell his daughter he'd rather stay in, when Honorata spoke.

"Stay in the neighborhood, Malaya. Just walk around here."

Malaya nodded, and Jimbo said, "Yes. Yes, I would like to take a walk."

Honorata felt lightheaded as she watched the two of them walk toward the front door. Jimbo wasn't frightening now, the way he had always seemed in her mind or the way he had been just weeks before. If she were meeting him for the first time, she would notice how self-conscious he was, how his hands trembled, how his voice was too high for his size. She would notice that he kept his head lowered slightly, as if anticipating a blow.

How could he have once been terrifying? He was rich. He looked rich. And he was big. But he was the opposite of frightening. He looked like someone who would always have time to read at Sunday Mass, to help with the ushering, to replace the bulletins in the pews. When she lived with him—it was amazing that she could have that thought without fear—when she lived with him, he had talked and talked and talked. So many words that washed over her, that she could not remember, even then, even an hour after he stopped talking, and she thought now that he must have noticed she did not remember, that she did not pay attention, and this hadn't mattered, because—and how could this be the first time she had realized this?—because nobody ever listened to him. He was used to being ignored.

It didn't change what he had done. It didn't change the horror of what her uncle had done, of those months in Chicago, of all the memories that had played over and over again in her mind all these years, but it did somehow relieve her. The money she had won, the daughter she adored, her whole life: it was connected to this. To Jimbo's loneliness. To the way he seemed as if he thought he were about to be struck. This was an idea that surprised her. That Malaya had come not from violence but from sorrow.

Coral backed out of her garage slowly. There were people walking in the street, and she looked down at her phone, to see if she had any messages, while they walked by. She clicked through the list—Ada's riot of emoticons and a cat video from Isa—and then she backed her car onto the street.

It was Malaya walking. Malaya and an older man, quite large. They were straight ahead of her, and in her rearview mirror, she caught sight of Honorata standing near her mailbox, watching the two. Something about her pose alerted Coral, and she looked again. Was that Malaya's father?

His head was tipped down, listening to his daughter. He was a big man, but he walked lightly. Beside him, Malaya Begtang's face was lit up. She was talking, and her hands were moving, and while Coral watched her, she took a little skipping step, either to catch up with her father's stride or out of pleasure—Coral couldn't tell. She looked young, younger than she had seemed in a long time, and Coral thought of the little girl who would stop by to show Trey her artwork, or to ask if she could give the little boys some *suman* her grandmother had made. That little girl had been so beautiful, so full of light.

For a second, Coral imagined she saw that light shining off Malaya's rainbow hair, reflecting on her father's navy suit. She thought of her own boys, of the way they still curled into her lap or into Koji's, like animals claiming their owned territory. She thought of Trey, and of her husband standing on his tiptoes to rest an arm around his nephew's shoulders. She thought of her brother telling everyone at school that she was a 100 percent Jackson. She thought of her mother, holding her hand as they sang at Macedonia Baptist on Sundays. And here was Malaya, looking into the face of the father she had thought she might never know.

Malaya and her father reached the corner. As they turned to walk toward the park, the girl looked back, past Coral in her car, to her mother still standing near the mailbox. The girl looked, and she smiled, and she waved. Tiny in the rearview mirror, Honorata waved back.

36

Coral had lived in Las Vegas for nearly all of her forty-nine years, but she had never set foot in the El Capitan. It was ironic that she would be headed there now—nearly two years after it had been scheduled for demolition, more than three decades since her father had died, now that her brother no longer owned it.

But Engracia worked at the El Capitan—had apparently worked there before her son had died—and she had been so reluctant to meet with Coral, so reluctant to discuss that day or what she had done, Coral wasn't about to complicate things by not accepting the first place she suggested. Engracia would come to the Midnight Cafe at nine in the morning, just after her shift ended. Coral had intended to be there early, but Isa couldn't find his baseball mitt, and Gus had yelled that if he were late, he wouldn't get to play and why did Isa always lose his things, and so Coral had stopped to help Isa find his glove, and Koji had given her a quick kiss; she could catch up with them later.

She was on her way to the El Capitan to meet Engracia at the request of Honorata.

Her neighbor had knocked on the door a few weeks after the incident and asked if she had time for some tea. She had made a cake, if Coral wanted to come down. So Coral, who wondered why Honorata had not called first, raised her eyebrow to Koji, ruffled the top of Isa's hair, and told them she'd be back in an hour or so.

Honorata's house was very clean. There were several pieces of furniture made of black lacquered wood, and, as usual, there was not a speck of dust showing. There were embroidered pillows on each chair, and embroidered curtains in the kitchen; Honorata had made these. It was a cheerful room, very light, and Honorata's mother was there, playing something on an iPad.

"Hello, Mrs. Navarro. It's nice to see you."

Honorata's mother stopped playing her game long enough to stand up and give her neighbor a hug. "Hello, hello," she said. Coral had never heard her speak much more English than this, but Nanay had been sending Malaya down with plates of *lumpia* and *pancit* for years. Coral knew that Nanay appreciated how Malaya felt about them: had noticed the hours Keisha spent playing with her when she was a toddler, had observed Trey's gentle teasing when she was eight, knew how much Gus and Isa had loved their babysitter.

Honorata motioned for Coral to sit down, and then she brought out a cake, decorated with coconut and set on a clear glass cake stand.

"It's a beautiful cake."

Honorata's mother nodded approvingly.

"Good cook. My daughter good cook."

Coral thought of Augusta, who had lived in her own house to the very end. She had never been sick enough to leave it, though Coral had always thought that her mother would one day live with her, and that she would have the chance to care for Augusta in the way her mother had cared for her. But it wasn't to be. At seventy-six, which wasn't so old, her heart gave out. They'd always known it would be her heart.

Honorata sliced the cake, poured some tea, and placed three sections of tangerine on each plate before handing one to Coral and another to her mother.

"Is Malaya home?"

"She's asleep. I want to talk before she comes down."

"Of course."

Coral had thought Honorata might want to explain about Malaya's father, but she didn't say anything about James Wohlmann. She must have known that Malaya had told Coral everything, but Honorata didn't give Coral any more information. This also made Coral think of Augusta, and how her own mother had never felt the need to explain herself. Still, Coral had just seen Malaya walking down the street with her father; she wondered how things were going.

"My housekeeper, Engracia . . ."

"Yes."

"I'm worried."

"Malaya told me about her son."

"Yes. But that's not why I'm worried."

"Oh."

Honorata did not continue right away, so Coral took another bite of cake. The grandmother patted her arm in an encouraging way. Finally, her neighbor continued.

"She's nice person, this housekeeper. Wise person. Even though she's very young."

Honorata wiped some crumbs off the counter, added some more cake to her mother's plate, picked up a napkin that had fallen to the floor.

"She might not be legal. Immigrant, I mean."

"Right. Well, I don't think what happened here will matter. The police don't turn that sort of stuff over to Immigration. And she didn't do anything."

"Yes. I see."

"Is she still working for you? Is she worried Immigration will find her?"

"No. She hasn't come back to work here."

Coral could have predicted that Honorata would not tell her why. Her neighbor didn't have ordinary conversations with people. Talking with her was like throwing a ball against a cracked wall: it bounced back, but not necessarily the way you predicted.

"She took the gun."

"What?"

"She took Jimbo's gun. She hid it in her pocket. The police didn't search her."

"Wow."

"That took a lot of courage. To take a gun when she's not legal. Right?"

"Well, courage is one word. It was definitely a risk."

"She just did it. She understood the problem. She understood how everything was going to go bad, how it was going to go bad for Malaya's father. She just fixed it. She fixed the problem, all by herself."

"I guess. I'm not sure. I mean, if Malaya's father had had a gun, they would have arrested him. I'm sure of that."

"Maybe he wouldn't have let them take him."

"Oh. Yeah. That would have been bad."

"It would have been bad for Malaya," Honorata said. "She would never recover from this. In her own house. After she found him. So mad at me."

"Yeah. I think you're right. I think that would have been terrible for Malaya."

"So. Engracia. This young woman. Who lost her child. She saved mine."

Coral's eyes watered. It was true, probably. If Engracia had gotten the gun away from Malaya's father. If it was because of her that the whole thing hadn't exploded.

"Does Malaya know this?"

"No. Malaya doesn't know her father had a gun."

"She told me about Engracia's son. How Engracia told you and her father about him."

"Yes, she knows that."

"So, what are you thinking?"

"I'm thinking that a very nice woman has a gun, and is not legal, and also, her son has died."

Yes. Coral agreed. The gun was dangerous in anyone's hands, and certainly in Engracia's. She'd be deported in a minute if she were caught with it. And, too, she was awfully vulnerable right now. A gun could be dangerous in so many ways.

"Have you talked with her? Asked her about the gun?"

"No."

"Do you think you could do that?"

"No."

Coral waited.

"Engracia doesn't like me, I think. She doesn't like that I didn't tell Malaya's father about her."

"She said this?"

"No."

"Well, okay. But you're just going to call her and ask about the gun. See if she got rid of it. Where it is."

"Maybe the police are listening to my phone."

"I doubt it."

"Maybe her number doesn't work anymore."

"Her phone? Did you try it?"

"Yes. It's disconnected."

"Well, I don't know how we would find her. Do you know her last name?"

"Montoya."

"Okay. Engracia Montoya. Illegal immigrant. We're not finding her."

"I worry about it every night. I worry about her. I want to help her."

"Well. How did you hire her? Do you know someone that knows her?"

"Father Burns. From Saint Anne's church. He asked me to hire her. He knows her."

"Okay. Well. Call him."

This was getting a little frustrating. Why was Coral here?

"No. I can't call. She won't take my call, and Father Burns won't tell me about her."

"So?"

"You could call Father Burns. You could talk with Engracia."

"Me? That doesn't make any sense at all."

"It does. You're a teacher. People feel safe with teachers. I want to give her some money." Honorata pulled out an envelope thick with cash. "For saving my daughter. You can give this to her. And you can tell her about the gun; about how they will deport her."

Honorata pushed the envelope of cash across the table, and Coral was looking at it, thinking this felt weirdly wrong, like a drug deal or something.

"I don't know anything about deportation. Nothing."

"Your husband's an immigrant."

Coral couldn't think of anything to say. Koji had been an American citizen for years. And Honorata was an immigrant too. Her neighbor could be so odd. It was kind of her to want to give this money to Engracia, Coral appreciated that, but it wasn't anything Coral could do for her. The boys wanted to see a movie today. She had hoped to bag items for the Salvation Army to pick up. It was time to go.

"Please, Coral. I trust you. Just call her. Find a way to give her the money. Get the gun. Make sure she doesn't have the gun. I can't sleep at all. I think of her every night, and I need your help."

Coral wasn't sure what to say. She didn't want to get in the middle of this. But the truth was that she'd been thinking about Engracia too. She hadn't known about the gun, of course, but she remembered the housekeeper sitting in her car, wanting to go to the church, looking for a place that was safe. Malaya had said her son was ten years old. So was Isa.

Oh, what the hell. Augusta would have said yes.

"Okay. Honorata, I'll try. I'll see if I can find her, if she'll talk to me. I don't know when. But I'll work on it. I'll let you know."

She regretted it the second she said it.

But it was too late. Honorata's face was transformed. Coral rarely saw her neighbor look unguarded in this way. Her eyes were bright, and she was smiling, and she reached out to take Coral's hand.

Well, all right. This would be awkward, but she would do it.

Coral didn't do anything about the envelope of cash for several days. She told Koji what Honorata had asked, and he raised his eyebrows when he saw how much money it was, but he told Coral it wouldn't hurt to try. For sure, Engracia could use the money.

On Wednesday, she looked up the number for Saint Anne's and left a message with the receptionist asking the priest to call her.

"Hello?"

"Coral Jackson? This is Father Burns."

"Father, thanks for calling. I appreciate it. Listen, I'm looking for a woman. She did some housekeeping for my neighbor. Her name is Engracia Montoya?"

"Oh, Engracia. Yes. She isn't working as a housekeeper now. I'm sorry."

"Oh no, I don't want her to clean my house. I wanted to talk with her. I wondered if you had a phone number."

"Well, um . . ."

"I gave her a ride home one day. Something happened in the neighborhood, and I gave her a ride. And I've been worried about her. I know about her son. I know she lost her child."

"Yes. Engracia has had a difficult time."

He sounded like an old man, rather formal, like someone with money. Not quite the way she imagined a priest.

"I just want to make sure she's okay. And there's something else. Something I want to talk to her about. I have something to give her."

"Well, I can see. Perhaps I can call Engracia. She'll have to call you."

"Sure. Here's my phone number. If she wants, all three of us can talk. If that would make her feel better."

"Well, I'll see. She'll probably be here tonight, and I'll ask her. Okay?"

"Thank you, Father."

Of course, Engracia did not call. Coral had to call twice more, feeling a little more foolish each time, but she had this stupid envelope of cash, and there was still the question of the gun. Coral was not about to ask Father Burns if he knew about the gun. She did say that she knew someone who wanted to give Engracia a gift.

She almost missed the call when it came.

It was early on a Saturday morning, not even light. She didn't recognize the number, and she was just about to roll over and fall back to sleep when she thought of Engracia.

"Hello?"

"Hello," Engracia's voice was very quiet. "I'm Engracia Montoya."

"Engracia, thank you for calling. This is Coral. I drove you home, awhile ago, after the thing . . . the thing with the police."

"*Si.*"

"How are you?"

She didn't reply.

"I mean, uh, I hope you're doing well. I called you because I was hoping we could meet. Ms. Navarro wants to give you a gift. She appreciates what you did that day. She's very grateful. And she'd like to give you something."

"I don't want anything."

"I understand. I do. But maybe we could just talk. Ms. Navarro is worried about something else. She wants to be sure you're okay."

"I'm okay."

"Do you think we could just meet? Just for ten minutes? I can meet you anywhere. At your house? At work?"

"I don't want anything."

"Engracia. You saved a whole family. You saved Ms. Navarro's daughter from a lot of pain. She's grateful. Please, just meet with me."

There was a long silence.

"Please. Don't hang up."

"I work at the El Capitan."

Coral's heart skipped. She would never be free of that place.

"I could meet you after my work. In the Midnight Cafe. I get off at nine."

"Today?"

"Yes."

"That's great. Thank you, Engracia. I'll be there."

She didn't say good-bye. Coral heard the phone click, checked for the number. It looked like a hotel. She had probably called from a room in the hotel.

So here she was now, racing to make it to the El Capitan before nine, and wondering what exactly she was going to say to Engracia Montoya. She had the money with her, but mostly there was the issue of the gun. Engracia might not reveal the truth about the gun, but maybe Coral could just tell her some of the risks of having it. How much more difficult Immigration would be if she were caught with that gun.

Thank God she was alive.

She figured Father Burns would have told her if something had happened, but he didn't give away much information. Each time she called, he just said that he would give Engracia the message again.

Coral took a shortcut to the back side of the casino, but a fence blocked the road a short ways from the hotel, so she pulled her car onto a patch of gravel and made her way around the fenced area on foot. Construction had stopped so fast on the Strip, when the money dried up a few years ago, that nobody had bothered to even move the trucks or the cranes or the lifts off the lots where the new casinos were to have been built. They just sat there, hulking, rusting beasts, and behind this array of them stood the faded façade of the El Capitan, with its arched entry and its old-fashioned neon and some of the letters missing in the sign: "C–me On In! Ge– Rich!"

The Midnight Cafe was just to the right of the main entry, in an older part of the casino. The whole place looked dilapidated, though the newer half had a tropical 1980s feel, whereas the older part was darker and lower, with wood paneling on the walls and a deep red fabric above it. The cafe sign was an old-fashioned marquee with a 1950s pin-up girl splayed across the letters M-i-d-n-i-g-h-t, and Coral gathered that the room had once been a nightclub. She took a booth on the side, facing the door, so that she would see Engracia when she entered. It was 8:55. Her shift had not yet ended.

Coral looked around to be sure Engracia wasn't there. Then she picked up the heavy leatherette binder that held the menu.

"What'll you have, honey?"

The waitress looked at least sixty, with bouffant hair and a big, smothering bustline and a Southern accent, though she might have lived in Vegas for decades.

"Coffee, please. I'll order when my friend arrives."

"No problem. Cream and sugar?"

"Just cream."

The cafe must have been remodeled shortly before the economic crash. Enormous black-and-white photos ringed the wall; they looked like they might be pictures taken at the El Capitan in its early years. She could see a line of showgirls, a group of men standing around a roulette table, and what might be Del Dibb posing with a little girl and smoking a big cigar.

Coral looked down at the menu. Her stomach did a small flip. She wished that Engracia worked somewhere else. This casino meant nothing to her, and yet in a way, maybe *she* meant something to *it*. She didn't like being in here. Didn't like that photo of Del Dibb.

The menu told the story of the cafe. It had started as a nightspot, the Midnight Room, and in the heyday of the El Capitan, it had been one of the premier clubs in town. Sammy Davis Junior had played there. And Jimmy Durante. Marlene Dietrich had stopped by to see Eddie Knox, and sung a duet with him. They'd kept it a nightclub even after they had expanded the casino, ran small local shows in it: revues of past hits, things like that. After June Dibb retired, her son Marshall had turned the nightclub into a cafe and decorated it with these enormous vintage photos from a starrier past.

Coral looked around for Engracia. It was 9:10. She probably had a time clock to punch.

"More coffee, honey?"

"Sure."

"Want a pastry? Tide you over?"

"No, thanks. She'll be here any minute."

But she wasn't there any minute.

Ten minutes passed, then twenty. It was 9:40. Obviously Engracia wasn't coming. Coral had upended her whole morning, was going to miss Gus's game, and then just sat here, drinking cup after cup of pretty good coffee.

"You sure you don't want something to eat, honey? It's on me. I won't charge you."

"Oh, thank you. No. I'm going to go. I was really hoping my friend was still coming."

"She doesn't have a phone?"

"No. But she works here. She's a maid. Do you know if there's anyone I could ask?"

"Well, you could try Arturo. Over at the cashier desk. This is payday, and a lot of the maids cash their checks when they get off."

"Okay. Thanks."

Coral paid her bill, left a large tip, and walked over to the cashier. Arturo was an old man, wearing a brocaded vest and a shirt with silver tips on the collar.

"Hi. I'm looking for someone who works here. A maid?"

"I might know her. I don't know."

"Her name's Engracia. Engracia Montoya. She got off at nine today?"

Arturo gave her a funny look.

"You know Engracia?"

"Yes. A little. She called me this morning, about five. She asked me to meet her at nine."

"Well, she's gone."

"Oh. Do you know where?"

"She cashed her check."

The man seemed to hesitate.

"I'd really like to see her. I have a gift."

The man looked carefully at Coral. Finally, he spoke.

"She wasn't wearing her uniform. Maybe she's not coming back."

Coral thought about this.

"Because she has to give back her uniform if she quits?"

"Yes. I work here a long time. And the maids cash their checks

with me. But when they're not wearing their blue dresses, sometimes they're not coming back."

"Did you talk with her?"

Arturo was quiet. He looked down as if he was not sure whether
to say something or not.

"Please," Coral said. "I want to help her."

"I don't know anything. She didn't tell me she was leaving.
Maybe she comes back tomorrow."

"Okay. Did she say anything?"

"No. But Engracia and I . . . When I see Engracia, I say a prayer.
We say it together. Because of her son."

Arturo's eyes were very sad, and Coral felt her own throat
tighten. Poor Engracia.

"Thank you. Thanks for your help. My name is Coral. If she
comes back."

"If she comes back," he said.

Coral was about to leave the casino and hike back across the abandoned construction lot to her car when she realized she had left
her sunglasses on the table at the cafe. She walked in, and immediately, the waitress called to her from across the room.

"Your sunglasses?"

"Yes. Did you find them?"

"I have them. On my way. Let me just drop this plate."

Coral turned and looked at the large black-and-white photo
nearest to her. It was Del Dibb, of course, Del Dibb as large as
life, standing with a big grin on his face, his hand resting on the
shoulder of his wife, who was seated in a chair below him. June
Dibb was a slight woman. Coral remembered the one time she'd

seen her, when Augusta took her to Del's funeral: more than thirty years ago, the day she first learned who her father was. June had worn a hat and sunglasses, and Coral still remembered her motionless small foot in a high heel.

She looked at June now, mostly to look away from Del. She was very pretty, with curly, dark hair and a long, pale neck. She sat with one knee crossed over the other, and Coral recognized the slim foot in the high sandal that she had fixated on so many decades before. June had her hands in her lap. She was wearing a big diamond ring. But it was the oddest thing. Her hand was so familiar. It looked exactly like someone else's hand. Like a hand she knew.

And with a sudden, sickening jolt, Coral realized that June's hand looked exactly like her own. Long narrow fingers with wide shell-like nails and the wrist unnaturally thin, the bones on the top of the hand visible and the thumb with its disproportionately large first joint. With something like horror or exaltation or maybe just shock, Coral followed the line of that hand, of those fingers, of June's laughing, delighted face, right to where she was looking: to the third figure in the photo, a man, who looked back at June, and there was no mistaking the feeling in his eyes. The man was Eddie Knox, and here they were: her parents.

37

Engracia had stayed in Las Vegas because she could not leave Diego there alone. Juan had to go back to Mexico. It was dangerous for him in the States. He could end up in jail for much longer than a month. And her mother, her father, her brothers, they had not been able to come to the funeral. Juan had offered to bring them, but it was harder than one imagined it would be. They didn't have passports. They didn't even have identification cards. There was no way to get them there in time. Her mama could not come with a coyote.

So the padre had been there. And Juan. And Engracia. And Mary from the El Capitan, with a whole group of maids. And the man who cashed her check. One of the nurses from the hospital came too. And the mother who had given Diego breakfast each day, and Mateo, the boy with the gun. Pilar drove up from Pomona with Maria and Javier and Oscar. When Pilar saw Engracia, she started to keen: "I'm sorry, I'm so sorry, I should never have told you to go."

And through all of that, Engracia had been numb.

She had said hello and accepted their hugs, and even answered as to whether she had eaten, or whether she was cold in the air conditioning, and as to how beautiful the flowers from the ICU team were. None of it was real.

It had been real in the hospital.

It had been real after she and Juan had said the doctors could stop the machine, after the nurse had explained that Engracia could stay with Diego, could get in the bed and hold her son, but that as soon as he died, as soon as his heart stopped beating, they would have to take him away fast. Because of the organs. Because Juan and Engracia had said they could take their son's organs.

It was Padre Burns who said that would be okay. Who said he thought it would help. He said that child-sized organs were so rare, they would probably keep another child alive. Juan had said no, he would not allow it, but Engracia had said yes. Somewhere there was another mother, so she had said yes.

"No, Engracia. No, not this!" Juan had cried.

"*Si, mi amor. Si.*"

And so she was all by herself in a city she barely knew and hated deeply. Now that Diego was not with her, the street in front of her apartment did not frighten her. The sounds of the sirens, the shouts, people running at night—these felt right now. The world should be falling apart. There should be shouts and sirens and wails in the night. How else could the world be?

At first, she had not been able to imagine returning to the El Capitan. So the padre had found her some work in people's homes. And then there had been the strange day at Ms. Navarro's house, and after that, she had not gone back to those jobs. She wanted to be home with her mama, with Juan—who was fixing her uncle's abandoned house for them. He wanted her to return to Zacatecas, to her village. Juan no longer wanted to have his own business and make a lot of money in the States; he wanted to stay on the dry hot land, grow beans and eat tortillas, and play in a mariachi band as his father had done.

Yet Engracia could not leave Diego, the only American in the family. So she had returned to the El Capitan. She rarely spoke to anyone. She went to Mass every day, and sometimes she went twice. Most days, the padre came and offered her some tea, and they talked about the Mass, or the way it was taking so long to get cold this year, and sometimes, but not enough, they talked about Diego.

But now it was done.

She would have to leave.

She couldn't face the teacher. She didn't want to know anything about Ms. Navarro or her daughter or the man with the gun. She didn't care about a gift. She had called the woman named Coral because the priest had asked her to, and she had agreed to meet with her because she didn't know what else to say. But as soon as she had done it, she knew that she would leave. She would finish her shift, cash her check, and go to Padre Burns. Then she would say good-bye to her son, lie down on his grave and eat some of the dirt, and she would go home. To her mother. To Juan.

A few days later, she stood talking with the padre while a sedan idled nearby.

"I've paid them already," he explained. "They'll take you all the way."

"*Si.*"

"Do you have any money?"

"*Si.*"

"Engracia, I will pray for you every day of my life. Wherever you are, know this. I am praying for you."

"Gracias, padre."

The young woman's eyes filled, and she turned to give him a last hug. Father Burns reached his arms around her, and as he did, he slipped a roll of tightly wound bills covered in a pink casino receipt into the pocket of her coat.

"*Vaya con Dios, amiga. Vaya con Dios.*"

The woman opened the door of the sedan and stepped in. She didn't roll down the window, and she didn't wave good-bye. She was heading south. To her *familia*, to the life she had abandoned, to the row of stucco houses on a dirt road where she would wear a *huipil* and wrap a *reboza* over her shoulders, and where she would stay even if her younger brothers decided to go north. Perhaps there would be a day when nobody who met her would suspect that she had ever left, that she had run away and become a mother and had a son, and left him all alone in *los Estados Unidos.* Padre Burns said that she had not left him: that Diego came with her and would go with her wherever she was, as his blessings for her would, as the grace of Dios would. These things were not geographic.

What she did not yet know was that she and Juan would have another child, and then another. She didn't yet know that her youngest brother would go north and go to college, and then would come home and be the doctor who cared for those children. She didn't know that her papa would die shortly after she arrived in the village, and that she would be with him, and that before he died, he would tell her of his own years in the United States, when she was a little girl, and when all she knew of him was that he sent the money that her mama collected when she made the long walk to Jerez.

He would tell her that if he had been able to write, and that if her mother had been able to read, he could have stayed in the

North. That's why he had insisted Engracia go to school, even when it was such a long walk, even when her mother needed her help at home. It had been too hard to be away from his *esposa* and his daughter all those years, to rely on the news that came from other Zacatecans—news passed from one to another, shared carefully with everyone who might someday meet someone who wanted to know. He had not been able to do it. He had been ashamed to come home, to not have enough money, but he was glad he had done so.

He had said that Engracia belonged to this land as well. He wished that he could stay longer and help her to know this. But now he was going to meet his grandson, and he would hold Diego for her. He would make sure her son knew how much he was loved. He and Diego would have some fun.

38

Today I had a brain scan. An MRI.

It was Marshall's idea, of course. I have seen lots of doctors, and they suggest different diagnoses. Alzheimer's. Senility. A form of Parkinson's. I don't quite fit any of these. Aphasia. For sure, I have aphasia, though I am not sure Marshall or the doctors understand this as clearly as I do.

Anyway, there is a new clinic in town. A brain center. And Marshall has given them money in my name, and now I have to do more tests. With the brain doctors. Though I've been seeing doctors all along. I don't mind, if it makes Marshall feel better, though I don't think these tests are going to help. Maybe there is a medicine for me, but it seems more likely that I'll be one of the ones that help the doctors figure things out for the next generation. That's okay. That pleases me.

I had a good life. A long life. And we all have to die.

I don't want to die, though. I wish I could have been like my Aunt Ruth, who died last year at ninety-nine and lived on her own, without help, until just before. But Ruth was extraordinary. Most of us aren't like Ruth. I'm not. It's a funny thing. To know there is nothing left but to die. To know that one has already gotten the good life, already missed all the things that might lead to an early death, and still, for life to seem so short. Still to want more. Even with an existence like mine. When I can't do anything I mean to do. When I spend my days with people who are paid to take care of me. Yet I still like it. Living, I mean.

I still hear the birds sing. I still notice the sunlight dappled on the table, the way the light moves when the leaves tremble. I still love music. I still have memories. I dream. In my dreams, I sometimes see them all. Del and my father and my mother. Marshall and a tiny, pink-swathed girl. Even if I am not dreaming, even when I am just remembering, it's all so vivid. My life comes back strongly. So many sounds: music and laughter and tears and Marshall's toddler voice: "This way, Mommy! Let's go this way." The feelings come back. All of them. Excitement and rage and contentment and fear. I'm not ready to give it up. I don't suppose I ever will be. And even now, it still seems like there must be something I could do, there must be some way to slow it down. But of course there's not. There never was.

Helen took me to the appointment. We had to be there early, before seven. And Helen couldn't figure out how to get into the place, though we could see it from a long way off. A bizarre, curving building, with a metal roof folded in on itself, and the walls appearing to tip, as if it were all about to slide, or implode, or collapse upon itself. No wonder Helen couldn't figure out how to get to it. It was disorienting to look at. Which is kind of funny, for a brain center. Like when some of the newer casinos piped in oxygen to get rid of the smell of cigarette smoke, they said, but really, because it made people feel good, and so it was just one more way to keep them inside the place. Maybe this crazy-looking building makes its patients feel a bit crazy, like they belong there more than they had thought they did. I laughed, and Helen said,

"It's not funny. Marshall told me not to be late." Which, of course, was funny to me.

The technician took me into a little room with Helen, and explained that I would have to wear nothing but the robe, and that the most important thing was for me not to move during the testing. Was I claustrophobic? Had the doctor given me something to take? What time had I taken it? Helen explained that I had taken something to relax me at six—I didn't know that—and also that it was best for him not to tell me what to do. It would be better not to give me instructions. Maybe it had something to do with whatever Helen had given me at six, but this made me laugh too. It was true, of course. Giving me instructions was a disaster. But then, my mother would have said the same thing. I laughed and laughed. Helen looked a bit exasperated; she was still upset about not being able to find her way into the parking lot, and the technician started reading the notes on his clipboard. Maybe it was notes about me; he stopped telling me what to do.

His name was Ahmad, and he helped me lie down on a narrow table in a room that was glaringly white, and he placed my head on a pillow, and fit some earphones over my ears, and put something in my hand to hold. It was all very easy. My body didn't jerk or cramp. I just lay there and he silently positioned me, and pulled a sort of metal frame over my head. Then I heard a small motor, and the bed on which I was lying slid slowly backward until I was encased in a white tube.

"Mrs. Dibb, are you feeling all right?"

The voice came through the earphones, but I did not reply. I felt sort of woozy, like I was about to fall asleep.

"This first test will last about thirty seconds, and you'll hear some funny noises. Okay?"

It sounded like a lawnmower, swooshing toward me and back, not quite touching my toes.

"Good, Mrs. Dibb. Thank you. This next test is longer. It's the longest one. It will take nine minutes and thirty seconds."

He gave such oddly specific times. As if I had a watch or could see a clock. All I saw was white. A white metal frame twelve inches above my head, and, beyond that, a white metal tube, like being inside a fluorescent bulb.

The nine-minute test was a spring being sprung—*twang thump*—at regular intervals, and I imagined a circus tent lifting slowly into the air, each *twang thump* the sound of another tether breaking loose. *Twang thump*, and a red-striped corner lifts. *Twang thump*, I can see sky beneath the flapping section. *Twang thump*, the fabric dances in the wind. *Twang thump*, round and round the tent, until finally, nine minutes and twenty-seven seconds later, the tent lifts: a soaring, spinning candy cane sphere, bright against the blue sky. And just before Ahmad asks how I am doing, I see a little girl, dark-haired as I was, looking up and pointing at the sight.

The other tests are less relaxing. For four minutes, there is a high-pitched series of whirs and clicks that remind me of my grandson playing video games at the beach house, and then there are three or four more tests, all identified for me by their duration: this one three minutes and thirty seconds, that one forty-five seconds, the next one five minutes. I have lived long enough to hear the sound of magnets taking photos of my brain, and I am pleased about this, and I wish I could live longer, to see all of the other things we will discover.

Afterward, I am very tired. Helen takes me home, and I go to the sunroom, where I like to take a nap in the afternoons. I don't know how long I'm there, a few minutes, a few hours, but I wake to the sound of the doorbell ringing, and then of Helen telling someone—someone she doesn't recognize, I can tell—that I am not available, that I do not take callers without an appointment, that the woman can call my son, Marshall, if she wishes to see me.

"Please. My name's Coral. I just want to say hello. I think she'll want to see me."

"No. I've asked you to leave, and if I have to, I'll call the police."

"Of course. I understand. You're doing your job, and I know Ms. Dibb is not well, I know I'm asking a lot. It's just, I really want to see her. And I think she'll want to see me."

By this time, I have gotten up and headed for the door. Whatever Helen gave me this morning makes me loopy, but it also seems to help me do what I want. I crack sharply into a hutch. Well, at least it sort of helps me. I am headed to the door, if not in a very direct way.

"Oh! Oh! Oh!" I call.

"Miss June, it's okay. You're all right. There's nothing you need to worry about out here."

Helen is annoyed. At me, at whoever is at the door.

"Oh!" I call louder.

"Ma'am, you'll have to go. I'm busy."

I can't see what is happening, but I don't hear the door close. I can't hear what the woman who is there says.

"*Let it snow, let it snow, let it snow,*" I sing, bizarrely.

"Everything's all right, Miss June. I'm coming."

"*Rockin' robin. Tweet, tweet, tweet! Rockin' robin.*" I am coming full speed now. I've taken a route through the dining room, instead of straight to the front door, but the singing is helping me get there.

"*Hopping and a-bopping and a-singing his song.*"

I come around the corner and catch sight of my visitor. She's a black woman, maybe fifty, wearing a well-cut suit and good shoes and holding a leather bag. I don't know her, which is disappointing, because I thought she said I would want to see her.

"There was no reason to get up," Helen says to me.

"Hello, Mrs. Dibb," says the woman in a strangely strained way.

"*Tweet, tweet, tweet!*" I sing.

The woman looks toward Helen, who isn't about to explain anything to her. Helen tells me to go back to the sunroom—I really don't like Helen very much—and then she tells the woman that I have had a very long morning and cannot be disturbed.

"I'm sorry to bother you. I'd like to come back. Maybe another day this week? I'd just like to talk with Mrs. Dibb for a little bit."

"I told you to contact Mrs. Dibb's son. If he says it's okay, then that will be fine."

I flail my right arm wildly, and it knocks against the entryway table, which hurts, and which also causes a picture frame that is standing there to fall over. Helen comes over to steady me, and the woman looks at me intently. I think about Matt, I think about him singing "S'wonderful," and the way the sun helps me stretch when we do our therapy sessions outside. I concentrate on Matt as hard as I can, and sure enough, I say what I want to say.

"Please stay. Please stay now."

"Miss June, I don't think that's a good idea."

"Helen, go in the kitchen."

"I'll stay with you, Miss June."

"No!"

My voice is sharp, and the woman listens to the two of us quietly, without saying anything, and then she says, "What about if Mrs. Dibb and I just sit down, right over there? Mrs. Dibb?"

And she reaches out her hand, and I take it, and, miraculously, we just walk over to the two chairs arranged by the fireplace, and I sit down, without a jolt or a jerk or a pull in the wrong direction. The woman holds my hand lightly, but she does not let it go when I sit down. She looks at it; she looks at my hand as if it means something to her, so I look at it, and I look at hers, darker than mine, but similarly long and slender. We both have shell-shaped nails. I never liked my nails, but they look sort of nice on her.

Helen rustles over, impatience brimming.

"Tea," I say.

I'm feeling really proud of myself, which is a mistake, because it will almost certainly put an end to this little moment where my body seems to be listening to me. The woman sits down in the chair next to mine.

"My name's Coral Jackson. I teach choir at Foothill High School."

Oh darn. I hope she's not here to ask for money.

"But that lucky old sun got nothin' to do but roll around heaven all day." I'd rather sing than talk about money. If I wanted to do something with my money, I wouldn't be able to do it. Marshall handles all that, and I can't even tell him that I want a bite of dinner.

I've already stopped thinking about Coral Jackson, but she surprises me by picking up my song.

"Fuss with my woman, toil for my kids, sweat 'til I'm wrinkled and gray."

She has a beautiful voice. Beautiful. I stomp my feet and shake my head a bit. And she keeps singing.

"While that lucky old sun has nothin' to do, but roll around heaven all day."

"Roll around heaven all day," I sing back.

She smiles.

"I'm sorry to come without calling. I was going to call your son, Marshall."

She knows Marshall.

"But . . . but I . . . I didn't do it."

Is this about Marshall? Is he okay? How does she know Marshall?

"I mean, I will call him. I'm happy to call him and tell him that I want to visit you. I just . . . I was nearby. I just stopped."

I wish she would sing again. I try. *"Would you like to swing on a star? Carry moonbeams home in a jar?"*

Something about my singing bothers her. I see her lip tremble, and her forehead crease. She looks down at her hands.

"My mother is Augusta Jackson."

It's a familiar name. But, of course, there could be a lot of Augusta Jacksons. Who was Augusta?

"She worked for your husband a long time ago."

Augusta Jackson! Of course. Ray's wife.

"No, no, no," I say, nodding my head and smiling.

"You remember her?"

She understands that I meant yes. This is Augusta's daughter. She's coming to say thank you. All those years that Del took care of that family. And Leo kept it up after, whatever it was that Del had arranged.

"My mother told me a story."

It's nice of her to come and see me, an old woman. I wonder if Augusta's still alive. She was about my age. A little older, maybe.

"She told me a story about your husband."

Are those tears? There are tears running down Coral Jackson's face. But she keeps talking, as if they aren't even there.

"It was 1960."

So Augusta's daughter is a teacher. She dresses nicely for a teacher. It's great to think that Del helped her somehow. He loved Ray so much. This must be Ray's youngest, the one that was the same age as Marshall.

The woman is looking down at her lap. She seems to be having trouble speaking. I want to pat her on the knee, tell her it was really so little. That money. She shouldn't feel a debt, because her father had been so important to Del. Del would have given Ray much more than that if he'd lived. And also, nobody had ever really known what happened when Ray died.

I don't like to think of those days. How naïve I was. How little I understood. I sing to stop thinking.

"Ol' man river. That old man river. He just keeps rolling. He just keeps rolling along."

She doesn't join me this time.

She keeps looking down, and I can hear the teakettle whistling, and I know Helen is making some tea for us.

"I get weary, and sick of trying. I'm tired of living, and feared of dying."

I hear Helen pick it up in the kitchen. She can sing too, though she almost never sings with me. *"And ol' man river, he just keeps rolling along."*

The woman looks up. She is clearly crying; she seems really upset. I feel bad for her, and I want so much to tell her that it is okay. That things will be okay. Whatever is wrong. Things will work out. I really believe that. If you just get lucky and stay alive, a lot of things work out.

"Augusta wasn't really my mother."

I wish I could nod my head, look like I'm listening to her. I am listening, but for some reason, I have decided to do a little bebop rhythm in my chair. My shoulders are shaking, and my head is bobbing, and I feel lucky just to be able to see her face out of the corner of my eye.

"Odell Dibb brought me to her as a baby. When I was just a few days old."

What?

"He didn't tell my mother . . . Augusta . . . where I came from. He just asked her to take care of me."

I have flung myself out of the chair, and I am banging my head against the fireplace. Helen comes running.

"What's going on here? Miss June, stop! What did you say to her?"

Coral Jackson is on her feet, and she is trying to capture me in her arms, she is trying to keep me from banging my head—pound, pound—on the wall. My head really hurts, and my stomach is sick, and I can't get my body to stop convulsing, but I am trying to look at her, I am trying to look at Coral Jackson. Coral! Of course. Coral!

Helen comes and pushes Coral out of the way.

"You need to leave. You need to leave this house right away!"

And I can hear Coral trying to catch her breath, crying, and saying, "I'm sorry. I'm so, so sorry. I just had to see you. I've been looking—"

And at that, I wrench myself away from Helen, and just by accident, I am facing Coral, I am looking at my daughter, at the person I never once stopped dreaming about, at the person I did not think I would ever see, and I can't say anything I want to say, I can't control my expression, I can't tell her in any way how fervently I hunted for her, how I didn't know where to look, how Del died, how she wasn't in Alabama, how there was no one to ask. How I hoped. Until there was nothing left to hope for. Until I could not imagine any wild, serendipitous, impossible way that I could find her. How had she found me? And really, how could it be that I would never be able to tell her how much I had wanted to find her?

Tears stream down her face, and I can see that she is about to leave. That she doesn't know what else to do. That it is all too much. And I think of Eddie, her father, and how she looks more like me than like him. But her voice. It's beautiful. She has Eddie's voice.

"In this world of hope, in this world of fear."

Just like that, the song comes to me.

"I'll be your rock. And you'll be my cheer. Every moment with you is so dear."

Eddie's song.

She knows it.

I see it on her face. She knows the song. She knows why I am singing it. She knows that I know.

And like that, my daughter steps forward and takes my wayward, truculent, unruly body into her arms.

So that we can dance.

ACKNOWLEDGMENTS

The correct answer to who made it possible to write this book is everyone I ever loved, and everyone who ever loved me. My editor, wise soul, suggests I make the list a bit shorter.

So I'll start at the top of the marquee. My husband, Bill Yaffe, for his great stores of patience, kindness, and humor (I noticed). And my editor, Trish Todd, for her counsel, her insight, and her commitment. Without her, no dream comes true.

There are others. My spirited agent Stephanie Cabot. All the cool kids at Touchstone—*if this is our ride, then my hands are up and my eyes wide open*—especially Susan Moldow, Tara Parsons, David Falk, Shida Carr, Kelsey Manning, Meredith Vilarello, Kaitlin Olson, Leah Morse, Cherlynne Li, Loretta Denner, and Philip Bashe (plus a coolest-of-all button for Wendy Sheanin). Those brave first readers: Jamie Jadid, Jodi McBride, Deb Newman, Vicki McBride, Randee Kelley, Tracy Conley, and Maya McBride. The College of Southern Nevada, for championing my journey. Dawn Stuart, whose Books In Common so enriched my author life. The Gernert Company, particularly Ellen Coughtrey. For meaningful favors: Grace McBride, Yolanda Hernandez, and Third Chan. And for delighting me: Leah Deborah and Noah Max.

To publish a novel is to find oneself suddenly immersed in a new world. To the readers who shared their deeply felt experiences. To the authors, who encouraged and allowed and celebrated, without hesitation. (In particular, Joanna Rakoff, Patry Francis, Margot Livesey.) And to the booksellers, those fairy godparents. Thank you. Two small words that do not begin to say all I feel.

ABOUT THE AUTHOR

Laura McBride is also the author of *We Are Called to Rise*. A graduate of Yale and a Yaddo fellow, she teaches at the College of Southern Nevada and lives in Las Vegas with her family.

IN THE MIDNIGHT ROOM

Spanning the six decades during which Las Vegas grows from a dusty whistle-stop into a melting-pot metropolis, *In the Midnight Room* tells the story of four women whose lives intertwine after each experiences a transformative moment in the El Capitan nightclub in Las Vegas.

FOR DISCUSSION

1. Describe the El Capitan. What does June love about it? How and why is it significant to the other characters in this novel? Does the nightclub change over time?

2. Why do you think McBride introduces the principal characters as falling in love, getting lucky, and so on? How do those descriptions affect your reading of their stories?

3. When June Stein first appears, the narrator says, "She was bad for the neighborhood. Things happened to other girls because of June Stein." What were your initial impressions of June? Did you like her? Were you surprised by the way her story ends?

4. At the end of June's section, Del examines the choices he made. What were they? Were they bad?

5. When Honorata arrived in the United States, she thought, "The Honorata who had lived in Manila did not exist anymore." How has she changed?

6. Augusta tells Coral: "'Life is long. There's a lot of ways for a secret to come out.'" What secret has Augusta been keeping? Do you agree with her decision to do so?

7. When Coral tells Ada she's afraid to share news of her pregnancy, Ada instructs her to "'give up that . . . Coral thing. That everything-has-to-be-right, my-life-isn't-messy thing.'" Do you think Coral is a perfectionist, needing to control everything around her? How have her experiences shaped her? Why is she afraid to tell Koji about her pregnancy?

8. Nanay tells Honorata that Malaya is "'an American,'" who "'should do American things.'" What does she mean? Do you think Malaya and Honorata are alike despite coming of age in different cultures?

9. In the aftermath of June's pregnancy, she believes that "Del was not the one who had made the mistake. It was not Del who had risked Marshall's world." Do you agree? What mistakes have been made? How does Del handle this situation?

10. Do you think Del's actions are justified? What effect do they have on both Del and June?

11. Coral sees her relationship with Gerald as "a private shame." Do you think any of the romantic relationships in this novel are healthy?

12. Cora believes that, ultimately, marrying Del "was going to be the best decision June ever made." Do you agree? Is June's marriage to Del beneficial to her? Did you find any aspects of their relationship surprising?

13. Moving to Las Vegas was "not the hardest thing [Engracia] had done. It was easy to do hard things for her son." What other sacrifices, if any, does Engracia make for him? Do you think she's a good mother? Do any of the other characters make sacrifices for their children? Were there any that you found particularly moving?

14. Once Coral was older, "she sometimes imagined Odell Dibb differently than Augusta had described him." What did you think of Odell? Did you like him?

15. Eddie, speaking to June about their relationship, says, "'For you, it's fun. For me, it's the end.'" Is the friendship dangerous for each of them? Do they also support each other?

16. In chapter 26, the narration switches from third person to first, with June telling her own story. What is the effect of the change in narration? Why do you think McBride does it?

17. Why does Coral choose to share the story of her upbringing with Malaya? Does it help Malaya? What effect does sharing the story have on Coral?

ENHANCE YOUR BOOK CLUB

1. When Augusta asked Coral to host the family Christmas celebration, telling Coral that hosting was becoming too much for her, "Coral knew that this wasn't true. Moving Christmas to her house was Augusta's way of anointing Coral's home." Why is it important that Augusta anoint Coral's home? Who hosts major holiday meals in your family?

2. Read *We Are Called to Rise* with your book club and compare it to *In the Midnight Room*. Has the author's writing style changed since the release of her first novel?

3. Las Vegas has occupied a special place in American mythology. To June, "Las Vegas was the future." For Honorata, it is the first place in the United States she has been treated with kindness and where she can make a home. Have you visited Las Vegas? If so, what are your impressions of it? And, if not, how do you imagine it?

4. To learn more about Laura McBride and read more about her other books, visit her website, http://lauramcbrideauthor .com/.

A CONVERSATION WITH
LAURA McBRIDE

Your first novel, *We Are Called to Rise*, was a critical success. *Booklist* proclaimed you "without question . . . a truly commanding literary presence." Did you feel added pressure while writing your second novel? If so, how did you handle it?

There were times when I wondered if I would have the persistence to write another novel, and days when I worried that I had charged into the story without giving it enough consideration in advance. Looking back, I see those were confidence fears. In fact, I'm dogged when I want something, and I had considered many possible stories, some at length, before feeling electrified about this one.

When the novel clicked together in my head—that I would use these characters, that the plot would develop in this particular way—I was just racing to get it on paper. I couldn't write fast enough or get enough writing time to lay it down while it was all in my mind. That was the pressure that never left me through the whole writing period: this thrum of anxiety that I might not have enough time to write it out, or to go back and make of it what I wanted.

We Are Called to Rise **has been a book club favorite since it was published, and you often speak to book clubs. What have you found most rewarding about that?**

I love the stories readers share with me—of their children,

their losses, their hopes. It's quite moving, the way that talking about a book can catapult people into these honest and personal revelations. It's a privilege. Also, book group folk are nice. I am showered with compliments, which is not at all good for one, but feels wonderful. And many book groups serve dessert.

Can you tell us about your writing process? When you started writing this novel, did you know how all of the characters' stories would fit together?

I had a short period to get the book going, and then I had to write it in all these weird moments and places: on planes, in hotel rooms, between classes. And it drove me crazy not to be able to concentrate for long periods of time in a quiet place. But in the end, it still got written. Which feels unbelievable to me. I half expect to wake up and find I never did finish that novel.

In general, though, I like to have a strong conception of the story before I begin. I want to know the first page and the last page, and I want to know some of the ways that it is going to get from the one to the other. Writing something as long as a novel is a process of discovery—characters and circumstances grow—but I choose to twist those curling vines around a strong branch. So while I had a plan and a conception for the whole story, I also followed the book where it led. I let the characters evolve, I let the plot change course. That's the fun of it, really.

Do you have any advice for aspiring writers? Is there anything that you wish you had been told at the start of your writing career?

I wish that I had not abandoned writing when I was younger and waited until I was fifty to take it up again. I quit because I didn't see a path to publication. I thought about what I was doing as "writing a book," and if I couldn't get that book produced and into the world, I didn't see the value in doing it. So I stopped writing and turned outward. I started teaching, I did a lot of volunteer work, I focused on my community.

When I'm in the thick of a story, when I'm writing feverishly and surely and intuitively, I am a pure form of myself. I'm both conscious and unconscious of what I'm doing, like a basketball player in the zone. Perhaps we aren't blank slates when we are born, perhaps we inherit certain kinds of knowledge—as salmon born in a particular river do—and given the chance to be the people we are born to be, we should take it. I turned my back on the person my seven-year-old self knew I was, and I wish I hadn't.

I hope I haven't given the wrong impression. I don't mean that my writing is inspired or even good; I mean that it's part of me, that it's natural to me, that I knew I could do it as soon as I was introduced to words on the page. I have always made sense of the world through story.

So, my advice. Write if you love it. Write if it's your natural gift. Write if it makes you feel as if you are in a conversation with the ages. But don't write for publication. Don't write for anyone else at all. These things are out of your control, and they poison the well.

Your descriptions of Las Vegas are so vivid that it becomes another character in the book. Did you base any of the descriptions of the city and its inhabitants on people or things that you encountered? Did you conduct any research to create the historical scenes?

Well, I call my research a novelist's research, which means that I read idly and listen in on conversations that are not my own and ask people random questions about the details of things they have casually mentioned. I think my friends are on to me—they suspiciously say, "Is this going in a novel?"

I've lived in Las Vegas for three decades, and in a city that has changed as much as this one has in that time, that's a lot of acquired but not necessarily verifiable information. So I often write from what I think I know, and later I try to verify that my memories are correct (they aren't always), and I try not to let this whole question of perfect accuracy get in my head. I want my novels to be grounded in truth, but they aren't textbooks; and as a fiction writer, I am seeking the subjective, not objective, view.

Joanna Rakoff praised this book, saying "I'm not one to pull out the term 'Great American Novel,' but Laura McBride's sublime book demands nothing less." Were you inspired by any "Great American Novels" when you were writing? Can you tell us about them?

I think that anything I could say in response to such a glorious comment would just be piling on. But I love that you asked me a question that included it. I wish everyone would ask me a question that included Joanna's comment. If I get to meet her in person, I'm going to give her a crushing hug.

Your second book spans many generations and many points of view. Was it difficult to switch between time periods and characters' viewpoints as you were writing? Did you write the characters' sections consecutively?

I wrote the story in the order one reads it, and the structure of this novel allowed me to generally be in one character's head at a time.

I did spend a lot of time trying to immerse myself in the particular area of the Philippines where Honorata grew up, and in the area of Mexico Engracia is from. I wrote pages and pages based on these explorations, and then deleted nearly all of them. That writing was self-conscious in its effort to prove I knew what I was writing about. It interrupted the story; those painstakingly acquired details were things the characters would neither notice nor report. So I would have four or five pages that took me a week to put together, and I would keep one tiny detail about the sound of a particular frog, and be back to the story in my head.

I finally just had to laugh about it. Working that hard freed me. Knowing that information, even if I didn't include it, gave me the confidence to keep imagining. It's really scary to write about the other—and a novelist has no choice but to do so. The essence of fiction, to my way of thinking, is the empathetic journey that writer and reader take. But making that imaginative leap into an other requires an assertion of the self that I, and perhaps many women, have learned to quell. The decision to write about people whose lives are different from mine was daunting. I could only begin by accepting that I might fail.

What would you like your readers to take away from this book?

I hope it's a pleasure to read. I hope they care about the characters and immerse themselves in an imagined world. That's what I was doing. I was caught by the idea of these four women: one rich, one poor, two American-born, two immigrants, four mothers. (Actually, I wanted Coral not to have children; I didn't want four mothers, but the life that she happened to live without children took me down a different path and away from this story, so I rewrote it.)

I wanted to write about the intensity and intimacy of women's lives; I wanted to capture some of those voices I hear when I walk in the park, talk with people in my college, or work on a community project. I'm interested in experiences that are different from mine, in people who see the world differently, and who believe things that counter my own beliefs. In the world of possible questions, I like *why*.

Is there anything that you have found particularly gratifying?

On my end, I could hardly breathe for wondering what my editor would think. It was inexpressibly thrilling to have her first response be, "Thank you very much for writing a new novel, and thank you extremely much for writing this one."

I didn't know that I would be even more thrilled the second time, or that I would have an even clearer sense of how lucky I am to have this creative opportunity. All through writing this book, I told myself that lightning doesn't strike twice, that the act of writing was the point, and that I must not count on anyone wanting to read it. I think that was a legitimate way to think about what I was doing, and yet, lightning did strike twice.

Are you working on anything now? Can you tell us about it?

I hope so! I'm answering this question eight months before my second book comes out, and at this point, I'm not much past daydreaming. I spent the summer plotting out a new book, but I think I've dropped that idea. For me, preparing to write happens on two levels: I have to choose the story and I have to make a plan for when I will write the book. It's hard to predict how long the first takes—I'm letting my mind spin and trusting that the characters and the situation will emerge—but I have a plan for the second. I'll be ready to go when the story hits!

TURN THE PAGE TO READ
AN EXCERPT FROM

LAURA MCBRIDE'S

We Are
Called
to Rise

1

Avis

THERE WAS A YEAR of no desire. I don't know why. Margo said I
was depressed; Jill thought it was "the change." That phrase made
me laugh. I didn't think I was depressed. I still grinned when I
saw the roadrunner waiting to join me on my morning walk. I still
stopped to look at the sky when fat clouds piled up against the
blue, or in the evenings when it streaked orange and purple in the
west. Those moments did not feel like depression.

But I didn't desire my husband, and there was no certain reason
for it, and as the months went by, the distance between us grew.
I tried to talk myself out of this, but my body would not comply.
Finally, I decided to rely on what in my case would be mother wisdom, or as Sharlene would say, "to fake it till you make it."

That night, I eased myself out of bed carefully, not wanting
to fully wake Jim. I had grown up in Las Vegas, grown up seeing women prance around in sparkling underwear, learned how to
do the same prancing in the same underwear when I was barely
fifteen, but years of living in another Las Vegas, decades of being
a suburban wife, a mother, a woman of a certain social standing,

had left me uneasy with sequined bras and crotchless panties. My naughty-underwear drawer was still there—the long narrow one on the left side of my dresser—but I couldn't even remember the last time I had opened it. My heart skipped a little when I imagined slipping on a black lace corset and kneeling over Jim in bed. Well, I had made a decision, and I was going to do it. I would not give up on twenty-nine years of marriage without at least trying this.

So I padded quietly over to the dresser, and eased open the narrow drawer. I was expecting the bits of lace and satin, even sequins, but nestled among them, obscenely, was a gun. It made me gasp. How had a gun gotten in this drawer?

I recognized it, though. Jim had given it to me when Emily was a baby. He had insisted that I keep a gun. Because he traveled. Because someone might break in. I had tried to explain that I would never use it. I wouldn't aim a gun at someone any more than I would drown a kitten. There were decisions I had made about my life a long time ago; firing a gun was on that list. But there were things Jim could not hear me say, and in the end, it was easier just to accept the gun, just to let him hide it in one of those silly fake books on the third shelf of the closet, where, if I had thought about it—and I never did—I would have assumed it still was.

How long had the gun been in this drawer? Had Jim put it there? Was he sending a message? Had Jim wanted to make the point that I hadn't looked in this drawer for years? Hadn't worn red-sequined panties in years? Had Jim been thinking the same way I had, that maybe what we needed was a little romance, a little fun, a little hot sex in the middle of the kitchen, in order to start over?

I could hear Jim stirring behind me. He would be looking at me, naked in front of our sex drawer. Things weren't going exactly the way I had intended, but I shook my bottom a little, just to give him a hint at what I was doing.

He coughed.

I stopped then, not sure what that cough meant. I didn't even want to touch the gun, but I carefully eased the closest bit of satin out from under the barrel, still thinking that I would find a way to slip it on and maybe dance my way back to the bed.

"I'm in love with Darcy. We've been seeing each other for a while."

It was like the gun had gone off. There I was, naked, having just wagged my fifty-three-year-old ass, and there he was, somewhere behind me, knowing what I had been about to do, confessing to an affair with a woman in his office who was almost young enough to be our daughter.

Was he confessing to an affair? Had he just said he was in love with her? The room melted around me. Something—shock, humiliation, disbelief—perhaps just the sudden image of Darcy's young bottom juxtaposed against the image I had of my own bottom in the hall mirror—punched the air out of me.

"I wanted to tell you. I know I should have told you."

Surely, this was not happening. Jim? Jim was having an affair with Darcy? (Or had he said he was in love?) Like the fragment of an old song, my mother's voice played in my mind. "Always leave first, Avis. Get the hell out before they get the hell out on you." That was Sharlene's mantra: get the hell out first. She'd even said it to me on my wedding day. It wasn't the least surprising that she'd said it, but still, I had resented that comment for years. And, look, here she was: right. It took twenty-nine years. Two kids. A lot of pain. But Sharlene had been right.

It all came rushing in then. Emily. And Nate. And the years with

Sharlene. The hard years. The good years. Why Jim had seemed so distant. The shock of Jim's words, as I stood there, still naked, still with my back to my husband, my ass burning with shame, brought it all rushing in. So many feelings I had been trying not to feel. It seemed suddenly that the way I had been trying to explain things to myself—the way I had pretended the coolness in my marriage was just a bad patch; the way I had kept rejecting the signs that something was wrong with Nate, that Nate had changed, that I was afraid for Nate (afraid *of* Nate?); the way that getting older bothered me, though I was trying not to care, trying not to notice that nobody noticed me, trying not to be anything like Sharlene— it seemed suddenly that all of that, all of those emotions and all of that pretending, just came rushing toward me, a torpedo of shame and failure and fear. Jim was in love with Darcy. My son had come back from Iraq a different man. My crazy mother had been right. And my whole life, how hard I had tried, had come to this. I could not bear for Jim to see what I was feeling.

How could I possibly turn around?

I AM NINE YEARS OLD, and inspecting the bathtub before getting in. I ignore the brown gunk caked around the spigot, and the yellow tear-shaped stain spreading out from the drain; I can't do much about those. No, I am looking for anything that moves, and the seriousness with which I undertake this task masks the sound of my mother entering, a good hour before I expect her home from work.

"Yep. You sure have got the Briggs girl ass. That'll come in handy some day."

She laughs, like she has said something funny. I am frustrated that my mother has walked in the bathroom without knocking, and I don't want to think about what she has just said. I step in the bathtub quick, bugs or not, and pull the plastic shower curtain closed.

"Should you be taking a bath? What if Rodney walked away?"

"He won't," I say, miffed that she is criticizing my babysitting skills. "He's watching *Gilligan's Island*."

"Okay," she says, and I hear her move out of the bathroom and toward the kitchen. She is going to make a peanut butter and banana sandwich. Sharlene is twenty-seven years old, and she loves peanut butter and banana sandwiches.

"I'M SORRY, AVIS. I NEVER wanted to hurt you."

I was still standing naked at the drawer, my back to Jim, the red satin fabric in my hand. I didn't know what to say to that. I couldn't seem to think straight, I couldn't seem to keep my mind on what was happening right that moment. Did Jim just say he was in love with Darcy? Why had I opened this drawer?

And still I was racing toward Jim's apology, grateful for it, hopeful. One of the first things I ever knew about Jim was that he was willing to apologize.

I AM TWENTY-ONE YEARS OLD, and working at the front desk of the Golden Nugget casino. It's taken years to get where I am, years to extricate myself from Sharlene, years to create the quiet, orderly life that means so much to me. That day, Jim is just one more man flirting with the front desk clerk, one more moderately drunk tourist wanting to know if I am free that evening; I barely register that he has said he will be back for a real conversation at four. And, of course, he is not back. But at ten to five, he rushes up, carrying a bar of chocolate, and tickets to *Siegfried and Roy* at the Frontier. I hear his very first apology.

"I'm sorry. I know you thought I wasn't serious, but I was. I couldn't get here at four. I was hitting numbers at the craps table, and if I'd left, I would have caused a small riot. Please forgive me. You don't even have to go to the show with me. You can take a friend."

That's how he apologized. All straightforward and a bit flustered and as if he meant it, as if I were someone who deserved better from him.

I WAS WONDERING WHY THE gun was in the drawer. I was thinking that I would have to turn around. I was acutely aware of being naked. I didn't know which one of those problems to address first. Turning around. Being naked. Figuring out how the gun got in the drawer. And, of course, none of those were the real problem.

"I didn't mean to fall in love with her. It just happened. We've been spending a lot of time together at work. You've been so distant. I don't know. I didn't plan it."

He just kept talking. He seemed to think that I was listening. That he should talk. As if the fact that he didn't plan it could make it better. He said he was in love with her. Was that supposed to make me feel better? I wanted to get angry—I wanted to grab at the lifeboat of anger—but instead, my mind kept repeating—*cover your ass, where did the gun come from, always get the hell out first, did he say he was in love*—as if I were on some whirling psychotropic trip.

I AM SEVEN YEARS OLD, and Sharlene and Rodney and I have been living in and out of Steve's brown Thunderbird for a year. We fill the tank with gas whenever my mom can pick someone's pocket or Steve can sell some dope, and then get back on the road, driving until we are almost out of gas, until Sharlene sees a place where we can camp without the cops catching us, where there is a park bathroom we can use if we are careful not to be seen. We have criss-crossed the country, even driven into Canada. That was a mistake, because the border patrol might have stopped us. But they didn't.

The craziest thing about that year in Steve's car is that there are thousands of dollars crammed under the front seats. Steve has stolen the money, stolen it from a casino, and we are on the lam because he is afraid of getting killed, because he knows the owner of the casino will have him killed the instant he knows where he is, and Steve has decided the bills are marked, that the casino owner—some guy Steve calls Big Sandy—has written down the numbers on the bills and has banks looking for them. So he is afraid to spend any of it, not one dollar of it. Even when we are hungry, even when Rodney cries and cries because his ear hurts, Steve does not give in; he does not spend any of that cash, any of those bills. They sometimes waft up when the car's windows are open, and Rodney and I try to catch them, and Steve slams on the brakes and swerves the car and screams at us that not one bill can fly out the window.

"AVIS, I'VE BEEN TRYING TO figure out how to tell you. I didn't mean for it to be like this. I didn't mean . . ."

His voice trailed off. He didn't mean for me to be stark naked and totally exposed when he told me? Then why had he told me?

Oh, yeah, things were about to get awkward.

Awkward if you were in love with your girlfriend.

I lifted my hand to put the bit of satin back in the drawer, and I touched my fingers to the cold, hard metal of the gun barrel. I had never liked guns. I was afraid of them. Afraid of the people who had them.

IT TAKES SHARLENE A LONG time, all of the year I might have been in second grade, but finally she has had enough. She waits until Steve is passed out stoned, and then she grabs huge fistfuls of the cash under the seats, and she grabs us—I remember being grateful that she had grabbed us, that she had not left us with Steve—and we walk to an all-night diner. We hitch a ride with a truck driver, and after Sharlene and the truck driver are done in the bed in the back of the cab, we get a real hotel room, and a shower. Sharlene stays in that shower until the water goes cold, and each time that the water warms up, she showers some more, and after a night and a day and a night of her showering—with Rodney and me watching television sitting under the pebbled pink comforter, pretending it is a teepee, watching all through the day and the night, whatever shows come on—after that, on the second day, we take a bus, and we are back in Las Vegas.

"WHY IS THERE A GUN in this drawer?"

It was the first thing I had said since Jim started talking. I realized it must have sounded incongruous. It was the only thing I could make my mouth say.

"What?"

"The gun. Our gun. It's in this drawer."

I was still naked. My back was still to him.

"I don't know. The gun?"

He sounded shaken. He was wondering if I had heard him. He didn't know what I was talking about.

WE STAY IN A SHELTER when we first get back to Vegas, where I sleep on a cot near a man who burps rotgut whiskey and we line up for breakfast with a lady who screams that Betty Grable is trying to kill her. After a couple of nights, we move to a furnished motel where Sharlene can pay the rent weekly. That motel is not too far from the motel we lived in before Sharlene met Steve, though it is not the same one we lived in when Rodney was born, and it is not the same one we lived in when Sharlene first came to Vegas—when Sharlene came to Vegas with me, just a baby, and the boyfriend who owned the 1951 Henry J. The Henry J broke down in Colorado, and Sharlene and I and the boyfriend had to hitchhike the rest of the way to Vegas. That's what Sharlene told me anyway, that's what I know about how I got to Vegas—that, and that the Henry J was a red car without any way to get into the trunk.

But they were mostly the same, those furnished motels. They all had rats, which didn't even scurry when I stamped my small foot, and mattresses stained with urine and vomit and blood. In all of them, the neon lights of dilapidated downtown casinos blinked through the kinked slats of broken window blinds.

"THIS GUN USED TO BE in the closet. Did you put it in this drawer?"

I didn't know why I was asking these questions. I didn't care why the gun was in the drawer. I just had to say something, and nothing else that occurred to me to say was possible.

"I put it there. I forgot. I mean, I forgot until just now."

I waited. Still naked. Was he still looking?

"It was a long time ago. At least a year. I had it out. I was looking at it. And you came in the room. I just wanted to put it away before you saw it. I meant to go back and get it, but I forgot about it. Until just now."

I thought about this. The gun had been in the drawer for a year. Jim was looking at it. He didn't want me to see him looking at it.

"Is it loaded?"

I heard Jim move, quickly. I almost laughed. I didn't know why I had asked if it was loaded, but I had no intention of shooting it. And suddenly, it was not funny. Did my husband just imagine that I would aim the gun at him? That I was asking him if it was loaded so that I could hurt him?

What had happened to us?

WE DIDN'T STAY IN THAT furnished motel very long. Sharlene got the shakes. She said she couldn't be alone, not with Rodney and me anyway. So we went to live with a friend from the bar where Sharlene used to work. We lived there for four months, and while we were there, Sharlene smoked and talked and cried, night after night, with her friend. And then she stopped crying and she started laughing. And when Sharlene and her friend had collapsed on the floor, laughing about Steve and the bills and the wind from the windows, for the third time, I knew we would be leaving the friend's house, and we would be going somewhere else. Eventually there would be another man, and another apartment, and if I were lucky, another school. I would go back to school.

"IT'S NOT LOADED. AVIS, PLEASE. Turn around. Just look at me."

I didn't care that I was naked anymore, and I didn't care that Jim had apologized, and I wasn't even thinking about what he had said about Darcy. I had reached some sort of disembodied state, and what I was thinking about was whether the gun might be loaded after all, and why Jim had been looking at it a year ago, and if there was still any way to get my life back.

I picked up the gun, and it was heavy for something that looked like a toy. I remembered this from the one time Jim had showed me how to shoot it. It took me a second to open the chamber, to hold the gun so that the slide would move back properly. I felt oddly pleased at the automatic way that I had opened the bottom of the gun, released the magazine, checked it for bullets. As Jim had said: no bullets.

No bullets. What about all those stories? All those guns that weren't supposed to be loaded? All those toddlers killed, eyes shot out, lives broken? Bullets could hide.

I AM TWENTY-FIVE YEARS OLD, in the parking lot of the Boulevard Mall at an Opportunity Village fund-raiser. Emily is done walking, wants none of her stroller, sits perched on Jim's shoulders. Small grubby fingers cling to his hair, his ear, his nose, as she rocks there. Jim sees the truck, so I buy the ice cream, the simplest one I can find, but still a swirl of blue and yellow dye.

Emily is amazed at this experience. At the truck, at the kids clustered next to it, at the excited chortle of their voices choosing treats. And then the ice cream itself. Cold! Her tongue laps in and out.

"Jim, her eyes are like a lemur's. She can't believe she gets to eat that thing."

She kicks her small feet into his collarbone.

"Whoa there, pardner," he says.

"Oh, I'm afraid it's getting in your hair."

"I can feel it."

In fact, the ice cream drips along his ear and down his neck, and before she has eaten half of it, Emily has dropped the whole soggy thing on his head. And then she puts her hands in his hair, lays her cheek on the ice cream, and says, as clear and sweet as those ice-cream truck chimes, "Good daddy."

So what can he do? Except walk around in the heat with a

cream-streaked child on his head, blue and yellow stripes dripping down his shirt, and me laughing.

And later, just weeks later, when Emily's fever hasn't responded to the Tylenol, when we have raced to the ER, when the nurse has plunged her in a tub of water, when the fever will not abate, when the doctor says it is meningitis, when he says it sometimes comes on fast like this, when thirty-seven hours and twenty-eight minutes and a hundred million infinite seconds pass, when Emily lies there, tiny in the ICU bed, her breathing labored, then faint, then fluttery (like a little bird), then gone, then a single heart-stopping gasp, and then, again, gone. And no gasp. Later, after all of it, I am so glad we bought that ice-cream treat.

"AVIS, I KNOW YOU ARE upset. I promise I will do right by you. We can figure this out."

"What about Nate?"

"Nate? I don't know. We'll have to tell him. Avis, I don't know. I haven't thought about this. I don't know what we're doing. What about Nate?"

"There's something wrong with Nate. He's different. You know he's different. Something happened to him. And he's not getting better. I know you've seen this."

"Avis. We're not talking about Nate right now."

"But we are. We are talking about Nate. What you are talking about is everything. Me, you, Nate, Emily, everything. We are talking about everything."

I had always known that I would never stop loving the man who left that little girl asleep on his head in the sun. But Jim must have held no equivalent debt to me. There was no image that kept him from falling out of love with me, no matter what happened, no matter how many times. No equivalent moment to a soggy ice-cream-stained child glued to his hopelessly knotted hair.

He stood up and moved behind me. I startled, and he breathed in. Jim was still thinking of the gun. He had said it was not loaded, but it bothered him anyway: the gun, and that I was holding it, and that I had not yet turned around. Then he pressed my bathrobe against my shoulders, offering it to me without quite touching me, his cheek very near my hair.

And I folded. I slipped to the ground with the bathrobe around me, and the tears began. I could not stop them. Awkwardly, Jim put his hand on my back, but I shrugged him away. He stood up and went out. Then I cried harder. Because I wanted Jim to hold me. Because how could I want Jim to hold me?

STRONG
to the CORE

H. NORMAN WRIGHT

HARVEST HOUSE PUBLISHERS

EUGENE, OREGON

STRONG TO THE CORE
Formerly published as *With All My Strength* (Servant Publications, Ann Arbor, MI)
Copyright © 1996 by H. Norman Wright
Published 2011 by Harvest House Publishers
www.harvesthousepublishers.com

Library of Congress Cataloging-in-Publication Data
   Wright, H. Norman.
   [With all my strength]
   Strong to the core : dynamic devotions for men of God / H. Norman Wright.
      p. cm.
   Originally published: With all my strength. Ann Arbor, Mich. : Vine Books, © 1996.
   ISBN 978-0-7369-2450-4 (pbk.)
   ISBN 978-0-7369-4199-0 (eBook)
   1. Men—Prayers and devotions. 2. Men—Religious life. 3. Devotional calendars. I. Title.
   BV4843.W75 2011
   242'.642—dc22

                                     2011008836

Printed in the United States of America

11 12 13 14 15 16 17 18 / LB-SK / 10 9 8 7 6 5 4 3 2 1

To a man who truly is strong to the core:

GARY JACKSON OLIVER

Gary, you have been the closest friend a man could have in times of joy and delight as well as adversity and despair. You've enhanced my life in so many ways, as well as the lives of so many throughout the world. You were my student, but I've learned from you.

We taught together, hunted pheasants together, fished too many places to count (I always caught more), challenged one another to grow, shared insights and laughed. (Oh, how we laughed—especially with your bizarre sense of humor.)

We've also grieved and cried together over the losses of our sons named Matthew, as well as the deaths of our wives. We didn't choose or like the journey of grief, but like so many experiences, it drew us closer together. We grew in our faith and dependence upon our heavenly Father. God allowed us the privilege of performing one another's second marriages (although I still can't believe you said what you did at mine!).

Thank you for being a man of prayer and for your deep commitment to Jesus. You have been a positive model and challenged me to grow. Thank you for teaching others how to live life to the fullest, as well as how to navigate the final stages of life.

So for the whole world to know, I thank you for being you. I love you.

Your brother and friend in Christ,

Norm

Have nothing to do with godless myths and old wives' tales;
rather, train yourself to be godly (1 Timothy 4:7).

You know what it's like to sweat. You're playing an intense game of racquetball or working in the yard. At first small beads of water ooze from your pores. Then, as though a pump were turned on, water pours down your face and body. Your shirt absorbs the perspiration, but soon it's so wet and sticky that it's in the way. You strip it off. The harder you work or play, the more you sweat. And for most of us, the better we feel.

The word *train* that Paul uses in today's verse literally means *naked*. In ancient Greek athletic contests, the athletes competed without clothing so they wouldn't be hampered by it. The word *train* meant "to exercise naked." And whenever you train, there is sweat.

Do you catch what Paul is saying in today's verse? He's saying to train (exercise, work out) for the purpose of godliness. Paul is calling for spiritual sweat. As the Greeks rid themselves of clothing that got in their way, Paul is calling us to get rid of any habit, relationship, or practice that keeps us from being godly men. The writer of Hebrews put it this way: "Therefore, since we are surrounded by such a great cloud of witnesses, let us throw off everything that hinders and the sin that so easily entangles, and let us run with perseverance the race marked out for us" (Hebrews 12:1).

After Paul said to train, he noted that we need to labor and strive for it. Labor means "strenuous toil." The Christian life isn't an easy walk in the park. It takes effort, energy, and sweat![1] One man put it this way: "The successful Christian life is a sweaty affair. No sweat, no sainthood."[2] Is anything holding you back from being godly? Ask the Lord to show you what to do about it. Then put forth all your energy to train for godliness.

It is God's will that you should be holy (1 Thessalonians 4:3).

The Bible says we are to be holy. What does that mean? And how do we do that? Perhaps a good place to begin is...with lust. Yes, lust—an issue we all struggle with in one way or another. Paul says, "Train yourself to be godly" (1 Timothy 4:7). In 1 Thessalonians 4:4-6, he says, "Each of you should learn to control his own body in a way that is holy and honorable, not in passionate lust like the heathen, who do not know God; and that in this matter no one should wrong his brother or take advantage of him. The Lord will punish men for all such sins, as we have already told you and warned you."

That's strong language, but it's important to heed. As Christians, we're called to be different. We're called to purity in our sexual lives. Impossible? No. A struggle? Yes. And that's why we need God's presence and power in our lives—to enable us to use our sexual passion in a positive way. How can we control raging hormones?

- Be accountable to someone you can be honest with.
- Pray specifically for your purity in thought and action.
- Memorize the Word of God. "I have hidden your word in my heart" (Psalm 119:11).
- Watch your thought life and what you focus your eyes on.

Job said, "I made a covenant with my eyes not to look lustfully at a girl" (Job 31:1). Did you know that was in the Bible? We need to be careful what we focus on. A minister said, "One look of recognition, one look of appreciation, and no more looks!" Holiness takes on new meaning when applied to everyday struggles, doesn't it? But it is possible![3]

*Wounds from a friend are better than kisses
from an enemy! (Proverbs 27:6 TLB).*

"Give it to me straight, I can take it." Is there anyone in your life who will tell it to you like it is? Have you got someone who will level with you and with whom you can level? And the relationship is stronger because of the honesty? That's what Proverbs 27:6 is talking about. We may not want to hear the truth, but we're better off because of what was said. Proverbs 17:10 (TLB) states: "A rebuke to a man of common sense is more effective than a hundred lashes on the back of a rebel." Oh yeah, it feels good to have someone flatter you, but it can cause problems. "Flattery is a trap" (29:5 TLB).

What I'm talking about here is candor—being open and honest so the truth builds the relationship. Candor comes because of our care and love for the other person. We have his well-being in mind. Ephesians 4:15 (TLB) says "speak the truth in love." This creates a healthy relationship. How many of those do you have? One? Several? If so, you're fortunate. Mutual candor is a sign of close friendship. You'll be a better person and so will your friend when candor is present. Proverbs 27:17 (TLB) reveals the result: "A friendly discussion is as stimulating as the sparks that fly when iron strikes iron."

Keep in mind that your response to the candor of your friend (it could even be your wife!) will make a difference. Defensiveness kills candor. Responses like "Let me think about that" or "That's something for me to consider" keep a relationship going.

So…can you take it? Should you take it straight? Why not? Will you build better relationships with candor? Definitely. One last thought: If you really want to have someone give it to you straight, take a look at God's Word.[4]

*The Lord is my shepherd, I shall not be in want. He makes me lie
down in green pastures, he leads me beside quiet waters (Psalm 23:1-2).*

Have you watched a marathon or experienced running those 26 miles under a hot, baking sun or a cold, driving rain? Mile after mile you lift one foot, slam it down on the concrete, and do the same with the other foot. How many times does each foot slam into that unyielding surface? Thousands upon thousands!

Sometimes microscopic cracks begin in the outer layers of the bones in the feet or legs. If the running continues and the lower body continues to receive punishment, those crevices enlarge. Soon they're large enough to create pain. These are called stress fractures. You may think stress fractures are limited to the bones, but they are not. We pound our bodies in other ways. Our schedule piles up, as do the bills; we take on a coaching job, learn to eat on the run (usually junk food), try to satisfy the boss, spouse, and church. Before long our nerves have microscopic cracks. We're on edge like a tightly wound rubber band ready to snap at whatever gets in our way.

Your spirit and your heart can be stress-fractured from taking on and doing too much by yourself. You were not called to go through life alone. That approach will break you. There's a Shepherd waiting to help you. Why don't you let Him?

> He lets me rest in the meadow grass and leads me beside the quiet streams. He gives me new strength...Even when walking through the dark valley of death I will not be afraid, for you are close beside me (Psalm 23:3-4 TLB).

Read this psalm aloud each day for a month, and then check your stress level.

*I went past the field of the sluggard, past the vineyard of the
man who lacks judgment; thorns had come up everywhere,
the ground was covered with weeds, and the stone wall
was in ruins. I applied my heart to what I observed and
learned a lesson from what I saw (Proverbs 24:30-32).*

This is a strange verse, isn't it? The writer is talking about a person who is basically inefficient. Some versions describe the person as a "sluggard." The Amplified Bible calls him "the lazy man." You may be thinking, *Just a minute here. That's not me! I'm an efficiency wizard. There's not a lazy bone in my body. You ought to see my smoke at work. They call me "Mr. Efficiency."* That's great, and that's consistent with Scripture. Everything we do ought to be done for our Lord's sake.

But let's take a detour away from work and go to the home front. What does your garage look like? What about the workroom, the backyard, and the catch-all drawer in the kitchen? If you're married, how would your wife rate you on efficiency around the homestead? Yeah, you're right. Bad question—but necessary to ask. Why? Simply because a number of men have MPP—Multiple Personality Problem. They're super-charged workhorses on the job, but at home they function like sluggards. And to make matters worse (much worse!), if their wives know they're giving it their all at the office, they will not be happy receiving only the leftovers at home.

So what's the answer? Consistent efficiency—at work and at home. Don't try to catch up or do it all at once. Space out the chores in an orderly fashion and watch the change—in you and your wife.

To him who is able to keep you from falling and to present you before
his glorious presence without fault and with great joy (Jude 24).

It's embarrassing. You're walking along and trip or miss a step. Splat! Down you go. If your friends are around, you know you're going to hear about it for a long time.

At many camps and conference grounds throughout the country there is a new activity. They call it "The Wall." It's a fifty-foot simulated rock climb, a wall of wood with rock-shaped fingerholds jutting out all over. It's safe though. You wear a harness around your waist that is attached to a rope that runs through a pulley. Someone holds onto the rope and secures it for you as you climb. If your fingers and hands tire and you happen to fall (which happens to many), the rope saves you.

This is a good metaphor for life because we fall in other ways too. We've slipped on promises, commitments, and even convictions. Max Lucado describes the result:

> Now you are wiser. You have learned to go slowly. You are careful. You are cautious, but you are also confident. You trust the rope. You rely on the harness. And though you can't see your guide, you know him. You know he is strong. You know he is able to keep you from falling.
>
> And you know you are only a few more steps from the top. So whatever you do, don't quit. Though your falls are great, his strength is greater. You will make it. You will see the summit. You will stand at the top. And when you get there, the first thing you'll do is join with all the others who have made the climb and sing this verse: "To him who is able to keep you from falling…"[5]

How can a young man keep his way pure? By living according to your word...I have hidden your word in my heart that I might not sin against you (Psalm 119:9-11).

I've got a confession to make. When I was a teenager I got into something—memorizing Scripture. And it helped me more times than I can remember. On several occasions when I was fleeing a temptation and struggling with a decision, guess what happened? Yep, you can figure it out. A Scripture I'd memorized just happened to "pop" into my mind right at that moment. And usually it was 1 Corinthians 10:13: "No temptation has seized you except what is common to man. And God is faithful; he will not let you be tempted beyond what you can bear. But when you are tempted, he will also provide a way out so that you can stand up under it." That passage was a lifesaver.

In my adulthood I really didn't make any consistent attempt to memorize God's Word...until a few years ago. A friend of mine at a family camp shared a session based on his book *Seeking Solid Ground*. It's all about Psalm 15. At the end he gently challenged us to memorize that psalm. It talks about how to get the most out of life.

I decided to do it. One thing I found is that the synapses of the brain cells at my current age aren't quite as alive as they were back in my younger days. It took more work, but just two or three minutes each morning and...eventually it was mine. Sometimes when I wake up at night I quote it silently. I quote it when I'm driving. The words are reassuring. They keep me alert, on track for God. But why not—it's His Word!

I wrote my friend and said, "Thanks for the push." I'm working on a longer psalm now. Then a passage in Colossians. I don't want to stop. Why not give it a shot yourself?

The tongue of the wise commends knowledge, but the
mouth of the fool gushes folly (Proverbs 15:2).

How many times are the words *tongue, mouth, lips,* and *words* mentioned in Proverbs? (I'll reveal the answer soon.) Proverbs is the finest, practical guide we'll ever have on how to communicate. Consider these principles on what not to say:

- How about boasting? "Like clouds and wind without rain is a man who boasts of gifts he does not give" (Proverbs 25:14). Boasting is useless, ridiculous, and can be profane. Paul admonishes: "Do not let any unwholesome talk come out of your mouths, but only what is helpful for building others up" (Ephesians 4:29).

- How about flattery? "He who rebukes a man will in the end gain more favor than he who has a flattering tongue" (Proverbs 28:23). Flattery is all about using insincere compliments to deceive someone.

- How about being verbose and running off at the mouth? Look at Proverbs 10:19 TLB: "Don't talk so much. You keep putting your foot in your mouth. Be sensible and turn off the flow!" That's graphic. You've met people like this. They fill the air with words—empty words of no significance. They don't know the meaning of listening.

- How about angry, argumentative words? "An angry man stirs up dissension, and a hot-tempered one commits many sins" (Proverbs 29:22). Purposeful, constructive debates are healthy, but many "talks" turn into battles. Avoid arguing.

To check out more powerful passages on communication, read Proverbs 14:16-17; 15:4; 17:14,22,24-25. (The answer to the first paragraph question? More than 150!)

*Listen to me, you who pursue righteousness and who seek the
LORD: Look to the rock from which you were cut and to the
quarry from which you were hewn; look to Abraham, your
father, and to Sarah, who gave you birth. When I called him he
was but one, and I blessed him and made him many. The LORD
will surely comfort Zion and will look with compassion on all
her ruins; he will make her deserts like Eden, her wastelands
like the garden of the LORD. Joy and gladness will be found in
her, thanksgiving and the sound of singing (Isaiah 51:1-3).*

How do you resemble your father and mother? Do you resemble them physically? Do you have a similar personality? Do you have the same mannerisms? As you age, have you caught yourself doing and saying things your dad did? That's common.

Isaiah, God's prophet, told a nation to look back at Abraham and Sarah and the heritage they passed on. And there's a heritage passed on to us too, whether we want it or not. Sometimes the only way we can understand ourselves is to look to who raised us. There's good and bad in us, and so there was in our parents. Sometimes our actions are based on liking what our parents did…or the opposite—reacting against it.

Some men don't want to look at their fathers because they weren't really dads to them. Perhaps you've been blamed for being the way you are because of your dad. Or it could be you're praised for who you are because of him. Isaiah pointed the people back to their roots, back to parents who were imperfect but also did much good. He said that by doing so, the people would find joy and gladness. We too have a choice. We can focus on what our parents didn't do, on what they did wrong, or we can concentrate on what they did correctly. There's a different result for each choice. What will your choice be?[6]

Though a righteous man falls seven times, he rises again,
but the wicked are brought down by calamity (Proverbs 24:16).

Some people seem to get all the breaks. Whatever they do turns to gold. They look like they're *always* successful. You do what they do, but it doesn't come out the same. They know the right people, have the right connections, or just happen to be in the right place at the right time, right? Well, not exactly...and not usually. It's easy for us to see people's successes. What we rarely see are their failures or even their humiliations.

Most people who are successful have been knocked down again and again like prize fighters. But they bounce back with the words "next time." For instance, you probably take your telephone for granted. You use it every day at home, in the car, and you may carry one around in your pocket. Thank Alexander Graham Bell for that convenience. But this man knew what it was like to be dumped on. He spent years going back and forth throughout New England trying to raise enough seed money to get his new invention off the ground. Mostly what he got was laughter and ridicule. But he kept saying, "Next time I'll get the funding." And eventually he did!

If you're a father, you've probably gone to Disneyland or Disney World with your kids. Did you know they almost didn't exist? Years ago a man had an idea for a cartoon called "Steamboat Willie." He kept trying to get backing, but it was difficult. He was bankrupt, and many people thought he was a failure. But Walt Disney kept at it! He kept said, "Next time." And the rest is a legend. Steamboat Willie became Mickey Mouse!

We've all failed at times, and through failure we've grown. Not succeeding only stops us when we see it as the final chapter. If we view it as a detour only, we can learn from it and go on.

*Call to me and I will answer you and tell you great and
unsearchable things you do not know (Jeremiah 33:3).*

It's impossible. I'd never be able to share my faith with someone."
"Me, coach that team of little tigers? It's impossible."

Impossible is used often today as the great escape, the ultimate excuse, the absolute final foot-stomping refusal. Who can argue with it? The only problem is, the word is usually employed *before* we make an attempt to do what we're calling "impossible." One hundred years ago no one would have believed someone could jump from a great height and have a canopy of cloth open above that would carry the person to the ground gently and safely. But it happened. The parachute came into being because someone was willing to try again and again and again. Sure, a number of attempts failed, but the inventors didn't cry "It's impossible." They went back to the drawing board, came up with more solutions, and today parachutes are used even for sport.

Several years ago a boy was born in Southern California. By the age of five he could tie his shoes and use a computer. That's not really spectacular except he had no hands or arms or legs. When he graduated from high school he had a 3.5 grade-point average, was a top cross-country track star, and was skillful in using a welding torch. This young man didn't know the meaning of the word *impossible.*

What *seems* to be impossible to you? Is it really impossible? Maybe there's a different way to try it? And if you try something and it doesn't work, that doesn't mean you have to quit. You can use it as a learning experience. As believers we're called to do the impossible, and why shouldn't we? We worship and serve the Lord of the impossible!

*Fathers, do not exasperate your children; instead, bring them up
in the training and instruction of the Lord (Ephesians 6:4).*

Are you a father? If so, today's verse is for you. If you aren't a dad, it's still for you because you may be a substitute father someday. God's Word has some practical guidelines for dads. The first is a "do not." Loosely translated, it says, "Don't be a big pain in the neck." Don't make your children so angry they seethe with resentment. The New English Bible says, "You fathers, again, must not goad your children to resentment."

How might a dad goad his children? Focusing exclusively on what a child has done wrong can break his spirit. Criticism includes tone of voice, silent stares, and body language. Being overly strict and controlling is sure to create rebellion.

Scripture also tells dads what to do. Bringing a child up in the training and instruction of the Lord can be summed up in three words: *tenderness, discipline,* and *instruction.*

- *Words of love and your gentle touch*—your *tenderness*—will send a message of love to both your wife and your children.

- *Discipline* isn't the same as punishment. Discipline's purpose is to create change for the better. Wise discipline takes into account the uniqueness of each child.

- *Instruction* can be translated "to place before the mind." But keep in mind that your children *watch* your actions to see if they jibe with what you say. We teach by word *and* example; we teach by praying and worshiping with our children.

Being a father is not a chore—it's a challenge and a blessing![7]

A desire accomplished is sweet to a soul (Proverbs 13:19 NKJV).

Accomplishments. Most of us like to be able to list a few. Even when we were kids we liked to receive ribbons, trophies, and awards to show we were successful. But to accomplish something, we've got to stick with the job against the pain and the odds. How does a guy who started out as a dishwasher at seventeen, right out of high school, get to be CEO of that same restaurant chain at thirty-five? By hard work. He didn't give up. He attracted attention because of his devotion.

How does a couple make it to their fiftieth wedding anniversary? (And that's some accomplishment in today's world!) They stick with it.

To accomplish anything, we have to do it completely. We don't leave loose ends. We don't complete to a 97-percent level and never get back to what's left. We're thorough. Webster defines *accomplishment* this way: "Done through to the end, complete, omitting nothing; accurate; very exact."[8] When we do something in this way it reflects a pattern of excellence.

In what area of your life do you need to follow through more thoroughly? If you need some help figuring that out, ask a friend. Ask one of your children. Better yet, ask your wife! And the next time you tackle a task, keep this in mind: "Whatever you do, work at it with all your heart, as working for the Lord, not for men, since you know that you will receive an inheritance from the Lord as a reward. It is the Lord Christ you are serving" (Colossians 3:23-24).

Your accomplishments can draw someone to your Lord. That's an excellent reason to be thorough!

*Again I tell you, it is easier for a camel to go through
the eye of a needle than for a rich man to enter
the kingdom of God (Matthew 19:24).*

For years pack animals have been used to carry the excess baggage people take with them on trips to remote areas. If you've ever been backpacking on a hunting or fishing trip into the high country, you're glad to have those mules or burros along to carry the gear. And if you're fortunate, you've got a guide who knows how to load and unload the animals and does it for you. It's a lot of work. To add to that, sometimes the animal is in a foul mood and either kicks or tries to take a bite out of its handler.

In the Far East, camels are the mainstay for desert travelers. And in Jesus' day they were very common. His statement in today's verse has more significance than first meets the eye. One of the gates in the wall around Jerusalem was actually called the *Needle's Eye Gate*. It was very narrow—just barely wide enough for a camel. The problem was the baggage. It wouldn't fit. The merchants had to "downsize" their camels' loads. They had to unload the beasts, walk through the gate with the camels, carry the baggage through, and, if they had farther to go, load the beasts back up. Only when the camels were unloaded could they get through the gate.

Jesus said, "Enter through the narrow gate. For wide is the gate and broad is the road that leads to destruction, and many enter through it" (Matthew 7:13). Are you carrying any baggage or burdens that might make it difficult to enter the narrow gate? Like the loaded camel, something may need to be stripped off. Take a look and get rid if any encumbrances.[9]

*In all this, Job did not sin by charging God
with wrongdoing (Job 1:22).*

Every day counselors listen to people's stories. So do bartenders and manicurists. Most stories have one thing in common—bad news. Sometimes the story is a continuing saga of one bad item after another. The listeners wonder how the storyteller keeps on keeping on. Some of the losses people experience are right up there with Job's life. Remember him? He was the man who lost most of his money, his herds of livestock, his crops, and his servants. And then he lost not one but all ten of his children! Usually the loss of one child tears a family apart. But ten! And finally his health crumpled. He didn't deserve all this. He was an honest, God-fearing man. He was a man of integrity.

Job survived. Have you ever wondered how? Is there something he did that can help us today? Take a look. "He replied, '...Shall we accept good from God, and not trouble?'...In all this, Job did not sin in what he said" (Job 2:10). Job accepted that God was in control. He acknowledged God's sovereignty. He didn't lash out in anger at God or curse Him. He accepted something that's difficult for most people to accept today: God is who He is. He's in charge even if we don't understand why things happen the way they do. "I know that my Redeemer lives, and that in the end he will stand upon the earth. And after my skin has been destroyed, yet in my flesh I will see God" (19:25-26).

Job knew that one day there would be a Messiah. No doubt that hope of the future helped Job handle the present (see Job 42:2-4). He did something that's vital to successful living. Basically he said, "God, I don't understand." He quit trying to figure life out by himself. He looked to the only One who could bring him to that place. That's not a bad plan to follow when life seems to be one bad-news day after another.

*If it is possible, as far as it depends on you, live at
peace with everyone (Romans 12:18).*

Why not pray this today?

Heavenly Father of peace and love,

I ask for You to bring Your peace to our world. Take away from our cities the violence of gang war, from our nations the suspicions and mistrust of one another, from our world the domination and exploitation of the powerful over those who are weak.

Give us the wisdom, strength, and grace to overcome the suspicious attitudes and prejudices we have carried and nurtured for years. Instead, help us show the love and acceptance that You extend to all of us.

Father, send Your peace to our cities and our nation. Help those in public office to set aside their political ambitions and humble themselves in private before You. May we learn to live in peace with those at work, on the expressway, in the checkout line, with the cantankerous neighbor, the difficult relative, and our family members.

Help me get rid of bitterness and unforgiveness. I need control over my impulses, my desires, my tongue, my eyes, and my temper. Help me not to retreat into silence and solitude when others need to talk. Help me lower my voice rather than raise it when I don't agree. Take away the worries that plague my mind. Help me feed my faith through You. I pray for a pure heart in my motives and my ambitions. Help me be more content with what I have and to thank You for it, rather than focusing on what I don't have.

I pray for inner peace.

I thank You for Jesus, Your Son.

In His name I pray.
Amen.

A voice from heaven said, "This is my Son, whom I love;
with him I am well pleased" (Matthew 3:17).

The world's standard of manhood is warped. Consider this definition of masculinity:

> Jesus' personality had several facets, but he did not hide them from anyone. He could chase the corrupters out of his temple in righteous anger, displaying his manhood in what might be called "masculine" ways—and yet later he wept over Jerusalem, displaying what is considered a "feminine" side.

> He met the challenge of the enemy and faced them in open debate; and yet he could hold children on his knees in a moment of tenderness and express how precious they were to him and the kingdom of God. On more than one occasion, he lashed out with a sharp verbal lance, even calling the religious leaders a bunch of "vipers," thus taking the wind right out of them and leaving them dumbfounded; and yet he dealt mercifully with a frantic father who honestly confessed his inability to believe that Jesus could heal his son, touching the boy in tenderness, compassion, and power—making him whole.

> He had all the legions of heaven on his side and could have, in one master stroke of his manliness, wiped out his enemies. Yet he stood mute before the Roman court, refusing to give dignity to a mob. Here is the Son of God, Jesus, the Man, who was not asexual, but who never used his sexuality to prove his manhood. Here is the king of the universe, sweating blood during the deep revulsion he felt in Gethsemane concerning the death that faced him, and yet pressing on to take that death on the cross without wilting.

> There is no greater picture of the "whole man"—a man who was "masculine" in terms of strength, muscle, sinew, and courage, and yet was not ashamed to show his "feminine" side in terms of tears, compassion, gentleness, and peace.[10]

*Now I want you to know, brothers, that what has happened to me
has really served to advance the gospel. As a result, it has become
clear throughout the whole palace guard and to everyone else
that I am in chains for Christ. Because of my chains, most of the
brothers in the Lord have been encouraged to speak the word of
God more courageously and fearlessly (Philippians 1:12-14).*

Archaeologists look for stuff everyone else has forgotten. Old—really old—stuff. They love to find the bones of animals that lived thousands of years ago. You're full of bones too. You need all your bones, but there are three "bones" that are more important than the others. These will get you through life—especially when tough times roll in. Do you know the three I'm talking about? The backbone, the wishbone, and the funny bone.

Your *backbone* stands for the strength and courage you need to make it through life. Paul showed backbone when he described his plight in 2 Corinthians 11:24-25—he was beaten, stoned, shipwrecked, and the list goes on. But he made it, and so can you.

Your *wishbone* is linked to your dreams and goals. Paul had a dream of spreading the gospel. Today's verses describe how that was being realized. Is your wishbone working? Are you working toward making your goals a reality? Or has your wishbone been buried and begun to petrify? Don't wait for an archaeologist to find it. Bring it to life and let God guide your dreams.

Last but not least, your *funny bone* may keep the other bones going, especially when life is at its most difficult. Let it do its job. Keep your sense of humor alive and well. The joy you experience will enrich your life.[11]

[Jesus said,] "Take courage! It is I. Don't be afraid" (Matthew 14:27).

We're a lot like the disciples, aren't we? We spend time with Jesus, experience His strength, and then quickly forget. Matthew 14 tells us Jesus healed the sick, fed the multitudes, then went away to pray. The disciples took off in a boat and a storm arose. Amid the thrashing waves and intense wind, Jesus walked on the water toward His friends. They thought He was a ghost and were afraid, but Jesus responded, "It is I. Take courage. Don't be afraid." Peter got out of the boat, started toward Jesus, saw the wind pick up, and panicked. One author gave this interesting analysis and application:

- *Uncertain circumstances*—Almost every time I deal with fear, I face uncertain circumstances—just like the disciples did… My boat is rocking. My favorite Captain does not seem to be on board. My future is unknown.

- *Wrong conclusions*—In the middle of my panic…instead of seeing Jesus supernaturally at work in the middle of my storm, I see all kinds of ghosts represented by my personal fears… "Where is Jesus when I need him most?"

- *Impulsive conduct*—Peter's "jump out of the boat" behavior reminds me of myself. Sometimes I cry, "Lord, if you are *really* here, in the middle of my panic and my frightening situation, prove yourself…Do something so I know it's you!"

- *Desperate call*—When I, like Peter, step out in trust, I sometimes take my eyes off Jesus and focus on my terrorizing circumstances…I cry, "Lord, save me!"

- *Immediate calm*—Without delay he reaches out…, "You of little faith…why did you doubt?" And in the security of his compassionate gaze and warm, affirming grip, my heart begins the measured, careful journey toward accepting his perfect love.[12]

*Blessed is the man who does not walk in the counsel of the wicked or
stand in the way of sinners or sit in the seat of mockers (Psalm 1:1).*

"That's righteous." Remember that phrase? People used it to describe
something good, positive, or outstanding. Psalm 1 describes something God wants from us that will benefit us and change our society. It's
called the "righteous" or "godly" life. In our society, how can this happen?

First, the psalmist tells us what *not* to do, and then he tells us what *to*
do. In verse 1 we find the conditions for spiritual erosion. "Walk" suggests
hanging around too closely to those who are living a lifestyle counter to
Scripture. The phrase implies the idea of a person who *does not* imitate
the wicked. We're called to live differently—to be set apart.

"Stand in the way of" implies an even closer relationship with those
living an ungodly lifestyle. When we get too close to the fire, we get
burned. And once we get this close we can end up with the final condition, which is "sitting" with the ungodly. This suggests a *permanent* stay.
From walking to standing, we slip *into* the lifestyle of the unrighteous.

Fortunately, the psalmist tells us what to do to avoid this. It's basic. It's
life-changing. In a nutshell, we're to occupy ourselves with God's Word.
It gives us direction, guidance, insight, strength, and can serve as a deterrent to getting involved in wrong lifestyles. How? First, we meditate on
God's Word. We think. We discover what it really says and means. Second, we memorize it. "How can a young man keep his way pure? By living according to your word…I have hidden your word in my heart that
I might not sin against you" (Psalm 119:9,11). Immersing ourselves in
God's Word works. Just check with someone who's tried it! He'll tell you
the good news.

*Man shall not live by bread alone, but by every word that
proceeds from the mouth of God (Matthew 4:4 NKJV).*

There is a whole range of eating disorders today: overeating, eating the wrong types of food, under eating, not eating, anorexia, bulimia, and so forth. They all have their own set of problems. Usually we think of eating disorders associated with women, but men engage in anorexia and bulimia just like women. Some men are diet freaks. But usually men manifest eating disorders in a different way—a spiritual way. Anorexia is body emaciation because of a physical aversion to food and eating. Bulimia is the binge-and-purge disorder. Steve Farrar describes these two disorders in the spiritual realm.

> Spiritual anorexia is an aversion to feeding from the Word of God. It is impossible for a man to stand and fight in spiritual warfare if he is spiritually malnourished. This is why the enemy will do whatever is necessary to keep us from reading and meditating on the Scriptures. Jesus put it this way…: "Man shall not live by bread alone, but on every word that proceeds from the mouth of God."

> …There is another disorder that is even more dangerous. Bulimia is an eating disorder that is commonly known as the binge-and-purge syndrome. Spiritual bulimia is knowing the Word of God without *doing* it…Spiritual bulimia is characteristic of those who binge on truth…through books, tapes, good Bible teaching, listening to a favorite communicator on the radio. That's why the spiritual bulimic appears to be so righteous. There's just one problem. The bulimic knows the truth, but he doesn't apply it.[13]

When we're undernourished spiritually, the answer is to eat more of God's Word!

*Be joyful always; pray continually; give thanks in all circumstances,
for this is God's will for you in Christ Jesus (1 Thessalonians 5:16-18).*

D r. Lloyd Ogilvie addressed the problem of whether prayer is always answered in his insightful daily devotional *God's Best for My Life:*

"If I thought," said John Baillie, "that God were going to grant me all my prayers simply for the asking, without even passing them under His own gracious review, without even bringing to bear upon them His own greater wisdom, I think there would be very few prayers that I would dare to pray."

All prayers are answered, but not always the way we had hoped or in the time we anticipated. We often judge the efficacy of prayer by how much it produces the results we prayed for. We make God our celestial errand-boy. Because God can see what we cannot see and knows dimensions which we can never understand, He works out our answers according to a higher plan than we can conceive. We are to tell Him our needs and then leave them with Him. It's only in retrospect that we can see the narrowness of our vision and can see that His answer was far better than what we could ever have anticipated.

Prayer is not just the place and time we tell God what to do, but the experience in which He molds our lives. In the quiet meditative prayer, we begin to see things from a different point of view and are given the power to wait for the unfolding of God's plan.

Elton Trueblood was right: "Prayer is not some slick device according to which, when we say the right words, we are sure of the outcome. The promise, fundamentally, is not that the Father always does precisely as we ask, but rather that He always *hears*."[14]

It is not good for the man to be alone (Genesis 2:18).

There it is again!
A twinge of pain?
Forget it. It will go away,
In the business of my day.
I've places to go and things to do...
A round of meetings with entrepreneurs,
Planes to catch and taxis to hail,
I have life by the tail.
But what is this painful wail?
From the depths of me I ache.
It greets me when I wake.
Even in a crowded room of people
I can hear a haunting toll from the church bell steeple.
There's nothing wrong with me.
I'm a success, as anyone can see.
I—I hurt. I feel an emptiness.
This feeling, is it loneliness?
Loneliness?
I'm married with children, three.
Yet at times I feel so alone.
Maybe it's time to come down from my throne.
It's not good for a man to be alone.[15]

If you're lonely, reach out to God, to your wife, to a friend. If you don't feel this way, reach out anyway. Someone else is lonely and needs you.

He who is slow to anger is better than the mighty, and he who rules his [own] spirit than he who takes a city (Proverbs 16:32 AMP).

Anger can kill. Strong words, but true. When we get angry our body prepares for action. Our blood clots more quickly, additional adrenaline is released, our muscles tense. Our blood pressure may increase, and our hearts beat faster. People have strokes and heart attacks during fits of anger. What happens if the anger isn't released? The results can be physically harmful.

Look at the result of anger in the life of the wealthy Nabal (1 Samuel 25). David sent some of his men to Nabal to get food supplies. They wanted some food for the troops, but Nabal gave them a rebuke and sent them away. Upon hearing of this insult, David gathered his men together and set out to fight Nabal. But Abigail, Nabal's wife, heard what her husband had done. She gathered together a large store of food and then went out, met David and his men, and appeased them with her gift of food and wise words.

> And Abigail came to Nabal…And [his] heart was merry, for he was very drunk; so she told him nothing at all until morning light. But in the morning, when the wine was gone out of Nabal, and his wife told him these things, his heart died within him and he became [paralyzed, helpless as] a stone. And about ten days after that, the Lord smote Nabal and he died (1 Samuel 25:36-38 AMP).

Nabal may have had a stroke or a heart attack because he reacted angrily to his wife's disclosure. Think about that the next time you get mad.

Drink water from your own cistern, running water from your own well...May your fountain be blessed, and may you rejoice in the wife of your youth. A loving doe, a graceful deer—may her breasts satisfy you always, may you ever be captivated by her love (Proverbs 5:15-19).

In *A Celebration of Sex,* Douglas Rosenau offers insights on today's verses:

> We could paraphrase this for wives:
>
> Rejoice in the husband of your youth. A gentle stag, a strong deer—may his hands and mouth satisfy you always, may you ever be captivated by his love.
>
> The Bible often uses water as a very powerful and fitting metaphor for cleansing, healing, and rejuvenating...What a tremendous portrayal of the dynamic nature of lovemaking to compare it to a cistern, a well, a stream, and a fountain of water. It is like a cool, refreshing drink from your own safe supply...
>
> Your sex life is like a cistern in which you have stored many amorous memories and a sexy repertoire of arousing activities. You can dip into it again and again in your fantasy life and lovemaking for excitement and fun. In another way, making love is like a stream or spring of water. Sex in marriage has an ever-changing, renewing quality to it. A routine sex life is not God's design. Renew your minds and attitudes, and get sexy and playful. You can make love four times a week for the next fifty years and still never plumb the surprising depths of this mysterious sexual "stream" of becoming one flesh.
>
> I appreciate the words *rejoice, satisfy,* and *captivated* in the Proverbs passage. Pleasure and fun are an intended part of making love... We can rejoice with the mate of our youth. Our creativity, imagination, and love allow us to remain ever enthralled sexually with the lover of our youth. We can be ever satisfied and captivated.[16]

*He whose walk is blameless and who does what is righteous, who
speaks the truth from his heart...will never be shaken (Psalm 15:2,5).*

We need men of integrity today, but integrity is a costly virtue. You can count on that. What will it cost you? Just a few things—like time, effort, money, and perhaps popularity and respect. *Integrity isn't popular.* It makes some people uncomfortable.

The word *integrity* means to be "sound, complete, without blemish, crack, or defect." In the construction business, the concept of integrity means adhering to building codes to ensure the building will be safe. Webster's dictionary has a simple word for it: *honesty.* So why practice integrity? Let's look to God's Word for the answers!

Integrity gives you direction. "The integrity of the upright guides them, but the unfaithful are destroyed by their duplicity" (Proverbs 11:3).

Integrity gives you a solid footing. "The man of integrity walks securely, but he who takes crooked paths will be found out" (Proverbs 10:9).

Integrity provides a blessing for your children. "The righteous man leads a blameless life; blessed are his children after him" (Proverbs 20:7).

Integrity gives you riches. "Better a poor man whose walk is blameless than a fool whose lips are perverse" (Proverbs 19:1).

Integrity pleases God. "I know, my God, that you test the heart and are pleased with integrity" (1 Chronicles 29:17).[17]

Get used to the word *integrity.* It's the hallmark of a righteous man.

After he left there, he came upon Jehonadab son of Recab...
Jehu greeted him and said, "Are you in accord
with me, as I am with you?"
"I am," Jehonadab answered...
Jehu said, "Come with me and see my zeal for the LORD." Then
he had him ride along in his chariot (2 Kings 10:15-16).

Jehu loved to drive. Today he'd be racing funny cars, off-road vehicles, or tearing down the street in a Corvette. Some men come alive behind the wheel. With gleams in their eyes, they put their foot to the pedal. Speed limits and stop signs? Those are for the other guys. Look at the description of Jehu's driving: "He has reached them...The driving is like that of Jehu son of Nimshi—he drives like a madman" (2 Kings 9:20). Do you relate to that? What does your driving say about your faith, your relationship with the Lord? If you speed a bit, enhance your enjoyment by singing these songs while you drive:

At 50 mph: "God Will Take Care of You"
At 60 mph: "Guide Me, O Thou Great Jehovah"
At 70 mph: "Nearer, My God, to Thee"
At 80 mph: "Nearer, Still Nearer!"
At 90 mph: "This World Is Not My Home"
At 100 mph: "Lord, I'm Coming Home"
Over 100: "Precious Memories"

Remember that the way you drive and how you respond to other drivers says a lot about your relationship with the Lord.[18]

A man's heart plans his way, but the LORD
directs his steps (Proverbs 16:9 NKJV).

I f you struggle to discover God's will for your life, perhaps you're not going about it in the best way. Dr. Lloyd Ogilvie shares an interesting perspective on this issue.

> Dr. James Dobson, in his helpful book *God's Will*, tells a penetrating story of Rev. Everett Howard, a veteran missionary to the Cape Verde Islands for twenty-six years. His call to the mission field has implications for all of us.
>
> After finishing college and dental school, Howard was still uncertain about God's will for his life. One night he went into the sanctuary of the church where his father was serving as pastor. He knelt down at the altar and took a piece of paper on which he wrote all the things he was ready to do for God. He signed his name at the bottom and waited for some sign of God's affirmation and presence but nothing happened. He took his paper again, thinking he might have left something out—still no response from the Lord. He waited and waited. Then it happened. He felt the Lord speaking within him. The Lord told him to tear up the sheet.
>
> "You're going about it all wrong," He said gently. "Son, I want you to take a blank piece of paper, sign it on the bottom, and let Me fill it in."
>
> Howard responded, and God guided a spectacular missionary career from that day forward.
>
> God is not as interested in our commitment to what we decide to do for Him as He is in what we will allow Him to do through us. Our task is not to list our accomplishments or our plans for service, but to give Him a blank sheet and let Him fill it in.[19]

The Lord has sought out for Himself a man after
His own heart (1 Samuel 13:14 NASB).

When Christ gave His farewell message to His disciples in the Upper Room (John 13), He knew His death was at hand. What was the most important message He wanted to leave with them? He told them what would identify them as followers. Interestingly, it was not an absence of mistakes or weaknesses, the number of things they abstained from, or their net worth. Instead, it was an emotion expressed through behavior: "A new commandment I give to you, that you love one another, even as I have loved you, that you also love one another. By this all men will know that you are My disciples, if you have love for one another" (John 13:34-35 NASB).

Yes, He calls them to have love. Not the ability to be witty and clever nor to win debates. God has designed us so that our emotions influence almost every aspect of our lives. And He speaks to us through our emotions. Emotions are to our personality what gasoline is to a car. They are the sources of our passion and intensity. They help us monitor our needs, make us aware of good and evil, and provide motivation and energy.

When God told Saul his kingdom would end, God revealed His priorities. Through Samuel He said, "Your kingdom shall not endure. The Lord has sought out for Himself a man after His own heart, and the Lord has appointed him as ruler over His people, because you have not kept what the Lord commanded you" (1 Samuel 13:14 NASB). Notice God's primary criterion. He did not seek someone "after His own head." No, God sought someone after His own *heart.* Yes, David made mistakes. He was fallible. But he had a quality God admired. David was a passionate man who had a heart for God.[20]

Cast all your anxiety on him because he cares for you (1 Peter 5:7).

You're driving along on the expressway with the nearest exit three miles away. Your car's engine misses a beat and then another. You notice that little light on the dashboard that indicates "empty." The gas tank is almost bone dry and you're running on fumes. Your engine misses another beat and the car jerks. Your body tenses up. You slow down to conserve gas (a lot of good that will do now), and you pray for one more gallon of gas to appear miraculously in the tank.

It's interesting how many people run around town with their vehicles' gas tanks on empty. It's as though they enjoy flirting with disaster. Well, a car isn't the only thing that people try to run on empty. We men do it in our personal lives as well. Spiritually we may be running around with our tanks bordering on empty. When nothing is left in the spiritual tank, we can make some major mistakes. This is often when our resistance is low and temptation hits. We all know the results.

Are we flirting with spiritual emptiness when we fail to fill up? Yes. Sometimes we just go through the motions of filling up when we attend church, talk to God, and read Scripture. Instead of merely attending church, we need to go there and *worship* the living God. Worship is focusing on God as the center of our lives instead of focusing on ourselves. Instead of just talking to God, we need to *listen* to Him. Instead of reading the Scriptures, we need to study and memorize them.

You don't have to run on empty.

You don't have to run out of gas.

Like everything else in life, you have a choice. [21]

When others are happy, be happy with them. If they are sad, share
their sorrow. Work happily together. Don't try to act big. Don't
try to get into the good graces of important people, but enjoy the
company of ordinary folks. And don't think you know it all! Never
pay back evil for evil. Do things in such a way that everyone can
see you are honest clear through. Don't quarrel with anyone. Be at
peace with everyone, just as much as possible. Dear friends, never
avenge yourselves. Leave that to God (Romans 12:15-19 TLB).

Today's verses were not created as a United Nations manifesto. Nor were they new policies created by the current government. These words were *inspired by God and given to us* to help us get along with others. Can you imagine what would happen if:

- everyone at your place of employment made a commitment to live by these guidelines within the company as well as when interacting with customers? Furthermore, you all sat down for lengthy discussion on how you could put these principles into practice in simple ways?

- your entire family decided to memorize this passage and each evening for a month evaluated how everyone was doing in applying its principles? They agreed to pray for each other and to implement the teaching in their own lives?

You may be saying, "Yes! If all these people would live by this teaching, it would be great. Now how do we get them to do it?" I thought you'd never ask! It's simple. *Do it yourself!* Live it. Show it in your life consistently. Make the Holy Spirit your source of power. People need a model, an example of this Scripture in action...and you're it!

*A glad heart makes a cheerful countenance, but by sorrow
of heart the spirit is broken (Proverbs 15:13 AMP).*

Being around some men is a downer. They're full of gloom. They have no joy, no laughter, no life. Sure, life is tough, but there is also a lot to smile about—a lot to laugh at. Do you ever wonder what made Jesus laugh? Probably a lot of the same things we enjoy, and quite possibly there are some things we laugh at that He wouldn't.

Humor is everywhere. Look for misprints in church bulletins or on signs: "This being Easter Sunday, Mrs. Jones will lay an egg on the church altar" or "Due to the Rector's illness, the healing service is postponed." What about outdated rules and regulations? In Seattle it's illegal "to carry a concealed weapon of more than six feet in length." In the state of Oklahoma, "any vehicle involved in an accident which results in the death of another person shall stop and give his name and address to the person struck."[1]

How do people view you? Do you laugh easily? Do you exude joy? Or are you a gloom machine? God is the author of smiles, joy, and laughter. He wants us to experience these gifts and infect other people with their positive potential. It's one of His prescriptions designed to make life more bearable. Think about these words of Elton Trueblood:

> The Christian is joyful, not because he is blind to injustice and suffering, but because he is convinced that these, in the light of the divine sovereignty, are never ultimate...The humor of the Christian is not a way of denying the tears, but rather a way of affirming something which is deeper than tears.[2]

A man of strength has a cheerful heart.

Let us fix our eyes on Jesus, the author and perfecter of our faith, who
for the joy set before him endured the cross, scorning its shame, and
sat down at the right hand of the throne of God (Hebrews 12:2).

When God called Moses to lead the Israelites out of Egypt, Moses argued with Him. *Really argued. Debated.* In essence he said, "God, You don't know what You're talking about! You don't know what You're asking me to do." Have you done that with God? Exodus 3 and 4 records Moses' arguments, which must have seemed perfectly logical to him. He said, "I'm not the person for a job like that!" (Exodus 3:11 TLB). Have you ever felt that way or said that to God? Or how about when Moses essentially tells God, "I don't know what to say or how to answer questions the people might have" (see 3:13). Has that thought ever kept you quiet? It keeps a lot of men from speaking out for their faith, sharing in church, or praying out loud with their wives. We need to let God be the determiner of what we say as well as the source of our words.

Moses said, "They won't believe me!" (4:1 TLB). Have you said that? Well, you won't know until you try. Moses said, "I'm just not a good speaker. I never have been, and I'm not now, even after you have spoken to me, for I have a speech impediment," Moses said (4:10 TLB). If that's true for you, does it really have to be a problem? With God's help and practice, who knows what you can do! And Moses said, "O Lord, please send someone else to do it" (4:13 NIV). He is essentially saying, "Anyone else can do this better than I can." If you say this, you really don't know that's true. Let God use you.

Moses looked at things through his own eyes. When he looked through God's eyes and stepped forward in faith, he accomplished remarkable things. So can you.

All have sinned and fall short of the glory of God (Romans 3:23).

Some of the most famous incidents in history have been acts of treason. Books have been written and movies made recounting the incidents and their effects upon the countries involved. Some people are still referred to as "that traitor." *Treason* is "a betrayal of trust or faith; violation of the allegiance owed to one's sovereign."³ *We are all guilty of treason.* That's not a pleasant thought, is it? But it's true. Are you aware of what most countries do to traitors? Public hangings and firing squads are still the norm in some countries. The treason we've committed is called *sin*. Everyone has violated God's law.

Have you considered the many ways we describe sin today? Consider these words: *unlawful, lawlessness, ungodliness, disobedience.* Each word is formed by negating another word. When you sin you fall short of the mark. And that's exactly what the word means in the original Greek of the New Testament—missing the mark.

Sin is all around us. Once we've committed treason, we cannot *not* be a traitor. In our human world, traitors are rarely given a pardon. It's different with God! "The wages of sin is death, but the gift of God is eternal life in Christ Jesus our Lord" (Romans 6:23). *What a reprieve!* Eternal life is undeserved, but God gives it anyway.

> God so loved the world that he gave his one and only Son, that whoever believes in him shall not perish but have eternal life (John 3:16).

Not only are we forgiven, not only has the slate been wiped clean by God, but He still wants us for Himself...forever!⁴

It is for your good that I am going away. Unless
I go away, the Counselor will not come to you; but
if I go, I will send him to you (John 16:7-8).

You've got a power source that will outlast any battery. It's more intense than what powers a nuclear submarine. And it's an actual person! The Holy Spirit isn't an "it." Scripture calls Him "the Spirit of truth." "The world…neither sees him nor knows him. But you know him, for he lives with you and will be in you" (John 14:17).

The Holy Spirit has knowledge of God's thoughts (1 Corinthians 2:11), a will (1 Corinthians 12:11), a mind (Romans 8:27), and love (Romans 15:30). We can lie to Him (Acts 5:3), insult Him (see Hebrews 10:29), and grieve Him (Ephesians 4:30). John calls Him "the Helper" (NCV). He is God inside of us to help us be men of integrity. You don't have to handle temptation and problems yourself. The Holy Spirit is with you!

- *He comforts anyone who is a Christian.* "When I go away, I will send the Helper to you" (John 16:7 NCV). Have you felt the comforting hands of God when your life seemed shattered? That was the Holy Spirit.

- *He convicts those who don't know Him.* "When the Helper comes, he will prove to the people of the world about sin, about being right with God, and about judgment" (John 16:8 NCV). Remember that time of conviction…or when something prodded you about what you had said or done? That was the Holy Spirit.

- *He conveys the truth.* "When the Spirit of truth comes, he will lead you into all truth" (John 16:13 NCV). Have you ever had a new spiritual insight or had Scripture speak to your heart? That was the Holy Spirit!

Let this power source—this person—run all of your life.[5]

*I have told you these things, so that in me you may have
peace. In this world you will have trouble. But take
heart! I have overcome the world (John 16:33).*

Hardship comes in several packages. One is physical suffering. "My life is consumed by anguish and my years by groaning; my strength fails because of my affliction, and my bones grow weak" (Psalm 31:10). The older we get, the more we identify with David in this passage. It may not have hit you yet, but because of age, illness, or accident we all become limited in our physical abilities at some point. David's body went through some changes as he got older. Let's face it. Even if we take care of ourselves, decay and deterioration set in. How will you handle it?

Hardship also happens because of people. They can cause some of the greatest grief in our lives. David knew this. "Because of all my enemies, I am the utter contempt of my neighbors; I am a dread to my friends— those who see me on the street flee from me. I am forgotten by them as though I were dead; I have become like broken pottery. For I hear the slander of many; there is terror on every side; they conspire against me and plot to take my life" (Psalm 31:11-13).

Sound familiar? Maybe you've been there, or perhaps that's where you are now. How do you handle people like this? Whether your problems are caused by physical limitations or other people, how you handle these problems of life say a lot about you.

Some men get sullen, grouchy, cantankerous, depressed, or withdrawn. Other men accept what can't be changed, change what they can, adjust, adapt, and learn from each hardship. Which man "makes it" in life, continuing to grow and really reflecting Jesus Christ? And which one are you?

I will rejoice in the LORD, I will be joyful in God my Savior. The Sovereign LORD is my strength; he makes my feet like the feet of a deer, he enables me to go on the heights (Habakkuk 3:18-19).

You get into your car, put the key in the ignition, turn it, and…nothing. The battery is dead, drained. There is not an ounce of electricity left to turn the engine over. You're not going anywhere. Some mornings you may feel like that dead battery. The alarm goes off and you're supposed to roll out of bed…but you never make it. You don't have what it takes. You're a depleted, disengaged, dead power source.

Why do batteries die? Sometimes they've simply lived out their life expectancy. They've given all they were meant to, and now there's nothing left to recharge. Others die because someone left the car lights on, which drained the battery of its strength.

We're a lot like a car battery. We keep running and running without stopping to rest and recharge. All too soon we can't function. We've run out of strength.

If you want strength, go to the power source—your Lord God. The phrase "I will rejoice in the Lord" really means "to leap for joy and spin around in exultation." Not too many of us do this literally but perhaps it wouldn't be a bad idea.

Do you know the difference between the words *joy* and *happiness* as they're used here? The latter is based on having no problems or concerns. Joy means having faith in God no matter what happens. When you trust in God rather than in your circumstances, you'll discover that God will give you the strength you need. And His strength will keep you moving ahead. So go to your power source—go to God!

*Here is my servant whom I have chosen, the one I
love, in whom I delight (Matthew 12:18).*

Servants have one job to perform: to serve. And that's what the Bible calls us to do. In some positions of serving we are recognized and appreciated; in others we feel taken for granted. If that's the way you feel at times, remember that someone else came to serve and was unappreciated. One of the more than 100 names and titles of Jesus was "servant." This role was a fulfillment of prophecy (Isaiah 52:13; 53:11).

The New Testament gives many examples of transformed people who called themselves servants. In Romans 1:1, Paul introduced himself as "a servant of Christ Jesus." In 2 Peter 1:1, Peter introduced himself as "a servant and apostle of Jesus Christ." Judas, the brother of Jesus, said the same, as did John (Jude 1; Revelation 1:1). Why, then, aren't we more ready to serve since we too are followers of Christ? Perhaps because our society doesn't value the servant role. We'd rather get than give, take than share, grasp than release. We have to learn to be "other centered." Are we afraid of what being a servant might cost us? Yes. But let's choose to focus on service as a privilege![6]

Astronaut James Irwin shared that while "lunar walking" he realized that people might consider him a celebrity. He records, "As I was returning to earth, I realized that I was a servant, not a celebrity. I am here as God's servant on Planet Earth to share what I have experienced, that others might know the glory of God."

If Christ, the Lord of the universe, became a servant for us, can we do any less for Him?[7] Consider how each person in your family could be more of a servant today. Why not discuss it with them and figure out how to put it into action?[8]

A wife of noble character who can find? She is worth far more than rubies. Her husband has full confidence in her (Proverbs 31:10-11).

In *Mystery of Marriage,* Mike Mason shares some great thoughts on marriage.

A marriage is not a joining of two worlds, but an abandoning of two worlds in order that one new one might be formed.

The call to be married bears comparison with Jesus' advice to the rich young man to sell all his possessions and to follow Him. It is a vocation to total abandonment. For most people, in fact, marriage is the single most wholehearted step they will ever take toward a fulfillment of Jesus' command to love one's neighbor as oneself. For every marriage partner begins as a neighbor, and often enough a neighbor who has been left beaten and wounded on the road of love, whom all the rest of the world has in a sense passed by.

The marriage vows give glory to God. While it is true that a man and a woman on their wedding day take a step toward a unique fulfillment of the commandment of love, it is even more true to say of matrimony that it is a sacramental outpouring of God's grace enabling such love to take place. The human couple indicates humbly a willingness to give themselves to this love; but it is the Lord who makes love possible in the first place, and therefore it is He who promises that His gift of love will not be taken away.

Marriage, even under the very best of circumstances, is a crisis— one of the major crises of life—and it is dangerous not to be aware of this. Whether it turns out to be a healthy, challenging, and constructive crisis or a disastrous nightmare depends largely upon how willing the partners are to be changed, by how malleable they choose to be.[9]

The precepts of the LORD are right, giving joy to the heart. The commands of the LORD are radiant, giving light to the eyes. The fear of the LORD is pure, enduring forever. The ordinances of the LORD are sure and altogether righteous. They are more precious than gold, than much pure gold; they are sweeter than honey, than honey from the comb. By them is your servant warned; in keeping them there is great reward (Psalm 19:8-11).

Rules, rules…and more rules. We live in a culture that wants as much freedom as possible, yet we enact so many rules. There are even rules for the rules. But laws provide necessary boundaries. Granted, some human laws are ridiculous, but God's laws never are. What are some of God's rules you resist? Some of us resist only in our minds, some flagrantly break God's laws, while others devise clever schemes to get around them.

God's laws are not given to restrict our lives and freedom. Newscaster Ted Koppel shocked people when addressing a graduating class at Duke University some years ago:

> We have actually convinced ourselves that slogans will save us. Shoot up if you must, but use a clean needle. Enjoy sex whenever and with whomever you wish, but wear a condom. No! The answer is No! Not because it isn't cool or smart or because you might end up in jail or dying in an AIDS ward…In its purest form, truth is not a polite tap on the shoulder. It is a howling reproach. What Moses brought down from Mount Sinai were not the Ten Suggestions.[10]

Are you treating some of God's laws as suggestions?

*A man who refuses to admit his mistakes can never be
successful. But if he confesses and forsakes them, he
gets another chance (Proverbs 28:13 TLB).*

Blame is pointing your finger at another person to get the focus off you. And blame isn't new; it started way back in the Garden of Eden:

> [God] said, "…Who told you that you were naked? Have you eaten from the tree that I commanded you not to eat from?"
>
> The man said, "The woman you put here with me—she gave me some fruit from the tree, and I ate it."
>
> Then the LORD God said to the woman, "What is this you have done?"
>
> The woman said, "The serpent deceived me, and I ate" (Genesis 3:11-13).

We blame people, circumstances, and even God. Most often, the blaming statements aren't very original. Read through this list and note which ones you have used:

- Well, I didn't start this. It wasn't my fault.
- What I did could have been worse. Besides, they provoked me.
- Everybody at work was doing it, so I couldn't be the odd one.

Blame doesn't build relationships or resolve differences. It pushes people apart and creates endless arguments. There are better ways to handle mistakes. Try saying:

- You're right.
- I am responsible.
- I'm sorry.
- I will choose a different response next time.

God said, "It is not good for the man to be alone" (Genesis 2:18).

Intimacy is the foundation for love and friendship. It's a close emotional bond that involves mutual sharing and understanding. Please note the word *mutual.* Each person in an intimate relationship wants to know the other's deepest dreams, wishes, concerns, hopes, and fears, while at the same time being an open book himself. Intimacy leads to deep feelings of closeness, warmth, and trust. It eliminates the pain of loneliness. If you're going to have intimacy, you must have the confidence to expose the private, vulnerable portion of your life. Intimacy means you can't remain isolated.

Yes, intimacy can hurt. It includes the risk of being real with another person. When a man relates closely to others, he discovers a greater awareness of himself. His fears can be dissolved, which lets self-acceptance develop. Some men approach intimacy by saying, "If I want to confront my fear of intimacy and open up, I need to see there are more benefits in opening up than in staying closed. I need to see it's safe. I don't want any negative value judgments about what I'm sharing. I don't want others telling me their opinions of what I think or feel. I need others to tell me it's okay to do this."

Men, be encouraged that others are hesitant about developing intimacy in relationships. It is a slow journey that takes work, time, and involves discomfort at times. It means learning more about your feelings. It may involve participating in a small group of men who will embark on this journey with you.

Now that you have a clearer idea of what true intimacy entails, how do you think your partner would rate the level of intimacy in your relationship?

He...speaks the truth from his heart (Psalm 15:2).

The heart is an important organ. We make reference to it all the time. When we're scared we say, "My heart almost stopped with fright." If we know someone who's generous we describe him as "having a big heart." When we describe a person as having a broken heart, we are talking about grief. When we were kids, to emphasize the fact that we were telling the truth, we'd say, "Cross my heart and hope to die."

The heart is also referred to when we talk about convictions: "I know deep in my heart." When we say "that person has a good heart" we could be talking about a person's character or ability to keep commitments. When David says in today's verse, "speaks the truth from his heart," he's saying a man of character is truthful and can be depended on to speak the truth regardless of the consequences. There's the key word: *regardless*...

Regardless of how much it costs him he speaks the truth.

Regardless of how much it makes him look bad.

Regardless of how much difficulty he gets into.

Regardless of how much others don't like to hear what he has to say.

Telling the truth is rare today. Who can you count on to consistently tell you the truth? Anyone? If you are a truth teller, you're different from a lot of men. But you'll also be trusted. Telling the truth benefits you, and it's a way to bring honor and glory to God in today's society![11]

*We pursue the things which make for peace and the
building up of one another (Romans 14:19 NASB).*

Do you want your marriage to last forever? Here's how to do it.

People in long-term marriages tend to take each other for granted.
The most common of the "takens" include:

You will always be here for me.

You will always love me.

We will always be together.

Making these assumptions in a marriage is living more in Fantasy-
land than on Reality Ridge. People who take things for granted
are seldom appreciative of the everyday blessings in their lives...
They seldom say thank you for anything. When you take someone
for granted you demean him or her. You send the unspoken message, "You are not worth much to me." You also rob this person
of the gift of human appreciation. And to be loved and appreciated gives all of us a reason to live each day...In long-term marriages where one or both spouses are continually taken for granted,
a wall of indifference arises between them...The way out of this
is simple but crucial:

- Start saying thank you and showing appreciation.

- Be more consciously tuned in; become more giving and
  affirming.

- Specialize in the little things that mean a lot: bring each
  other flowers...hold hands in public and walk in the rain,
  send caring and funny cards...[12]

Husbands, love your wives (Ephesians 5:25).

I f you're married, here are today's Ten Commandments for loving your wife:

- *Silence is not always golden,* especially between husband and wife. Ask your wife when she'd like to set aside time just to talk.

- *Take your wife's feelings and viewpoints seriously.* When they differ from yours, tell her, "I see things differently, but maybe I can learn from you." Believe it!

- *Tell your wife how much you value her.* "A wife of noble character who can find? She is worth far more than rubies" (Proverbs 31:10).

- The best way to tell your wife about something you don't like is to tell her about something you do like: "I really like it when you try out new recipes on me."

- *When your wife lets you know you've hurt her, think about your goal.* Will you be defensive? Resentful? Humble? If you want to be close, the choice is clear.

- *Be your wife's companion.* When your wife is upset, exhausted, or overwhelmed, do you know what she needs most of all? Usually it's simple companionship. Be there for her. Your presence, patience, and prayers will help her feel loved.

- *If you love someone you will be loyal to her no matter what the cost.* You always believe in her, expect the best of her, and defend her (1 Corinthians 13:7).

- *Complaining about your wife won't improve your marriage.* Instead, tell her what you like about your marriage and make positive suggestions for *both* of you.[13]

*Do not worry about your life, what you will eat or drink; or
about your body, what you will wear. Is life more important
than food, and the body more important than clothes?...
Seek first his kingdom and his righteousness, and all these
things will be given to you as well (Matthew 6:25,33).*

During the Great Depression of the 1930s, the unemployment rate in the United States soared. Men and women waited for hours to get loaves of bread or bowls of soup. Jobs that seemed secure disappeared overnight. Today job security seems to be a thing of the past too. Workers at all levels have lost their jobs. How secure is your employment? If you were to lose it tomorrow, how would you and your family survive? How would you feel about yourself as a man? Have these thoughts plagued you?

- They don't need me anymore.

- Someone else can do it better.

- It could be I'm too old.

- I can't cut it anymore.

Some people live in constant fear of these messages—even when their jobs are secure. They work harder and longer than others. They give 110 percent, which leaves a deficit for home. We get in this bind because we use work as our security. We forget that our security is in God! Sure, we can worry about it, but why not make the choice listed in today's verses? Don't you think one is a much better choice than the other?

Clothe yourselves with the Lord Jesus Christ (Romans 13:14).

O God, our Father, we thank you that you sent your Son Jesus Christ into this world to be our Savior and our Lord. We thank you that he took our body and our flesh and blood upon himself, and so showed us that this body of ours is fit to be your dwelling place.

We thank you that he did our work, that he earned a living, that he served the public, and so showed us that even the smallest tasks are not beneath your majesty and can be done for you. We thank you that he lived in an ordinary home, that he knew the problems of living together, that he experienced the rough and smooth of family life, and so showed us that any home, however humble, can be a place where in the ordinary routine of daily life we can make all life an act of worship to you.

Lord Jesus, come again to us this day. Come into our hearts, and so cleanse them, that we being pure in heart may see God our Father. Come into our minds, and so enlighten and illumine them that we may know you who are the way, the truth, and the life. Touch our lips, that we may speak no word which would hurt another or grieve you. Touch our eyes, that they may never linger on any forbidden thing. Touch our hands, that they may become useful with service to the needs of others.

When we are sad, comfort us; when we are tired, refresh us; when we are lonely, cheer us; when we are tempted, strengthen us; when we are perplexed, guide us; when we are happy, make our joy doubly dear…Help us so to live that, whenever your call comes for us, at morning, at midday or at evening, it may find us ready, our work completed and our hearts at peace with you, so that we may enter at last with joy into your nearer presence and into life eternal; through Jesus Christ our Lord. Amen.[14]

*Husbands, love your wives, just as Christ loved the
church and gave himself up for her (Ephesians 5:25).*

Commitment is costly, especially if you're married. When Dr. Robertson McQuilken announced his resignation as president of Columbia Bible College to care for his wife, Muriel, who was suffering from the advanced stages of Alzheimer's disease, he wrote:

> My dear wife, Muriel, has been in failing mental health for about eight years. So far I have been able to carry both her ever-growing needs and my leadership responsibilities at CBC. But recently it has become apparent that Muriel is contented most of the time she is with me and almost none of the time I am away from her. It is not just discontent. She is filled with fear—even terror—that she has lost me and always goes in search of me when I leave home. Then she may be full of anger when she cannot get to me. So it is clear to me that she needs me now, full-time.

> Perhaps it would help you to understand if I shared with you what I shared at the time of the announcement of my resignation in chapel. The decision was made, in a way, forty-two years ago when I promised to care for Muriel "in sickness and in health...till death do us part." So, as I told the students and faculty, as a man of my word, integrity has something to do with it. But so does fairness. She has cared for me fully and sacrificially all these years; if I cared for her for the next forty years I would not be out of debt. Duty, however, can be grim and stoic. But there is more; I love Muriel. She is a delight to me—her childlike dependence and confidence in me, her warm love, occasional flashes of that wit I used to relish so, her happy spirit and tough resilience in the face of her continual distressing frustration. I do not have to care for her, I get to! It is a high honor to care for so wonderful a person.[15]

Get rid of all bitterness, rage and anger, brawling and slander, along with every form of malice. Be kind and compassionate to one another, forgiving each other, just as in Christ God forgave you (Ephesians 4:31-32).

Getting along with others is not always the easiest task. It takes work and requires the *absence* of four spirits.

The competitive spirit. Whenever there are several people involved in any task, it's important to work together. The group will get more accomplished when everyone functions as partners. This is difficult for men because we were raised to be competitors—to look out for ourselves, disparage the successes of others, and focus on winning. It's possible to do our best without it being at the expense of others.

The critical spirit destroys not only others and the person possessing it. Often it comes from being perfectionists. No matter the reason, it's not a good way to live. God's Word says, "Therefore let us stop passing judgment on one another. Instead, make up your mind not to put any stumbling block or obstacle in your brother's way" (Romans 14:13).

Some men struggle with *a vain spirit.* We're enamored with ourselves, and our calling in life seems to be to impress others. Our goal is to capture people's attention and live off their applause. When this spirit overtakes us, it's difficult to reflect the presence of Jesus in our lives. The two can't live together.

The adversarial spirit is destructive. When we're at odds with another person and feelings linger, bitterness and resentment come into play. Perhaps you've resented your parents, your wife, and your coworkers. God's Word tells us there's a better way to live. Read today's verses again and let the spirit of them indwell your heart and run your life.[16]

For God so loved the world... (John 3:16).

Do you want to be loved and accepted in a consistent way? Only One being can do that: God. Note what the Scriptures say about Him by meditating on these verses:

- He is the loving, concerned Father who is interested in the intimate details of our lives (Matthew 6:25-34).

- He never gives up on us (Luke 15:3-32).

- He sent His Son to die for us though we were undeserving (Romans 5:8).

- He stands with us in good and bad circumstances (Hebrews 13:5).

- He gives all races and sexes equal status (Galatians 3:28).

- He is available to us through prayer (John 14:13-14).

- He is aware of our needs (Isaiah 65:24).

- He created us for an eternal relationship with him (John 3:16).

- He values us and causes our growth (1 Corinthians 10:13).

- He comforts us (2 Corinthians 1:3-5).

- He strengthens us through His Spirit (Ephesians 3:16).

- He cleanses us from sin (Hebrews 10:17-18).

- He is always available to us (Romans 8:38-39).

- He is a God of hope (Romans 15:13).

- He provides a way to escape temptation (1 Corinthians 10:13).

*God created man in his own image, in the image of God he
created him; male and female he created them (Genesis 1:27).*

Harry Hollis, Jr., in his book *Thank God for Sex,* writes:

Thank you, O Redeemer, for letting me express love through sex.
Thank you for making it possible for things to be right with sex—
that there can be beauty and wonder between woman and man.

You have given us a model for love in Jesus. He lived and laughed
and accepted his humanity. He resisted sexual temptations which
were every bit as real as mine. He taught about the relationship
of husband and wife by showing love for his bride the church.
Thank you that he gives me the power to resist temptations also.
Thank you that real sexual freedom comes in being bound to the
true man Jesus.

Everywhere there are signs that point to the sex god: Books declare
that sex is our savior; songs are sung as prayers to sex; pictures
show its airbrushed incarnations; advertisers hawk its perfume
and aftershave libations. Help me know that sex is not salvation.
Help me see instead that there is salvation for sex. For the exciting
sensations of erotic love, I offer you my thanks.

Lord, you replace sexual boredom with joy; you point past sexual slavery to the hope of purity; you enable sexual lovers to be
friends; you teach how to replace lust-making with lovemaking.
Would I have any hope for sexual responsibility without the power
you give? Would I ever be a covenant keeper without the fidelity
you inspire?

Thank you, Lord, for a love that stays when the bed is made.
Help me to keep my marriage bed undefiled—to see it as an altar
of grace and pleasure. Keep sex good in my life, through your
redeeming love. Teach me to say: "Thank God for sex!"[17]

Grace and peace to you from God our Father and
the Lord Jesus Christ (Ephesians 1:2).

Grace is the unmerited favor of God. He gives us what we don't deserve. There are four aspects of grace. The first is described in the word *prevenient,* which means "beforehand." God's grace is extended to you before you even ask. His acceptance is given before you feel acceptable, forgiveness is offered before you ask, and God chose you before you responded to Him. Jesus said, "You did not choose me, but I chose you" (John 15:16). "God demonstrates his own love for us in this: While we were still sinners, Christ died for us" (Romans 5:8). When a man accepts the Lord he says, "I found God!" It may seem that way, but it's actually the opposite. God chose him. This is grace as well.

Second, God's grace is an *initiative* grace on His part. He is always pursuing a deeper relationship with you, even if you're in a holding pattern. Isaiah said: "As the days of a tree, so will be the days of my people; my chosen ones will long enjoy the works of their hands. They will not toil in vain or bear children doomed to misfortune; for they will be a people blessed by the LORD, they and their descendants with them. Before they call I will answer; while they are still speaking I will hear" (Isaiah 65:22-24).

Third, God's grace is *inexhaustible.* You can't drain the supply. You can't even diminish it. The container is *always* full.

And fourth, God's grace is *all-sufficient*—not partial but totally. Jesus said to Paul at his time of need, "My grace is sufficient for you" (2 Corinthians 12:9).

With this in mind, go out and do what you have to do today with a new sense of assurance and power. That's what grace can do for you![18]

*So when you, a mere man, pass judgment on them and yet do the same
things, do you think you will escape God's judgment? (Romans 2:3).*

Dr. Lloyd John Ogilvie had this insight to share about judging others:

A father paced the bedroom floor while his daughter took what
he thought was far too long to say good night to her boyfriend...
"I don't see why it takes that young man so long to say good night.
I don't know about this younger generation!" he said.

"Oh, come to bed," his wife said. "Weren't you young once?"

"Yes, I was, and that's just why I'm worried and can't come to
bed!"...

The humor of this story enables us to consider a very serious truth.
The over-worried father's statement expressed real insight into
himself. His judgment of his daughter and her young man was
based on his own memories of what he had done in living rooms
a generation before. The problem was that he had projected these
memories into worry in the present. His judgment did not fit the
new situation but was based on his own concern.

Judgments often are exposures of our own needs. The things we
judge in others are often the things which are troubling us deeply
within. Righteous indignation may be caused by something not
so righteous in us. Something we have done or wished we had had
the courage to do, something unresolved or unforgiven, something hidden or unhealed will cause the judgment of someone else.

Whenever we are overly critical we should ask ourselves, "Why
does that bother you?" There are some things which need to be
questioned in loving concern for another person, but when our
judgments are rash or emotional or severe, it usually indicates that
part of the problem is still within us.[19]

*I can do everything through him who gives
me strength (Philippians 4:13).*

It's been one of those days—a bad day, a fur-ball day, a rotten day. The kind of day where nothing goes well. People are late, they don't follow through, dinner is cold, everyone wants something without giving appreciation, and the expressway is a joke. You're irritated and discouraged. You may even be a bit depressed.

When days like this occur, sometimes we compound the problem by trying to fix everything ourselves. This is the time to say "God, please help me." And He will! One of the best ways to handle these days is to dwell on God's Word. Read these passages out loud during your dark days. Reflect on them and then note the difference in your day.

> I have set the LORD always before me. Because he is at my right hand, I will not be shaken (Psalm 16:8).

> You, O LORD, keep my lamp burning; my God turns my darkness into light (Psalm 18:28).

> The LORD is my light and my salvation—whom shall I fear? The LORD is the stronghold of my life—of whom shall I be afraid? (Psalm 27:1).

> God is our refuge and strength, an ever-present help in trouble (Psalm 46:l).

> Create in me a pure heart, O God, and renew a steadfast spirit within me (Psalm 51:10).

> Cast your cares on the LORD and he will sustain you; he will never let the righteous fall (Psalm 55:22).

> My soul finds rest in God alone; my salvation comes from him (Psalm 62:l).

Always keep on praying (1 Thessalonians 5:17 TLB).

H ere is another thought about praying together as a couple.

Prayer is an awareness of the presence of a holy and loving God in one's life, and an awareness of God's relations to one's husband or wife. Prayer is listening to God, a valuable lesson in learning to listen to one another. In prayer one searches the interior life for blocks to personal surrender to God, evaluating one's conduct in the quiet of prayerful meditation. At times prayer may be rich with confession and self-humbling, or with renunciation and higher resolve to fulfill God's best.

Praying together shuts out the petty elements of daily conflict and anxiety, permitting a couple to gain a higher perspective upon their lives, allowing their spirits to be elevated to a consideration of eternal values and enduring relationships.

Prayer helps a couple sort out unworthy objects of concern and helps them to concentrate on the nobler goals of life. All the threatening things that trouble a pair can find relief in the presence of God; humbling themselves before Him, they humble themselves before one another…Unbecoming self-assurance and stubborn independence give way before the recognition of their inadequacy to meet divine standards of life; thus, two people are led to seek God's help and the support of each other.[20]

Scripture also tells us to pray:

You haven't tried this before, [but begin now]. Ask, using my name, and you will receive, and your cup of joy will overflow (John 16:24 TLB).

Admit your faults to one another and pray for each other (James 5:16 TLB).

Jesus stood and said in a loud voice, "If anyone is thirsty, let him come to me and drink. Whoever believes in me, as the Scripture has said, streams of living water will flow from within him" (John 7:37-38).

You've been walking across the desert for two days now. Your car broke down, and you had no other choice but to hoof it to civilization. You know it will take at least four days to get there. The quart of water you started out with is gone. Your mouth feels as dry as the desert you're walking on and your tongue has swelled. The gritty sand feels like rocks between your teeth. All of a sudden you see a well. You run up to it and pump the handle. Soon there's a flow—but it's not water. It's sand. Then you notice a sign: "Two feet over and two feet down you'll find a jug of water buried. Dig it up and use the water to prime the pump. Drink all the water you want, but when you are done, be sure you fill the jug again for the next person and then bury it!"

You dig down, one foot, eighteen inches, and then your hand hits the jug. You bring it up and hear the water sloshing around. What do you do? Your mouth and throat are crying out for water. But the well could provide enough for you to drink to your heart's content, fill your containers, and make it to safety. But what if you prime the pump with the water and it doesn't work?

What would you do? It's a risk, isn't it? That's what life is all about. That's what faith is all about too. It's trusting the writer of the sign. It's following the instructions. It's living on the edge. God wants us to be faithful. Hebrews 11:6 says, "Without faith it is impossible to please God, because anyone who comes to him must believe that he exists and that he rewards those who earnestly seek him."[21]

*You have made known to me the path of life; you
will fill me with joy in your presence, with eternal
pleasures at your right hand (Psalm 16:11).*

Pleasure is an interesting word. The dictionary defines it as "a pleased feeling; enjoyment; delight; satisfaction; something that gives these. Gratification of the senses; sensual satisfaction."[22] Slogans use the word incorrectly. Tobacco companies use ads that say, "Come to where the pleasure is." A chewing gum company says, "Double your pleasure, double your fun." And the ads work. We all want to be satisfied.

Some pleasures are all right. Some violate other people. Some violate us and lead to addiction. Have you ever thought about what you do that gives you the most pleasure and what gives you the least pleasure? When your pursuit of pleasure is in balance and stays within ethical boundaries, it's all right. You're still in control of it. But many men become slaves to their pleasures, and seeking it becomes their primary drive.

If you struggle with this, you're not the only one! It's always been a temptation. Look at Solomon. This king went overboard in his desire for pleasure and so did his kingdom. He didn't know the meaning of the word *moderation*. He lost his focus on God and God's standards and his kingdom failed. True, a nation may not be destroyed by your pursuit of pleasure, but your family can be…and so can your career.

God is not against pleasure; He provides it. Ask Him what kind of pleasure He has in store for you. "Delight yourself in the LORD and he will give you the desires of your heart" (Psalm 37:4). And acknowledge "who satisfies your desires with good things so that your youth is renewed like the eagle's" (Psalm 103:5). The pleasures God provides are not like the fleeting pleasures promised by commercials. God really satisfies!

*He who listens to a life-giving rebuke will be at home among the
wise. He who ignores discipline despises himself, but whoever
heeds correction gains understanding (Proverbs 15:31-32).*

How do you handle it when someone takes you to task, criticizes
you, or offers "constructive suggestions"? Do you enjoy it? Does it
make you feel better? Do you usually say, "You're right. Thanks"? Probably not. But, really, we need all the help we can get. The Bible talks about
reproof. It uses a Hebrew word that means "to correct or to convince."
God's Word and the Holy Spirit also correct us. A needed slight course
correction now may prevent disaster later on. If an airliner is off course
by just half a degree, several hundred miles later it's way off course. It's
the same way with our lives.

Too often we do what Solomon talks about in Proverbs 1:23-24,28:
"If you had responded to my rebuke, I would have poured out my heart
to you and made my thoughts known to you. But since you rejected me
when I called and no one gave heed...[you] will call to me but I will not
answer." The word *rejected* essentially means "a direct digging in of the
heels and saying, 'Don't confuse me with the facts. My mind is made up.'"

When Solomon says, "No one gave heed," it's as though people are
ignoring what is said or are being insensitive. Verse 25 says, "Since you
ignored all my advice and would not accept my rebuke." Two problems
jump out. Neglecting counsel implies indifference: "Hey, don't bother
me!" This attitude doesn't build close and loving relationships. And when
it says "would not accept my rebuke," what word comes to mind? You're
right! *Defensiveness.* The defensive person says, "You're wrong; I'm right.
I won't consider it."

The next time someone offers a reproof, what will your response be?

Now when Joshua was near Jericho, he looked up and saw a man
standing in front of him with a drawn sword in his hand. Joshua
went up to him and asked, "Are you for us or for our enemies?"

"Neither," he replied, "but as commander of the army of the LORD *I*
have now come." Then Joshua fell facedown to the ground in reverence,
and asked him, "What message does my Lord have for his servant?"

The commander of the LORD'S *army replied, "Take off your*
sandals, for the place where you are standing is holy."

And Joshua did so (Joshua 5:13-15).

Joshua's mentor, Moses, was dead so there was no more help from that direction. Joshua was the newly appointed commander of the army of Israel. They were ready to go to battle to claim the Promised Land, but the results were uncertain. Then Joshua sees this imposing figure with a sword and challenges him. He is confronting a commander of the Lord's army! If you were Joshua, how would you have responded? Joshua's response gives us a model of what to do. He threw himself on the ground. He probably had a sense of relief as well, and thought, *Now God is going to give me the battle plan! Yes! Now we can overwhelm our enemy.* Was he right? Not at all.

Joshua was told something quite simple: Recognize that God is holy. Surrender to Him. Humble yourself before Him. It's the same for us today. Our battles are different, but they are the same in some ways. There's an enemy for us to fight. Before we engage him, let's go to God and be humble before Him. That's the secret source of strength. Then we can face our enemies with confidence. [23]

"Where is your faith?" [Jesus] asked his disciples (Luke 8:25 NASB).

Have you had days when you wondered where your faith went? It seemed lost and you wondered how to find it? Martyn Lloyd-Jones said something interesting about that:

> Faith is not something that acts automatically, faith is not something that acts magically. We seem to think that faith is something that acts automatically. Many people, it seems to me, conceive of faith as if it were something similar to those thermostats which you have in connection with a heating apparatus: you set your thermostat at a given level and it acts automatically. If the temperature is tending to rise above that, the thermostat comes into operation and brings it down; if you use your hot water and the temperature is lowered, the thermostat comes into operation and sends it up, etc. You do not have to do anything about it, the thermostat acts automatically and brings the temperature back to the desired level automatically.
>
> Now there are many people who seem to think that faith acts like that. They assume that it does not matter what happens to them, that faith will operate and all will be well. Faith, however, is not something that acts magically or automatically. If it did, these men would never have been in trouble, faith would have come into operation, and they would have been calm and quiet and all could have been well. But faith is not like that and those are utter fallacies with respect to it.
>
> What is faith? Let us look at it positively. The principle taught here is that faith is an activity, it is something that has to be exercised. It does not come into operation itself, you and I have to put it into operation. It is a form of activity.[24]

Remind yourself of what Scripture says about faith and act on it. God will help you!

*I know that there is nothing better for men than to be happy and
do good while they live. That everyone may eat and drink, and find
satisfaction in all his toil—this is the gift of God (Ecclesiastes 3:12-13).*

These interesting verses from the book of Ecclesiastes talk about four gifts God has given to us. The first gift is the *ability to rejoice and enjoy life*. To what extent are you doing that? Is there something to rejoice in that you're overlooking? Being a Christian means we have the capability of enjoying life *regardless. Regardless* of what is or isn't happening. Proverbs 15:15 AMP says, "All the days of the desponding and afflicted are made evil [by anxious thoughts and forebodings], but he who has a glad heart has a continual feast [regardless of circumstances]."

The second gift is the *ability to do good independently* from what others do for us. God helps us develop hearts of generosity and helpfulness. *Regardless!* There's that word again. If you wait for someone else to do good before acting, you're letting them control what you do. Does that put a new light on it? You don't have to explain why you're being helpful or help in a way that gains recognition. Do good for the sake of God's kingdom!

The third gift is the *appetite to eat and drink*—yes! The *ability to enjoy our food*. If that sounds basic and mundane, just remember that it's one of God's gifts to you and purpose to savor what He has provided.

The fourth gift is the *ability to see good in our labor*. Do you see it that way? Some of our work is boring and routine, but do you look for God's purpose in all you do?

There's a purpose in all of God's gifts. Reflect on the four gifts we've just discussed. Will they make a difference in how you view life?

Some people like to make cutting remarks, but the words
of the wise soothe and heal (Proverbs 12:18 TLB).

Frustration! That teeth-grinding, steering-wheel-pounding feeling! We've all been there and done that. But think about these facts:

- *Frustration is a normal response.*
- *Anger is also a normal response.*
- *You will, at times, be irritated, disappointed, and frustrated with other people.*
- *Accepting your frustration is healthy; denying it can be disastrous.*

Frustration doesn't always lead to anger. If another person is doing something that bothers you, you may feel frustrated, but you can control your response. Frustration doesn't have to lead to an angry reaction. Your response is your choice! Two events during the 1976 Olympic games in Montreal illustrate frustration responses. In the two-man sailing event, the British team came in fourteenth in a field of sixteen. The British sailors were so frustrated they set fire to their yacht and waded ashore. Olneus Charles, a Haitian runner, also experienced frustration. He was lapped nine times in the 10,000-meter race. He came in last, but he didn't quit or let frustration get the best of him.

Here are three smart tactics for handling frustration. First, commit today's verse to memory. The next time frustration hits, delay your response. Slow down and take a few deep breaths. Finally, plan your response to frustration in advance. You'll be able to change only if you *plan* the change. Go for it! The results can be very constructive.

*The LORD spoke to Moses face to face, as a man
speaks to his friend (Exodus 33:11 AMP).*

Remember the story of Gale Sayers and Brian Piccolo? Gary Oliver describes it so well in his book *Real Men Have Feelings, Too:*

> Both were running backs with the Chicago Bears; Sayers was black and Piccolo was white. When they became roommates for away games in 1967 it was a first for race relations in the NFL. Between 1967 and 1969 their relationship developed into one of the most memorable in the history of professional sports. During the '69 season Brian Piccolo developed cancer. Though he fought as hard as he could to complete the season, he was in the hospital more than on the football field.
>
> Sayers and Piccolo and their wives had planned to attend the annual Professional Football Writers' Banquet in New York where Sayers was to receive the George S. Halas award as "the most courageous player in professional football," but Brian Piccolo was too ill to attend. As the strong and athletic Sayers stood to receive the award, tears began to flow that he couldn't hold back. He said: "You flatter me by giving me this award, but I tell you here and now that I accept it for Brian Piccolo...I love Brian Piccolo and I'd like you to love him. Tonight, when you hit your knees, ask God to love him too."
>
> Healthy men are men who aren't afraid to need other men. Real men aren't afraid of what people will say about them if they have close male friends. Godly men aren't afraid to risk learning how to love another man.[1]

Do you have a male friend you talk to face-to-face, heart-to-heart, from the gut? If so, you're fortunate. If not, it's worthwhile to develop such a relationship. Sure, it takes time and involves risks, listening, sharing, and honesty. But it's worth it!

Whatever you do, work at it with all your heart, as working for the Lord, not for men (Colossians 3:23).

Sixty thousand people in one stadium. They all paid good money to attend this game. Look at them! Row after row of people jammed together for three hours. They're not the players in the game; they're there to watch and enjoy their favorite sport. They cheer, boo, and second-guess the coaches, players, and referees. If they were out there on the field they'd do it differently—but they're not out there in the game. They're in the stands. They wouldn't dare to get out of the stands and go on the field. They'd get kicked out. They're supposed to be in the stands. But spectators do make a difference in games at times. Their enthusiastic cheering encourages the players. The money they spend for the tickets helps to pay the bills for the team. They may even take pictures of their hero and wear a shirt with the team name on it. But that's all they do. They're spectators.

There's another place where there are a lot of spectators—church. People file in, take their places in the pews, sing rather than cheer, pray rather than stomp their feet, and sit and listen quietly to a message. Then when it's over, they get up and leave. But wait. Where was the team—the players? They're supposed to be here too. Guess what? They were! But they were sitting in the wrong place. They were in the pews. The players had turned into spectators. In the church it's all right to climb out of the stands to get on the playing field. Not only is it all right, it's a necessity. *Christianity is not a spectator sport.* It's for players only. There's a game being played and the stakes are high—eternal life. But others won't know about God and the salvation available through Jesus unless the players are active. What about you? Are you in the game or just watching?

I became greater by far than anyone in Jerusalem before me.
In all this my wisdom stayed with me (Ecclesiastes 2:9).

Your name is printed on the program for everyone to see. So are your accomplishments. In fact, not only are your family and your company aware of what you've accomplished, so is everyone else at the convention—2000 delegates, all in the same field you're in. And because of that, doors and opportunities are now open to you.

Your company just offered you a new position. It comes with more money, status, responsibility, two secretaries, and a spacious office with windows. You've arrived! Life is full of perks with this new position.

The pursuit of position in our society is accepted as normal. We all want to move up the ladder. Each rung gets us closer to the top. But as we climb, we need to ask ourselves several questions. First, what rung of the ladder does God want us on? If you become the "best" in your field, how will you feel when someone else eventually takes your place? Keep in mind that if you aren't available, you'll be replaced immediately! We are called to live lives of excellence. That's great. But that doesn't always mean we'll get the best position.

What's the cost of striving for that position? Solomon went after prestige, power, and position, and he knew what it was like to reach the top. He couldn't go any higher. He was top dog. He was even greater than his father. But it cost him his nation and negatively influenced his son. Scripture says, "[Rehoboam] did evil because he had not set his heart on seeking the LORD" (2 Chronicles 12:14). That's a high price to pay for being on top.

*Husbands ought to love their wives as their own bodies. He
who loves his wife loves himself. After all, no one ever hated his
own body, but he feeds and cares for it, just as Christ does the
church—for we are members of his body (Ephesians 5:28-30).*

Do you want to know how to love your wife? Those forty-six words
in Ephesians sum it up. A husband loves his wife as himself. Her
body is his body. Her comfort is his comfort. Her need for care and concern is his. Richard Selzer explains it this way:

> Her young husband is in the room. He stands on the opposite side
> of the bed, and together they seem to do well in the evening lamp-
> light, isolated from me, private. *Who are they,* I ask myself, *he and
> this wry-mouth I have made, who gaze at and touch each other so gen-
> erously, greedily?* The young woman speaks. "Will my mouth always
> be like this?" she asks. "Yes," I say, "it will. It is because the nerve
> was cut." She nods and is silent. But the young man smiles. "I like
> it," he says. "It is kind of cute…" Unmindful, he bends to kiss her
> crooked mouth, and I, so close, can see how he twists his own lips
> to accommodate to hers, to show her that their kiss still works.[2]

That's love. That's care. That's adapting and sacrificing.

Love in everyday living means not only noticing that your wife may
be very different in personality and temperament, but accepting it—
praising her uniqueness and learning how she will help you become a
more complete and fulfilled man because of it![3]

It means treating your wife as you treat yourself. For instance, if you
give yourself extra time for fun, you give her the same. Kent Hughes
wrote, "What a challenge Ephesians 5 presents us—*sacrificial* love (love
is like death!), *sanctifying* love (love that elevates), and *self-love* (loving
your wife as much as you love your own body). If it calls for anything, it
calls for some holy sweat!"[4]

*Whatever you do, whether in word or deed, do it all
in the name of the Lord Jesus, giving thanks to God
the Father through him (Colossians 3:17).*

Have you ever watched a hummingbird or a bumblebee? They're quite similar. They're active, busy, and never spend very much time in one place. They hop from one flower to another. It seems like they dabble in one and then another and another. There are men and women who fit this pattern too. They jump from one thing to another, never settling in for any length of time. They dip into activities and beliefs, never concentrating on any one thing. Are you one of them? Have you ever listed all the various activities or causes you're involved with? Ask yourself why you do what you do and what the results are. This may help you gain a better perspective on your life.

Dabblers engage in quantity rather than quality. Some remind me of the college student who signed up for forty different courses in one semester. When asked if he were crazy, his answer was, "I just want to have a varied education. I go to class for fifteen minutes then leave and go to another one. I've got it worked out so I can hit every class and pick up a little from each one." A little is right! There was no depth of learning, no thorough education—just a frantic pace.

Does all that you do bring satisfaction to you?

Does all that you do bring honor and glory to God?

Are you living your life the way God wants? Or are you exhausted trying to live up to the demands and expectations of others? Are you at peace with the way you go about living your life? Doing less, when it is done thoroughly and enjoyed, will often bring you more satisfaction—and may reflect upon the Lord in a better way too.[5]

*I keep asking that the God of our Lord Jesus Christ, the
glorious Father, may give you the Spirit of wisdom and
revelation, so that you may know him better (Ephesians 1:17).*

It's right in front of your nose. Are you blind? Can't you see it?" Most
kids hear that from their parents at some time or another, and it's true.
You can be looking at something and not see it. It happens to us men too.

William Randolph Hearst, the world-renowned newspaper publisher,
invested a fortune in collecting great works of art. You can still see some
of them at Hearst Castle in California. One day he heard about a piece of
artwork that was very valuable. He wanted to find it and add it to his collection. His art agent searched all over the world in the various art galler-
ies and couldn't locate it. Months later he did find it…in one of Hearst's
own warehouses. It had been stored there, right under his nose, but he
couldn't see it!

This happens to us too. Some Christians are continually searching for
something more in life. They're just not fulfilled. They don't understand
who they are and what they have in Christ. Paul knew about this. That's
why he prayed what he did in today's verse. He wanted us to understand
the fullness of our inheritance. It is difficult for us to imagine or fully
comprehend all God has done for us. There will always be some part of
what we have been given that will remain a mystery. But sometimes we
don't stop to think about all that we have. And when we do we can say,
"It is there right in front of me."[6]

Praise be to the God and Father of our Lord Jesus
Christ, who has blessed us in the heavenly realms with
every spiritual blessing in Christ (Ephesians 1:3).

You're at work and a coworker comes up to you and says, "What's this stuff I hear about you being a Christian? Are you? What do you have being a Christian that you didn't have before?" So what do you say? You might say, "It's not too pleasant to think about when I wasn't a Christian. I was in bondage to evil, spiritually dead, and had no hope whatsoever! (See Romans 3:10-12; 1 John 5:19; Romans 1:18; Ephesians 2:1; 4:17-18; Ephesians 2:12.) I decided that kind of life wasn't for me. The benefits of being a Christian are so much better. Do you want to hear about them?"

Your coworker didn't realize what he was in for, so he might stammer and say, "Sure, why not?" That's your opportunity to share the gospel with him! "When I became a believer my life with God changed. It took a lot longer for my attitudes and behavior to change, but instantly here's what I received. I became a new creation in Jesus Christ. All these changes are stated in the Word of God. They're not just my idea. I became fully alive, and would you believe I now possess the righteousness of Jesus Christ? That's right—the righteousness of the Son of God. And I'm going to share in everything He receives (see 2 Corinthians 5:17; Ephesians 2:5; Romans 6:22; 2 Corinthians 5:21; Romans 8:16-17).

"How's that for benefits? Aren't you glad you asked me that question? So what about you? Does that sound like something you'd like too?"

Live in harmony with one another; be sympathetic, love
as brothers, be compassionate and humble. Do not repay
evil with evil or insult with insult, but with blessing...
that you may inherit a blessing (1 Peter 3:8-9).

Some men have a real gift when it comes to the fine art of insults. That's not unusual because our style of humor is different from women's. We use gentle insults, poke fun at one another, emphasize each other's goofs and mistakes, and throw in some sarcasm from time to time. Men enjoy putting each other down. There's nothing wrong with any of this—when it's in fun, when it's mutual, and when it's between men. Often it occurs because we care for these men. They are our friends.

Sometimes, though, our tendency to use insults and putdowns seeps into our family life. Then it becomes destructive. It's easy to fall into this trap because we know our family members better than anyone else. They make easy targets. Within a family, insults and sarcasm hurt. You may make a wisecrack to your teenage daughter that seems funny to you. You laugh and so do her siblings, but she runs off crying to her room. You may wonder, *What did I say?* Keep this question in mind: Does my insult, comment, or sarcasm fit within the wisdom of 1 Peter 3:8-9? Use that as your guide. It will help.

Often we learn sarcasm from the sitcoms and comedy shows we watch. Putdowns and comments that hurt seem to be an accepted part of our culture. But as Christians, this culture is not to be our culture. If sarcasm and insults are the norm in your family, the most powerful way to change that is to have every family member memorize today's verses. Make it a family project. Make sure you note the changes that take place when you put these verses into practice.

*Do not forget my teaching, but keep my commands
in your heart, for they will prolong your life many
years and bring you prosperity (Proverbs 3:1-2).*

The frog sat in the cool water enjoying himself. He was happy swimming around. He was also oblivious to the fact that underneath the pan was a Bunsen burner with a flame so small the water was being heated at .017 of a degree Fahrenheit per second. The water temperature was rising so gradually that the frog wasn't aware of the change. The minutes went by and then about two-and-a-half hours later the frog was dead. He'd boiled to death, not knowing for a long time what was happening because it was so gradual.

Changes can happen to us in the same way. There can be an erosion in our lives that is so subtle it's like the slippage of a hillside that loses a few grains of soil a minute. A year later there is no hill. Deterioration is all around us. A building suddenly crumbles, and people are injured and killed. "What went wrong today?" we ask. It didn't just happen today. It started to give way years ago, but it was so slight that no one noticed.

Character doesn't erode overnight. Morals don't change suddenly. A marriage doesn't "suddenly" fall apart. Children don't "go wild" out of the blue. A company doesn't "suddenly" go bankrupt. Enough said?

*If you think you are standing firm, be careful
that you don't fall! (1 Corinthians 10:12).*

Years ago the television-viewing audience was captivated by the cop show *Hill Street Blues*. After their morning briefing and just before they hit the streets, the sergeant would say to the officers, "Let's be careful out there." He was warning them to keep their guard up because the unpredictable could and would happen. That's good advice for us as well.

You're faced with issues in the world that are just begging you to leave behind your Christian values and standards. Scripture warns again and again to be on guard. Jesus said be on guard against hypocrisy (Matthew 16:6-12), greed (Luke 12:15), persecution (Matthew 10:17), false teaching (Mark 13:22-23), and spiritual slackness and unreadiness for the Lord's return (Mark 13:32-37). "Be careful or your hearts will be weighed down with dissipation, drunkenness and the anxieties of life" (Luke 21:34).

Listen to these warnings: "Be careful that you don't fall" (1 Corinthians 10:12). "Be careful to do what is right" (Romans 12:17). "Be careful that none of you be found to have fallen short" (Hebrews 4:1). "Be careful to do what the LORD your God has commanded you" (5:32). "Be careful that you do not forget the LORD" (6:12). "Be careful to obey all that is written in the Book of the Law of Moses" (Joshua 23:6). "Give careful thought to your ways" (Haggai 1:5).

There's a reason for all these warnings and more. We need to be reminded of temptation areas and who we get our strength to resist from. If you're struggling with an issue, read these passages out loud every morning for a month. Before long you'll know them from memory. That's the best safeguard when temptation strikes.[7]

*Each of you should learn to control his own body in a way
that is holy and honorable (1 Thessalonians 4:4).*

Just when you think you're in control of your life and you've got all the walls up against attack, something breaks through. It's embarrassing when you've got your guard up and something slips by. Defensive linesmen in football face this constantly. A runner slips by and is off to the goal line. A boxer is told by his trainer time and time again, "Don't let your guard down."

Even countries let their guard down from time to time. On May 29, 1987, Russia was celebrating "Border Guards' Day." They prided themselves on their ability to let no one in or out. That is, until Matthias Rust, a West German computer analyst, took off from Helsinki in a single-engine Cessna and flew through four hundred miles of heavily guarded airspace. He not only passed borders, he buzzed through them.

The "impenetrable" borders weren't impenetrable! The guards weren't guarding, and you can bet some heads rolled. Especially as this little plane buzzed Leningrad, barely cleared the walls of the Kremlin, and landed in Red Square a few feet from the tomb. Adding insult to injury, the whole world knew about it! Red Square turned into red faces and some made a trip to the Siberian salt mines. This teenager gained fame and a four-year trip to a society labor camp. But he caught the Russian nation with their guard down.

Have you ever been caught with your guard down? It doesn't just happen to football players, boxers, and border guards. It happens to us too if we're not careful. Hear the warning of Scripture; heed the teachings of Scripture. Be careful out there.

*Why, you do not even know what will happen tomorrow. What
is your life? You are a mist that appears for a little while and
then vanishes. Instead, you ought to say, "If it is the Lord's
will, we will live and do this or that" (James 4:14-15).*

What happened in the yesterdays of your life? Think about it. In
the past twenty years, what are the three most significant events of
your life? How did they impact you? How did they affect you spiritually?
Sometimes it pays to stop and take stock of the past to keep on course in
the present. But we can also get caught up in remembering the past too
much, spending excessive time reliving the good times. It's safer to stay
in the past, especially when you read today's verses from James.

James has an unnerving notification for us: Life in the future is uncertain. What we have to look forward to is not the certainty of the events
of the past, but the inevitability of the unexpected in the future. In fact,
the best-case scenario could occur as easily as the worst-case scenario. Life
has always been uncertain. It's brief and challenging. The Bible says we're
not to live in fear of the future or constantly ask "What if?" That attitude
can rob us of our joy. Chuck Swindoll puts James 4:14-15 in perspective:

> *Life is challenging.* Because it is short, life is packed with chal-
> lenging possibilities. Because it is uncertain it's filled with chal-
> lenging adjustments. I'm convinced that's much of what Jesus
> meant when He promised us an abundant life. Abundant with
> challenges, running over with possibilities, filled with opportuni-
> ties to adapt, shift, alter, and change. Come to think of it, that's
> the secret of staying young. It is also the path that leads to opti-
> mism and motivation.[8]

*Here I am! I stand at the door and knock. If anyone
hears my voice and opens the door, I will come in and
eat with him, and he with me (Revelation 3:20).*

Heavenly Father, You stood at the door of my heart and knocked. I am thankful that I opened the door to let You in. Please walk through all the rooms of my life and fill them with Your presence. Give me ears that hear You calling me to live for You in a world that has gone deaf to Your voice. May I not only hear but also respond to Your summons, even though it may be costly. Help me hear the silent cries of suffering in the vacant eyes of the abused in families and in the shuffling walk of the homeless on the streets of my city. Guide me and help me act with a heart of compassion.

Give me an open mind to hear something new from my family, my coworkers, and my pastor. Don't let my past experiences keep me frozen against the newness of today and tomorrow. Give me the courage to change my mind and be a man of unpopular conviction when necessary. Give me open eyes to see the greatness of what You have created as well as the needs of the lost who have not heard about Jesus. Lift the covering from my eyes and forgive me for my self-imposed blindness to the concerns around me. Help me see the person who needs the door opened, the sack lifted, the wave of recognition, and the "well done" touch on the shoulder.

Give me open hands to lift the hurting and tired, to share the blessings that You have given to me. Give me an open heart to be receptive to who You want me to be and to do all You want me to accomplish.

I praise You for being a giving God.

In Jesus' name.
Amen.

You shall not commit adultery (Exodus 20:14).

One of the best books written for couples on the sexual relationship is Doug Rosenau's *A Celebration of Sex.* Hear what he has to say about today's verse:

> A great marital partnership has room for only two people in it. Commitment is vital to intimate companionship, and the creation of good boundaries is irreplaceable for a fantastic marriage and sex life. *Adulterate* means "to contaminate by adding a foreign substance or watering down a product." You can adulterate your marital companionship in many ways other than by having a sexual affair. You can adulterate your marriage by over-committing to work, children, or church. God's injunction of "thou shalt not commit adultery" is often portrayed in terms of a protective fence that guards the beautiful marital and sexual garden…The no-adultery fence is there so you can have the intimacy to create… a deeper level of emotional and sexual connecting that can occur and flourish only in an intimate marriage. It protects you from contaminating elements that can threaten the quality of your companionship.
>
> The more important commitments to your mate come in a series of daily choices. Every day when you say, "I love my mate," and refuse to entertain thoughts about someone else, you are reaffirming your commitment. You are allowing sex to be relational and setting good boundaries as you choose to control your sexual impulses and preserve sexual integrity. These little commitment choices to preserve and deepen intimacy pop up in all areas of marriage. It could mean calling off a lunch with a colleague, deciding whether to have that third child, going to a bed-and-breakfast for weekend renewal…These choices are not always huge and obvious, but they create the glue that keeps a marriage and sexual relationship together.[9]

We want you to know about the grace that God has given the Macedonian churches. Out of the most severe trial, their overflowing joy and their extreme poverty welled up in rich generosity. For I testify that they gave as much as they were able, and even beyond their ability. Entirely on their own, they urgently pleaded with us for the privilege of sharing in this service to the saints. And they did not do as we expected, but they gave themselves first to the Lord and then to us in keeping with God's will (2 Corinthians 8:1-5).

It's good to be seen as a giver by your family members. And in giving to your church it's good to be seen as a giver by God. Some men are known as givers and some aren't. But that doesn't mean the unknown ones are not givers. Some of the most generous men keep it private. Today's passage from 2 Corinthians has several suggestions regarding the way we are to give. The first is *anonymity*. No one needs to know what you give. Sometimes we run into people who are very quick to let you know they tithe a huge amount. And you don't have to wonder why they're telling you either.

The second is to *give voluntarily*. Sometimes we may resent "having to give" or we keep our money as long as possible. But money (and anything else we have), isn't ours. It belongs to God. "Each man should give what he has decided in his heart to give, not reluctantly or under compulsion, for God loves a cheerful giver" (2 Corinthians 9:7).

The third suggestion is to *give generously*. Paul described the people in Macedonia as overflowing in generosity. This doesn't have to be just with money, but with time and ability as well. Generosity is deciding what you're going to give and then giving more. Develop generosity as a natural part of your life by practicing it until it becomes habit.

You, my brothers, were called to be free. But do not
use your freedom to indulge the sinful nature; rather,
serve one another in love (Galatians 5:13).

Who me? I didn't do it."
"You asked for it."
"I didn't mean to."
"It was their fault."

Blame is the projection of responsibility onto the other guy. One of the best lines I've heard was an accident report someone had filled out: "No one was to blame for the accident, but it never would have happened if the other driver had been alert." People get away with a lot today. An FBI agent embezzled $2000 from the government and blew it all in one afternoon of gambling. He was fired but then was reinstated. Why? The court ruled he had a gambling addiction and was protected under federal law because of his "handicap." Or what about the man who applied for a park attendant job? The park people ran a background check and discovered the man had been convicted many times for indecent exposure. He wasn't hired, so he sued. After all, he'd never flashed in a park—only libraries and Laundromats. The man blamed the park for not hiring him even though his actions made him unsuitable. The man won his job discrimination suit.

Blaming is how people avoid personal responsibility. It cripples the atmosphere in the workplace. It tears apart churches. And too many couples follow the pattern of Adam and Eve and put the responsibility for problems onto one another. Proverbs suggests a better way: "A man who refuses to admit his mistakes can never be successful. But if he confesses and forsakes them, he gets another chance" (Proverbs 28:13 TLB).[10]

*Trust in Him at all times, O people; pour out your heart
before Him; God is a refuge for us (Psalm 62:8 NASB).*

D o you ever get angry? Ridiculous question, isn't it? We all get mad. Some people show it, others stow it. Some people use it, others abuse it. Some people see it as a tool from Satan, others see it for what it is…a gift from God. Have you ever heard it put that way before? Anger is a gift. We need the emotion of anger to counter injustice.

We tend to view anger as a problem, but the problem is in *how* we use it and *express* it. Often anger is a cover-up for other feelings, such as hurt, fear, and frustration. When you're angry, ask if you're frustrated or hurt or afraid. Then deal with the real issue.

God's Word can help you use anger wisely. "Better a patient man than a warrior, a man who controls his temper than one who takes a city" (Proverbs 16:32). Following this advice helps you direct anger's energy. "Do not be quickly provoked in your spirit, for anger resides in the lap of fools" (Ecclesiastes 7:9). If you take time to consider the issue at hand, you can make progress even if you're upset. Why not pray about your anger?

> Dear Lord, Thank you for creating me in your image with the ability to experience and express the emotion of anger. I know sin has damaged and distorted anger in my life. I thank you that you have promised to be at work within me both to will and to work for your good pleasure. I thank you that you can cause all things to work together for good and that I can do all things through you because you give me strength. I ask you to help me to change my anger patterns. Help me to experience and express this emotion in ways that are good and that bring honor and glory to you. Amen.[11]

*Speaking the truth in love, we will in all things grow up
into him who is the Head, that is, Christ...Each of you must
put off falsehood and speak truthfully to his neighbor, for
we are all members of one body (Ephesians 4:15,25).*

G od's Word calls us to be people of truth. And not just for His benefit—for ours as well. John Trent and Rick Hicks suggest four benefits to being truthful.

First, you won't have to put forth the energy to maintain a facade.
Putting up a false image to...get what you want puts pressure and
strain on you. When people interact with you, they want a situation where "what they see is what they get."

Second, you will have freedom from being found out. When you tell
the truth, you don't have to remember what you said for fear of
contradicting yourself. Politicians live with this fear, or at least
they should! We've seen too many people who say one thing
before they're elected and then change later on. That doesn't sit
well with us.

Third, you will have freedom from guilt. Unfortunately, some people
have practiced lying so much that their consciences are damaged,
and they're not sure where lies and truth part company. But most
of us know what guilt feels like. It's miserable. Perhaps David
described it best when he said: "When I kept silent, my bones
wasted away through my groaning all day long. For day and night
your hand was heavy upon me; my strength was sapped as in the
heat of summer" (Psalm 32:3-4). When there's a clear conscience,
there's peace of mind too.

The last benefit is that *our truthfulness honors God...*God wants
truthful hearts. He helps us speak the truth and then when we do
we're drawing attention to him and his character. Telling the truth
benefits everybody.[12]

The fruit of the Spirit is...peace (Galatians 5:22).

Here is a slightly different way to look at peace. Perhaps you can relate.

Jon Johnson quotes from a humorous article titled "Five Ways to Have a Nervous Breakdown" in *Walls on Bridges*:

- *Try to figure out the answer before the problem arises.* "Most of the bridges we cross are never built, because they are unnecessary." We carry tomorrow's load along with today's. Matthew 6:34 says: "Do not worry about tomorrow, for tomorrow will worry about itself."

- *Try to relive the past.* As we trust him (God) for the future, we must trust him with the past. And he can use the most checkered past imaginable for his good. (See Romans 8:28.)

- *Try to avoid making decisions.* Doing this is like deciding whether to allow weeds to grow in our gardens. While we're deciding, they're growing. Decisions will be made in our delay. Choice "is a man's most godlike characteristic."

- *Demand more of yourself than you can produce.* Unrealistic demands result in "beating our heads against stone walls. We don't change the walls. We just damage ourselves." Romans 12:3 says, "Do not think of yourself more highly than you ought, but rather think of yourself with sober judgment."

- *Believe everything Satan tells you.* Jesus described Satan as the "father of lies" (John 8:44). He's a master of disguise, masquerading as an angel of light. But our Lord declared that his sheep follow him because they "know his voice" (John 10:4). They have listened to it in his Word.[13]

MARCH 22

*I saw that wisdom is better than folly, just as light
is better than darkness (Ecclesiastes 2:13).*

Do you know what real success is? Listen to the world's view:

Aristotle Onassis, tycoon: "It's not a question of money. After you reach a certain point, money becomes unimportant. What matters is success. The sensible thing would be for me to stop now. But I can't. I have to keep aiming higher and higher...for the thrill."

Barbra Streisand, recording artist: "Success for me is having ten honeydew melons and eating only the top half of each one."

Ted Turner, media mogul: "I think it's kind of an empty bag...I've always said I was more an adventurer...I mainly did CNN just to see if it would work. And the same with the superstation...just out of personal curiosity to see if it could be done."[14]

Dr. Gary Rosberg has a much better perspective:

Success is not just a matter of money, power, and ego, but also issues of the heart—like compassion, kindness, bravery, generosity, love. It's an issue of character, not performance. It's an issue of being the person God designed you to be, not how much salary you can pull down in a year. It's an issue of who you really are, not how many notches you can rack up on your resume or the shape of your car's hood ornament.

There's a shift now in our culture. Success hasn't cut it. But significance has more meaning. Who makes us significant?...Not your boss, kids, parents, or even you. What makes you and me significant is the Person of Jesus Christ. He created us in order to glorify Himself. That's our job in life, to bring honor and glory to Him.[15]

*Let no debt remain outstanding, except the continuing
debt to love one another, for he who loves his
fellowman has fulfilled the law (Romans 13:8).*

How are you and your bank getting along? You know, the place where you go and deposit your weekly check—just to turn around and draw it out again, along with additional funds. How would you feel if you were at a restaurant with friends and the loan officer of your bank walked by, said hello, and suggested you stop in to talk about your account? What would be your comfort level? Your guilt level? It's interesting the amount of tension that arises when you're in the presence of someone you owe money.

One of the greatest sources of tension happens when money is loaned between family members. Perhaps you loaned your brother-in-law some money to help him save up for the down payment on his house. The next time you see him, he drives up in a new BMW purchased with the money you loaned him! It sticks in your throat, doesn't it? You feel ripped off, and you'd like him to pay back every cent right now.

Friendships have been lost over the loaning of money.

Families have been torn apart over the loaning of money.

Bankruptcies have occurred over the borrowing of funds.

Keep this in mind: When you owe on your credit cards, you've become a servant to the one you owe. Does that make you feel comfortable? Proverbs states it even more strongly: "The rich rule over the poor, and the borrower is servant to the lender" (22:7). When you're tempted to borrow—delay, wait, pray. Look at your current bills. If you wait until you've saved the money to buy the item, it may take longer to get it, but you'll have a greater sense of freedom.

What good is it for a man to gain the whole world, and
yet lose or forfeit his very self? (Luke 9:25).

An interesting paraphrase of this verse is "What good is it for a man to gain the whole world and lose his children?" Even generations ago there was concern over putting career above family. In 1923, Edgar Guest wrote words that are still applicable today:

I have known of a number of wealthy men who were not successes as fathers. They made money rapidly; their factories were marvels of organization; their money investments were sound and made with excellent judgment, and their contributions to public service were useful and willingly made. All this took time and thought. At the finish there was a fortune on the one hand, and a worthless and dissolute son on the other. WHY? Too much time spent in making money implies too little time spent with the boy.

When these children were youngsters romping on the floor, if someone had come to any one of those fathers and offered him a million dollars for his lad he would have spurned the offer and kicked the proposer out of doors. Had someone offered him ten million dollars in cash for the privilege of making a drunkard out of his son, the answer would have been the same. Had someone offered to buy from him for a fortune the privilege of playing with the boy, of going on picnics and fishing trips and outings, and being with him a part of every day, he would have refused the proposition...

Yet that is exactly the bargain those men made, and which many men are still making. They are coining their lives into fortunes... and great industries, but their boys are growing up as they may...A little less industry and a little more comradeship with the boy is more desirable. Not so much of me in the bank, and more of me and of my best in the lad...To be the father of a great son is what I should call success. [16]

*Lord, who may go and find refuge and shelter in your
tabernacle up on your holy hill? (Psalm 15:1 TLB).*

Have you seen someone who appears to "have it made" and wished you were him? We look at people who have money, position, security, fame, and wonder, *Why them? Why not me? I've got what it takes. They just lucked out.* The problem is that we tend to see their "up" times and not the downs. Their lives could be an elevator ride just like yours. A lot of men have ridden the elevator of life...like David, the writer of many of the psalms as well as a man "after God's own heart." Think about his life for a moment.

At one point he was the classic example of a gladiator. He stood up to the giant Goliath and gave him a major migraine. Later he covered up two major sins—murder and adultery. A king rewarded him for his military exploits by giving him his daughter to marry. Later she ridiculed him in front of his friends as his marriage crumbled.

David experienced the delight of becoming a parent but also the devastation of having a baby die. He faced a corporate takeover attempt— by two of his grown children who tried to topple his kingdom and kill him. He had a close friendship with a man who risked his life for him, but other friends dropped him when he needed them most. His employer tried to make him a wall ornament using a spear—twice! He was hunted like a common criminal in the wilderness. He stepped from the up elevator to the down elevator and then back to the up elevator again and again. Yet no matter how down he was, no matter how desperate he was, no matter how devastated and discouraged he was, he never lost his inner core of strength. His source of strength was not himself or his abilities. It was God. David's repeated response, in spite of what was going down was, "Yet will I trust you."[17]

*There is no fear in love. But perfect love drives out fear, because fear
has to do with punishment. The one who fears is not made perfect
in love. We love because [God] first loved us (1 John 4:18-19).*

Have you ever tried to control a cat? It's a losing battle. Some men keep trying though. They don't seem to get the message about control. They can't control everything, but they keep persisting. Why? Because they feel they *must* be in control of every aspect of their lives. They push, pull, persuade, manipulate, and withdraw. Yes, withdraw. Silence and withdrawal are great ways to control others. What prompts this lifestyle?

Control is a camouflage for fear. Who wants to be afraid or even admit he is? Not me; not you. Fear makes us feel vulnerable. If people knew we were afraid they might take advantage of us. So we strive to hide our fear by going on the offensive.

Control is a cover-up for insecurity. A secure man doesn't need to always be in control. He can defer, ask for advice, and be comfortable when someone else leads. To feel safe, many men go overboard by trying to control everything and everyone. There's an emptiness within us when we're insecure. We're like a bucket with a hole in it. We can never get filled up enough, but we keep trying to get that way through control.

Control is also a cover-up for low self-esteem. When we feel down on ourselves, worthless, lacking, we don't want others to know. We may even blame them for helping to create the problem. What better way to overcome this than by making others pay through control? But control never fulfills or solves the problem. It pushes people away.

Give God the reins of your life. Let Him control you. When God is in control, you'll be amazed at how much better your relationships with others will be.

Come, follow me...I will make you fishers of men (Matthew 4:19).

I have confidence in you. I believe you have the ability and the wisdom to do what I'm asking you to do. Go for it!" Great words of encouragement, aren't they? Well, these statements are made to every believer by Jesus. He is saying, "Tell others about Me. You can do it." But many Christians hesitate. It's a bit scary to tell others about Christ. But there are three "I will" statements in Scripture that can give us courage.

"I will make you fishers of men." Luke 5:10 says, "Don't be afraid; from now on you will catch men" (NKJV). The Aramaic word for *catch* means "to take alive." This passage defines our call and tells us Christ will help us. "But what will I say?" you ask.

"I will give you a mouth and wisdom." Luke 21:13-15 tells us that God will give us the words when we need them: "It will turn out for you as an occasion for testimony. Therefore settle it in your hearts not to meditate beforehand on what you will answer; for I will give you a mouth and wisdom which all your adversaries will not be able to contradict or resist." What a promise! You don't have to struggle or plan what to say. Ask God for opportunities as well as the words to say and know He will give them to you.

The third "I will" is an encouragement and alarm. "Whoever acknowledges me before men, *I will also acknowledge him before my Father in heaven.* But whoever disowns me before men, *I will disown him before my Father in heaven"* (Matthew 10:32-33).

Jesus doesn't want us to be silent about Him. Being silent is a form of denial. The more we confess Jesus to others, the more He attests that we belong to Him. He empowers us to share and then proclaims we are His. He has confidence in us. When you think about it, doesn't that make it a lot easier to share your faith?[18]

*There is a time for everything, and a season for every
activity under heaven (Ecclesiastes 3:1).*

You're probably quite conscious of time. Most of us are. Our lives are regulated by it. When you get up, eat, begin work, leave for church... it's all regulated by time. Some of us control it, and others are controlled by it. What would it be like to live in a society where there was no such thing as time? No seconds, minutes, or hours. You wouldn't have to keep checking your wristwatch to see what time it was. Unfortunately, this scenario wouldn't work. We'd have chaos. And we'd use the stars and the sun to create some other time framework.

Do you struggle with time? You know—do you usually run late? Do you feel your stomach muscles tighten up when you're running behind? Does irritation creep in when your wife keeps you waiting for twenty minutes?

There are a few things to remember about time. It is limited. You have 1440 minutes a day—no more, no less. Every day is the same. No twenty-three-hour days or twenty-five, only twenty-four. Once you use time, it's gone forever. There's no retrieval system.

Time needs to be used wisely. As one man put it, "The great use of life is to spend it for something that will outlast it."[19] How do you use your time? Wait a minute. Let's correct that. It's not our time. It's God's. He's given it to us. So how are you using God's time?

Be kind and compassionate to one another (Ephesians 4:32).

What makes a marriage work today? Affection is a key component.

Being consistently affectionate—and not just at those times when one is interested in sex—is a must in a marriage. Sometimes nothing is shared verbally. It can be sitting side by side and touching gently or moving close enough that you barely touch while you watch the sun dipping over a mountain with reddish clouds capturing your attention. It could be reaching out and holding hands in public...

Years ago I heard the story of a couple who had been invited to a potluck dinner. The wife was not known for her cooking ability, but she decided to make a custard pie. As they drove to the dinner, they knew they were in trouble for they smelled the scorched crust. Then when they turned a corner, the contents of the pie shifted dramatically from one side of the pie shell to the other. He could see her anxiety rising by the moment.

When they arrived, they placed the pie on the dessert table. The guests were serving themselves salad and then went back for the main course. Just before they could move on to the desserts, the husband marched up to the table, looked over the number of homemade desserts and snatched up his wife's...He announced, "There are so many desserts here and my wife so rarely makes my favorite dessert, I'm claiming this for myself..."

...Later his wife said, "He sat by the door eating what he could, mushing up the rest so no one else would bug him for a piece, and slipping chunks to the hosts' Rottweiler when no one was looking. He saw me looking at him and gave me a big wink. What he did made my evening. My husband, who doesn't always say much, communicated more love with what he did than with what any words could ever say."[20]

Are you this kind of man?

*How long, O Lord? Will you forget me forever? How
long will you hide your face from me? (Psalm 13:1).*

There are times when we feel like the psalmist did—forgotten because
of the way our lives are going, especially when we fall flat. Have you
ever fallen on your face—literally? You're walking down some stairs and
miss the last step or trip over a threshold you didn't see and—splat! You're
on your face. A few years back, U.S. runner Mary Decker, who had trained
for years to get to the Olympics, fell during the competition. Years of training—and one slip spelled defeat. There is agony in defeat. It hurts. [21]

Perhaps you've fallen flat on your face in a figurative way. You feel
defeated. God is in the business of raising men from the ashes of defeat!
He gives us more than one chance. Peter Drucker, a management con-
sultant, offered these suggestions for recovering from a fall:

- Watch what you focus on. Pick the future rather than the past.

- Instead of concentrating on the problems, go after opportunities.

- Choose your own direction.

- Aim for something that's going to make a difference.

Perhaps the answer to defeat—and to the psalmist's question in
today's verse is found in Psalm 139-17-18 TLB: "How precious it is, Lord,
to realize that you are thinking about me constantly! I can't even count
how many times a day your thoughts turn toward me. And when I waken
in the morning, you are still thinking of me!" [22]

*The LORD God took the man and put him in the Garden
of Eden to work it and take care of it (Genesis 2:15).*

The term *junkie* has come to be associated with drug users or people addicted to a substance. They live for the high or feeling of euphoria. Many men today are work junkies. They work for a "rush" of feeling, for their identity, for determining their adequacy. They've distorted something God gave as a blessing before the fall. What part does work play in your life? Use these questions to help you evaluate your view:

- Do you spend a lot of time thinking about the satisfaction you're receiving from your job or what you wish would happen?

- Can you articulate clearly what you need out of your job compared to what you want from your job?

- In what way is your job furthering the kingdom of God? If your job were taken away from you for the next six months, how would you feel about yourself?

- If someone asked you to explain how you experience God's pleasure in your work, what would you say?

Remember Olympian runner Eric Liddell? Everything he did was for God's glory. His sister felt he was neglecting his calling as a missionary to China. One day when she was upset, Eric said, "Jennie, you've got to understand, I believe God made me for a purpose—for China. But He also made me fast! And when I run, I feel His pleasure." Can you say that about what you do?

*Whatever you do, whether in word or deed, do it all
in the name of the Lord Jesus, giving thanks to God
the Father through him (Colossians 3:17).*

I almost made it. Not quite, but almost."

"I'm almost finished."

"I was just a bit behind but it should be good enough—for now."

Some people live by the "almost" creed. They never quite get in line. They're a step behind. We do this in our Christian walk too. "I almost lived for the Lord today," "I was almost a loving husband this weekend," or "I almost made it to church Sunday, but we got home late, and, well, you know how it goes." We become proficient at creating and using excuses. We become "almost Christians." As Tim Hansel put it,

> What would [it] have been like if Jesus had done the same thing? What if God had almost revealed himself in Jesus Christ? What if Christ were almost born and almost lived and almost died? What if he would have said, "Ask and it will almost be given you; seek and you will almost find; knock and it will almost be opened to you?" What if he would have said, "Come to me, all who labor and are heavy-laden, and I will almost give you rest?" And what if Jesus had told his disciples, "For whoever would save his life will lose it, and whosoever loses his life for my sake will almost find it?"[1]

Are you living your life as an "almost disciple"? It's easy to do, especially in our prayer lives. We "almost" believe, but not enough to live by faith. *Almost*—a simple word by itself, but put it with faith and it just doesn't belong there. It belongs with incompleteness. The life and work of Jesus were definite, and thorough. And that means the benefits of His life, death, and resurrection for you are complete—not "almost."

"Come, follow me," Jesus said (Mark 1:17).

Years ago Tim Hansel wrote some thoughts that might challenge your ideas about what it means to follow Christ:

> When God chose to reveal himself uniquely, he did it through a person, through a lifestyle—because he knew then, as now, that what we are is far more potent than what we say. Two thousand years ago God declared unambiguously in the life of Jesus Christ that human flesh is a good conductor of divine electricity—and, as far as I understand, he hasn't changed his mind.
>
> The great problem with Jesus' message is not that it cannot be understood, but that it can. The difficulty is…whether or not we can translate what we know into a lifestyle. Almost Christianity will reveal itself in countless subtle ways. I know many who claim that "with Christ *all* things are possible"—except to help them lose weight. I know those who extol the benefits of quiet time—but don't have enough time for contemplation themselves. Others lecture on the resurrection—and try to do everything on their own power. I know people who give sermons on the Lordship of Christ—but who can't slow down, because they think the world would collapse without their activities. Some people applaud the security we have in Christ—but are unwilling to take any chances. And still others glorify the freedom that is ours—but are still enslaved to their work.
>
> It is merely my contention that we are living in an age…that demands first of all a deep, quality relationship with Jesus Christ. This era's pace of life has changed so radically that it demands we take a solid look at our lifestyles, including both work and leisure. We cannot afford to simply try to keep up with the new pace. But we must constantly remind ourselves that we are a part of the permanent, and that we are called to be holy, which means to be different and to have a distinct identity in Christ.[2]

*Unless the LORD builds the house, its builders labor
in vain. Unless the LORD watches over the city, the
watchmen stand guard in vain (Psalm 127:1).*

Work! Work! Work! Now and then you meet someone who reminds you of a hamster frantically running around inside the exercise wheel. He believes that unless he lives in a frantic frenzy he's wasting time. *Hurry* is his byword, which fits our fast-paced society. Take computers—technology is changing so fast we just get our system up and it's outdated. Everything has to be now: instant success, instant happiness, instant sex.

Sometimes Christians fall into the same trap. We become frantic in wanting our lives and our churches to be perfect and complete. Ever met a Christian workaholic? They never stop, and through guilt and the misuse of Scripture they try to get you to hop onto their frantic treadmill. It's not very relaxing or enjoyable to be around frantic people, even if they are Christians. We weren't called to live like this. Tim Hansel puts it well:

> We are called to be faithful, not frantic. If we are to meet the challenges of today, there must be integrity between our words and our lives, and more reliance on the source of our purpose…"It is in vain that you rise up early and go late to rest, eating the bread of anxious toil; for he gives to his beloved sleep" [Psalm 127:2].

> Almost Christianity reveals itself in feverish work, excessive hurry, and exhaustion. I believe that the Enemy has done an effective job of convincing us that unless a person is worn to a frazzle, running here and there, he or she cannot possibly be a dedicated, sacrificing, spiritual Christian…We need to remember that our strength lies not in hurried efforts and ceaseless long hours, but in our quietness and confidence. The world today says, "Enough is not enough." Christ answers softly, "Enough *is* enough."[3]

*Rejoice with those who rejoice; mourn with
those who mourn (Romans 12:15).*

You may not agree with what's written here. If not, good! That means you're thinking. Here's today's focus: *Men and women tend to handle their losses differently.* Let's see if you fit the pattern. The difference is that women *talk* their way through things, and men *think* their way through things. Women lighten their load by sharing the weight. They talk about it with somebody. It stands to reason that women are going to spend more time with other people when they have something important to deal with.

Men, thinking alone, never really get at what is troubling them because they're not talking, not explaining, not asking questions, not using someone else to help figure out their feelings. Of course, they can't do that unless they are going to fully share all of what they are thinking, and men just don't do that with their friends. We men tend to think it's the manly thing to carry all the weight ourselves. What do you think? Is this you? Are you comfortable with the way you respond to loss?

We men face another problem. Not too many people bother to ask how we're feeling. And often when we tell them, they don't know how to handle it, so our silence is reinforced. Years ago, I wondered if I should bring up my feelings about the loss I felt over Matthew, my severly impaired son. I learned to just come out with them, which helped my wife, Joyce (now deceased), and me strengthen each other. Few people over the years ever asked how I felt when they learned about our son's condition. Fortunately, when Matthew died, people asked me about my feelings as much as they did Joyce.

I've made the leap from silence to sharing. And yes, I feel better. So will you.

*Two men went up to the temple to pray... The Pharisee stood
and prayed about himself: "God, I thank you that I am not like
other men—robbers, evildoers, adulterers—or even like this tax
collector. I fast twice a week and give a tenth of all I get." But the
tax collector stood at a distance. He would not even look up to
heaven, but beat his breast and said, "God, have mercy on me, a
sinner." I tell you that this man, rather than the other, went home
justified before God. For everyone who exalts himself will be humbled,
and he who humbles himself will be exalted (Luke 18:10-14).*

Two men were praying. One to God, and the other? He was basically
having a dialogue with himself. Dr. Lloyd Ogilvie has quite an insight
on these two men:

> God does not hear a comparative prayer. The Pharisee took the
> wrong measurements, comparing himself with the tax collector.
> He was looking down on another human being rather than up
> to God. He grasped an opportunity to lift himself up by putting
> another down. But our status with God is not based on being bet-
> ter than others. We are to be all that God has gifted us to be. God
> has given us the only acceptable basis of comparison: Jesus Christ.
> God does not hear the prayer that is based merely on externals.
> The Pharisee's prayer was built on the unstable foundation of *what
> he had done*, not *what he was*...What he did and abstained from
> doing were on the surface. He had accomplished it all himself. He
> had no dependence on God for his impeccable life.

Jesus wants us to understand how pride twists and distorts our
capacity for self-scrutiny. Our minds were meant to be truth-
gathering computers. But prayers such as that of the Pharisee
make us ignore reality...[They] delude us into thinking that we
can be right with God because of our own accomplishments and
goodness. The purpose of prayer is to see things as they are: ourselves as we really are, and God as He has revealed Himself to be.[4]

Young men, in the same way be submissive to those who are older. All of you, clothe yourselves with humility toward one another, because, "God opposes the proud but gives grace to the humble." Humble yourselves, therefore, under God's mighty hand, that he may lift you up in due time. Cast all your anxiety on him because he cares for you (1 Peter 5:5-7).

Most of us want to be successful. In fact, all men want to succeed in some way. It's much better than tasting the fruits of failure. Why do we work? Why do we play? Why do we compete? We live in a success-saturated society. There are books, classes, CDs, and seminars…promising to teach us a new approach that will enable us to taste success. The problem with success is the cost. Who counts it in advance? *The Executive Digest* said, "The trouble with success is the formula is the same as the one for a nervous breakdown." That's sobering, uncomfortable, and too often true. But there's a way to gain success other than by pushing, striving, promoting, and being slick and aggressive. It's a simple way; it's God's way. It's found in today's verses. It involves authority, attitude, and anxiety. Read 1 Peter 5:5-7 again. What can you do? First of all, submit to those who know more than you. Ask for and listen to their advice, their wisdom, the lessons they've learned, and their guidance. Find a mentor and let this man help shape your life.

Next, be humble, especially before God. Let Him bring the success to you in His way and in His time. You can pull strings and manipulate or let God work. A humble attitude doesn't offend or repulse people. It attracts them because you are different.

Finally, take the anxieties that come and throw them to God. Let Him deal with them. Success is waiting for you! So is God's plan. They go hand in hand![5]

*Jesus called in a loud voice, "Lazarus, come out!" The dead
man came out, his hands and feet wrapped with strips of
linen, and a cloth around his face. Jesus said to them, "Take
off the grave clothes and let him go" (John 11:43-44).*

Judson Edwards wrote a fascinating statement about the play *Laughing with Lazarus:*

> Eugene O'Neill's play *Laughing with Lazarus* begins with Jesus'
> raising of Lazarus from the dead and deals with the change this
> miracle makes in Lazarus' life. After he has been raised, Lazarus
> becomes fearless. Try as they might, the Jewish leaders cannot sti-
> fle his gladness. Laughter is his trademark, and everywhere he goes
> people are warmed and enlivened by his presence. Because he has
> learned that even the Final Enemy cannot defeat him, Lazarus is
> eternally infected with joy…
>
> We are like Lazarus!…[We] walk in newness of life…[We] insist
> that the hope of the resurrection affects us profoundly the moment
> we choose Jesus. Every last one of us who claims to be a Christian
> has an inheritance, the same joy Lazarus experienced after his mir-
> acle…The same fearlessness. The same contagious freedom.
>
> The only bucket of water hanging over the fire is our unbelief. At
> heart, you see, we are unbelievers. We refuse to accept all of the
> incredible implications of Calvary. We believe the lie that God is
> not for us. Though the prison door stands wide open, we huddle
> in self-imposed chains…We cannot get our hearts to believe that
> laughter is our birthright. But, thank God, it is never too late! The
> door stands eternally open. And our joy and peace are the surest
> indicators we have walked through it.
>
> So, if you want to know just how Christian you really are, don't lis-
> ten to your creeds or your prayers…Listen, instead, to your laugh-
> ter. It comes from your soul and reflects your heart. Your laughter
> will tell you unfailingly of your faith in God.[6]

The fruit of the Spirit is love, joy, peace, patience,
kindness, goodness, faithfulness (Galatians 5:22).

Do you really understand what *joy* is? Most people don't. And yet, as followers of Christ, it is one of our main benefits. It's available to all of us. Some people think joy is a good feeling. But that's not joy. To some, joy comes from what happens to them. That's not joy—that's happiness. Happiness is based on circumstances that go our way. *Joy is a choice,* a sense of gladness. Here are some more definitions of joy for you to consider:

- "Joy does not depend on outer circumstances but on the reality of God."[7]

- Joy is "believing the reasons to be excited about life are greater than the reasons to get discouraged and negative."[8]

- Joy at its highest meaning calls for the vertical, or spiritual, dimension that translates superficial happiness, productive adjustment, and self-help techniques into an encounter with God. Joy becomes the power of God's grace, the process of God's Spirit, and the presence of God's nature in our lives. In the biblical sense, joy then becomes a spiritual balance between expectations and achievements—the ability to approach problems objectively by accepting things as they are and working toward solution and adjustment…Joy is a sense of imperturbable gladness that sings when rejected, praises when persecuted, and stands when attacked…Joy is seeking first the kingdom of God and His righteousness. It is knowing full well that all things we need…will be given to us as we live in the knowledge that God loves us.[9]

When you live based on these perspectives of joy, good things happen.

We preach Christ crucified, to the Jews a stumbling
block and to the Greeks foolishness, but to those who are
called, both Jews and Greeks, Christ the power of God
and the wisdom of God (1 Corinthians 1:23-24 NKJV).

Power failure. The lights dim and then go out. The sounds of machinery, such as the refrigerator and air conditioners come to a halt. An eerie silence hangs in the air. Usually it happens when there's an overload of circuits. It could be a short in the system or a transformer that wore out. Sometimes it's as simple as tripping over a cord and unplugging something. A power outage is no fun. If it goes on for an extended time, food rots in the refrigerator, heat rises along with tempers, and life is thrown off course.

Consider these two important questions. First, who's *your* power source? You? Your spouse? Your friends? The Lord? Some of us go through life connected to a real power source, and others run their lives on a portable battery pack of their own doing. Naturally, they run out of juice after a while. But when your source is the Lord, there's never any lack of energy. In Acts 2:32-33 we read, "God has raised this Jesus to life… Exalted to the right hand of God, he has received from the Father the promised Holy Spirit and has poured out what you now see and hear." He gives us the gift of power—the Holy Spirit!

The second question? Are you plugged in? An electric saw won't work by running the blade back and forth by hand over wood. It's got to be connected. We're connected when we pray, listen, and read God's Word. Busy? Yes, we all are. We can pray lying down, sitting, standing, walking, or driving. We can read any time even if only for a minute or two. People who begin their day with Jesus realize they are connected to a power that won't overload or run out! [10]

*You are awesome, O God, in your sanctuary; the God of Israel
gives power and strength to his people (Psalm 68:35).*

P*ower.* What a feeling! We come into the world looking for power. One of our first experiences is a power struggle between our parents and us. One of our first words is *"No!"* Why should we be surprised at that? The first couple on earth engaged in a power struggle with God. He created us with free will—the ability to choose. Well, Adam did choose. And he messed it up for the rest of us because of his failure to follow God's way.

We equate power with security and control. We hear about power brokers. Books are written in the leadership arena telling us how to gain power, retain power, and use power. The feeling of power can be addictive. It gives an adrenaline rush. Take a minute to listen to some ads. We buy into what they're selling because they promise to give us power.

The misuse of power in marriage usually manifests itself as domination. In fact, some men demand that their wives be submissive because "Scripture says they're supposed to." How sad. *Any time a man demands submission, he's lost it.* He's failed. Instead of bringing up what his wife is supposed to do, all a husband really needs to do is follow God's instructions for *him*—love his wife as Christ loves the church. Power isn't a problem unless we make it our god. Power isn't the problem unless we misuse it. David gives us perspective on this issue:

> It is God who arms me with strength and makes my way perfect (Psalm 18:32).

> The LORD is my light and my salvation—whom shall I fear? The LORD is the stronghold of my life—of whom shall I be afraid? (Psalm 27:1).

*When Jesus had finished saying these things, the crowds were
amazed at his teaching, because he taught as one who had authority,
and not as their teachers of the law (Matthew 7:28-29).*

Tension. We don't enjoy it, and we don't want it. We try our best to get rid of it. But then we go and become Christians. We invite Jesus Christ into our lives as Lord and Savior and set out to live for Him. And what do we get? Tension.

When Jesus taught the people, He spoke directly against the religious leaders of His day (Matthew 5–7). He said, "Do not be like [the pagans]" (Matthew 6:8). Don't be like the hypocrites. And therein lies the tension. When we follow Jesus, there will be tension because we live in a society that has a multitude of beliefs and values, most of them contrary to the teachings of Scripture. We're pressured at work, at play, and even in our families to fit in with the world. But Jesus is asking us to be misfits. He's calling us to be different to the extent that others will notice. And this will make them uncomfortable.

Take time to read Matthew 5:21-44 where Jesus says repeatedly, "You have heard…but I say to you…" It's the call not to fit in but to be different. It's the call that will increase the tension in our lives. But it's a great calling! Ask:

- "How do I fit in where it would be best not to fit in?"

- "In what ways am I obviously different so I draw others to Jesus?"

- "In what way does God want me to be different this week?"

And remember, when God calls you to be different that's a good thing.

*Give ear to my words, O Lord, consider my sighing...In the
morning, O Lord, you hear my voice (Psalm 5:1,3).*

Are you a morning person or are you married to one? You know what
they're like. They wake up bright-eyed and bushy-tailed at six o'clock
(or earlier!). They're ready to face the day and can't wait to start talking—
even before coffee! Some of us are just not wired that well for morning. We
feel the day ought to begin at ten o'clock, not six! Sometimes people who
are early-morning "alerts" are insensitive to other people and need to heed
the admonition found in Proverbs: "If you shout a pleasant greeting to a
friend too early in the morning, he will count it as a curse!" (27:14 TLB).

Whether you fit the six o'clock crew or the ten o'clock one, keep in
mind there is something good that can come out of the morning: time
alone with God. That's what David said, according to today's verses. And
it's mentioned other times in Scripture as well:

> Evening, morning and noon I cry out in distress, and he hears my
> voice (Psalm 55:17).

> I cry to you for help, O Lord; in the morning my prayer comes
> before you (Psalm 88:13).

> Because of the Lord's great love we are not consumed, for his
> compassions never fail. They are new every morning; great is your
> faithfulness (Lamentations 3:22-23).

Is there a better way to begin your day? Not really. If you're down and
the day looks dim and dreary, you can make a choice to look up. You'll
be amazed at what you see.

My tears have been my food day and night, while men say
to me all day long, "Where is your God?" (Psalm 42:3).

"I am at a loss for words." We all say this when we've heard unbelievably shocking news. Our brains go into reverse, and we become tongue-tied. What can we say? Sometimes nothing at all. It's probably good that our bodies and minds help us at that time by shutting down and turning off. When we don't know what to say and we go ahead and say something anyway, it's usually the wrong thing. Open mouth, insert foot.

When words fail us, there is something else that helps us express what we're experiencing—tears. Tears are God's gift to all of us—men and women—to release our feelings. When Jesus arrived in Bethany following Lazarus' death, He wept (John 11:35). Ken Gire describes the scene beautifully in *Incredible Moments with the Savior:*

> On our way to Lazarus' tomb we stumble on still another question. Jesus approaches the gravesite with the full assurance that he will raise his friend from the dead. Why then does the sight of the tomb trouble him?

> Maybe the tomb in the garden is too graphic a reminder of Eden gone to seed. Of Paradise lost. And of the cold, dark tomb he would have to enter to regain it…It is remarkable that *our* plight could trouble *his* spirit; that *our* pain could summon *his* tears.

> The raising of Lazarus is the most daring and dramatic of all the Savior's healings. He courageously went into a den where hostility rages against him to snatch a friend from the jaws of death. It was an incredible moment. It revealed that Jesus was who he said he was—the resurrection and the life. But it revealed something else. The tears of God.

> And who's to say which is more incredible—a man who raises the dead…or a God who weeps?[11]

*When he saw the crowds, he went up on a mountainside
and sat down. His disciples came to him, and he began
to teach them, saying: Blessed are the poor in spirit, for
theirs is the kingdom of heaven (Matthew 5:1-3).*

Have you ever wondered what would happen if Jesus were here today and gave the Sermon on the Mount in person? Picture Him in the L.A. Coliseum, or Mile High Stadium in Denver, or at the Superdome with thousands of people waiting for Him to teach. And teach He does. He says, "Blessed are the poor in spirit." What? That's not what we're taught to be in our society. You're right. We're not. That's okay. Many people have tried it society's way. It won't hurt to try the biblical model. The Living Bible spells it out in a practical way: "Humble men are very fortunate!" Why? Because "the Kingdom of Heaven is given to them."

Jesus is asking every believer to be humble. We can't be strong-willed if we plan to be humble. We can't promote ourselves and call attention to our achievements if we're humble. We can't carry around our box scores to show everyone how we've done if we're humble. We can't rely upon ourselves if we're humble.

"Poor in spirit" also means that we admit we are lacking spiritually. We have a condition known as spiritual poverty. When we admit this and acknowledge our need of God, we find permanent happiness. When we put all of our trust in God, the kingdom of heaven is ours. Do you hear anyone else making such an offer?

*Blessed are those who mourn, for they will
be comforted (Matthew 5:4).*

How can someone be blessed when they mourn? Sitting at a graveside with a long face hurts. It's the pits. What in the world was Jesus talking about anyway? It's one thing to be different, but I'm not going to go around in sackcloth and ashes!" That's what one man thought this passage meant. But it's much more than that. *Mourn* is a heavy word. When we think of someone mourning, we think of an aching heart or a mind torn apart with anguish. There is a lot to mourn over in life because it is full of losses. The people who don't mourn are the ones who end up with problems. We mourn over our losses and the losses of others. We also mourn over the state of affairs of our country and the world.

Mourn also includes the idea of caring for the needs and hurts of others. We are called to weep with those who weep. Perhaps one way of translating this passage is "You are fortunate when your heart is broken by all the suffering you see around you and by your own sinful condition. Out of this sorrow you will discover the fullness of life and the joy that comes from God."

So what have you mourned for recently? What do you need to mourn for? In what way can your compassion be used to minister to a hurting person? When you can truly mourn, you will receive the benefits of today's passage.

The earnest (heartfelt, continued) prayer of a
righteous man makes tremendous power available
[dynamic in its working] (James 5:16 AMP).

Oh God, I'm full of questions about me today. I thank You in advance for hearing my confusion and my concern. I ask for wisdom and clarity as I talk with You about what is on my mind and heart. Lord, I just want to talk out loud with You and ask some questions.

Have I been living in the way You want me to live to fulfill the reason that I'm here? Have I been seeing the ways You want me to serve You and others? Have I done anything that defeats calling myself a Christian? Have I been lazy or neglectful or passive in any way that would frustrate others and cause them difficulty? Have I failed You and those I love by my thought life? Have I been honest in my work and given my full energy and dedication to my employer? Have I cheated my family in any way by bringing home my work in my briefcase or my mind? Have I been a peacemaker at home or work? Or have I been more of a pain in the neck? Have I learned the fine art of rationalizing so well that I fail to see my faults and stagnation, thus stifling growth and change? Have I been rude to those I love rather than being loving?

Lord, these are hard questions for me to ask. Help me to answer honestly, to hear Your clear answers, and then to be open to the Holy Spirit's work in me.

In Jesus' name, I pray.
Amen.

*My son, if you accept my words and store up my commands
within you, turning your ear to wisdom and applying your heart
to understanding, and if you call out for insight and cry aloud
for understanding, and if you look for it as for silver and search
for it as for hidden treasure, then you will understand the fear
of the LORD and find the knowledge of God (Proverbs 2:1-5).*

Choices—your life is full of them. Have you ever read the entire book of Proverbs? Have you studied its teachings in depth? If you do, it will help you handle the stresses and strains of everyday life because it talks a lot about making choices.

Look again at today's passage. Notice the "ifs" and the "thens." An "If…then" structure in a sentence (Groan! Back to basic English class) is a *conditional* clause. And that's just what it means. The outcome *depends* on the person doing or taking certain steps. The result is not guaranteed. You have to choose to do what it says to do if you want the results. And choosing means you also accept the responsibility for your choice.

The way you and I turn out as adults is our choice. It's kind of ridiculous to see a forty-year-old man blaming his parents for the way he is now. As you read through Proverbs, note your options. You can choose to be wise or you can act the fool. You can be angry or calm, be liked or disliked, be lazy or productive, tear down others or be an encourager, be righteous or evil, bring honor to your parents or disgrace, be pure or sleep around.

Proverbs is old wisdom that has never grown stale. It changes lives. It could change yours.

Where your treasure is, there your heart will be also (Matthew 6:21).

Purity. Ethics. Commitments. Standards. Where do these begin? Scripture says they begin in our hearts. Consider some strong statements about this from Dr. Gary Oliver:

> Moral and ethical purity start in the heart. Only the passionate love of purity can save a person from impurity. That's why Proverbs tells us, "Above all else, guard your affections. For they influence everything else in your life." It goes on to warn us, "Spurn the careless kiss of a prostitute. Stay far from her. Look straight ahead; don't even turn your head to look. Watch your step. Stick to the path and be safe. Don't sidetrack; pull back your foot from danger" (Proverbs 4:23-27 TLB).
>
> Are there any prostitutes in your life? Hear me out before you answer…a prostitute can be any person, habit, or activity that promises short-term pleasure for a high price, that makes you forget the most important for the least important, that increases your vulnerability.
>
> Let me ask the question a different way. Are there any thoughts, habits, possessions, or activities in your life that are more important to you than God, that make you more vulnerable to compromise and sin? If so, giving in to that is like giving in to the careless kiss of a prostitute. Proverbs warns us to stay as far away from these things as possible.
>
> How do you do that? By looking for and focusing on all the potential pitfalls? No! The only solution is to set your mind on things above, to fix your eyes on Jesus. When Christ met Peter on the seashore after His resurrection, He didn't bawl him out for his lack of faith in denying Him. Three times He asked Peter the simple question, "Do you love Me?" A growing affection for our Lord Jesus Christ is the only antidote for the kind of apathy that leads down the primrose path to compromise.[12]

This, then, is how you should pray: "Our Father in heaven, hallowed be your name, your kingdom come, your will be done on earth as it is in heaven. Give us today our daily bread. Forgive us our debts, as we also have forgiven our debtors. And lead us not into temptation, but deliver us from the evil one" (Matthew 6:9-13).

The Lord's Prayer, or the Disciple's Prayer as it is also called, is often one of the first passages of Scripture most children memorize. It's one of the few passages of Scripture that many adults know. It's used in church services and either said or sung in unison. But that's not its purpose. That wasn't the reason it was given to the disciples. They didn't ask Jesus for a prayer to memorize or recite each day. They asked Him to teach them to pray, and that is exactly what He did. What He gave them was a general pattern for all prayer.

There are six things this prayer teaches us to ask God for. One is that His name be honored. Second, that He bring His kingdom here to earth; third, that He do His will; fourth, that He provide for our daily needs; fifth, that He pardon our sins; and sixth, that He protect us from temptation. Did you catch that sixfold pattern? Read the prayer again. Do your prayers fit this pattern? All of these requests contribute to the ultimate good of prayer—to bring glory to God.

When you follow this pattern of prayer, remember that you are following Jesus' teaching, and He will do whatever you ask in His name. You may want to write out some of your prayers. It's an easy way to develop this pattern of praying. Go ahead. Follow these six steps for prayer.[13]

Blessed are the meek, for they will
inherit the earth (Matthew 5:5).

A mistranslation of this passage is "Blessed are the wimps, for they shall be doormats and walked on." The word *meek* brings up that image. It's not a favored word in our culture. A more correct definition of the word is "yieldedness." It's not easy to yield either. Have you ever watched two men approach an intersection with signs saying "yield to oncoming traffic"? Too often neither yields and they end up with fractured fenders. We see yielding as a negative. In reality, to yield shows strength and control. It says, "Hey, I don't care what others think. No one has forced me to do this. I'm *choosing* to do it."

Yielding can put you in the driver's seat in many situations. A number of Bible versions use the word *gentle* instead of *meek*. We use *gentle* in many ways. We talk about gentle words. A horse that has been broken and tamed has been "gentled." Chuck Swindoll offers a great description of what today's verse means:

> Gentleness includes such enviable qualities as having strength under control, being calm and peaceful when surrounded by a heated atmosphere, emitting a soothing effect on those who may be angry or otherwise beside themselves, and possessing tact and gracious courtesy that causes others to retain their self-esteem and dignity. Clearly, it includes a Christlikeness, since the same word is used to describe His own makeup: "Come to Me, all who are weary and heavy-laden, and I will give you rest. Take My yoke upon you and learn from Me, for I am gentle and humble in heart; and you will find rest for your souls" (Matthew 11:28-29 NASB).[14]

Good sense makes a man restrain his anger, and it is his glory to overlook a transgression or an offense (Proverbs 19:11 AMP).

Anger can be used for good or bad. Unfortunately, it's often used negatively in families. Saul's anger toward David and Jonathan is an illustration of destructive anger: "The women responded as they...frolicked, saying, Saul has slain his thousands, and David his ten thousands. And Saul was very angry" (1 Samuel 18:7-8 AMP).

Jealousy and envy toward David progressed to anger and hatred, and not far behind was action—attempts to take David's life. Later Saul's anger turned toward his own son.

> [Saul] said to him, You son of a perverse, rebellious woman, do not I know that you have chosen the son of Jesse to your own shame and to the shame of your mother who bore you?...Saul cast his spear at him to smite him, by which Jonathan knew that his father had determined to kill David (1 Samuel 20:30,33 AMP).

When a person lets himself be governed by emotion instead of fact, he may react in destructive ways. Thousands of children are abused physically because a parent's anger gets out of control. Many parents and spouses live with overwhelming regrets because of actions made in anger toward family members.

When you're angry, try taking the four-step approach:

- Delay—put the wisdom of Proverbs into practice.
- Discover the cause—it's usually fear, hurt, or frustration.
- Say what you're feeling in a calm voice.
- Let the person know what you want. It works. Really, it does.

Blessed are the merciful, for they will be shown mercy (Matthew 5:7).

You've seen it in movies and perhaps even in live television trials. It's the courtroom scene and the perpetrator has been convicted. There's only one thing left for him to do: throw himself on the mercy of the court and hope the judge will be lenient. We have a misconception of what it means to show mercy. We think it's just a matter of giving kindness to others. Cutting a bit of slack for someone who owes us, giving someone more time to pay off a debt, or giving a little more in the special missions offering to help the poor. This is our idea of being merciful. But that misses the mark.

The original word for *mercy* in today's verse is a bit difficult to translate. We know that it doesn't simply mean to feel sorry for someone in trouble. It's the ability to get inside the other person's skin and see life with his eyes and feel things with his feelings.

Mercy will cost you. It's empathy—experiencing with another person what he (or she) is going through. You're with him. It means reaching out to others in need to the extent that it costs you. You get involved. *Involved* is a key word. Listen to God's Word:

> If you have a friend who is in need of food and clothing, and you say to him, "Well, good-bye and God bless you; stay warm and eat hearty," and then don't give him clothes or food, what good does that do? (James 2:15-16 TLB).

> If someone who is supposed to be a Christian has money enough to live well, and sees a brother in need, and won't help him—how can God's love be within him? (1 John 3:17 TLB).

Who needs you to get involved in their lives today?

Blessed are the pure in heart, for they will see God (Matthew 5:8).

M atthew 5:8 is a problem verse if we're honest about it. Who has a truly pure heart? How is it possible to have a pure heart? How can we tell if a person's heart is pure? It's not easy. We seem to have an array of masks in our closets that we put on, depending on the occasion. We sometimes choose to fool people. We say what we think they want to hear.

Being pure in heart means our motives are clean, uncontaminated, uncorrupted. Our motives aren't mixed. It means looking at what we do and trying to discover the purpose. It's having the same attitude, behavior, and speech at home and at work that we display at church. This is a big order. But that's what pure in heart is all about. It's being consistent. Purity of heart means not wearing a mask. Jesus said,

> Settle matters quickly with your adversary who is taking you to court. Do it while you are still with him on the way, or he may hand you over to the judge, and the judge may hand you over to the officer, and you may be thrown into prison. I tell you the truth, you will not get out until you have paid the last penny. You have heard that it was said, "Do not commit adultery." But I tell you that anyone who looks at a woman lustfully has already committed adultery with her in his heart (Matthew 5:25-28).

No masks. No hidden agendas. Check your motives.

Blessed are the peacemakers, for they will be
called sons of God (Matthew 5:9).

There are a number of misconceptions about what a peacemaker is. Some think that to be a peacemaker you should…

- avoid all arguments and conflict

- be passive and non-confrontational

- be easygoing and let others always have their way

Not quite. The peace today's verse is talking about doesn't happen because of avoidance. Just the opposite. A peacemaker forces problems to the surface and settles them. In the last century, one of the weapons used in the Old West was a revolver called "The Peacemaker." It served its purpose, but the peacemaking this passage talks about doesn't blow people away! Look at God's Word and the emphasis on living in peace:

> If it is possible, as far as it depends on you, live at peace with everyone (Romans 12:18).

> Let us therefore make every effort to do what leads to peace and to mutual edification (Romans 14:19).

To be a peacemaker you've got to be at peace with yourself. A peacemaker doesn't add fuel to the fire when there is a conflict. He looks for the positive and brings it out. He looks for solution-oriented alternatives. He doesn't bait others to lure them into an argument. He knows how to arbitrate to settle disputes.

Are you a peacemaker? What can you do to become a more effective peacemaker?

*Blessed are those who are persecuted because of righteousness,
for theirs is the kingdom of heaven. Blessed are you when
people insult you, persecute you and falsely say all kinds of evil
against you because of me. Rejoice and be glad, because great
is your reward in heaven, for in the same way they persecuted
the prophets who were before you (Matthew 5:10-12).*

Persecuted? Not likely in the United States, at least. But why not? Many men live their faith like they belong to the Secret Service. No one knows about it. Being a Christian costs. Being a Christian in the business world today cuts counter to the values of our society. When you follow what Scripture says in your work, you may hear:

- "Hey, slow down. Don't work so hard. You're making us look bad."

- "Everyone around here does it. Don't rock the boat. We've got a good thing going."

- "This is convention time. Your wife will never know. These shows will turn you on."

- "It's no big deal to pad expenses. If you don't, how do we explain ours?"

You're pressured to be one of the guys, to go with the flow, to not disrupt the pattern. When you don't just go along, you'll feel the heat. But this kind of persecution isn't much compared to what the first Christians endured. Their faith disrupted their work, their social lives, their home lives, and their families. Many were killed for their faith.

We're called to take a faithful, loving stand for our faith—not to be obnoxious about it. A simple statement of our beliefs and a consistent pattern of behavior will get through to others in time. In the meantime, expect flak. When the heat rises, read today's verses again. There are some benefits to being persecuted for your faith. Keep those in mind.

What good is it for a man to gain the whole
world, yet forfeit his soul? (Mark 8:36).

Yes, we're going to talk about money again. We can't afford not to. Most of us have never thought much about, let alone developed, a "money lifestyle." We all have four choices regarding that lifestyle. Some choices have better consequences than others.

You can live *above* your means—that's easy. We look rich to other people. We accumulate as much as we want in goods…and pay more than we should in high interest rates. We indulge our insecurities with material goods. The problem is, it's never enough. It takes more…and more…and more. *Question:* How does this lifestyle glorify God?

Living *at* your means is a better choice, but still not a good one. It comes in one hand and goes out the other at the same rate. There's not much debt, but there are no savings either. The focus is on gathering rather than planning for the future. Things occupy our thoughts. The problem? There's not much room left for God. *Question:* How does this lifestyle glorify God?

Living *within* your means follows the scriptural teaching of being a good steward of what God has entrusted to you. The man who lives within his means thinks about today and the future. He uses his money for God's kingdom. Tithing is a part of this man's life, even when he can't afford it. *Question:* How does this lifestyle glorify God?

Living *below* your means is not a typical choice. It requires unusual self-discipline and a deliberate choice not to move up. The gift of giving rather than acquiring is this man's joy. He simply uses only what's necessary.

Which of these four styles describes your life? And…is it by choice?[15]

The LORD God said, "It is not good for the man to be alone.
I will make a helper suitable for him."...Then the LORD
God made a woman from the rib he had taken out of the
man, and he brought her to the man (Genesis 2:18,22).

You've probably had the experience of working long and hard on a project that turned out great. You stand back and say, "That's great. I did a good job." That's not pride, it's fact. You now know a little about how God felt when He created the earth.

The first daylight burst forth and He said, "It is good."

Then there was land and sea and He said, "It is good."

When the land produced trees and plants He said, "It is good."

When two great lights were formed He said, "It is good."

When the sea creatures and birds were created He said, "It is good."

When the animals came into being He said, "It is good."

When man was created He said, "It is *not* good...for man to be alone."

Aloneness and isolation—not good. If you're married, you need your wife more than you realize. The greatest hurt in marriage is feeling like you're a married single. Isolation has no place in marriage. It's the first step toward adultery. Couples need intimacy, which includes talking, listening, and sharing. Dr. John Baucom makes an interesting observation about how we've moved away from intimacy:

> With the appearance of the two-bathroom home, Americans forgot how to cooperate. With the appearance of the two-car family, we forgot how to associate, and with the coming of the two-television home, we will forget how to communicate.[16]

If you have been given a special helper, ask her if there are times when she feels lonely and, if so, what she would like you to do to help. Whatever she says, just reply with, "Thank you for letting me know. I'll begin to work on that." Your answer and your action will do wonders to cure the loneliness.[17]

*Husbands, love your wives, just as Christ loved the
church and gave himself up for her (Ephesians 5:25).*

If you're married, do you pray together as a couple? If not, you can learn to do so. It will take a while to develop a comfort level, so don't give up. Charlie and Martha Shedd have helped thousands of couples with their prayer lives. They shared this:

> We would sit on our rocking loveseat. We would take turns telling each other things we'd like to pray about. Then holding hands we would pray each in our own way, silently. This was the beginning of prayer together that lasted. Naturally, through the years we've learned to pray in every possible way, including aloud. Anytime, anywhere, every position, every setting, in everyday language… Plain talk, ordinary conversation. We interrupt, we laugh, we argue, we enjoy. We hurt together, cry together, wonder together. Together we tune our friendship to the Friend of friends.
>
> Do we still pray silently together? Often. Some groanings of the spirit go better in silence. "I've been feeling anxious lately, and I don't know why. Will you listen while I tell you what I can? Then let's pray about the known and unknown in silence."
>
> …Negatives, positives, woes, celebrations, shadowy things—all these, all kinds of things we share in prayer. Aloud we share what we can. Without the vocals we share those things not ready yet for words…
>
> Almost from the first we knew we'd discovered an authentic new dimension. In becoming best friends with each other, we were becoming best friends with the Lord. And the more we sought his friendship, the more we were becoming best friends with each other.[18]

Let the word of Christ dwell in you richly as you teach and admonish
one another with all wisdom, and as you sing psalms, hymns and
spiritual songs with gratitude in your hearts to God (Colossians 3:16).

One of the best descriptions of the Bible came from an old-time evangelist and baseball player named Billy Sunday. He talked about entering the "Wonderful Temple":

> I entered at the portico of Genesis, walked down through the Old Testament art galleries, where pictures of Noah, Abraham, Moses, Joseph, Isaac, Jacob and Daniel hung on the wall. I passed into the music room of Psalms, where the Spirit swept the keyboard of nature until it seemed that every reed and pipe in God's great organ responded to the tuneful harp of David, the sweet singer of Israel. I entered the chamber of Ecclesiastes, where the voice of the preacher was heard; and into the conservatory of Sharon, where the Lily of the Valley's sweet-scented spices filled and perfumed my life. I entered the business office of Proverbs, and then into the observatory room of the Prophets, where I saw telescopes of various sizes, pointed to far-off events, but all concentrated upon the bright and morning star. I entered the audience room of the King of Kings, and caught a vision of His glory from the standpoint of Matthew, Mark, Luke and John, passed into the Acts of the Apostles, where the Holy Spirit was doing His work in the formation of the infant church. Then into the correspondence room, where sat Paul, Peter, James, and John penning their epistles. I stepped into the throne room of Revelation, where towered the glittering peaks, and got a vision of the King sitting upon the throne in all His glory, and I cried:
>
> > All hail the power of Jesus' name, let angels prostrate fall, Bring forth the royal diadem, and crown him Lord of all.[19]

Six days you shall labor and do all your work (Exodus 20:9).

Are you a workaholic? You know, that person who is a blur as he rushes by, talking on the phone, checking his watch, and grabbing something to eat while running to catch a cab. Hustle and hassle is his life. It's a trap many of us fall into.

Workaholics work hard, but not all hard workers are workaholics. Hard workers work to gain a promotion, earn more money, or please someone. Workaholics think about work constantly. They love working! Many are happy, but those around them often aren't. Workaholics are rarely at home, and when they are, they don't participate very much.

Workaholics are intense, energetic, competitive, and driven. They wake up in the morning and can't wait to get started. They drive themselves and compete with others, including how many hours per week they work. Workaholics also have strong self-doubt. You wouldn't suspect this by looking at them because they cover it well. They suspect they are inadequate, so they work hard to compensate. "The workaholic trades sweat for talent." He thinks the way to overcome feelings of inadequacy is to do more.

Workaholics prefer work to leisure. There is no holiday season for them. Their homes may be a branch office or extension of their profession. Saving time is a goal, and they glance at their watches frequently. They sleep less, and their meals are functional (mealtimes are for eating, not socializing). They make schedules well in advance, punch the walk button several times at street corners, and plan, plan, plan.

It wears me out to read this description. How do they work in a wife, children, church, prayer, and waiting on the Lord? Is there a better way to live? Yes. It's called *balance:* enjoying life, enjoying yourself, and enjoying God.

Your attitude should be the kind that was shown us by Jesus Christ, who, though he was God, did not demand and cling to his rights as God (Philippians 2:5-6 TLB).

The world's motto is "Look out for number one." Many people live by this phrase. They believe it's the only way if you plan to get ahead in life, so they use this philosophy to fight and claw their way to the top. Bodies are strewn along the way—the casualties of war. Everyone wants to get to that top position to enjoy the office with windows, your own parking space, a personal secretary, and a private phone line. Rank has its privileges.

Have you met men like this? You know, the ones who have "arrived." They have status, they have power—and they let everyone know it. You feel overwhelmed by them because whatever they have they flaunt.

Jesus' example is such a sharp contrast to this pattern. If ever anyone had status, He did. If ever anyone had power, He did. If ever anyone had the right to say, "Listen to Me and do what I say," He did. After all, He was and is the Son of God. But Jesus didn't do it that way. He wanted to leave us a model to follow, an example that would confuse, irritate, and convict the world around us. It's called *servanthood,* and it goes counter to the world around us. If you follow Jesus' words to His disciples, you won't have to call attention to yourself. You will be noticed.

"But among you it is quite different. Anyone wanting to be a leader among you must be your servant. And if you want to be right at the top, you must serve like a slave. Your attitude must be like my own, for I, the Messiah, did not come to be served, but to serve, and to give my life as a ransom for many" (Matthew 20:26-28 TLB).[1]

*Let us run with perseverance the race
marked out for us (Hebrews 12:1).*

Many men are into running. Some run in marathons, others compete in sprints and shorter races, while some spend their time running from the couch to the refrigerator during commercial breaks. Running can be enjoyable, but it's hard work. Are you aware that both feet leave the ground for an instant during each stride? And there's a risk involved when your feet come down in unfamiliar territory.

If you run, what can you expect? Your heart will pound, you'll gasp for air, your lungs will feel tight, your mouth will dry up, and your muscles will ache. It's grueling. Stand at the end of a marathon and watch the racers. Some are dead on their feet.

If you decide to get into running, you're faced with a multitude of choices: what kind of running or race you want to be in, why you run, how long you run, how fast, and how often you'll run. Once you select the race to run, you're stuck. You can't deviate from the prescribed course. If you want to run on flat land, don't go into cross-country running! You now have two goals—to finish the course and, hopefully, to place first.

We also run a spiritual race, based on the way we live. Some men run the race of life on a treadmill. They'll get exercise, but they don't go anywhere. Others run a race that destroys them. It's called the "rat race." It's easy to enter and difficult to get out of. Keep in mind that the only one who wins a rat race is a rat.

Hebrews 12 tells us that God has a different race for us to run, and when we run His race we're not alone. "Those who hope in the LORD will renew their strength. They will soar on wings like eagles; they will run and not grow weary, they will walk and not be faint" (Isaiah 40:31).[2] How fast or slow you run isn't important—only that you finish.

> *A certain man was preparing a great banquet and invited many*
> *guests. At the time of the banquet he sent his servant to tell those*
> *who had been invited, "Come, for everything is now ready." But*
> *they all alike began to make excuses. The first said, "I have just*
> *bought a field, and I must go and see it"...Another said, "I have just*
> *bought five yoke of oxen, and I'm on my way to try them out"...Still*
> *another said, "I just got married, so I can't come" (Luke 14:16-20).*

It was party time. But no one wanted to come. They had more excuses than you could imagine. The host was probably shocked, just like God is shocked when He hears our excuses for not coming to His party. One man couldn't come because he had to look at a field...*after* he bought it? Another couldn't come because he had to look at his oxen...*after* he bought them? And the man with a new wife...he had all year, according to Jewish custom, to tend to her with no responsibilities. What flimsy excuses! The people just didn't want to come. Lloyd Ogilvie has an interesting thought about it:

> Jesus is telling us that the people's longing for the Messiah was not authentic. And in telling us this, He has drawn us into the parable. We find ourselves in those three reluctant guests. Do we really want the kingdom of God if it means the absolute rule of the Lord in our lives? We talk a great deal about our need for Christ in our lives. How much do we want Him? Why are we so quick to make excuses when He invades our lives and wants to take charge of our minds and hearts? Is it possible that we want our relationship with Him on our own terms? What's the real reason we stay away from the feast?[3]

There's a party—a feast!—waiting. The invitations have gone out. Will you come?

After David had finished talking with Saul, Jonathan
became one in spirit with David (1 Samuel 18:1).

David and Jonathan were close friends. In fact, they're a great model for what it means to have a close friend. We need men, and they need us. Real friendship is deeper than acquaintances (those we work with, work out with, or share a mutual fence with).

"One in spirit" means you're on the same wavelength. You connect, you relate, and you share similar values and life view. When you're both Christians, you know the same God, want the same things for your life, and can open your hearts to each other in prayer.

There was an intense bonding of love: "And [Jonathan] loved [David] as himself" (1 Samuel 18:1). It's difficult for some men to say they have love for another male friend. But if it's there, why not admit it? Friendship involves a deep commitment to the other person and a willingness to be vulnerable. "Jonathan made a covenant with David because he loved him as himself" (18:3-4).

Friendship involves loyalty, sticking to the other person during times of difficulty. Jonathan's father, Saul, wanted to kill David, but "Jonathan spoke well of David" (19:4). True friends do that when they're not together. They focus on the positives.

Close friends encourage each other. When David was discouraged and hiding from those who wanted to hurt him, Jonathan came through. "Saul's son Jonathan went to David at Horesh and helped him find strength in God" (23:16). This is a reflection of Proverbs 17:17: "A friend loves at all times, and a brother is born for adversity."

Friendship involves mutuality, love, commitment, loyalty, and encouragement. Do you have a friend who reflects these qualities? As a friend do you reflect them as well?[4]

Let everything that has breath praise the LORD *(Psalm 150:6).*

This is a test—yes, again. Take out a piece of paper and write your definition of the word *hallelujah.* Well, many of us would probably fail this test even though we use the word again and again. It's a simple word. It means "praise the Lord." So whenever you say "Praise the Lord," you're saying "Hallelujah."

Did you know there are four groups of psalms that are called "Hallal Psalms"? That's because they have the word *hallelujah* in them. They are Psalms 104–06; 111–18; 135–36; and 146–50. Psalm 150 is the conclusion to the last group of these psalms. It's a wonderful psalm because it answers four questions about praising God: *Where? What? How?* and *Who?* Take a moment and read Psalm 150 right now.

You've probably figured out the answers to these questions by now.

Where do we praise God? We praise Him in His sanctuary and in His heavens. Praise Him no matter where you are.

What do we praise Him for? What *don't* we praise Him for? Verse 2 says to praise Him for His deeds, His greatness, who He is, and what He has done in the past.

How are we to praise Him? Through a vast array of worship experiences. Perhaps you've been in a worship service where they have every instrument, from the soft melodious flute to the trumpets and drums, and creative worship dance as well. That's what the psalm is talking about. It may be different from your worship, but it's okay.

Who is to praise God? Everything and everyone. No one is to be left out. And who does our worship center on? It's not the pastor, the choir, the special singers and dancers, or us. True worship centers on God. He's the object of our attention in worship.[5]

*Whatever is true, whatever is honorable, whatever is right,
whatever is pure, whatever is lovely, whatever is of good
repute, if there is any excellence and if anything worthy of
praise, dwell on these things (Philippians 4:8 NASB).*

If you want a verse to keep you on track each day, here it is. Read it; memorize it!

The word *true* means just what it says. There are many concepts, New Age teachings, and assumptions that are deceptive.

Honorable refers to something that has the dignity of holiness about it. The idea is that we set our minds on things that are serious, dignified, and have substance.

Right means a state of right being or right conduct. It also describes people who are faithful in fulfilling their duty to God and to men. Our thoughts ought then to be on those things which would lead us to act in a way that reflects our relationship with Jesus Christ.

Pure means moral and free from defilement and contamination. It's so easy for our thoughts to deteriorate when we dwell on negative. We need to keep our thoughts clean.

The word *lovely* means "pleasing, agreeable, or winsome"—our thoughts and actions toward others are full of kindness, love, and acceptance, as opposed to vengeful or bitter.

Good repute means "of good report" or "fair-speaking." Perhaps it implies that the words that go though our own minds should reflect fairness. They should also be words we wouldn't be hesitant for God or others to hear.

The words *dwell on* mean "to consider or ponder." Colossians 3:2 advises that we should keep our minds on what is above—the higher things, heavenly things.

So there's the plan. Workable? Yes, but don't try it by yourself. Let the Holy Spirit work with you, and you'll see a big difference in your thought life.

When I call to remembrance the genuine faith that is in you,
which dwelt first in your grandmother Lois and your mother
Eunice, and I am persuaded is in you also (2 Timothy 1:5 NKJV).

D r. Lloyd Ogilvie tells this moving story about his mother:

Some years ago I had an experience I will never forget. It was a
gala occasion. I had just finished preaching in the church where
I began my ministry. It was a time for memories and reflection.

Suddenly I was face to face with a gracious, radiant woman in her
early seventies. She had tears of joy in her eyes, and somehow a
handshake was not enough for us. She embraced me and drew
me close. Then she kissed me and whispered in my ear, "Pay no
attention to me. You belong to these people tonight." I kept an
eye on her throughout the evening, catching a glimpse every so
often through the crowd. She sat alone, greeted every so often by
some of the people. She waited until most of the people had left.
We looked long and hard at each other…and then laughed with
joy. "Mother, how are you?" I said.

She had come to attend the service from a nearby community
which had been my hometown, and to have a few hours together
before I returned home. The memory of the visit has lingered
pleasantly, but her words to me in the crowd have persisted for
deep thought and reflection. She did not know all that she had
said, but the true meaning of Christian motherhood was affirmed:
"Pay no attention to me; tonight you belong to these people." In so
speaking, she proclaimed the true essence of Jesus' message about
the family and the special calling of mothers to prepare their children for service and then give them away to follow Him.[6]

*Honor your father and your mother, so that you may live long
in the land the LORD your God is giving you (Exodus 20:12).*

The sound from the television is deafening as shouts erupt from 80,000 people. Many are jumping up and down. A spirit of mayhem rules on the field. An electrifying play has vaulted the home team to an overwhelming lead. One of the defensive backs intercepted a pass, cut through an army of opposing players, and sprinted across the goal line. That was the easy part. Now he is fighting his way back to the sideline through an exuberant crowd of players and coaches who are hopelessly out of control.

Finally the hero of the moment makes it to the bench and takes off his helmet, rivulets of sweat pouring down his face. He grabs an oxygen tank, takes a few whiffs to get his wind back, and grins broadly to acknowledge the congratulations of the other players. Suddenly he senses that the TV camera is focusing on him. He turns his six-foot five-inch muscular frame toward the camera, smiles, waves, and says, "Hi, Mom!" Soon his friends stick their heads in the camera and echo his words: "Hi, Mom! Hi, Mom!"

On the battlefields of the Civil War, the World Wars, Iraq, and others, soldiers cry out in their native tongues: "Mother!" "Madre!" "Mom!" "Mama!" Why do men, in times of ecstasy and agony, so often call out to their mothers? Because mothers are connected to sons in a special way. Perhaps it's because Mom was the first one to love and comfort us.

How is your relationship with your mom? What might she need from you? A note of appreciation? Do your children hear more positives than negatives about your mom from you? How does your relationship with your mother affect your responses to your wife?

Just a few questions for you to think about today.

To all who received him, he gave the right to become children of God.
All they needed to do was to trust him to save them (John 1:12 TLB).

Do you think of yourself as a son of God? Not too many of us consider this, but it's reality. You are. Not only did John say this, but so did Paul: "For now we are all children of God through faith in Jesus Christ" (Galatians 3:26). That's kind of a frightening thought, isn't it? It's full of responsibility. How did we get to be God's sons? We were adopted! "Long ago, even before he made the world, God chose us to be his very own through what Christ would do for us; he decided then to make us holy in his eyes, without a single fault—we who stand before him covered with his love" (Ephesians 1:4).

If you know Jesus Christ as Savior, you were adopted into God's family. The apostle John wrote: "To all who received him, to those who believed in his name, he gave the right to become children of God" (John 1:12). Understanding the fullness of your spiritual adoption can redirect your thinking and responses to life. Your adoption is a gift of grace. This is how you have been chosen for blessing.

In Roman law during New Testament times it was common practice for a childless adult who wanted an heir to adopt an adult male as his *son.* We too have been adopted by God as His heirs. The apostle Paul wrote, "Now if we are children, then we are heirs—heirs of God and co-heirs with Christ" (Romans 8:17). "So you are no longer a slave, but a son; and since you are a son, God has made you also an heir" (Galatians 4:7).

When you received Jesus Christ as your Savior, you were adopted into God's family and received *all* the rights and privileges of a full heir. There are no limitations.

*He has rescued us out of the darkness and gloom of Satan's kingdom
and brought us into the Kingdom of his dear Son (Colossians 1:13 TLB).*

How do you feel about being adopted by the King of the universe and being delivered from the kingdom of darkness? You've been taken into God's family and established as His heir. You may have come from a dysfunctional home, but God is a Father who can fill the gaps in your life because you are now part of His immediate family. Closeness, affection, and generosity are the basis of your relationship with Him. He loves and cares for you. Your relationship as an heir is the basis for your Christian life and the foundation for all the other blessings you receive in your day-to-day experience.

Your relationship as an adopted child of God has a number of implications for the way you live. Just as a child grows up imitating his parents, so you can become more and more like your Father God. For example, in the Sermon on the Mount Christ calls you to *imitate* your heavenly Father: "Love your enemies and pray for those who persecute you...Be perfect, therefore, as your heavenly Father is perfect" (Matthew 5:44,48).

You are also called to *glorify* your Father in heaven: "Let your light shine before men, that they may see your good deeds and praise your Father in heaven" (Matthew 5:16).

As you imitate and glorify your heavenly Father, you will sense the thrill of participating in the destiny for which you were created. You'll enjoy the blessings of being God's child and realize the benefits that come from *behaving* as God's child. As your knowledge of God grows, so does your awareness of His love for you. You'll be transformed, blessed with the understanding that you are fulfilling His purpose.

How can you honor and please your Father in heaven today?

*Whatever you do, whether in word or deed, do it all
in the name of the Lord Jesus, giving thanks to God
the Father through him (Colossians 3:17).*

Pastor Joe Brown, a former Navy officer, shared this story about doing our best:

> As a young man, President Jimmy Carter graduated from the Naval Academy and served as an officer on a nuclear-powered submarine. However, before he was able to assume that position, he had to have a personal interview with Admiral Hyman Rickover, the man considered to be the father of the nuclear navy. Carter was understandably nervous, knowing how much was at stake...
>
> When he stood before Rickover, it was soon obvious to the young officer that the wise admiral knew more about nearly every subject discussed than did he. Finally Rickover came to the last question on his seemingly never-ending list. "Where did you finish in your class, young man?"
>
> Pleased with his accomplishments and thrilled to finally be presented a question he was sure of, Carter informed the Admiral that he had finished 59th out of a student body numbering 820. Then he waited for a commendation from the old sailor...
>
> "Did you always do your best?" was the question that broke the uncomfortable silence between the two men.
>
> Carter thought and then cleared his throat. "No, sir, I did not," was his hesitant reply.
>
> Rickover turned his chair around...and asked, "Why not?"

It's a good question—"Why not?" How do you evaluate what you do? Poor, so-so, adequate, good, very good, outstanding? We are called to be people of excellence, to fulfill our potential. It's easy to coast along rather than make that extra effort. Some men are pretty good at that. But if you can do better, why not?[7]

*The lips of the wise spread knowledge; not so
the hearts of fools (Proverbs 15:7).*

Would you like to be a man whom others respect, admire, go to for advice, and consult for solutions? You can! The principle can be summed up in one word—*communication.* The book of Proverbs offers great wisdom on effective communication.

First, be a man who gives good advice and wisdom. "Plans fail for lack of counsel, but with many advisers they succeed" (Proverbs 15:22). Follow the wisdom in Proverbs.

Second, when you are on the receiving end of another person's exhortation or reproof, listen, evaluate, and accept. Don't react. "Wounds from a friend can be trusted, but an enemy multiplies kisses" (Proverbs 27:6).

And when someone needs correction, do it lovingly and sensitively. "He who rebukes a man will in the end gain more favor than he who has a flattering tongue" (Proverbs 28:23). Discernment, patience, and prayer on your part will be needed. "A word aptly spoken is like apples of gold in settings of silver" (Proverbs 25:11).

Have a sense of humor. We need men who can be serious but also laugh and help others lighten up. "All the days of the oppressed are wretched, but the cheerful heart has a continual feast" (Proverbs 15:15). The words *continual feast* literally mean "to cause good healing." Don't laugh at the expense of others, but do look for the funny side of life.

One other guideline is essential. Be an encourager, a cheerleader. Show your sincere appreciation and people will want to be around you. "A man finds joy in giving an apt reply—and how good is a timely word!" (Proverbs 15:23).

That's the plan. It's workable…and the best place to put it into practice is at home.

*Seek first [God's] kingdom and his righteousness, and all
these things will be given to you as well (Matthew 6:33).*

Jugglers look so smooth and cool. As the dishes fly through the air, the
juggler's hands move in perfect rhythm and balance. It looks so effort-
less. We don't realize the endless hours of practice, the stacks of broken dishes, or the pursuit of missed balls that are part of the struggle to
become proficient. We probably identify more with the failures than we
do with the achievements of the juggler.

We're all jugglers in one way or another. We try to juggle the demands
of marriage, parenting, career, continuing education, church, community service, our parents, and perhaps even a little time for ourselves now
and then. And at times we feel like we're on the "rack" with ropes around
each limb pulling in opposite directions. Everybody wants a piece of us.
Sometimes there is not enough to go around. So what's a guy to do? Prioritize. Regroup. Cut and trim. Here are some suggestions to get you started.

First place in your life is for the Lord. Ask Him, "What do you want
from me?"

Second place in your life is for your wife. Ask her, "What do you want
from me?"

Third place in your life is for your children. You and your wife determine what is needed for them.

Fourth place in your life is your career. What can you give to it?

Ask, "Why am I doing all that I do? For what purpose? For whose
glory?" Then make a list of every activity in your life. Evaluate them
under the following formula: Anything "important" could either stay
or go, and anything simply "good" goes! Think about it and then trim.
You'll be glad you did.

*Better one handful with tranquillity than two handfuls
with toil and chasing after the wind (Ecclesiastes 4:6).*

I n the book *Becoming Soul Mates,* the Parrotts offer stories of how couples developed spiritual intimacy in their marriages. Here's one to
encourage you if you're married.

> Our friends introduced us to the "principle of reintroduction."
> Simply put, this principle acknowledges that every day we change
> as individuals based on our experiences that day. In order to build
> a growing relationship as a couple, then, we must make time to
> "daily reintroduce" ourselves to each other. We share the mundane
> and the profound. We disclose what's going on in our lives and
> genuinely inquire about each other's life.
>
> Frankly, this was fairly easy to do when we were first married and
> had few distractions. We had lots of time for meaningful dia-
> logue, cups of coffee, and sharing activities together. But as chil-
> dren came and other adult responsibilities began to crowd our
> schedules, we were grateful we had established the habit early on
> and that it still prevails. For no amount of reading the Bible or
> praying together genuinely builds our relationship if we haven't
> bared our lives with each other on a regular basis and feel con-
> vinced that we are "naked and unashamed" with each other in the
> fullest sense of that biblical definition of intimacy.
>
> Now our daily reintroduction habit usually takes the form of a
> long walk, an extended cup of coffee (decaf, now), or a long phone
> call if I'm out of town. But we keep very short accounts, and we
> can testify that we depend on this habit to keep us growing, both
> as individuals and as a couple. [8]

If anyone competes as an athlete, he does not receive the victor's crown unless he competes according to the rules (2 Timothy 2:5).

The cry of the Olympic athlete is "Go for the bronze!" No? Well, what about "Go for the silver"? Not quite? How about, "Go for the gold"? Yes! That's what they're after! What we see in the competitions are the result of years of sacrifice. To get there athletes have to be disciplined. They undertake a vigorous training schedule. It's essential if they want a chance to make it to the Olympics. Do you know what they go through?

They begin training as young as possible. Their trainer knows the value of early training.

They develop all the muscles in their body, not just a few. Ice skaters take dance and gymnastics as well as skating lessons. Some of the men in pairs skating build their upper bodies so they can lift their partners.

They master the fundamentals of their sport before hitting the competitions. Learning the basics prevents later disaster.

They know their equipment inside and out. They have to if they're going to use it.

They learn from the many mistakes they make. They view their performances on recordings again and again. They ask others for advice and learn from their experiences. They're teachable and get back on their feet after a fall. They build on their successes.

They have learned how to focus. They concentrate and practice the same thing again and again, refining their techniques.

As Christians, if we applied these principles to our lives, we'd quickly move from being Christians to being disciples. Isn't that a great thought?[9]

Then a teacher of the law came to him and said, "Teacher, I will follow you wherever you go." Jesus replied, "Foxes have holes and birds of the air have nests, but the Son of Man has no place to lay his head" (Matthew 8:19-20).

Have you felt like you didn't fit in? You know, sort of part of a group, but not really? It's an uncomfortable feeling, but it's normal if you're a Christian. When you follow Jesus, you won't really feel like you fit in... or at least you shouldn't. There's a good reason for that. You're an alien... a stranger just visiting this world for a while. Earth may be where you're living, but it's not really your home. Again and again God's Word says:

> If you belonged to the world, it would love you as its own. As it is, you do not belong to the world, but I have chosen you out of the world. That is why the world hates you (John 15:19).

> Dear friends, I urge you, as aliens and strangers in the world, to abstain from sinful desires, which war against your soul (1 Peter 2:11).

> Our citizenship is in heaven. And we eagerly await a Savior from there, the Lord Jesus Christ (Philippians 3:20).

We are here on a visit and we have a purpose: to enjoy God as well as to love Him forever, but also to help enlarge the kingdom of God. If you want an opportunity to introduce others to the kingdom, the next time someone asks you where you live, just tell them you're an alien on a visit and they wouldn't believe where your real home is. Go ahead, try it! And get set for some strange reactions. Once you've gotten their attention, share the Good News of Jesus!

*In view of God's mercy, to offer your bodies as living
sacrifices, holy and pleasing to God—this is your
spiritual act of worship (Romans 12:1).*

Dear God,
I'm praying today for wisdom to know what I need to be doing in this world.

Help me to overcome my not wanting to face the truth, which I need to face.

Help me to overcome my laziness that keeps me from learning the truth.

Help me to overcome my prejudices that keep me from seeing what is truth.

Help me to overcome my stubbornness that keeps me from accepting the truth.

Help me to overcome my pride that keeps me from looking for the truth.

Keep my eyes and ears open so I can hear my conscience. Take away my arrogance, which keeps me from accepting advice. Open my locked-up mind, which resists even the Holy Spirit…

Give me the grace and power to do what I know I ought to do. Lord, keep me from the weakness of my will that gets off course now and then. Save me from my lack of resistance, which causes me to give in to temptation all too easily…

Lift from my life the fears that have immobilized me in the past…

Give me strength to tackle the hard things of life in place of settling for the easy.

Give me courage to let others know that I know and love You. So now once again I ask for wisdom to know Your will and do it.

In Jesus' name.
Amen.[10]

*"Let him who boasts boast about this: that he understands
and knows me, that I am the* Lord, *who exercises
kindness, justice and righteousness on earth, for in these
I delight," declares the* Lord *(Jeremiah 9:24).*

Part of our American dream is enjoyment. Everyone wants a good time. Advertisements cry out to us to enjoy ourselves. From car ads to food ads they appeal to our desire for fun. There's nothing wrong with enjoyment…unless it becomes our god.

A document written in 1647 set out to instruct readers in the dogmas of the church. It was called *The Westminster Shorter Catechism*. In it is the question, "What is man's chief end?" And the answer is, "To glorify God and enjoy him forever." That's a shocker for some. Worship Him? Yes. Fear Him? Yes. Pray to Him? Yes. But enjoy Him? How?

Enjoyment comes when we are more knowledgeable about something. The closer we get, the more familiar we are, the more we can enjoy whatever it is. Enjoyment means liking, relaxing in something's presence, and delighting. And when we enjoy God we're more apt to glorify Him by serving Him.

But there's one other thing to know: *God enjoys you!* How does that grab you? It's a foreign thought to some. They're more likely to think of all the reasons why God couldn't enjoy them. Remember there are things He doesn't enjoy about us, such as sin, failure, and drifting from Him. But He delights in you as a person. His enjoyment and love for you is not conditional.

Think about these two ideas today: Your purpose is to enjoy God, and He enjoys you. That ought to do something for your outlook.[11]

Where can I go from your Spirit? Where can
I flee from your presence? (Psalm 139:7).

Do your thoughts ever drift away when you're praying? Dr. Lloyd Ogilvie addresses this problem.

Meditation: "What do I do about wandering thoughts when I pray?" I've been asked that question repeatedly. A wandering attention simply tells us that our minds are on other things. Why not talk to God about what's really commanding our attention? Whatever our minds drift off to is an indication of what we really need to ask for help or solve or conquer.

But what about abhorrent thoughts or fantasies? They indicate a deeper need beneath the surface. Allow God to gently probe the cause. We are like a ball of yarn with one strand protruding. The Lord gets hold of that and begins to unravel us. Since He knows all about us, He's never surprised. Why do we think we can hide anything from Him? There is no place we can go, even into the depths of ourselves, where He's not there waiting for us.

How many times should I ask God for something in my prayers? Here is a formula that works for me: ask God once, and thank Him a thousand times. God is not hard of hearing, nor does He forget the requests we've made of Him. Thanks that He has heard is an effective method of recommitting the need to Him. The Lord knows what we need and will act when it is according to His plan and timing for us. Remember that prayer is not an argument with God to persuade Him to move things our way, but an exercise by which we are enabled by His Spirit to move ourselves His way.[12]

I do not consider myself yet to have taken hold of [perfection].
But one thing I do: Forgetting what is behind and straining
toward what is ahead, I press on... (Philippians 3:13).

D o you know what God wants to do with you today? Let me tell you. First of all, He wants to renew your mind. In 1 Corinthians 2:16 Paul states that "we have the mind of Christ." Romans 12:2 tells us that we can be "transformed by the renewing of your mind." In Philippians 2:5 we are challenged, "Your attitude should be the same as that of Christ Jesus." How will your life and your relationships be different when this happens?

After God renews your mind, He wants to heal your emotions. In 1 Corinthians 14:1 we are commanded to "pursue love" (NASB). In Ephesians 4:26 we see that with God's help we can be angry and not sin. In Ephesians 5:1-2 we are told that we can be imitators of God as we "walk in love, just as Christ also loved [us]" (NASB). How will your life and your relationships be different when this happens?

God also wants to direct any choices you make. Romans 13:12 instructs us to "lay aside the deeds of darkness and put on the armor of light." Ephesians 4:22-24 tells us that we can choose to "lay aside the old self" and "put on the new self, which in the likeness of God has been created in righteousness and holiness of the truth." In Philippians 3:13 we are encouraged not to dwell on the things of the past but to choose to reach forward to what lies ahead.

That's quite a plan for your life, isn't it? The good news is that it's workable. Have you had a better offer today? Probably not. And there won't be a better one tomorrow either.[13]

[Anyone who] keeps a promise even if it ruins him...
shall stand firm forever (Psalm 15:4-5 TLB).

When your name is mentioned, what do you want people to think about you? Better yet, what do you want them to *say* about you? How about that you're honest? Honesty probably ought to be put on the endangered species list. It's harder and harder to find an honest person. Our society has learned to cut corners, shade the truth, leave out information (like on tax reports), and present the image that will get us what we want. It's not really profitable to be honest, especially if we're competing with others who aren't honest. Even Plato said, "Honesty is for the most part less profitable than dishonesty."

Fortunately, there are some honest people around. They are sincere, frank, and free from deceit or fraud. They are genuine. They are who and what they say they are. Others can trust and depend on them. Our first president, George Washington, said, "I hope I shall possess firmness and virtue enough to maintain what I consider the most enviable of all tides, the character of an honest man."

Think about it. Can you give examples as to why others see you as an honest man? Are you thought of as someone who keeps his word? If you are married, does your wife see you as someone who listens, says yes to a request, and then follows through? When you tell the kids you'll be there, can they count on you? Honesty is a great way to say that you're a Christian. Who knows, someone may ask why you're the way you are...and they could be introduced to your Lord![14]

When justice is done, it brings joy to the righteous
but terror to evildoers (Proverbs 21:15).

"There ain't no justice anywhere." Yeah, it's easy to think that way today. Criminals caught in the act are released because of technicalities. Innocent people are sued and their lives ruined by those who lie on the witness stand. In Washington it seems the special interest groups with the most money end up with laws going their way.

In the Old West a different form of fairness emerged now and then. In frontier justice, vigilantes would catch a horse thief or cattle rustler, go to the nearest tree, and hang him on the spot. Who needed courts when the thief was caught with a branding iron in hand?

We all want justice. Right should prevail, and wrong should be punished. But justice is easily hindered and sometimes destroyed by powerful and angry people. Politicians, lynch mobs, business owners, and even those in the church have been known to prevent it. God wants justice to prevail. He wants us to be just and fair:

> To do what is right and just is more acceptable to the LORD than sacrifice (Proverbs 21:3).

> The violence of the wicked will drag them away, for they refuse to do what is right (21:7).

> When justice is done, it brings joy to the righteous but terror to evildoers (21:15).

> Many seek an audience with a ruler, but it is from the LORD that man gets justice (29:26).

We honor God when we act in a just and fair way. Yes, it's tough—but possible.

*Do not eat the food of a stingy man, do not crave his delicacies; for he
is the kind of man who is always thinking about the cost. "Eat and
drink," he says to you, but his heart is not with you (Proverbs 23:6-7).*

Your attitude and how you think about your problems impact how you feel and behave. Two men were confined to the same hospital room for an extended period. They were quite ill and, unfortunately, didn't have the typical diversions such as books or TV. They just had each other, so they engaged in a lot of conversation. They talked about everything, including their personal histories. Through this they became close friends.

Neither could leave his bed, but one man was next to a window. Each day for part of his treatment he would sit up for an hour. During this time he brought the outside world to his friend by describing everything he saw. He talked in great detail about the people, the trees, the lake, the birds, the dogs, the color of the clouds and the sky.

In time, though, his friend began to think it wasn't fair for the other to have all the access to the world, while all he saw was the room. He didn't like thinking this, but with the abundance of time available to him he began to think this way more and more. Soon thoughts of jealousy and envy dominated his thinking and his mood.

One night the man closest to the window woke up, coughing and choking. He tried to push the button to call the nurse but it dropped out of his hand. His bitter, jealous friend listened to the struggling but did nothing. When the nurse arrived, the man was dead. After a few days, the envious man asked to have that bed and was moved. As soon as the nurse left the room, he rose up on one elbow to look out. The window through which his friend had filled his life with wonderful sights showed nothing except...a blank wall![15]

*Jesus replied, "No one who puts his hand to the plow and looks
back is fit for service in the kingdom of God" (Luke 9:62).*

When would you like to retire? Dr. Lloyd Ogilvie shares a new twist
on this issue:

> Some time ago, a full-page ad appeared in the *Wall Street Journal*
> entitled "How to Retire at 35." I read the advertisement immedi-
> ately. Though I had long passed 35, I wanted to know what I had
> missed. This is what it said:
>
> > It's so easy. Thousands of men do it every year. In all walks
> > of life. And it sets our economy, our country, and the
> > world back thousands of years in terms of wasted human
> > resources. But worst of all, it is the personal tragedy that
> > almost always results from "early retirement."
> >
> > It usually begins with a tinge of boredom. Gradually a
> > man's work begins to seem endlessly repetitious. The rat
> > race hardly seems worth it any more. It is at this point that
> > many a 35-year-old boy wonder retires. There are no testi-
> > monial dinners or gold watches. He goes to work every day,
> > puts in his forty hours, and even draws a paycheck. He's
> > retired, but nobody knows it. Not at first, anyhow.
> >
> > The lucky ones get fired in time to make a fresh start. Those
> > less fortunate hang on for a while—even decades, wait-
> > ing and wondering: waiting for a raise or promotion that
> > never comes, and wondering why. With life expectancy
> > approaching the century mark, 65 years is a long time to
> > spend in a rocking chair.
>
> I began to think of people I knew like that—not just in their work,
> but in their discipleship. Christ never allows us to take an early
> retirement. In fact, He recalls us today into active service.[16]

Still think it's time to think about retirement? Perhaps not.

A simple man believes anything, but a prudent man
gives thought to his steps (Proverbs 14:15).

Do you believe everything you hear? I mean, how do you respond to some of those TV commercials or infomercials? Do you believe the outrageous stories some people tell? And how about all that rhetoric from politicians? Today's verse provides a warning that may help us stay out of difficulty. In The New American Standard Bible it says, "The naive believes everything, but the sensible man considers his steps."

In Hebrew, the word for *simple* or *naive* presents the idea of "open-mindedness" or "inexperience that leaves a person open to being conned." One writer describes the naive as "a person of undecided views and thus susceptible to either good or bad influences."[17] Do you know anyone like this?

Simple people are way too trusting. They are gullible and believe just about anything. They lack a discerning spirit. The Bible says they like the way they are. A proverb asks, "How long, O simple ones [open to evil], will you love being simple?" (Proverbs 1:22 AMP). Perhaps the reason is they rarely consider the consequences of what they do. They enjoy being open-minded. They also lack good moral sense. They're lousy judges of character, and they often develop friendships with people like themselves. They don't seem to recognize evil. "A prudent man sees the evil and hides himself, but the simple pass on and are punished [with suffering]" (Proverbs 22:3 AMP).

Is there hope for this person? How will he turn out? Well, wait until tomorrow for the rest of the story.

Only a simpleton believes everything he's told! A prudent man understands the need for proof (Proverbs 14:15 TLB).

I s there any hope for the simpleton?" Well, first look at what Proverbs says about the outcome of naiveté: "That is why you must eat the bitter fruit of having your own way and experience the full terrors of the pathway you have chosen. For you turned away from me—to death; your own complacency will kill you. Fools! But all who listen to me shall live in peace and safety, unafraid" (Proverbs 1:31-33 TLB).

The naive may be satisfied with what they do, but it comes back to haunt them. Proverbs 14:18 TLB says: "The simpleton is crowned with folly; the wise man is crowned with knowledge." The fool doesn't learn from what he does. He doesn't improve. He gets worse. Is there any hope? Only the Lord God can save them from themselves. "The LORD protects the simplehearted; when I was in great need, he saved me" (Psalm 116:6 NIV).

The naive can change but not without some pain. "Strike a scoffer and the naive may become shrewd" (Proverbs 19:25 NASB); "when the scoffer is punished, the naive becomes wise" (Proverbs 21:11 NASB). Since the naive are so influenced by others, when they get into trouble they learn from their friends' mistakes.

There is a second way the naive can learn and that is from the Word of God:

> The law of the LORD is perfect, restoring the soul; the testimony of the LORD is sure, making wise the simple (Psalm 19:7 NASB).

> The unfolding of your words gives light; it gives understanding to the simple (119:130).

That is the rest of the story.[18]

No one can serve two masters. Either he will hate the one and love the other, or he will be devoted to the one and despise the other. You cannot serve both God and Money (Matthew 6:24).

People die for it and lie for it. They curse it and save it. They spend it or lend it. You work all your life for it, but you can't take it with you when you die. You can use it for the kingdom of God and save people from the wages of sin or let it enslave you and lead you into sin. Our world revolves around who has money and how it's used. Poor people have the illusion money will make them happy; rich people discover it can't.

There are more than 2300 verses on handling money in the Bible. Jesus summed up the problem in today's verse. Read Patrick Morley's additional insights into this verse:

> The word *serve* translates "to be a slave to, literally or figuratively, voluntarily or involuntarily."
>
> It is not a question of *advisability,* "You *should* not serve both God and money." That would be a *priority* choice. It is not a question of *accountability,* "You *must* not serve both God and money." That would be a *moral* choice.
>
> Rather, it is a matter of *impossibility,* "You *cannot* serve both God and money." *There is no choice;* we each serve one, and only one, master. We are either a slave to God or a slave to money.[19]

What is your perspective on money? What did you learn about money and possessions while growing up? Money itself isn't bad. We need it, and it's useful. But we also need a financial guide. Why not read the book of Proverbs? Read one chapter a day and write down what it says about money. This might change your financial future.

Have nothing to do with godless myths and old wives' tales;
rather, train yourself to be godly (1 Timothy 4:7).

I f you believe in something—really believe in it and want it—
you'll persist no matter what. The obstacles may seem overwhelming or you may not feel fully equipped, but if you're
convinced that this is for you, you go for it…like Christopher
Columbus did. Columbus must have been so convinced of his
dream that he became a super persuader. His idea of a transatlantic voyage in the 1400s was kind of far-out. Centuries of supersti-
tion and traditions had to be overcome. Beside that, even though
Columbus had been to sea several times, it had only been as a passenger, never as captain. To top it off, he was a foreigner (Italian)
living in Portugal and then Spain. Then there was another minor
problem: He didn't have the money to fund such a journey. And
the only one who could legally fund an exploratory voyage was
the head of a country, such as a king or queen. That certainly narrowed the possibilities.

And then…what Columbus wanted personally from this voyage
wasn't pennies. He wanted a 10-percent commission on all new
commerce between the mother country and the new land, the
title of "Admiral of the Ocean Sea," and the permanent position
of governor of the newly discovered lands.

He asked again and again for what he wanted. For seven years
he asked King John of Portugal for the funds. Nothing. No luck.
Then he worked another seven years on Ferdinand and Isabella of
Spain. Again and again he asked. One day the answer was yes! And
you know the rest of the story. Persistence pays.

Is there something you need to be persistent about in your life?
What obstacles have to be overcome? Go for it as a team—you and
your heavenly Father![20]

Husbands, love your wives, just as Christ loved the
church and gave himself up for her (Ephesians 5:25).

"Who does a woman marry when she marries?" Sound like a dumb question? Perhaps the answer is obvious: She marries a man. Unfortunately, however, some don't. They find they have simply married a paycheck. Their husbands rationalize, "Hey! I'm working hard for us. I want to build a better life for you, to give you everything you want. Now, just be patient. This big deal at work will be over in three to six months and then we'll have some time together. In fact, I may even take you away for a weekend."

The only thing that might be over in three to six months, however, is the marriage if this has become a pattern! I've seen it happen time and again. A wife wants a man, not things. She wants him to love her as Christ loved the church, sacrificially. And that doesn't mean working all the time.

Many men say all the work is to provide for their wives, but there are other reasons. It could be more comfortable at work, or he could be building his identity through work, or avoiding conflict or intimacy at home. While men are off working and providing, their wives could be getting emotionally colder. If deep freeze is in process, it's because we (husbands) are not functioning too well as the thermostat. That's our role, you know. A wife needs our warmth, our time, our eyes, and ears to listen, our emotions.

Sure, you could work and work and work like some men and have everything external but have nothing on the home front. Consider how Jesus loved the church. He gave *Himself* for it. That's the key word for us too.

The fruit of righteousness will be peace; the effect of righteousness will be quietness and confidence forever. My people will live in peaceful dwelling places, in secure homes, in undisturbed places of rest (Isaiah 32:17-18).

Let's talk about noise pollution. We can't even go into a nice restaurant for dinner without having to contend with loud music. Radios, TV, horns, airplanes, people talking and yelling, electric lawn mowers and blowers, freeways. Isn't there any place where there's no sound? Chuck Swindoll has a few words to say about quietness:

> That wonderful, much-needed presence has again come for a visit—*quietness.* Oh, how I love it…need it. The last time it was this quiet was a few weeks ago when I was walking with a friend along the sandy shore at Carmel. The silence of that early dawn was broken only by the rhythmic roar of the rolling surf and the cry of a few gulls floating overhead. The same thought I had then I have now: *I cannot be the man I should be without times of quietness.* Stillness is an essential part of our growing deeper as we grow older. Or—in the words of a man who helped shape my life perhaps more than any other: "We will not become men of God without the presence of solitude."
>
> Those words haunt me when I get caught in the treadmill of time schedules…when I make my turn toward the homestretch of the week and try to meet the deadline of demands, just like you. [21]

Can you handle the stillness of solitude? Is it unnerving to sit and listen to…nothing? Are you an activity addict? Are the noises in your head so loud you can't hear God? His still, small voice won't try to out-shout the noise. He's waiting for you to be quiet, to listen, to relax, so that you can be restored.

Jesus asked, "Do you see anything?" He looked up and said, "I see people; they look like trees walking around" (Mark 8:23-24).

I'm partially blind. So are you. We may have 20-20 or 20-40 vision, but in some ways we're blind. Our view of life is distorted. Our ability to perceive life is similar to a camera. Photographers can alter the image of reality through the use of various lenses or filters. A wide-angle lens gives a broad panorama, but the objects appear distant and smaller. A telephoto lens has a narrower, more selective view. It can focus on a beautiful flower, but shuts out the rest of the garden. Happy and smiling people seen through a fish-eye lens appear unreal. Filters can blur reality, bring darkness into a lighted scene, or even create a mist. Thus a photographic view of the world can be distorted.

It's easy to view life in a distorted way. And sometimes we contort how we view our spouses, children, coworkers, ourselves, and even God. Blindness can be selective, and there can be degrees of it present in our lives. We need what the blind man received:

> Taking the blind man by the hand, [Jesus] brought him out of the village; and after spitting on his eyes and laying His hands on him, He asked him, "Do you see anything?" And he looked up and said, "I see men, for I see them like trees, walking around." Then again He laid His hands on his eyes; and he looked intently and was restored, and began to see everything clearly (Mark 8:23-25 NASB).

There is One who can open our eyes in many ways, especially spiritually:

> I will lead the blind by a way they do not know, in paths they do not know I will guide them. I will make darkness into light before them and ragged places into plains (Isaiah 42:16 NASB).

*Live such good lives among the pagans that, though they
accuse you of doing wrong, they may see your good deeds
and glorify God on the day he visits us (1 Peter 2:12).*

When you're not around and other people bring up your name, what's the first thing that comes to their minds about you? Better yet, what do they say about you? Most of us will never know for sure, but it might be interesting to find out. What others are thinking and saying about us is based on what we've let people know about us as well as how we've acted around them. We have reputations that represent us in the minds of others when we're not around. Webster's defines *reputation* as "estimation in which a person or thing is commonly held, whether favored or not; character in the view of the public."[1]

Sometimes people don't give you the time of day until you've established a good reputation. Artists have discovered this, as have sports figures, writers, and ministers.

Everyone has a reputation, whether or not we want one. A good reputation is made, is earned. It takes hard work and consistency of word and deed.

How's your reputation? Why not check it out? If you're brave (or crazy, as some people would say) you could ask! To your coworkers: "In your eyes, what is my reputation?" To your wife: "In your eyes, what is my reputation?" To your children: "In your eyes, what is my reputation?" To the Lord: "In Your eyes, what is my reputation?" May you be well thought of!

*O LORD, answer me, so these people will know that
you, O LORD, are God, and that you are turning
their hearts back again (1 Kings 18:37-39).*

C an you imagine a guy who was on top of the world with everyone in his country and thinking he was the greatest man alive? And what does he do? He comes down with a good case of depression. It doesn't make much sense, does it? But it happened. God's prophet Elijah got so depressed he wanted to die. (Read 1 Kings 18–19.) Elijah misinterpreted a situation by seeing only certain elements of it. His misperceptions concerning God, other people, and himself were caused partly by the tremendous emotional and physical exhaustion he suffered. Have you ever felt that way?

Elijah had an intense emotional experience when he was used by God to demonstrate His power on Mount Carmel. Perhaps he expected everyone to turn to the true God after that and was disappointed when Queen Jezebel was still so hostile. He was physically exhausted because of the encounter on Mount Carmel and his twenty-mile race before the king's chariot. When Jezebel threatened his life he became frightened. He forgot about God's power that had just been dramatically demonstrated. Fearing for his life, Elijah left familiar surroundings and cut himself off from his friends. Have you ever done that?

All of these factors led to his depression. His distorted thinking is evident in his lament that he was the only one left who was faithful to God. He was convinced the world was against him. Self-pity caused him to lose further perspective. Sound familiar?

When you get down, discouraged, or even depressed (they're all normal responses), take a look at what you've been doing and thinking. It could be the "Elijah Pattern." God straightened out Elijah's thinking and behavior, and He can do that for you too.

The fruit of the Spirit is love, joy, peace, patience, kindness, goodness, faithfulness, gentleness and self-control (Galatians 5:22).

Perspective can make a big difference in how you view what happens to you. For example, take the case of Fred, a landscape contractor. His first job was to remove a huge oak stump from a field. Fred had to use dynamite. The only problem was that he'd never used any before. He was kind of nervous, especially with the old farmer watching every move he made. So he tried to hide his jitters by carefully determining the size of the stump, the precise amount of dynamite, and where it should be placed to get the maximum effect. He didn't want to use too small an amount and have to do it over, nor did he want to use too much. He went about it scientifically.

When he was ready to detonate the charge, Fred and the farmer went behind a pickup truck where a wire was running to the detonator. He looked at the farmer, said a prayer, and plunged down the detonator. It worked...too well. The stump broke loose from the ground, rose through the air in a curving arc, and then plummeted down onto the cab of the truck. Fred's heart sank, and all he could think of was the ruined cab. Not the farmer. He was full of amazement and admiration. Slapping Fred on the back he said, "Not bad. With a little more practice you'll get it into the bed of the truck every time!"

Some of us are like Fred, and some of us are like the farmer. We hit hard times and give in to discouragement or we see how close we came to making it work and say, "Next time I'll get it right!" The fruit of the Spirit includes joy. It's realistic optimism, not the absence of hardship. It's a choice we make. Why not smile when the stump lands on your truck and say, "It could be worse. I'll do it better next time!" [2]

*If, when we were God's enemies, we were reconciled to him
through the death of his Son, how much more, having been
reconciled, shall we be saved through his life! (Romans 5:10).*

Most of us have done it at one time or another. We've made a mistake in the checkbook. All of a sudden we realize we're still writing checks but the well is dry. The money is used up. We hurriedly transfer funds into our checking account and heave a sigh of relief. We're saved. There's money to cover the checks. Of course, we wish the bank would just pour extra money into our account, but that's not going to happen.

Some people think of God as being generous. That's why He overlooks our sins and forgives us, right? Wrong. God is holy and can't overlook our sins. Exodus 34:7 talks about God "maintaining love to thousands, and forgiving wickedness, rebellion and sin. Yet he does not leave the guilty unpunished; he punishes the children and their children for the sin of the fathers to the third and fourth generation." God doesn't let a guilty person go unpunished. Sin has to be paid for.

So if you're guilty and I'm guilty, how can we get rid of the guilt and our responsibility for sin? Through the work of Jesus, who was willing to die for our sins. Because He took our sins upon Himself we can live. His righteousness was put upon us. This is similar to what happened at the bank. There was a transfer. This time, though, it wasn't money. This transfer is referred to as *imputation*. Our sins and sinful natures were *imputed* to Jesus, which makes us innocent. But in God's eyes we need to be seen as righteous. That's why it was necessary that Jesus' righteousness also be *imputed* to us.

Do we earn it? No. Do we deserve it? No. Praise God for this transfer![3]

*He picked up the cloak that had fallen from Elijah and went
back and stood on the bank of the Jordan (2 Kings 2:13).*

Imagine that you've been working with a man for years. He's had a
highly responsible job. He's known by many, but he hasn't always
been appreciated because of his brutal honesty. He never allowed any
slack and wouldn't let much slide by. He had high standards and held to
them even when others didn't. He spoke out against the majority—the
immoral majority of his time.

But now it's time for him to leave. He's going to die, to go into the
presence of the Lord. The man who has been your mentor wants *you* to
succeed *him*. This man always wore a specific article of clothing that set
him apart from others and designated who he was. When he dies, that
cloak will be ready for you to take up as you assume his position. It will
designate who and what you are…but it will also bring some hostility
from others. You won't always be liked, accepted, or popular. Picking up
that cloak will bring you some grief. But you will know you're doing the
right thing. So what will you do?

That's the dilemma Elisha faced with Elijah. You can read about it
starting in 2 Kings, chapter 1. Elisha knew if he were going to follow Elijah he would need an abundance of God's strength, and that's what he
asked for. When Elijah was taken up to heaven, the cloak was left behind.
Elisha looked at it a while…and then picked it up.

We may not have a cloak to pick up and wear, but we do have the
cross of Christ. If you think it's heavy and that carrying it is hard, remember what happened on it. It changed the world. It changed lives. It can
change your life.

*These commandments that I give you today are to be upon
your hearts. Impress them on your children. Talk about them
when you sit at home and when you walk along the road, when
you lie down and when you get up (Deuteronomy 6:6-7).*

Do you know what the calling is of a father? In what specific ways is a father to be involved with his children? Having a son is an opportunity to lead him to another father—our heavenly Father. A dad who is in a right relationship with God will have the greatest opportunity to be in a right relationship with his wife and his children.

I am the father of a daughter and a son. I wish I had known thirty years ago what I know today. Part of my parenting challenge was the limited resources and information available. Today there's plenty of information, but it still needs to be read, applied, and implemented. Here's a strong, graphic statement of the father's importance:

> Fathers leave a lasting impression on the lives of their children. Picture fathers all around the world carving their initials into their family trees. Like a carving in the trunk of an oak, as time passes the impressions fathers make on their children grow deeper and wider. Depending upon how the tree grows, those impressions can either be ones of harmony or ones of distortion.

> Some fathers skillfully carve beautiful messages of love, support, solid discipline, and acceptance into the personality core of their children. Others use words and actions that cut deeply and leave emotional scars. Time may heal the wound and dull the image, but the impression can never be completely erased. The size, shape, and extent of your father's imprint on your life may be large or may be small but it is undeniably there. [4]

What kind of imprint are you leaving as a father?

Moses' father-in-law replied, "What you are doing is not good. You and these people who come to you will only wear yourselves out. The work is too heavy for you; you cannot handle it alone" (Exodus 18:17-18).

Have you ever had an in-law make a suggestion to you? If so, how did you take it? Most of us don't want to take advice, much less from our in-laws. Look at Moses. He was busy working for the Lord by handling disputes, making decisions, giving out advice, and listening to concerned complaints from dusk until dawn. He was doing his job all day long and half the night—and do you think he was appreciated by his father-in-law? It didn't seem so. Jethro sounded critical: "Moses, what in the world are you doing?"

So Moses told him and ended with a statement that ought to put anyone in his place, "I was doing the Lord's work, Jethro" (Exodus 18:15). Maybe Moses thought, *That ought to get him off my back and put him in his place.* But it didn't faze Jethro. In essence he said, "Moses, lighten up. You're wearing yourself out. You need help! You can't do it all by yourself" (see today's verses). Blunt. Direct. Confrontational. Necessary.

Has anyone ever told you something like this? It's not easy to hear, especially when you're conscientiously working to provide for your family and serve the Lord. But wait a minute. Can we really do it all?

Jethro simply suggested that Moses get other people to help him. Do you need help? Can you ask for it? Would you?

By the way, take a look at verse 24. Moses listened to Jethro and followed his advice. He asked for help, and his life changed for the better. Will you?

*I give them eternal life, and they shall never perish; no
one can snatch them out of my hand (John 10:28).*

Pets add a lot of enjoyment to our lives…as well as additional work. Most families end up with at least a dog or a cat. Sometimes these creatures teach us valuable lessons. For instance, have you ever noticed how a mother cat carries her kittens? She's not like a kangaroo, whose baby rides in a pouch or a baby monkey who grasps its mother with its little paws and holds on for all it's worth. A baby monkey's security depends on itself. That's risky. A kitten doesn't have to hang on. The mother grasps the baby by the neck with her teeth and carries it around. The kitten's security depends on the mother.

What does your sense of security depend on? Work, ability, money, reputation, athletic ability? What about your spiritual security—your salvation? Does it depend on your ability to hang on like a baby monkey or does it depend on who God is and what He does? What do you believe? Better yet, what does Scripture teach? Sometimes we let our life experiences shape what we believe rather than trust in what Scripture says.

Reread today's verse and consider its truth. God gave you to His Son, and your security is complete in Him. Christ paid the price in full for your sins. Nothing is owed (see Ephesians 1:7); God is satisfied with the payment (see Romans 3:25). Jesus is continuing His work for you by constantly praying for you (see Colossians 2:13). How often do you think about that fact? When you accepted the Lord, at that moment you were sealed with the Holy Spirit. God owns you (see 2 Corinthians 1:22).

So, if there is a day when you feel insecure for any reason, remember that your security in Christ is permanent.[5]

*Do not seek revenge or bear a grudge against one of your
people, but love your neighbor as yourself (Leviticus 19:18).*

This is a message from one of America's favorite pastors, Max Lucado:

Relationships. America's most precious resource. Take our oil, take our weapons, but don't take what holds us together—relationships. A nation's strength is measured by the premium it puts on its own people. When people value people, an impenetrable web is drawn, a web of vitality and security.

A relationship. The delicate fusion of two human beings. The intricate weaving of two lives: two sets of moods, mentalities, and temperaments. Two intermingling hearts, both seeking solace and security.

A relationship. It has more power than any nuclear bomb and more potential than any promising seed. Nothing will drive a man to a greater courage than a relationship. Nothing will fire the heart of a patriot or purge the cynicism of a rebel like a relationship.

What matters most in life is not what ladders we climb or what ownings we accumulate. What matters most is a relationship. What steps are you taking to protect your "possessions"? What measures are you using to ensure that your relationships are strong and healthy?…

Do you resolve conflict as soon as possible, or do you "let the sun go down when you are still angry"? Do you verbalize your love every day to your mate and children? Do you look for chances to forgive? Do you pray daily for those in your life?

Our Master knew the value of a relationship. It was through relationships that he changed the world. His movement thrived not on personality or power but on championing the value of a person…And what was that he said about loving your neighbor as yourself? It's a wise man who values people above possessions.[6]

*Each man should give what he has decided in his heart
to give, not reluctantly or under compulsion...God
loves a cheerful giver (2 Corinthians 9:7).*

There is a rival to Almighty God in our lives. For some it's the god of money. This god propels us, drives us, dominates us, controls us, punishes us, and is never satisfied. Often we feel there is never enough cash. And when there is, we still want more.

The great reformer Martin Luther had an interesting observation about the term *conversion*. He said, "There are three conversions necessary: the conversion of the heart, the mind, and the purse." The latter is difficult for some because of their attitude. Jesus confronted a group of people who used their giving as a cover-up for their selfishness. They tithed all right, but they were so picky and ritualistic about it that they missed the whole point of giving. Hear what Jesus said about them:

> Woe to you, teachers of the law and Pharisees, you hypocrites! You give a tenth of your spices—mint, dill, and cumin. But you have neglected the more important matters of the law—justice, mercy, and faithfulness. You should have practiced the latter, without neglecting the former. You blind guides! You strain out a gnat but swallow a camel (Matthew 23:23-24).

One of the opportunities we all have is to give as much as we can. Les and Leslie Parrott, the authors of *Becoming Soul Mates,* say they changed their perspective from asking "How much of our money should we give to God?" to "How much of God's money should we spend on ourselves?"

By the way, do you know how to get rid of the god of money? Give your money away. It works.[7]

Having eyes, do you not see? And having ears,
do you not hear? (Mark 8:18 NASB).

You're not listening to me." "Didn't you hear what I said to you?" We've all heard similar words—and we didn't enjoy it. One reason is because often they're true. We didn't really hear or, more accurately, we tuned out. We filter out the negatives and then say, "But I didn't hear you."

> An Indian was in downtown New York, walking along with his friend, who lived in New York City. Suddenly he said, "I hear a cricket."
>
> "Oh, you're crazy," his friend replied.
>
> "No, I hear a cricket. I do! I'm sure of it."
>
> "It's the noon hour. You know there are people bustling around, cars honking, taxis squealing, noises from the city. I'm sure you can't hear such a small animal."
>
> "I'm sure I do." He listened attentively and then walked to the corner, across the street, and looked all around. Finally on the other corner he found a shrub in a large cement planter. He dug beneath the leaf and found a cricket.
>
> His friend was duly astounded. But the Indian said, "No, my ears are no different than yours. It simply depends on what you are listening to. Here, let me show you."
>
> He reached into his pocket and pulled out a handful of change— a few quarters, some dimes, nickels, and pennies. And he dropped it on the concrete.
>
> Every head within a block turned. "You see what I mean?" the Indian asked as he picked up his coins. "It all depends on what you are listening for."[8]

What are you listening for? Who do you have difficulty hearing?

If any of you lacks wisdom, he should ask God, who gives generously to all without finding fault, and it will be given to him (James 1:5).

D o you like owls? They are fascinating creatures with their ability to see and fly at night as well as their heightened sense of hearing. Owls are mentioned in Scripture in a very unique way. In the Bible, the owl is mentioned usually in connection with desolation foretold for nations and their proud cities. Zephaniah prophesied that Nineveh would be left "utterly desolate and dry as the desert" and that the call of the desert owl and the screech owl would "echo through the windows" (Zephaniah 2:13-14). Isaiah also mentioned birds regarding the downfall of Edom: "The great owl and the raven will nest there" (Isaiah 34:11). Because owls lived in the ruins and caves of desolate, forsaken places, the psalmist said when he was feeling alone and distressed, "I am...like an owl among the ruins" (Psalm 102:6). In the Bible the owl is also associated with God's judgment on unbelief because its haunting sound in the night can scare us (see, for example, Micah 1:3-8).[9]

We tend to refer to the owl as wise. We're told to take this wisdom to heart. But there's a better place to get your wisdom—God's Word. Proverbs 1:7-8 says, "The fear of the LORD is the beginning of knowledge, but fools despise wisdom and discipline."

We all need wisdom—the ability to accurately discern and make good decisions. All you have to do to get it is seek God, and you'll find Him. Then ask Him for wisdom, and you will receive it.

*The LORD is my shepherd, I shall not be in want. He
makes me lie down in green pastures, he leads me beside
quiet waters, he restores my soul. He guides me in paths
of righteousness for his name's sake (Psalm 23:1-3).*

In the midst of the noise and the hustle and bustle of everyday life,
what would you like to see God doing in your life? Think about it for
a minute. Some have said, "I'd like to see that God cares. I'd like to see
Him do something good…for a change." Well, He's always doing good
things for us.

One of the ways God does things for us is best explained by a hobby
that many men enjoy—restoring old cars. They take an old wreck with
the metal rusting, the tires flat, the spark plugs all chewed up, and the
upholstery torn to shreds. But often after several months of painstaking
effort, sanding, polishing, ripping out, and putting in, the car begins to
look like it did the day it rolled off the assembly line. Instead of looking
like a wreck, it is restored.

There will be times in all our lives when we want to be restored, when
our goals are shattered and our dreams have turned into nightmares. Not
only do we make mistakes and fail, but sometimes people pull the rug
out from underneath us. Our God is a God who restores. Our God is a
God who heals. Our God is a God who can reverse our fortunes from bad
to good. Imagine that! The psalmist describes what God does so well:[10]

> The LORD is close to the brokenhearted and saves those who are
> crushed in spirit (Psalm 34:18).

> [The LORD our God] raises the poor from the dust and lifts the
> needy from the ash heap; he seats them with princes, the princes
> of their people (Psalm 113:7-8).

A father to the fatherless, a defender of widows,
is God in his holy dwelling (Psalm 68:5).

What were your parents like? Can you remember back to being a preschooler? What did you think of your parents? When you were ten, what were your thoughts about them? When you became a teenager, your perception of your parents had probably changed radically.

Perhaps you haven't thought about your parents very much. When you were younger and defenseless you needed them to nourish and protect you. There were times when you went running to them because you were afraid or hurt. They probably came through for you…most of the time. But sometimes they were lacking. They weren't perfect. No parent is. You may have wanted them to listen to you more, love you more, or help you more.

Then you became an adult. If you think you outgrew your need for a parent, you didn't. We still need a parent—and we have one…God. Psalm 103:13 says that "as a father has compassion on his children, so the LORD has compassion on those who fear him." The way He cares for you is far superior to anything you could ever imagine. He never makes mistakes. Time is not a problem for Him. He is not limited by anything our parents were limited by.

If there is a cry inside of you for something your parents couldn't give you or do for you, that cry can be silenced. The needs of your life can be and have been met by your heavenly Father. You have been adopted by Him with all—*not some, but all*—the benefits. If you're in need of parenting, you've got it. If you're in need of acceptance, you've got it. If you're in need of love, you've got it.

You then, my son, be strong in the grace that is in Christ Jesus. And the things you have heard me say in the presence of many witnesses entrust to reliable men who will also be qualified to teach others (2 Timothy 2:1-2).

All fathers are unique. They respond differently to the challenges of fatherhood, but they all leave imprints on us. My father didn't talk very much. One day I asked him if he loved me, and he said of course he did. And I knew it—but I wanted to hear it from him.

I am an avid reader. I love to read Western and adventure novels. I grew up going to the library every week and reading practically every book in the children's section. Why? Because Dad, who only finished the eighth grade, read two books a week and was constantly at the library. I had a positive role model.

Dad did something else for me that totally influenced my life. As a child I didn't like going to church. I found every excuse possible to get out of going. When I was twelve, my dad said he would like me to go with him to a new church. We would take the new members' class, and then join the church together. That started my involvement at the First Presbyterian Church of Hollywood, where I practically lived throughout my junior and senior years in high school. I was eventually influenced toward the ministry by Dr. Henrietta Mears in the college department.

Dad had his faults and his strengths, but who doesn't? Sons have a choice as to which of their fathers' characteristics they will focus on. I appreciate my dad for who he was as a person and for the years we had together. I hope you appreciate your dad. If so, if he's still living let him know. And make sure you don't waste the time to do things with and for your children now so they will appreciate you.

Whatever is true, whatever is noble, whatever is right, whatever is pure, whatever is lovely, whatever is admirable—if anything is excellent or praiseworthy—think about such things (Philippians 4:8).

Lord Jesus, I come to You today asking for power, strength, and the grace that I need to overcome the temptations that are all around me and appeal to a man.

I need a pure heart that will slam the door of my heart to the wrong thoughts that seem to come in uninvited.

I need Your strength for my willpower so I can be strong to fight against the temptations at work and on the television screen.

I ask for an abundance of love to replace all bitterness, to serve as You served and to forgive as You forgave.

May I be faithful so others, especially my family, can rely on my word. Help me to stick to my commitments and projects to see them through. When I tend to be lazy, please give me a shove in the right direction.

Give me clarity of mind to make the right decisions. When I don't know what to do, give me the willingness to ask for help—and to listen to the advice.

I pray that I won't wallow in regrets over the past nor live in the dreams for the future. Keep me in the real, present world so I don't overlook what You have for me or want me to do.

As Your Word says, help me to fight the good fight as Paul did. May I be a race finisher and not just a starter. Help me to keep the faith and at the end receive the crown of righteousness You have promised.

Thank You for hearing me and for being faithful.

> In your name.
> Amen.[11]

*I made a covenant with my eyes not to look
lustfully at a girl (Job 31:1).*

We all struggle with lust at times, so let's talk about it. Most men and women don't really know what God's Word says about it. For example, did you know there are four Hebrew and three Greek words translated into the English word "lust" or "to lust after"? When Moses and the people of Israel praised God after their deliverance from Egypt, they sang, "The enemy said, 'I will pursue, I will overtake, I will divide the spoil; my *desire* shall be gratified against them; I will draw out my sword, my hand will destroy them'" (Exodus 15:9 NASB). The word *desire* is translated "lust" in other Bible versions.

Hedonism comes from the Greek word *hedone,* translated "lust" in James 4:1 and 3 (KJV). In each instance in Scripture where the word *hedone* is used, whether translated "lust" or "pleasure," the emphasis is on gratification of natural or sinful desires.

God designed sex to be part of a relationship. When whole persons interact with each other as objects, lust becomes a problem. Without a relationship as a foundation for sexual intimacy, people treat each other as objects to gratify their lust rather than as whole persons. Within God's design, *desire,* even strong desire, is not wrong; it is good. The Greek word *epithumia* illustrates this. It denotes strong desire of any kind. Since marriage is God's design, strong desire within marriage is not only natural, it is blessed. Even anticipative desire that precedes marriage is natural and blessed.

So what, then, is lust? Lust is not noticing that a woman is sexually attractive. Lust is born when we turn simple awareness into preoccupied fantasy. When we invite sexual thoughts into our minds and nurture them. Luther put it this way: "We cannot help it if birds fly over our heads. It is another thing if we invite them to build nests in our hair."[12]

*God said to Moses, "I AM WHO I AM. This is what you are to
say to the Israelites: 'I AM has sent me to you'" (Exodus 3:14).*

Who is the God you worship? Let's explore your beliefs to see if what you believe is really who God is or if you have created your own image of Him. It happens, you know. Remember when you were first born and an infant? Of course you don't. But when you were that young, you were completely dependent. You couldn't do a thing. Your parents had to care for you. You were dependent on them for life and nourishment. Animals are dependent on other animals, vegetation, and water for survival. Trees and plants are dependent on sun, rain, and good soil for their survival. Everything in this world is dependent upon something else in order to survive.

All, that is, except God. God is the only One who is truly independent. As men we might think we are, but we're not. God doesn't need to be dependent on anything else in order to survive because *He is God.* He has life in Himself.

Perhaps you wonder what God meant when He said "I AM WHO I AM." It's a strange statement. He was saying to the people then and to you and me now that He is the One who has always existed. You and I are bound by time. *God isn't.* You and I have a beginning, and we will have an end. *God doesn't.* He always exists. You and I have a past, present, and future. For God, everything is in the present. His name emphasizes His self-existence.

That's a lot to comprehend. And think about this: Isn't it even more amazing that an independent, timeless God reaches down to love us?[13]

I am the LORD, *I do not change (Malachi 3:6* NKJV*).*

We live in a world full of rapid change. And it's occurring faster and faster all the time. There is one thing, though, that doesn't and won't change—God. Change has a purpose. It's either for better or for worse. However, it's impossible for God to change. What does that actually mean?

His *life* doesn't change. Created things have a beginning and ending, but God doesn't. He has always been. There wasn't a time He didn't exist. He doesn't grow older. He doesn't get wiser, stronger, or weaker. He can't change for the better; He's already there.

> They shall perish, but you go on forever. They will grow old, like worn-out clothing, and you will change them like a man putting on a new shirt and throwing away the old one! (Psalms 102:26 TLB).

> Listen to me…I alone am God. I am the First; I am the Last (Isaiah 48:12 TLB).

> God's *character* does not change. He doesn't become less or more truthful, or merciful, or good than He was or is. James talks about God's goodness, generosity, and holiness. He says God "does not change like shifting shadows" (James 1:17).

> God's *truth* doesn't change. He doesn't have to take back anything He's ever said. God still keeps the promises found in His Word.

> God's *purposes* do not change. What God does in the context of time, He planned from eternity. All that He has committed Himself to do in His Word will be done. Nothing takes God by surprise so that He has to revise His plan.

> It's difficult to comprehend everything about God with our human minds. And that just highlights what a difference there is between us and God.[14]

*It seems to be a fact of life that when I want to do what is
right, I inevitably do what is wrong (Romans 7:21 TLB).*

Would you like to be successful? What man wouldn't? How to be successful is no mystery; in fact, it's simple. All you have to do to succeed is fail. That's right, fail…and then learn from your failures. Failure is not the enemy of success; it's the first step toward success. Failure is a stern but helpful teacher. Have you heard the story about the young executive who asked the company president how he became successful? The man replied, "By making good decisions." The young man then asked how he learned to make good decisions. The president answered, "By making bad ones."

When you hear the name Babe Ruth, you probably think of his record 714 home runs. Few people know he also set the record for striking out. He failed a lot; he also succeeded. In 1978, the first transatlantic balloon flight finally became a reality. What made the difference? One additional crew member and experience. One of the crew said, "I don't think you can fly the Atlantic without experience, and that's one reason it hasn't been flown before. Success in any venture is just the intelligent application of failure."[15]

We have a choice in how we will respond to failure, a choice that can make a big difference in our struggle toward success. Dr. Gary Oliver says,

> Failures can leave many different scars—hurt feelings, wounded relationships, wasted potential, broken marriages, shattered ministries—but they can also be used by God to sharpen the mind, deepen the spirit, and strengthen the soul. Those people who have learned to view failure through God's eyes emerge with a softer heart, stronger character, and a fresh awareness of God's grace.[16]

Be strong and courageous (Joshua 1:6).

We admire courage. Sometimes we say, "That took a lot of guts!" That means the same thing. It takes courage today to survive, and even more to live the Christian life. God wants men of courage, and He gave us some great examples in His Word. Remember Joshua? Twice Moses told him to be courageous, and four times God said the same thing. Even the leaders of the people said it!

If people kept telling you to be courageous, wouldn't it get to you after a while? After all, Joshua was no wimp! He had led the army for forty years. Why all the push to be courageous? Was it because of what was facing him? Did he know he needed to hear those words again and again. He was being asked to lead Israel—a huge group of people—on a military campaign to take over land and also to provide moral leadership.

What about you? If you're married, how are your leadership skills in your family? How are they expressed in the financial area? The spiritual?

Joshua was asked to be courageous because he had to obey God's law. "Be strong and very courageous. Be careful to obey all the law my servant Moses gave you; do not turn from it to the right or to the left, that you may be successful wherever you go" (Joshua 1:7). Not everyone followed it back then, and not very many follow God's law today. It will take courage on your part to follow it, especially at work.

God told Joshua one more thing about courage: "Be strong and courageous. Do not be terrified; do not be discouraged, for the LORD your God will be with you wherever you go" (1:9).

God is your source of courage too. He's waiting to respond to you. Just ask![17]

It is for your good that I am going away. Unless I
go away, the Counselor will not come to you; but
if I go, I will send him to you (John 16:7).

Max Lucado, an insightful writer, helps us understand the Holy Spirit:

The Holy Spirit is not an "it." He is a person. He has knowledge (1 Corinthians 2:11). He has a will (1 Corinthians 12:11). He has a mind (Romans 8:27). He has affections (Romans 15:30). You can lie to him (Acts 5:3-4). You can insult him (Hebrews 10:29). You can grieve him (Ephesians 4:30).

The Holy Spirit is not an impersonal force...He is God within you to help you. In fact John calls him the Helper.

Envision a father helping his son learn to ride a bicycle, and you will have a partial picture of the Holy Spirit. The father stays at the son's side. He pushes the bike and steadies it if the boy starts to tumble. The Spirit does that for us; he steadies our step and strengthens our stride. Unlike the father, however, he never leaves. He is with us to the end of the age.

What does the Spirit do?

He comforts the saved. "When I go away, I will send the Helper to you" (John 16:7).

He convicts the lost. "When the Helper comes, he will prove to the people of the world the truth about sin, about being right with God, and about judgment" (John 16:8).

He conveys the truth. "I have many more things to say to you, but they are too much for you now. When the Spirit of truth comes, he will lead you into all truth" (John 16:12).

Is John saying we don't need the book in order to dance? Of course not... "God is spirit, and those who worship him must worship in spirit and truth" (John 4:24).[18]

*Only be careful, and watch yourselves closely so that you do
not forget the things your eyes have seen or let them slip from
your heart as long as you live. Teach them to your children
and to their children after them (Deuteronomy 4:9).*

D r. Dave Stoop talks about a father's influence in his book *Making
Peace with Your Father.* He suggests that a father's role includes nur-
turer, lawgiver, protector, and spiritual mentor. When a father nurtures
his son, the son feels secure and valued and can bond with his dad. But he
needs to see his dad approach life with competence and confidence as well.
Lawgiving isn't being authoritarian. It means being involved in a son's life,
as well as clarifying the rules and enforcing discipline. Stoop writes:

> When lawgiving is balanced with nurturing, a father helps his
> children learn to make decisions about right and wrong for them-
> selves. It is not just a matter of "following orders." When it comes
> to rules and standards of behavior, children operate on a "show
> me, don't tell me" basis. They need to see morality modeled, strug-
> gled with, confronted, and dealt with realistically and honestly. A
> father who is comfortably balanced in his lawgiving role is able
> to *demonstrate* his sense of integrity and morality by the way he
> relates to his children, not just proclaim it to them.[19]

As a protector, a father needs to stand with his son during the adolescent years, when they face changes that can affect them both. This is
a time to help a child prepare to battle effectively with life. Being a spiritual mentor means drawing the child into the future and helping him
dream realistically. It means helping a son learn to live a life of faith.[20]

*Ask and it will be given to you; seek and you will find;
knock and the door will be opened to you. For everyone
who asks receives; he who seeks finds; and to him who
knocks, the door will be opened (Luke 11:9-10).*

Prayer has many elements. Too often, though, we focus on what we want, need, or expect. We focus on ourselves. Why not turn our focus to the One we're praying to—God? Dr. Lloyd Ogilvie talks about the importance of this essential element of prayer:

> *All great praying begins with adoration.* God does not need our praise as much as we need to give it. Praise is like a thermostat that opens the heart to flow in communion with God. Hallowing God's name is enumerating His attributes. When we think magnificently about God's nature we become open to experience afresh His glory in our lives. I once took a course in creative conversation. The key thing I discovered was that there can be no deep exchange with another person until we have established the value of that person to us. Just as profound conversation with another person results from our communicating that person's worth to us, so too, we become receptive to what God wants to do in our lives when we have taken time to tell Him what He means to us. Don't hurry through adoration. Everything else depends on it. Tell God what He means to you, pour out your heart in unhurried moments of exultation. Allow Him to remind you of aspects of His nature you need to claim…He is the leader of the conversation. The more we praise the Lord, the more we will be able to think His thoughts after Him throughout our prayer. He loosens the tissues of our brains to become channels of His Spirit.

> Praise is the ultimate level of relinquishment. When we praise God for not only all He is but what He is doing in our lives, we reach a liberating stage of surrender.[21]

These words of wisdom can change your relationship with God. Adore Him today.

Your love is more delightful than wine (Song of Solomon 1:2).

Have you considered the sexual benefits of being a Christian? That's quite a question, isn't it? But think about it. Are there any benefits sexually?

God is for sex. It was His idea. He created not only the pleasurable drive but the best and proper context for its total expression. For many Christians, their faith and their sexuality have existed like a double set of train tracks, paralleling one another as far as one can see and going off into the distance. But they never come together. What *are* the benefits? Consider these:

- Negative attitudes toward our body and sex can be overcome by accepting what God has said about our body and sex.

- When we come to the realization that God and Christ are aware of our love-making as a married couple and are saying, "That is as was intended!" We can relax and rest in His approval...

- The presence of Christ in a person's life can give him the ability to love another with agape love. Because of His unconditional love, we can move toward that love which brings a greater sexual life...

- Jesus also assists a person to communicate in an open and honest manner. Vulnerability can occur and hidden hurts and concerns can come to the forefront. These barriers once eliminated help to create a closer relationship...

Romans 8:1 states there is "no condemnation for those who are in Christ Jesus." For many, this has meant no condemnation *except in* sexual matters. Not so.[22]

Sex is God's idea. It has a purpose and a place. Thank Him for it and... enjoy.

*[God] in these last days has spoken to us in
His Son (Hebrews 1:1-2 NASB).*

Has God ever spoken to you directly? I don't mean necessarily in an audible voice, but in some way? Today's verse tells us that God reveals Himself to people in a variety of ways. One of the interesting means God used to reveal Himself in the Old Testament was through theophanies. Have you ever heard of this before? A theophany is when God shows Himself in and through some created thing. When God revealed Himself to Moses, how did He do it? It was through a bush burning with divine glory. But God also revealed Himself through dreams—and quite frequently too. Have you ever experienced this? Remember some of these occasions in the Bible? There were Jacob, Joseph, Nebuchadnezzar, and Zacharias. In the New Testament, God spoke to Joseph and to Pilate's wife through dreams. Others saw visions. Ezekiel, Isaiah, and Peter were awake when they experienced God speaking to them in this way.

Have you ever wondered how the people responded to those who saw a theophany or had a dream or vision? We know how people would view us today—skeptically!

How does God speak to us today? I've experienced God's direction through a sermon or message that I felt was just for me. His Word speaks to us. And He speaks to us through prayers.

[Jesus said,] "Follow me" (Matthew 8:22).

We often ask, "What's it going to cost me?" It's a good question. We need to know the cost before we commit. Dr. Lloyd Ogilvie addresses this in the Christian life:

> Scripture shows us several responses to the cost of commitment. Jesus' mood is determined and decisive: He is on the way to Jerusalem, and He wants followers who can count the cost. The three different levels of commitment represented in people He met along the way expose the ways Christians relate to their discipleship today.

> The first man made a grand, pious commitment that went no deeper than words. He promised to follow the Master wherever He went. Jesus challenged the man to count the cost. So often we come to Christ to receive what we want to solve problems or gain inspiration for our challenges. He gives both with abundance, but then calls us into [ministries] of concern and caring. We are to do for others what He has done for us. Loving and forgiving are not always easy.

> The second man had unfinished business from the past. He wanted to follow Christ, but a secondary loyalty kept him tied to the past. In substance, Christ said, "Forget the past; follow Me!" We dare not misinterpret His words to suggest a lack of concern for life's obligations, but rather a call to be concerned about His call to live rather than worry about what is dead and past.

> The third person wanted to say goodbye to his family. Jesus' response to him stresses the urgency of our commitment. He was concerned about competing loyalties in the man. Our commitment must be unreserved to seek *first* His kingdom. We are left with a question about ways that we have one hand on the plow of discipleship and the other reaching back to the past or to lesser commitments. In what ways are you looking back?[23]

*God will meet all your needs according to his glorious
riches in Christ Jesus (Philippians 4:19).*

There is an old legend about three men with sacks. Each man had two sacks, one tied in front of his neck and the other tied around his back. When the first man was asked, "Hey, what's in the sacks?" he said, "Well, in the sack on my back are all the good things my friends and family have done. That way they're out of sight and hidden from view. In the front sack are all the bad things that have happened to me. Every now and then, I stop, open the sack, take the things out, examine them, and think about them." Because he stopped to concentrate on the bad, he really didn't make much progress in life.

The second man was asked, "What have you got in those two sacks?" He replied, "In the front sack are all the good things I've done. I like them; I like to see them. So quite often I take them out to show them off to everyone around me. The sack in the back? Um, I keep all my mistakes in there and carry them with me all the time. Sure, they're heavy. It's true that they slow me down. But you know, for some reason I can't put them down."

When the third man was asked about his two sacks, his answer was, "The sack in front is great. In this one I keep all the positive thoughts I have about people, all the blessings I've experienced, and all the great things other people have done for me. The weight isn't a problem. It's like the sails of a ship. It keeps me going forward. The sack on my back is empty...I cut a hole in the bottom of it. So I put all the bad things in there that I think about myself or hear about others. They go in one end and out the other."

What are you carrying around in your sacks? Who are you carrying around in your sacks? Which sack is full—the one full of blessings or the one in back?[24]

In Him you have been made complete (Colossians 2:10 NASB).

Remember the TV miniseries *Roots?* Perhaps you've read the book by Alex Haley. It was the fascinating story of an African-American man searching for his roots, for his heritage. His journey took him back to Africa. Many of us are interested in our genealogy. Doing a historical search of your family's heritage can help you understand yourself in a new way. But as Christians we enjoy an additional heritage. Our roots are found in the fact that we were created in the image of God. And God wants His work to be complete in us. Enjoy the following description of your heritage in Christ:

> This, then, is the wonder of the Christian message: that God is this kind of God; that He loves me with a love that is not turned off by my sins, my failures, my inadequacies, my insignificance. I am not an anomalous disease crawling on the face of an insignificant speck in the vast emptiness of space. I am not a nameless insect waiting to be crushed by an impersonal boot. I am not a miserable offender cowering under the glare of an angry deity. I am a man beloved by God Himself. I have touched the very heart of the universe, and have found His name to be love. And that love has reached me, not because I have merited God's favor, not because I have anything to boast about, but because of what He is, and because of what Christ has done for me in the Father's name. And I can believe this about God (and therefore about myself) because Christ has come from the Father and has revealed by His teaching, by His life, by His death, by His very person that this is what God is like: He is "full of grace."[25]

For as [a man] thinks in his heart, so is he (Proverbs 23:7 NKJV).
Do not let your heart be troubled (John 14:27 NASB).

Did you know that most stress comes from ourselves—our thought lives and our attitudes? That's right, our inner responses are the culprit. What we put into our minds affects our bodies. Consider one way in which your thoughts are affected daily: what you hear on the radio or see and hear on TV—especially if it's the news. What is the first thing you listen to on the radio in the morning? What is the last TV program you watch at night before you go to sleep? There may be a correlation to the stress you feel.

What you think about when you're driving can stress you out too. If you're stuck on the freeway and have an appointment in twenty minutes you know you won't make on time, what do you say to yourself? Do you fuss and say things like "I can't be late!" "Who's holding us up?" Do you lean on the horn and glare at other drivers? That's why you are getting upset—it's caused by your thoughts and the way you are responding to a situation over which you have no control. You're butting up against a brick wall.

In a situation over which you have no control and there is nothing you can do, quit fighting. Go with the flow. Give yourself permission to be stuck in traffic, to be late. Tell yourself, "I would rather not be stuck here and would rather not be late, but I can handle it. I give myself permission to be here, and I can make use of the time." Instead of fussing you can pray, read a book, put in an inspiring CD, smile at the other drivers, or sit back and relax. By doing this, you take control of the situation— and your inner responses—and your stress drains away. You may not be able to take this attitude in every situation, but in many you can. Why not try it today? It may keep your heart from being troubled.

Call to me and I will answer you and tell you great and unsearchable things you do not know (Jeremiah 33:3).

We can plod along in our Christian lives, using our ideas, plans, and strength or we can let God amaze us. With His help you may surprise yourself by what you're able to do, just like a certain woodpecker I heard about in a book called *Battle Fatigue.*

> He went through life much as the other woodpeckers, bouncing from tree to tree, drilling holes, searching for grubs, occasionally running from a hungry cat…Then it happened! One afternoon, as he was going about his business of boring into tree trunks—suddenly, unexpectedly, without announcement or warning—a bolt of lightning zapped that tree, splitting it right down the middle. The poor woodpecker was thrown several feet into the air and out over the forest. When he landed, he was belly up on the forest floor. He slowly opened his eyes. Dazed, feathers smoking, beak tingling, he shook himself. As he surveyed the demise of the mighty oak, he rubbed his smoldering beak and raised a skeptical eyebrow. Then he stood straight up, thrust out his charred chest feathers, and strutted off through the woods saying, "My, I didn't I know I had that in me!"

> How many Christians are like that woodpecker? We spend our appointed days in the doldrums of the ordinary, frightened by the unscheduled, content to walk in the familiar, well-worn ruts of life. Then suddenly God intervenes in our lives, moves us out of the mundane, changes our routine, lifts us above the forest floor for a brief moment—by doing something which takes us totally by surprise—and we look at our smoking beaks, dust ourselves off, and say, "Did I do that? I didn't know I had that in me."[1]

What would you like to be doing in your Christian life? Talk to God about it. Why not let Him take you by surprise so you can say, "I didn't know I had that in me!"

Moses was a very humble man (Numbers 12:3).

Is there a meek man in your life? Perhaps there's one at work, in the family, or at church. What do you think of him? Is he a man you'd like to be like or would rather stay away from? Are there any meek men on the Dallas Cowboys football team or the Los Angeles Kings hockey team? We tend to equate meekness with being a wimp! Not so. Moses wasn't passive. He took on an Egyptian overseer, stood up to Pharaoh, and hiked the desert for forty years. It's kind of hard to see him as a wimp.

Meek doesn't mean what we think. Bottom line, it's being humble before God. It's a choice. It's deliberately harnessing your strength and tempering it to use in a controlled way. Meek is believing and obeying God…even when we don't particularly want to.

Moses wasn't always enthusiastic about what God wanted. Nor did he feel capable. Sort of like us at times. When God called him to lead the people out of bondage he didn't exactly say, "Right on!" It was more like "Me? You've got to be kidding. Try someone else" (see Exodus 4:10-13).

God's response? "I will be with you."

When you're debating whether to teach that Sunday school class, feeling hesitant and inferior, God says, "I will be with you." When you wonder whether you can make it another day with the stress of your job, He says, "I will be with you." When you're faced with a tough decision and wondering what to do, He says, "I will be with you."

You may be a bit reluctant. So was Moses. But he obeyed God. Moses believed Him, did what He said, and said what He was told. And God was with him.

So can you…and that's being meek. [2]

*What profit is there if you gain the world—and
lose eternal life? What can be compared with the
value of eternal life? (Matthew 16:26 TLB).*

How do we balance the demands of family, job, and the teachings of Scripture to arrive at success? Perhaps the best way is to ask and answer these questions:

- In what way am I putting God first in my life? "Seek first his kingdom and his righteousness, and all these things will be given to you as well" (Matthew 6:33).

- In what way am I in the center of God's will? "It is God who works in you to will and to act according to his good purpose" (Philippians 2:13).

- In what way am I constantly seeking after the will of God? "Do not conform any longer to the pattern of this world, but be transformed by the renewing of your mind. Then you will be able to test and approve what God's will is—his good, pleasing, and perfect will" (Romans 12:2).

- In what way should I be a husband, father, and provider? "If anyone does not provide for his relatives, and especially for his immediate family, he has denied the faith and is worse than an unbeliever" (1 Timothy 5:8).

- In what way am I seeking to be financially responsible? "Whoever can be trusted with very little can also be trusted with much, and whoever is dishonest with very little will also be dishonest with much. So if you have not been trustworthy in handling worldly wealth, who will trust you with true riches? And if you have not been trustworthy with someone else's property, who will give you property of your own?" (Luke 16:10-12).[3]

Well, what did you learn? And what will you do about what you've learned?

*If the LORD is pleased with us, he will lead us into that land, a
land flowing with milk and honey, and will give it to us. Only
do not rebel against the LORD. And do not be afraid of the
people of the land, because we will swallow them up. Their
protection is gone, but the LORD is with us (Numbers 14:8-9).*

Kids look for ways to avoid doing their chores, especially if the chores
are difficult. Some carry this pattern into adulthood. If it's difficult,
risky, or a challenge, they think of creative ways to avoid the task. Fortunately, only a few men are like that. Most are like Caleb. Remember him?
He and Joshua were the only men who survived the forty years of wandering in the wilderness and were allowed to enter the Promised Land.
Caleb once made an unusual request of Joshua. Here is the last portion
of what he said:

> So here I am today, eighty-five years old! I am still as strong today
> as the day Moses sent me out; I'm just as vigorous to go out to bat-
> tle now as I was then. Now give me this hill country that the LORD
> promised me that day. You yourself heard then that the Anakites
> were there and their cities were large and fortified, but, the LORD
> helping me, I will drive them out just as He said (Joshua 14:10-12).

This man was ready to take on the Anakites, who were giants! Caleb
still believed God wanted His people to possess the land. Caleb still had
confidence in God. He didn't give excuses. He wanted the challenge. And
he rose to it. Do you have friends who see life in this way? Do you see
life this way? Full of challenges and opportunities? You may have giants
facing you, but it's amazing…when you face them they seem to shrink.
There may be a giant you have to face today. Do it with the Lord![4]

*Do not withhold good from those who deserve it, when
it is in your power to act (Proverbs 3:27).*

Often at funerals and memorial services one or more family members or friends deliver a eulogy. They share the positive qualities, characteristics, and accomplishments of the deceased. They extol the person's virtues and go into detail as to why the person will be missed. Everyone there hears the kind and affirming words except one—the person they are talking about. Sometimes you wonder how much of what was shared at the memorial service was told to the person directly. In most cases, it probably wasn't.

Today's verse gives us clear directions. There are some families who have taken this to heart in a dramatic way. They conduct *living* eulogy services with a family member who is terminally ill. The family members and friends come together with the person in his or her hospital room or home, and each one shares what they would say if they were giving a eulogy. This is better than waiting until someone is gone, but what a difference it might have made had such statements been made throughout that person's life!

So many parents and children end up saying, "If only I had told him how much I loved him, what I appreciated, how much he meant to me." "If only"…words of sadness over missed opportunities. The presence of positive words can motivate, encourage, and lift up. The absence, well, perhaps the person would never know what he missed. Or he could have been living with the longing for a few well-chosen and positive words.

We can't change the times we've missed, but we can uplift our family members' lives now and in the future. Who needs words of love and encouragement today? And who do you need to hear from? What others hear from you may help them do likewise. [5]

A man of many companions may come to ruin, but there is a
friend who sticks closer than a brother (Proverbs 18:24).

Y ou can't depend on anyone. They let you down when you need them
the most." Have you ever felt that way? Whether it happens to you
in business or with a friend, it's disappointing. You look for predictability in other people, yet when they let you down, it's irritating. The best
description of this dilemma is found in Proverbs: "Like a bad tooth or a
lame foot is reliance on the unfaithful in times of trouble" (25:19).

When you encounter unfaithfulness in a friend, you feel like the rug
has been pulled out from under you. And it often happens when you're
the most vulnerable. Scripture is filled with examples of this. David was
more wounded emotionally by his friends than by his enemies. He shared
this hurt in a psalm: "If an enemy were insulting me, I could endure it;
if a foe were raising himself against me, I could hide from him. But it is
you, a man like myself, my companion, my close friend, with whom I
once enjoyed sweet fellowship as we walked with the throng at the house
of God" (Psalm 55:12-14).

You expect friends to keep their word as well as your confidences.
Faithful friends do that. When this trust is violated, the relationship is
often severed. Proverbs states: "A perverse man stirs up dissension, and a
gossip separates close friends" (16:28).

Is it worth it to have close male friendships? You bet! Relationships
involve risk. We can let a bad experience poison us against people, concentrate on what others have done, become gun shy, or isolate ourselves.
Or we can learn from the experience and move on.

Regardless of what someone has done to you, be a faithful friend
yourself. Other people need your friendship, your faithfulness. Everyone will benefit. It's worth the risk.[6]

The LORD said, "Rise and anoint him; he is the one" (1 Samuel 16:12).

How do you handle it when you see one of those guys? You know, the kind who has everything—looks, muscles, brains, voice, ability, smarts? It almost seems immoral for anyone to have so much. Sometimes you wonder why everything was poured into one person. Couldn't God have spread it around a bit? Where's the fairness?

Well, perhaps there were people in David's time who felt the same way. David was good-looking and without a fault physically (1 Samuel 16:12). To be a shepherd took a tremendous amount of intelligence and skill. How would you like to take on a bear and a lion—and not with a 30.06, a .270, or a double-barrel shotgun with slugs, but with a spear? Talk about giving the animals an edge! David did. He was also one of the most gifted musicians of his time…and a prolific poet.

He was brilliant as a politician, military leader, and guerilla fighter. He was also able to unite the tribes of Israel into a nation. It wasn't easy. They had as many differences culturally and politically as many countries do today.

Sure, David was gifted. So are you. Maybe not in the same way, but you have abilities. Have you discovered them? Better yet, are you using them for God's glory? That's why you have them.

By the way, if you're tempted to compare yourself with some outstanding guy like David, keep in mind we've all got our failings. David did. After all, he murdered a man and committed adultery. That's a bit sobering. We're all a mixture of strengths and weaknesses. The good news is that God uses us regardless.

Take the helmet of salvation, and the sword
of the Spirit... (Ephesians 6:17).

For hundreds of years, battles were won or lost by the use of the sword. Even after guns were introduced, swords still had their place. And they still do today in the life of a Christian. Paul describes the armament we need in this life, and he states that the Scriptures are our sword. (He was referring to a dagger used in hand-to-hand combat.)

When you and I encounter Satan, we have the Holy Spirit with us who will bring to mind the right passages of Scripture to help us confront the problem. For example:

- When you're exhausted and need strength: "Those who hope in the LORD will renew their strength. They will soar on wings like eagles; they will run and not grow weary, they will walk and not be faint" (Isaiah 40:31).

- When you're struggling with fear: "This is what the LORD says—he who created you, O Jacob, he who formed you, O Israel: 'Fear not, for I have redeemed you; I have summoned you by name; you are mine. When you pass through the waters, I will be with you; and when you pass through the rivers, they will not sweep over you. When you walk through the fire, you will not be burned'" (43:1-2).

- When you feel like you're dealing with life all by yourself: "Surely I am with you always, to the very end of the age" (Matthew 28:20).

- When you feel boxed in with all sorts of impossibilities: "Call to me and I will answer you and tell you great and unsearchable things" (Jeremiah 33:3).

Why not commit these verses to memory? You'll soon see the difference they make in your struggles with the problems of life. [7]

Do not be anxious about anything, but in everything,
by prayer and petition, with thanksgiving, present
your requests to God (Philippians 4:6).

Have you ever felt wound up and you're being turned tighter and tighter? If so, that's stress. *Stress* is a common, catchall word to describe the tension and pressure we often feel. But do you know what stress is? It's the irritation you feel in any bothersome life situation. Stress is anything that places conflicting or heavy demands upon you.

What do stressful demands do to you? They cause your equilibrium to be upset. Your body contains a highly sophisticated defense system that helps you cope with threatening situations and challenging events. When you feel pressure, your body quickly mobilizes its defenses for fight or flight. In the case of stress, we are flooded with an abundance of adrenaline, which disrupts normal functioning and creates a heightened sense of arousal.

A stressed person is like a rubber band that is being stretched. When the pressure is released, the rubber band returns to normal. But if stretched too much or too long, the rubber begins to lose its elastic qualities, becomes brittle, develops some cracks, and eventually breaks. That's what happens to us if there is too much stress in our lives.

What is stressful to one individual may not be stressful to another. Some get stressed about future events that can't be avoided or events after they've occurred. For others stress means simply the wear and tear of life. They're like pieces of stone that have been hammered for so long they begin to crumble.

How are you feeling right now? Are you relaxed? Uptight? If you're feeling stressed, take out your Bible and read Philippians 4:6-9. Read it, practice it, and experience your stress getting an eviction notice.

*Let the word of Christ richly dwell within you, with
all wisdom teaching and admonishing one another with
psalms and hymns and spiritual songs, singing with
thankfulness in your hearts to God (Colossians 3:16).*

What are your relationships like with other people? Are they deep relationships, or just, well, you know…so-so? There are four levels of relationships. Let's consider them.

Minimal relationships. Minimal relationships involve surface-level verbal interaction, which is generally pleasant. People do not give or receive help, emotional support, or love from each other. They just speak and listen to each other when it is necessary.

Moderate relationships. A moderate relationship contains the characteristics of a minimal relationship but adds emotional attachment. You want emotional support and are willing to give it. Openness enables both parties to listen to each other's hurts, concerns, joys, and needs. Ideally, this openness is a two-way street, but when it's not, believers are called to respond with openness. These relationships occur by taking the initial steps of emotional openness and support. The other person may follow suit or back away.

Strong relationships. The difference between a moderate relationship and a strong one is found in the word *help.* Strong relationships develop when you really become involved with people by reaching out to minister to them in tangible ways. You're ready to provide help when they need it, and you accept help from them when you need it.

Quality relationships. These include the elements of the other levels but adds loving trust. You feel safe with these people and reveal your inner needs, thoughts, and feelings. You invite them to share their needs, thoughts, and feelings, and they feel safe doing so.

Who are the people in your life today that fit each classification? What are your feelings about them? How often do you pray for them and *how* do you pray for them?

*If I rise on the wings of the dawn, if I settle on the far
side of the sea, even there your hand will guide me, your
right hand will hold me fast (Psalm 139:9-10).*

Nobody likes to face a crisis. We'd rather walk on water than face
the flood. In fact, we reason that godly men should be so on top of
things that they just don't have the same problems as others. The truth is,
all people face the water, the fire, and the flood. There are, however, some
special conditions in which God's children face these. Isaiah 43:1 NASB
reads: "Do not fear, for I have redeemed you; I have called you by name;
you are mine!" That's a promise that helps you face your trials.

And don't forget, my friend, God loves you. And He may well have
allowed the experience that has you backed up to the wall or lying on a
hospital bed. He wants to do something in your life or makeup that just
wouldn't and couldn't happen apart from the circumstances facing you.
God explained that He allowed the circumstances to happen because His
children are "precious in his sight" (Isaiah 43:4). He then describes what
He's going to do because of the deep waters He's allowed His people to
pass through. More than ten times the phrase "I will" appears in the Isaiah 43 passage. God says that He will give other people in exchange for
your life. He will bring your offspring from the east and the west. He will
not remember your sins, which is a New Testament picture of God's forgiveness. He says He will pour out water on thirsty land and His Spirit
on their offspring. He promises to go before them and make rough places
smooth, and more.

Can you take these promises personally? Without a doubt! He will
meet you at the point of deepest trial, and, as Isaiah whispered long ago,
you will hear Him say, "I will be with you!" (Isaiah 43:2). How much
more important to know this than to be exempt from trials and wonder if the bridge over which we must cross is strong enough to hold us.[8]

*As occasion and opportunity open up to us, let us do good [morally]
to all people [not only being useful or profitable to them, but also
doing what is for their spiritual good and advantage]. Be mindful to
be a blessing, especially to those of the household of faith [those who
belong to God's family with you, the believers] (Galatians 6:10 AMP).*

Life is full of choices, and there are just as many opportunities to do good as to do evil. Neil Anderson shares some of these opportunities gleaned from an unknown author:

- People are unreasonable, illogical and self-centered. Love them anyway.
- If you do good, people will accuse you of selfish, ulterior motives. Do good anyway.
- If you are successful, you will win false friends and true enemies. Succeed anyway.
- The good you do today will be forgotten tomorrow. Do good anyway.
- Honesty and frankness make you vulnerable. Be honest and frank anyway.
- The biggest people with the biggest ideas can be shot down by the smallest people with the smallest minds. Think big anyway.
- People favor underdogs but follow only top dogs. Fight for the underdog anyway.
- What you spend years building may be destroyed overnight. Build anyway.
- People really need help, but may attack you if you help them. Help people anyway.
- Give the world the best you've got and you'll get kicked in the teeth. Give the world the best you've got anyway.[9]

That's not a bad game plan, is it?

*Be joyful always; pray continually; give thanks in all circumstances,
for this is God's will for you in Christ Jesus. Do not put out
the Spirit's fire; do not treat prophecies with contempt. Test
everything. Hold on to the good. Avoid every kind of evil. May
God himself, the God of peace, sanctify you through and through.
May your whole spirit, soul and body be kept blameless at the
coming of our Lord Jesus Christ (1 Thessalonians 5:16-23).*

Remember when you camped out as a kid? Perhaps you were in the Boy Scouts. Campfires were part of those times, and when the evening came to a close, someone had to douse the fire and make sure it was out. It had to be *quenched*.

There are times when quenching something is not the best step to take. That's what Paul is talking about in today's passage. Sometimes we can stifle the fire that God builds in our hearts or the hearts of others. We can stagnate our life by what we think. Look at the "Seven Steps to Stagnation." Have you ever thought or voiced any of them?

1. We've never done it that way before.

2. We're not ready for that.

3. We're doing all right without it.

4. We've tried that once before.

5. It costs too much.

6. That's not our responsibility.

7. It just won't work.[10]

Resistance statements inhibit, limit, and stagnate. Paul's words will expand your life. Go back and reread the passage for today. Then open your life to opportunities.[11]

*I can do everything through him who gives
me strength (Philippians 4:13).*

Sometimes we let what others say about us limit us. Sometimes we let setbacks limit us too. We can give up or we can press on. Consider where we would be today if these people had given in and given up!

"As a composer, he's hopeless." That's what Beethoven's music teacher said about him.

When Isaac Newton was in elementary school, his work was evaluated as poor.

One of Thomas Edison's teachers told him he was unable to learn.

Caruso's music teacher told him he didn't have any voice.

Einstein didn't speak until he was four, and couldn't read until seven. He struggled with dyslexia.

Walt Disney was fired by a newspaper editor because he didn't have any good ideas.

Louisa May Alcott's editor told her that her writings would never appeal to anyone.

Someone once evaluated Henry Ford as having "no promise."

Admiral Richard Byrd had been evaluated as "unfit for service."

Guess who failed the sixth grade? Winston Churchill.

The Royal College gave Louis Pasteur an evaluation of "mediocre" in chemistry.

Fortunately, these people pressed on. So did those in the Bible who faced obstacles that included people who didn't believe in them. God can take our failures and mistakes and make them learning experiences. [12]

*The Son is the radiance of God's glory and the exact
representation of his being, sustaining all things by his
powerful word. After he had provided purification for sins, he
sat down at the right hand of the Majesty (Hebrews 1:3).*

Dear God,
You have shown Your love for us by sending Your Son Jesus Christ and because of this our lives have been changed. Thank You for this wonderful gift.

I thank You for the years Jesus spent living among us.

I thank You for every act of love that He did.

I thank You for the words and teaching He left for all mankind.

I thank You for His obedience unto death and then His triumph over death.

I thank You for the presence of His Spirit with me now.

Help me to remember…His eagerness to help others rather than to be helped Himself,

> His sympathy to those suffering,
> His willingness to suffer on my behalf,
> His meekness to turn the other cheek, which is so difficult
>   for me to do,
> His simple lifestyle and willingness to mix with those
>   who were different from His own people,
> His complete reliance upon You.

I want this for my own life and ask for wisdom and discernment to do this.

I ask for grace so that in each of these ways I can follow Jesus.

May today be a day of patient understanding of those around me, a day of doing what You want, and a day when Your Word is seen in what I do.

In Jesus' name.
Amen.

How long, O LORD? Will you forget me forever? How long
will you hide your face from me? How long must I wrestle
with my thoughts and every day have sorrow in my heart?
How long will my enemy triumph over me? (Psalm 13:1-2).

You think you've had a hard day? David was probably in even worse shape when he wrote this psalm. He was the king-elect, but he was living and hiding like an animal in the desert and forest, because Saul was trying to kill him. That's when he wrote this psalm. It's a prayer, but the first two verses reflect the fact that he's overwhelmed by life.

Have you ever been there? You probably haven't had the king's hit-men tracking you down, but it could be the crying kids, a broken water heater, unpaid bills, the IRS, bill collectors, and guess who's coming for a two-week visit! You feel like David when he says, "God has forgotten me—forever!" When you don't have any relief, you tend to lose hope. You wonder if you haven't been abandoned by God.

And when you feel abandoned you end up feeling that God doesn't even care about you. "How long will you hide your face from me?" We call this self-pity.

Later in the psalm David says he's going to have to take matters into his own hands and find solutions himself if God won't help. The Hebrew term *take counsel* means "to plan." Perhaps the result of trying to do it his way is the reason for the phrase "having sorrow in my heart all the day." Proverbs 3:5 offers a better choice: "Trust in the LORD with all your heart and lean not on your own understanding."

Did David stay in this condition? Fortunately, no—emphatically no. He found an answer, and so can you. Why not read about it in Proverbs 13:3-6? If it worked for David, it will work for you.[13]

*God spoke all these words: "I am the L*ORD *your God, who brought you out of Egypt, out of the land of slavery" (Exodus 20:1-2).*

Laws! We are a country filled with laws. We have no idea how many laws are on the books. There are even laws to help in formulating new laws. Some laws are good, while others need to be dropped from the system. There are probably some you'd like to get rid of. Our lives are regulated by laws, but it doesn't mean we always keep them, especially traffic laws. (Sorry if I'm meddling now.)

Laws come from God. He is the originator. He gave them so that we would get the most out of life. Consider the Ten Commandments, for example. Do you remember them? Can you list them? Take a minute and think about them. They were applicable when they were given, and they still are today.

It's true that as Christians we live under the grace of God and we're saved by grace. But we still need the laws of God. There are benefits to the law. Law and grace are not at odds with each other. The law actually reveals God's grace. The law was founded on God's grace. The Ten Commandments passage from Exodus reveals this. Because of His grace the children of Israel were to follow the Ten Commandments, not for the purpose of gaining salvation but out of thanksgiving for what the Lord had done for them. God's grace brought them out of slavery.

That's why you and I are to follow the teachings in the New Testament. Following them won't save us but it will reflect the fact that we are followers of Jesus. Jesus fulfilled the law, and when we come to know Him we have an opportunity to reflect Him by following the law. Even the Ten Commandments.[14]

*I have not come to abolish [the Law or the Prophets] but
to fulfill them. I tell you the truth, until heaven and earth
disappear, not the smallest letter, not the least stroke of
a pen, will by any means disappear from the Law until
everything is accomplished (Matthew 5:17-18).*

We live in a world of lawbreakers. Some believe that laws were made to be broken. Some rules are fair; some are unfair. They restrict, they confine, they regulate, but they also provide structure and order. There are laws that you would like to see changed. But what about the laws that God has given us? How do you feel about them? Do you see them as restrictive or beneficial? Hampering you or making your life better? Difficult to keep or easy? Or have you even thought about God's laws? His laws will bless you if you follow them. David gave us a thorough description of the benefits of this:

> The law of the LORD is perfect, reviving the soul. The statutes of the LORD are trustworthy, making wise the simple. The precepts of the LORD are right, giving joy to the heart. The commands of the LORD are radiant, giving light to the eyes. The fear of the LORD is pure, enduring forever. The ordinances of the LORD are sure and altogether righteous. They are more precious than gold, than much pure gold; they are sweeter than honey, than honey from the comb. By them is your servant warned; in keeping them there is great reward (Psalm 19:7-11).

What does the law do? It reveals God's holiness. It invites you to be holy. Its purpose is to help you know the Lawgiver better and to make your life full.

*I am the LORD your God, who brought
you out of Egypt (Exodus 20:2).*

Have you ever wondered what it would have been like to have been there when God gave the Ten Commandments? Read what happened. Picture it in your mind. See it. Hear it. Smell it. Feel it. Have you been in a thunderstorm that was so intense the sounds rolled and roared? Have you seen lightning flash from peak to peak? Have you felt the rumble and shake of an earthquake? Put all these together and you have the scene:

> On the morning of the third day there was thunder and lightning, with a thick cloud over the mountain, and a very loud trumpet blast. Everyone in the camp trembled. Then Moses led the people out of the camp to meet with God, and they stood at the foot of the mountain. Mount Sinai was covered with smoke, because the Lord descended on it in fire. The smoke billowed up from it like smoke from a furnace, the whole mountain trembled violently, and the sound of the trumpet grew louder and louder. Then Moses spoke and the voice of God answered him (Exodus 19:16-19).

The giving of the law is a description of God's gracious nature. His grace in action. When the law was given the second time, Moses reminded the people:

> The LORD did not set his affection on you and choose you because you were more numerous than other peoples...But it was because the LORD loved you and kept the oath he swore to your forefathers that he brought you out with a mighty hand and redeemed you from the land of slavery (Deuteronomy 7:7-8).

That's what He does today because He loves you. The children of Israel couldn't earn God's love, and neither can we. He paid the way for His people then, and He pays it now.

You shall have no other gods before me (Exodus 20:3).

Nothing, absolutely nothing is to come before God. The first commandment is plain and simple…and easy to break. Today gods have multiplied. Some worship the earth. Many worship Elvis and his memory. Everyone today has a god, whether they call it god or not. Famous preacher G. Campbell Morgan said:

> It is as impossible for a man to live without having an object of worship as it is for a bird to fly if it is taken out of the air. The very composition of human life, the mystery of man's being, demands a center of worship as a necessity of existence. All life is worship… The question is whether the life and powers of man are devoted to the worship of the true God or to that of a false one.[15]

What you place first in your life may be your god. It could be your job, wife, golf, an accumulation of the things that make up the good life, or sex. Anything that takes priority over God has removed Him from the throne. When God said "you shall have no other gods before me," He was saying you shall have *Me!* Do you understand what it means to have God, to love Him? Everything you do is to be done to honor and glorify Him. It's your life's calling. It's expressed best by David:

> O God, my God! How I search for you! How I thirst for you in this parched and weary land where there is no water. How I long to find you! How I wish I could go into your sanctuary to see your strength and glory, for your love and kindness are better to me than life itself. How I praise you! (Psalm 63:1-3 TLB).

How can you fulfill this commandment today?[16]

*You shall not make for yourself an idol in the form
of anything in heaven above or on the earth beneath
or in the waters below (Exodus 20:4).*

This commandment is not the same as the first one. The first one forbids the *existence* of other gods. This commandment forbids the *making* of other gods. In other words, we are not to purposely create other gods. Verse 5 takes this commandment even further: "You shall not bow down to them or worship them; for I, the LORD your God, am a jealous God, punishing the children for the sin of the fathers to the third and fourth generation of those who hate me" (Exodus 20:5). This commandment may disturb you because we have pictures and statues in our churches. It's all right to use them as visual reminders created by man's perception. But the commandment does forbid the use of objects such as pictures and statues of Jesus and of God in *private* and *public worship*.[17]

Images limit God, yet He is limitless. Images obscure God's glory. They are made to reveal God, but they actually do the opposite. They hide the real God. Did you know that it's possible to buy a machine-washable Jesus doll? There are also plans to bring out a God doll that is a white-haired, white-bearded, white man in a rainbow colored robe with all the animals of creation flowing from him. When we create an idol it is to give ourselves something. Not only does it not do that, it *takes away* from what we have.

The God who created the universe—the God who created us—cannot be confined in a man-made image. When we try to create something to represent Him, we detract from the worship of who He really is. We cannot see Him. He is above being seen. That adds to His holiness and majesty. What about it? Are there images of any kind in your life? What about in your church? Think about it.

You shall not misuse the name of the LORD your God, for the LORD
will not hold anyone guiltless who misuses his name (Exodus 20:7).

This commandment must be a joke considering the way it is ignored, mistreated, and violated today. You can hardly find a movie or TV show that doesn't violate this commandment. And who bothers to think about it anymore? Times sure have changed.

The children of Israel had such reverence for some of the names of God that they wouldn't even use them. The name *Jehovah* was so sacred that it was said only once a year by the priest when he gave the blessing on the Day of Atonement (Leviticus 23:27).

There are many ways we misuse God's name these days. We use God's name in insincere or empty ways. We may take an oath in God's name and break it. Leviticus 19:12 says, "Do not swear falsely by my name and so profane the name of your God." Scripture is clear that when we use God's name irreverently, we violate the commandment. What do you say when you hit your thumb with a hammer? "Ouch" or something not so innocuous? Some men have a highly developed swearing skill. Lord Byron said, "He knew not what to say, so he swore." Another violation is using God's name to curse others. This is misusing and abusing God's name.

Read today's verse again. Now read Matthew 12:36-37:

I tell you that men will have to give account on the day of judgment for every careless word they have spoken. For by your words you will be acquitted, and by your words you will be condemned.

That's sobering, isn't it?

Remember the Sabbath day by keeping it holy. Six days you shall labor and do all your work, but the seventh day is a Sabbath to the LORD your God. On it you shall not do any work, neither you, nor your son or daughter, nor your manservant or maidservant, nor your animals, nor the alien within your gates (Exodus 20:8-10).

R*est.* God is saying that once a week we need to take a break. He is saying there is more to life than work. He is also urging us to follow His pattern: "In six days the LORD made the heavens and the earth, the sea, and all that is in them, but he rested on the seventh day. Therefore the LORD blessed the Sabbath day and made it holy" (Exodus 20:11). Since God is God, He didn't *need* to rest as we know it. He certainly wasn't worn out. He just decided to. And He wants us to do the same.

We need rest physically. There is a rhythm to the seventh day of rest that is the best balance of work and rest, even though people have tried other plans and failed. Spiritually we need this time to refocus our lives. For the children of Israel this was a day to celebrate their redemption and liberation. God wanted the people to spend one day looking to Him and thanking Him for being liberated. Listen to what the Lord said to Isaiah: "If you keep your feet from breaking the Sabbath and from doing as you please on my holy day, if you call the Sabbath a delight and the LORD's holy day honorable, and if you honor it by not going your own way and not doing as you please or speaking idle words, then you will find your joy in the LORD" (Isaiah 58:13-14).

So what do you do on the Sabbath? Some of us work; some of us play. It's a day that belongs to God. So who comes first on that day? Evaluate how you are using the Sabbath.

Then God issued this edict: "I am Jehovah your God who liberated you from your slavery in Egypt" (Exodus 20:1-2 TLB).

Kent Hughes has written an exceptional book titled *Disciplines of Grace*. In it he gives a provocative summary of the first four commandments (Words of Grace):

> What a remarkable enabling bouquet we have…[to help us love] God with all we have. Each of the words is magisterial and foundational, and each is uniquely powerful. But like a floral bouquet, their maximum effect comes when they are held together, for then comes the sweet power to love God. Consider the bouquet:
>
> *The First Word of Grace—the primacy of God:* "You shall have no other gods before me." That is, "You shall have Me! I must be in first place." If God is first, if there is nothing before Him, you will love Him more and more! Is He truly first in your life?
>
> *The Second Word of Grace—the person of God:* "You shall not make for yourself an idol in the form of anything…" That is, you shall not make a material image or dream up a mental image of God according to your own design. God wants you to see Himself in His Word and in His Son, because if you do, you will love Him more. The clearer your vision, the greater your love. How is your vision?
>
> *The Third Word of Grace—reverence for God:* "You shall not misuse the name of the Lord your God." That is, "You shall reverence God's name." Reverently loving Him in your mind and with your mouth will elevate and substantiate your love. Honestly, do you misuse or reverence His name?
>
> *The Fourth Word of Grace—the time for God:* "Remember the Sabbath day by keeping it holy." This tells us to keep holy the Lord's Day. Are you week by week offering it up in love to Him?[18]

*Honor your father and your mother, so that you may live long
in the land the LORD your God is giving you (Exodus 20:12).*

The emphasis of the fifth commandment is on loving others. The first
four are on loving God, which makes it possible to fulfill the next six.
If you have a right relationship with God, you can have a right relationship with others. And it begins with your parents.

Honor is not a word we use much today or practice. The Hebrew word
comes from a verb that means "to be heavy." In a sense you give weight to
a person you honor or hold in high esteem. You elevate him or her. You
see that person as important.

As an adult, how can you honor your parents? You *reverence* them.
Here are four ways you can do this:

> *You can respect them.* "Each of you must respect his mother and
> father, and you must observe my Sabbaths. I am the LORD your
> God" (Leviticus 19:3). How? Quite simple. *Respect* means you
> speak kindly to them and about them.

> *You can provide for them.* Don't neglect your parents when they are
> older. Give them time, attention, love, your listening ear, as well
> as help with their physical needs.

> *You can treat them with consideration.* Make their remaining years
> easier. Encourage them to spend your inheritance on themselves!

> *You can honor them by the way you live your life.* Give them some-
> thing to be proud of. "The father of a righteous man has great
> joy; he who has a wise son delights in him. May your father and
> mother be glad; may she who gave you birth rejoice!" (Proverbs
> 23:24-25).[19]

You shall not murder (Exodus 20:13).

"Don't kill!" Life is precious. "God made man like his Maker. Like God did God make man; man and maid did he make them" (Genesis 1:27 TLB). If you live in the United States, you live in a country where the future is excellent—for murder. American culture kills. Violence of all types, including murder and terrorist attacks, are on the rise. The atrocity and mayhem of 9/11 and the Oklahoma City bombing, as well as the rise of the murder of families and then perpetrators committing suicides stare us in the face.

Life is sacred. We've been called to cherish, honor, and protect our own lives and the lives of others. Matthew 22:39 says, "Love your neighbor as yourself." The Scriptures say no to homicide. It says no to suicide too, which is violence toward oneself. It also would include violence against family members and friends, such as involvement in medically assisted suicides for the ill and elderly. Suicide is wrong, regardless of what society says. The Scriptures say no to *feticide*—abortion. It's a direct sin against God. We all will have to take a stand on this issue sometime. God's Word comes first.

You may be thinking, "This is for someone else. I'm no murderer." Consider these words from Jesus, which apply to all of us: "You have heard that it was said to the people long ago, 'Do not murder, and anyone who murders will be subject to judgment.' But I tell you that anyone who is angry with his brother will be subject to judgment...Anyone who says, 'You fool!' will be in danger of the fire of hell" (Matthew 5:21-22).

Haven't we all had anger and contempt in our hearts for others? Haven't we all had thoughts of murder in our hearts for others? That's where it all begins—and thoughts sometimes lead to actions. [20]

You shall not commit adultery (Exodus 20:14).

This commandment is laughed at—even by some Christians. They don't take it seriously, but God does. The frequency of adultery mentioned in the Old Testament is second only to idolatry. In the New Testament its frequency is second to none.

Adultery violates the sacredness of marriage by breaking the marriage covenant, which God created. It's also a sin against one's own body. "Flee from sexual immorality. All other sins a man commits are outside his body, but he who sins sexually sins against his own body" (1 Corinthians 6:18). A Christian's body is a member of Christ:

> Do you not know that your bodies are members of Christ himself? Shall I then take the members of Christ and unite them with a prostitute? Never! Do you not know that he who unites himself with a prostitute is one with her in body? For it is said, "The two will become one flesh." But he who unites himself with the Lord is one with him in spirit (1 Corinthians 6:15-17).

Adultery is a sin, but like other sins, it is forgivable. Repentance, which means "to change and commit, to never repeat the offense," makes it so. What I recommend next won't be popular. If a man has committed adultery, he needs to confess to God, to his wife, and to the church. For his wife, since he has violated her, he should take a blood test for STDs. For the church, if he is in any position of service, he should resign and go through a time of healing and restoration before serving again.

Are you one who has never fallen? Then praise God! Here's a gentle nudge. Jesus said, "I tell you that anyone who looks at a woman lustfully has already committed adultery with her in his heart" (Matthew 5:28). How's your heart and thought life?

You shall not steal (Exodus 20:15).

If you lived in Old Testament times and took and disposed of a sheep or ox, you were required to give back four sheep or five oxen (Exodus 22:1-4).

What would happen today if a group of people were walking along and someone yelled, "Stop! Thief!" Most would probably stop. Haven't we all stolen something at one time or another? If the IRS had all the money it's been cheated out of and companies had the money stolen by employees, we'd be in great shape financially. In the book *The Day America Told the Truth,* the authors conclude:

> The so-called Protestant ethic is long gone from today's American workplace.
>
> Workers around America frankly admit that they spend more than 20 percent of their time at work totally goofing off. That amounts to a four-day work week across the nation.
>
> Almost half of us admit to chronic malingering, calling in sick when we are not sick, and doing it regularly.
>
> Only one in four give work their best effort; only one in four work to realize their human potential rather than merely to keep the wolf from the door. [21]

Stealing is not limited to shoplifting or taking all the cash out of a cash register. It's much easier to steal time—long breaks and lunch hours, being late to work and early to leave. Not working up to our full capacity is theft. What about misuse of the fax machine, photocopier, phone, or supplies for personal use? It happens all the time. We can steal a person's reputation, plagiarize someone's work, and cheat on our tax return.

So have we covered theft? No! God's Word says, "Will a man rob God? Yet you rob me...But you ask, 'How do we rob you?' In tithes and offerings" (Malachi 3:8). [22]

You shall not give false testimony against
your neighbor (Exodus 20:16).

We are a country of proficient liars. We cultivate and practice telling lies. We're good at it no matter how young or old we are. Research tells us that men do it more than women. Two out of three people in the United States see nothing wrong with lying.[23] But we can destroy another's reputation and cripple the ministry of a person or a church with lies. And worst of all we destroy ourselves before God: "The LORD detests lying lips, but he delights in men who are truthful" (Proverbs 12:22). "There are six things the LORD hates, seven that are detestable to him...a false witness who pours out lies and a man who stirs up dissension among brothers" (6:16,19).

We lie by adding to and embellishing stories. We leave out information to create another impression. We tell the truth so that it destroys, countering God's Word that says to speak the truth so that it cements our relationships: "Speaking the truth in love, we will in all things grow up into him who is the Head, that is, Christ" (Ephesians 4:15).

We can make insinuations about others or situations and then back out of it by saying we didn't mean it. "Like a madman shooting firebrands or deadly arrows is a man who deceives his neighbor ands says, 'I was only joking!'" (Proverbs 26:18-19). We lie by spreading gossip—information that may be true...or not. God's Word says, "The words of a gossip are like choice morsels" (18:8).

Pray that God will help you to be a man of truth. And remember: "An honest answer is like a kiss on the lips" (Proverbs 24:26). "Set a guard over my mouth, O LORD; keep watch over the door of my lips" (Psalm 141:3).

You shall not covet your neighbor's house. You shall not covet
your neighbor's wife, or his manservant or maidservant, his ox or
donkey, or anything that belongs to your neighbor (Exodus 20:17).

We want more. We think we're satisfied, and then we see something better, bigger, flashier, or more beautiful. Then we covet, which means we desire it. Coveting also means "lust" or "passionate longing." We live in a culture that promotes dissatisfaction and coveting. And coveting leads to the violation of other commandments: "All day long he craves for more, but the righteous give without sparing" (Proverbs 21:26). Jesus warned us about it: "Watch out! Be on your guard against all kinds of greed; a man's life does not consist in the abundance of his possessions" (Luke 12:15).

We live under the misbelief that more is better and possessions make us happy. We find it hard to rejoice in what others have because we want it ourselves. We envy the rich who have it all—but they don't really. Most are missing peace and satisfaction.

Have you coveted? Probably. We all have. Often it's the big three we want: possessions, position, and people. We can covet and we can possess, but there's a better way. Jesus said, "Seek first [God's] kingdom and his righteousness, and all these things will be given to you as well. Therefore do not worry about tomorrow, for tomorrow will worry about itself. Each day has enough trouble of its own" (Matthew 6:33-34). When you're content, you won't covet. Paul said, "I have learned to be content whatever the circumstances" (Philippians 4:11). He also said, "God will meet all your needs according to his glorious riches in Christ Jesus" (Philippians 4:19). If you want to do some "good" coveting, desire the best for someone else, such as your wife or a friend. [24]

*I am the LORD your God, who brought you out of
Egypt, out of the land of slavery (Exodus 20:2).*

Is it possible to follow the Ten Commandments? Paul talked about the law:

> Is the law sin? Certainly not! Indeed I would not have known what sin was except through the law. For I would not have known what coveting really was if the law had not said, "Do not covet." But sin, seizing the opportunity afforded by the commandment, produced in me every kind of covetous desire (Romans 7:7-8).

Kent Hughes said, "If one knows Christ, it is possible, through discipline, to live within the spiritual parameters, the borders of the Law. How so? Because Jesus Christ fulfilled the Law (Matthew 5:17):

- Jesus never put any god or, indeed, anything before his Father.
- Jesus never constructed materially or mentally an idol...
- Jesus never misused the Father's name but instead "hallowed" it.
- Jesus kept the Sabbath day holy.
- Jesus unfailingly honored his earthly father and mother.
- Jesus never indulged in a murderous, hateful thought.
- Jesus never engaged in mental adultery, much less physical adultery.
- Jesus never stole or even had a larcenous thought.
- Jesus never once bore false testimony...
- Jesus never coveted anything except another's spiritual well-being."[25]

No one perfectly lives the law, but we can strive to live within its spiritual borders.

How blessed is he whose transgression is forgiven, whose sin is covered! How blessed is the man to whom the LORD does not impute iniquity, and in whose spirit there is no deceit! (Psalm 32:1-2 NASB).

Have you had the experience of finally overcoming a habit or problem that plagued you for years? When that problem has been laid to rest (with no resurrection), that's an occasion to celebrate. And that's what David is doing in today's verses. He's overjoyed! Read the verses again and look at the four words or terms used for wrongdoing.

The first is *transgression.* The Hebrew word means "to rebel or revolt." It's when you know the rule, you know what's right, and you deliberately violate it.

The second term, *sin.* means "to miss the mark." You deviate from God's way.

The third term is *iniquity* or guilt. We know we sinned and guilt is the payoff.

The fourth term, *deceit,* means "treachery, self-deception, and deception." Self-deception sets in when we override the guilt and refuse to face and overcome the sin.

In today's verses, David is saying, "When these four things are gone, what a relief!" If a friend said to you, "I've been transgressing and sinning. I feel full of guilt and I'm deceiving myself," what would you suggest? Here are some clear answers to share:

I acknowledged my sin to you and did not cover up my iniquity... and you forgave the guilt of my sin (Psalm 32:5).

He who conceals his sins does not prosper, but whoever confesses and renounces them finds mercy (Proverbs 28:13).

If we confess our sins, he is faithful and just and will forgive us our sins and purify us from all unrighteousness (1 John 1:9).[1]

He who covers his transgressions will not prosper, but whoever confesses and forsakes his sins shall obtain mercy (Proverbs 28:13 AMP).

Are you fed up hearing people trying to get off the hook by giving lame excuses? No one wants to take responsibility for the problem. Even in marriage it happens: "Yeah, my marriage would be better if she would get with it." Perhaps you've heard some of these excuses or even…Naw, you wouldn't have used these:

Some men blame their health or feelings:
- I have migraine headaches and…
- I'm just tired all the time.
- I've been depressed.
- The kids make me so upset.

Some men blame their nature:
- I'm just this way, that's all. I always have been. I can't change.
- I'm a phlegmatic—you know what they're like.

Some men blame others:
- Her mother is always…
- It's the darn kids. They just never go to sleep at the right time.
- My boss just gets to me.
- If my wife would only listen to me.

Some men blame the past:
- She has always been that way.
- My mother always used to put me down.

Some men blame "Why":
- If only I could understand why she does…
- Why can't she stay home on Saturdays and not shop?

There's a better way. Take responsibility. Admit you can do better. Then do so.

You made all the delicate, inner parts of my body and knit
them together in my mother's womb. Thank you for making
me so wonderfully complex! It is amazing to think about. Your
workmanship is marvelous—and how well I know it. You were there
while I was being formed in utter seclusion! You saw me before I
was born and scheduled each day of my life before I began to breathe.
Every day was recorded in your book! (Psalm 139:13-16 TLB).

Do you ever feel like you don't exactly fit in—you know, your image or the way you act or dress is a bit different from the people at work or at church? In many ways we're continually fighting an "image syndrome." We feel the pressure to wear the right suits, tennis shoes, and underwear. We need to act a certain way to fit in with everyone else. *Conformity* is the word, and clones are the result. If you try to do things a different way at church or in a work presentation, you get flak because you didn't match up to "the image." People say there's a right way and a wrong way to be, but is that true? Have you ever wondered how some of the prophets or John the Baptist fit in with their societies? Probably not too well at times!

The truth is, you are you! You are who God created you to be. Have you discovered who that is? Have you discovered your unique characteristics and talents? Probably not if you're still trying to fit in. Keep in mind that you were created by God and then the mold was broken. No one else is like you. You're unique. You're special. It's all right to be you. Don't let others shape you—or what you do, say, or think. That's God's task. He started with you, and He will finish with you. And He really does want you to be you.[2]

*Everyone who hears these words of mine and puts them into practice
is like a wise man who built his house on the rock. The rain came
down, the streams rose, and the winds blew and beat against that
house; yet it did not fall, because it had its foundation on the rock.
But everyone who hears these words of mine and does not put them
into practice is like a foolish man who built his house on sand. The
rain came down, the streams rose, and the winds blew and beat
against that house, and it fell with a great crash (Matthew 7:24-27).*

Is this the real thing? How do you know it's authentic?" These are questions we're all asking today. What you see isn't always what you get. Labels can even be misleading. You buy an expensive piece of clothing, shoes, or even furniture, and then, as you more closely examine it, discover it wasn't what you thought at all. You feel ripped off.

Sometimes Christians aren't what they seem either. They say one thing but act another way. They behave one way at church and another way at work. They're not real; they're not authentic. They're bluffers! You've seen them at work. They have no depth.

There's an area in our lives that needs to be authentic. It's called faith. Do you know what *authentic faith* is? It's a mixture of joy and conviction. It's not afraid to ask questions—hard questions—that may expand your faith. Have you asked any recently?

Authentic faith is honest and is expressed so others can understand you. It doesn't use clichés or confusing terminology. Who have you shared your faith with recently?

Authentic faith is not centered on you, but on Jesus Christ.

Authentic faith admits you struggle, but finds its solution in Jesus. Who have you asked to pray for you recently?

Your faith may help someone else discover faith. Let's keep that in mind.[3]

If you really knew me, you would know my Father as well. From now on, you do know him and have seen him (John 14:7).

How you and your father connected as you were growing up impacts how you respond as a man in your adulthood. How was your relationship? Did you really know your dad? What he thought? What he believed? What he felt? Many men say, "Yes, I knew my father," until they are faced with these questions.

A lot of men have a father hunger. It's often activated when they have sons of their own, when they hit mid-life, or when they experience a loss. Look at the themes of fathers and sons in films. Do you remember the shock Luke Skywalker experiences meeting his father Darth Vader in *The Empire Strikes Back?* Or the newfound strength Indiana Jones discovers as he talks with his aging father in *The Last Crusade?* In *Backdraft* a firefighter's sons follow in his footsteps; and in *Field of Dreams* a man plays baseball with his father in the spirit realm, which frees him emotionally.

There are popular songs like Paul Overstreet's "Seein' My Father in Me," Chet Atkins' "My Father's Hat," and "A Boy Named Sue" by Johnny Cash. All of these have the same message of portraying a man's boyhood and his longings as an adult to be connected to his father.

Is your father living? If so, what is your relationship like? If he's deceased, you may still long for something from him. Sometimes our dads can't give us what we wanted or still want. But there is a Father who *can* fill all our needs. Have you met Him? He's always available and accessible. And He wants a relationship with you more than you do with Him…or it may seem that way. Your Father is waiting. Talk to Him today.[4]

I have brought you glory on earth by completing the work you gave me to do (John 17:4).

Why was Jesus so effective in dealing with people? His ministry involved helping them achieve fullness of life, assisting them in developing their abilities to deal with the problems, conflicts, and burdens of life. We too have been called to minister in this way.

Foremost in Jesus' life was obedience to God. There was a definite relationship between them. "I did not speak on My own initiative, but the Father Himself who sent Me has given Me a commandment as to what to say" (John 12:49 NASB).

Jesus lived a life of faith. He saw life through God's eyes. How about you? In what way does your faith need to be strengthened?

Jesus lived a life of prayer. "Large crowds were gathering to hear Him and to be healed of their sicknesses. But Jesus Himself would often slip away to the wilderness and pray" (Luke 5:15-16 NASB). Is prayer a daily event for you?

Jesus spoke with authority. "He was teaching them as one having authority, and not as their scribes" (Matthew 7:29 NASB). When you realize the authority you have in Jesus, you will become more effective in talking about Him.

Jesus was involved. He wasn't aloof; He was personal, sensitive, and caring. Are these qualities seen in your life?

Jesus had the power of the Holy Spirit. We see how His ministry began when Jesus received the power of the Holy Spirit in Luke 3:21-22: "When all the people were being baptized, Jesus was baptized too. And as he was praying, heaven was opened and the Holy Spirit descended on him in bodily form like a dove. And a voice came from heaven: 'You are my Son, whom I love; with you I am well pleased.'"

Each of us will give an account of himself to God (Romans 14:12).

We're all accountable to someone—our employers, our spouses, the government. We're definitely accountable for our money through the kind auspices of the IRS. And we're accountable to God. But what about the accountability we can choose? I'm talking about accountability to other Christian men. I don't mean friendship and fellowship—I mean accountability, a relationship in which they can ask you and you can ask them hard personal questions so you all stay on track.

Why is accountability necessary? When we don't answer to someone, we're more likely to blow it. We all like to be in charge of our own lives, but we're also oblivious to some of our areas of need. Accountability people can challenge, support, confront, and encourage us. Answering to someone helps us reflect God in our lives in a genuine way:

> Brothers, if someone is caught in a sin, you who are spiritual should restore him gently. But watch yourself, or you also may be tempted. Carry each other's burdens, and in this way you will fulfill the law of Christ (Galatians 6:1-2).

> Two are better than one, because they have a good return for their work: If one falls down, his friend can help him up (Ecclesiastes 4:9-10).

> Wounds from a friend can be trusted, but an enemy multiplies kisses (Proverbs 27:6).

> As iron sharpens iron, so one man sharpens another (verse 17).

What about it? If you don't have an accountability group of men in your life, think about it and pray about it. Reach out to others, and your life will never be the same.

The poor will eat and be satisfied; they who seek the LORD will praise him—may your hearts live forever! (Psalm 22:26).

"Man, am I filled up." You've said it and so have I—usually following a Thanksgiving or Christmas feast. Sometimes it's a good, satisfying feeling. Other times our skin feels so tight we think we're going to explode. The phrase "filled up" is used in many settings. We drive into a gas station and say, "Fill 'er up"—or we used to! There's nothing worse than driving around and having that "E" dash light come on. Driving on empty is no fun, and eventually you have to stop.

Going hungry isn't very pleasant either. Your body begins to hurt after a while. But perhaps it isn't all that bad to feel the pangs of hunger. It helps us anticipate what is to come. Our hunger pangs can cause us to think about the One who one day will have us sit with Him at a huge banquet. We won't be hungry again. Read two of the promises found in God's Word as the psalmist talks about God filling our needs:[5]

> [The LORD] satisfies the thirsty and fills the hungry with good things (Psalm 107:9).

> [The LORD] upholds the cause of the oppressed and gives food to the hungry. The LORD sets prisoners free, the LORD gives sight to the blind, the LORD lifts up those who are bowed down, the LORD loves the righteous. The LORD watches over the alien and sustains the fatherless and the widow, but he frustrates the ways of the wicked (Psalm 146:7-9).

*"In your anger do not sin": Do not let the sun go down
while you are still angry (Ephesians 4:26).*

Let's consider the positives of anger. You need to be angry. That's right and okay. Ephesians 4:24 tells us to not sin in our anger. The word *angry* in this verse means an anger which is an abiding, settled habit of the mind that is aroused under certain conditions. The person is aware and in control of it. There is a *just* occasion for the anger. Reason is involved, and when reason is present, anger such as this is usually legitimate.

Christians do and should get angry at injustices and other problems we see in the world around us. *Righteous anger* is not sinful when properly directed. What are the characteristics of righteous anger? First, it is controlled; it is not heated or unrestrained. Even if the cause is legitimate and directed at an injustice, uncontrolled anger can cause errors in judgment and increase the difficulty of the situation. "In your anger do not sin."

Second, there must be no hatred, malice, or resentment. Anger that harbors a counterattack complicates the problem. Jesus' reaction to the injustices against Him is a great example of staying in control. When He was reviled and insulted, He did not revile or offer return insults. When He was abused and suffered, He made no threats of vengeance; He trusted Himself and the situation to God, who judges fairly (1 Peter 2:23).

A third characteristic of righteous anger is that its motivation is unselfish. When the motivation is selfish, usually pride and resentment are involved. Anger should be directed not at the wrong done to oneself but at injustice done to others.

So…how can you use your anger constructively today?

*Knowing their thoughts, Jesus said, "Why do you entertain
evil thoughts in your hearts?" (Matthew 9:4).*

I've come to see life more and more as a war. Ultimately, our battle is
with the forces of evil, but on a daily level war involves a struggle with
time, money, priorities, health, and unplanned crisis. Can you relate?

If you and your wife are to fight as allies, then you both must grow
in greater intimacy. To this growth I suggest you set aside some special
time. Perhaps before or after dinner? Consider this time sacred and non-
negotiable. It is your R&R before returning to the fight. This may require
repeated instructions to your children not to interrupt. It will require you
to let the phone ring, to let guests wait for their hosts to return, and it
may offend some who see your committed time together as selfish. But
this is a refueling time that will help you engage with your world with a
clearer loyalty to one another, a deepened passion for what is good and
right, and a sense of rest.

Make the time at least a half-hour, with the option of stretching it to
an hour. Begin by catching up on the events of the day. Those events will
become the springboard for conversation about what was provoked in us
that caused distress or delight. If you keep a journal, share your thoughts
with each other. Reading out loud together helped my wife and I crystal-
lize our vague struggles and gave us an opportunity to record our progress.

Keep the structure loose, letting your focus move from events to feelings, from a struggle to joy, or from reading to prayer. When concluding,
call on God to deepen your hearts for Him. You'll return to your family
and world refreshed in your sense of being intimate allies.[6]

*God made him who had no sin to be sin for us, so that in him we
might become the righteousness of God (2 Corinthians 5:21).*

We all make some questionable choices in life. One of the most questionable is the decision to live with guilt rather than without it. Why choose to live with guilt? Since we can opt for forgiveness, why not do that? Let's take a look at the basics of forgiveness.

First, you can be forgiven regardless of what you've done or thought. Moses, a murderer, was forgiven. David, an adulterer, was forgiven. Saul, who had Christians killed, was forgiven. We can all be forgiven in the same way.

Second, forgiveness comes through Jesus Christ alone—not through self-punishment. You can't do it yourself, and neither can another person. Only the Son of God can. He faced our problem (sin) and paid the penalty for it.

Third, forgiveness can't be purchased or bargained for. It's a *gift*. And it can eliminate your guilt forever. "If we confess our sins, [God] is faithful and just and will forgive us our sins and purify us from all unrighteousness" (1 John 1:9).

Fourth, forgiveness is not limited. It's forever. It lasts. It's hard to conceive of *what forever* means, but it's a long time. "As far as the east is from the west, so far has he removed our transgressions from us" (Psalm 103:12).

If we choose to live with guilt, we've made a choice that God says doesn't have to exist. Guilt drives people to insanity, drinking, drugs, addictions, abuse, and abandonment. If those are the results, why choose to live with it? God is in the business of creating solutions, not problems. Forgiveness can set you free. Who in their right mind wants to live life as a captive?[7]

*Do not eat the bread of a miser, nor desire his delicacies; for
as he thinks in his heart, so is he (Proverbs 23:6-7 NKJV).*

I t is interesting how Scripture talks so much about heart. Perhaps
because it can determine who we are and what we do in life. Norman
Vincent Peale told the story of his experience on the streets of Kowloon in
Hong Kong. He walked by a tattoo studio and stopped to notice the sam-
ples displayed in the window. Among the typical ones was an unusual
expression: "Born to Lose." He went into the shop and, pointing to the
words, asked the tattoo artist if anyone actually had that tattooed on
his body. The man replied, "Yes, sometimes." Dr. Peale said he couldn't
believe that anyone in their right mind would do such a thing. The Chinese man tapped his forehead and said in broken English, "Before tattoo
on body, it on mind."[8]

Arnold Palmer is well known for being one of the greatest golfers.
He's won hundreds of trophies and awards. In his office you will find
two items—the cup for his first professional win in 1955 and a plaque
on the wall that says:

> If you think you are beaten, you are. If you think you dare not,
> you don't. If you'd like to win but think you can't, it's almost cer-
> tain you won't. Life's battles don't always go to the stronger or
> faster man, but sooner or later, the man who wins is the man who
> thinks he can.[9]

One thing I do: Forgetting what is behind and straining toward what
is ahead, I press on toward the goal to win the prize for which God
has called me heavenward in Christ Jesus (Philippians 3:13-14).

"Pay attention!" Those words echo in my mind from childhood. Teachers, piano teachers, and parents gave me that message time and time again. Did you hear it too? Sometimes we get distracted when we're listening, when we're praying, or when we're setting out to accomplish a goal. Some distractions can be fatal. Sometimes we paralyze our progress by trying to accomplish several things at the same time or else we put our energy into doing a task that isn't very important and neglect something that's vital.

A number of years ago an Eastern Airlines jumbo jet crashed in the Florida Everglades. Flight 401 carried a full load of passengers and had taken off from New York bound for Miami. As the plane began its approach in Miami, the pilots noticed that the light indicating the landing gear was down wasn't lit. They flew in a large looping circle over the Everglade swamps while they worked on the problem. The landing gear could be improperly deployed or it could have been a defective light bulb.

The flight engineer tried to remove the light bulb but it was stuck. The other members in the cockpit tried to help him loosen the bulb. While they were distracted, they failed to notice that the plane was losing altitude. It flew right into the swamp. Dozens of passengers were killed. The cockpit crew had a job to do, but they were distracted by a seventy-five cent light bulb.

What distracts you from doing your job? And what distracts you from your relationship with God? That's the major question![10]

*Do not worry about what to say or how to say it. At that time you
will be given what to say, for it will not be you speaking, but the
Spirit of your Father speaking through you (Matthew 10:19-20).*

W hat in the world will I say?" At some time in life we're all confronted with this challenge. We struggle for the appropriate words
to share a thought or concern with someone. And when pressure situations occur, sometimes our minds shut down and we don't know what
to say.

In today's passage, Jesus is talking about our concern over what to say
when we are faced with giving testimony about Him in a setting hostile
to the Christian faith. He assures us that the Holy Spirit will give us the
thoughts, the words, and the courage we so often lack. When we are concerned about sharing our faith in Christ with someone or when we are
challenged in our faith by other people, we can rely on the fact that God
is the source of our thoughts and words. Dr. Lloyd Ogilvie said:

> Our only task is to open our minds in calm expectation of wis-
> dom beyond our own capacity. We were never meant to be ade-
> quate on our own. It is when we think we are adequate that we
> get into trouble. A Christian is not one who works for the Lord
> but one in whom and through whom the Lord works. We are not
> to speak for God but to yield our tongues to express the thoughts
> the Lord has implanted.[11]

What can we draw from these words? Listen to the Lord before you
speak, and after you have heard Him, speak with confidence and concern.
Perhaps today you can identify an area of concern in your life regarding
something you need to say to someone. Pray for this situation and ask
God for the words and the confidence you need.[12]

*May your fountain be blessed, and may you rejoice
in the wife of your youth (Proverbs 5:18).*

Doug Rosenau has some words of wisdom about sex. Consider his thoughts:

Fun sex depends on a husband and wife who have learned to love themselves. This means you take care of your health and exercise your body to keep it in shape. You should also enjoy and accept the body God gave you. Self-acceptance, self-esteem, and a good body image are healthy parts of sexiness and Christian self-love...

Psychological research has shown us that the people and things we are more familiar with, we tend to like more...As you get more comfortable with seeing your body and allowing it to be in your thoughts without negative criticism, you will start to like it more.

An important part of love is respecting and unconditionally accepting your mate. If you want to find and focus on flaws, you will put a damper on your partner's sexiness and the whole love-making process. First Corinthians tells us that true love protects, forgets, and doesn't keep a record of wrong (13:4-7). Allowing your mind to become preoccupied with the size of body parts or age is very destructive.

You reap the benefit (or the destructiveness if you stay obsessive) of nurturing and helping your love revel in sexual appeal. Every time you affirm some particular aspect of masculinity or femininity that you admire and enjoy, you lovingly increase your mate's sex appeal. It is such a growth-producing process when you are unconditionally committed to accepting your own sexiness and affirming the sexiness of your partner. It creates the environment for a comfortable, safe, sexual greenhouse in which playfulness and risk-taking blossom. Unconditional love and acceptance and affirmation set the temperature for some fantastic sex.[13]

Hear my prayer, O LORD! (Psalm 102:1).

God, You made everything. It was Your creative power that created this earth. When You first created light You looked on the first morning and saw it was good. It is still good, and I thank You for it. I praise You for another day to experience You. I praise You for the life within me.

I praise You for the world around me. Help me to discover the unseen good that I overlook.

I praise You for the clouds and sky which I tend to ignore by walking through life so fast with my head down.

I praise You for the work You've given me and for being able to work. I praise You for my friends.

I praise You for the things I enjoy. Help me to keep them in perspective and to never compete with You.

There are others who have difficulty praising You or even believing in You because of the pain and turmoil of their lives. Make me sensitive to them and to those in whom the pulse of life is weakening; to those who have to lie in bed all day; to those who cannot see the light of day because of blindness; to those who are overworked and cannot experience the pleasure of play; to those who have no job and are discouraged; to those who are deep in grief. Empower me to help as best I can.

Lord, don't let anything that I do darken my life and keep me from experiencing You. May the Holy Spirit rule my heart and life.

In Jesus' name.
Amen.[14]

*So overflowing is his kindness toward us that he took
away all our sins through the blood of his Son, by
whom we are saved (Ephesians 1:7 TLB).*

*His presence within us is God's guarantee that he really
will give us all that he promised; and the Spirit's seal upon
us means that God has already purchased us and that he
guarantees to bring us to himself. This is just one more
reason for us to praise our glorious God (1:14 TLB).*

Do you feel forgiven? Are you experiencing the benefits of being forgiven? Remember the death of Jesus was the *complete* payment for everything you've done wrong. The penalty for our sins had to be paid. God spared nothing to secure for you an eternal identity in Christ. He willingly gave His cherished Son in order to give you the right to be with Him forever. Not only that, you are also safe in His care for eternity!

Perhaps the best way to explain the security we enjoy is to describe how I feel when I go to my bank and ask to see my safety deposit box. I have to sign in to prove my ownership, have my signature evaluated, and produce the proper key. Only then will the attendant allow me into the vault, take out the bank's key, and use both our keys to let me access my box. When I leave, my box is locked up and the outer doors of the safe are locked as well. I leave feeling comfortable and confident that my valuables are protected. My sense of security for what's in my box is based on human standards and structures. And even the most securely guarded banks and locked vaults can be robbed.

You and I have been *sealed* by the Holy Spirit! We are totally secure in Jesus Christ. We have been purchased by His blood. We don't have to be concerned about being tossed out, kicked out, or rejected. We are permanently sealed as God's possessions.

Only be careful, and watch yourselves closely so that
you do not forget the things your eyes have seen or let
them slip from your heart (Deuteronomy 4:9).

"Don't forget!" You've probably heard those words time and time again as a child. But sometimes even as adults we hear these words. Now they come from our spouses, children, and employers. Is it easy for you to remember? It should be. As a man you are called "the remembering one." Genesis 1:27 says we were made in God's image. The Hebrew word for "man" is *zakar* which means "the remembering one."

Perhaps it means that we were created to recall the past, to benefit from what we have experienced, and then pass the knowledge on so other people can profit as well. Are there events in your life that are significant, and yet very few people, if any, know about them? Perhaps by sharing them, your family members and others will have a more complete picture of who you are.

Have you ever stopped to recall the spiritual events or milestones in your life that have shaped you? Or are the memories dim and faded?

When you're having a difficult time, it helps to remember how God has worked in the past so you can anticipate how He will work with you in the future. Take some time to reflect on your memories today. What memories can help where you are now? What passages from God's Word were you more familiar with back then than you are today?

You can't recreate the past or its experiences, but you can benefit from them and move to a stronger, fresh relationship with the Lord. Jesus wants you to remember who He is, what He has done for you, and what He will do for you! These remembrances make the present livable.[15]

For you must worship no other gods, but only Jehovah, for he is a God who claims absolute loyalty and exclusive devotion (Exodus 34:14 TLB).

We all experience jealousy at times. That we can accept. But how can God be jealous? That's a human malady, isn't it? It sounds contradictory for God to be jealous. We see it as something negative because envy is part of it in the human experience. But there can be a positive jealousy. The Hebrew word for *jealousy* can also be translated as *zealous*. This means "a strong emotion expressing desire or possession of an object."

Why is God jealous? How could He be jealous? Well, He's jealous for His name. He wants to be the One we worship, and He deserves it. The Israelites got into deep trouble because they made idols and worshiped them: "They angered him with their high places; they aroused his jealousy with their idols" (Psalm 78:58). That wasn't a very bright move on their part! They ended up going to Babylon as indentured guests of the Babylonians. "Then at last my fury against you will die away; my jealousy against you will end, and I will be quiet and not be angry with you anymore" (Ezekiel 16:42 TLB).

God is jealous for His people. He wants our complete, not our half-hearted, devotion. "What? Are you tempting the Lord to be angry with you? Are you stronger than he is?" (1 Corinthians 10:22 TLB).

Basically, God is jealous when we are not giving Him what is His to begin with—our complete attention, devotion, and worship. We belong to Him. But let's turn this around. Are you jealous for Him? When you hear His name taken in vain and misused, how do you respond? When you see His teachings violated, how do you feel? Perhaps you've never considered this before. This may be a good time to do so.[16]

O Lord, you have examined my heart and know
everything about me (Psalm 139:1 TLB).

What comes into your mind when you think of God? Can you describe or list His qualities or characteristics? Can you describe Him for someone else? Hard questions? Perhaps, but important ones. What comes into your mind when you think about God could be the most important thing about you. It will affect your worship *and* your daily living. That's why we need to take a close look at God's Word to see who God is.

If you would like to amaze people at work, church, or anywhere else for that matter, walk into a room and announce: "Let me tell you something about God that you may already know or perhaps you don't. God doesn't ever learn a thing. He knows all things. He doesn't have to go around spying on people to discover what's going on. He already knows. Remember when you were in school and struggled in some class trying to learn something? Well, God cannot learn and has never learned. He doesn't need to. He knows everything instantly. He knows everything equally well. He never wonders about anything, never discovers anything, and is never amazed by anything. He also knows all the possibilities that can happen."[17]

I can't guarantee or predict how others will respond to your statement. But it's a summation of the fact that God is all-knowing (omniscient). What's the significance of it to you and me? It's a comfort. He knows all of our troubles and struggles. And He knows everyone's heart, everyone's thoughts. He knows everything about you…and still loves you and me and the whole world. That too is amazing.[18]

*I can never be lost to your Spirit! I can never get
away from my God! (Psalm 139:7 TLB).*

*Can anyone hide from me? Am I not everywhere in
all of heaven and earth? (Jeremiah 23:24).*

We attend church for the purpose of worshiping God. Why? Is that where He is? You've probably been in a service or a meeting and the person praying says, "Oh God, as we come into Your presence…" Is that right? Not really. God is everywhere, not just in a building or outside that building. He is in all places. He is at the same time near as well as far off. There isn't any place that anyone can get away from him.[19]

We live in a world where people disappear. Spouses leave a marriage never to be seen again. Children are kidnapped and disappear forever. Some people change their names and start new lives. Our government provides a witness protection program and gives those who testify against powerful crime figures new identities. It's as though the earth just swallowed them up. But no one disappears from God.

David talked about this in Psalm 139. He knew he couldn't hide from God. He could go to heaven or Sheol, or he could take wings and fly, or go to the depth of the sea, but God would be there. It's hard to grasp these thoughts about God. Perhaps it's good that we find the idea overwhelming. It may help us have more respect, more reverence, and more awe.[20] The knowledge that God is everywhere is a comfort. Jesus taught this to bring encouragement to His disciples: "Surely I am with you always, to the very end of the age" (Matthew 28:20). So when you're at work or at home or playing golf, serving God and living for Him, remember He is *always* with you. He supports and loves you.

Ah, Sovereign Lord, you have made the heavens and
the earth by your great power and outstretched arm.
Nothing is too hard for you (Jeremiah 32:17).

Power. We're enthralled by it. We like to feel powerful. We enjoy sitting in the cab of a truck with hundreds of horsepower revving up under that hood and just waiting to be unleashed. And if you've tied into a 500-pound tuna while deep-sea fishing, you know about power.

There's someone who is so all-powerful that we can't even imagine it—God. The word *almighty* helps us understand His power. Do you realize that when you begin a prayer with "Almighty God," in a sense you're saying "All-powerful God"? God can do whatever He pleases (Psalm 115:3). Nothing can hinder Him. What He is going to do, He will do.

Remember what He has already done! He made a ninety-nine-year-old man a father (Genesis 17:1-6). Jesus said He could appeal to His Father to send 72,000 angels to rescue Him. He didn't do that, you know, but that's something He could have done. Perhaps the greatest display of God's power was the resurrection of His Son Jesus. That has implications for you.

Do you realize there *are* some things God cannot or will not do? There are. Do you know what He can't do? Think about it for a minute. God can't associate with sin. That's clear (see Habakkuk 1:13). God can't go back on His Word (see 2 Timothy 2:13). God can't lie (see Hebrews 6:18).

Remember, there's nothing—absolutely *nothing*—too difficult for your God![21]

*God "will give to each person according to
what he has done" (Romans 2:6).*

Do you ever get disgusted with our justice system? There are times when the innocent seem to get punished and the guilty are set free. Open-and-shut cases against the criminal element are tossed out of court on minor technicalities, and the criminals are free to prey on society again. Sometimes a first-time offender for a minor crime gets a longer sentence than a hard-case repeat crook. Is there any justice anymore?

But wait. There is still some justice out there—God. He is the only One who is just in everything He does. God is correct, consistent, and fair. When He punishes, it's not too much or too little. It's just right.

There are times when we don't see the justice of God. We wonder where He is and why He's silent. We think He ought to be intervening. In those times, we need to remember that His timing is not ours and that we don't see the whole picture. Some ask, "How is God just?" Well, God rewards those who love Him over the generations. They do what He's asked. Paul looked to the "righteous Judge" to reward him for having fought the good fight (2 Timothy 4:7-8). God does punish those who break His laws (Romans 2:9). In Revelation 16, it states He will judge this world at the end of the age.

God is just, and He's also good. He can look at the lawbreaker and see his sin, but when the person confesses his sin and acknowledges Jesus as Lord and Savior, that individual will experience God's forgiveness. There is no more payment required for what he did. Someone else has already paid the price—Jesus. This puts a new word alongside justice. It's called *grace*.

[The Lord] said to me, "My grace is sufficient for you, for my power is made perfect in weakness." Therefore I will boast all the more gladly about my weaknesses, so that Christ's power may rest on me (2 Corinthians 12:9).

What's your handicap? If you're a golfer you understand. In some sports, a handicap means a weight or impediment put on an outstanding athlete. It's used to balance the odds. Winning horses are weighted down to even the other horses' chances of winning. In golf, a high-scoring player has a high handicap while a low-scoring player has a low one.

So, back to the question. What's your handicap? "I'm not a golfer," you say, "and I don't play the horses, so I'm off the hook." Not so. Every one of us is handicapped. There's something in our lives or background that limits us in some way or another. With some people it's visible and obvious. In others, it's hidden. If you don't see yourself as handicapped in any way right now, consider the words of Pastor R. Scott Sullender:

> Sooner or later each of us will become handicapped in one way or another. Sooner or later each of us will have to deal with one or several major losses in our health. Then we will travel down the same path that the handicapped person currently walks. Then we will know their pain, frustration and sufferings. Perhaps if we could learn from them now, whatever our age, we would be better prepared for our own future.[22]

That puts a different light on your life, doesn't it? Someday we will all be crippled and broken. Perhaps it reminds you of something someone did many years ago. Christ's body was broken, bruised, and battered for us. Our brokenness will come from age; His was a choice. And He made it out of love. Keep that in mind.

You were dead in your transgressions and sins, in which you used to live when you followed the ways of this world and of the ruler of the kingdom of the air, the spirit who is now at work in those who are disobedient. All of us also lived among them at one time, gratifying the cravings of our sinful nature and following its desires and thoughts (Ephesians 2:1-3).

Paul is talking about the living dead. A contradiction? Not at all. Many people are spiritually dead even though they're walking around. You've heard the expression, "Man, that's living!" But when do we use that phrase? Usually when we see a pretentious home, a couple lounging on a yacht, or someone having Maine lobster and caviar for dinner.

The extreme of this style of living is told in a story about two gravediggers who had to dig a grave fifteen feet long and eight feet wide. They didn't know why and complained constantly. When it was done, a crane rolled up followed by a trailer carrying a gold-plated Rolls Royce. The funeral director arrived in a hearse, directed the removal of a casket, and placed it by the Rolls Royce. Opening the door of the car and the casket, he lifted the body out, placed it in the car behind the steering wheel, put the hands on the wheel, molded the face into a smile, and opened the corpse's eyes. The crane swung around, a worker hooked a cable to the car, and it was lifted, swung around, and lowered into the grave. One gravedigger turned to the other and said, "Man, that's living!"

Isn't it interesting what we think the good life is all about? There is a better life—a life that is *really* living. The definition is found in Ephesians: "Because of his great love for us, God, who is rich in mercy, made us alive with Christ even when we were dead in transgressions—it is by grace that you have been saved" (Ephesians 2:4-5).[23]

*How good and pleasant it is when brothers
live together in unity! (Psalm 133:1).*

I magine you are college-age and not yet married. You're with a group of students at a meeting and everyone is very involved. But why not! The subject is marriage and how to find the right mate. The speaker asks each person to take several minutes to write down all of the qualities and characteristics of the person they would like to marry. They do so, and a number are asked to share their lists with the group.

After a while the speaker makes a simple comment and asks a question: "You've all had the opportunity to describe the person you would like to marry. Let's say you meet this person. What would there be *about you* that would cause this person to fell in love with you?" That's a thought-stopper! Most people are looking for the right one instead of working on *becoming* the right person.

This question carries over into marriage as well. What about you keeps your wife in love with you? We often assume our partners are going to stay in love with us, so we coast along. Keep in mind it's in the process of being a certain person and doing things for your partner that she fell in love with you. It's in the very process of being a certain person and doing things for your partner that she'll stay in love with you!

Once you marry you don't stop being who you were or let up on the attentive responses to your wife. Continue to develop your character qualities and your loving behaviors toward her. That is—if you want her to stay in love with you!

Brothers, I do not consider myself yet to have taken hold
of [that for which Christ Jesus took hold of me]. But
one thing I do: Forgetting what is behind and straining
toward what is ahead, I press on (Philippians 3:13).

Some men are content with a few things in life. Some men want it all. Everything! Some have a hard time removing the clutter from their lives even though it hurts them. They can't seem to eliminate what they don't need. They're like the Englishman who was with a group of climbers preparing to tackle Mont Blanc in the French Alps. The night before the climb the guide met with the group and gave them some simple instructions. He told them it would be a hard climb; if they wanted to get to the top, they should bring only what was necessary.

In the morning the Englishman showed up with the necessary gear, plus much more. His gear included a heavy blanket, cheese, a bottle of wine, several bars of chocolate, and two cameras with multiple lenses. The guide took one look and said, "You'll never make it with all that stuff."

The Englishman was a bit stubborn and went ahead of the group to prove it could be done. The rest of the group followed the guide's instructions. As they climbed they saw articles scattered along the way—a blanket, bottle of wine, cheese, etc. Eventually, when they reached the top, they found the Englishman, tired but wiser. He shook his head and said, "It would have been easier if…"

Your life might be easier if you cleaned house. [24]

*We were under great pressure, far beyond our ability to
endure, so that we despaired even of life. Indeed, in our hearts
we felt the sentence of death. But this happened that we might
not rely on ourselves but on God (2 Corinthians 1:8-9).*

There are days when you feel like throwing in the towel. You're wiped out, exhausted, crushed, and devastated. Even Paul felt this way. He said there was a time when there was so much opposition that he was worn out. Not just worn out—he was so tired of what had gone on that he wished he were dead. Perhaps you've felt that kind of weariness. It could be the opposition is coming from people at work, at church, or even in your own family. When you have to face opposition from others over a period of time, your defenses and resolve slowly erode until nothing is left to face the onslaught.

Paul wasn't the only one to face this. David's son Absalom "stole the hearts of the men of Israel" (2 Samuel 15:6) and created conditions so bad that David was forced to leave his home, his throne, and Jerusalem, the city he built. Then a distant relative of Saul came by and attacked, cursed, and stoned David. That was rubbing salt in his wound. David was bone weary when they arrived at their destination: "The king and all the people with him arrived at their destination [Jordan] exhausted" (2 Samuel 16:14).

Opposition exhausts. At times like this, I suggest practicing the three Rs:

Remember. You're not alone; there is One who is with you.

Rest. There is no substitute for allowing your body and mind to heal. Look to the One who gives you rest.

Resolve. When your strength is back, try to resolve the differences between you and your opponent. Your adversary may not change, but at least you went the second mile.

*Be strong and very courageous. Be careful to obey all the law my
servant Moses gave you; do not turn from it to the right or to the
left, that you may be successful wherever you go (Joshua 1:7).*

Forty years of dreaming. That's probably how long Joshua dreamed about going into the Promised Land. Then one day God said:

> You and all these people, get ready to cross the Jordan River into the land I am about to give to them—to the Israelites. I will give you every place you set your foot, as I promised Moses…No one will be able to stand up against you all the days of your life. As I was with Moses, so I will be with you; I will never leave you nor forsake you. Be strong and courageous, because you will lead these people to inherit the land I swore to their forefathers to give them. Be strong and very courageous (Joshua 1:2-3,5-7).

And move into the land Joshua did. But there were obstacles. He was older, the report by the spies was negative, the land was filled with giants. They had to work the land and fight the enemies, as well.

Some days you may feel like Joshua. You hit one obstacle after another. But that's life, and life isn't easy. But the more we believe it should be easy, the more likely we are to give up when it gets tough. Turning back from difficulty wasn't in Joshua's makeup, and it doesn't have to be in yours either. Sure, you may have to back up and regroup, but that's all right. There is something you can do to help you press on. It's in God's instructions to Joshua: "Do not let this Book of the Law depart from your mouth; meditate on it day and night, so that you may be careful to do everything written in it. Then you will be prosperous and successful" (Joshua 1:8).

*God is our refuge and strength, an ever-present help in
trouble...We will not fear, though the earth give way and the
mountains fall into the heart of the sea...The LORD Almighty
is with us; the God of Jacob is our fortress (Psalm 46:1-2,7).*

Let's consider some of Scripture's guidelines by asking three important questions.

When should we pray? "Pray continually" (1 Thessalonians 5:17). We're invited to talk to God anytime, anywhere, about anything. He is available always. In every decision, we need to include Him. Every move we make is to be with His guidance. We can pray during a meeting, while driving, and when we wake in the night. "I have set the LORD always before me. Because he is at my right hand, I shall not be shaken" (Psalm 16:8).

Where should we pray? "I want men everywhere to lift up holy hands in prayer, without anger or disputing" (1 Timothy 2:8). Every experience we are involved in is an invitation to pray. Psalm 139:7-8 describes David's experience of everywhere: "Where can I go from your Spirit? Where can I flee from your presence? If I go up to the heavens, you are there; if I make my bed in the depths, you are there." God is inescapable. Don't limit Him. It can't be done. Take the initiative. Pray all the time and everywhere!

What should we pray about? "Rejoice in the Lord always...The Lord is near. Do not be anxious about anything, but in everything, by prayer and petition, with thanksgiving, present your requests to God. And the peace of God, which transcends all understanding, will guard your hearts and your minds in Christ Jesus" (Philippians 4:4-7). You may find some things difficult to pray about—that's even more reason to talk to God!

Why not make a note to remind yourself how to pray, using the "when? where? and what? questions." This could change your life![25]

Do not be anxious about anything, but in everything,
by prayer and petition, with thanksgiving, present
your requests to God (Philippians 4:6).

Worry is a result of the fall of mankind. It distorts our minds—one of God's gifts to us. Scripture has much to say about the results of worry and the benefits of a calm mind:

I heard and my heart pounded, my lips quivered at the sound; decay crept into my bones, and my legs trembled (Habakkuk 3:16).

Anxiety in a man's heart weighs it down (Proverbs 12:25 AMP).

A calm and undisturbed mind and heart are the life and health of the body (14:30 AMP).

A happy heart makes the face cheerful, but heartache crushes the spirit (15:13 NIV).

Worrying intensely about the possibility of an event happening doesn't prevent it from happening—and it might actually help bring it about! People who worry about having an accident while driving are accident prone. They are more likely to have accidents than others because they constantly visualize it. Worrying about a problem or potentially dangerous situation usually exaggerates the chances of it occurring. Why? The energy used in worrying isn't directed toward solving the problem. A classic example is the person who worries about getting an ulcer—and soon is rewarded for his efforts.

If you focus on yourself as a failure or as failing, you will likely follow that example in your performance. You condition yourself with your negative thinking. But if you spend time and energy planning how to *overcome* those anticipated mistakes and visualize yourself being successful, your performance will probably be far better. Proverbs 23:7 says, "As [a person] thinks in his heart, so is he." It doesn't pay to worry.

*Do not conform any longer to the pattern of this world, but
be transformed by the renewing of your mind. Then you
will be able to test and approve what God's will is—his
good, pleasing and perfect will (Romans 12:2).*

D o you want to be your own man? Sure! But instead of creating who
we want to be, often we allow ourselves to be shaped and conformed by society, which says we are:

- to *be* something
- to *own* something
- to *do* something
- to *achieve* something
- to *prove* something

All of these imply we have to be successful to be acceptable. Who sets
the criteria for success? We can follow society's standards or we can follow God's. Society says take more, make more, spend more, and above
all get more! Sometimes we equate God's blessings with affluence. Is driving a BMW a sign of blessing or of caving in to society's standard of success? It's something to consider.

It's easy to get caught up in the wants and shoulds. And sometimes it's
the pressure of another family member that pushes us. Go back to those
five statements society defines as success and ask these questions: What
do I want to be? What do I want to do? What do I want to own? What
do I want to achieve? What do I want to prove?

You don't have to do anything, prove anything, own anything, or
achieve anything. Jesus Christ has done all of this for you! So relax. Jesus
asks you to follow Him and let Him live life for you. Didn't He say,
"Seek first [your heavenly Father's] kingdom and his righteousness, and
all these things will be given to you as well" (Matthew 6:33)?[1]

*The Lord is compassionate and gracious, slow to anger,
abounding in love…He does not treat us as our sins deserve
or repay us according to our iniquities (Psalm 103:8,10).*

How does God see our failures? They don't ever surprise Him. He knows we will fail, and He loves us anyway. That's good news in this competitive world! When we fail, we may be tempted to blame someone or something, but let's leave God out of the loop. He doesn't cause our failures; He allows them to occur. Some failures involve sin; some don't. Regardless, God promised to never leave us, forsake us, or turn His back on us:

> The Lord is close to the brokenhearted and saves those who are crushed in spirit (Psalm 34:18).

> The Lord upholds all those who fall and lifts up all who are bowed down (145:14).

Did God dump Adam and Eve after their disobedience that affected the entire human race? No. Did He turn His back on Moses after he murdered the Egyptian? No. Did God reject David after his adultery and scheme to kill his lover's husband? No. God is the God of second chances…and third and fourth…He fully understands what we can learn from our failures. He wants us to know that in each failure lies a seed of growth.

The great news is that He sees beyond our failures.[2] We say, "Look how I've blown it. I can never be used by God again." God says, "You've blown it. Let's discover what you can learn and then put it to use for My kingdom." We look at our lives through a microscope. God looks at us with binoculars and says, "I wish you could see what I see for you in the future." If that doesn't give you hope, nothing will!

The fruit of the Spirit is love, joy, peace, patience, kindness, goodness, faithfulness, gentleness and self-control (Galatians 5:22-23).

Most skills are built on proper technique. Take baseball, for example. The players spend hours mastering their technique in hitting the ball. They work on getting the bat off their shoulders at the proper time, keeping their heads down, stepping into the ball, using the strength of their legs, keeping their swings level. Hours go into mastering form. But this won't make any difference in the score of the game or the amount of the player's salary unless he hits the ball consistently. Technique is one thing; results are another.

Theology is the same way. You may know some guy whose theology is exacting and correct. They can quote chapter and verse for their beliefs as well as the doctrines of John Calvin and Martin Luther. But unless this theology is translated into something else, it's not worth much. What you and I believe is important, but not as much as who we are as people and the way we behave.

You can have correct theology, but no joy.

You can have correct theology, but no peace.

You can have correct theology, but have no self-control.

If that's the case, what good is your theology? It's not what's in your head that counts—it's what's in your heart and what you actually do. Correct theology by itself won't draw others to the Lord, but the fruit of the Spirit will. What others see in you has more impact than what you tell them you believe.

In baseball it's easy to have a good technique and still strike out. It's the same with faith. If you're striking out, it's time for a change, isn't it?[3]

One day the angels came to present themselves before the
LORD, and Satan also came with them (Job 1:6).

S atan. What do you think when his name is mentioned? Is Satan real?
Do you have an image of him in your mind? Do you believe he exists?
I hope so. He would love for you not to believe he exists. That would give
him easier access to your life.

We need to be aware of the devil's reality and what he does. He was
created as one of the angelic beings. He was one of God's angels, but there
was a problem. He fell with others into a state of rebellion. Now, keep in
mind he is just that—a fallen angel. He is *not equal* to God. He doesn't
have the power or presence of God. And he doesn't live in hell. That's an
idea people have created. At the last judgment he and all the wicked will
be sent there. Where does he live now? Right here on earth. In the book
of Job, when God asks Satan where he has been, Satan says he was roaming the earth. He still is. He's got work to do. He's got a job to do…and
it's against us.

Do you know what the word *Satan* literally means? "Slanderer" or
"accuser." His job is to accuse us against God. He tempts us to sin, but his
main job is to accuse us. Take a look at Job, chapters 1 and 2. Satan is hard
at work slandering Job. He likewise loves to give us believers a bad name,
and not just before God, but before others on earth as well.

Then the devil goes a step further. He tries to get you to accuse yourself.
He throws doubt in your mind and may even sow doubts about your salvation. Watch out for him! What can you do about it? Fill your life with
the presence of God. Saturate your mind with the teachings of Scripture.
Memorize God's Word. When you have doubts, don't feed on them. Ask
some questions and get some answers…from the Source—God!

*Love bears up under anything and everything that comes, is
ever ready to believe the best of every person, its hopes are
fadeless under all circumstances (1 Corinthians 13:7 AMP).*

If married, do you believe nothing can improve your marriage? If so,
test this belief. Look your relationship and clarify the problems. Select
one that appears easy to change and work on it. One husband wanted to
have discussions with his wife without defensive arguments. He learned
how to stay out of the arguments and eliminate defensiveness:

- He chose to believe his wife wasn't out to get him or simply to
  argue with him out of spite. She might have some good ideas.

- He committed to not interrupting, arguing, debating, or
  walking out on her.

- He would respond to what she said with such statements as:
  "That's interesting," "I hadn't considered that," "Tell me more,"
  and "I'd like to think about that."

- He chose to think, *If this doesn't work the first time, I'll try it at
  least five times.*

- He determined to thank her for each discussion, and when
  her response was even 5 percent less defensive, to compliment
  her for the way she responded.

Five weeks later he said, "The fourth discussion was totally different…
My belief that nothing can improve our relationship is destroyed. There's
a bit of hope now."

To counter negative beliefs, read Scriptures that are future-oriented
and positive: "'I know the plans that I have for you,' declares the LORD,
'plans for welfare and not for calamity to give you a future and a hope.'"
(Jeremiah 29:11 NASB). So what would you like to change in your marriage? The first step may be to change your beliefs.[4]

*Make every effort to add to your faith goodness; and to goodness,
knowledge; and to knowledge, self-control; and to self-control,
perseverance; and to perseverance, godliness; and to godliness,
brotherly kindness; and to brotherly kindness, love (2 Peter 1:5-7).*

You don't have much time left. In fact, it has to happen immediately. If you don't act now, the opportunity is lost…gone forever. And you could end up feeling regret because you missed it. What am I talking about? The opportunity on a split-second's notice to be kind to someone. When you see an opening unfold before you, there may be no time to debate what to do. You need to act or the window could be shut forever.

Consider the TV filmmaker who has to shoot a scene set up by his producer. It's a forty-story building he found that was going to be demolished. What a chance! The explosion expert has planted the material so the building will implode (instead of explode, hopefully). It will take perhaps ten seconds. The filmmaker takes hours to set up several cameras and consider the lighting. Why? He's got *one chance* to capture the collapse. After that, it's gone. There's no second chance. Only possible regrets. Just like acts of kindness.[5]

A woman drops her groceries coming out of the store and they scatter. It's a chance to show kindness. The homeless vet is asking for a meal. Sure, you could take the position that he shouldn't be smoking, or he could get a job if he tried, or you'll encourage his begging behavior if you help. Do you feed him? I think Jesus would have. I encourage you to listen to people, give them words of encouragement, even write someone a thank-you note. Kindness counts.

*I looked for a man among them who would build up the wall
and stand before me in the gap on behalf of the land so I would
not have to destroy it, but I found none (Ezekiel 22:30).*

The book *Real Men Don't Eat Quiche* sold almost a million copies within a few days of its release. It was a spoof rather than a serious book, but the title raises a unique question: What is a real man?

What would God see as a real man? Looking at us (me included), the word *macho* wouldn't be used. Physical strength, boasting, domination, strutting, chasing, and conquering one woman after another are not on God's list of qualities for a man. God is looking for men who are authentic and genuine. They have the inner strength to stand alone when they need to. They know who they are. Their security doesn't come from conquests or whiskey, but from inner qualities. They are secure because they know who they belong to and who they reflect—God. They're strong enough to control or dominate others, but their strength is displayed in choosing not to. They don't try to prove themselves to the world. They're capable of doing things contrary to the way culture and society dictate.

Real men are willing to learn. They can admit "I'm wrong" or "I don't know how, but I'm willing to learn." They know what humility is too. There are a lot of these men around. We don't hear about them in the press or on TV, but they are noticed by those who know them—and especially by God![6]

The LORD God said, "It is not good for the man to be alone.
I will make a helper suitable for him" (Genesis 2:18).

David, an honest man, shared it like it was. In Psalm 142 he really cut loose. He says to God: "I cry," "I pour out my complaint," "my spirit grows faint," "no one is concerned for me" (verses 1-4). Cries of pain; cries of loneliness. Sometimes when a man feels lonely, he feels ashamed. We take loneliness as a sign of failure and inadequacy. Webster's Ninth Collegiate Dictionary defines *loneliness* as "a sadness from being alone…producing a feeling of bleakness or desolation."[7] When you're lonely you feel like no one is there for you and no one cares.

God did not create us to live in isolation. He created us for relationships and fellowship. Sometimes when we feel lonely we expect other people to know this and reach out to us. They ought to be able to read our minds and know our situation, we think. "But," you say, "what's so bad about being lonely? I like my solitude!" Loneliness and solitude are not the same. Solitude can give us rest, strength, and provide a sense of renewal. It builds and refreshes. Loneliness leads to stagnation and alienation. Have there been times in your life when you've been lonely? Some people just resign themselves to being lonely. That won't work. Some people wait for others to rescue them. That won't work either. Some people face their loneliness and say, "I don't have to be lonely. I'm going to reach out to God and other people." That works.

God can use your loneliness to draw you into a deeper relationship with Him and other people. Use your loneliness as a motivational tool to do something new with your life. If loneliness hurts, why stay in pain? There's a better way to live. It's your choice.

All glory to him who alone is God, who saves us
through Jesus Christ our Lord (Jude 24 TLB).

Have you ever seen a person walking along a congested sidewalk with his or her gaze glued to the ground? No? Look around. You'll find people like this everywhere. And if you observe them long enough, you'll wonder about them. Their behavior is kind of odd. Most of us look ahead when we walk, but not this group. Do you wonder why?

Some people are so insecure they just can't face others. Some are afraid of tripping or stumbling so they concentrate on looking toward the ground for obstacles. They want to make sure they place their feet in the right places. It seems strange, but these are the people who end up tripping or stumbling more than most people. They concentrate so much on what they don't want to do that they end up doing it.

Karl Wallenda, one of the greatest high-wire artists of all time, involved his family in his acts. They performed all over the world. In 1978 he was walking a seventy-five-foot tightrope (wire) between two structures when he lost his balance and fell to his death. Later his wife said that for the previous three months Karl had done something he had never done before. He constantly thought about falling. It's as though his entire focus was on falling rather than on walking across the wire successfully.

Have you ever found yourself concentrating on what you want to avoid rather than on what you want to accomplish? If so, watch out. The very thing you want to avoid may become a reality. There's a better direction to look to and focus on. It's Jesus Christ. Our eyes focused on Him will keep us from stumbling no matter what situation we're concerned about.

*May God himself, the God of peace, sanctify you through and
through. May your whole spirit, soul and body be kept blameless
at the coming of our Lord Jesus Christ. The one who calls
you is faithful and he will do it (1 Thessalonians 5:23-24).*

It's a nightmare. Or you hope it is. A rope is tied around each arm and each leg—four ropes—and you're being pulled in different directions. You've got so much coming at you, so much to decide, and so much to do that you feel fragmented and wrenched apart. Paul understood. He describes your situation graphically:

> When I want to do good, I don't; and when I try not to do wrong, I do it anyway. Now if I am doing what I don't want to, it is plain where the trouble is: sin still has me in its evil grasp. It seems to be a fact of life that when I want to do what is right, I inevitably do what is wrong. I love to do God's will so far as my new nature is concerned; but there is something else deep within me, in my lower nature, that is at war with my mind and wins the fight and makes me a slave to the sin that is still within me. In my mind I want to be God's willing servant, but instead I find myself still enslaved to sin. So you see how it is: my new life tells me to do right, but the old nature that is still inside me loves to sin. Oh, what a terrible predicament I'm in! Who will free me from my slavery to this deadly lower nature? Thank God! It has been done by Jesus Christ our Lord. He has set me free (Romans 7:19-25).

You can be free from this frantic state. Rest in the promise of Scripture to give you clarity of thought, vision, and direction. Jesus is at work! He can make you whole and complete. The power is yours through Him. There is wholeness in Him, as well as peace.[8]

[Heaven] will be like a man going on a journey, who called his servants and entrusted his property to them. To one he gave five talents of money, to another two talents, and to another one talent, each according to his ability. Then he went on his journey. The man who had received the five talents went at once and put the money to work and gained five more…His master [said,] "Well done, good and faithful servant! You have been faithful with a few things; I will put you in charge of many things" (Matthew 25:14-16,21).

Would people call you an ambitious person? *Ambition* is an interesting word. It comes from a Latin word that means to "go around." It's a movement around the opportunities to reach a goal. The man described in today's verses was ambitious for his master. He made a good investment on his master's behalf. You need ambition to be successful, to get ahead, to make a mark in this world. An ambitious person is someone who's on the move. He or she is not standing still.

Which direction are you moving? Is it toward God…or the opposite way? Sometimes ambition takes us in the wrong direction. Remember Paul? He very ambitiously persecuted the Christians. And God didn't put a damper on his ambition. Paul was going the wrong way, so God changed his direction. What about you? Are you making good investments for the Lord? Do you see your walk with Him and your faith growing? Are you ambitious in your work, your family, and for the kingdom of God?

You may be a mover and a shaker. If so, God can use you. He can direct you. He wants you to be ambitious for Him and make an investment for Him. What's a new way you can be ambitious for the Lord? If you want adventure in life, this is the way to get it. [9]

Where there is no revelation, the people cast off restraint;
but blessed is he who keeps the law (Proverbs 29:18).

Every now and then a swimmer steps off the shore of England and sets out for France. Can you imagine swimming the English Channel? It's difficult enough completing a few laps in a calm, heated pool, let alone fight the waves, treacherous currents, and icy water of the Channel. But many try. Some fail; some make it.

One swimmer started out and immediately ran into rough seas. Since he'd trained in the ocean, he was in peak physical condition so he continued. The next problem was the temperature—icy cold and each mile the water seemed to get colder. The rigorous training and the oil used to grease his body became a form of insulation. The swimmer's trainers were in a boat alongside, and now and then they handed over some hot soup.

Hour after hour, arm over arm, the swimmer put mile after mile behind him. Then a fog bank descended, cutting off visibility and filling the air with a chilling mist. The swimmer continued to push ahead, but the waves seemed larger and now cramps were beginning in his arms and legs. The swimmer's muscles were in agonizing pain, and with less than two miles to go he asked to be pulled from the water.

Later the swimmer was asked, "Didn't you know you were almost there?" He replied, "No, I didn't. I didn't have it clearly in mind. I lost sight of my goal. I guess I just lost sight of that other shoreline on the horizon. I didn't have a vision for it anymore."

What's the vision that keeps you going in life? Is it clear or has a fog drifted in? What are you keeping in your mind's eye? Don't let the waves of life blot out your vision or throw you off course.

His mouth is his undoing! His words
endanger him (Proverbs 18:7 TLB).

"Y ou fool!" How many times have we said this about someone or even to his or her face? We use the word, but do we know what a fool really is? Fools were in school with you. Did you recognize them? You may work with them. Can you identify them? You may even have some in your family!

Fools must be a problem. Why else would the word *fool* be used around seventy times in the book of Proverbs? There are three Hebrew words translated *fool* in the Old Testament. One of them is used almost fifty times. It means a person who is dull and obstinate, and it's a choice he has made. He is not willing to search patiently for wisdom. He feels it should be handed to him. He shares his opinions with people quite freely, but they're not worth much. "A wise man thinks ahead; a fool doesn't and even brags about it!" (Proverbs 13:16 TLB) And what he says falls flat or comes back to haunt him.

The problem is that the fool doesn't learn from his mistakes. "In the mouth of a fool a proverb becomes as useless as a paralyzed leg" (Proverbs 26:7 TLB). "A rebel will misapply an illustration so that its point will no more be felt than a thorn in the hand of a drunkard" (26:9 TLB). "A rebuke to a man of common sense is more effective than a hundred lashes on the back of a rebel" (17:10 TLB).

A fool likes the way he is. He returns again and again to his folly. Avoid this guy! "Be with wise men and become wise. Be with evil men and become evil" (Proverbs 13:20 TLB). To be blunt, a fool is a menace. He's a loose cannon. Don't waste your time with a fool. "If you are looking for advice, stay away from fools" (14:7 TLB). It's kind of sobering, isn't it? But we're not finished with the fool. There's more to come tomorrow.

Even a fool is thought to be wise when he is silent. It pays
him to keep his mouth shut (Proverbs 17:28 TLB).

Yesterday you learned about one of the words in Scripture that is translated *fool*. There are two more. The second Hebrew word is used nineteen times. It suggests "stupidity and stubbornness." This word is darker, more serious than the first. How do you identify a fool? It's easy. As today's verse suggests, as soon as he opens his mouth, he gives himself away. He quarrels. Boy, does he quarrel! He doesn't have any restraint or self-discipline. He goes for his goal, regardless. "It is an honor for a man to stay out of a fight. Only fools insist on quarreling" (Proverbs 20:3 TLB). You're in real difficulty if you're stuck with such a person at work—or anywhere else, for that matter.

The last Hebrew word translated *fool* occurs just three times. It's similar to the others except it adds the quality (if you can call it that) of being a bore. The fool's mind is closed to God as well as to reason. That doesn't leave him with much, does it?[10]

There is one characteristic to keep in mind about the fool. He hates learning, clear and simple. It's not for him. " 'You simpletons!' [Wisdom] cries. 'How long will you go on being fools? How long will you scoff at wisdom and fight the facts?' " (Proverbs 1:22 TLB). Give the fool a warning sign and it doesn't register. He won't learn from what you say or do for him. "Wisdom is a fountain of life to those possessing it, but a fool's burden is his folly" (16:22 TLB). He knows it all. He's right. Don't confuse him with the facts! "A fool thinks he needs no advice, but a wise man listens to others" (12:15 TLB). He just won't respond to reason. This makes you shudder a bit, doesn't it? But wait until tomorrow. It gets worse. The problem is his mouth!

Wisdom is the main pursuit of sensible men, but a fool's
goals are at the ends of the earth! (Proverbs 17:24 TLB).

For any family or organization to ran smoothly, you've got to have good, healthy communication. That involves controlling two things: your tongue and your temper. James talks about the problem graphically: "No human being can tame the tongue. It is always ready to pour out its deadly poison. Sometimes it praises our heavenly Father, and sometimes it breaks out into curses against men who are made like God. And so blessing and cursing come pouring out of the same mouth" (James 3:8-10).

The fool knows no limits. He violates boundaries. Self-control is a dirty word to him. "A rebel shouts in anger; a wise man holds his temper in and cools it" (Proverbs 29:11 TLB). What a fool says weighs heavy on those around him: "A rebel's frustrations are heavier than sand and rocks" (27:3 TLB). This person is an out-and-out troublemaker. He loves to quarrel. "To quarrel with a neighbor is foolish; a man with good sense holds his tongue" (11:12). He expresses everything without regard to the impact it may have on others. Some people know when to speak and when to shut up. The fool? Forget it. It never crosses his mind to be quiet and gain from it. "A wise man doesn't display his knowledge, but a fool displays his foolishness" (12:23).

The fool is a classic gossip. He loves to talk about others, whether the information is true or not. He's got an opinion for anything and everything. He's a self-proclaimed expert! "The wise man is glad to be instructed, but a self-sufficient fool falls flat on his face" (Proverbs 10:8 TLB). "To hide hatred is to be a liar; to slander is to be a fool" (10:18 TLB). "His mouth is his undoing! His words endanger him" (18:7 TLB).

What do you do with a fool? What can you do? Tomorrow, it will all come together.

God doesn't listen to the prayers of those who
flout the law (Proverbs 28:9 TLB).

What can you do with someone who's a fool? Proverbs has some guidelines:

- *If you talk with a fool, be careful and firm.* "When arguing with a rebel, don't use foolish arguments as he does, or you will become as foolish as he is! Prick his conceit with silly replies!" (26:4-5 TLB).

- *Don't bother giving a fool responsibilities.* It won't work. "To trust a rebel to convey a message is as foolish as cutting off your feet and drinking poison!" (26:6 TLB).

- *It's useless to spend your time trying to educate a fool.* "In the mouth of a fool a proverb becomes as useless as a paralyzed leg" (26:7 TLB). He doesn't want to learn.

- *Don't honor the fool.* I don't know why anyone would want to, but it does happen. "Honoring a rebel will backfire like a stone tied to a slingshot!" (26:8 TLB).

- *Don't give work to a fool.* "A rebel will misapply an illustration so that its point will no more be felt than a thorn in the hand of a drunkard. The master may get better work from an untrained apprentice than from a skilled rebel!" (26:9-10 TLB).

The last two guidelines may seem harsh and unforgiving, but they are necessary.

- *Don't expect a fool to change.* His character is set.

- *Stay away from a fool because you might be influenced by him.* "Be with wise men and become wise. Be with evil men and become evil" (13:20 TLB).[11]

*A wise man's heart guides his mouth, and his lips
promote instruction (Proverbs 16:23).*

Many men die of heart trouble. Some die of troubled hearts. "Troubled heart" won't be listed on a death certificate, but it ought to be. Has a friend said, "You look like your heart is troubled"? This kind of pain usually shows in your face and body language. What are the symptoms of a troubled heart? Anxiety—that sense of tension and feeling wired. It's often brought on by worry, and it does a real number on us. "An anxious heart weighs a man down, but a kind word cheers him up" (Proverbs 12:25). You feel as though a hundred-pound weight is pressing on your heart…and it's not indigestion.

And then there's depression, the feeling that hope has disappeared and everything is seen through a veil of gloom. Solomon talked about a "sorrowful" heart as well. "Even in laughter the heart may ache, and joy may end in grief" (Proverbs 14:13).

Or maybe the troubled heart belongs to a friend, spouse, fellow worker, or employee. They may smile and laugh, but on the inside they are anxious or depressed. They might need your permission to talk about what's troubling them. They may need you to draw it out of them: "The purposes of a man's heart are deep waters, but a man of understanding draws them out" (Proverbs 20:5). Help them talk. Listen to what they say without commenting. As it says in James, "Be quick to hear [a ready listener]" (James 1:19 AMP).

Look back at the verse for today. The next verse gives you additional help in ministering to others. "Pleasant words are a honeycomb, sweet to the soul and healing to the bones" (Proverbs 16:24). Troubled hearts can be healed. If yours is troubled, seek out a friend. If someone else is troubled, be a friend to him.

The prayer of a righteous man is powerful and effective (James 5:16).

Lord, I thank You for pursuing me with Your love even when I wasn't interested. Thank You that You give me thoughts to guide me and that You strengthen my will through Your Holy Spirit. Sometimes I think some things happen by chance, but I am learning that with You there is no "chance" or "accident." Thank You for the way Your Spirit leads me. Keep me from being blind to Your Spirit's direction. I pray that each day I will grow more into the man You would have me to be. I pray that I would become more like that man of men, Your Son Jesus.

But I want to pray for more than just me…

I pray for those struggling with temptations right at this moment.

I pray for strength for the people who have tasks that are overwhelming them.

I pray for wisdom for the men and women who are struggling with decisions difficult to make.

For those overcome by debt or poverty;

For those experiencing the consequences of behavior done a long time ago and forgiven by You;

For those who at an early age were abused or never had a chance to experience life;

For families torn apart by divorce or death;

For those serving You in countries I don't even know about.

I pray that the concerns of my prayers would be less focused on me and more on the others You love, as well.

In Jesus' name.

Amen.[12]

The LORD God said, "It is not good for the man to be alone.
I will make a helper suitable for him" (Genesis 2:18).

You're sitting at home with the family. It's hot, so in addition to the TV, the stereo, the computer, the fridge, the stove, and the iron, you turn on the air conditioner. All of a sudden nothing is on. You're in semi-darkness and sudden silence until everyone starts shouting, "What happened? What's wrong?" No more electricity. Why? Because the circuits were overloaded. It was too much for the circuit board to carry. It shut down. Sometimes wires actually burn up. Homes have caught on fire because of this and been destroyed…along with the people inside.

It happens at home in other ways too. Sometimes a wife collapses emotionally. Her feelings for her husband dry up. Or she doesn't get out of bed because she's immobilized by depression.

In some cases it's because of her husband. He overloaded the circuits by putting too much of a load on her. Some guys act like drill sergeants with their wives, snapping orders left and right. Some are perfectionists and everything has to be in order before they go to bed at night. And guess who has to keep everything in order? One of the most common ways to overload a wife is to come home and do nothing at all except eat, watch TV, and sleep.

That's not the way God intended it. A wife is a *helper,* created to be suitable to her husband. She is not a slave or a servant. She was never meant to carry the burden. She needs a teammate, a lover, a provider, and an encourager. Enough said?

*Just as each of us has one body with many members, and these
members do not all have the same function, so in Christ we who are
many form one body, and each member belongs to all the others. We
have different gifts, according to the grace given us (Romans 12:4-6).*

Your church is like a body, with different members taking different
roles in order for the body to function. This happens in business, it
happens in the family, and it has to happen for the body to function
smoothly. Sometimes we switch roles to help out others and let them take
a breather. Perhaps the best way to demonstrate this is to look at the behavior
of geese. These birds help each other during the rough times of life.

When they fly, they do so in a V formation. As the bird flaps its wings,
it makes flying easier for the bird behind it by creating an uplift of air.
If one gets out of line it feels the resistance of the air. Flying in this way
allows the flock to add 70 percent more distance to its range. These birds
fly hundreds and even thousands of miles this way.

Every so often the leader falls back in the V, and another bird takes
over the lead. Flying at the front takes the greatest strength; the further
back you go, the easier it is because of decreased wind resistance. The
birds keep trading off and work in harmony.

And which geese do you hear honking? It's not the leader as you might
think. It's those in the back encouraging the others who are doing the
hardest job. If one bird becomes ill and has to drop out, two others follow
it down to protect it. When it recovers, the three take off and form
their own V until they rejoin the main group.

The birds cooperate, trade off the hard jobs, encourage, support, and
protect. It's a good example for all of us in the body of Christ.

I do not consider myself yet to have taken hold of [that for which Christ Jesus took hold of me]. But one thing I do: Forgetting what is behind and straining toward what is ahead, I press on (Philippians 3:13-14).

Sometimes when you travel on an airline, you end up with excess baggage. The problem is that you're only allowed to check so many bags. You can go ahead and check in the excess, but it will cost you. Many of us are going through life with some excess baggage that's costing us. Not only that, it's robbing us…of joy, of being productive, and of achieving our potential. Excess baggage contains numerous items. Some of us carry hurts from our past—maybe an embarrassing incident in adolescence that keeps us from experiencing life to the fullest. Some of us carry baggage from giving in to peer pressure when we were younger. We liked the result and it became a way of life. We compromise our beliefs and values for the momentary approval of those around us, and soon we discover we're not really in charge of our lives because others are.

There's another item of excess baggage. A lot of men carry it, and often it's evident to others. It's a little three-letter word: *ego*. Ego is nothing more than an inflated, distorted sense of importance. I've seen it in men, and so have you. They introduce themselves by their titles, their diplomas, by what they drive, what they've accomplished. They want you to identify them by what they've accomplished or accumulated rather than let you get to know them as they are. They want others to think they're unique, special. So they tell them. But it usually has the opposite effect.

Excess baggage. Who needs it? There's a better way to live—God's way. And it's free and clear!

"For I know the plans I have for you," declares the
LORD, *"plans to prosper you and not to harm you, plans
to give you hope and a future"* (*Jeremiah 29:11*).

There are three different kinds of men in this world. Which one are you? The first are those who just *get along in life.* They have no dreams and no plans. They live for what's going on right now. Their lives are full of the same routine day after day, week after week, year after year. You've met some of them. Sometimes you go back to your high school reunion and you come away amazed at the lives of some of your classmates. Nothing has changed—and they don't seem to want their lives to change either.

Other men are *full of dreams*...but that's about all. There's no action. They talk a lot and tell everyone what they want to do. But somehow those dreams never get translated into reality. If you press them on how they're going to make their plans work, you'll hear excuses and perhaps blame.

The third group of men have *dreams with action.* They are the accomplishers. They look to God for direction, strength, insight, and wisdom. If you want some examples of men like this, look in the Bible. Solomon had a dream to build a temple for God. He built it. Nehemiah had a dream to rebuild the walls of Jerusalem. He built them and made it possible for God's people to return and live there. Joseph interpreted Pharaoh's dream. He obeyed its message, and a nation was saved from starvation.

How about you? Do you have a dream? If not, ask God for one. He wants you to do something significant with your life...for Him. And you can if you put that dream into action![13]

*In peace I will both lie down and sleep, for You, Lord, alone
make me dwell in safety and confident trust (Psalm 4:8 AMP).*

Sleepless nights—you know what they're like, especially those nights
when you go to bed extra early because you have to get up at some
unearthly hour. You lie there telling yourself to go to sleep, but sleep is
an elusive phantom. The more you try, the worse it gets. You toss and
turn, disturbing your wife and causing her to wake up in a grumpy mood.
We've all had to deal with sleeplessness at one time or another. It's no fun.

When you sleep, is it restful? Is it a time of recouping your strength?
Or do you awake just as exhausted as when you went to bed? If so, why?
Some people have difficulty sleeping because they carry their fears and
worries to bed with them. Have you experienced the peace the psalmist
is talking about in today's verse? Do you give your fears and worries to
Jesus Christ each night before you lie down? Do you say, "Lord, here are
the burdens I have carried all day long. I should have shared them with
You earlier, but I do so now. I thank You for taking my cares so they won't
plague my sleep. Thank You for the promise that You will carry my burdens. Thank You for the promises found in Your Word." If you haven't
tried this before, why not do it tonight? What do you have to lose?

Here's another suggestion. If you watch the news on TV just before
you go to bed, it may be having a negative effect on your sleep. Watching the bad news of the world isn't conducive to rest. Talking about positive things, listening to soothing music, reading a book or passages from
Scripture, or making love may make a difference in the way you sleep.
What is your bedtime routine? How can you make it better?[14]

*Many are the plans in a man's heart, but it is the
LORD's purpose that prevails (Proverbs 19:21).*

Life is full of decisions—every day. Some decisions are easy, such as
what to eat for breakfast and whether to read the sports page or the
comic page first. Other decisions are difficult—how to spend the last
$100 in your checking account or how to tell your family you're not get-
ting the promotion you thought you were. When you're a Christian
there's another element involved in decision making—knowing God's
will. Proverbs 16:1-4 seems to reflect the process many of us go through
to get to God's will for our lives:

> "To man belongs the plans of the heart…" (16:1a). Sometimes we
> decide first what we're going to do and later we say, "Oh, by the
> way, God…" We finally tell Him about it (as if He didn't know).

> "But from the LORD comes the reply of the tongue" (16:1b). God
> responds to what we decide, and sometimes in ways that surprise
> us. Has that happened to you?

> "All a man's ways seem innocent to him, but motives are weighed
> by the LORD" (16:2). Have you ever pleaded with God to let you
> have what you want? Sometimes we beg and justify why we want
> what we want. But He knows what's going on inside us.

> "Commit to the LORD whatever you do, and your plans will suc-
> ceed. The LORD works out everything for his own ends" (16:3-4).

Give the decision to God. Tell Him His decision is your decision, and
you'll do what He wants…in His timing. Then wait on Him and listen
to Him. Let His desire become your desire. Are you facing an important
decision today? Get divine guidance!

A lazy man sleeps soundly—and he goes hungry! (Proverbs 19:15 TLB).

When you hear the word *sluggard,* what image comes to mind? Maybe the same image I see—a slug. A slimy, slithery, slow slug. They don't seem to get anywhere, do much, or have much purpose in life. Sometimes we even feel like stomping on the critters. The Hebrew word for this type of person is pretty much what I described—slow, hesitant, sluggish. I'd call him lazy and in low gear. This person seems to lack a battery—or if he has one, it's dead. He needs a jump-start. He is not a self-starter. "Some men are so lazy they won't even feed themselves!" (Proverbs 19:24 TLB).

Maybe they don't know what to do or they're low on fuel! You wonder if they can even take care of the basic necessities of life. "But you—all you do is sleep. When will you wake up?" (Proverbs 6:9 TLB). Lazy people rationalize and procrastinate. "'Let me sleep a little longer!' Sure, just a little more! And as you sleep, poverty creeps upon you like a robber and destroys you; want attacks you in full armor" (6:10-11 TLB).

This kind of person seems to go downhill. He wants things but lacks the oomph to go after them. "The lazy man longs for many things, but his hands refuse to work. He is greedy to get, while the godly love to give!" (Proverbs 21:25 TLB). And he's full of irrational fears. He thinks the worst of situations. "The lazy man is full of excuses. 'I can't go to work!' he says. 'If I go outside, I might meet a lion in the street and be killed!'" (22:13 TLB). He's his own worst enemy. "A lazy fellow has trouble all through life; the good man's path is easy!" (15:19 TLB). He's got a huge ego. He's a legend in his own mind. "He sticks to his bed like a door to its hinges! He is too tired even to lift his food from his dish to his mouth! Yet in his own opinion he is smarter than seven wise men" (26:14-16 TLB).

Not a pretty picture? No, but there's hope—tomorrow.[15]

A lazy man sleeps soundly—and he goes hungry (Proverbs 19:15 TLB).

The sluggard isn't pretty, is he? Perhaps you wish he'd go off somewhere and not get in your way. But what if you work with one? What if he is one of your students in school or Sunday school? What if he works for you? "A lazy fellow is a pain to his employers—like smoke in their eyes or vinegar that sets the teeth on edge" (Proverbs 10:26 TLB).

When you give this person a job, you think he's in a race with a snail—and losing! You'd like to get a cattle prod to move him along. There is an answer to this problem: Never hire a sluggard. If one works for you, write frequent reviews of his work so if needed you can fire him without fear of being sued. A sluggard can drive you up the wall because he leans on you for everything. He wants people to bail him out. "If you won't plow in the cold, you won't eat at the harvest" (Proverbs 20:4 TLB). He is dependent.

The consequences of this lifestyle, according to Proverbs, include poverty: "'A little extra sleep, a little more slumber, a little folding of the hands to rest' means that poverty will break in upon you suddenly like a robber and violently like a bandit" (Proverbs 24:33-34 TLB). If you're lazy now, you pay later—with interest. And the worst consequence is death. "The lazy man longs for many things, but his hands refuse to work" (21:25 TLB). He could die of starvation. Many people make this choice even today! Whatever we put off doing comes back to haunt us. You can lose your job, your wife, and your children by getting stuck in the area of rationalization and procrastination.[16]

Is there hope? Yes! It's the same answer as for all our problems—an encounter with Jesus Christ. He can take the unmotivated and make them motivated. He can take the dependent and make them independent. It's happened before; it can happen again!

This, then, is how you should pray: "Our Father in heaven, hallowed be your name" (Matthew 6:9).

Hallowed is not a word we use much anymore, not even in church. Some who use it aren't even sure what it means. The word *hallowed* seems heavy, austere, almost…sacred. To simplify it, what Jesus was saying was, "God, may Your name be thought of or regarded as holy." God's name must be set apart and given the special place it deserves.

In God's Word, holiness is linked to things or persons that were set aside for God's service, such as the Sabbath or the priests. You and I are also to "be holy" because we belong to God, we "who through faith are shielded by God's power until the coming of the salvation that is ready to be revealed in the last time" (1 Peter 1:5).

What comes to mind when you think of the word *holy*? Something austere, unattainable, unreachable? God is holy but accessible. And that's amazing when you realize that *holiness* means "purity." We have contact with God because of His love for us. How does He show His holiness? Well, get ready for this—you may be surprised—He shows it through you! Yes, through you. You are an instrument through whom He displays his holiness. "Let your light shine before men, that they may see your good deeds and praise your Father in heaven" (Matthew 5:16). That's quite a responsibility. But we've been called to be holy, to be set apart, by the way we think, believe, speak, and behave. Don't think of it as a chore but as an opportunity to draw people to the Father. You can be that instrument.[17]

He who is slow to anger has great understanding (Proverbs 14:29 AMP).

Scripture has clear implications for men regarding the control of anger. The book of Proverbs, for instance, offers healthy guidelines for dealing with anger: "An angry man stirs up dissension, and a hot-tempered one commits many sins" (29:22). "Do not make friends with a hot-tempered man, do not associate with one easily angered" (22:24-25).

In *The Man in the Mirror,* Patrick Morley describes a scenario familiar to many men:

> Anger resides behind the closed doors of most of our homes. Personally, I have never lost my temper at the office. I would never want my colleagues to think I couldn't control myself. But rarely a week goes by in which the sparks of family life don't provide good tinder for a roaring fire of anger…
>
> At the end of a long, hard day at the office, when you pull up the drawbridge to your own private castle, your family gets to live with the real you.
>
> Anger destroys the quality of our personal lives, our marriages, and our health. Angry words are like irretrievable arrows released from an archer's bow. Once released, traveling through the air toward their target, they cannot be withdrawn, their damage cannot be undone. Like the arrows of the archer, our angry words pierce like a jagged blade, ripping at the heart of their target.
>
> When anger pierces the soul of the home, the lifeblood of the family starts to drain away. You may notice that a secretary seems to find you attractive. You reflect on how your wife no longer appreciates you. It never occurs to you that it may be you, that if that secretary knew the real you—the angry you that lives secretly behind the closed doors of your home—she would find you about as desirable as a flat tire.[18]

That's sobering, isn't it?

When someone becomes a Christian, he becomes a
brand new person inside. He is not the same anymore. A
new life has begun! (2 Corinthians 5:17 TLB).

You're somebody. You became a somebody when you accepted Christ. You became a new species. Your body didn't change (maybe you hoped it would!), your hair and eye color didn't change, you look and feel the same—but you're different. You were given a new identity at that time. In your old identity you lived under a set of rules designed to help you get the most out of life. But with a new identity comes a new lifestyle. You have a new set of directions for the way you behave. Here are a few of them:

> Don't just pretend that you love others: really love them. Hate what is wrong. Stand on the side of good. Love each other with brotherly affection and take delight in honoring each other. Never be lazy in your work, but serve the Lord enthusiastically. Be glad for all God is planning for you. Be patient in trouble, and prayerful always. When God's children are in need, you be the one to help them out. And get into the habit of inviting guests home for dinner or, if they need lodging, for the night.

> If someone mistreats you because you are a Christian, don't curse him; pray that God will bless him. When others are happy, be happy with them. If they are sad, share their sorrow. Work happily together. Don't try to act big. Don't try to get into the good graces of important people, but enjoy the company of ordinary folks. And don't think you know it all! Never pay back evil for evil. Do things in such a way that everyone can see you are honest clear through. Don't quarrel with anyone. Be at peace with everyone, just as much as possible (Romans 12:9-18 TLB).[19]

Let the peace of Christ rule in your hearts, since as members of one
body you were called to peace. And be thankful (Colossians 3:15).

Here is the story of one couple's adventure in developing spiritual intimacy.

For Esther and me, the best way to describe our life together is a covenant of love. We are both committed to walk as disciples of Christ, and this covenant binds us together in spirit, in purpose, and with integrity. Because of this common covenant, we have always been able to trust each other and to respect each other…

Support for spirituality in our lives has come from reading the Word, from prayer, from worship, but especially from the dynamic of small-group relationships. Over the past twenty-five years we have shared in three such groups. These have enriched us and stretched our spiritual resources by offering fellowship and demanding accountability. This has been especially true for the past thirteen years working in the inner city…We've shared everything from personal issues to a careful review of…financial resources and patterns of stewardship. We must be willing to be vulnerable with others and to search all the corners of our spirits.

Once, during a time of deep anguish over a problem in our family, three persons from our group came and asked us to permit them to do the praying for us during the next week; we were to relax and unhook from the emotional burden of prayer on this issue! This was a level of participation in the Spirit that provided therapy for our own spirits.

In our ministry we frequently meet ourselves in other persons while studying, counseling, and serving. We have sought to avoid a professionalism that makes the spiritual into an expression more than an experience, and have regularly sought the infilling of the Spirit to enable us to walk together in the fellowship of Christ.[20]

*If you make the Most High your dwelling—even the
LORD, who is my refuge—then no harm will befall you, no
disaster will come near your tent (Psalm 91:9-10).*

Years ago a TV program called *The Fugitive* captured the imagination of the nation. In the early 1990s it was made into a movie starring Harrison Ford and Tommy Lee Jones. It's the story of a man falsely convicted and escaping from a prison bus. It's a very intense film with a train wreck scene that brings people out of their seats.

Today there are people in our society who are fugitives for one reason or another. We see some of them on the streets, while others have hidden so well they are almost invisible. What's interesting, though, is the number of men who are fugitives, even though they've remained at home. They may be living there physically, but their hearts and minds are miles away. They pretend to listen to their families and participate in family routines. These fugitives go through the motions, but they're on the run. The energy and effort it takes to be a functioning family member has been diverted elsewhere. Often it's been used up at work or in sports, hobbies, or, sometimes, on another woman.

Have you been or are you now a fugitive? If so, you're a member of a very elite group. Moses was a fugitive for forty years and finally got his life straightened out. Look at how God used him! David was a fugitive off and on because many people wanted to separate his head from his body. God still used him. Then there was Jonah. Who was he running away from? Yep—God. Do you identify more with Jonah than the other two?

Are you running from God? If so, stop, turn around, and go home. He's not punitive. He's loving. Read Luke 13:31-35 and you'll see.

*Whatever you do, whether in word or deed, do it all
in the name of the Lord Jesus, giving thanks to God
the Father through him (Colossians 3:17).*

How will you leave this world? No, I'm not asking how you will die. Rather, will you leave this world a better place or the opposite?

The world is a better place because Michelangelo didn't say,
    "I don't do ceilings."

The world is a better place because Martin Luther didn't say,
    "I don't do doors."

The world is a better place because Noah didn't say,
    "I don't do arks."

The world is a better place because David didn't say,
    "I don't do giants."

The world is a better place because Peter didn't say,
    "I don't do Gentiles."

The world is a better place because Paul didn't say,
    "I don't do letters."

The world is a better place because Mary didn't say,
    "I don't do virgin births."

The world is a better place because Jesus didn't say,
    "I don't do crosses."

What will be your legacy? Dwight L. Moody heard these challenging words, and a new era began in his life: "The world has yet to see what God will do, with, and for, and through, and in, and by, the man who is fully and wholly consecrated to Him." *He said "a man," thought Moody. He did not say a great man, nor a learned man, nor a rich man, nor a wise man, nor an eloquent man, nor a "smart" man, but simply "a man." I will try my utmost to be that man.*[1] Will you try your utmost to be that man too?[2]

Taking with Him Peter and the two sons of Zebedee,
[Jesus] began to show grief and distress of mind and
was deeply depressed (Matthew 26:37 AMP).

Years ago there was a phrase that went "Real men don't eat quiche." We found out that wasn't true. There's another myth that's been placed upon us as men: "Real men don't get depressed." That's a lie too. Men—even Christian men—get depressed. Too many men pretend their depression isn't there. It's difficult for them to admit they have it. They see it as a weakness rather than a symptom of something else. They may try to work harder to make it go away, but that doesn't work. If you're depressed or have been, you're not alone. Look at some of the great men of history who experienced depression:

Vincent van Gogh: first great impressionistic painter

Peter Tchaikovsky: composed the classic *Nutcracker Suite* and other symphonies

Wolfgang Amadeus Mozart: the musical genius of his day

Ernest Hemingway: author of *The Old Man and the Sea* and other great novels

Fyodor Dostoyevsky: wrote *Brothers Karamazov* and *Crime and Punishment*

Theodore Roosevelt: president of the United States

F. Scott Fitzgerald: American novelist, wrote *The Great Gatsby*

Charles Spurgeon: great expository preacher

In God's Word you'll find many others who experienced depression: Jonah, Joseph, Jeremiah, and Elijah.[3] Depression is simply a message system telling you something is going on. Listen to that message. Depression admitted is the first step to recovery. Find a trusted friend and share what's been going on. Who knows, he may struggle with depression too. Jesus knows what you're going through. He's been there also.

*Now it is God who makes both us and you stand firm in
Christ. He anointed us, set his seal of ownership on us, and
put his Spirit in our hearts as a deposit, guaranteeing
what is to come (2 Corinthians 1:21-22).*

You and your wife are out looking for a new car. You find a car mart—one of those places where there are new car dealers one after another. You look. You start with Toyota, then Honda, then Buick, and finally end up at the BMW dealer. (If you do, let's hope you're making plenty of money!) You inspect, you discuss, you barter, you quibble, you decide, and then you buy...on time, of course. The first big step is the down payment. A down payment is a pledge that the rest of the amount will be paid. This could range from 5 to 20 percent of the total cost. You pay it and now you have something to look forward to in addition to driving away in this quality car—four or more years of monthly payments. Great.

Well, a down payment was made on you too. When you became a Christian, you received a gift—the Holy Spirit. The Holy Spirit represents God's down payment to you. It's a promise that there are more payments to come—the reality of heaven. You will be going there. God is saying in this verse that there is a guarantee that you will receive all you have coming. That's your assurance. You don't have to worry (like the BMW dealer) that God might renege on His payment. You don't have to worry that your salvation will be repossessed. It's set. It's safe. It's sure. Full payment is waiting for you. It's got a good sound to it too...it's called eternal life!⁴

You also were included in Christ when you heard the word of truth,
the gospel of your salvation. Having believed, you were marked
in him with a seal, the promised Holy Spirit (Ephesians 1:13).

Seals are interesting—and I don't mean those ocean-going animals. Sometimes when you purchase a quality vase or art object there is a seal impressed on the base to indicate its authenticity—it's the real thing. You find seals like this on many objects, including cattle. The owners of the herd have a roundup each year. They bring in all the new calves, heat up the iron in the coals, and brand each one. This seal is a sign of ownership.

You too have been branded (if you want to look at it that way). You've been sealed, as the Scripture states, with the Holy Spirit. In a sense this seal is God's mark of ownership on you. You belong to Him, not to yourself, your wife, your parents, or your work. This seal does something else: It gives you security. No one else can put their brand or seal on you as rustlers used to do to cattle. You are branded by God for ever. No one can take that seal off. What happened to you took place on the inside.

Think about this: If you have a seal on you that comes from God, it means that what He has done for you is real. It's authentic. Your new birth is actual. You have heaven to look forward to.

And one more item. Remember the cattle owner? He dictates where the cattle go and what happens to them. He has authority over them. God has authority over you as well. As you go through this day, rest in the security of being sealed! It puts a new perspective on the troubles of this life.[5]

Submit to one another out of reverence for Christ (Ephesians 5:21).

If you're married, you and your wife are not compatible. That's a fact of life. You may be becoming more compatible, but when you were first married, the differences were quite apparent. That's all right. They enhance a marriage relationship. These differences can be resolved if you listen, lighten up, and not withdraw. Remember the turtle? He only makes progress when he sticks his head out!

Conflicts are a given. It's how you handle them that's important. Attacks and defensiveness aren't good strategies for marriage. Listen to your partner's point of view and respond with "That's a different way to look at this" or "Let me think about that for a minute." Here are some helpful Scriptures. How can you apply them to *your* marriage?

> Correct, rebuke and encourage—with great patience and careful instruction (2 Timothy 4:2).

> Speaking the truth in love…putting away lying, "Let each one of you speak truth with his neighbor"…Do not let the sun go down on your wrath (Ephesians 4:15,25-26 NKJV).

> No chastening seems to be joyful for the present, but painful; nevertheless, afterward it yields the peaceable fruit of righteousness (Hebrews 12:11 NKJV).

> Encourage one another daily…so that none of you may be hardened by sin's deceitfulness (Hebrews 3:13).

> Make straight paths for your feet, so that what is lame may not be dislocated, but rather be healed…[Look] carefully lest anyone fall short of the grace of God; lest any root of bitterness springing up cause trouble, and by this many become defiled (Hebrews 12:13,15 NKJV).

Rejoice in the Lord always (Philippians 4:4).

D o you ever want to resign from life? You know, the days that "Murphy's Universal Laws" are in effect? Remember those laws?

"Nothing is as easy as it looks."

"Everything takes longer than you think it will."

"If anything can go wrong, it will."

Have you had a day when…

> …during the night, to help out your wife, you change the baby's diaper, take it into the bathroom to drop it in the diaper pail, and it lands on your bare foot?

> …you discover the dog is eating your baby's food, and the baby is eating the dog's?

> …you go to work and at the end of the day discover your zipper was down?

This list could go on and on! (By the way, all these happened to me!) At times like these, you pray for patience—immediately. Speaking of patience, J.I. Packer wrote,

> Patience means living out the belief that God orders everything for the spiritual good of his children. Patience does not just grin and bear things, stoic-like, but accepts them cheerfully as therapeutic workouts planned by a heavenly trainer…

> Patience, therefore, treats each situation as a new opportunity to honor God in a way that would otherwise not be possible, and acts accordingly. Patience breasts each wave of pressure as it rolls in, rejoicing to prove that God can keep one from losing his or her footing.[6]

*Do not take revenge, my friends, but leave room for
God's wrath, for it is written: "It is mine to avenge; I
will repay," says the Lord (Romans 12:19).*

Have you ever wanted to get back at someone who's hurt you? Sure. We all have at one time or another. Some men get a great deal of satisfaction out of revenge. Did you hear about the cranky old guy who was bitten by a dog? Not only that, it appeared the dog might have rabies. So the man was rushed to the hospital for treatment and was kept there to see if further care was needed. An intern walked by the man's room and saw the man muttering to himself and staring into space. But he was also writing something on a piece of paper, and the intern thought at first that he was writing a will. The man said, "Now, in case I get rabies, I'm making a list of the people I want to die before I kick off." This man was poisoned, all right—by hate and revenge. And he didn't get it from a dog bite.

Settling the score is not our right. In fact, vengeance comes from bitterness, which can kill us. At one time or another we all may feel we have a right to get back at someone. If anyone has felt that way it was Joseph. His brothers sold him into slavery (see Genesis 37–50). But when they were finally reunited, Joseph explained what he was going to do: "'Don't be afraid. I will provide for you and your children.' And he reassured them and spoke kindly to them" (Genesis 50:21).

Let God be who He is and do what He does. Read and take to heart today's verse (Romans 12:19). What God wants from us is to forgive. It's the only sure way to resolve issues.[7]

By faith [Moses] left Egypt, not fearing the king's anger; he
persevered because he saw him who is invisible (Hebrews 11:27).

Many of the Old Testament men had character traits worth imitating. This doesn't mean they were perfect. Far from it. We can breathe a sigh of relief for that. But we can still learn from them.

What would you think about a guy who was so stubborn that even when the ruler of his country started hassling him, he wouldn't budge? He stood his ground. What would you think about a man who wouldn't budge from what he believed in and wanted to do, even when thousands of people he was supposed to lead disagreed with him? And they weren't silent in their disagreement. They were verbal! They griped and complained and blamed, and finally…rebelled. And to make it worse (maybe you've been in this pressure cooker), his own family—his brother and sister—got on his case and became critics. But this guy wouldn't budge even one inch. Talk about stubborn…or was he?

Scripture uses another word to describe Moses. He *persevered.* He wouldn't cave in or throw in the towel. When someone is having a hard time we often say, "Hang in there." That's what Moses did. The Living Bible says, "Moses kept right on going." The New American Standard says, "He endured." Chuck Swindoll said we should…

> Stand firm when conspirators seem to prosper. Stand firm when the wicked appear to be winning. Stand firm in times of crisis. Stand firm even when no one will know if you compromised. Stand firm when big people act contemptibly small. Stand firm when petty people demand authority they don't deserve. Stand firm…keep your head…stay true…endure![8]

Treat others as you want them to treat you...Never criticize or condemn—or it will all come back on you. Go easy on others; then they will do the same for you. For if you give, you will get! Your gift will return to you in full and overflowing measure, pressed down, shaken together to make room for more, and running over. Whatever measure you use to give—large or small—will be used to measure what is given back to you (Luke 6:31,37-38 TLB).

Interesting verses, aren't they? The "rubber band principle" is there: What you do and give to others is going to come back to you. It's like a boomerang. You get ticked off at that guy who cut in front of you on the freeway and you make a threatening gesture (or worse). You know what will happen. Did you really think he'd be sorry, wave happily, or apologize? In your dreams! He'll dish out what you gave right back.

It works that way all the time. If you frown and scowl around other people, guess what? You'll get the same back. If you want the people you work with to be critical and rude, griping and complaining, all you have to do is treat them that way. People tend to mirror back what they experience. They're like parrots repeating what they hear.

You can exert a tremendous amount of influence on others by your words and behavior. We're called to model the behavior that we want in others. That's what today's verses are all about. So, why don't you describe the kind of people you want around you? Be specific. Identify the responses you're looking for. Just remember, they're waiting for you to set the tone. Go ahead; you can do it. After all, if God called you to model right behavior, it is possible to do. He's the one to make it happen.

*I will give them an undivided heart and put a new spirit
in them; I will remove from them their heart of stone
and give them a heart of flesh (Ezekiel 11:19).*

The picture on the TV monitor wasn't pretty. It showed a cavity in the man's chest where his heart had been. The surgeon had just lifted it out and placed it in a steel dish. The heart was worn out, defective; and now dead. It was going to be discarded. The medical team had taken a new heart from a special container and was placing it in the chest cavity. Soon it would be sewn in place.

Some men don't want to hear about this process. But let's face facts. Some of us will have heart attacks. Some of us will have bypass surgeries. And a few will have a heart transplant (if hearts are available). Half a million adults and 6000 children will die this year because of defective hearts. And of those whose hearts are so bad they need a transplant, 90 percent of them will die before they receive one. There are just not that many available. Many men sit around waiting, hoping that someone will choose to be a donor while they are alive. They want their defective hearts replaced by healthy, beating, massive muscle that will successfully adjust to their bodies.

Actually, we all need heart transplants. Ours has a disease called sin that destroys our lives and keeps us separated from God. Jesus died, but in His death He essentially said, "I want to give you a new heart, a clean heart, a healthy heart, free from sin!" And when you accept this, there is no fear of this transplant being rejected. It's a perfect fit! We have a new lease on life.[9]

Conduct yourselves in a manner worthy of
the gospel of Christ (Philippians 1:27).

As a follower of Jesus Christ, are you doing what today's verse advocates? Are you following Christ in how you respond to others? Consider these four attributes.

Jesus had compassion. Jesus said, "I have compassion on the multitude, because they have now continued with Me three days and have nothing to eat" (Mark 8:2 NKJV). He wanted to alleviate suffering and meet people's needs. How can you show compassion?

Jesus accepted people. He accepted people and believed in them and what they would become (see Luke 19; John 4; 8). When He met the woman at the well, He accepted her as she was without condemning her. He did the same with the woman caught in adultery. He accepted Zacchaeus, the dishonest tax collector, as well. Who needs your acceptance?

Jesus gave people worth. People were His top priority. He put their needs before the rules the religious leaders had constructed. Jesus got involved in the lives of people who were considered the worst of sinners. He met them where they had needs, revealing how important they were to Him. Jesus showed people their value in God's eyes: "Are not two sparrows sold for a cent? And yet not one of them will fall to the ground apart from your Father...You are more valuable than many sparrows" (Matthew 10:29,31 NASB).

Jesus encouraged people. "Come to Me, all who are weary and heavy-laden, and I will give you rest. Take My yoke upon you and learn from Me, for I am gentle and humble in heart, and you will find rest for your souls. For My yoke is easy and My burden is light" (Matthew 11:28-30 NASB).

One of the ways we can encourage others is to introduce them to Jesus!

*Don't grumble against each other, brothers, or you will be
judged. The Judge is standing at the door! (James 5:9).*

Does griping get to you? Some people are never satisfied or grateful. They perpetually complain. They want more, less, or something different. You've probably heard plenty of griping at work and at home. You're not alone. Even Moses got an earful: "The people were soon complaining about all their misfortunes" (Numbers 11:1 TLB). You may have to hear the griping of one, three, or even a small group of people. Moses had a couple million to contend with. So what did he do? He complained! He said to the Lord:

> Why pick on me, to give me the burden of a people like this? Are they my children? Am I their father? Is that why you have given me the job of nursing them along like babies until we get to the land you promised their ancestors? Where am I supposed to get meat for all these people?...I can't carry this nation by myself! The load is far too heavy! If you are going to treat me like this, please kill me right now; it will be a kindness! Let me out of this impossible situation! (Numbers 11:11-15 TLB).

Well, God fed the people with quail...but He also sent a plague. Have you ever wanted to do something like that because of complaining people? What can you really do when others gripe and grumble? It's simple:

- Don't follow their example.

- Ask God for wisdom.

- When people complain, let them know you hear them. Then ask them for two possible solutions to the problem. Who knows? They may solve it themselves!

The good man is covered with blessings from head to foot,
but an evil man inwardly curses his luck (Proverbs 10:6 TLB).

Have you used the word *wicked*? We use it to describe all kinds of situations, such as "He's got a wicked left hook," "He throws a wicked curve ball," "We live in a wicked world." Yes, our world is full of wicked people—no less than it was during Solomon's time. How would you describe a wicked person? Think about it for a minute. In the Old Testament the words used to describe this kind of person include: rejecting God, idolatrous, abusing others and property, violent, greedy, oppressive, oppressing the poor, and thinking nothing of murder. Morals? They don't know the meaning of the word.

Take a look at the daily paper. It's full of events just described. But do we call these events wicked? Not usually. There's a lot more emphasis on rationalizing the behavior, blaming others for the cause, or looking for ways to sugarcoat what was done. Some people are blatantly wicked, but others are clever about it. They know what to say, when to say it, and how to say it. They're subtle. Proverbs 21:29 NASB says, "A wicked man shows a bold face." Wicked people have the ability to portray themselves as people they really aren't. They're deceptive.[10] You've heard the phrase "all things to all people." That's the way the wicked operate. "Blessings crown the head of the righteous, but violence overwhelms the mouth of the wicked" (10:6).

Did you catch that? They're able to cover up violence. Sometimes their lifestyle seems attractive. Sometimes they seem to get away with so much that it doesn't seem fair. But remember this: "Don't envy the wicked. Don't covet his riches. For the evil man has no future; his light will be snuffed out" (Proverbs 24:19-20 TLB).

*When a good man speaks, he is worth listening to, but the
words of fools are a dime a dozen (Proverbs 10:20 TLB).*

You see them on TV all the time. They're interviewed on gossip shows
and in the tabloids, and even on *Entertainment Tonight* and other
shows. Fools talk about their business deals, their eight marriages, and
how they were caught with a hooker or someone's spouse. People shrug
their shoulders and accept their actions as part of life—not really acceptable but tolerable. We seldom call their actions wicked—but God would.

There are a lot of people in small and large businesses, in the government, and in the entertainment industry, just to name a few, who would
do anything and use anyone to get what they want. They seem to have
no sense of morality. What can we do about them?

First, don't think of joining them. Don't envy them. "Don't do as the
wicked do. Avoid their haunts—turn away, go somewhere else" (Proverbs 4:14-15 TLB).

Second, don't let them get to you or worry you. "You need not be
afraid of disaster or the plots of wicked men, for the Lord is with you; he
protects you" (3:25-26 TLB).

Third, remember they will get what they deserve. "Reverence for God
adds hours to each day; so how can the wicked expect a long, good life?"
(10:27 TLB).

Fourth, you (as a righteous man) will survive. They won't. "Evil men
shall bow before the godly" (14:19 TLB).

Fifth, take a stand. Speak out and speak up. When you see sin, confront it. You may not be popular, but who needs human adulation anyway?

Some of what goes on today occurs because we've let it. Remember
Proverbs 24:25: "Blessings shall be showered on those who rebuke sin
fearlessly" (TLB).

*Do not merely listen to the word, and so deceive
yourselves. Do what it says (James 1:22).*

Lord, I praise You for understanding me and my struggles. I admit that I
have numerous faults that still interfere with living my life as You
want. Forgive me for my conscious and purposeful acts of sin, as well as
those which seem to creep in even though I'm fighting against them.

Help me not to say one thing with my words and another with my
actions.

Help me not to criticize others for the same faults I see in myself.

Help me not to demand standards from others that I make little or
no effort to fulfill.

Help me not to play with and skirt around temptations that I know
are my weakness.

Help me to deal with the inability to say yes or no and to be definite
in my commitments.

Help me with my stubbornness and reluctance to give up habits I
know are wrong and break my relationship with You.

Help me to quit trying to please both worlds; forgive me for pleasing
others and myself first rather than You.

Help me to be consistent and live the week the way I live on Sunday
morning.

Help me to kick out anything in my life that keeps me from giving
You all of me.

Thank You for hearing, for responding, and for working in my life.

In Jesus' name,
Amen.[11]

*You made [man] a little lower than the heavenly beings
and crowned him with glory and honor (Psalm 8:5).*

Most of us like to be successful. Some of us, however, turn success into a requirement. When this happens, we become preoccupied with the pursuit, not of excellence, but of perfection. The greater the degree of pursuit, the lesser the degree of joy. Perfectionism becomes a mental monster.

To prove they are good enough, perfectionists strive to do the impossible. They set lofty goals and see no reason why they should not be able to achieve them. Soon they are overwhelmed by the arduous tasks they've set for themselves. The standards of a perfectionist are so high that no one could consistently attain them. Yet their worth, they think, is determined by attaining these goals.

We, as believers in Christ, are called to be perfect. But it is really a call to *continue to grow and mature*. This call does not mean never making a mistake. It means looking at ourselves objectively and accepting and recognizing our strengths and talents as well as the areas of our lives in which we are lacking.

One author said, "We must stop being picture straighteners on the walls of life before we can find and bring joy in life."[12] It's not so terrible to be average. In fact, the world is full of mostly average people. We can be average and yet be adequate. Adequacy is a free gift to us and always has been. Any shortage in our lives has been paid for by God's free gift. Let's express ourselves from of our sense of adequacy instead of striving to become adequate. Let's let go of the criterion of human performance because God calls us to be *faithful* instead of being without flaws. This is the standard—faithfulness!

*Then Job replied: "I have heard many things like these; miserable
comforters are you all! Will your long-winded speeches never
end? What ails you that you keep on arguing? I also could
speak like you, if you were in my place; I could make fine
speeches against you and shake my head at you" (Job 16:1-4).*

You're having a lousy day. Nothing has gone right. One thing after
another piles up. How could anyone have so much difficulty at one
time? It's like your world is crumbling around you. Fortunately, you have
some friends to comfort you. Or at least you thought they were your
friends. At first they didn't say anything. They were just there, silent, in
support of you. That helped. Then they began to talk, and you wished
they hadn't! One of them told you to remember the advice you gave to
others in the past. That didn't help much, but this friend went on with
a clincher. He had the audacity to tell you that he'd had a vision showing him that your suffering was the result of sin in your life. Isn't that
just great? Then he told you that you sounded like a fool and what you
needed to do was repent! To make matters worse, he said these problems
were also blessings in disguise.

Just when you need comfort, empathy, and support, what do you get?
Theology. And as you argue with your friends, their insensitivity grows.
It's as though you are arguing with their theology. Well, if this has happened to you, you're not alone. Remember Job? You can read about his
friends in the book of Job, chapters 4 and 5.

When a friend is hurting he needs comfort, not theology. He needs
you to listen, not give advice. "Understand [this], my beloved brethren.
Let every man be quick to hear [a ready listener], slow to speak, slow to
take offense and to get angry" (James 1:19 AMP). He needs encouragement. Be there. Be silent. Be available. Be sensitive.

*How I long for the months gone by, for the days when God
watched over me, when his lamp shone upon my head and
by his light I walked through darkness! (Job 29:2-3).*

One of the worst experiences we can have is to be or feel abandoned. When this happens to us as children we live with the fear of abandonment for a long time. Have there been times when you felt God abandoned you? Job felt that way. He lost everything—property, servants, livestock, children, and health. He experienced intense pain. But the worst experience of all was God withdrawing the assurance of His presence.

We all experience this at some point. Some call this "the dark night of the soul." Many believe God deserted them. Does God desert anyone? No, He doesn't. But in the midst of our suffering we might begin thinking God has left us just like Job did. But God hasn't. What He does is make us sensitive to His absence so we look for Him with greater intensity and cry out for Him.

Job accused God of forsaking him (Job 30:21). This was like saying, "God, You're unfair!" Have you ever asked God "why" again and again as Job did? Your "why" question is probably more of a cry of protest against what has happened. Was God obligated to answer Job's questions? No. Is He obligated to answer your questions? No.

Elihu gave Job some good advice that's applicable for us today (Job 32–37). We can focus on what we think God hasn't done and what we think He should do *or* we can dwell on who He is and His majesty. You may even think God's ways are wrong. They're not; they're just different and mysterious to us humans. Consider the dark days greater opportunities to trust Him more.[13]

*My God, my strength, in whom I will trust; my shield and the
horn of my salvation, my stronghold (Psalm 18:2 NKJV).*

All of us would like to be strong. It's part of being masculine. When
you think of strength, what comes to mind first? Probably physical strength. We usually measure strength from a physical perspective.
Pumping iron, running laps, doing curls, walking fifteen miles in three
hours. We measure ability in terms of endurance and strength.

Physical fitness is a big business. Just check out the sports club ads
in the Monday edition of the paper for examples of strength and perfect
proportions. But to look like that (and some of us never will, no matter
what we do) takes time.

There are other kinds of strength: strength of character, emotional
strength, spiritual strength. What are your personal strengths? Have you
ever identified them? How are they being used? In what ways would you
like to be stronger?

The psalmist states that God is his strength. The word *stronghold*, as
used in the Old Testament, meant "a place of refuge" where a person
would be secure. No one could break in and penetrate this place. David
spoke frequently of God as his stronghold. It's a descriptive term for God.
And David did the one thing with God that gave him strength. It's the
same step that will give each of us the strength we need to continue. He
spent time alone with God. We must do the same, clear the clutter from
our minds, and reflect upon Him.

If you want real strength—spiritual strength—go to the trainer who
can get you into condition. The Stronghold. Invest your time with Him.
You'll discover a strength that will amaze you.

*I am speaking in human terms because of the
weakness of your flesh (Romans 6:19 NASB).*

We're weak. We've all got Achilles' heels that we don't like to admit. We try to compensate for physical weakness by working out hour after hour, joining health clubs, taking vitamins, going to the health food store for supplements. Even with our preparations, defenses, and walls of resistance, there are things that can bring us to our knees.

We're like Superman. Remember him? The man of steel, faster than a locomotive, leaper of tall buildings. Nothing could get to him…except kryptonite, a substance from his home planet. It weakened him and even could kill him with prolonged exposure. Many times he tried to use his super strength or fly and couldn't because of kryptonite.

If even Superman had a weakness, is there any hope for us? There are many varieties of kryptonite out there. Some of it appears attractive too. More money, a bigger house, the BMW, popularity with the guys, glances from attractive women. We've all got our weaknesses. What's yours? When you admit it, face it, confess it, and ask Jesus Christ to help you, it loses its power. And that weak area of your life begins to diminish.

There is a state of weakness that is positive though. It's when we acknowledge we are insufficient and weak in the flesh and choose to lean on Christ for strength. Paul wrote,

> [The Lord] said to me, "My grace is sufficient for you, for my power is made perfect in weakness." Therefore I will boast all the more gladly about my weaknesses, so that Christ's power may rest on me. That is why, for Christ's sake, I delight in weaknesses, in insults, in hardships, in persecutions, in difficulties. For when I am weak, then I am strong (2 Corinthians 12:9-10).

Be still before the LORD and wait patiently for him (Psalm 37:7).

Would you like to get more out of your life? Enjoy it more, feel relaxed, and be productive? If you said yes, consider these suggestions. This is the program type A men learn to follow to change their lives. We'll consider these today and tomorrow.

Begin each day by asking God to help you prioritize those items that need to be done. Do only those items for which you really have time. If you feel you can accomplish five during the day, do only four. Try to accomplish only one thing at a time. Each day think about the cause for any potential time urgency. Write down one of the consequences of being in a hurry. If you feel pressured about completing your tasks, ask: *Will completing this matter three to five years from now? Must it be done now? Could someone else do it?*

Make a conscious effort to become a "ready listener" (see James 1:19 AMP). Ask questions to encourage others to continue talking. When someone is talking, put down your newspaper, magazine, or work and give that person your full attention.

Reevaluate your need for recognition. Instead of looking for the approval of others, tell yourself in a realistic way, "I did a good job, and I can feel all right about it."

Relax without feeling guilty. Give yourself permission to enjoy yourself. Play some soft music at home or at the office to create a soothing atmosphere. Read magazines and books that have nothing to do with your vocation.

Look at the type A behavior of others. Ask: "Do I like that person's behavior and the way he or she responds to people? Do I want to be that way?"

Plan your schedule so you drive or commute when traffic is light. Drive in the slow lane of the highway. Reduce your tendency to drive fast. Let others pass you!

Be still before the LORD *and wait patiently for him (Psalm 37:7).*

Begin your day fifteen minutes early and do something you enjoy. If you tend to skip breakfast or eat standing up, sit down and take your time eating. Look around the house or outside and fix your interest upon something pleasant you've been overlooking.

Think about what your values are. Where did they come from and how do they fit into the teaching of Scripture?

Each day try to spend a bit of time alone. Whatever you do at this time, do it slowly in a relaxed manner. And develop some interests and hobbies that are totally different from what you do for a living. Experiment a bit.

Periodically decorate your office or work area with something new. Take pride in what you do to express yourself and run the risk of being different.

As you play games or engage in sports, whether it be racquetball, skiing, or cards, do it for the enjoyment. Don't make it a competition. Look for the fun of a good run, an outstanding rally, and the positive feelings that come with recreation.

Allow yourself more time than you need for your work. Schedule ahead of time and for longer intervals. If you usually take half an hour for a task, allow forty-five minutes. You may see an increase in the quality of your work.

Evaluate what you do and why you do it.

Dr. Lloyd Ogilvie, a chaplain of the U.S. Senate, raised two interesting questions that relate to what we are doing and how we are doing it: "What are you doing with your life that you couldn't do without the power of God?" and "Are you living life out of your own adequacy or out of the abundance of the riches of Christ?" Think about it.

I do not understand what I do. For what I want to do
I do not do, but what I hate I do (Romans 7:15).

Failure! The word we dread. Some of us don't allow it in our vocabulary. Failure is what happens to others, or so we hope, but it hits all of us at times. The word *failure* means "to deceive or disappoint." The words *fallacy* and *fallible* come from the same source. Webster's Dictionary says failure is "the condition or fact of not achieving the desired end."[14] But is failure just the absence of success? Is it simply a matter of bombing out, of not completing what we set out to attain? Perhaps not.

Many men have achieved significant goals, but found no satisfaction in them. The end result really didn't matter after all. This is one side of failure. It's like climbing a path up a mountain and making it to the top, only to find you climbed the wrong mountain! Failure is not just the pain of loss but the pain of a new beginning as well.

When you experience failure, do you judge yourself as having failed or what you did as having failed? The difference is crucial. We can let failure devastate and cripple us or we can look at Scripture and see how God used people who failed, such as Noah, Abraham, Jacob, Moses, and others to accomplish His purposes. Think about this perspective on failure from a Promise Keeper speaker, Dr. Gary Oliver:

> What apart from God feels like a failure can, in His skilled hands, become a part of His provision for our growth. We can't be successful in the Christian life if we deny the existence of failure. If we learn how to value it, understand it, and take it to the foot of the cross, we can become wiser and stronger because of it.[15]

What can you do to reconstruct the way you view failure?

*There is no one righteous, not even one; there is no one who
understands, no one who seeks God. All have turned away, they
have together become worthless; there is no one who does good, not
even one. Their throats are open graves; their tongues practice
deceit. The poison of vipers is on their lips. Their mouths are
full of cursing and bitterness...the way of peace they do not know.
There is no fear of God before their eyes (Romans 3:10-18).*

This is a strong passage. It hits hard. It should. It describes a man who has no reverence for God. *Reverence* doesn't mean being quiet and reserved in worship service. *Reverence* is standing in awe of who Almighty God really is. It's recognizing that He is all powerful, not us. In Exodus 3:4-6, God called Moses by name, and what did Moses do? He hid his face. He was afraid to look at God. He had a godly fear, a reverence.

There are benefits in reverencing God. Are you aware of that? First of all, it's the beginning of wisdom: "The fear of the LORD is the beginning of knowledge, but fools despise wisdom and discipline" (Proverbs 1:7).

Second, it will give you greater confidence in life: "He who fears the LORD has a secure fortress, and for his children it will be a refuge. The fear of the LORD is a fountain of life, turning a man from the snares of death" (Proverbs 14:26-27). When you have confidence in God, your confidence grows because you're not going through life alone.

Third, reverencing God gives you a more exciting, longer life: "The fear of the LORD adds length to life, but the years of the wicked are cut short" (Proverbs 10:27). "The fear of the LORD leads to life: Then one rests content, untouched by trouble" (19:23).

Men spend lots of money and put in hours and hours to keep in shape. That's great. But they're missing one element—reverencing God. That's the ultimate workout.[16]

Even the Son of Man did not come to be served, but to serve,
and to give his life as a ransom for many (Mark 10:45).

"This is a test. Take out a pencil and a piece of paper. You've got ten minutes to complete it." Remember those hated words in high school and college? Those sneak quizzes teachers and professors would drop on you the days after the night you didn't crack a book? Well, guess what? Today you get to take a quiz. But good news! There will be no grade or penalty.

There are three words for you to define. The first is *ransom*. Do you know what it means? *Ransom* is built on the concept that something has been lost or taken and now has to be paid for in order to be set free. That's what Jesus did for us in a voluntary way.

Watch out for the next word. It's *propitiation*. This denotes an appeasement. God's wrath against sin needed to be appeased. This was done by Jesus' suffering and death on the cross for our sins. God is a just and holy God, and the penalty needed to be paid. God stepped in and sent His Son as the payment to appease His wrath.

The last word may get you. It's *expiation*. This sounds like a combined English/Theology class, doesn't it? True, but it's important to understand what took place to give us the freedom we have. When Jesus suffered and died, His suffering *purged* our sins. That is what expiation is all about. The act of removing our guilt by paying the penalty for sin. Your penalty and mine were put on Jesus. He took our punishment; God has been satisfied.

Did we deserve it? No. Was God satisfied? Yes. And one other thing: God didn't have to do this for us. He chose to because He loves us![17]

Give thanks in all circumstances (1 Thessalonians 5:18).

How do you handle the "gifts" life gives you? Like when you get an ugly sweater for Christmas instead of the power saw. Or you plan to play golf and it rains for three hours so you stay in the clubhouse visiting. Or the doctor tells you your arthritis will get worse.

Paul said to give thanks in *all* circumstances. He's talking about *gratitude*: "I am glad to be a living demonstration of Christ's power...I am quite happy about 'the thorn,' and about insults and hardships, persecutions and difficulties; for when I am weak, then I am strong—the less I have, the more I depend on him" (2 Corinthians 12:9-10 TLB).

If you want happiness, be grateful for what you receive. A soldier put it well:

I asked God for strength that I might achieve.
I was made weak that I might learn humbly to obey.
I asked God for health that I might do greater things.
I was given infirmity that I might do better things.
I asked for riches that I might be happy.
I was given poverty that I might be wise.
I asked for power that I might have the praise of men.
I was given weakness that I might feel the need for God.
I asked for all things that I might enjoy life.
I was given life that I might enjoy all things.
I got nothing that I asked for but everything I had hoped for...
Almost despite myself my unspoken prayers were answered.
I am among all men most richly blessed.

—Unknown Confederate soldier

"I know the plans I have for you," declares the LORD,
"plans to prosper you and not to harm you, plans to
give you hope and a future" (Jeremiah 29:11).

Some days you'll feel as if life is crumbling around you. That's when you question God. The three questions most often asked in hard times are "Why, God, why?" "When, God, when?" "Will I survive, God?" Of these three, the most common is "Why?" Why me? Why now? Why this? Why, God, why? You're not the first person in crisis to ask why, and you won't be the last. Remember Job, the man who lost everything in one day? One devastating crisis after another everything went—his family, possessions, wealth, and health. After several days of silence he began asking the questions many of us ask: "Why didn't I die at birth?" "Why can't I die now?" "Why has God done this to me?"

He threw the "Why?" questions at God sixteen times. Each time there was silence. And you know, silence was probably the best answer. That sounds strange, but if God had given Job the answers to his questions right away, would he have accepted it? Would we? Or would we argue against God's replies? We probably wouldn't understand God's reason at the time. By not having the answer, we have the opportunity to live by faith.

God doesn't explain all the suffering in the world or the meaning of each crisis. What He allows us to experience is for our growth. He arranged the seasons of nature to produce growth, and He arranges our experiences for growth also. Some days bring sunshine; some bring storms. He knows the amount of pressure we can handle. First Corinthians 10:13 tells us He will "not let you be tempted beyond what you can bear." But He does let us be tempted, feel pain, and experience suffering. Instead of asking why, let's thank God for loving us and discover what He wants us to learn in our situation.

When you were dead in your sins and in the uncircumcision
of your sinful nature, God made you alive with Christ.
He forgave us all our sins (Colossians 2:13).

Harold Sala shares a fascinating story of how Jesus changed lives.

Things didn't go quite as airline officials had planned on that July morning when American Airlines inaugurated their new flight #673. They were to have company dignitaries along with several public officials honor the first passenger with a news photo and speeches. Everything was fine until they handed passenger Ron Rearick a plaque commemorating his flight. Here the script fell apart.

Upon receiving the presentation, Rearick presented the airline official with a copy of *Iceman*, the story of his life. The official took a quick glance; then was horror-struck. On the cover was a block of ice on which was pictured the profile of the man who stood on the platform that day. The back cover was a photo of Rearick and these words: "In 1972 Iceman hijacked United Airlines for one million dollars. He was sentenced to 25 years at McNeil Island Federal Prison. No one wanted him out. Not the state! Not the FBI! Not the public! But Iceman was freed by a higher court! Read the true story of Ron Rearick. He was the Iceman!"

Suddenly the politicians moved from view of the TV cameras. The airline officials went into a huddle. This was the man, all right... Rearick walked over. "By the way, I'm not in the business anymore. I'm on your side now."

...The real story is that this hardened criminal had met Jesus in prison and his life was transformed. After a twenty-five-year career in crime, Rearick, alias Iceman, became Ronald Rearick, B.A. (born again). Today he's an ordained minister and speaks before thousands, telling them about his changed life. God is no respecter of persons. What he's done for Rearick, he'll do for you. He's still in the business of changing lives.[18]

The older son was in the field. When he came near the house, he heard music and dancing. So he called one of the servants and asked him what was going on. "Your brother has come," he replied, "and your father has killed the fattened calf because he has him back safe and sound." The older brother became angry and refused to go in (Luke 15:25-28).

The elder brother was all business. He was a serious guy working in the fields. And there's a good reason for that. He was the oldest son. He would receive two-thirds of the inheritance. The land would become his, and he treated it as such.

Was he ever indignant when he learned the reason for this big party! His brother, the playboy who wasted his inheritance, had come home, and now his father was treating him like nothing had happened. In verse 30 he accuses his brother of squandering the father's property on prostitutes, which no one had mentioned. Is the brother making up sordid details?

Look at the self-righteous brother. His status with his father was based on how well he served and obeyed. He was proud of who he was and what he'd done. Pride leads to arrogance, which leads to becoming judgmental. The proud look down on the less fortunate. If they haven't worked as hard as we have, they don't deserve what we have.

How do you feel when someone you think is undeserving is elevated, like the younger son was? Do you resent missing out on living the life of a prodigal? Is there an "elder" brother lurking within you? Sure, there are many prodigals in life. They're obvious. But anyone can be a prodigal and not even show it, even an elder brother.[19]

Many waters cannot quench love; rivers cannot wash it away. If one were to give all the wealth of his house for love, it would be utterly scorned (Song of Songs 8:7).

One of the discoveries I've made regarding marriage is that developing spiritual intimacy is part of the foundation for a long-lasting relationship. This is more than doing activities together; it's an *attitude* or an *atmosphere* within the marriage relationship. It's the feeling of freedom that you can connect with your spouse at any time and in any way about spiritual matters or issues. You don't walk on eggshells about sharing or raising a question. You live together with the confidence that you are connected spiritually.

In terms of the specifics of spiritual growth, my wife and I each maintain our personal devotional lives. This involves prayer with a specific list of prayer requests. We read from both the Old and New Testaments as well as devotional reading. Some days we read separate material, but on others it is the same. Our worshiping together at church is very important, and frequently we talk about our responses to the music and message as we drive home.

Sharing mutual grief over the losses in life also bring us together spiritually. We've learned to share our hurts, concerns, frustrations, and joys. What has ministered to us both at these times was worship—not only at church, but at home through worship music from a multitude of Christian artists and numerous musical and inspirational videos. We've found that our personal and corporate walk with the Lord must be a priority and commitment just as much as our wedding vows.

*Whatever is true, whatever is noble, whatever is right, whatever
is pure, whatever is lovely, whatever is admirable—if anything is
excellent or praiseworthy—think about such things (Philippians 4:8).*

The label is everything. We're taught to check the labels of food items in the store. We won't buy clothes or golf clubs if they don't have the right labels. We depend on labels, and they have their place…except in marriage. Negative labels never provide a full picture of your wife. They are limited and biased and interfere with an essential ingredient in marriage for change and progress. It's called *forgiveness*. Seeing your wife in a new light enables forgiveness to occur. Negative labels block forgiveness. Can you forgive a person you label selfish, controlling, insensitive, manipulative, or crazy?

Labels are false absolutes. They're used to make it easier to justify ourselves and to keep us from thinking through the situation. If we used our minds constructively, we would be able to see both sides of a person. Labels limit our understanding of what is occurring because we see "the label" as the cause of the problem so why look elsewhere?

Labels keep us from looking at our part in the problem. They help us avoid looking in the mirror. When we treat our wives as if they are certain ways and possess particular negative qualities, they may begin to act that way. Our negative expectations can become self-fulfilling prophecies. We cultivate what we don't want to grow.

Do you and your spouse label each other? Are the labels positive and motivating or negative and debilitating? Are there generalizations attached to descriptions, such as *always* or *never*? If you do use labels, why not change them in your heart and mind to give her opportunities to be different? It could revolutionize your marriage.[1]

Husbands, love your wives, just as Christ loved the church and gave himself up for her (Ephesians 5:25).

We need men today who are leaders—leaders in the home, the workplace, the community, and the church. Since there are different ways to lead and different styles of leadership, let's see what we can learn from leaders about leadership. British Field Marshall Bernard Montgomery describes it this way: "Leadership is the capacity and will to rally men and women to a common purpose and the character which inspires confidence."

Former U.S. president Harry Truman said, "A leader is a person who has the ability to get others to do what they don't want to do and like it." If you can do that, what an ability! It means overcoming resistance and defensiveness. It means creating an openness on the part of a person to consider what you are suggesting and substitute it for what he believes or does. To be this kind of leader you need to listen, believe in what you feel needs to be done in a non-obnoxious manner, and show the positive benefits of what you are suggesting.

Another leader, Fred Smith, said simply, "Leadership is influence." There are some people in positions of leadership who don't lead. If you're not affecting the thoughts and actions of others, you're not leading. Someone said, "He who thinks he leads and has no one following him is only taking a walk."

True leadership is modeling. It's leading the way, showing what to do in a sacrificial way. That's the biblical way. That's God's way.[2]

My times are in your hands (Psalm 31:15).

Take a look at your hand. What do you see? Is it smooth or calloused, squat or long, strong or weak? Can you imagine going through life without the use of one or both of your hands? We depend on our hands. The word *hand* has great significance in Scripture. "The hand of the Lord" is used frequently. Do you know what it means? It's a figure of speech that uses the word *hand* for the "providence, presence, and power of the Lord."

We use *hand* as a compliment: "I've got to *hand* it to you." Many of the statements we make about a person's ability and activity relate to hands: "Will you lend me a *hand*?" In naval war movies we've heard the phrase "All *hands* on deck." We ask someone to help us by saying, "Can you take this off my *hands*?" We refer to a worker as a "hired *hand*." We see someone begging and say, "He wants a *handout*." Hands can be used for good or evil. The same hand that gently caresses a wife's face can deliver a stinging slap.

One day on the Sabbath Jesus met a man with a withered hand. "And a man with a shriveled hand was there" (Matthew 12:10). The original Greek indicates it wasn't a birth defect, but perhaps a burn or an accident. He couldn't use his hand. It had become a burden, a restrictive portion of his body that limited his life. He looked to Jesus for healing—and he got it. Jesus said, "Stretch out your hand." The man did and "it was completely restored, just as sound as the other" (Matthew 12:13).

Are your hands complete? Are they handicapped in any way? Do they hinder you? Are they being used to further Christ's kingdom? Is there any way in which they are withered? If so, reach out and allow Jesus Christ to touch you so that your hands can be instruments of healing to other people.[3]

"Love the Lord your God with all your heart and with all your
soul and with all your mind and with all your strength." The
second is this: "Love your neighbor as yourself." There is
no commandment greater than these (Mark 12:30-31).

L*ove is a choice.* Yes, there may be feelings of love at times, but they come and go. It is a choice—especially *agape* love. This word is used in one form or another more than 200 times in Scripture. If you're married, it's the type of love that will make your marriage come alive. You can't do it on your own though. It's too difficult. You need God infusing you with this love and the strength to be consistent with it. If you want to know what it's like, look at Jesus. There are three words that describe how Jesus loves us and how we're to love others.

Jesus loves us unconditionally. He loves us with no conditions, no restrictions. No matter how wild we are, how bad we are, how mad we are, how vile we are, He loves us. Remember this! How we behave doesn't earn us any more of God's love. The man who murdered his wife and three children? Jesus loves him as much as He loves you and me. That's unconditional love.

Jesus loves us willfully. He loves us because *He wants to love us.* He wasn't forced to go to the cross for us; He chose to. He chose to touch lepers, He chose to heal the sick, He chose to die. How do we love others? By choosing to. And when that's difficult, which it will be at times, pray for a change of heart and attitude.

Jesus loves us sacrificially. Sacrificial love gives all expecting nothing in return. It's a costly love. It takes something from us. It takes us out of our comfort zones.

How could you love someone like Jesus does today? When you've decided, go ahead and do it. In doing so, you become a bit more like Him.[4]

We love because he first loved us (1 John 4:19).

A*gape* means self-giving love, the love that goes on loving even when the other person becomes unlovable. In a marriage, agape can keep erotic love alive or rekindle erotic love that has been lost. Agape love is not just something that happens to you; it's something you make happen. When the Bible states that God is love, it uses the word agape. John wrote, "God so loved [agape] the world that he gave his one and only Son" (John 3:16). Agape gives. Agape sacrifices. Agape initiates. Agape loves whether or not the object deserves that love. "God demonstrates His own love toward us, in that while we were yet sinners, Christ died for us" (Romans 5:8 NASB).

Let's get practical and consider what agape is all about in a marriage. Agape is kindness. It's being sympathetic, thoughtful, and sensitive to your spouse. It's…

- squelching the urge to ask whether she's eating more chocolates lately
- listening when she wakes up and wants to talk at 2:35 AM
- helping put the children to bed, even during the fourth quarter of the Super Bowl

Agape is forgiving. It's being content with things that don't live up to expectations:

- being patient when she squeezes the toothpaste tube from the wrong end for the 837th time
- not making nostalgic comments about your mother's fine cooking
- learning to love all her relatives—even Uncle Howard

*The fool says in his heart, "There is no God." They
are corrupt, their deeds are vile; there is no one
who does good…[The sons of men] have turned
aside, they have together become corrupt; there is no
one who does good, not even one (Psalm 14:1,3).*

Have you been on the receiving end of slander? It can hurt you and your reputation for years to come. Slander demonstrates graphically the proverb "Death and life are in the power of the tongue" (Proverbs 18:21 NASB). Slander destroys reputations, friendships, and trust, as well as a person's potential for the future. It's a twisting of the truth to do in another person, usually for the slanderer's benefit.

Slander is all around us. Listen to the news or read tabloid headlines. Character assassination happens frequently. The slanderer looks at the person as if through a microscope. What is the slanderer looking for? Imperfections, weaknesses, cracks in the person's character. The plan is to turn the microscope into a verbal magnifying glass and share it with the world. Even if there isn't an ounce of truth to what is said, the damage is still done. It's the same thing that happens when a judge in a trial says to the jury, "Disregard that last comment." The damage has already been done.

A man after God's heart doesn't give in to the temptation to elevate himself by demeaning another person. The wise man looks for truth. He looks for the person's positive character qualities and talks about those rather than the defects. When he hears others bad-mouthing someone, not only does he refrain from passing it on, he challenges the one who's talking to verify that what is being said is accurate.[5]

Nobody needs slander. When you learn something good about another person, share it. When you learn something bad about someone, forget it.

The rich man's wealth is his only strength. The poor man's poverty is his only curse (Proverbs 10:15 TLB).

Would you like to be wealthy? Let's be honest. Who wouldn't? Somewhere within us is that dream of having all the money we want so we will never be in need and can buy whatever we want. We don't want to wait for wealth. We want it now. I see this all the time when I counsel young couples before they marry. They want to start out economically at the same level as their parents—even though it took their parents twenty-five or so years to get there. The reality is that when they marry, they will probably have to step down a notch or two economically.

Proverbs has much to say about wealth. Its teachings go a bit counter to how people usually think today. If you're interested in becoming wealthy, heed the advice in Proverbs: "Lazy men are soon poor; hard workers get rich" (10:4 TLB). Make money by earning it…working for it. But don't forget another way to garner wealth: "True humility and respect for the Lord lead a man to riches, honor and long life" (22:4 TLB).

Humility doesn't seem to fit the profile of society's wealthy, especially when you consider the ones who made their money through the sports and entertainment industries. It's just the opposite. Or is it? Those who get press are the ones we know about. There are many others we don't see who have found that the wisdom from the book of Proverbs is true. And speaking of wisdom, that's another way to be wealthy: "Any enterprise is built by wise planning, becomes strong through common sense, and profits wonderfully by keeping abreast of the facts" (Proverbs 24:3-4 TLB). This gives you something to consider.[6]

If you must choose, take a good name rather than great riches; for to be held in loving esteem is better than silver and gold (Proverbs 22:1 TLB).

Imagine with me for a moment that you're on a major TV quiz show and you're on a winning streak. One question to go and you make it to the top. The question is asked, you give the answer. It's correct! You've done it!

All of a sudden the announcer says, "We have one more question for you."

You're shocked! It shows on your face.

The announcer continues. "You've won, but now you've got a choice of prizes. You can have all this wealth—the money, the boat, the new car, the European trip—or you can have integrity. Which do you want?"

Silence. Perhaps you're wondering even now which you would take. You may even ask, "Why not both?" But if you had to choose, which one would you take? This could be tough, especially if you look at your bills, the house, what the kids need, and so forth.

We need money, but sometimes we place too high a value on getting ahead. Does wealth bring us closer to God? Or might it help us drift away from Him? It's easier to trust our abilities when we're financially comfortable—unless we remember that all we have belongs to God. It's not wrong to have money; God never condemns wealth. Many wealthy people give a lot to the Lord's work. They've discovered wealth *and* integrity.

Proverbs offers much wisdom about wealth: "Better to be poor and honest than rich and a cheater" (28:6 TLB). "Better [to] be poor and honest than rich and dishonest" (19:1 TLB). "A little gained honestly, is better than great wealth gotten by dishonest means" (16:8 TLB).

Anyone who oppresses the poor is insulting God who made them. To help the poor is to honor God (Proverbs 14:31 TLB).

What does God think about that guy in tattered, dirty clothes standing on the corner with a scrawled sign that reads "Homeless—will work for food"? What do you think of him? Good question, isn't it? Few of us have been that poor. We don't know what it's like, so let me be blunt: God is for the poor. He looks out for them. "Don't rob the poor and sick! For the Lord is their defender. If you injure them, he will punish you" (Proverbs 22:22-23 TLB). "Everyone enjoys giving good advice, and how wonderful it is to be able to say the right thing at the right time!" (15:23 TLB).

If God is for the poor, then what is our responsibility? Sometimes the poor are victimized because many can't defend themselves well. Other people rip them off. Perhaps we do too…in a different way. Like when we give them a dollar knowing it won't buy a meal. Or perhaps we hire them but don't pay as much as we would someone else. Proverbs says, "They devour the poor with teeth as sharp as knives" (30:13-14 TLB).

There's just one thing to do. We have to take responsibility to help the poor. "Happy is the generous man, the one who feeds the poor" (Proverbs 22:9 TLB). "When you help the poor you are lending to the Lord—and he pays wonderful interest on your loan!" (19:17 TLB). "He who shuts his ears to the cries of the poor will be ignored in his own time of need" (21:13 TLB). "If you give to the poor, your needs will be supplied! But a curse upon those who close their eyes to poverty" (28:27 TLB).

Take a minute to read Matthew 25:31-46. It may shed new light on the poor for you.

"But even if [God] does not... (Daniel 3:18).

Three men were in deep trouble. King Nebuchadnezzar told Shadrach, Meshach, and Abednego that if they didn't bow down and worship his gods, he would cook them—crank up the heat in the furnace and invite them in. How did they respond?

> We do not need to defend ourselves before you in this matter. If we are thrown into the blazing furnace, the God we serve is able to save us from it, and he will rescue us from your hand, O king. But even if he does not, we want you to know, O king, that we will not serve your gods or worship the image of gold you have set up (Daniel 3:16-18).

Each of us has our own dreams, desires, expectations, and hopes. If these come about we say, "Everything is all right. I can handle life, and I'm content. I have peace and stability." For many of us, our faith is dependent on getting God to do what we want. This is not the biblical pattern. It's all right to say, "I hope it turns out that way," "I hope the escrow doesn't fall through," and "I hope he pulls through the operation." But we must also say, "I hope...but even if it doesn't turn out that way, it will be all right."

We all face "fiery furnaces" at times. When such a time hits, we'll experience the normal emotional responses that are part of the healing process. And then, with God's strength and stability, we'll face the results. God doesn't always send in a rescue squad or bring along a fire extinguisher. He says, "Let's go through this together." He gives us the grace to live— the assurance that our lives can be all right when everything seems wrong. Saying "even if it doesn't" means we willingly leave the results up to Him.

*The eye is the lamp of the body. If your eyes are good, your whole
body will be full of light. But if your eyes are bad, your whole
body will be full of darkness. If then the light within you is
darkness, how great is that darkness! (Matthew 6:22-23).*

"Dream on!" That's a common expression we use to let people know what they're saying is not possible. When we say someone is a "real dreamer," it's not usually a compliment. But there's nothing wrong with having dreams for yourself or for others. We need vision and often that comes from dreams.

Perhaps you've seen *Man of La Mancha,* the musical about Don Quixote, a crazy old man. The story takes place about 100 years after the age of chivalry. Even though there were no more knights, Don Quixote thinks he is one. So he puts on a suit of armor and rides out into the world to fight evil. He wants to protect those who are weak. He has a servant whom he takes along as his squire. When they stop at an inn used by mule traders, Don Quixote calls the innkeeper the lord of the castle. In this inn he meets a pathetic, abused girl who cleans up after everyone and is misused by the profane mule traders. Our hero renames her Dulcinea and begs for her handkerchief to carry with him as a token into battle. You probably remember scenes of Don Quixote on his horse charging windmills and trying to slay them with his lance.

At the end of the play, as he's dying, Quixote no longer has delusions. In a gripping scene, every person he's renamed comes to his bedside. They plead with him not to change. Why? The excitement he had about their futures transformed them into the people he imagined. His strange dreams shaped their lives. That's what dreams can do!

Let marriage be held in honor...
[and] let the marriage bed be undefiled (Hebrews 13:4 AMP).

Sex—we think about it a lot. And why not? We were created as sexual beings. Sex wasn't man's invention but God's idea. So why not thank Him for it in a prayer like this:

> Lord, it's hard to know what sex really is—
> is it some demon put here to torment me?
> Or some delicious seducer from reality?
> It is neither of these, Lord.
> I know what sex is—
> it is body and spirit,
> it is passion and tenderness,
> it is strong embrace and gentle hand-holding,
> it is open nakedness and hidden mystery,
> it is joyful tears on honeymoon faces, and
> it is tears on wrinkled faces at a golden wedding anniversary.
> Sex is a quiet look across the room,
> a love note on a pillow,
> a rose laid on a breakfast plate,
> laughter in the night.
> Sex is life—not all of life—
> but wrapped up in the meaning of life.
> Sex is your good gift, O God,
> to enrich life,
> to continue the race,
> to communicate,
> to show me who I am,
> to reveal my mate,
> to cleanse through "one flesh"...
> Thank you that I feel free to say: "Thank God for sex!"[7]

*Let your eyes look straight ahead, fix your gaze directly
before you. Make level paths for your feet and take only
ways that are firm. Do not swerve to the right or the
left; keep your foot from evil (Proverbs 4:25-27).*

Keep your eyes straight ahead. There are good reasons for that admonition. You've seen guys at the beach with their wives. Some husbands strain their necks and turn their heads frequently, checking out the abundance of bikini-clad bare skin. Have you noticed the wives' faces? Their expressions range from deep hurt to "You check out one more woman and you're dog meat, fella." One of the greatest insults a husband could lay on his wife is gazing at another woman, especially in her presence! It sends plenty of messages to his wife—the wrong kind. Those glances should be reserved for her!

There's another reason why our eyes stray. It's called envy, and this isn't just a problem for women. Men struggle with it too. When you're envious, you're not content. "More" is the byword. "Better and bigger" is the theme song. If you have a computer, what kind is it? How many gigabytes? How do you react when you see a guy with one that computes circles around yours? Did your level of satisfaction go down? Did "I want what he's got" come into play? When envy hits, rationalization is refined. We have the "best" reasons in the world for having what others have—all but the good reasons.

Whether it's golf clubs, power equipment, or the make and year of our cars, the potential for envy is there. And when it hits, remember you're allowing yourself to be dominated and controlled by what the other guy has. That's worse than envy. And it wouldn't happen if we were looking ahead rather than to the side. Don't fix your eyes on what others have; fix your eyes on Jesus, the author and finisher of your faith.

No servant can serve two masters. Either he will hate the one and love the other, or he will be devoted to the one and despise the other. You cannot serve both God and Money (Luke 16:13).

When I was a kid, I lived in the hills of Hollywood, California. It was a long way up that steep road to get to my house. So as soon as the school bus dropped me off, out came my thumb to snag a free ride. It beat walking. And it usually worked. Back then we knew most of the people in our neighborhood and it was safe. I rode in Model A's with rumble seats or stood on the running board of a car, hanging on to a window and hoping my parents wouldn't find out. You may not even know what a rumble seat or a running board is! If not, ask a "mature" (older) man who's in the know.

Times have changed. It's too dangerous now to hitch a ride or to pick up a hitchhiker. But consider the hitchhiker for a moment. He wants a free ride. He has no responsibility at all for the vehicle. He doesn't have to buy a car, pay for insurance, upkeep, or gas. Have you ever met a hitchhiker who volunteered to chip in for gas? Not likely. He wants a free ride, a comfortable ride, a safe ride, and sometimes imposes upon you to take him even if it's out of your way. It's as if he expects you to do this.

There are a lot of spiritual hitchhikers today. They know the Lord, but they want a free ride. They want all the benefits of being Christians but none of the responsibilities or the costs. No accountability, no commitment, no willingness to serve. And if it begins to cost, or decisions have to be made to give up the free ride, they bail out.

The decision to serve God or serve themselves is a big one. We can't serve both. We can hitchhike in our faith or we can serve God. And actually, the ride is better with Him. [8]

*Live by the Spirit, and you will not gratify the desires of
the sinful nature. For the sinful nature desires what is
contrary to the Spirit, and the Spirit what is contrary
to the sinful nature...(Galatians 5:16-18).*

Lord, You have given me everything good in my life. Remind me that
I haven't done it and that I'm not You. I pray now for a greater sense
of responsibility...

Help me never to do anything that I would spend the rest of my life
regretting.

Lord, I want to always remember my responsibility to my friends, to
those I love, and to those who love me and those who don't.

I want to be faithful so I don't disappoint those who love me.

Help me not to fail anyone who depends on me.

Keep me from being a source of grief to others.

Lord, sometimes it's difficult to be faithful, but I know that You can
keep me faithful. Thank You that it's not just up to me!

Help me not to be a man who remembers my rights and forgets my
responsibilities.

Help me not to be a man who wants to get everything out of life without putting anything into it.

Help me not to be a man who doesn't care what happens to others.

Remind me that I am responsible to You and will answer to You for
the way I use what You have given to me.

And help me each minute of the day to remember how much You
love me and how Jesus died for me.

I praise You.
Amen.[9]

The LORD is my shepherd, I shall not be in want (Psalm 23:1).

Y ou've heard the hyped-up announcements on TV offering you great deals. And you believe every word the ads say, right? Only if you're gullible. If someone said, "I want you to have this gift: rest, peace, restoration, guidance, courage, companionship, constant comfort, protection, power, abundance, and security," would you believe the offer? This one you can trust! Here is the way Chuck Swindoll describes the promises of Psalm 23:

I shall not lack rest or provision—why? *He makes me lie down in green pastures.*

I shall not lack peace—why? *He leads me beside quiet waters.*

I shall not lack restoration or encouragement when I faint, fail, or fall—why? *He restores my soul.*

I shall not lack guidance or fellowship—why? *He guides me in the paths of righteousness.*

I shall not lack courage when my way is dark—why? *Even though I walk through the valley of the shadow of death, I fear no evil.*

I shall not lack companionship—why? *For Thou art with me.*

I shall not lack constant comfort—why? *Thy rod and Thy staff, they comfort me.*

I shall not lack protection or honor—why? *Thou dost prepare a table before me in the presence of my enemies.*

I shall not lack power—why? *Thou hast anointed my head with oil.*

I shall not lack abundance—why? *My cup overflows.*

I shall not lack perpetual presence—why? *Surely goodness and mercy shall follow me all the days of my life.*

I shall not lack security—why? *I will dwell in the house of the LORD forever.*[10]

*Enter [the LORD's] gates with thanksgiving and his courts with
praise; give thanks to him and praise his name (Psalm 100:4).*

Thanksgiving Day. But wait a minute. Every day is a thanksgiving day. Every day of our lives is to be a day of gratitude. Thanksgiving is more than a day of football games, reunions, and eating turkey.

Gratitude is a quality or feeling of being grateful or thankful. It's being appreciative of what you have received. Have you ever made a list of all you've received that you are thankful for? I mean an extensive list that you keep adding to daily for a month. It's a great family activity for Thanksgiving Day. You could also record the family conversation to capture all the interaction. That will give you choice memories for years to come.

Wouldn't it have been an experience to be there on that first Thanksgiving Day? The pilgrims knew what gratitude was—at least those who were still alive. Many died on the voyage and in the harsh new country. The survivors were grateful because now they were free. They weren't oppressed anymore for what they believed. Sure, they faced hardships we don't know anything about. But we've got our own hardships too. Being thankful doesn't happen without difficulties; being thankful happens in the midst of difficulties.

God can give us a grateful heart if we ask. And He does want to hear about our gratefulness to Him. After all, He gave His all for us.[11]

Though an army besiege me, my heart will not fear (Psalm 27:3).

There is something we don't want to admit: *Fear.* Men aren't supposed to be afraid. Whoever started that myth didn't understand human nature. We're all afraid at some time. Those who say they're never afraid, take their pulse. They could be cadavers!

What are you afraid of? If you need some help identifying your fears, here are some suggestions: failure, heights, crowds, disease, rejection, macho men, wimpy men, strong women, unemployment, death, a call from the IRS, a summons from your boss, financial reversal, war...and the list goes on. Fear hits us at the worst time, at our weakest point, and works on our minds. It's like a sickness that won't go away. Chuck Swindoll has some helpful words about fear based on Psalm 27:

> With broad, bold strokes, the monarch of Israel pens a prescription guaranteed to infuse iron into our bones. He meets Fear face-to-face...with two questions: Whom shall I dread? Whom shall I fear?
>
> He slams the door in Fear's face with the declaration:
>
> My heart will not fear...in spite of this I shall be confident (v. 3).
>
> He then whistles and hums to himself as he walks...reminding himself of the daily dosage required to counteract Fear's repeated attacks:
>
> *Prayer:* I have asked from the Lord (v. 4).
>
> *Vision:* I behold the beauty of the Lord (v. 4).
>
> *God's Word:* I meditate in His temple (v. 4).
>
> *God's protection:* In the day of trouble He will conceal me/hide me/lift me (v. 5).
>
> *Moment-by-moment worship:* I will sing (v. 6).
>
> *Rest:* I had believed...wait for the Lord (vv. 13-14).
>
> *Determination:* Let your heart take courage (v. 14).[12]

Never avenge yourselves. Leave that to God, for he has said
that he will repay those who deserve it (Romans 12:19 TLB).

Anger is mentioned 455 times in the Old Testament. And 375 times it refers to God's anger! In the New Testament six different Greek words are used for anger. One of them is found in Ephesians 4:26, where we are advised not to let the sun go down on our wrath. The word in that verse refers to anger that is accompanied by irritation, exasperation, and embitterment. It can be easily expressed in attitude, speech, and behavior. Out of it can come a resentment that will hurt you more than it hurts others.

Resentment carries with it a tinge of revenge—wanting to get back at another person or get even. This type of anger needs to be gotten rid of quickly. In Dr. S.I. McMillen's book *None of These Diseases*, the story is told of a visit Dale Carnegie made to Yellowstone National Park. While observing the grizzly bears feeding, a guide told him that the grizzly bear could whip any animal in the West with the exception of the buffalo and the Kodiak bear. That night as the people sat watching a grizzly eat, they noticed there was only one animal the grizzly would allow to eat with him—a skunk. Now the grizzly could have beaten the skunk in any fight. He probably resented the skunk and wanted to get even with it for coming into his feeding domain. But he didn't attack the skunk. Why? Because he knew the high cost of getting even! It wouldn't be worth it.

Many of us spend time dwelling on our resentments and even plotting ways to strike back. That's to our detriment. The price for this kind of anger can be high, including severed relationships with God and people (even those to whom the anger is not directed), strokes, heart attacks, high blood pressure, hypertension, ulcers. Is it worth it?

*We have different gifts, according to the grace given us. If a man's gift
is prophesying, let him use it in proportion to his faith (Romans 12:6).*

Take heart. There are many different styles of responding to life. You
don't have to be a replica of all the other men you've known. God
wants you to have the freedom to express your unique personality in
what you do. Let's consider for a moment how your spiritual gifts may
be reflected in your life. Romans 12:6 says "having then gifts…" The
word *gift* in Greek is *charisma*. The root of this Greek word means "joy"
or "gladness." The seven gifts described in Romans 12 are to be considered gifts of joy. So if you are aware of your gift and use it, the result is you
will be a person bringing joy and gladness. And your gift is just that…a
gift from God. There are seven such gifts.

The first gift mentioned is *prophecy*. It means to "speak out" or to
"declare." It also has the connotation of proclaiming in a very direct manner. A person reflecting this gift will be seen as one who is telling, declar-
ing, or speaking out about something. This could be your gift—or it
could be your wife's or a friend's. A person with the gift of prophecy
doesn't waver. The truth is spoken without much hesitation. The pro-
phetic person acts on whatever is right, sometimes without concern over
the consequences. Other people know where the prophet stands and can
trust that person's word because he or she doesn't vacillate. The prophet
is usually a person of action—persuasive, even competitive.

People with the gift of prophecy attract other people, but they can
also push them away. They have strong convictions and the unusual
capacity to stand alone.

Is prophecy your gift? Someone else's in your family or circle of
friends? If so, how can it be used to bring honor and glory to God? Why
not talk about it?[13]

*We have different gifts... If it is contributing to the needs
of others, let him give generously (Romans 12:6,8).*

G*enerosity.* Perhaps that's the best word to describe a person with the gift of giving. In many Bible translations the verse is translated "he who gives, with liberality" (i.e., NKJV). The original Greek word means "to share a thing with anyone, or to impart." Once again Webster's dictionary gives us food for thought. Some of the definitions for *giving* are "to be the source, produce; supply; as, cows give milk."[14] A cow cannot *not* give milk. That's its function. And it's the same with any person with this gift. They can't help but give. His whole lifestyle is that of giving. It's a natural habit and is built in.

Giving means something a bit foreign to the thinking in our culture today. A person gives by turning over possessions or control of something to another person with no strings attached. There is no cost. There is no bartering. It's given freely. Givers look for ways to give without drawing attention to themselves. And they gain enjoyment in giving without the pressure of an appeal. A husband looks for ways to give to his wife without his wife demanding, expecting, or using some ploy to get her way.

Giving sets a wonderful example for children because they can gain an understanding of God generosity. Parents usually encourage their children to give and to express gratitude for what they've received. There is also contentment on the part of givers to be satisfied with whatever they have in life, whether a little or a lot.

If neither parent has the gift of giving, they can find someone who has it and is willing to be involved with their children to model this gift. All gifts have a purpose; one isn't better than another. Even if generosity isn't our gift, we can all learn to give.[15]

We have different gifts... If it is encouraging,
let him encourage (Romans 12:6,8).

Are you an exhorter? "A what?" You know, a man who gives advice and warnings. No yelling, pushing, or prodding—just the facts. Most people don't understand what the gift of exhortation is. Frequently it's equated with preaching, but that's not the case.

Various translations of the Bible express it differently. The Berkeley version describes an exhorter as an "admonisher." In the Williams version the person with this gift is described as "one who encourages others." J.B. Phillips, in his modern English version, describes this gift as one used in "stimulating" the faith of others. Elsewhere in the New Testament it's used to convey the idea of consolation, comfort, and entreaty.

So if a man has this spiritual gift, he'll be admonishing, advising, encouraging, and stirring up the faith and self-worth of others. Family members will feel affirmed and cheered by his encouragement. They will feel fortified because of his noncritical listening as well as his belief in their capabilities. They know that he's available whenever needed.

This gift is often manifested by taking the time to explain, amplify, or clarify situations for others. A balanced exhorter is one who knows enough not to get so personally involved that it jeopardizes his time, knowledge, or...finances. He also knows not to allow others to develop an unhealthy dependency upon him.

Is this your gift? Your spouse's? Your child's? All of us, especially those of us who are parents, need to be people of encouraging words. "Anxiety in a man's heart weighs it down, but an encouraging word makes it glad" (Proverbs 12:25 AMP). If this is your gift, it will come naturally. Use it to build up others and glorify the Lord.[16]

*[He whose gift is] practical service, let him give
himself to serving (Romans 12:7).*

A person whose gift is serving has an approach to life that is devoted
to meeting the needs of others. In fact, some who have this gift seem
to anticipate and care for some needs even before they're evident. Some
people don't particularly care for this gift. They'd rather be served!

The word *practical* has rich and deep connotations. It means "designed
for us; utilitarian; concerned with the application of knowledge to useful ends; or concerned with, or dealing efficiently with everyday activities."[17] While all Christians might reflect some of the meaning of this gift,
for some their entire lives are devoted to this calling. Various Bible translations all convey the idea of "giving assistance or advantage to another
person." And it is done with a sense of joy and delight (not grudgingly).
Those who live with a person who has this gift will see an example of
cheerfulness in meeting needs. Verbalizing concerns may be a part of this,
but *doing* is their forte.

All of us need to be givers in some way. This is the calling to everyone who claims Jesus as Lord of their lives. But a spiritual gift is different.
There needs to be both *joy in giving* as well as *knowing how not to neglect
your own needs.* Who do you know with this gift? If it's yours, how can
you use it for the glory of God?[18]

We have different gifts...If it is showing mercy,
let him do it cheerfully (Romans 12:6,8).

D o you know someone who enjoys informal social gatherings? Or someone who is sensitive to the atmosphere of a get-together? Or perhaps he or she likes to listen to a speaker who is very emotional compared to someone more calm. Have you run into a highly sympathetic person, one who may cry easily? What about the one who is very tactile, always touching others? This person reflects empathy, compassion, sympathy, and is highly attentive while listening sincerely. These people have the gift of mercy.

People with this gift seem to have an antenna that picks up the emotional responses of others. They want harmony in their homes and at work. They go out of their way to soothe people in disasters. Physical contact is highly valued in all of their relationships. They seem to be able to read the body language of others very well.

There are some limitations, as with the other gifts. Being so caring can make it difficult to discipline, confront, or correct. Sometimes there is too much toleration of situations that could result in more hurt. They are often swayed and influenced easily.

Family members of those gifted with mercy know they are loved, understood, and accepted because their feelings are validated and accepted. Mercy means "to console or to succor one afflicted." The Amplified Bible says, "He who does acts of mercy, with genuine cheerfulness and joyful eagerness" (Romans 12:8). Mercy leaps from people's hearts. There's no resistance to doing, and they don't begrudge. Sometimes people with different gifts ask, "How can you keep doing that?" Well, they can't by themselves. Mercy is a gift from God, and He gives the strength to use it.[19]

*We have different gifts... If it is teaching, let
him teach (Romans 12:6-7).*

S ome men instill within others a quest for knowledge and a thirst for
learning. It could be with their children or with people at work. It's
as though they are able to turn every situation into a classroom. These
individuals have been given the gift of teaching. For them it's very natural and happens constantly. The word *teach* means "to train...to give lessons to (a student or a pupil); to guide the study of; to instruct...to give
lessons in...to provide with knowledge, insight."[20]

If you have this gift, you are usually sharing information or knowledge with a joyful attitude. It's easy. It's normal. The opportunities are
unlimited. A child raised in this type of home will have an abundance of
stimuli such as books, recordings, and other research material. An executive will provide the same for his employees. These men usually surround
others with what assists them in learning.

Wise men know the value or strength of their gift as well as the weakness of its overuse. For example, a wise teacher does not overburden
others with too many details and douse their enthusiasm. When a person asks the time, don't tell them how the watch was made! A wise man
allows for individual differences within others and looks for teachable
moments. He also works with others to help them discover their own
uniqueness and giftedness. If this is your gift, rejoice in it and use it.[21]

We have different gifts...If it is leadership,
let him govern diligently (Romans 12:6,8).

We all want to rule to some degree, but the one with this spiritual gift is quite obvious. He is usually organized, structured, and gets things done. Others may refer to the person with this gift as "the boss" or even "bossy." Leadership is a biblical gift and quite necessary. The Amplified Bible says, "He who gives aid and superintends, with zeal and singleness of mind" (Romans 12:8).

The gift of leadership or governing is a managing approach. Men like this. Think "take the lead, to superintend, to preside over." But conflict may arise in a marriage if both husband and wife have this gift. Hopefully they quickly discover the importance of delegating and give and take. A parent with this gift orchestrates the household and organizes the life of each child and often each pet! Leaders are good jugglers and can balance many things at once. Managers who don't have this gift wish they did. If this is you, find someone who does and follow his or her lead. (It could be your wife.)

A man with the gift of administration determines the abilities of other people and channels them. He helps them make the most of their gifts. The way this gift is manifested is crucial. Avoid being a controller. A loving tone of voice that gives suggestions rather than directives is a must. Men with this gift value reliability and responsibility. They are tenacious, remaining steadfast even when problems arise.

If you have this gift, you need the gifts of others to bring a balance into the tight ship you run. You want your gift to be seen as a plus, a benefit, an asset—not a liability. At this point in time, is your leadership gift helping or hindering others? [22]

Whoever claims to live in [Jesus] must walk as Jesus did (1 John 2:6).

Some men walk through life burdened by a load of baggage. Sometimes it's in the form of a label that's been slapped on them such as "slow," "inept," "stupid," "irresponsible," or "loser." It's as if someone wrote this word on a tag, attached it to their chests, and now it determines what happens to them for the rest of their lives.

During the Vietnam War, a mobile army surgical hospital (M.A.S.H.) would prepare for the incoming helicopters with their loads of wounded and dying soldiers. A system of triage was used to categorize the soldiers by the severity of their injuries. One color tag was placed on the dying to indicate they could not be saved. They were hopeless. They would not recover. A second color tag was used for those with superficial wounds. They would receive medical attention and would recover. The last color tag was placed on those who were critical but could make it with medical care. They might recover.

A critically wounded man was brought to one mobile hospital, and after examination he was tagged with "critical—will not recover." He was given a painkiller and left to die. A nurse came by, saw he was conscious, and talked with him. After a while she felt he could probably make it. So she reached down, took off the tag, and replaced it with one that read "salvageable." Because she changed the tag, he's alive today.

Are you walking through your life with the wrong tag? How do you see yourself? Critical and unsalvageable? Or do you have hope for your recovery? If you have a tag on you, who placed it there? Did you? The tag God puts on you has just one word: salvageable. Let Him work on any wounds you have and give you full recovery.[23]

Be of one mind, live in peace (2 Corinthians 13:11 NASB).

What's the status of your bank account? Is there a surplus or are you in the red? One of the metaphors used to describe a couple's interaction is that of a bank account. There are variations of this, but one is called a Relational Bank Account. As is true of any bank account, the balance in the Relational Bank is in flux because of deposits and withdrawals. Relationship deposits vary in size just like our monetary deposits. They could be a kind word or action or a very large gift of love. Withdrawals also vary. A minor disagreement could be a small withdrawal, and a major offense could drain the account. Zingers are definitely a withdrawal, and so is defensiveness.

When you think of your relationship in this way, you become more aware of deposits and attempted deposits, as well as what constitutes withdrawals. The larger the balance, the healthier the relationship. And like a monetary account, it's best to have sufficient reserves. Unfortunately, many couples live with their balances at debit levels.

There are two types of currencies in relational accounts—his and hers. Each may have a different valuation and fluctuate often. One major difference in this type of bank account is that the "teller" or receiving person sets the value of a deposit or withdrawal.

If there is a large balance in the account, a few small withdrawals won't impact the account that much. But if the balance is relatively small or hovers around zero, a small withdrawal is definitely felt. The ideal is to keep the deposits high and the withdrawals low. Each partner needs to be enlightened by the other as to what he or she perceives as a deposit or a withdrawal. What is a deposit for you? For your wife? What is a withdrawal for you? For your wife? It may help you to discuss this concept for clarification.[24]

*My grace is sufficient for you, for my power is made
perfect in weakness (2 Corinthians 12:9).*

My only son was handicapped—the diagnosis was "profound mental retardation." When he died at age twenty-two, he had never progressed mentally to more than eighteen months old. Through Matthew I learned about life. He taught me to experience my emotions, to listen with my eyes, to appreciate each small step of progress. But why shouldn't he have taught me this? He was a gift. His name means "gift from God." He was and still is.

You too can learn from the disabled and handicapped. R. Scott Sullender wrote:

> Handicapped persons also can teach us how to suffer and how to rise above bodily limitations. Sometimes pain cannot be fixed, nor can all limitations be conquered. Most of us will have to deal with pain and limitations, at first in minor ways and later in major ways. We will learn new meanings for the word "courage." Either we will rise above our limitations and learn to live with them or we shall sink to new lows of despair, bitterness, and helplessness. The choice depends largely on the strength of our courage.
>
> In a sense, then, a handicap or a loss of health can become a gift. It never starts out that way. Initially it is a horrible loss. If through the loss, however, we can learn to nurture our spiritual qualities and learn the art of suffering well, then we will have transformed our loss into a gain. We will have grown in and through our loss. We will have risen above our loss precisely by not letting it defeat us, but by letting it propel us forward…The loss of health in later life, as horrible as it seems, can be the opportunity for growing toward an even greater level of spiritual maturity.[25]

*God chose the foolish things of the world to shame the wise; God chose
the weak things of the world to shame the strong (1 Corinthians 1:27).*

There are times in every man's life when he feels ordinary, perhaps even useless. Such times can be very discouraging, especially when you try to turn your life around. Moses went through the same experience. When he finally took his first steps toward maturity, his performance wasn't warmly received. His first attempts were responded to with rejection and sneers rather than success. He was still young and had a lot to learn.

His impulsivity, immaturity, and inability to handle his anger led to forty years in another country. When I was younger, I viewed those as "wasted" years. But almighty God used that time to refine Moses and transform him into a strong leader. When Moses returned to Egypt, he was changed. He chose to learn from his mistakes, and God used him in mighty ways. But Moses also learned the high cost of not learning. From an early age, he struggled with anger. Remember, that's what got him in trouble in the first place. While he gained some control, he never allowed God to help him master it. Eventually his inability to learn from his repeated failures cost him a trip into the Promised Land.

In Philippians 3:10, Paul expressed his desire to know Christ and the power of His resurrection and the fellowship of sharing in His sufferings. Through the struggle and suffering that come from big and little failures, however, we're reminded of who we are and who He is. When you feel weak, powerless, discouraged, frustrated, limited…when you feel ordinary, you are prime material for God to use. Time and again, the Bible clearly tells us that our God deliberately seeks out the weak and the despised things because it's from them that He can receive the greatest glory.[26]

Come to me, all you who are weary and burdened,
and I will give you rest (Matthew 11:28).

Busy, busy, busy. That's a characteristic of our lives. And if we're accomplishers, those around us reinforce it by saying, "I don't know how you do all you do. It's amazing!" And we beam with pride. You may be busy, but are you exhausted? You may be busy, but are you enjoying what you do? You may be busy, but what is it costing you?

Most busy people struggle with weariness. And without rest work suffers, the desire to continue diminishes, tempers flare, patience becomes nonexistent, and we give up. We get tired of being tired. And this is not a new problem. More than fifty years ago the author of *Springs in the Valley* shared this interesting tale from African colonial history:

> In the deep jungles of Africa, a traveler was making a long trek. Coolies had been engaged from a tribe to carry the loads. The first day they marched rapidly and went far. The traveler had high hopes of a speedy journey. But the second morning these jungle tribesmen refused to move. For some strange reason they just sat and rested. On inquiry as to the reason for this strange behavior, the traveler was informed that they had gone too fast the first day, and that they were now waiting for their souls to catch up.

The author concludes with this penetrating exhortation:

> This whirling, rushing life which so many of us live does for us what that first march did for those poor jungle tribesmen. The difference: they knew what they needed to restore life's balance; too often we do not.[1]

Let's hope we do!

*Do not be surprised at the painful trial you are suffering, as
though something strange were happening to you. But rejoice that
you participate in the sufferings of Christ (1 Peter 4:12-13).*

We don't like suffering. We beg and plead with God to remove it. We question His sense of fairness and try to convince Him there's a better way. When we compare our lives with the lives of others, we think we've accomplished more. We're better than others so we deserve better. Or perhaps we wish we were someone else. We see their easy lives and wish we had it that good. But remember Psalm 49:16-17: "Do not be overawed when a man grows rich, when the splendor of his house increases; for he will take nothing with him when he dies, his splendor will not descend with him."

When we suffer, some of us move into self-pity. Discouragement sets in and our favorite passage of Scripture becomes Psalm 73:12-14: "This is what the wicked are like—always carefree, they increase in wealth. Surely in vain have I kept my heart pure; in vain have I washed my hands in innocence." Then we get angry. At ourselves? No, at God. "Why? Why? Why?" we ask. And we begin to doubt Him. How can He allow this to happen and stay absent? Discouragement overwhelms us because we're trying to figure out everything ourselves.

These thoughts and feelings are normal. To get on track, go to God's Word: "Do not fear, for I am with you; do not be dismayed, for I am your God. I will strengthen you and help you" (Isaiah 41:10). The solution to suffering is to learn how to enjoy the fellowship of sharing in Christ's suffering—to not falter in times of trouble, to be anxious for nothing, to endure patiently, and to walk in the power of the Holy Spirit. [2]

If I rise on the wings of the dawn, if I settle on the far side of the sea, even there your hand will guide me (Psalm 139:9-10).

Have you had a good crisis lately—you know, when a whirlwind sweeps through your life, throws you around, and disrupts all of your best-laid plans? Those crises make us feel like we're being tossed about in a barrel rolling downhill. All of us will have crises come into our lives. Except for adrenaline addicts, not very many of us like having our lives invaded by troubles. Before they come, it's important to burn into your memory the fact that you will have opportunities for more spiritual growth during a crisis than at most other times. During a time of crisis God wants to do something in your life.

The promise of today's passage is that no matter where you are, God will lead you. In Isaiah 43, the Lord declares that He will be with you through your times of crisis. Turn to that chapter right now and read it aloud.

Did you notice the number of times God said "I will"? If not, go back and notice what the "I will" statements apply to. A comforting thought is that God will not remember our sins. That is encouraging, since for some of us there's a lot for God to forget! Many people feel that one of the most comforting "I wills" is in verse two: "I will be with you." Will you remember that when you are discouraged? Will you remember it when you're faced with a difficult ethical dilemma at work? Will you remember it when you feel you have nothing left to give in your marital relationship? Will you remember it when you feel that you're all alone and no one cares? These words of comfort can lift us at any time.

*Come to me, all you who are weary and burdened, and I will give
you rest. Take my yoke upon you and learn from me, for I am
gentle and humble in heart, and you will find rest for your souls.
For my yoke is easy and my burden is light (Matthew 11:28-30).*

Look at your calendar. What's it saying to you? Is there any white space available or is every hour filled in? Some men's calendars are like that day after day, week after week. They'd like a calendar that has sixty days in a month and 48-hour days because they're trying to cram too much into their lives. The problem is that their new calendar would soon be overfilled too. The issue isn't the calendar, it's who's in charge of it.

Alexander Berardi, in his book *Never Offer Your Comb to a Bald Man*, wrote:

> We're all too busy for our own good. Most of us live as if we will be judged at our final reckoning according to the number of crossed-off items on our cosmic to-do list. I'm not sure what it is that causes otherwise rational people to think that, by working harder, faster, and longer, they'll get everything done, when they know by experience the exact opposite is true.

The calendar isn't the enemy—we are. We wear ourselves out. Jesus has some words for us about our hectic lives. Read today's verses from Matthew again and consider what you'll do with them.[3]

For the lips of a prostitute are as sweet as honey, and smooth flattery is her stock in trade. But afterwards only a bitter conscience is left to you, sharp as a double-edged sword. She leads you down to death and hell. For she does not know the path to life (Proverbs 5:3-6 TLB).

Solomon doesn't mince any words. He shoots from the hip. He needs to because it's a dangerous world out there. You see, many women don't know the first thing about boundaries, nor do they care to. If they see men they want, they go after them. Some men are this way too when they see desirable women. There's no respect for wedding rings.

Anyone can commit adultery. We're all one step away from it. It doesn't take character to commit it. In fact, person who commits adultery is showing *a lack* of character. And the cost of adultery is terribly high. The consequences are devastating. And it will be found out. In fact, it's immediately known by you and God.

Are there safeguards to protect you? You bet. First, remember your fantasy life belongs to your wife. Don't play around with another woman in your mind. Second, if you're attracted to a woman other than your wife, avoid contact. That may take effort, especially if you work with her. Third, if there is temptation, never be alone with her. Always make sure another man is present—or your wife. Fourth, be aware of danger signals. If you're thinking of different excuses to call her or see her, you're in quicksand. Get out now! Finally, go to men you trust and ask for help. You need them, and they've probably been there too. Let them walk with you. "Confess your sins to each other and pray for each other…The prayer of a righteous man is powerful and effective" (James 5:16). Adultery can be avoided. Let Jesus guard your mind and heart.

*Do not conform any longer to the pattern of this world, but
be transformed by the renewing of your mind. Then you
will be able to test and approve what God's will is—his
good, pleasing, and perfect will (Romans 12:2).*

Do you "go along" in order to "get along"? Strange question? Sure, but it needs to be asked. Many people play to the crowd to get what they want. They conform. Jesus gives us permission to be nonconformists. Just look at what a nonconformist He was. He went counter to what people believed. He lived differently. You know how others saw Him. They thought He was a heretic because He refused to join the self-righteous hypocrite club of the religious leaders of His day.

People tried to entice Him to sell out and compromise, but He didn't. Satan really went after Him, just like he does us. Satan said, "Look, be practical. Turn these stones into bread. Doesn't everyone love a man who can give out free bread?" He also said, "Let's join forces. Be a negotiator. And together we can rule the world. After all, isn't it the deal makers who get ahead in life?" The devil also said, "What You need to do is be sensational and get everyone's attention by jumping off the top of the temple. When You're sensational everyone wants to follow You."

Everything Jesus was asked to do went back to conformity. Play to the crowd; go along to get what you want. We all face this kind of temptation. The best response is the one Jesus gave. It was short, simple, and definite: "No!"

*Encourage one another and build each other up, just
as in fact you are doing (1 Thessalonians 5:11).*

Have you heard the story of Johnny Lingo, a man who lived in the South Pacific? The islanders all spoke highly of him. He was strong, good-looking, and intelligent. When it came time for him to find a wife, the people shook their heads. The woman Johnny Lingo chose was plain, skinny, and walked with her shoulders hunched and head down. She was hesitant and shy. She was also older than the other unmarried women in the village.

What surprised everyone most was Johnny's offer. In order to obtain a wife in that village, the prospective groom paid for her by giving her father cows. Four to six cows was considered a high price. The other villagers thought he might pay two or even three cows at the most, but he gave eight cows for her! Everyone chuckled about it because they believed Johnny's father-in-law put one over on him. Some thought it was a mistake.

Several months after the wedding, a visitor came to the Islands to trade and heard the story about Johnny Lingo and his eight-cow wife. Upon meeting Johnny and his wife, the visitor was totally taken back because she wasn't a shy, plain, and hesitant woman anymore. She was beautiful, poised, and confident. The visitor asked about the transformation, and Johnny Lingo's response was very simple. "I wanted an eight-cow woman, and when I paid that for her and treated her in that fashion, she began to believe that she was an eight-cow woman. She discovered she was worth more than any other woman in the islands. And what matters most is what a woman thinks about herself."

When you encourage people around you, something amazing happens. You increase their value, and they value themselves more. And that's what God did for us, didn't He?

Perseverance, character; and character, hope (Romans 5:4).

Have you ever wondered how a person's character is formed? Are we born with it, do we inherit it, or does it just develop? First, let's define what we mean by *character*. It's a combination of features and traits that forms the nature of a person. It can include qualities such as honesty and courage. It also includes reputation, ethical standards, and principles. It's what makes people distinctive. And believers in Jesus Christ are called to be people who stand out, who are different in a positive way.

How does character develop? In the book *Just So Stories*, Rudyard Kipling reveals how the camel got its hump. This animal had a disposition that wasn't too nice. It had attitude! It wouldn't cooperate with the other animals. When asked to do so, all it said was "Humph!" The animals complained to a genie, who then appealed to the camel to cooperate. But all it said was "Humph!" Finally, after hearing this again and again, that's what the genie gave him—a "humph" on his back.

When you say something or do something long enough, it becomes a habit. It might be a good habit or a negative one. And that's what makes up character. Plutarch said character is simply "habit long continued." We can end up carrying our habits around the rest of our lives…like a camel.

One of the great evangelists of the past, Dwight L. Moody had an interesting thought about character. He said that character is what we are in the dark. What makes up your character?[4]

Then I saw a new heaven and a new earth, for the
first heaven and the first earth had passed away, and
there was no longer any sea (Revelation 21:1).

Everyone seems to be interested in either knowing what's going to happen in the future or predicting the future. Some use computers, astrology, or psychics to try to figure out what may happen. In 1960, the Rand Corporation, a scientific think tank, made some predictions in a magazine article. They offered some wild speculations such as manned space flight, photos of Mars and Venus by 1978, direct energy laser weapons by 1980, drugs that bring about major personality changes by 1983, regional weather control by 1990, synthetic protein foods that can be commercially created by 1990, and so forth. Perhaps the years are off, but some of these have become realities and others are in process.

The world of science seems to be expanding, and we're able to create more and more. In some ways we've become scientific giants, but in other ways we've become ethical and moral infants. New ways are being created to take life, such as abortion and euthanasia, rather than sustain it. Something is wrong, and we wonder where it will end. We'd like a preview.

Perhaps what we need to do is what we do when reading an intense, exciting novel. When we can't wait to see how it turns out, what do we do? Turn to the last chapter and read it. You can if you want to. It's all right. You'll find an ending you like. It's in the book of Revelation.[5]

Lord, who may go and find refuge and shelter in your
tabernacle up on your holy hill? (Psalm 15:1 TLB).

Today's verse asks a great question, and David answers with 11 characteristics of a godly person:

1. Verse 2: A person of integrity is solid and wholesome and blameless. It's who you are as well as where you go. You live the truth.

2. Verse 2: A person of rightness keeps his nose clean. He's honest and doesn't compromise.

3. Verse 2: When you speak truth in your heart, it's also how you think. Your attitudes and reactions reflect truth.

4. Verse 3: Slander is not part of a righteous man's life. Verbal poison and sharing or listening to gossip are inappropriate...

5. Verse 3: He doesn't do in his neighbor. He doesn't create problems for him.

6. Verse 4: He doesn't say sharp and cutting things about his friends.

7. Verse 4: He doesn't cultivate a close association with someone who is disinterested in spiritual matters. This one is a real challenge in today's world.

8. Verse 4: He honors those who follow the Lord. These are the people to spend time with and build close relationships with.

9. Verse 5: He's a man of his word...When he makes a promise he keeps it. You can trust him.

10. Verse 5: If a believer needs money, he doesn't charge interest. Be discerning about money, and if you loan it, do so out of concern and compassion.

11. Verse 5: He doesn't take a bribe against the innocent. This speaks for itself.

On a scale of 0 to 10 on each one, where are you?[6]

God is our refuge and strength, an ever-present help in trouble (Psalm 46:1).

Are you depressed? Here are a few reasons men have identified for depression.

- Men get depressed when they continue to work at a job they hate.
- Men get depressed when they see their bodies change.
- Men get depressed when they realize they can't accomplish the goals they've set for themselves or that another person has set for them.
- Men get depressed when their marriages fail to meet their deepest needs.
- Men get depressed when they realize their children see them only as a meal ticket.
- Men get depressed when their friends move away or die.

Do any of those statements hit home? Knowing the reasons for depression may enable you to help yourself or a family member when it hits. Depression comes because of past deprivations, inadequate food and rest, reactions to medication, chemical imbalances, guilt over sin, self-pity, low self-esteem, and patterns of negative thinking.

There are two other causes to consider. One is *repressed anger*. When anger is bottled up, there is energy displacement. Depression is one of the outcomes. A second cause of depression is *loss*. The loss could be tangible, imagined, abstract, or threatened. Too much change or a crisis might cause depression.

Every loss needs to be faced. Is there loss in your life you've never fully grieved over? Take it to Jesus. "Cast your cares on the LORD and he will sustain you" (Psalm 55:22). Sharing with a trusted friend also helps.[7]

I the Lord do not change (Malachi 3:6).

One of God's characteristics is His immutability; He doesn't change. He is consistent and constant. We need to pray in harmony with His character. Let's consider some of God's character traits and how they should affect the way we pray.

- God is holy, so we must never pray for anything that would compromise his holiness or cause us to be unholy (Psalm 99:9; Isaiah 6:3; Revelation 15:4).

- God is love, and our prayers should invoke the love of God for others and reflect the love of God in our own attitudes (Jeremiah 31:3; John 3:16; Romans 5:8).

- God is good, and the results of our prayers must bring goodness into the lives of all concerned (Psalm 25:8; 33:5; 34:8; Nahum 1:7; Matthew 19:17; Romans 2:4).

- God is merciful, and our prayers should reflect that we have received his mercy and we are willing to be merciful (Psalm 108:4; Lamentations 3:22; Joel 2:13).

- God is jealous, and we dare not ask for something that would take first place in our hearts over God (Exodus 20:5; Deuteronomy 4:24; 1 Corinthians 10:22).

- God is just, and we cannot expect him to grant a request that would be unjust or unfair to anyone (Psalm 103:6; Zephaniah 3:5; John 5:30; Romans 2:2).

- God is so patient with us so we shouldn't be impatient in our prayers or waiting for his answers (Isaiah 48:9; Romans 9:22; 1 Peter 3:20).

- God is truth, and our prayers must never seek to change or disguise truth (Deuteronomy 32:4; Romans 3:4; Hebrews 6:18). [8]

As God's chosen people, holy and dearly loved, clothe
yourselves with compassion, kindness, humility,
gentleness and patience (Colossians 3:12).

Here's another story from the book *Becoming Soul Mates* by Les and Leslie Parrott.

[We] realized early in our marriage that a prerequisite to intimacy of any kind was a foundation of respect for each other and for our relationship...

- Not discussing problems in harsh, angry tones, but in attentive conversation, while working toward solutions that genuinely satisfy both of us.

- Not joking cuttingly about each other, especially in front of others.

- Never kidding about divorce.

- Saving constructive criticism for when we're alone and in a receptive frame of mind.

- Being willing to give in to each other's preferences, and developing a language for conveying when that is really needed...[We] reserve the simple phrase "this is really important to me" for those times when we most need to be heard and respected.

- Regularly giving verbal and nonverbal encouragement to each other for who we are as well as for what we do. This includes...dinner dates, gifts, massages, prayers, and time alone together without distractions.

- Fostering [this] attitude..."I'd rather die than hurt or bring shame on you. You're the one precious person to whom I've committed my love for the rest of my life."

These actions and attitudes have helped us to build a strong foundation for our marriage.[9]

*Trust in the Lord with all your heart and lean not
on your own understanding (Proverbs 3:5).*

How do I know God's will?" Before this question can be answered, another question should be asked: "Am I willing and ready to do God's will?" If the answer is yes, then ask the first question. What God has in mind may surprise you. Isaiah 55:8 says: "'My thoughts are not your thoughts, neither are your ways my ways,' declares the Lord." To discover and do God's will, keep these three words in mind.

Initiative. "Jesus gave them this answer, 'I tell you the truth, the Son can do nothing by himself; he can do only what he sees his Father doing, because whatever the Father does the Son also does'" (John 5:19). Let God take the initiative and then join Him in the walk. The closer you are to Jesus, the easier this will be to understand.

Timing. "There is a time for everything...He has made everything beautiful in its time. He has also set eternity in the hearts of men; yet they cannot fathom what God has done from beginning to end" (Ecclesiastes 3:1,11). God's timing is perfect. He is never too early or too late. Waiting may be the best step you can take until all the indications say, "Yes, this is the time." Praying for wisdom in timing is essential.

Submit. "Trust in the Lord with all your heart and lean not on your own understanding; in all your ways acknowledge him, and he will make your paths straight" (Proverbs 3:5-6). To know and do God's will there can't be any power struggle. He wants our will to be submissive to Him. The more we value control and power, the greater struggle we'll have. Along with God's will being dependent on His initiative and His timing, He also needs to be in charge.[10]

There is a time for everything, and a season for every
activity under heaven (Ecclesiastes 3:1).

Solomon's comparison of opposites, a profound description of life, says there's an appointed time for everything. "There is a time to be born; a time to die" (Ecclesiastes 3:2). But we forget time is out of our hands. Have you considered when you might die? We avoid thinking about it, but it's already set in God's timetable. Two questions are vital: "Will I be ready to die?" "What do I want to accomplish for Him before then?"

There's also "a time to plant and a time to harvest" (verse 2). If we plant and harvest at the wrong time we're throwing away money and crops. Our timetables don't always work out. Perhaps God's timetable is different from ours. We can ask Him about changes in our lives. When our ideas match His timing, things happen for the best.

There's also "a time to weep and a time to laugh" (verse 4). We look forward to laughter and fun, but we also need times to weep. C.S. Lewis said, "Pain is God's megaphone. He whispers to us in our pleasure (when we laugh), but He shouts to us in our pain (when we weep)."[11] Another person wrote:

> Contrary to what might be expected, I look back on experiences that at the time seemed especially desolating and painful with particular satisfaction. Indeed, I can say with complete truthfulness that everything I have learned in my 75 years in this world, everything that has truly enhanced and enlightened my existence, has been through affliction and not through happiness, whether pursued or attained.[12]

Has this been your experience? If not, it will. Fortunately, when we experience affliction we're not alone because God is with us! It's all part of His timing.

Do not judge, or you too will be judged. For in the same way you judge others, you will be judged, and with the measure you use, it will be measured to you. Why do you look at the speck of sawdust in your brother's eye and pay no attention to the plank in your own eye? How can you say to your brother, "Let me take the speck out of your eye," when all the time there is a plank in your own eye? You hypocrite, first take the plank out of your own eye, and then you will see clearly to remove the speck from your brother's eye (Matthew 7:1-5).

Dear God, sometimes I get so bothered about other men—what they do and how they think. Politicians, those in authority, public employees, friends, and even relatives get to me at times. Help me think and feel toward them as You would. Help me to act in loving ways so that they may begin to think about You.

Lord, before I criticize and judge others, remind me of what it feels like to be criticized and judged. Before I find fault with others, especially my family, help me remember what it's like to have stones thrown at me.

Help me make the allowances for others that I want for myself. I want to be as understanding and accepting of others as I expect them to be of me. Help me to verbally and prayerfully encourage others. Give me the strength to forgive others as I would like them to forgive me. Help me not to keep score of what others have done to me but have the ability to erase those incidents from my memory.

I want to live and love as Jesus did. He did good to others, He served others, and He forgave even as He died on the cross. I want to be a man full of His love.

In His name I pray.
Amen.

All these people were still living by faith when they died. They
did not receive the things promised; they only saw them
and welcomed them from a distance (Hebrews 11:13).

Archibald Hart shared a fascinating story about a pastor's message at the conclusion of a retreat. The sermon title was "I pray that you will all die before you are finished":

> As he began to unfold his understanding of God's plan, his point became perfectly clear. He was not giving a prayer for an early demise; it was a prayer for a very long and fruitful life. It was a reminder that God's plan is never finished, His work never done...
>
> Of course, there was a reason why these people died before they were finished. God is not a kill-joy or a sadist who would rob us of final victory just for the fun of it. "For God wanted them to wait and share the even better rewards that were prepared for us" (Hebrews 11:40 TLB).
>
> What makes us think we will finish all we want to do before we die? A neurotic need to prove something to ourselves? Some memory of rejection by a parent who said, "You'll never amount to anything"? Some uncomfortable inner drive to prove that we're perfect? A hope that people will respect us more if we are successful and powerful? I suspect that the more we want to finish before we die, the more likely we'll die before we're finished. Life is, unfortunately, a chain of incompletes.
>
> A successful life will always be unfinished, and the more successful it is, the more will be left undone. This is how life works. It may seem sad, but the positive side to all of this is that God is with us in our incompleteness and gives us permission to stop trying to accomplish everything in one brief period of existence. It is liberating to realize that we don't have to finish. All we have to be is faithful.[13]

Be strong and courageous. Do not be afraid or terrified because of them, for the LORD your God goes with you (Deuteronomy 31:6).

I n his book *Today Can Be Different,* Harold Sala offers some wise words about trials:

Trials are not an indication that God has singled you out for special punishment or proof that you're not a victorious believer. Trials happen…

1. Trials never leave you where they find you. Like a whirlwind that picks something up, when you finally hit the ground you are not in the same place; you're not even the same person.

2. Trials will cause you to grow better or bitter…Hopefully, you'll learn the lesson the trial has to offer without having to take the test all over again. A certain fellow saw an ad for an ocean cruise at a phenomenally low price, so he promptly bought the adventure. But, immediately upon boarding the liner, the floor opened and he tumbled down a chute, finding himself in a little rowboat out on the ocean all by himself. Toward evening, another individual came by in a rowboat…He called out, "Do they serve meals on this cruise?" The other replied, "They didn't last year!"

3. Trials produce growth and maturity.

4. Trials are of limited duration…eventually God leads us to the other side.

5. Trials cause you to know His presence and power…A Chinese friend, who spent nine months in total darkness in a Communist prison, wrote after he left China for the West: "What I miss more than all else are the intense, quiet moments with Christ that I have not known since the anguish of the days while I was in solitary confinement!"

Don't curse your trials: realize God is with you through them.[14]

*Do not conform any longer to the pattern of this world, but
be transformed by the renewing of your mind. Then you
will be able to test and approve what God's will is—his
good, pleasing and perfect will (Romans 12:2).*

Where are you going? What are you going to do? What will you accomplish? Has anyone asked you these questions recently? Some years ago, Lawrence Appley, chairman of the board of The American Management Association, spoke at a large convention. Afterward a young student asked, "What are your ten-year goals?" The speaker replied, "Do you know how old I am? I'm seventy-five!" The student said, "Yes, I knew that. What are your ten-year goals?" He made his point. We are never too old to dream.

Some men react negatively to this idea of setting goals. They say, "I like my freedom. I'm a spontaneous man. I don't want to be limited." Well, who said setting goals limits you? It's just the opposite. You need to give some thought to the future. We weren't created to drift or to bounce off the walls of life.

God wants you to experience the fullness He has for you. Consider these questions: What are your personal goals for the next three months? Six months? The next year? The next five years? The next ten years? In that time, where will you be in accomplishing the things you (and no other person) was born to do?[15] Consider Lloyd Ogilvie's words:

> There are few things which give life more verve than knowing "what is that good and acceptable and perfect will of God" (Romans 12:2) in the short- and long-range goals for our lives. We know where we are headed and can react with spontaneity to everything which brings us closer to our destiny and destination as persons. And the Holy Spirit will guide us each step of the way![16]

Do not conform any longer to the pattern of this world, but be transformed by the renewing of your mind. Then you will be able to test and approve what God's will is—his good, pleasing and perfect will (Romans 12:2).

Do you remember the movie *The Elephant Man*? It's the story of a deformed man who eventually achieves dignity. Although his body stayed the same, he changed, gaining a sense of personal worthiness, of purpose. There are many men today who aren't deformed in the physical sense, but they are in other ways. Some have deformed attitudes that are negative and pessimistic. This deformation is curable. Some have habits that have deformed into addictions. This is also curable.

There is one deformity that mars every person alive. It's called sin. It's a spiritual deformation, distorting our values and our minds. It can even cripple our abilities. You may not be able to see it from the outside, but it's there. The worst part is that the image of God, in which we were created, has been marred by sin. Look around you, read the paper, watch the news. You'll see the results of sin's deformity.

But, praise God, He intervened to change this deformity. It wasn't an external patch job either. It's called *regeneration,* being born again, which gives us new life in Christ. The word used to describe this change is *transformation,* which means "changing." This is not anything we can bring about; it's the Holy Spirit causing a major renovation.

Regarding the key words for today: *Deformation*—In what areas do you still feel deformed? *Regeneration*—When did you experience this in your life? *Transformation*—What area of your life needs this today? *Renovation*—In what ways would you like to be renovated?[17]

For to me, to live is Christ and to die is gain (Philippians 1:21).

The question "Why, God?" is as old as humanity itself. From the beginning people have been trying to reconcile the basic goodness of God with some of the calamities that befall us. A lot of sincere, trusting individuals pondered the answer to that question when Paul Little died as the result of injuries sustained in an automobile accident. He directed InterVarsity Christian Fellowship, a student organization with a worldwide impact.

Then there was the untimely death of Dawson Trotman, founder of the Navigators—an organization emphasizing the study of God's Word that has touched millions of lives. When he drowned, many asked why. The list of lives cut short while serving God includes Willis Shank, missionary pilot and Christian statesman whose plane went down in the Arctic; Paul Carlson, a medical doctor who gave his life in the Congo rebellion; Nate Saint, Jim Elliot, and Ed McCully—missionaries who died in Ecuador; Clate Risley, evangelical leader and educator who was murdered; Chet Bitterman, whose bullet-riddled body was found wrapped in a revolutionary flag in Colombia; Don Bowers, essential radio engineer and technician in Saipan who drowned; and many, many more.

Of these people several things need to be said. First, each would immediately endorse the words of Paul, who wrote that his desire was that Christ should be glorified in his body, whether by life or by death (Philippians 1:20). Then we know that God can use the untimely death of one of His servants to speak to the hearts of many, who will then step out and serve Him. Third, our faith in Christ doesn't make us immune to disasters, but it gives us the assurance that death opens the door to eternal life: "[For] to be absent from the body and to be present with the Lord" (2 Corinthians 5:8 NKJV).[18]

*I thought in my heart, "Come now, I will test
you with pleasure" (Ecclesiastes 2:1).*

"I thought in my heart" is an interesting concept. That's where everything begins—in our hearts. It's the source of our attitudes and beliefs. When Solomon looked at his heart he made an important discovery that might help us avoid pitfalls!

> I wanted to see what was worthwhile for men to do under heaven during the few days of their lives…I built houses for myself and planted vineyards. I made gardens and parks and planted all kinds of fruit trees in them. I made reservoirs to water groves of flourishing trees. I bought male and female slaves and had other slaves who were born in my house. I also owned more herds and flocks than anyone in Jerusalem before me. I amassed silver and gold for myself, and the treasure of kings and provinces. I acquired men and women singers, and a harem as well—the delights of the heart of man. I became greater by far than anyone in Jerusalem before me. In all this my wisdom stayed with me.

> I denied myself nothing my eyes desired; I refused my heart no pleasure. My heart took delight in all my work, and this was the reward for all my labor. Yet when I surveyed all that my hands had done and what I had toiled to achieve, everything was meaningless, a chasing after the wind; nothing was gained under the sun.

> Then I turned my thoughts to consider wisdom, and also madness and folly…I saw that wisdom is better than folly, just as light is better than darkness. The wise man has eyes in his head, while the fool walks in the darkness; but I came to realize that the same fate overtakes them both. Then I thought in my heart, "The fate of the fool will overtake me also. What then do I gain by being wise?" I said in my heart, "This too is meaningless" (Ecclesiastes 2:3-15).

DECEMBER 23

Mary was pledged to be married to Joseph, but before
they came together, she was found to be with child
through the Holy Spirit (Matthew 1:18,21).

Have you ever wondered what it was like for Mary to rear Jesus? Max Lucado, in his book *God Came Near,* raises twenty-five questions for Mary that will make you think. Here are some of them:

What was it like watching him pray?

How did he respond when he saw other kids giggling…at the synagogue?

When he saw a rainbow, did he ever mention a flood?

Did you ever feel awkward teaching him how he created the world?

When he saw a lamb being led to the slaughter, did he act differently?

Did you ever see him with a distant look on his face, as if he were listening to someone you couldn't hear?

How did he act at funerals?

Did the thought ever occur to you that the God to whom you were praying was asleep under your own roof?

Did you ever try to count the stars with him…and succeed?

Did he ever come home with a black eye?

How did he act when he got his first haircut?

Did he have any friends by the name of Judas?

Did he do well in school?

Did you ever scold him?

Did he ever have to ask a question about Scripture?

What do you think he thought when he saw a prostitute offering to the highest bidder the body he made?

Did he ever get angry when someone was dishonest with him?

Did you ever catch him pensively looking at the flesh on his own arm while holding a clod of dirt?

Did he ever wake up afraid?

Who was his best friend?

When someone referred to Satan, how did he act?

Did you ever accidentally call him Father?[19]

After Jesus was born in Bethlehem in Judea...(Matthew 2:1).

C hristmas each year weaves its magic spell on our hearts. Carols float on the air, and there is a surge of love and kindliness not felt any other time of the year. Crèches appear reminding us of the miracle in the manger. In that feeding trough in lowly Bethlehem, a cry from an infant's throat broke centuries of silence. For the first time God's voice could be heard coming from human vocal cords. C.S. Lewis called that event—the coming of Christ at Christmas—"the greatest rescue mission of history."

During each Christmas season the words of Micah resonate throughout the world. He was inspired to give the prophecy that named the birthplace of the Messiah: "But you, Bethlehem Ephrathah, though you are small among the clans of Judah, out of you will come for me one who will be ruler over Israel, whose origins are from of old, from ancient times" (Micah 5:2). Micah was telling those who were proud, powerful, rich, and self-righteous that God's great ruler would not come from their stately environs. He would come forth from the nondescript hamlet of Bethlehem. More than 700 years after the prophecy, when the wise men searched for Jesus, the scribes had to brush off the dust from the book of Micah to direct them to the location where He would be born.

The One who would come was from ancient times (verse 2). This literally means "from days of eternity." This speaks of the eternal existence of Christ. His providence and preeminence are also prophesied as One who will "stand and shepherd his flock...[and] his greatness will reach to the ends of the earth. And he will be their peace" (Micah 5:4-5). What beautiful and precious promises Micah shares, this plowman who became God's mighty penman.[20]

*[Mary] gave birth to her firstborn, a son. She wrapped
him in cloths and placed him in a manger, because
there was no room for him in the inn (Luke 2:7).*

O God, our Father, we remember at this Christmastime how the eternal Word became flesh and dwelt among us.

We thank you that Jesus took our human body upon him, so that we can never again dare to despise or neglect or misuse the body, since you made it your dwelling-place.

We thank you that Jesus did a day's work like any working man, that he knew the problem of living together in a family, that he knew the frustration and irritation of serving the public, that he had to earn a living, and to face all the wearing routine of every-day work and life and living, and so clothed each common task with glory.

We thank you that he shared in all happy social occasions, that he was at home at weddings and at dinners and at festivals in the homes of simple ordinary people like ourselves. Grant that we may ever remember that in his unseen risen presence he is a guest in every home.

We thank you that he too had to bear unfair criticism, prejudiced opposition, malicious and deliberate misunderstanding.

We thank you that whatever happens to us, he has been there before, and that, because he himself has gone through things, he is able to help those who are going through them.

Help us never to forget that he knows life, because he lived life, and that he is with us at all times to enable us to live victoriously. This we ask for your love's sake. Amen. [21]

Jesus said, "Follow me" (Matthew 4:19).

D o you follow Jesus? There are many good reasons to do so.

Christ said to follow Him because following anyone or anything else gets us lost.

Christ said to know who we look like because drawing our self-image from any other source but God poisons our souls and spirits.

Christ said to love our neighbor as ourselves because we grow the most when committed to fostering another's growth, not just our own.

Christ said to clean the inside of the cup because that is the only way to develop true character and avoid a shallow existence.

Christ said to stop fitting in with our culture because our culture is sick, and adapting to it will make us sick, too.

Christ said to get real because wearing masks makes our lives empty and our relationships unfulfilling.

Christ said to stop blaming others because taking responsibility for our own problems is essential for true maturity and health.

Christ said to forgive others because unforgiveness…hurts others as well as ourselves.

Christ said to live like an heir because to live like an orphan leads to settling for far too little in life.

Christ said to solve paradoxes because it is often that which seems contrary to common sense that is the healthiest route of all.

Christ said to stop worrying because worry only drains us of the energy we need to work on the things that we can do something about.

Christ said to persevere because the fruit of our labor won't ever show up if we grow tired of doing what it takes to bear it.

Everything Christ tells us is in our best interest. His counsel wasn't designed to burden us, but to set us free. His counsel will meet our deepest needs if we follow it. [22]

Isn't this the carpenter? (Mark 6:3).

M ost of us don't spend much time thinking about Jesus as a carpenter. It doesn't seem very significant. And yet, maybe it is. A carpenter fashions and creates. Jesus did this in the expression of His divinity and humanity. He created the universe: "Through him all things were made; without him nothing was made that has been made" (John 1:3).

He also fashioned furniture. There were no electric drills and saws. It was muscle-pushing, rough-hewn tools that were basic and caused calluses. His hands were probably bruised and cut from handling the wood and the crude saw or hammer. You wouldn't believe the amount of time and energy spent back then to make a chair or table.

But what does Jesus being a carpenter have to do with us? Consider these thoughts:

> As the Carpenter, Christ forever sanctified human toil...Our tasks are given dignity by the One who worked amid the wood shavings at the carpenter's bench for the greater part of His life. His labor enabled the oxen to plow without being chafed by their yokes, children to take delight in the hand-carved toys, families to live in the comfort of a home built by the Carpenter.

> Today, the Carpenter of Nazareth, who once smoothed yokes in His skillful hands, would take a life that is yielded to Him and fashion it into a beautiful and useful instrument of God's eternal kingdom.[23]

All your effort and toil as a parent also has purpose and merit. As Jesus is fashioning your life, let Him work through you to fashion your child's life.

> Carpenter of Nazareth, take my life and smooth the coarseness of its grain, work out the flaws and imperfections, make me a worthwhile and useful instrument.[24]

DECEMBER 28

*The weapons we fight with...have divine power to
demolish strongholds. We demolish arguments and
every pretension...and we take captive every thought to
make it obedient to Christ (2 Corinthians 10:4-5).*

Problems—we've got them in all sizes. Solving them is based mostly on how we think about them. Dr. William Mitchell shared five possible ways of viewing them:

Curse the problem. This, in essence, means adding a negative opinion to the negative facts of the situation—in other words, compounding the negativity.

Nurse the problem—focusing time and attention on the problem itself rather than on its solution.

Rehearse the problem—replaying the problem until the person is actually thinking about very little other than the problem.

Disperse it. A technique used in tackling scientific problems is to break a problem down into its component parts and then to work at each part until an answer is reached. As the component problems are solved, the big problem is also solved. This principle holds true for all of life. One of the most effective things a person can do about what seems to be an overwhelming problem is to...break it down into its smaller component problems...

Reverse it. Seek out the positive...There is always some glimmer of hope, some ray of light. Recognize negativity for what it is—a distraction from a positive solution. Dismiss the negativity. Of course, you do not ignore the problem in hopes that it will go away. To the contrary! Disposing of the negative thought means... making a conscious decision that the negative response is going to do nothing to solve the problem, and in that light, refusing to dwell on the negative and turning instead to the positive. [25]

*[The LORD] guards the course of the just and protects
the way of his faithful ones (Proverbs 2:8).*

When Prince Charles was four years old, his mother (Queen Elizabeth) decided to rear him as a normal child. And the little boy thought all the kids were just like him, and every child's mother was a queen. But in spite of his mother wanting him to be like any other boy, he had to make some major adjustments as he reached adulthood. You see, life doesn't always turn out the way we think it will.

Did Joseph of the Old Testament dream of being a ruler in Egypt? Not likely. He probably had visions of settling down with a local girl and owning a few head of cattle. When Jeremiah was a young man, do you think he wanted to end up being a doom-and-gloom prophet? Probably not. But Joseph and Jeremiah made the shift.

Think of some others who made major changes in their lives—such as Martin Luther. He was encouraged to be a lawyer. Can you imagine his reaction if he had known what was coming: "Me, be a monk and lead the Protestant Reformation? I don't think so." But it happened because he adjusted.

Herbert Hoover was raised a Quaker and went to Stanford University to be a minister. Can you imagine his response if someone had said, "Hey, Herb, how would you like to be president of this country someday?" It happened. He adjusted.

How well do you adjust to changes, to new plans? They're going to happen whether you want them to or not. We live in a changing world. Those who make the adjustments are those willing to change. It could be that God wants you retrained for something. Wonder what it is? Just wait on Him. You'll see soon enough.[26]

There are six things the Lord hates—no, seven: haughtiness, lying, murdering, plotting evil, eagerness to do wrong, a false witness, sowing discord among brothers (Proverbs 6:16-19 TLB).

I nteresting, isn't it? Several of the things the Lord hates in today's passage are the misuse of words. Words have tremendous power. "Those who love to talk will suffer the consequences" (Proverbs 18:21 TLB). One well-placed word with the proper tone of voice and look can have more impact than an entire sermon. The way something is said can be a source of healing or hurt. Did you know that in face-to-face conversation, the way your words are packaged makes all the difference in the world? Your words make up 7 percent of the message, your tone 38 percent, and your nonverbal 55 percent!

Our words can lacerate a person's feelings. "Some people like to make cutting remarks" (Proverbs 12:18 TLB). But "telling the truth gives a man great satisfaction, and hard work returns many blessings to him" (12:14 TLB). Our words can lift people and even give them health. "Anxious hearts are very heavy, but a word of encouragement does wonders!" (12:25 TLB). "Kind words are like honey—enjoyable and healthful" (16:24 TLB). We can damage someone's self-esteem by flattering them. "Flattery is a trap; evil men are caught in it, but good men stay away and sing for joy" (29:5-6 TLB).

The good news? Your words can be so productive that what you say not only comes back to benefit you, but others as well. That's not a bad proposition. "Gentle words cause life and health; griping brings discouragement" (Proverbs 15:4 TLB).

Often we hear the phrase "They're known by their words." What do your words tell others?[27]

*No one can lay any foundation other than the one already laid,
which is Jesus Christ. If any man builds on this foundation using
gold, silver, costly stones, wood, hay or straw, his work will be
shown for what it is, because the Day will bring it to light. It will
be revealed with fire, and the fire will test the quality of each man's
work. If what he has built survives, he will receive his reward. If
it is burned up, he will suffer loss; he himself will be saved, but
only as one escaping through the flames (1 Corinthians 3:11-15).*

Someday you will retire. What's it going to be like? Exciting and fulfilling or empty and dull? Many men find what they're doing right
now fulfilling. There are business deals to make, mergers to arrange, golf
lessons to take to lower that handicap, children to raise and marry off,
meetings to attend—the list goes on. Life is full…for now. But when
you retire, where are the mergers and business deals? Will those muscles
stand up to 18 rounds of golf or a softball game? What if the kids live
3000 miles away? Or what if your divorced daughter and her three children come home to live?

Much may be going on now…but how about later? Can you continue your activities into your retirement? Athletes have said that for
years their lives were consumed by their sport. One of the greatest baseball players of all time made the statement, "You know, for years I ate
baseball, I slept baseball, I talked baseball, I thought it and lived it. One
day it was over. I found out then when you get beyond those years, you
can't live on baseball!"

Many men live their lives as though what they do will be extended
until they die. But it might not be. There is one thing we can do now
and all our days. It's called living the Christian life. It's here now, and it
will stay with you!

ACKNOWLEDGMENTS

Thank you to those who granted permission to reprint their material:

Neil and Joanne Anderson. *Daily in Christ*. Eugene, OR: Harvest House Publishers, 1993. Used by permission.

Bill Austin. *How to Get What You Pray For*. Reprinted by permission.

William Barclay. *A Barclay Prayer Book*. London: SCM Press. Permission for rights in the U.S. granted by Trinity Press International.

Joe E. Brown, *Battle Fatigue*. Nashville: Broadman and Holman Publishers, 1995. All rights reserved. Used by permission.

Randy Carlson. *Father Memories*. Chicago: Moody Press, 1992. Used by permission.

Lloyd Cory. *Quotable Quotations*. Wheaton, IL: Victor Books/SP Publications, Inc., 1995.

Judson Edwards. *Regaining Control of Your Life*. Minneapolis: Bethany House, 1989. Reprinted by permission.

Paul Enns. *Approaching God*. Chicago: Moody Press, 1991. Used by permission.

Henry Gariepy. *100 Portraits of Christ*. Wheaton, IL: Victor Books/SP Publications, Inc., 1987.

_____. *Light in a Dark Place*. Wheaton, IL: Victor Books/SP Publications, Inc., 1995.

Ken Gire. *Incredible Moments with the Savior*. Grand Rapids, MI: Zondervan Publishing House, 1990. Reprinted by permission.

Tim Hansel. *When I Relax I Feel Guilty*. Colorado Springs: David C. Cook Publishing, 1979. Used by permission.

R. Kent Hughes. *Disciplines of a Godly Man*. Wheaton, IL: Good News Publishers/Crossway Books, 1991. Used by permission.

James L. Johnson. *What Every Woman Should Know About a Man*. Copyright © 1981. Permission granted by Mrs. James L. Johnson.

Jon Johnston. *Walls or Bridges*. Grand Rapids, MI: Baker Books House, 1988. Used by permission.

Carol Kent. *Tame Your Fears*. Colorado Springs: NavPress, 1994. Used by permission. All rights reserved.

Max Lucado. *A Gentle Thunder*. Dallas: Word, Inc., 1995. All rights reserved.

_____. *God Came Near*. Sisters, OR: Multnomah Books/Questar Publishers, 1987. Used by permission.

_____. *On the Anvil*. Wheaton, IL: Tyndale House Publishers, Inc., 1985. Reprinted by permission. All rights reserved.

D. Martin Lloyd-Jones. *Spiritual Depression*. London: HarperCollins, 1965. Permission granted for North American rights.

Mike Mason. *The Mystery of Marriage*. Portland, OR: Multnomah Books/Questar Publishers, 1985. Used by permission.

Dean Merrill. *Wait Quietly, Devotions for Busy Parents*. Wheaton, IL: Tyndale House Publishers, Inc., 1994. Used by permission. All rights reserved.

W.P. Moody. *The Life of Dwight L. Moody*. Uhrichsville, OH: Barbour & Company, Inc., 1985.

G. Campbell Morgan. *The Ten Commandments*. New York: F.H. Revell, 1901. Used by permission.

Patrick Morley. *The Man in the Mirror*. Brentwood, TN: Wolgemuth and Hyatt, 1989. Used by permission.

Malcolm Muggeridge. *A Twentieth Century Testimony*. Nashville: Thomas Nelson Publishing, 1978. Used by permission.

Lloyd John Ogilvie. *God's Best for My Life.* Eugene, OR: Harvest House Publishers, 1981. Used by permission.

_____. *Silent Strength for My Life.* Eugene, OR: Harvest House Publishers, 1990. Used by permission.

Gary Oliver. *How to Get It Right When You've Gotten It Wrong.* Wheaton, IL: Victor Books/SP Publications, Inc., 1995.

_____. *Real Men Have Feelings Too.* Chicago: Moody Press, 1993. Used by permission.

J.I. Packer and Sangwoo Youtong Chee, "A Bad Trip," *Christianity Today,* March 7, 1986. Reprinted by permission of James I. Packer.

Les and Leslie Parrott. *Becoming Soul Mates.* Grand Rapids, MI: Zondervan Publishing House, 1995. Used by permission.

James Patterson and Peter Kim. *The Day America Told the Truth: What People Really Believe About Everything That Really Matters.* New York: Simon & Schuster, 1991. Used by permission.

Tim Riter. *Deep Down.* Wheaton, IL: Tyndale House Publishers, Inc., 1995. Used by permission. All rights reserved.

Gary Rosberg. *Guard Your Heart.* Sisters, OR: Multnomah Books/Questar Publishers, 1994. Used by permission.

Douglas E. Rosenau. *A Celebration of Sex.* Nashville: Thomas Nelson Publishing, 1994. Used by permission.

Harold Sala. *Today Can Be Different.* Ventura, CA: Regal Books, 1988. Used by permission.

Charlie and Martha Shedd, *How to Start and Keep It Going,* cited by Fritz Ridenour, "Praying Together," *The Marriage Collection.* Grand Rapids, MI: Zondervan, 1989. Used by permission.

Richard Selzer. *Mortal Lessons,* © 1976. Used by permission. All rights reserved.

Dwight Small. *After You've Said I Do.* Grand Rapids, MI: Fleming H. Revell/Baker Book House, 1968. Used with permission.

Lewis B. Smedes. *Forgive and Forget.* New York: HarperCollins Publishers, Inc., 1984. Reprinted by permission.

Jim Smoke. *Facing 50.* Nashville: Thomas Nelson Publishing, 1994. Reprinted by permission.

R.C. Sproul. *Pleasing God.* Wheaton, IL: Tyndale House Publishers, Inc. 1988. Used by permission. All rights reserved.

David Stoop. *Making Peace with Your Father.* Wheaton, IL: Tyndale House Publishers, Inc., 1992. Reprinted by permission. All rights reserved.

R. Scott Sullender. *Losses in Later Life.* New York: Paulist Press, 1989. Used by permission.

Charles Swindoll. *The Finishing Touch.* Dallas: Word, Inc., 1994. Used by permission. All rights reserved.

_____. *Growing Strong in the Seasons of Life.* Sisters, OR: Multnomah books/Questar Publisher, 1983. Reprinted by permission of Charles R. Swindoll.

_____. *Improving Your Serve.* Dallas: Word, Inc., 1981. Used by permission. All rights reserved.

_____. *Living Beyond the Daily Grind.* Dallas: Word, Inc., 1988. Used by permission. All rights reserved.

Chris Thurman. *If Christ Were Your Counselor.* Nashville: Thomas Nelson Publishing, 1993. Reprinted by permission.

H. Norman Wright. *How to Really Love Your Wife.* Ann Arbor, MI: Servant Publications/Vine Books, 1995. Used by permission.

_____. *Quiet Times for Parents.* Eugene, OR: Harvest House Publishers, 1995. Used by permission.

NOTES

January

1. Kent Hughes, *Disciplines of a Godly Man* (Wheaton, IL: Crossway, 1991), 15-16, adapted.
2. Ibid., 17, adapted.
3. Ibid., 29-31, adapted.
4. David W. Smith, *Men Without Friends* (Nashville: Thomas Nelson, 1990), 79-80, adapted.
5. Max Lucado, *A Gentle Thunder* (Dallas: Word, 1995), 80-81.
6. David Stoop, *Seeking Christ* (Nashville: Thomas Nelson, 1994), 2-3, adapted.
7. Hughes, *Disciplines of a Godly Man,* 53-56, adapted.
8. Webster's New World Dictionary (New York: Prentice Hall, 1994), s.v. *accomplishment.*
9. Judson Edwards, *Regaining Control of Your Life* (Minneapolis: Bethany, 1989), 157, adapted.
10. James Johnson, *What Every Woman Should Know About a Man* (Grand Rapids, MI: Zondervan, 1981), 104-05.
11. Charles R. Swindoll, *The Finishing Touch* (Dallas: Word, 1994), 72, adapted.
12. Carol Kent, *Tame Your Fears* (Colorado Springs: NavPress, 1994), 28-29, adapted. Also from H. Norman Wright, *Quiet Times for Parents* (Eugene, OR: Harvest House, 1995), Sep. 19, adapted.
13. Bill McCartney, ed., *What Makes a Man* (Colorado Springs: NavPress, 1992), quoting an article by Steve Farrar, 58-59.
14. Lloyd John Ogilvie, *God's Best for My Life* (Eugene, OR: Harvest House, 1981), Jan. 16.
15. Ken Olsen, *Hey Man! Open Up and Live* (New York: Fawcett, 1978), 147-48.
16. Douglas E. Rosenau, *A Celebration of Sex* (Nashville: Thomas Nelson, 1994), 21.
17. John Trent and Rick Hicks, *Seeking Solid Ground* (Colorado Springs: Focus on the Family, 1995), 58-60, adapted.
18. Charles Swindoll, *Growing Strong in the Seasons of Life* (Sisters, OR: Multnomah, 1983), 27-28, adapted.
19. Lloyd John Ogilvie, *Silent Strength for My Life* (Eugene, OR: Harvest House, 1990), 308.
20. Gary J. Oliver, *Real Men Have Feelings, Too* (Chicago: Moody, 1993), 60-61.
21. Gordon MacDonald, *Restoring Your Spiritual Passion* (Nashville: Thomas Nelson, 1986), 59-60, adapted.

February

1. Swindoll, *Finishing Touch,* 64-65, adapted.
2. Elton Trueblood, as quoted in Swindoll, *Finishing Touch,* 65.
3. Webster's New World Dictionary, 3rd college ed. (New York: Simon & Schuster, 1994), s.v. *treason.*
4. R.C. Sproul, *Before the Face of God,* bk. 3 (Grand Rapids, MI: Baker, 1994), 242-43, adapted.
5. Lucado, *Gentle Thunder,* 68-69, adapted.
6. Henry Gariepy, *100 Portraits of Christ* (Wheaton, IL: Victor, 1987), 95-96, adapted.
7. Ibid., 96.
8. H. Norman Wright, *Quiet Times for Parents* (Eugene, OR: Harvest House, 1995), Sep. 13, adapted.
9. Mike Mason, *The Mystery of Marriage* (Portland, OR: Multnomah, 1985), 91, 97-98, adapted.
10. Quoted in Dean Merrill, *Wait Quietly* (Wheaton, IL: Tyndale, 1994), 49.

11. Trent and Hicks, *Seeking Solid Ground,* 79, adapted.

12. Jim Smoke, *Facing 50* (Nashville: Thomas Nelson, 1994), 40-41, adapted.

13. H. Norman Wright, *How to Really Love Your Wife* (Ann Arbor, MI: Servant, 1995), 93.

14. William Barclay, *A Barclay Prayer Book* (London: SCM Press Ltd., 1963), 8-9.

15. Hughes, *Disciplines of a Godly Man,* 35-36.

16. MacDonald, *Restoring Your Spiritual Passion,* 96-104, adapted.

17. Harry Hollis, Jr., *Thank God for Sex* (Nashville: Broadman, 1975), 109-10.

18. Lloyd John Ogilvie, *Enjoying God* (Dallas: Word, 1989), 22-24, adapted.

19. Ogilvie, *God's Best for My Life,* August 27.

20. Dwight Small, *After You've Said I Do* (Grand Rapids, MI: Revell, 1968), 243-44.

21. Neil Anderson with Joanne Anderson, *Daily in Christ* (Eugene, OR: Harvest House, 1993), July 31, adapted.

22. New World Webster Dictionary of the American Language, 2nd college ed. (New York: Simon and Schuster, 1980), s.v. *pleasure.*

23. Gordon Dalbey, *Fight Like a Man* (Wheaton, IL: Tyndale, 1995), 2-3, adapted.

24. D. Martyn Lloyd-Jones, *Spiritual Depression* (London: HarperCollins, 1965), 142.

March

1. Oliver, *Real Men,* 160-61.

2. Richard Selzer, *Mortal Lessons: Notes on the Art of Surgery* (New York: Simon & Schuster, 1976), 45-46.

3. Hughes, *Disciplines of a Godly Man,* 40-41, adapted.

4. Ibid., 42.

5. Edwards, *Regaining Control,* 78-79, adapted.

6. John F. MacArthur, *Drawing Near* (Wheaton, IL: Crossway, 1993), Jan. 22, adapted.

7. Gary Rosberg, *Guard Your Heart* (Sisters, OR: Multnomah, 1994), 15-17, adapted.

8. Swindoll, *Finishing Touch,* 281.

9. Rosenau, *Celebration of Sex,* 8-9.

10. Les and Leslie Parrott, *Becoming Soul Mates* (Grand Rapids, MI: Zondervan, 1995), 144, adapted.

11. Oliver, *Real Men,* 138.

12. Trent and Hicks, *Seeking Solid Ground,* 80-84, adapted.

13. W.T. Purkiser, "Five Ways to Have a Nervous Breakdown," *Herald of Holiness,* October 9, 1974, as quoted in Jon Johnson, *Walls or Bridges* (Grand Rapids, MI: Baker, 1988), 176-77, adapted. Purkiser was commenting on J.L. Glass's, "Five Ways" list.

14. As quoted in Rosberg, *Guard Your Heart,* 134-35.

15. Rosberg, *Guard Your Heart,* 138-40.

16. Edgar Guest, *My Job as a Father* (Chicago: Reilly & Lee, 1923), 83.

17. Trent and Hicks, *Seeking Solid Ground,* 20, adapted.

18. Lloyd John Ogilvie, *Climbing the Rainbow* (Dallas: Word, 1993), 114-19, adapted. Also H. Norman Wright, *Quiet Times for Parents,* May 21, adapted.

19. William James, *Quotable Quotations,* Lloyd Cory, ed. (Wheaton, IL: Victor, 1985), 181.

20. H. Norman Wright, *Secrets of a Lasting Marriage* (Ventura, CA: Regal, 1995), 52-53.

21. Harold Ivan Smith, *Changing Answers to Depression* (Eugene, OR: Harvest House, 1978), 95, adapted.

22. Peter F. Drucker, *The Effective Executive* (New York: Harper & Row, 1966), 111, adapted.

April

1. Tim Hansel, *When I Relax I Feel Guilty* (Colorado Springs: David C. Cook, 1979), 51.
2. Ibid., 53-54.
3. Ibid., 55, adapted.
4. Ogilvie, *God's Best for My Life,* May 8, adapted.
5. Swindoll, *Finishing Touch,* 60-61, adapted.
6. Edwards, *Regaining Control,* 47-48.
7. John Sanderson, "The Fruit of the Spirit," as quoted in Tim Riter, *Deep Down* (Wheaton, IL: Tyndale, 1995), 59.
8. Tim Riter, *Deep Down* (Wheaton, IL: Tyndale, 1995), 52.
9. Paul Walker, *How to Keep Your Joy* (Nashville: Thomas Nelson, 1987), 17.
10. Lloyd John Ogilvie, *The Loose Ends* (Dallas: Word, 1991), 43-47, adapted. Also Wright, *Quiet Times for Parents,* May 24, adapted.
11. Ken Gire, *Incredible Moments with the Savior* (Grand Rapids, MI: Zondervan, 1990), 96-97.
12. Gary J. Oliver, *How to Get It Right When You've Gotten It Wrong* (Wheaton, IL: Victor, 1995), 171.
13. John F. MacArthur, *Drawing Near* (Wheaton, IL: Crossway, 1993), Jan. 23, adapted.
14. Charles R. Swindoll, *Improving Your Serve* (Dallas, TX: Word, 1981), 105.
15. Patrick Morley, *Seven Seasons of a Man's Life* (Nashville: Thomas Nelson, 1990), 90-91, adapted.
16. As quoted in Dean Merrill, *Wait Quietly,* 63.
17. Ibid., 62-63, adapted.
18. Charlie and Martha Shedd, *How to Start and Keep It Going,* cited by Fritz Ridenour, "Praying Together" in *The Marriage Collection* (Grand Rapids, MI: Zondervan, 1989), 442-43.
19. Billy Sunday, *Standing on the Rocks,* as quoted in Parrott and Parrott, *Becoming Soul Mates,* 111-12.

May

1. Merrill, *Wait Quietly,* 13-15, adapted.
2. Joe E. Brown, *Battle Fatigue* (Nashville: Broadman & Holman, 1995), 30-36, adapted.
3. Lloyd John Ogilvie, *The Heart of God* (Ventura, CA: Regal, 1994), 202.
4. Hughes, *Disciplines of a Godly Man,* 62-65, adapted.
5. Sproul, *Before the Face of God,* 446-47, adapted.
6. Ogilvie, *God's Best for My Life,* May 9.
7. Brown, *Battle Fatigue,* 116-17.
8. Parrott and Parrott, *Becoming Soul Mates,* 17.
9. Neva Coyle and Zane Anderson, *Living by Chance or by Choice* (Minneapolis: Bethany House, 1995), 95-97, adapted.
10. Barclay, *Barclay Prayer Book,* 28-29, adapted.
11. Ogilvie, *Enjoying God,* 4-5, adapted.
12. Ogilvie, *God's Best for My Life,* Jan. 27.
13. Oliver, *Real Men,* 72, adapted.
14. James S. Bell and Stan Campbell, *A Return to Virtue* (Chicago: Northfield, 1995), 97, adapted.
15. G.W. Target, "The Window," in *The Window and Other Essays* (Mountain View, CA: Pacific Press, 1973), 5-7, adapted.
16. Ogilvie, *Silent Strength for My Life,* 275.

17. A. Cohen, ed., *Proverbs, Soncino Books of the Bible* (London: Soncino Press, 1946), 2.

18. Robert Hicks, *In Search of Wisdom* (Colorado Springs: NavPress, 1995), 35-41, adapted.

19. Patrick Morley, *The Man in the Mirror* (Brentwood, TN: Wolgemuth & Hyatt, 1989), 130.

20. John C. Maxwell, *Developing the Leader Within You* (Nashville: Nelson, 1993), 119-20, adapted.

21. Swindoll, *Growing Strong*, 82, adapted.

June

1. Webster's New World Dictionary, 3rd college ed. (New York- Prentice Hall, 1994), s.v. *reputation.*

2. Riter, *Deep Down*, 52, adapted.

3. Sproul, *Before the Face of God*, 220, adapted.

4. Randy Carlson, *Father Memories* (Chicago: Moody, 1992), 13, 62.

5. Paul Enns, *Approaching God* (Chicago: Moody, 1991), Aug. 15, adapted. Also Wright, *Quiet Times for Parents*, Dec. 20, adapted.

6. Max Lucado, *On the Anvil* (Wheaton, IL: Tyndale, 1985), 69-70. Used by permission.

7. Parrott and Parrott, *Becoming Soul Mates*, 178, adapted.

8. Hansel, *When I Relax I Feel Guilty*, 146-47, adapted.

9. Rudolph F. Norden, *Each Day with Jesus* (St. Louis: Concordia, 1994), 216, adapted.

10. Dan Allender and Tremper Longman, III, *The Cry of the Soul* (Colorado Springs: NavPress, 1994), 250-51, adapted.

11. Barclay, *Barclay Prayer Book*, 14-15, adapted.

12. R.C. Sproul, *Pleasing God* (Wheaton, IL: Tyndale, 1988), 79.

13. Enns, *Approaching God*, January 5, adapted.

14. J.I. Packer, *Knowing God* (Downers Grove, IL: InterVarsity, 1973), 68-73, adapted.

15. Cited in *National Geographic*, December 1978, 858-82.

16. Oliver, *How to Get It Right When You've Gotten It Wrong*, 27.

17. Sproul, *Before the Face of God*, bk. 3, 284-85, adapted.

18. Lucado, *Gentle Thunder*, 69-70, adapted.

19. David Stoop, *Making Peace with Your Father* (Wheaton, IL: Tyndale, 1991), 60-61.

20. Ibid., 55-76, adapted.

21. Lloyd John Ogilvie, *Praying with Power* (Ventura, CA: Regal, 1987), 25-26.

22. H. Norman Wright, *Holding on to Romance* (Ventura, CA: Regal, 1987), 178-80, adapted.

23. Ogilvie, *God's Best for My Life*, March 14.

24. John Mark Templeton, *Discovering the Laws of Life* (New York: Continuum, 1994), 247-48, adapted.

25. Joseph Cooke, *Free for the Taking* (Old Tappan, NJ: Revell, 1975), 29.

July

1. Brown, *Battle Fatigue*, 51-52, adapted.

2. Sproul, *Before the Face of God*, bk. 3, 148-49, adapted.

3. Morley, *Seven Seasons*, 270, adapted.

4. William Mitchell, *Winning in the Land of Giants* (Nashville: Thomas Nelson, 1995), 20-21, adapted.

5. Wright, *Quiet Times for Parents*, March 25, adapted.

6. Smith, *Changing Answers to Depression*, 75-76, adapted.

7. Ogilvie, *Enjoying God*, 198-201, adapted.

8. Harold Sala, *Today Can Be Different* (Ventura, CA: Regal, 1988), July 10, adapted.

9. As quoted in Anderson with Anderson, *Daily in Christ,* May 31, author unknown.

10. "Seven Steps to Stagnation," Robert H. Franbe Association, Chicago.

11. Lloyd John Ogilvie, *Life As It Was Meant to Be* (Ventura, CA: Regal, 1980), 91-92, adapted.

12. Mitchell, *Winning in the Land of Giants,* 36, 49, 50, adapted.

13. Charles R. Swindoll, *Living Beyond the Daily Grind* (Dallas: Word, 1988), 39-41, adapted.

14. Kent Hughes, *Disciplines of Grace* (Wheaton, IL: Crossway, 1993), 15-18, adapted.

15. G. Campbell Morgan, *The Ten Commandments* (New York: Revell, 1901), 18-19.

16. Hughes, *Disciplines of Grace,* 34-39.

17. Packer, *Knowing God,* 39, adapted.

18. Hughes, *Disciplines,* 93-94.

19. Ibid., 98-104, adapted.

20. Ibid., 116-20, adapted.

21. James Patterson and Peter Kim. *The Day America Told the Truth: What People Really Believe About Everything That Really Matters* (New York: Simon & Schuster, 1991), 155.

22. Hughes, *Disciplines of a Godly Man,* 142-47, adapted.

23. Patterson and Kim, *Day America Told the Truth,* 45, 49, adapted.

24. Hughes, *Disciplines of a Godly Man,* 172-81, adapted.

25. Ibid., *Disciplines,* 187-88.

August

1. Swindoll, *Living Beyond,* 110-11, adapted.

2. Swindoll, *Growing Strong,* 108-10, adapted.

3. Edwards, *Regaining Control,* 124-25, adapted.

4. Dalbey, *Fight Like a Man,* 31, adapted.

5. Allender and Longman, III, *Cry of the Soul,* 254-55, adapted.

6. Parrott and Parrott, *Becoming Soul Mates,* 92, adapted.

7. Sala, *Today Can Be Different,* June 27, adapted.

8. Norman Vincent Peale, *Power of the Plus Factor* (New York: Fawcett, 1988).

9. Maxwell, *Developing the Leader Within You,* 101-02, adapted.

10. Ibid., 32, adapted.

11. Ogilvie, *God's Best,* August 15.

12. Wright, *Quiet Times for Couples* (Eugene, OR: Harvest House, 1990) May 8, adapted.

13. Rosenau, *Celebration of Sex,* 26-27.

14. John Baillie, *A Diary of Private Prayer* (Toronto: Oxford University Press, 1979), 33, adapted.

15. Larry Crabb, *The Silence of Man* (Grand Rapids, MI: Zondervan, 1995), 79-85, adapted.

16. Enns, *Approaching God,* January 12, adapted.

17. A.W. Tozer, *The Knowledge of the Holy* (New York: Harper Brothers, 1961), 61-62, adapted.

18. Enns, *Approaching God,* January 14, adapted.

19. Tozer, *Knowledge of the Holy,* 79-82, adapted.

20. Enns, *Approaching God,* January 15, adapted.

21. Ibid., January 16, adapted.

22. R. Scott Sullender, *Losses in Later Life* (New York: Paulist, 1989), 142-43.

23. Ogilvie, *Enjoying God,* 64-65, adapted.

24. Maxwell, *Developing the Leader Within You,* 30, adapted.

25. Ogilvie, *Praying with Power,* 40-45, adapted.

September

1. Harold Ivan Smith, *Changing Answers to Depression,* 66-68, adapted.

2. Oliver, *How to Get It Right,* 66-78, adapted.

3. Edwards, *Regaining Control,* 48, adapted.

4. Wright, *Secrets of a Lasting Marriage,* 87, adapted.

5. Bell and Campbell, *Return to Virtue,* 133, adapted.

6. Sala, *Today Can Be Different,* June 30, adapted.

7. Webster's Ninth Collegiate Dictionary (New York: Simon & Schuster, 1991), s.v. *loneliness.*

8. Ogilvie, *Life As It Was Meant to Be,* 108, adapted.

9. Ogilvie, *Heart of God,* 240-43, adapted.

10. Derek Kinder, *The Proverbs* (Downers Grove, IL: InterVarsity, 1964), 41, adapted.

11. Hicks, *In Search of Wisdom,* 194-200, adapted.

12. Baillie, *Diary of Private Prayer,* 47, adapted.

13. Brown, *Battle Fatigue,* 117-18, adapted.

14. Wright, *Quiet Times for Couples,* May 22, adapted.

15. Hicks, *In Search of Wisdom,* 45-54, adapted.

16. Ibid., 56-58, adapted.

17. MacArthur, *Drawing Near,* March 17, adapted.

18. Morley, *Man in the Mirror,* 58-59.

19. H. Norman Wright, *Chosen for Blessing* (Eugene, OR: Harvest House, 1992), 40-43, adapted.

20. Parrott and Parrott, *Becoming Soul Mates,* 190.

October

1. W.P. Moody, *The Life of Dwight L. Moody* (Uhrichville, OH: Barbour & Co., 1985), 122.

2. Morley, *Seven Seasons,* 274-75.

3. Harold Ivan Smith, *Changing Answers to Depression,* 37, 133, adapted.

4. Enns, *Approaching God,* May 18, adapted.

5. Ibid., May 19, adapted.

6. J.I. Packer and Sangwoo Youtong Chee, "A Bad Trip," *Christianity Today,* March 7, 1986, 12. Wright, *Quiet Times for Parents,* April 20, adapted.

7. Sala, *Today Can Be Different,* Aug. 29, adapted.

8. Swindoll, *Finishing Touch,* 148.

9. Sala, *Today Can Be Different,* Aug. 24, adapted.

10. Hicks, *In Search of Wisdom,* 62-64, adapted.

11. Barclay, *Barclay Prayer Book,* 248-49, adapted.

12. John Roberts Clarke, *The Importance of Being Imperfect* (New York: David McKay, 1981), 11.

13. Sproul, *Before the Face of God,* 424-25, adapted.

14. Webster's New Riverside University Dictionary, 2nd ed., s.v. *failure*.

15. Oliver, *How to Get It Right,* 17.

16. Ronnie W. Floyd, *Choices* (Nashville: Broadman & Holman, 1994), 54-59, adapted.

17. Sproul, *Before the Face of God,* bk. 3, 218-19, adapted.

18. Sala, *Today Can Be Different,* August 30, adapted.

19. Ogilvie, *Heart of God,* 232, adapted.

November

1. Paul W. Coleman, *The Forgiving Marriage* (Chicago: Contemporary Books, 1989), 47, 52, adapted.

2. John C. Maxwell, *The People Person* (Wheaton, IL: Victor Books, 1989), 53-54, adapted.

3. Lloyd John Ogilvie, *Why Not Accept Christ's Healing and Wholeness?* (Old Tappan, NJ: Revell, 1985), 153-55, adapted.

4. Floyd, *Choices,* 38-41, adapted.

5. Trent and Hicks, *Seeking Solid Ground,* 111-14, adapted.

6. Hicks, *In Search of Wisdom,* 82-87, adapted.

7. Hollis, *Thank God for Sex,* 12-13.

8. Brown, *Battle Fatigue,* 32-33.

9. Barclay, *Barclay Prayer Book,* 254-55, adapted.

10. Swindoll, *Living Beyond the Daily Grind,* 71, adapted.

11. Bell and Campbell, *Return to Virtue,* 93, adapted.

12. Swindoll, *Growing Strong in the Seasons of Life,* 366, adapted.

13. Pat Hershey Owen, *Seven Styles of Parenting* (Wheaton, IL: Tyndale, 1983), 15, 27, 28, adapted; Wright, *Quiet Times for Parents,* Jan. 27, adapted.

14. Webster's New Twentieth Century Dictionary, Unabridged, s.v. *giving*.

15. Owen, *Seven Styles of Parenting,* 82-89, adapted; Wright, *Quiet Times for Parents,* Sep. 5, adapted.

16. Owen, *Seven Styles of Parenting,* 69-77, adapted; Wright, *Quiet Times for Parents,* Nov. 13, adapted.

17. Webster's New Twentieth Century Dictionary, Unabridged, s.v. *practical.*

18. Owen, *Seven Styles of Parenting,* 48-49, adapted. Wright, *Quiet Times for Parents,* Feb. 4, adapted.

19. Owen, *Seven Styles of Parenting,* 108-115, adapted. Wright, *Quiet Times for Parents,* April 24, adapted.

20. Webster's New World Dictionary, s.v. *teach,* adapted.

21. Owen, *Seven Styles of Parenting,* 59-60, adapted; Wright, *Quiet Times for Parents,* March 30, adapted.

22. Owen, *Seven Styles of Parenting,* 93-99, adapted; Wright, *Quiet Times for Parents,* July 6, adapted.

23. Brown, *Battle Fatigue,* 14-15, adapted.

24. Clifford Notarius and Howard Markman, *We Can Work It Out* (New York: G.P. Putnam's Sons, 1993), 70-73, adapted.

25. R. Scott Sullender, *Losses in Later Life,* adapted.

26. Oliver, *How to Get It Right,* 20-21.

December

1. Lettie Cowman, *Springs in the Valley* (Grand Rapids, MI: Zondervan, 1939), 196-97.

2. Morley, *Man in the Mirror,* 240-41, adapted.

3. Edwards, *Regaining Control,* 75-76, adapted.

4. Bell and Campbell, *Return to Virtue,* 15, adapted.

5. Sala, *Today Can Be Different,* Jan. 6, adapted.

6. Swindoll, *Living Beyond the Daily Grind,* 51-54, adapted.

7. Smith, *Changing Answers to Depression,* 134, adapted.

8. Bill Austin, *How to Get What You Pray For* (Wheaton, IL: Tyndale, 1984), 63, adapted.

9. Parrott and Parrott, *Becoming Soul Mates,* 25.

10. Floyd, *Choices,* 112-14, adapted.

11. C.S. Lewis, *The Problem of Pain* (London: Collins, 1962), 93.

12. Malcolm Muggeridge, *A Twentieth-Century Testimony* (Nashville: Thomas Nelson, 1978), 18.

13. Archibald Hart, original source unknown.

14. Sala, *Today Can Be Different,* July 11, adapted.

15. Ogilvie, *Life As It Was Meant to Be,* 100-03, adapted.

16. Ibid., 103.

17. Norden, *Each Day with Jesus,* 304, adapted.

18. Sala, *Today Can Be Different,* July 20, adapted.

19. Max Lucado, *God Came Near* (Sisters, OR: Multnomah/Questar Publishers, 1987), 43-44.

20. Henry Gariepy, *Light in a Dark Place* (Wheaton, IL: Victor, 1995), 250-51.

21. Barclay, *Barclay Prayer Book,* 16-17.

22. Chris Thurman, *If Christ Were Your Counselor* (Nashville: Thomas Nelson, 1993), 134.

23. Gariepy, *100 Portraits of Christ,* 78-79. These thoughts are from an officer of the Salvation Army.

24. Ibid.

25. Mitchell, *Winning in the Land of Giants,* 27-28.

26. Norden, *Each Day with Jesus,* 256, adapted.

27. Kinder, *The Proverbs,* 46-47, adapted.

More Great Books by
H. Norman Wright

101 Questions to Ask Before You Get Engaged

After You Say "I Do"

After You Say "I Do" Devotional

Before You Remarry

Before You Say "I Do"®

Before You Say "I Do"® Devotional

Before You Say "I Do"™ DVD

Coping with Chronic Illness

Finding the Right One for You

Quiet Times for Couples

Quiet Times for Every Parent

Reflections of a Grieving Spouse

Gift Books

My Faithful Companion (dogs)

Nine Lives to Love (cats)

Quiet Times for Couples

*"Let Norman Wright guide you together to God...
and your marriage will never be the same."*
MAX LUCADO

**Uplifting, insightful devotions to inspire,
encourage, and strengthen your marriage**

In these short devotions that promote togetherness, joy, and sharing your dreams, trusted Christian counselor and bestselling author Norm Wright offers...

- innovative ideas to establish and maintain a
  flourishing marriage
- insights for encouraging intimacy and harmony
- little and big things you can do to enhance
  your relationship
- specific suggestions for accommodating differences
  and handling conflicts
- great ideas for supporting and helping your spouse

Your relationship will become more loving, considerate, and united as the two of you experience these quiet "together times" filled with deep insights, powerful meditations, God's presence, and His truths and love.

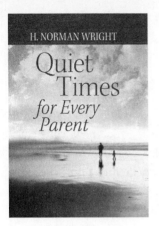

Quiet Times for Every Parent

Parenthood is wonderful, but finding quiet times for yourself can seem impossible. It's not! Bestselling author and noted Christian counselor Norm Wright provides encouragement, support, innovative ideas, and biblical wisdom in brief devotions to help you...

- encourage peace and joy at home
- know and provide what your children need
- grow in Christ even when days are hectic
- get revitalized when you're worn out
- cope on days when everything goes wrong

These short readings will provide an oasis filled with positive steps, uplifting hope, and moments of calm for your life as a busy parent.

Coping with Chronic Illness

Norm Wright and *Lynn Ellis*

Has chronic illness attacked you or someone you love? From fibromyalgia to arthritis, from constant back pain to frequent migraines, chronic conditions afflict more than 200 million people in the United States alone.

Respected counselor Norm Wright and Lynn Ellis, a researcher afflicted with chronic illness, share practical, doable steps you can take to accept and cope with an ongoing illness and the losses associated with it. You'll discover sincere encouragement, a solid foundation for hope, and proven strategies for...

- maintaining and improving relationships with family and friends
- interacting with the medical community, including finding health-care providers who care and setting up supportive networks
- managing and even allaying the stress, fear, and depression that often accompany chronic situations
- getting the most out of life in spite of the circumstances
- helping people around you understand what's happening and how they can assist you

God is with you always. As you explore what His Word says about suffering, you'll discover many of the ways He will love you, support you, and strengthen you during this difficult time.

An informative, comprehensive resource for chronic illness sufferers, their families and friends, and medical and counseling professionals.